"A deft, spicy,
and exciting
blend of fact
and fiction."
—*USA Today* on
*Citizen Washington*

# ★ CITIZEN ★
## *Washington*

### A Novel

# William Martin

FORGE®

$9.99
($11.99 CAN)

ISBN 978-0-7653-6361-9

9 780765 363619

50999

EAN

## Books by William Martin

*City of Dreams*
*The Lost Constitution*
*Harvard Yard*
*Citizen Washington*
*Annapolis*
*Cape Cod*
*The Rising of the Moon*
*Nerve Endings*
*Back Bay*

# Citizen Washington

A NOVEL

# WILLIAM MARTIN

FORGE®

A TOM DOHERTY ASSOCIATES BOOK
NEW YORK

CITIZEN WASHINGTON

Copyright © 1999 by William Martin

Originally published in 1999 by Warner Books.

A Forge Book
Published by Tom Doherty Associates, LLC
175 Fifth Avenue
New York, NY 10010

www.tor-forge.com

Forge® is a registered trademark of Tom Doherty Associates, LLC.

ISBN 978-0-7653-6361-9

First Forge Edition: July 2011

Printed in the United States of America

0  9  8  7  6  5  4  3  2  1

*for Chris,*
*at the start*
*of another twenty-five*

# Acknowledgments

One of the great pleasures of writing a novel like this is that I meet so many people willing to help me fashion fictional reality from our nation's history. Without their opinions, insights, expertise, and criticism, my work would be much less enjoyable. I thank all of them, from the nearest to the farthest away.

*In Massachusetts*: at the Massachusetts Historical Society—William Fowler, director; Peter Drummey, librarian; Celeste Walker of The Adams Papers; and the wonderfully helpful library staff; also Ned Downing; Christopher Keane; David and Nancy Sutherland; Dixie Whatley; and the staff of the Weston Public Library.

*In New York*: William Kuntz.

*In New Jersey*: Garry Wheeler Stone, historian, Shore Region, New Jersey State Park Service, and the staff at the Monmouth Battlefield State Park.

*In Virginia*: at The Papers of George Washington—Philander D. Chase, Jack D. Warren, Mark Mastromarino; at Mount Vernon—Barbara McMillan, librarian; Mary Thompson, research specialist; and all the staff and docents; at the City of Fredericksburg Department of Tourism—Karen Hedelt. Special thanks go to Ann Rauscher, former director of Media Relations at Mount Vernon, and to Dorothy Twohig, editor emeritus at The Papers of George Washington, a great friend to historians and historical novelists everywhere.

*In Paris, France*: Le Comte René de Chambrun.

In exploring the world that Washington walks in this book, I have visited dozens of historical sites—private, state, and federal—staffed by enthusiastic docents, interpreters, re-enactors, librarians, and park rangers who keep open the windows on a world all but gone. Consider that the scene set in the cornfields above Kips Bay, in Part Four of this book, unfolds on ground now crossed by Second Avenue and Thirty-second Street in Manhattan, and you can't help but appreciate the work of these people in saving the past. My thanks to them all.

*In Massachusetts*: at the Vassall-Craigie-Longfellow House in Cambridge, and all along Boston's Freedom Trail. *In New York*: at Washington Headquarters State Historic Park in Newburgh on the Hudson; at Fraunce's Tavern Museum in lower Manhattan; at the Jumel Mansion in Harlem. *In New Jersey*: at the Princeton Battlefield State Park; at the Old Barracks Museum in Trenton. *In Pennsylvania*: at the historic parks at Fort Necessity, Valley Forge, and Washington Crossing; and at the Independence National Historic Park in Philadelphia. *In Virginia*: at Colonial Williamsburg; at the Colonial National Historical Park and the Victory Center at Yorktown; at Carlyle House and the Gadsby's Tavern Museum in Alexandria; at the George Washington Headquarters in Winchester; at the Mary Washington House, the Ferry Farm site, and Kenmore in Fredericksburg; at Monticello in Charlottesville; and most important, at Mount Vernon, where the Mount Vernon Ladies Association has been preserving and studying George Washington's world since before the Civil War.

Finally, my thanks, as always, to my editor, Jamie

Raab; my agent, Robert Gottlieb; and my family, all of whom contributed in various capacities, as research assistants, proofreaders, opinion-givers, and general inspirations.

WILLIAM MARTIN
*October 1998*

# PROLOGUE

George Washington was dead, and all of America mourned . . . except perhaps for my uncle.

In Philadelphia, thousands marched behind an empty hearse. In New York, church bells chimed a sonorous requiem. In Boston, eulogies issued forth from every pulpit and every parlor. But from Alexandria, Virginia, Uncle Hesperus wrote: "Nothin' better than the death of a demigod to help sell newspapers."

He expressed this sentiment in a letter inviting me to come and work for him at the *Alexandria Gazette*. "The southern Drapers," he wrote, "should not be the only Drapers to benefit from our national sorrow."

I agreed, though between the Boston and Virginia branches of our family there was little agreement on anything, least of all national matters. But on one thing all Drapers agreed: Uncle Hesperus had known Washington for long enough, and intimately enough, and tempestuously enough, that nothing he said about America's first icon would surprise anyone, north or south.

So I headed for Virginia. I arrived in Alexandria in the last week of the last year of the last century, determined to learn all that I could about the business of newspapering.

Uncle Hesperus often said that in America, the man who owned the printing presses could protect himself as well as the man who owned the artillery . . . at least until the shooting started. He would then produce a brace of pistols, set them on his desk, and add that it was best to own both.

I can still recall my surprise at the vibrant presence behind his desk. My uncle was sixty-seven, brother to my father's father, which made him a great-uncle in fact, but he was no decrepit ancient. Here was a man who had fought Indians on the Monongahela, ridden at the front of the Continental line in the brutal heat at Monmouth, and sown a small empire in the rocky soil of American publishing. Those deeds were ageless, and so, it seemed, was he.

As he rose to greet me, he looked like a whip—long and thin and leathered, sheathed in a brown coat and lighter brown waistcoat that were no more than gradations of color complementing brown hair and tanned skin. As his hand snapped toward me, the rawhide face brightened, and he said, "Twenty-five and you still don't know what you want to do with yourself?"

"I want to be a writer, sir," I said eagerly.

He laughed at that. "When a man says he wants to be a writer, before he's been anything else, he's sayin' he doesn't really know *what* he wants to be."

"A harsh judgment, sir," I said, trying to meet his gaze rather than the tops of my shoes. "I did study the law for a time."

"The *law*. A barren desert of *wherefore* and *whereas*, of *thence*, *whence*, and *hence*, all in the service of pence. The last thing we need is more lawyers." He said this as much to the portrait on the wall as to me.

The portrait and the hearth above which it hung were the only elements of warmth in the office—a fine yellow flame jumping on the hearth and a fine yellow dress on the woman in the portrait. The woman I took to be his long-dead wife, Charlotte. The fire, I learned, was stoked high on the last Monday of the month to warm the young woman whose regular visits provided my uncle with one of his favorite forms of entertainment.

And she was even then arriving. My uncle's eyes brightened at something beyond my shoulder. And I turned to see her standing in the doorframe, head bowed beneath a hood, body shrouded in a dove-gray cape. Without a word from Mr. Stitch, the elderly doorkeep, she stepped into the room.

"So then," said my uncle, as if he had only moments before sent her on an errand, "is it true?"

The girl cast her eyes toward me.

My uncle told her I was a trusted confidant, a term that surprised me more than it enlightened her. Then he closed the door behind her and told her to sit.

She perched on the sofa by the fireplace and removed her hood. Her face—though pinched by the cold and a curious tension that suggested she was not entirely comfortable with the task before her—was finely structured and symmetrical in all its parts. What, I wondered, was my uncle doing with such a pretty young woman in the middle of the afternoon?

He sat beside her and said, "So . . . is it true, my dear? Has he been put into the vault?"

This question surprised me, considering the transaction I expected. Her answer, however, was in character with what I took to be her profession: "The whole world knows already, sir, but if you're payin' . . ."

"I knew 'twas true," said my uncle, "but you're my eyes and ears at Mount Vernon, darlin'. Till I hear it from you, all news is rumor, all gossip is falsehood."

The girl extended a hand. "The pay, then, sir."

My uncle gave her a gold coin; then he formally introduced me to Miss Delilah Smoot, daughter of a Mount Vernon overseer, one of the few white servants at the mansion house, and my uncle's spy. On the last Monday of each month she came to Alexandria and related all that had happened at Mount Vernon in the previous thirty days . . . for a price, of course.

That this made her the most unfaithful of domestics did not enter my mind. I was too taken by her beauty, and too intrigued by her story, which began on the day that Washington first took the chill that killed him.

" 'Twas the twelfth, a Thursday, I think. General went ridin' . . . visitin' his farms, like always. . . . It took to snowin' just after he left. Then the snow went over to rain, hard and cold. When the General come in, 'round three, his hat was drippin' wet. I asked him if he wanted dry clothes laid out, but he said the greatcoat kept him dry. Well, that greatcoat weighed ten pounds if it weighed a pennyweight, soaked right through."

"That proves it," said my uncle.

"Proves what?" said I.

"He didn't know enough to come in out of the rain."

"Mr. Draper," said the girl, "if you want me to keep tellin' this here story, stop sayin' mean things and sit quiet."

My uncle, to my surprise, folded his hands and sat back, as if he knew just how far to irritate a person before bowing to her anger.

And the girl went on: "The General never went out the next day. He had a sore throat and kept near the fire, 'cept when he went out on the piazza to watch the snow swishin' down. I 'member watchin' from a window and wonderin' what a man in his sixty-eighth year thinks when another winter comes on."

There was a fine bit of empathy.

"What he was thinkin'," she said, "was how to improve the view, 'cause he went across the lawn and marked half a dozen trees for cuttin'."

I could see Washington through her eyes, wearing his black greatcoat, gray hair tied at his collar, tricorne piled with snow. I could even see his footprints, the last he would ever leave, on the whitening lawn.

"The General sat up that evenin' with Mrs. Washington and Tobias Lear, his secretary. They read the papers and talked some, though he didn't say much with his sore throat. Mr. Lear asked if he'd take somethin' for it, but he said to let it go as it came. 'Twas what he always said."

"Had a strong constitution," said my uncle. "Survived more diseases than a New York rat. Why should a little sore throat do him in?"

"Just afore dawn," said the girl, "I went to their chamber to lay in a fire, and Mrs. Washington whispered that the General's throat had closed up. He'd been sick half the night, but he never let her get out of bed to get help, for fear she'd catch cold herself. Then the General tried to speak, and all I could hear was a funny croakin', like the words was caught in his throat.

"Finally he got it out that he wanted to be bled. Said to fetch Doc Craik—"

"Craik," grunted my uncle. "As land-hungry as his most famous patient."

"I'm warnin' you, Mr. Draper—"

"My dear, do not warn me again," snapped my uncle. "Just tell your story." While he knew how far to aggravate a person's emotions, he could play his own like a fine harpsichordist.

And Miss Delilah heeded his tune. " 'Fore the doctor come, I made the General a drink—molasses, warm vinegar, melted butter. A good cure for sore throat, but I feared I killed him with it. He started in to gaggin', turnin' blue . . . Couldn't get a drop down . . . Come nigh to stranglin' 'fore he spit it all up. . . ."

And so the story went, through the last fifteen hours of Washington's life.

Dr. Craik arrived, and after examining his old friend, he stepped into the hallway and told Mr. Lear, in a quavering voice, " 'Tis the quinsy. Throat infection. Most virulent sort. I fear 'tis mortal."

But he promised to do all he could. Then he did what every doctor does when in doubt: he bled the patient, to no avail. So he tried Spanish fly, applied to the patient's throat, in hope that the blisters it raised would draw the infection to the surface. But Washington's breathing only grew worse. So Craik dosed him with calomel, in hope that the sickness could be purged through the bowels. Still, there was no improvement. So Craik, in his wisdom, took another pint of blood.

More doctors arrived. More opinions were expressed. And their conclusion: do what medical science had taught from the time of Hippocrates: bleed him, blister him, and physic him yet again.

By four-thirty, Washington had been drained all but dry. And yet the inflammation had not been purged through any orifice, natural or man-made.

As night came on, breath came harder and harder for the old General.

"When it looked like nothin' would help him," said Delilah, "I heard him whisper to Mr. Lear, 'I'm just going. You'd better take no more trouble about me but let me go off quietly.'"

"A noble actor," said my uncle. "Even on his death-bed he was playin' a role, givin' the dyin' hero noble things to say."

I could not hold my peace. I told my uncle straight out that a man who died bravely deserved respect.

"Of course he died bravely," answered my uncle. "'Twas expected of him. And he never done but what was expected of him."

"Doctors wouldn't let him go quiet, though," said Miss Delilah. "'Round eight, they blistered his feet and put wheat-plaster poultices on him. But he kept slippin' . . . strainin' to breathe, tossin' about, askin' the time, till around ten."

My uncle said, "About his last words, Delilah. . . ."

"''Tis well'?"

"That's what we've heard. What did he mean? What was well?"

"'Twas well that Mr. Lear understood the General's last instructions. He told Lear, 'Don't let them put me in the tomb in less than three days.' Lear said he wouldn't, and the General said, ''Tis well.'"

"So," said my uncle, "he expected to rise from the dead but didn't think he'd have the strength to roll the stone back from the tomb."

"No stone in front of the Washington tomb," said the girl innocently.

I suggested he might have feared being buried alive. There were stories of men going to their tombs prematurely because of poor doctors or overzealous heirs.

Miss Delilah said: "Oh, he was dead when they buried him. I didn't see him go, but I was outside his door. I heard his breathin' get lighter. Then it stopped.

After a few seconds, I looked in. Dr. Craik was closin' the General's eyes.

"Lady Washington asked, 'Is he gone?' Dr. Craik nodded, so sad he couldn't speak. Lady Washington give out a sob and said, ' 'Tis well, 'tis well. All is over. I have no more trials to pass. I'll soon follow.' "

"Those words show a sensitive spirit," said my uncle.

"She's always been sensitive with me," said Miss Delilah. "After they brung the General's body down to the dinin' room and laid it 'fore the fire, she said she was givin' me the most sensitive task of the whole sad night."

"And what would that be?" asked my uncle.

"She took me back to the bedroom and told me to stoke the fire. Then she took two packets of letters from her desk. They was mostly yellowed, and some so old they was crumblin' 'round the edges. She give me a packet and stood over the fire with the other, and told me to feed the letters into the flames, one by one."

"One by one?" said my uncle.

"So they'd all burn good. She wanted them all gone, with nothin' left behind. 'Let them rise with his spirit,' is what she said to me."

"What was in 'em?" My uncle leaned closer. Here was a secret. And a man like my uncle thrived upon secrets. "What was in the letters?"

"Oh, I'm not . . . I'm not at liberty to say, sir," she answered.

"Delilah, tell me what was in the letters, or it shall be echoed back to Lady Washington that you visit me monthly, and the benefit of whatever piddlin' loyalty you're showin' now will go up in smoke with the letters."

Delilah was gripped with an involuntary shiver, as if realizing the degree of her perfidy against the Washingtons. She glanced at me, then at my uncle.

But however great was her guilt, it was not near so strong as my uncle's charm, or his money. He gently took one of her hands, placed a gold coin in the palm, then closed her fingers over it. "Now, darlin', what was in the letters that Martha burned?"

She opened her fingers, glanced at the coin, and with no further hesitation, she said, "They was the letters the General sent to her durin' their life together."

"Their *love* letters?" whispered my uncle, with all the awe that a man might muster had he found the true cross. "Their *private* letters?"

"Yes, sir."

"Did you . . . did you read any?"

"Oh, I never once read their mail, sir. That'd be dishonest."

At that, I could not stifle a laugh.

And Miss Delilah spoke to me directly for the first time, raising her chin as haughtily as a minister's daughter passing a whorehouse, "I beg your pardon, sir."

I might have answered with the truth: that I was subtracting a coin from her treasury for disingenuousness. But as she was quite lovely and I was quite susceptible to loveliness, I put on a soft voice and said, "On the contrary, it is *your* pardon that *I* beg, madam."

"If you beg it," she decided after a moment, " 'tis given."

My uncle chuckled. "Don't be tryin' to impress my nephew with your put-on Virginia airs, Delilah. He's from Boston. He sees through such things."

\* \* \*

When she was gone, Hesperus gave me an angry squint. "The daughter of a plantation overseer heaves her breast at you and you're ready to run off with her?"

"I . . . I . . ."

"No matter. Shows you've got some of the good Draper blood in you. Time with a servant girl can be time well spent. But never marry one. You want yourself a real lady, like my Charlotte." He went to the sofa and looked up at the portrait. "So, darlin', what do you suppose was in those letters?"

For a moment it was as if he actually expected her to speak.

I said, "Perhaps the letters contained terms of endearment . . . statements of purpose . . . the things that a man writes to the woman he loves."

" 'Twas a marriage of convenience," answered my uncle. "But if George did say endearin' things in his letters, why would Martha burn them?"

"Because they're private, and so much of their lives has been public that—"

"Maybe she burned them to hide somethin'."

"There's no evidence of that. What would she be hiding?"

"That's what I want you to find out." And as if stroked suddenly by genius, my uncle sat and scratched out a bank draft. "You have till October first."

I took the draft and almost staggered. Two hundred and fifty dollars. A small fortune. "Until October first . . . to do what, Uncle?"

"Find out what was in the letters."

"But the letters are gone."

"And before long, so will the truth about old George be gone. Up in smoke. Then Americans'll believe he truly *was* a demigod and not what he was."

"What was that, sir?"

"A man. No more. No less. A man who wrote letters to his wife. And she burned them. Find out why, and you may understand the man. Get started, and I'll keep you goin' with three more drafts between now and October."

"A thousand dollars? That's serious money, sir."

"I take this very seriously, son."

I weighed the draft in my hand. I could not imagine how much heavier a thousand dollars would be. I was not sure I was ready for the responsibility. So I said, "I came here to be a writer, sir, not some kind of snoop."

"Well, what do you think I want you to do with what you find, boy? Write it all down. Have it finished by October. We'll publish in time for the caucuses."

"The presidential caucuses?"

"That's right, son. I love a fight"—he smacked his hands together—"and this is the grand contest for the soul of a nation. Adams against Jefferson. Federalist against Republican."

These were our first political parties, born in the 1790s of the family feud that had gone on since the founding of the country.

Federalists believed that a strong central government—hands held firm to the reins of banking, finance, and human frailty—was a necessity if we were to control the mule team of competing interests we had harnessed into a nation. Republicans distrusted the concentration of power. They believed that the future of America lay with the yeoman farmer—an independent, uncomplicated, and altogether mythical creature who drew sustenance from the American earth, and by the simple act of drawing it, gave it back again.

My uncle said, "Adams will invoke the name of

Washington, because Washington swallowed all the Federalist foolishness that Adams and Alexander Hamilton poured down his throat. To beat Adams, we've got to show Washington with all his warts."

To beat Adams, I thought, all that was necessary was to show him with all *his* warts. And the Federalist foolishness, as my uncle so alliteratively put it, had created the stable banking system that allowed him to write out a draft with the knowledge that it would be paid at the bearer's request. But I didn't mention any of this. I was imagining the impact that I, Christopher Draper, a simple young scribbler, might make on the 1800 election . . . if I showed Washington with all his warts.

Still, I had to be honest. I said, "Uncle, I've never written anything of substance."

"Learn by doin', son. That's my motto. Learn by doin'."

# Part One

✧

## THE BOY
## AND HIS MOTHER

C.D.—*I took my uncle's advice to heart. I would learn by doing. I would go to Mount Vernon. I would see Martha Washington and state my case.*

*Young writers, afflicted as they are with the arrogance of naïveté, expect that anyone should be interested in talking with them, simply for the opportunity to have their words put down.*

*Why would Mrs. Washington refuse a writer setting out to tell her husband's story? For the same reason she had burned their letters, of course. But I did not consider the answer. I was too pleased with the plan.*

*So the next morning I headed south on a borrowed horse. The night's rain had frozen on every Alexandria rooftop and tree branch, giving the whole world the look of a delicious marzipan confection. And all along the river, sunlight shimmered like the silver coins that would soon be jangling in my pocket.*

*About nine miles downstream, the road rose from the river onto the winter-sere fields of the Muddy Hole Farm, one of five that Washington had established on his Potomac acreage. Each farm had its own buildings, its own slaves and overseers, its own part to play in Washington's grand scheme, though what that scheme was, I could not tell, nor did I care. My interest was the mansion house.*

*And if Washington was an actor, as my uncle had suggested, there was a true sense of the theatrical in the way that he had ordered his landscape to reveal his house. After a traveler left Muddy Hole behind, the piney woods thickened, dramatically absorbing the light until, like a curtain, they parted, revealing a wide meadow that rose to a promontory atop which sat the famous mansion.*

*I was struck first by the color of the roof. It was the red-orange of sunset, as painted by some artist whose canvases might be garish but whose taste in roofing colors was close to perfection. The house itself was a glorious white, and on that glorious morning I could not believe that I had ever seen anything so magnificent.*

*As I drew closer, I noticed the slave quarters, fine brick barracks under a row of trees; I admired the gardens on either side of the carriage turnaround; I counted no fewer than a dozen outbuildings flanking the mansion like honor guards. And the piece-by-piece nature of the mansion's construction became apparent.*

*Washington had expanded his home three times, permitting small though not displeasing asymmetries—a main entrance set a few feet left of center, a window on one side of the door but no balancing window on the other, a cupola rising from the ridge beam, several feet out of line with the peak of the gabled front. Or was it the gable that was out of line? No matter.*

*For all its majesty this was a house with a human*

face, quite unlike the cold and implacable visage that artists had given to its master as he grew in age and importance.

The house looked as if it had been built of sandstone blocks, but closer examination revealed that the siding was wood, paneled and coated with a sandtextured white paint. After a liveried slave admitted me to the passage, the hallway through the center of the house, I was embraced by the rich, warm woodwork of the paneling, the moldings, the arches above the doorframes. Then I realized that it was all like the exterior: simple American material—pine, perhaps—artfully painted to resemble something grander.

Was this foyer, this whole house, a symbol for the man who built it? A place of majesty hewn from coarser things?

My musing was interrupted by a tall and solemn gentleman appearing from one of the doorways on the passage. "Can I help you, sir?"

I introduced myself as Christopher Draper, son of the late Joshua Draper, former Federalist congressman from Massachusetts.

He told me he was Tobias Lear, the Washingtons' secretary, and he asked the reason for my visit.

"I'm a writer, sir, about to write a life of General Washington."

"Like half the writers in this country." His attitude was noncommittal if not downright hostile.

I had expected—again the arrogance of naïveté—a warm welcome, a seat in Mrs. Washington's parlor, a cup of tea. Washington hospitality was well known.

Instead, Mr. Lear demanded, "What is the theme of your work? The political intent? And who will print it?"

*I did not want to tell him the truth, so I fell back on something I had read in a pamphlet of advice: "Writers write, sir, to discover their themes. I want to discover Washington the man. As for political intent, I'm simply trying to write an . . . an honest book about a man who . . . who valued honesty."*

*And there I stopped. I was not so naive as to think that an honest answer to his third question would do me any good at all.*

*But Lear was not to be put off. "Yes . . . And the printer with whom you share a surname is best known for his opposition to the late General."*

*No amount of dissembling could change my name, so I decided to push ahead. " 'Tis true, sir, that Hesperus Draper will print what I write, but he cannot make me change the truth."*

*"You'll forgive me if I don't believe you," answered Lear. "You'll also forgive Lady Washington if she begs her indisposition. And I'll forgive you for showing the bad taste to appear at a house in mourning, unannounced, not three weeks after the master's death. Good day, sir."*

*And there I stood, in a puddle of my own embarrassment, trying to think of something to save the visit.*

*It was then that Miss Delilah Smoot appeared, bound for the downstairs bedchamber, her arms heaped high with linens. She went about her business with head down and eyes averted, but when she glanced at me from the corner of her eye, she stopped as if struck by a sash weight.*

*I felt my jaw drop at the sight of her, and my stomach dropped, too. I nearly spoke to her, which would surely have exposed us both to Lear's suspicion.*

*But after an instant of shock, Miss Delilah scurried into the bedchamber as though she had never seen me before and had barely seen me then.*

In the time it took for Tobias Lear to usher me out, and for my horse to carry me back to the edge of the woods, Miss Delilah managed to finish her chores, mount a horse in the stable, find her way through the trees to the south, and appear on the road just ahead of me.

"Mr. Draper. Mr. Trusted Confidant." The only thing more surprising than the sound of her voice was the sarcasm. "Your uncle promised he would never come here while I worked here. What are you doin' here?"

I spurred a little closer. "I came to see Mrs. Washington, so that she might help me write a book about the General. And I wanted to see you."

I hoped that last part would compliment her, but it served only to anger her. "You can't come here. It's—"

And we both heard a noise—the sound of someone humming nearby.

"It's a slave," whispered Delilah. "An honest slave always hums when he thinks he's come upon white folk in private talk . . . to let them know he's there."

She kicked her mount toward a curl of smoke rising from behind a clump of pines. And there was the slave, standing over a little fire. He was wearing a match-coat that looked new, patched breeches that looked old, and a slouch hat pulled so low that his face could harely be looked upon at all.

"Mornin', Miss Delilah."

"Jacob. What are you doin'?"

"Your pa, he send me out to pick up deadwood and

*what the ice take down. Burn the twigs, he say, and save the branches for kindlin'."* The old slave tugged at the brim of his hat and gave me a *"Mornin', suh."*

"Morning," I answered. Then, by way of making a bit of conversation, I said that he had probably seen many a winter at Mount Vernon.

*"Oh, yassuh, I see winters so cold your breath freeze 'fore it git out your mouth. And summers so hot, that big ol' river down there, it like to stop flowin'."*

"Mr. Confidant," said Delilah, "I think you should be goin'."

*Perhaps.* But what stories could this old slave tell? I dismounted and told Delilah, "I'll warm myself by the fire before I leave, and perhaps Jacob can tell me of bygone summers . . . to warm me better still."

She gave me a look to drive an iron nail through a two-inch plank. "If my pa finds you botherin' a slave, he'll whup the slave. Then he's like to whup you too, 'specially if he finds you're from Boston." She ordered me not to bother her or the Washingtons again. Then she kicked her horse and was gone.

"Spirited, ain't she?" said Jacob, giving me a sly look and a sly chuckle. The fire crackled and smoked, and we stood beside it for a few moments. Then he said, "So you makin' a book 'bout the General?"

"You heard us?"

"Slaves hear a lot."

I peered under the brim of the hat, into the ancient face. His skin was dark, though not the darkest I had seen among the slaves of Virginia. A hoarfrost of stubble covered his chin, and there were deep lines on either side of his flat nose, like furrows in a field. But it was in his eyes that his age was most apparent. They had no white. What was not brown was red—a hun-

dred tiny veins and vessels, bloodshot and broken—
and nothing in his sweet chuckle could drain them of
their sadness.

I asked him how long he had known the General.

"What year he born?"

I told him in 1732.

"Then I know him from 1732 right up till a few
weeks ago."

And I knew I had made the right choice in staying.
Where else breathed there a man who might say he
had seen Washington in his diapers and in his coffin . . . and be telling the truth?

I had been taught that, in general, the Negro was
not to be believed about anything that the white man
could not verify, as lying served his laziness, which
was as natural as his color. But Jacob's eyes bespoke
more honesty to me than I had heard in a lifetime of
Boston sermons, and even if his mouth delivered no
better than half-truths, I wanted to hear them.

"Could you tell me what you remember about the
General?" I asked.

"How long you got?" He dragged a log close to the
fire, angled it so that it was upwind of the smoke,
then plunked himself down.

"You have work to be doing," I said. "Won't you
be whipped if—"

"I'se a house slave in the President's mansion. I
been places. I seen things. If I wants to sit and speak
a bit 'bout the General, they ain't no overseer gonna
raise a hand to me." He smacked the log. "So jess set
here and ax me a question. I do the rest. I likes to
talk."

That was an understatement. As my uncle might
say, old Jacob could talk a dog off a meat wagon, and

*he did not stop talking until the December sun finally dipped toward the horizon.*

*That night, in my room in Gadsby's Tavern, I took a dozen sheets of rag bond from my trunk, along with a new bottle of ink and two sharpened quills, and I began to set down Jacob's story, leaving out those places where I had prodded him or questioned him, adjusting the words that he put into others' mouths so that they sounded appropriate, but keeping, as best I could, the peculiarities of his speech and pronunciation. It would be the first Washington story of many.*

# The Narrative of Jacob,
# Mount Vernon Slave:

I come into the world, near's I can figger, in the year 1728, on the Washin'ton tobacco farm on Popes Creek, jess 'bove where it run in the P'tomac.

My mama's name be Narcissa, and she a big woman, see, with big fleshy arms that jiggle when she laugh . . . jiggle when she mad, too. Truth is, she jiggle all over, and ain't nothin' make a boy feel happier 'n to have them arms 'round him.

She owned by a planter named Shields, down Williamsburg way, who decide to sell off some of his breedin' wenches. Tha's what them white massas call good women like my mama—breedin' wenches.

And tha's how Massa Washin'ton—the General's father—how he come to buy her. 'Course, he don't know he's gittin' hisself a two-fo'-one deal, 'cause I'se a-growin' in my mama's belly.

Now, my papa, him I never know. When I'se little,

mama tell me he go west and mebbe he come back someday. By and by, she tell me the truth—he run away from that Shields plantation right after they sell her. They track him six days 'fore they catch him, all hungry, tore up from brambles . . . snakebit, too.

When the overseer ax what to do with him, Massa jess say to hang the nigger, hang him from the nearest tree. Say he cause trouble for the last time, and no Shields gonna sell no troublemakin' nigger to no neighbor.

Yassuh . . . if they's one thing 'bout Tidewater folk, they's good neighbors.

Mama say she don't want for me to end up twistin' from no tree, so she ain't makin' Papa out to be no hero. Better for me to live my life workin' for the Washin'tons. They treat slaves good, and don't hang none of 'em, neither.

Now Massa Washin'ton, his name Augustine, but ever'body call him Gus. He be a big 'n—six feet, with shoulders like a big ox yoke, and one of them big heads, like a big ox head, see, kind of head he pass on to the General. And he be strong as a ox, too, like the General.

He git his land from his pa, who git it from his 'fore him. The Washin'tons, see, they been in Virginny since 1650 or so, but they ain't what you call first-rank folk. And Massa Gus ain't a man to sit still. Always itchin' for a bigger spread, for . . . for fatter fish to fry.

He have him two sons off to school in England, Lawrence and Augustine, and he spend time over there hisself, lookin' for them fat fish. And when he's away one time, his first wife die. I don't 'member her. But I sure do 'member the woman he marry 'bout a year later.

She have the name Mary Ball, but some slaves call her Mary Ball-and-Chain. Easy to see why she make it all the way to the age of twenty-three without a husband. I b'lieve she bring land as dowry. Mebbe tha's why Massa Gus marry her. Lord know, they ain't many other reasons.

She ain't no beauty, tha's for sure. She have what you call a strong face, see, and she need it to hold down that strong nose of hers. Same kind of nose the General git, come to think of it. And her eyes is wide apart, kind of eyes that don't give up much, one way or th'other. When she look at you, you don't know what she's thinkin' or even *if* she's thinkin' . . . and damn but if them ain't the kind of *eyes* the General git, too.

First I 'member of her come when her belly take to swellin', bout eight months after she come to Popes Creek. I'se in the kitchen with Mama, see. She be the house cook now, and she teachin' me how to make gingerbread. I like bein' in the kitchen. Warm in there, and it smell good. And Mama always let me lick the spoon once I'se done stirrin' the gingerbread.

Now, Mama step out back to lug in a few logs, so I'se all alone, stirrin' the gingerbread, stirrin' and smellin', and it smell *good*. So I takes a taste, see. I brings the spoon to my lips, and damn, but it *taste* good, too. Tha's what I'se thinkin' whilst commencin' to stir agin.

And all of a sudden, a shadow come over me. And I hears that voice, high and scratchy, like a gate needin' grease. Mary Ball-and-Chain Washin'ton herself. She say, "You 'spect me to eat that, now that it's got your spit in it?"

Well, I can't think of nothin' to say. I'se too scairt,

and that belly of hers, it's all but pokin' in my face, big and round, like it's 'bout to bust right there.

And she say, "What you starin' at, you nosy little pickaninny?"

Tha's when Mama come in and see Miz Washin'ton lookin' down like—this how Mama say it—like she lookin' at somethin' she jess step in, and I'se lookin' up like I'se 'bout to git stepped *on*. Mama start yellin', "He sorry, ma'am. He jess a young 'n. What all he done, he won't do it never agin."

Ball-and-Chain say, "Teach him his manners or keep him out the kitchen."

Mama whup me good after that. She say the Washin'- tons be good massas, and I'se never to do nothin' to make 'em want to sell me. Well, suh, I promise myself right then I ain't never crossin' that lady. Even when I git older, that woman scare me. Scare all the boys ... even the white boys. And tha's a fact.

Next I 'member of her be a few months later, a cold Febr'ary mornin'. I'se outside with a little hatchet, shavin' wood chips to throw on a smolderin' cook fire, so's it jump up hot. Safe job for a boy jess learnin' how to handle a hatchet. How a little shaver gits to be a big shaver, see.

Anyways, I hears a scream, and Mama come runnin' out the house and say, "Fetch some firewood, Jakie! Bring it t' Massa's bedroom! And be quick!"

I thinks, if tha's Ball-and-Chain doin' the screa- min', I don't want to be nowheres nearby. But I don't want to git whupped, neither, so I do what I'se told. And I learn two things: First, whatever Eve done in the Garden, women been payin' for it ever since.

Second, a slave can make hisself invisible jess by standin' still.

Ball-and-Chain layin' on the bed. Mama standin' to one side of her, moppin' her brow. A white neighbor lady be on th'other side, holdin' her hand. 'Nother white lady, the midwife lady, she standin' 'twixt Ball-and-Chain's legs.

I drop the logs and I'se backin' out the room when Ball-and-Chain start in to screamin' agin—a big loud scream that go up so high I reckon it might bust the windows. Then I hear the midwife say, "All right, darlin'. Push."

Well, push what? I'se thinkin'. So I stops in the corner and takes a peek.

This be somethin' new, seein' a white lady with her legs spread, lookin' like her insides be bustin' out of her. She scream and strain like somebody jess drop a mill wheel on her belly and she tryin' to lift it off 'fore it crush her.

I wants to run. But I don't. And long's I stand still, them white ladies don't even know I'se there. Then they's more screamin' from Miz Washin'ton and all kinds of nice words from the others, sayin' what a good job she be doin'.

Well, I'se wonderin' what in hell *could* she be doin' to make her scream so.

Then the midwife lady say, "Baby's crownin'," and I catch on. Foalin' season for the white folk. Now, I seen cows drop calves, and I seen bitches whelp pups, but I ain't never seen this. So I watch right the way through. She push and scream some more, and then I see hair, hair the color of a chestnut stallion. And 'fore long, I'se lookin' at a head. Then the midwife git in the way, and I hears one more big scream, and

Mama's the first one to say it: "Oh, Lordy, it's a boy!"

Midwife take the baby and hold him by th' ankles. He's blue, a little bloody, and drippin' this white, cheesy stuff, jess like all the babies I ever seen born since. And the midwife give him a slap, right on the ass, see. And that baby cry, high and screechy, like some 'coon treed by the dog pack.

I'se wonderin' why they hit that baby and make him cry so. But I learn soon 'nough, tha's how we all come in the world, white babies like li'l Georgie Washin'ton, and black babies like me.

We don't stay at Popes Creek long. Massa Gus buy some land from his sister, where Little Huntin' Creek reach the P'tomac, place called Epse . . . Epsewasson. Injun name, see.

By and by they call it Mount Vernon. But it ain't much when we git there, jess a little tenant house, which Massa Gus fix up, so he have four rooms downstairs, three up, and good, solid chimbleys, too. Slaves gits what you call push-away chimbleys, all mud and sticks. If they's ever a fire in one, you run out and push it away from your shack. But on the big house, they's still usin' the chimbleys we built back then, we build 'em so good.

But Massa Gus don't stay there much. He have a iron furnace near Fredericksburg, see—one of them fish that ain't never so fat on the plate as in the water—and he always down there. Wonder to me he git Ball-and-Chain big-bellied four times more. But he be the kind of pa what spend more time makin' his chilluns than makin' 'em happy.

'Course I don't have no pa, so I figger the world be workin' like it should. Slave chilluns and white chilluns play together nice, right up till the time come for ever'body to learn their place. Then they send the white chilluns to their tutors and the black chilluns to the overseers.

Well, one day—I'se ten and Massa Georgie is six— Massa Gus tell me his boy like to fish, and he know I like to fish, so mebbe I teach Georgie. . . .

Well, I teach that boy all I know—how to find a straight saplin' for a pole . . . where to find big night crawlers . . . how to put 'em on the hook. . . . Then we go down to the dock and dangle our lines. Catch catfish, bass, carp. . . . We fish all that summer. Ain't no better way to spend them hot days than settin' on the dock, danglin' a line. I figger I has a friend for life. Then somethin' happen.

We's settin' barefoot on the dock, see, and I'se splashin' my toes, but little Georgie, he can't reach. So he be stretchin' his leg, tryin' to git his toes down in the water, jess to prove to hisself how tall he gittin'.

And all the while, he talkin' 'bout his half brother Lawrence, who done schoolin' in England and be comin' home any day.

I ax Georgie if *he* want to go to England.

He say his pa tell him he goin' there for schoolin'.

I say, "I reckon I likes to stay here and fish."

He say, "Me too." Then he finely git that big toe down in the water and give 'er a splash and start a-shoutin', "Hey, Jake! I done it! I done it!"

But I don't care about that, 'cause somethin' pull at my line and damn near pull me in the water. That pole bend like a bow. I start in to screamin' and shoutin' and Georgie's jumpin' up and down, sayin' "C'mon, Jake! C'mon. It's a big 'n. A big 'n."

And tha's when we hears the plantation bell. Now, the bell ring for lots of things—to call the slaves to supper, call for help if they's a fire or somethin'—and Mama, she promise us she ring it soon's Lawrence come ridin' up the road. Well, 'tain't dinnertime, and we don't smell no smoke, so Georgie figures 'tis his brother. I'se callin' for him to help me bring in that fish, but he's gone runnin' up the path. . . .

I gits that fish up on the dock by myself—a catfish long's my leg. And it's twistin' and slitherin' and it's swallered the hook too deep to git out. Catfishes do that, see. So I decides I'll bring it up to Mama, let her gut it and cook it. I'se proud of that fish, and I'se hopin' ever'body gonna make a big thing out of it.

But when I gits to the house, they's a bunch of folks there—Massa Gus, Ball-and-Chain, the house slaves, little Georgie, and right in the middle of 'em is a tall gent wearin' a brown coat and waistcoat, all cut fine. He got a slave with him, and the *slave* dress better 'n most Virginny *massas*.

I thinks, This must be Massa Lawrence. He look at me and smile. He have kind eyes and one of them big jaws—a lantern jaw, they call it. And he have a fancy way of holdin' hisself, with his left hand pressed on his hip and his right foot stuck way out in th' other direction . . . how they teach 'em to stand in England, I reckon.

He smile at me, but he don't show no teeth, not a big horse grin. You can tell he be a kind massa, a massa you be glad to have.

I like him right away, so I hold up the catfish . . . to show him, see.

He say, "That's a fine fish." And he bend down to take a look, but jess then a hand tug at his coat. It's

Georgie. He say, in this big put-on voice, that he's growed tall enough to sit on the dock and dangle his toes in the water.

"Well, bravo, young George," says Lawrence . . . jess like that . . . like Georgie done somethin' special jess by growin'.

And now, 'stead of showin' off my fish, I'se *yesterday's* fish.

Lawrence give Georgie that butter-meltin' smile, and Georgie grin up at him through the big space where he lost his milk teeth.

Massa Lawrence throw his arm 'round little Georgie and say, "Come in, everyone. I brought presents for you all."

But you know what he mean by "ever'one"— ever'one but us.

Ball-and-Chain spit a few orders at us. Then she go in with the rest.

And all the slaves go runnin' off but me. I'se lookin' down at that fish, and I jess can't figger why I feel so bad, see. Thinkin' on it later, I reckon I jess want a man like Lawrence to look up to.

And then Mama's shadow come over me. She's smilin', and she say, "Honey, that jess 'bout the finest catfish I ever did see."

And that make me feel better. She show me how to clean it and bread it and fry it. And I eat it all. Then I feel fine.

But I knows Georgie 'n' me, we ain't gonna be such friends much longer.

Well, suh, George never git no schoolin' in England. Never git much schoolin' anywhere. 'Cause his pa die when he's eleven, see. After that, they ain't no money for no schoolin'. Ain't much money for much of nothin'.

Massa Gus, see, he leave his best land, which is Epsewasson, to his first son, which is Lawrence, who name it Mount Vernon. The second son, Augustine, git the second-best land, at Popes Creek. And the third son, George, git put in line for third-best land—a little spread jess across the Rappahannock from Fredericksburg, called Ferry Farm. Tha's where Ball-and-Chain and her young brood be livin' jess then. Massa Gus move 'em there to be close to his iron furnace. Ferry Farm's a workin' spread, see—small house, tough soil. No fortune comin' from there, jess a good life so long's a boy work hard.

But Massa George—tha's what I call him, now that I'se his personal slave—he tell me someday he gonna be a rich man, a gentleman, with fine horses and fine clothes. And I'se to be a gentleman's servant.

And you know what I thinks? I'se fifteen, damn near a growed man, with a man's beard and a man's . . . a man's dick, and his *voice* ain't even changed, and he 'spectin me to git all happy 'bout how I'se to serve him when *he* grow up. But I ain't so brave as to say it. I jess ax him, "Now that you ain't goin' to England, where you gonna learn to be a gentleman?"

"From Lawrence," he say. "Mount Vernon will be my school."

So when his ma let him, like when he do good with his tutor or somethin', we head up the road, 'bout thirty-five mile as the crow fly. And when we gits to where we can see the house, Massa George stop and look. It be smaller than today, but he say that someday he own somethin' jess as nice, so men respect him like they respect Lawrence.

Now, Massa Lawrence take what his pa give him and what brains he have, and he make somethin' of it. He fight for the king in a war in Jamaica. Git hisself 'lected to the House of Burgesses. Git named military adjutant of Virginny. And git married to a girl from the plantation next to Mount Vernon, a spread called Belvoir.

Yassuh, best thing Massa Gus ever do is move in next to Belvoir, 'cause the Fairfaxes live there, and they's the most impo'tant folk in Virginny. Lawrence's wife, Miz Nancy, she's daughter to Colonel Wil'lum Fairfax, who's cousin to Lord Fairfax, who hold what they call the Virginny Proprietary—all the land on the Northern Neck, stretchin' right the way to the head-waters of the P'tomac, all give to him by the king of England hisself.

The Fairfaxes, they be first-rank folk, and ever' Sunday they invites other first-rank folk for parties and dinners, and sometimes a foxhunt. Ladies always dress fine, and gents always show off how smart they is, and the talk's high-flown stuff 'bout Annapolis horse races and business at Wil'lumsburg, and when somebody makes even a *little* joke, ever'body laugh like hell.

Yassuh, they's the laughin'est bunch of folks you ever did see . . . And why not? If I own all that land and all them slaves to work it, I laugh too.

Massas bring slaves to them Belvoir shindigs, so I go plenty. The time I 'member most, I'se eighteen, and Massa George, he's fo'teen. 'Course, he's bigger 'n me—

over six foot already, all ganglin' long legs and arms, big hands, big feets, but scrawny up top, not much in the way of chest and shoulders.

He's wearin' a light blue coat his brother lend him, very fancy, with a lace stock and lace cuffs. I'se wearin' what they call livery—white breeches and coat and a red waistcoat. Them colors come from the Washin'ton coat of arms, see. I always feels funny, all fancied up like a plumed pony, but Massa George go sashayin' 'round the carriage 'fore we leave, actin' like his coat been made special for him. And you know, he look good in it, even if it be a little small in the back.

And when Massa Lawrence and his wife come out to git in the carriage, Massa George's eyes go buggin', 'cause Lawrence be wearin' his Virginny soldier suit, see—red coat, red breeches, red waistcoat, too. He say he wear it sometime to show the folks what a good servant of the king he be.

He stick his arm out and tell George to feel the cloth, and George run his hand up and down that red sleeve, like he feelin' the coat on a fine stallion, and he say that someday he gonna git hisself a uniform jess like it.

Lawrence ax him, "What would you say to wearing the blue-and-white of the Royal Navy, George?"

And Massa George stammer—he done that, see—he stammer, "R-r-royal Navy?"

Lawrence say he been considerin' it.

George say he ain't never consider it a'tall.

And Lawrence say, "Maybe you should."

Me, I don't like this talk, 'cause they ain't no slaves in no Royal Navy. If Massa George go sailin', I go to the fields and hoe tobacco for Ball-and-Chain.

But by the time they gits to Belvoir, they's dropped this talk, and they's goin' on 'bout who gonna be there and who be sweet on who, and all like that.

I'se ridin' up top, 'longside the reg'lar driver, a big-handed slave with the straightest face I ever see . . . never smile, never take his eye off what he doin', jess give a twitch ever' now and then to them fo' matched grays.

Massa Lawrence call this slave Homer. But Homer tell the slaves to call him what his mama call him when he's a boy back in Africa: Matchuko.

I say, "Well, you call yourself Matchuko if you wants, and I call you Matchuko 'cause you ax. But the massa call you Homer and dress you in that suit, and they's nothin' you can do to change it, so why don't you do what my mama'd tell you: smile a bit . . . Matchuko."

He gimme a look, like if I say more, he throw me right off'n that seat.

Not many with a mouth so quick as mine. All the respect in me git used up on my massas. I don't have none for no slaves, 'cept my mama.

Anyways, we rides on a while more. Then Matchuko say, "You been eyein' my daughter, boy, ain't you?"

And I say, "She a eyeful, Matchuko."

He say, "Well, you keep your paws to yourself. And you call her by what I named her. You call her Rwanda. Don't be callin' her no Alice."

See, he don't smile 'cause his family split up, 'twixt Mount Vernon and Belvoir. 'Course, mos' slave families is split. Most places, the idea of slaves bein' family at all is a joke. What you 'spect, when they call slave gals breedin' wenches, like they's prize mares?

Anyways, 'tain't long 'fore we's swinging up the drive to Belvoir and I hears the hounds. All in front of that big brick house they's bayin' and barkin', sniffin' and snuffin', and all them Virginny gents—and some ladies, too—they's all rarin' to git after a little fox they got caged up on the piazza, up where the dogs can't git at him.

Soon's our carriage pull up, I jump down to help Miz Nancy out. We's all extra nice to her, see. She's a skinny, frail thing, with skin so white you can see the blue veins underneath. This be only the second or third time she been out since her first baby die, jess four months after she born.

But 'fore I can help her, her papa, Colonel Fairfax, come ridin' up on his big black mare, all but knockin' me down, and he look inside the carriage.

Lawrence stick his head out, and in that fancy British way of talkin', he say, "My dear Colonel, a fox-hunt was not part of the invitation."

Fairfax answer, "Nor part of the plan, but we trapped a fox last night at the henhouse. Only sporting that we give him a chance to run for his life."

Well, Lawrence pop out of that carriage like he's on springs, sayin' how they's nothin' more excitin' than ridin' good horse after good hounds chasin' a good quarry. George pop out right after, sayin' the same thing, like he done it enough to know.

Colonel Fairfax look in at his daughter and say, "It seems these Washington men love the hunt more than good manners, my dear."

" 'Tis all right, Father," she say. "Let them have their fun."

Massa George git all red, like he done somethin' that ain't polite, and manners be the sign of a gentleman, see. So he offer his hand to her, and damn near trip over two dogs sniffin' 'round his feet.

Miz Nancy take his hand, but he have a funny look to his face. Then I see one of them foxhounds—nothin' but a overgrowed beagle, which be nothin' but a mouth and a nose and a asshole—and he be pissin' on the carriage wheel, and it be splatterin' back on Massa George's shoes, but he don't want to start twitchin' about and 'tractin' attention, see. Better to git pissed on than to look bad in front of all them fine folks. So he jess stand stock-still till Miz Nancy git out.

Then, with the dogs barkin' and the men shoutin' and the excitement buildin', Colonel Fairfax call out, "Mounts for the Washingtons!"

A slave bring out a big white geldin' and a nasty-lookin' roan stallion, too.

Lawrence say, "I'm familiar with that roan, Colonel. I'll take the gelding."

Colonel Fairfax look hard at George, "It seems you'll be riding Fiery Prince this afternoon, son. Are you up to it?"

And George, he jess give his left shoe a little shake and jump for the horse. When he do, the seam on his brother's blue coat split right in the middle, and it split loud—loud enough for ever'one to hear.

But Colonel Fairfax, he like George, like him a lot, and he turn quick to ever'one, 'fore they can laugh, and he say, "Young Washington may be just fourteen, but he bids fair to be the most accomplished horseman in Virginia."

Then he call for the slaves to handle the dogs, and the slaves go chasin' 'round, and the barkin' git louder, and the ladies git all oogly and googly, and the riders pull their mounts, and George handle his like it's a old cow, 'stead of some bad-tempered stallion.

Then Colonel Fairfax give a signal for to open the fox cage, and that scairt little fox stick his nose out and look 'round at all the people and horses and hounds, and he jess leap.

Then they loose the dogs, and they's like a brown-and-white wave, see, a wave of foxhound rollin' 'crost the lawn.

Then the bugler give a call, and Massa George hear it 'fore anybody else. He take off on that big horse with his coattails flyin' like wings. And tha's the way I see him a thousand times after . . . ridin' to hounds, and ever'body else on his heels.

Now, whilst they's off chasin' that fox, they's plenty for us slaves to do—waterin' the team, washin' the dog piss off the wheels—and when we's done, Matchuko say, "Come on in the kitchen . . . git us somethin' to eat."

So we go 'round back of the big house to the kitchen house. They's fires goin' inside and out and a big side of beef turnin' on a spit. I'se lickin' my chops, hopin' I gits a taste, and then I sees her—tall, slim, dark-skinned, and straight as a statue. She's in line with a whole row of gals, all dressed in white shirts and blue skirts, all headin' in the house with trays of food, see, for when the riders git back.

And Matchuko call to her, "Rwanda!"

She glare at her pa and shake her head, like to say, "Don't call me that." Then she gimme a big grin, like she always do.

And I grin even bigger. "Afternoon, Alice."

And if you think Matchuko don't smile 'fore this, you should see how much he don't smile now.

I keep clear of him the rest of the night, but I do what I can to git close to Alice. I help out in the kitchen, carry wood and such, and after a while she tell me how I shouldn't be gittin' my white suit all dirty. I say, "It don't matter, if I can help you." And she gimme another big grin. That gal, she light somethin' up inside me, and it ain't jess a twitchin' in the breeches, if you knows what I mean.

She say, "You ain't no scullion slave, so don't act like one. If you wants to help, carry a platter in the big house."

By now, folks is all finished eatin', see, and we's bringin' in sweets—cakes and cookies and such—and Colonel Fairfax be raisin' his glass, "To young George Washington, first to the fox."

Ever'body cheer. The colonel pull the foxtail from his pocket and hand it to George. They's another big cheer, and George turn red as his brother's breeches, 'cause the colonel say, "First to the fox leads the grand march!"

So Massa's stuck. He ain't had no dance lessons, and he start to stammer somethin', so Colonel Fairfax say, "Come along, George. There's many a fine beauty here tonight. Take one by the hand and lead us!"

And he look 'round, real nervous, till his eyes set on a pretty young gal with jet-black hair and skin so clear it make you see why white folks think they's the prettiest things God ever made. Her name's Fanny Alexander, from down Fredericksburg way, and not much older than George.

He give her his hand. She curtsy. And the players— two flutes and a drum—they start a march. And there be George, with his coat split and yellow splatters on his stockin's, hardly knowin' how to turn as he go down the room and back, and all the best folks in Virginny followin' him.

I wants to watch, but Alice nudge me and say, "You ain't one of the guests, Jacob. You's one of the servants. C'mon."

So we goes out, and in the shadows, I stop and give her a kiss. And she kiss me back. Yassuh, with all she got.

Music's playin' and night's all warm, and I'se gittin' feelin's and . . . well, I press myself to her, see, and . . . from out the corner of my eye I sees a white livery coat. Then I gits kicked right in the ass. It's Matchuko, but I can't turn 'round 'cause I don't want him to see the way my breeches is standin' up, like they's a tent pole in 'em.

So Alice whisper, real mad, "Pa, don't you kick him. I can kiss him if I wants."

Matchuko jess say, "You 'member that while you's kissin', they's folks 'spectin' you to be workin'. So 'less you wants to git whupped, git on to work."

And she don't argue no more, 'cause my tent pole's gone, and I'se goin', too.

But a little later Matchuko git me alone and he say, real soft, real hard, "Don't you kiss that girl agin, not till you jump the broom."

Jump the broom . . . tha's what slaves do when they wants to marry, see. Sometime a slave preacher hitch 'em, someone who know somethin' 'bout Jesus and 'bout how they do things in Africa, too. But sometime slaves jess go out to the woods and jump the broom, and no papa slave can say nothin', 'cause the papa don't own his daughter. The massa do. And I almost tell Matchuko that.

But he say, "She ain't jumpin' no broom till I say so. I won't see her made no breedin' wench 'fore her time. Y'unnerstand me, boy?"

I ain't no fool. Ain't nothin' to say to that but yas-suh.

I jess git on with bringin' platters of cake and sweetmeats in the big house.

Now, I 'spect Massa be havin' a fine time with Miss Fanny from Fredericksburg. And I see her laughin' and chatterin', lookin' like the center of a daisy, and all the young gents, and all the young gals with their fans a-flutterin', they's like the petals around her.

But Massa George, he be over on th'other side of the room, with Colonel Fairfax, Massa Lawrence, and the colonel's son, George Wil'lum. He listenin' hard to these gents, cockin' his head to let 'em know how interested he be in their talk. And their talk be 'bout land. Of all the things they talk 'bout, land be their most favorite. But ever' so often, George's eyes driff over to where Miss Fanny enjoyin' herself. He watch her for a bit, then look down at his shoes, then cock his head and pretend he be listenin' to the gents agin.

By and by, folks is leavin'. They's big torches burnin' all down the drive. Carriages pullin' up. And Massa spy Miss Fanny comin' out of the house. So he go up to her.

You never seen a boy more tongue-tied. He be fo'teen, so he ain't no smooth talker, jess all *um*'s and *ah*'s, and Miss Fanny jess stand there, smilin' up at him in the torchlight, waitin' for him to say somethin', and he's "A . . . um . . . so proud to have been priv'leged to have . . . um . . . ah . . . been give the opportunity to . . . to . . ."

Jess then one of the other boys come out, a skinny whippet of a thing, from down Chotank way . . . Hesperus Draper. He have a uncle in them parts who been invited to the Fairfax party. So he git to come, too.

He slip right in 'twixt George and Fanny, and without payin' George no mind, he say, "Miss Fanny, I had a fine time dancin' with you. If you'd do me the honor again, I'd surely like to take your hand and take another turn to the music."

Smoother 'n loose cow shit, that Hesperus Draper.

He go runnin' off to his uncle's carriage. And Fanny, she 'scuse herself 'cause her carriage comin', too. And my massa be left standin' there by hisself. He march down the steps and jump in his brother's carriage, and I think the damn thing like to tip over, the way he throw hisself down.


Well, suh, gatherin's like that teach him two things: he need some polish if he hopin' to impress gals and fancy-talkin' gents, and if he want to rise in Tidewater society, he need what matter most—not slaves or money, but land, and knowin' 'bout land.

So one day, back at Ferry Farm, he go out to the shed, out to where his pa leave some of his surveyin' tools—a compass, a tripod, some chains. He bring 'em out, set 'em in the sun, and very careful, he stretch out the chains, he oil the wooden legs on the tripod, and he polish up the brass compass. Then he go to a surveyor in Fredericksburg by the name of Byrne and ax for lessons.

Byrne say, "A boy with such fine tools, so well kept, he must be serious indeed."

And tha's a good word for Massa George: serious. And gittin' seriouser.

All summer he stay home to learn surveyin'. We never go once to Mount Vernon, so I never see Alice. Massa see Miss Fanny some 'round Fredericksburg, but he always say so many *um*'s and *ah*'s to her, and he git so mad at hisself after, he go home and jess lock hisself in his room and study his plats and charts all the rest of the day.

One day in September we's shootin' boundaries at Ferry Farm . . . for practice, see. Hotter 'n hell. Rappahannock's movin' slower 'n dirt.

Me and George's little brother Jack, we's the chainmen. George spend a lot of time with Jack. Not so much with the others. None of 'em be near so smart as George, nor so tall, and none of 'em dream no big dreams. S'like Massa come from the same *mother* as Lawrence, 'long with the same father.

So we's doin' this here survey, when who do we see comin' 'crost on the ferry barge but Colonel Fairfax and his son, George Wil'lum.

Massa git all flustered, wonderin' what they's comin' for. "Ferry Farm is n-n-no place to welcome them," he say. "I can't let them see how we live here."

So we run down to the landin' . . . head 'em off, see.

Now, Colonel Fairfax, when he ain't chasin' a fox, he be a nervous-lookin' gent. He have a skinny face and big eyes, like a deer's eyes, and he keep his upper lip pulled down over his lower lip like he's makin' sure nothin' slip out. Why he look like this, why he don't walk the length of Virginny like he own it, is 'cause . . . well, he don't. He jess a 'ministrator, like an overseer, workin' for his fat ol' cousin, Lord Fairfax. Lords is higher than colonels, see.

But still, he have some power to help Massa George. He bring two letters—one from Lawrence for George, the other from Lawrence for Ball-and-Chain.

Massa George look at the letters, kind of puzzled-like.

George Wil'lum say, "My father has exercised a bit of influence with the Royal Navy. A midshipman's warrant awaits you."

Massa George stammer, "Wh wh-when?"

The colonel say soon, but George's mother have to be convinced.

This Royal Navy ain't been talked 'bout these last few months. Now, I reckon, if George go to sea, I'se runnin' away. Jess like my papa done. 'Cause I ain't gonna be no field hand for Ball-and-Chain.

Massa George tear open his brother's letter, read it quick, and say, "Tell him I'll follow his advice. Tell him he's my best friend."

And Colonel Fairfax put his hand on Massa George's shoulder. "I started in the Royal Navy myself, George. 'Tis a fine beginning."

So Massa George ax the colonel, w-w-would he like to come up to the house for tea? The colonel say they have impo'tant business in Fredericksburg, and they has to be goin'. And I know Massa George be thinkin', Thank the Lord.


After Ball-and-Chain read her letter from Lawrence, you can hear her all the way to Reverend Marye's school, up the hill on th'other side of town. And for once I'se glad to hear her yell, 'cause it mean mebbe I don't has to run away.

"Royal Navy?" she say, like she sayin', "Hot poker up your ass?"

Massa George say, "Lawrence and Colonel Fairfax feel 'twould be a fine career, Mother. The colonel himself began as a midshipman."

She say, "I won't hear of it."

He say, "But, Mother—"

"We need you here. You can't be off rottin' on some ship."

He say, "I won't rot."

She say, "Because you won't go."

They's like two peas in a pod—pigheaded, quick-tempered. . . .

He say, "Lawrence thinks there'll be little opportunity for me here. But opportunity abounds in the navy . . . and I'll be an officer of the king."

She say, "Lawrence is not your father. Till you come of age, you won't go to sea without my signature." Then she say she'll write to her brother George in England. If brother George say it's a good idea, son George can join the Royal Navy.

He say, "But it could take nine months to get that answer."

She say, "If Colonel Fairfax is so high and mighty that he can get a warrant, he can get one that don't go bad in a week, like a bushel of damn peaches."

And that was that . . . leastways for a while.


Now, 'member how I spoke 'bout him gittin' some polish? Well, he ax his tutor to help him, and the tutor bring him a book put together by some French priests 'bout two hunnert years back, called *Youths Behaviour*. A book of rules, see, on how to act.

George take to copyin' it down and memberizin' it, and he bring it with him whenever we goes to Mount

Vernon, which ain't near so often enough for me, seein' how I feels 'bout Alice. And even when we's there, that Matchuko watch me like a cat watch a bird. He say if I goes nightwalkin' to Belvoir, he tell the overseer and git me whupped good.

Nightwalkin'—tha's when a slave sneak off to dally with a gal at some other plantation. Massas hate nightwalkin', but they don't do much to stop it, 'cause they know if we don't have a little fun, why, hell . . .

I tell Matchuko I stay awake longer and sneak off when he fall asleep, but when I'se there, that big Ebo not only don't smile, he don't sleep, neither, so I only see Alice at gatherin's, where slaves from different plantations git together on Sat'day nights to sing and dance and tell stories 'bout olden times in Africa.

When I'se away from her, I has a funny feelin' in my belly, like a knot. My mama call it love. I call it *lack* of love.

And it make me mad when Massa have me saddle up and I thinks we's headin' to Mount Vernon, and then he point us south to Chotank, way down the P'tomac. Chotank's mos'ly second-rank farms, see, workin' spreads. But he like goin' there 'cause tha's where his cousins lives and lots of boys his own age, who he ain't tryin' to impress, like that skinny little ferret Hesperus Draper. Down there George fish and play cards and sneak a drink of wine, too.

Now, this one night, they's a card game down in a Chotank barn. They's Cousin Lawrence—'nother gangly, overgrowed Washin'ton and Eli Stitch and that Hesperus Draper. They's at a table in the tack room, playin' loo. I'se in a stall, hunkered down in the straw to keep warm. Through the door, I can see them playin' and hear the cards shufflin' and flickin'. None of them boys have much money, and after 'bout a hour George git all of it.

So they stop for a spell . . . pass the bottle some. And Hesperus tell a story 'bout a gal in Fredericksburg, how she go with him, out behind her papa's barn, and she let him slip his hands under her skirt and she slip hers into his breeches and both of 'em have a grand time.

George act like he ain't interested. But I know he's wonderin' if it's Fanny Alexander that Hesperus be diddlin'.

Then Hesperus come out to the stalls and look me over like I'se some new colt, and he ax, over his shoulder, "Is he a good slave?"

Massa George say, "Serviceable and, on a long trip, companionable."

I thinks, I taught that boy to fish, and tha's the best he can say?

"Someday I'll have me a personal slave, too," say Hesperus. Then he look at me. "Is George a good massa, Jake?"

I say, "Yassuh . . . best a slave could want."

Cousin Lawrence say, "Hesperus, where you gonna get a personal slave? You're a farmer's son, with a pa who run off five years ago."

"Don't you speak 'bout my pa," say Hesperus, with a little mad gunpowder flash in his eyes. Then he go back to his normal snide-mouthed self. "We ain't talkin' 'bout me. We's talkin' 'bout Georgie here. He's jess a farmer's *orphan*."

"Yeah," Cousin Lawrence say, "but he got a important brother."

George give his cousin a nod. "*Half* brother . . . and best friend."

"I aim to be important too," Hesperus say. "I'll get me some land; then I'll get me a good slave."

Then I hears him pissin' in the next stall. And while he's pissin', he still talkin'. "You know, Washington, I was up to Fredericksburg last week . . . called on Fanny Alexander."

George look up and jess say, "Oh," calm as he can. He still sweet on her, see. He even writ her some poetry. But she ain't exac'ly invited him for tea.

Hesperus say, "Her and me had a fine chat. Didn't mention you till I brung up that pissin' foxhound. Remember him?"

And George stand up real slow. He be near full height by now, six-and-three, so he tower over Hesperus. Hell, he tower over everyone. But that Draper, he be a banty little rooster, and he come out the stall with a big smile on his face, buttonin' up his breeches.

George look at him, and his eyes git all small, like they do when he's mad.

Hesperus say, "Yes, sir. A good piss always reminds me of that dog. Me and Fanny had a fine laugh over it."

Then he strut back to the card table and say, "Let's play, boys. I'm winnin' my money back from Washington here. Then I'm winnin' that slave away from him, too." Then he straighten his pecker in his breeches, which sometimes a man have to do after he piss.

And Massa George jess say: "'When in company, Draper, put not your hands on any part of the body not usually discovered.' Rule Number Two."

And Hesperus say, "What in hell are you talkin' about, George?"

Massa George pull his book out: *Youth's Behaviour,*

*or the Rules of Civility and Decent Behaviour in Company and Conversation.*

"Oh," say Hesperus. "That damn thing."

"You'd do well to study it," say Massa George.

Hesperus sit down and shuffle the cards and give him a grin. "In or out, George? Tell me quick. I want to win that slave of yours."

George sit down again. "You'll win nothing."

But that ain't the truth. 'Cause all the while they's playin', Hesperus keep talkin', and Massa keep gittin' madder, so Hesperus keep winnin' more.

And ever' time he win, he give out a hoot and rake it all in, makin' a big show of countin' his coin, which a gentleman ain't ever s'posed to do.

Massa George glare at him, and finely Hesperus make a sad face, like he jess comin' back to his senses, and he say, "Sorry, George. 'Do not express joy before one sick or in pain, for that contrary passion will aggravate his misery.' Rule number forty-three."

And that jess make Massa all the madder.

Finely, Draper crane his neck so he can look out and see me. "I hope you brung your gear, Jake, 'cause I'm winnin' you next."

And I thinks, Like hell . . . Nobody gonna win me in no card game.

None of 'em seen me slip out the door.

The big moon, it look like the face of God. And the ground, it all look like silver. And I decides I'se runnin' north, I'se runnin' to see my Alice, and mebbe t'gether we run away. I ain't thinkin' too straight, but leastways I'se thinkin'.

I'se smart, too. I go on foot. I knows a horse be easier to track than a shoe-leather slave. So I jess head up the road. I move all night, steady and fast, and turn for the river near dawn. They's a dock I know where cargo sloops stop pretty reg'lar. I reckon to hide under it till I can sneak a ride up to Little Huntin' Creek, 'tween Belvoir and Mount Vernon. Then I get Alice and run.

I never figger out how they catch me. Guess I ain't so smart after all, 'cause 'bout a hour after dawn, this posse come gallopin' right up to the dock and drag me out like I'se a dog hidin' under a settee. They's Massa George and the card-playin' boys, a bunch of local fellers I ain't never seen, and Cousin Lawrence's pa, a big, bad-tempered Washin'ton who they call Second John of Chotank, like some damn dirt-farm royalty.

He say, "Whup him, George. Whup him now, and whup him here, or that nigger'll run off on you whenever you turn your back."

Massa George, he look 'round at all the folks watchin', and he say, "If it's the same to you, I'll . . . p-p-punish him in my own way."

And Second John git real mad. He say, "Listen, boy, we may not do things the way you're gettin' used to seein' 'em done up in Fairfax County, but we know how to keep our niggers. Now, whup him."

"Do it," say Hesperus, "or he'll never respect you."

"*He* won't," say Second John, "and none of the gentlemen who've helped you track him will either."

I'se thinkin', Oh, Massa, I'll respect you forever, if you *don't* whup me, but what Second John say, it carry weight. Not havin' the respect of a gentleman posse, even if the most genteel one of the bunch be a second-rank farmer with a secondhand name, tha's somethin' that ain't too good.

So Massa George, he give this tight little nod, and they truss me up, and Second John's overseer, he go to work.

And you know what it feel like to be lashed, even with a knotted rope? It *hurt*. It hurt in your skin, and it hurt in your bones, too, and it hurt in your heart. Tha's where it hurt most.

Best way not to feel it to be to think on somethin' else. So you think up some hate, so you hurtin' and hatin' at the same time. You know they can do this to you any time they wants. And that make you hate even more. And that hurt even more, 'cause the man you hatin', you like him, see. Leastways, I like Massa George.

And then, that lash hit a few more times, and you fergit the hate, 'cause the pain blinds out ever'thing else, and the lash ain't hittin' skin now. What it's hittin' be soft and wet . . . meat flesh, see, and . . . hell.

It hurt walkin' thirty mile home, too, with Massa George's eyes diggin' in me the whole way. When he finely say somethin', his voice sound so sad, you think he have *his* back stripped. "Why did you run, Jake?"

They's two answers to that. The first one he know already. But I say it. "I ain't no animal to be put up for wager."

And he stop his horse. "I told that to Draper after you run off. I treat you better than that. You disappointed me, Jake."

I reckon tha's s'posed to hurt me, too. It don't. I jess tell him, "I run 'cause I'se in love, Massa. I loves a girl from Belvoir."

And he ride on for a time, then he say, "In love?" like he don't think it can happen to a slave. "In love?"

"Yassuh."

"Have you . . . have you jumped the broom?"

"No, suh."

"Maybe you should, next time you go to Mount Vernon."

I give a little look over my shoulder and I say, "When that be, massa?"

"Sometime. Sometime soon. Until then, don't run away again."

Well, he don't ever treat me real warm after that. Always fair, but never quite the same. All spring, I'se a field hand, separatin' tobacco seedlin's, pickin' out the good ones, pinchin' off weak ones. 'Tis low work, but I does it and keeps my mouth shut, like my mama tell me.

Then, come Easter, Massa George say for me to saddle the horses. We's goin' to Mount Vernon. And I'se happier than a Christian.

When we gits there, on the night 'fore Easter, I tells Matchuko what I'se plannin' to do at the gatherin' with the Belvoir slaves. I say that I'se jumpin' the broom with his daughter, and he ain't stoppin' me.

He say, "I tol' you, my little girl ain't no breedin' wench."

I say, "She ain't no breedin' wench if I loves her."

And he snort. "Love's jess a word. What you do to prove it?"

And I pulls up my shirt, so's he can see my back. "This ain't no word."

Matchuko look at them scars, and he git up, real slow, go over to the corner and grab his old straw broom, and he say, "Let's go to the gatherin', boy."

Well, suh, me and Alice jump the broom aside this big bonfire burnin' out in a field. Afterwards we eat a fine big ham Massa Fairfax give to his slaves for Easter. Then one of the old men bring out some African drums. And Alice sing this African song, 'bout a lion and a lioness raisin' strong lion babies.

I look at her in the firelight, and I think she be the most beautifullest thing I ever seen. And I look up in that black spring sky, and I see the sparks from the fire risin' up . . . risin' up and flickerin' out, and I wonder if we's ever gonna be free to raise strong babies too.

Well, if you's a slave, and your massa's in Fredericksburg and your wife's at Belvoir, you ain't gittin' much chance to make no babies.

One day I ax Massa George why he don't sell me to Massa Fairfax.

He say, "You're the best slave I have, Jacob."

He say this like I'se s'posed to be proud to hear it. But I say, "What if you go in the navy? You won't need me then."

"But my mother will."

Tha's what worry me. Worry me plenty, till one day, in May or June, a letter come, and 'fore she even open it, Ball-and-Chain go to the front door and call George into the house, 'cause they's news from England.

I'se doin' some weedin', and I decide the garden by the big house need some hoein' . . . the garden by the window . . . the *open* window.

Ball-and-Chain start in readin' the letter from her brother. She come quick to the part 'bout the Royal

Navy. It say George be better off as a . . . a 'prentice to a tinker. It say a common sailor got no liberty, and if George go to sea—this be the part I 'member word for word—'they'll cut him and staple him and use him like a Negro, or a dog.' No, suh, dogs and Negroes . . . don't want to be none of them.

And George say, "But, Mother, I'll be a midshipman. An *officer*."

And she jess laugh. "The cull of a bad litter is what you'll be."

"I'm bigger and stronger and smarter than any other boy my age."

"It'll take more than that in the Royal Navy." And she read from the letter, 'bout how they's too many midshipmen graspin' for too few places, and George'll be at the bottom of the list.

I'se watchin' in the window, pretendin' to work the hoe. *Scritch-scratch-scritch*. Give a listen. *Scritch-scratch-scritch*. Take a peek.

Massa George have his back to the window, and his mama's in a chair. She sittin' up straight like a new-set fence post, and George standin' up the same way. And nobody givin' a inch. Like always.

He say, "But . . . but the Royal Navy is a pathway to becoming a gentleman."

"Be a good farmer and a good surveyor. That'll be gentleman enough."

"I won't be chained to here," he say, and his voice git higher.

She say, "My brother's a man of property, and he writes, 'Don't be hasty to get rich. Don't seek after being a fine gentleman too soon. Let time take its course at Ferry Farm, and you'll be happier than if ever you went to sea.'"

And Massa George, he yell, "I'm goin'."

And she yell, "You're stayin', and that's final."

Then the front door bang open, and George stalk out of the house, mad as hell. He go down the hill, down the path through the trees, down to the river-bank. And all the way he's kickin' at stones and whis-perin' to hisself 'bout how he damns that farm and damns his mother and damns hisself for not runnin' away.

He's fifteen, don't forget, and they's no better age for feelin' sorry for yourself, even if you got nothin' to feel sorry 'bout.

He pick up a stone, and he fling it out at the river. Now, the Rappahannock be slow, and not so pretty as the P'tomac, nor near so wide. But wide enough, 'bout seventy yards or so. And that stone jess drop and splash. Then he pick up another one and fling it harder, and I swear it split the difference 'tween the first splash and the far bank. Then he try again, and he git even closer.

I watch from behind a tree, and he jess put all his mad into throwin' them stones, till finely I swear he throw a apple-sized stone all the way 'crost that damn river. All the way. And I thinks, damn but he's strong.

'Tis as if he throw all the mad out of him. Then he jess stand there, lookin' all tuckered out. Then his head swivel 'round, like he's a sharp-eared buck who hear somethin' behind him. And he look right at me. "How long you been there, Jake?"

"Long enough," I say. "And nice throwin', Massa. But I . . . I has a question."

"What?"

"When your mama say we's stayin' here, do that

mean she ain't lettin' us go to Mount Vernon, neither?"

He say, "We'll go to Mount Vernon, Jake. And other
places, too. She won't hold us here forever. So go get
my compass and chains."

# Part Two

## Boy Soldier and Soldier of the King

C.D.—*It was not surprising that the old slave never mentioned Martha's letters, but he took me from the beginning of Washington's life to the end and by the time he was done, it was clear to me that the arc of that life across the American sky might be traced through five distinct sections, as would become readily apparent to the reader. Moreover, each name that Jacob mentioned promised yet another pathway to Washington.*

*So I went to my uncle's office with a list of those names, perhaps a dozen, like Dr. James Craik, Sally Fairfax, the Marquis de Lafayette, and I searched out their addresses. I had determined that I would send them letters and request interviews, even if my travels should take me all the way to France.*

*Naturally, when my uncle spied me at his files, he was filled with curiosity.*

*"You got all those names from old Jacob? The one we had to chase? Found him under a Chotank dock?" He chuckled, as if some ancient slave hunt were to be as fondly remembered as a first catfish . . . or a first kiss.*

*"He seems a smart old Negro," I said.*

"A sharp-eyed slave can tell you plenty. Especially if he has a sharp nose and can smell scandal. That's what counts in this, boy. The odor of impropriety. The stink of deceit. Find out what was in those letters, and I won't need to throw stones at the statue. I'll have a hammer to break it into pieces."

I said, "Will you tell me your story? Tell me why you want a hammer?"

"I told you," he said, "I'll hammer Washington because of all the damn Federalists who collected around him like ticks on a hairy dog . . . and because of his hunger for land, some of which should have been mine."

"Then, this was more than political. It was personal, too?"

"Isn't everything, son?"

He then announced that it was time for his daily stroll. Putting on his tricorne and taking his silver-headed walking stick, he led me out into the bright sunshine of the third day of a new century. He went briskly in the chill air, snapping his stick ahead of him, meeting the gaze of everyone who passed.

Most ladies gave him a smile or a nod, though a few looked pointedly away. As for gentlemen, the better-dressed offered him bows, others doffed their hats, and tradesmen gave out with booming loud greetings. And my uncle answered each of them in kind. He was clearly a man of wide reputation.

Between greetings, he lectured me: "Now, then, about the Federalists, I'll offer four words: Alien and Sedition Acts. Familiar with them?"

"My father was a prime supporter. I argued bitterly with him."

"We'll make you a Republican yet," he said as

we wended our way toward the riverfront. "Never thought the country I fought for would make a law prohibitin' public assembly—and I quote—'with intent to oppose any measure of the government.' But the Federalists did it two years ago."

"Because we were about to fight the revolutionary French government over freedom of the seas. We couldn't trust the Frenchmen in America."

"Believe that if you want, son, but here's the truth: the Federalists want to control dissent. They're the faction in power. And they want to keep it that way."

Up ahead I could see the bustling docks and the wide brown water.

"The Bill of Rights is supposed to guarantee freedom of the press," he went on. "But the Federalists' act makes it illegal 'to print, utter, or publish . . . any false, scandalous, or malicious writing' against the government.'"

"And you've done that?"

"What we said about Adams in the Philadelphia Witness was true. He wants to concentrate power in the hands of the moneyed interests, put on the trappings of royalty, and cozy up to England. Jefferson, for all his faults, doesn't."

"But Jefferson loves the French. And the French love the guillotine."

My uncle just grunted and quickened his pace. With his walking stick tapping out the rhythm of our steps, he led me out onto one of the docks. He did not stop until he was at the very end, with the wide Potomac before us.

"Son, the Federalists want to take government out of the hands of local folks and put it all there"—he aimed his walking stick north, toward the triangle of land where the Potomac forked—"the federal city. Washingtonopolis is what they called it to start. Now they're just callin' it Washington. I call it the swindle on the Potomac."

"But my father once told me you bought up half the land there."

"I'm not stupid. One man's swindle is another man's opportunity."

I had ridden through Washington on New Year's Day. And while there might have been stranger sights in the year of our Lord 1800, I would have had to see them to accept the premise.

It has been said that Rome was not built in a day, or even a century, but Americans were attempting to construct a new capital, after that ancient model, in a single decade. They had chosen to build it, with what has since come to be called typical American optimism, on land that was mostly malarial swamp, virgin forest, and muddy hillside. The allotted decade was nearly over, Congress would soon be arriving, and as yet, swamp, forest, and mud prevailed.

My uncle snorted. "Washington picked the spot. Said he did it for the good of the country. Always said that. But he wanted that city there because he was chairman of the Potomac Canal Company. Puttin' the new capital where he did was good for business."

I suggested that nothing I'd seen in the capital looked good for anything. Shanties, muddy streets, and half-baked wedding cakes of limestone block were not the stuff to inspire investors, or a nation. It seemed to me that Washington's capital was a failure.

My uncle said that Washington had always found a way to outlast his failures, and so it would be with the city named after him.

"Always?" I asked.

"I watched him do it for his whole life. . . ."

And he began his story. He talked for two days. And as I set down his words, I found that like the teeth of a dovetailed joint, they could be interlocked with Jacob's, and a picture of the young Washington might emerge.

## The Narrative of Hesperus Draper:

George didn't impress me. He was just like the rest of us—a boy who grew up on a backwater farm.

Now, when we were young, the geography of Virginia said as much about *who* you were as *where* you were. Top-rung people lived on the Tidewater. Got there first, got the best land, got the most land, too. As you went up the rivers, you went down the ladder. Near the fall lines, near places like Fredericksburg, the farms got smaller and life got harder. Then there was the frontier. Out there, you might work your hands to the bone and lose your scalp to maraudin' Injuns, but you could be whatever you made of yourself.

No matter where you lived in this world, though, you were supposed to know your place. You tipped your hat to the ones higher up and turned up your nose to the ones below.

And if you wanted to climb the ladder, you had to get your hands on some of that land. But how, when you had a king who gave charters to favored companies and land grants to favorite lords? You had to go lookin' for what was called ungranted lands, or go hat in hand, ready to pay Fairfax quitrents to get Fairfax patents.

Considerin' his Fairfax connections, George had a jump on me. And he was already puttin' on airs, tryin' to act like the folks up on the top rung. That's why he studied that book of rules. A lot of us read it, but he took it serious. Took himself serious, too.

After that card game, where he took himself so serious that I took all his money, I didn't see him again for a year. Spring of 1748, to be exact. We were both sixteen and both about as far away from home as we'd ever been. I was bringin' civilization to folks pressin' the frontier westward. George was bringin' the survey tools to do the pressin'. And both of us was tryin' to get rich.

My scheme was a pretty fair one. I had an uncle, Jonathan Draper, fattest Draper who ever put his foot into a shoe. Ran the tobacco inspectin' station at Huntin' Creek, where they built Alexandria a few years later. He did a little factorin', a little tradin', and I'd made a deal with him to expand his business out to the frontier, which he liked doin' about as much as he liked expandin' his waistline.

Convinced him to give me a wagonload of goods—consignments that Tidewater planters had turned down, damaged goods, overstock, stuff I could peddle to frontier tradin' posts. I reckon he liked my ambition, and since his brother had run out on me and my mother, he figured he owed me somethin'.

So he gave me a team of horses, two of his slaves, and a covered wagon, and off we all headed for the Blue Ridge. The slaves drove the wagon. I rode a horse. My friend Eli Stitch rode along, too. And him and me, we each carried a brace of pistols in leather holsters, just to keep the nigras in line and discourage anyone else who might want to trade some lead for whatever we had in our wagon.

Mostly we were bringin' things we thought the tradin' posts couldn't do without: wool blankets; china cups and plates, the heavy kind; a box of spectacles— some for readin' up close, some for seein' far off; crates of tea; cones of sugar wrapped in blue paper; cloves and pepper. Carried a few luxuries, too: three bolts of silk, a mantelpiece clock in a mahogany case, a set of French duelin' pistols, and the finest red-feathered hat you ever did see.

My uncle didn't demand collateral. I was takin' it all on consignment. Gettin' twelve percent of what I sold, like a factor. Bringin' back what I didn't sell. No excuses. Simple as that.

Along the Tidewater, spring was comin' in. Daffodils and tulips bloomin' in the dooryards. Dogwoods puttin' out flowers. And when we come out into the open country, where it rolls on to the Blue Ridge, the color of the grass was so light it looked almost yeller. Yes, sir, the color of youth it was.

We traveled northwest. Headed for a place called Ashby's Gap, 'bout fifty miles inland. Got colder as the land rose. The fresh color faded some. And once we started climbin' in the Blue Ridge, we saw more snow. Trail got damn muddy, too. Horses sunk to their fetlocks. Wagon wheels sunk to their hubs. Pushed that wagon more than we pulled it. But after two days, we reached the top, and I saw the Shenandoah Valley for the first time.

I knew right then why folks talked about it like they did. As far as you could see, 'twas good bottomland and stands of hardwood and wide meadows of grass that the Injuns had been burnin' clear for . . . well, for as long as there'd been Injuns to hunt in burned-off meadows. The river flowed through it like a pretty blue ribbon. And the Alleghenies made a wall to the west, protectin' it all like a mother protectin' her only child.

I said to Eli, "Let's go and make our fortune."

The next night we reached Winchester, in the hilly woodlands at the north edge of the valley. 'Twasn't much of a town, just crossroads in the wilderness, but there was a trader there, name of Hite. I done some business with him and made some money, which made me feel pretty proud. Then he told me if we pushed on to Cresap's tradin' post, about thirty miles northwest, on the Maryland side of the Potomac, we might catch up to the surveyors who come through Winchester a few days before.

Well, we'd heard down Chotank way about Washington goin' west with a Fairfax surveyin' party. He was helpin' to shoot boundaries, so that old Lord Fairfax could start puttin' down marker stones and puttin' off squatters and sellin' some of that five million acres of his.

I'd been considerin' a push to Cresap's. Hearin' that Washington was there, that made up my mind. I'd show him he wasn't the only boy around with ambition.

'Twas a small world we moved in, don't forget, and what people thought about you mattered. You might think I don't give two damns for what men think about me. But your reputation means everything.

It means more than sayin' you're good in a fight, or rich, or smart. It means you have the respect of the men around you. It means you know who you are and so does everybody else. It means your credit's good. Hell, it means you can say the cows'll come home at dawn instead of sunset, and no one's gonna get up early to prove you wrong.

I figured if I showed up all the way out there, ready to do business, George'd have to respect me and speak well of me, no matter what he thought about me. Then my reputation 'mongst my peers, the boys down Chotank, 'twould be solid as stone.

But gettin' to Cresap's was no midnight saunter out to the necessary. I couldn't have picked a worse time to be crossin' rivers, never mind haulin' a wagon. Spring runoff was roarin' out of the mountains. 'Twas rainin' like hell. But I was goin' to Cresap's. Told Eli, "I'll eat dirt 'fore I go back over the Blue Ridge with my wagon half full and my tail between my legs."

The slaves looked at each other and rolled their eyes, which I pretended I didn't see. Fact is, those two poor nigras—can't even remember their names, only that one was fat and one was skinny—I think they could see what lay ahead.


Now, when folks think of the Potomac, they think of that big, flat river down on the Tidewater. They forget that above the falls, way up in the backcountry, 'tis narrow and rocky and about as fast as a jackrabbit with the hounds on his tail. And no bridges.

So we traveled twenty miles northwest, and I bartered all my spices and the last of my tea to get two canoes from a feller that Hite told me about. Didn't have any more sugar, or he would've got that, too.

Then I asked him where the best spot was to cross.

By then that skinny little muskrat—name was Andrew Mensing—he'd pawed through everything in my wagon. Decided he wanted my mantelpiece clock. Said he'd guide us if we give it to him.

But his house was a miserable shack with a push-away chimney, settin' in the middle of those dark, wet woods, with the mud gettin' deeper by the minute. I said, "What in hell would you want with a mantelpiece clock when I don't reckon you even have a mantel?"

He just said, "I likes ze clock." He was one of those Dutch or Germans come down from Pennsylvania. Had a pretty heavy accent.

I shook my head and started to walk away. I was learnin' how to bargain.

So Mensing said, "Vat about ze hat? I seen a red-feathered hat. Give to me ze hat and I show you ze best crossing."

Now, this feller was wearin' rags. His own hat flopped down to his shoulders and poured rain right the way down his back. And from what I could see of his boots, the only thing keepin' his feet dry was the mud caked in the holes.

I said, "What in hell will you do with the hat?"

And he said, "Give it to my wife. A hat she vould like."

Just then she stepped out of the shack. She was yeller-haired and wide-hipped. Tall, too. Had bare feet, dirt on her face, livin' a mean life in a mean place, just 'cause she wasn't born up on one of them high Tidewater rungs. Fact was, she couldn't've been much older 'n me.

Seein' her, I went soft, right in my belly. . . . When I give her the hat, she smiled like I give her a bag of sunshine. 'Twas a good feelin', even if I was givin' up a lot for a little . . . damn little, as it turned out.

Mensing brought us to a spot on the south bank. River was about eighty feet across, with dark, wet woods on both sides. But in the quarter mile of water we could see, 'twas the only spot that wasn't swirlin' and roilin' and boilin' like a kettle on a four-log fire.

Mensing had to shout over the roar, just to say that this here was the reg'lar crossin'. "You cannot tell. Ze vasser iss six feet more zan it should be. But cross here. Zen take ze Maryland Road, jah? And stay on it. And don't take no cow paths. Zey get you lost quicker zan your niggers."

And with that, he was gone. Off to see how his wife looked in her new red-feathered hat . . . and bare feet.

I was glad to get rid of him. Could barely understand the son of a bitch.

I looked at that river, and Eli looked up at the rain, and the slaves looked at each other, and the only one who didn't look over his shoulder at the road headin' back was me. . . .

About two hours later we had both canoes filled.

Then I asked the slaves which of 'em knew how to handle a canoe. They just shrugged and rolled their eyes. I figured they was duckin' the work. I didn't know yet the difference 'tween shiftless and scared.

So Eli and me, we took the first canoe. Don't know how we ever got across. The river looked quiet in that spot, but the current pulled at us like Satan tryin' to pull a sinner down to hell. Halfway over, it got hold of us good. You never saw two boys paddle harder.

If the roar of that river is anything like the roar of

hell's fires, we should all repent. But the Lord favored us, if he favors anyone, and before long we were on the far bank, callin' to the slaves to follow us.

They shouted back that we should come and paddle the second canoe, we done such a good job with the first one.

I told 'em that if they ducked this work, I'd see that they were sent back to the fields. That made 'em take to the water like two bird dogs.

But the truth was, they didn't know a canoe from a cornstalk. I could see it as soon as they were off the bank. They paddled too fast. Kept swingin' the paddles from one side to th' other, with no rhyme or reason. And sure enough, they tipped over right in the middle of the damn river.

My goods was gone in a flash. And if those slaves drowned, I'd be payin' off my uncle for the rest of my life.

So Eli and me, we plunged in, rowed like hell, almost tipped 'fore we fished one of them out—the skinny one. Figured I'd lost the fat one, and a lot of money, too. But he had enough fat on him that he floated, and the current carried him back to the south bank. Found him clingin' to a tree, cryin' for his mama and cursin' all white men.

Well, now that we were down to one canoe full of goods, we didn't need the slaves. And we only needed four horses, which we swum across with ropes tied to their bridles and tails. We chained our wagon to a tree, and tethered the other two horses, and told the slaves we'd be back in a few days. Left 'em sittin' on a little outcrop of limestone, up where the riverbank reached the road. Warned 'em that if they run off, we'd come find 'em and throw 'em in the river again.

Couldn't have been two slaves anywhere happier to see the backside of a bad master than them two.

The trail to Cresap's was nothin' but a mud path through the dark, wet woods and the wide, wet meadows and back into the dark, wet woods again. The tradin' post sat in a clearin' on a promontory, above where the south branch of the Potomac met the north. A stockade surrounded it, with gates they could shut quick in case the Injuns got ugly.

But the only Injuns around was some Delawares. They were comin' home after a raidin' party on the Shawnees with nothin' to show but one measly Shawnee scalp. Must've been embarrassed by that, because they were stoppin' at Cresap's to load up on firewater. Made such a stir that nobody noticed me and Eli comin' through the gate right after them.

There was men everywhere inside the stockade, mostly from the Fairfax surveyin' party. I reckoned they couldn't work on account of the rain and the swollen rivers, so they were just killin' time. Some were whittlin'. One was sightin' a compass. Two young fellers were practicin' fencin' off in a corner. And all of them quit what they was doin' at the sight of those Injuns.

I knew the two fencers—Washington and George William Fairfax. Washington sheathed his sword and came closer to the Injuns. Don't guess he'd ever seen a war party before. He studied them close, cranin' his neck and cockin' his head. Then he started whisperin' with Fairfax.

They say Washington looked up to young Fairfax, but I never liked him. Struck me as a fop. Educated in England. Liked to wave his sword around but never fought a real fight in his life. Had a soft face and soft hands. Acted as if he was better than anybody he was likely to set eyes on without takin' a six-week sail to England. Wonder to me that he could keep his stockin's so white in the wilderness. But I figured that was what made a gentleman—havin' white stockin's while everyone else was caked with mud.

Their eyes were on the Injuns, of course. They couldn't give a care about two young traders leadin' a pack train, so I shouted over to them, "Any of you boys have any money to spend?"

And Washington looked at me like he was seein' his own dead father walkin' through the gate. "Draper?"

I give him a grin. "Surveyed any good plots, George?"

"Well, I . . . I"—he stammered sometimes, when he was nervous or surprised—"I've been through some beautiful groves of sugar trees. I've seen some r-r-rich land, some of it planted in good grain–hemp tobacco. . . . Good to see you, Draper."

I knew he was happier to see my blankets than me. He wanted to buy one right away. Said he'd slept on his share of bug-infested beds in the backcountry, and he'd took to sleepin' outside, so he could use another clean blanket.

I said, "Sorry, George. I come to do business with Cresap. He'll sell you the blankets I sell him." Felt good, leavin' him there with his money in his hand. I decided that whatever I'd been through to get there, 'twas worth it.

Cresap was the sort you'd expect to find runnin' a frontier tradin' post—bearded, buckskinned, smart, and strong-smellin', too, which was sayin' a lot in them parts, since everybody smelled like dried shit and rottin' leather. I was just a boy, and he could've skinned me good. But he give me ten beaver pelts for fifty blankets. I tried to sell him the mantelpiece clock too, but he just laughed.

I didn't want to carry the clock home, so I decided to give it to the Injuns. Figured I'd be back soon, with a long train of packhorses. And there'd be nothin' better than havin' the local Injuns think good thoughts about me.

So I went out to where they were drinkin' rum with the surveyors. Made a big show of holdin' the clock over my head, then put it into the chief's hands with all the ceremony I could muster. Told them, "This clock is a symbol of my friendship with great warriors."

When the Injuns saw that the clock made a tickin' sound and the pendulum moved, and the sound and movin' went together, I was their friend for life. I'd give them somethin' with magic in it, somethin' for them to take home. So they made sure me and Eli got all we wanted to drink.

After I had a little rum-dum buzz 'twixt my ears, I went over to where Washington and Fairfax were watchin' all this.

Fairfax give me this down-the-nose look. "Great warriors, you say? Great warriors bring more than one scalp."

"You ever *seen* a scalp before?" I asked him. "Or a war party?"

He raised his chin to give that uppity look those folks are so good at, and he said, "I've read enough about war parties to know that one scalp is a paltry haul."

I looked at George, "What about you? You read any books about Injuns?"

He shook his head. "Where did *you* learn about them?"

"The same place you're learnin' about land. On the frontier. Learn by doin', George. That's my motto."

And he gave me that flat stare, like he was tryin' to see through me. Later, people said that stare showed how smart he was. Said he'd look hard, think hard, say nothin' till he had everything straight. Others said his look showed just the opposite. Said that while he was lookin', he was tryin' to figure out what to think about the thing he was lookin' at.

What he really had, though, was one of those heavy minds, like a mill wheel, just sittin', waitin' for the river to rise so the keeper could throw the lever and engage the gears and the wheel could start to turn, and then 'twould turn so slow and steady you wouldn't be able to stop it.

Even if it took George a bit of time to get somethin' straight, he usually got it. And he was gettin' it straight about me, which meant all the boys in Chotank would, too. However much ambition he had, I had as much.

Now, the liquor'd made the Injuns so happy, they was startin' to raise a ruckus. Built a big fire out in front of the tradin' post. Made themselves a drum by stretchin' a deerskin across one of Cresap's kettles. Filled a couple of gourds with shot for noisemakers. And the chief stood in the middle of the circle givin' a speech, wavin' his legs and arms like a big bird.

Fairfax whispered somethin' in George's ear and made a funny flappin' motion with his elbows. Both of 'em snickered. I thought, These Injuns might be ignorant as all hell, but you won't get nowhere by laughin' at 'em.

'Twas pretty funny, though, seein' that chief do his storytellin' dance. Then another brave jumped up and started swoopin' about the circle like he was made of nothin' but arms and legs and feathers. Then all of them got up and started swoopin' and jumpin' and hoppin' from one foot to the other, like they all had bees in their breeches.

I was afraid to give Eli a glance, 'cause I knew we'd both start in to laughin'. Don't forget, we were just boys, and boys can be damn silly, 'specially boys who've had a few long swallers of rum.

But I think all of us wanted to laugh so we wouldn't feel so . . . so awed by those Injuns. They were half naked. They were childlike. They were mostly drunk. But if they wanted to, they could've turned on us and taken our scalps right then. Knowin' that, and feelin' the poundin' of those drums deep in your chest . . . 'twas all as strange and strong as them dark, wet woods. 'Twas somethin' you couldn't ignore. So you laughed to make it seem less powerful.

Next mornin' 'twas rainin' again, but I was bound to get back to that river crossin'. So I said good-bye to George and asked him what he was plannin' to do.

"I'll let the Indians amuse me some, then write about it in my journal."

I said, "Make sure you put down about a Chotank boy come west to trade with nothin' but a few packhorses and Eli Stitch to keep him company."

Just then George William Fairfax come runnin' out, wearin' fresh stockin's, white as snow against the mud. Had a letter in his hand, wavin' it at me. "I say there. I say there, Draper. You're heading back to

Hunting Creek, aren't you? Would you be so kind as to deliver this to Belvoir? My father will see that it's forwarded."

I said I'd do my best.

"You must *promise* me, Draper."

I told him he didn't have to say it twice.

George said, "Mr. Fairfax corresponds with a lady he's engaged to. She means a great deal to him. I know he'll favor anyone who delivers a letter to her."

I didn't give a fiddler's fart about Fairfax and who he favored and who he fondled. But I wasn't stupid. I knew what a Fairfax could do for me, or *to* me. So I plastered a foolish grin on my face and promised: "This letter will get to . . ."

"To Sally Cary, of Ceelys," said Fairfax. "It's a plantation down on the James. You may know of it."

I didn't and didn't care. But if love could make an old German river rat bargain for a fancy hat, 'twas no surprise it could turn a young fop into a chatterin' girl.

And chatter he did. "She'll be Sally Fairfax of Belvoir before Christmas. This is my first letter to her from the frontier, Draper. See that she receives it, and you shall get to meet her when she comes up the Potomac."

"Thank you, Mr. Fairfax. Thank you, sir." I gave my hat brim a polite little pull, feelin' like a hypocrite all the while.

But Fairfax just kept talkin': "I've already described her many times for George. Raven hair, brown eyes, elegant long neck, forehead so high and proud and redolent of intelligence . . ."

He really talked that way. I thought to warn him about intelligent women. My pa used to say they was like intelligent slaves. Too smart for their own good, too dumb to be left alone, and never to be trusted. But I wasn't sure 'twas true.

And when George William was talkin', he wasn't interested in listenin'. "I've painted so fine a portrait of Sally that I think Washington is already in love with her, even though he hasn't even met her."

At that, George's face got red. Talk of women could always bring a flush to his face. And talk of women was somethin' boys my age was glad to engage in, even if they didn't have anything truthful to say.

So I talked, too, like the boy I was, and I tweaked, like the troublemaker I've always been. "You don't have to worry, Mr. Fairfax. George won't be interested in your Sally. He's in love with a Fredericksburg gal."

And Washington's face burned as red as an andiron.

"Yep," I said. "Her name's Fanny Alexander, and George's even written poetry about her, or so I've heard."

After all I'd been through, just to show Washington that I was as ambitious as him, I had to go and rub his nose in all that. He brought his hand to the hilt of his sword, and his eyes—blue-gray they were—they got as cold as two little nuggets of ice in that flamin' hot face of his.

But I was too stupid to shut up. I threw my head back and declaimed his poetry, "'From your sparkling eyes I was undone; rays you have more transparent than the sun.' Written by George Washington. Surveyor and versifier, too."

He said, "Where did you hear those lines? Who read them to you?"

I'd heard them from Fanny herself, but I was smart

enough not to say so. I was also smart enough to be takin' to the trail right then. I give a wave over my shoulder, but I didn't turn around. Knew Washington wouldn't stab me in the back. Wasn't near so certain of what he might do if I looked him in the eye.

"You're a fool, Hesperus Draper. No two ways about it." That was Eli. Called me a damn fool for embarrassin' George. Called me a cursed fool. A *god*-damned fool. And once, he even called me a fuckin' fool.

I told him if he called me *that* again, I'd throw him in the river. So he went back to sayin' *damned* fool as many ways as he could. Stayed at it for two days.

He was still goin' on when we come up to the crossin' where we'd left the nigras. But I wasn't listenin' to him. I was listenin' to the river. Sounded louder somehow. And the banks seemed steeper, muddier, and there was more light, too. Couldn't figure that out.

When we looked out at the river, I thought we were at the wrong place.

By now Eli'd stopped chatterin'. He was lookin' hard across that brown water. Lookin' for somethin' familiar.

I said, "You got a good eye for landmarks, Eli. You see any?"

And he pointed to a honeycomb of limestone rock stickin' out of the ground at the place where the land dropped away.

And I knew. That was the outcroppin' where we'd left our two slaves a few days before. Now the earth all around it was gone. And the trees was gone. And the wagon chained to the trees was gone. And the horses tethered 'tween the wagon and the trees was gone. And the nigras was gone, too.

The river just came up and swept 'em all away. As quick as that.

Before I came 'round that bend and saw that lime-stone rock, Cresap's pelts had damn near turned my trip into a break-even operation. But when I got back to Huntin' Creek—minus two slaves, two horses, wagon, and goods—I was so deep in debt to my uncle that I had to work for him for the next four years.

And my reputation down Chotank . . . well, 'twas as muddy as the Potomac. But for the next four years, while I was workin' off my debt, I was thinkin' about that Shenandoah Valley and the land beyond and how someday, somehow, I'd get me a piece of it, even if I didn't have two pennies to my name.

## Jacob, Mount Vernon Slave:

I always 'member Christmas of '48.

We go up to Mount Vernon, see, and I go night-walkin'. And Alice waitin' for me at her cabin door. When she see me, she don't need to say nothin'. She jess glow. Tha's the only way I can say it. She glow. I'se to be a papa. That make me so happy I jess cry.

Even ol' Matchuko smile.

As for Massa George, he be a real surveyor by now. He have enough money to start buyin' nice clothes and take dancin' lessons, too, so's he know what to do when the music start and all the ladies and gents go tippy-toein' and tappin'.

And they's plenty of dancin' at Belvoir that winter,

'cause George Wil'lum Fairfax marry a fine-lookin'
long-necked gal ever'body call Sally.

We's there the first night she meet ever'one. House
all trimmed with laurel leaves, music playin', candles
glowin', drinks flowin' like the river. And I'se sweatin'
like a stump-pullin' donkey in my livery and white
wig.

But Massa George go right up to George Wil'lum
and his new wife. He ain't no skittish colt no more. He
give 'em both a deep bow, like he learn it in England
'stead of with the music massa down Fredericksburg.
They chitchat some, and when the music start in to
playin', he offer Sally his hand.

And she know jess what to do. She been well bred,
see. She rest her hand on top of his, like hers be a little bird and his be the nest, and they go tippy-toein'
and tappin' onto the floor.

Massa George dance with plenty of gals. And near
every time he come away lookin' like he jess fall in
love. Sometime he send letters to the gal he dance
with, and sometime he write her poems, too. But most
gals don't take to George. Mebbe he too big for 'em.
Or he don't say the right things. 'Tis true that he still
dance better than he chitchat.

This Sally Fairfax be eighteen and married to his
best friend, but he struck with her, too. They curtsy
and bow, and she flash him these little smiles, and all
the while they dance he have this happy look on his
face, like he been drinkin' too much punch. He only
dance with her once, but he never quit lookin' at her
the rest of the night.

After, we's back at Mount Vernon, and Massa
George's sittin' up with his brother. I pour sherry for
'em and listen to 'em talk. And George say how much

he envy Mr. Fairfax, which is what he still call George Wil'lum.

Lawrence ask him, "Why, beyond the obvious?"

"Because of his new wife," George say. "What an amiable beauty, possessed of mirth, good humor . . . What else?" He just plain tongue-tied by that gal.

Lawrence start in to say somethin', but a fit of coughin' git him, bad coughin' that make a big crackin' in the middle of his chest. After he take a drink of sherry, it settle down some, but he got no mo' color than the snow outside.

George say, "Is that cough the reason you've taken leave from the House of Burgesses?"

Lawrence say the cough ain't nothin'. Jess a cold. He come home, he say, on account of his wife.

'Member Miz Nancy, how she lose her first baby? Well, she have 'nother, a boy named Fairfax. And she lose him after two months. And then she have a girl, named Mildred, three month old, and awful sickly, too. That Mount Vernon be a sad house.

So we stay there that whole winter. Massa George want to be close, in case somethin' happen to the new baby, or his brother don't stop coughin', which he don't. But it ain't all gloom. They go plenty over to Belvoir. They's chitchattin' with George Wil'lum and Miz Sally, card playin', dancin', foxhuntin' with the colonel. And I gits to sleep with Alice all winter.

Come springtime, Massa start surveyin' agin, and his first job's a big 'n—layin' out lots for the town of Alexandria, which they's buildin' that year up on Big Huntin' Creek, by the tobacco 'spection station.

And Lawrence go to England. He hope them doctors can make his cough go away. But he don't go jess for that. Him and bunch of other rich gents got a charter, see, to start somethin' they call the Ohio Company of Virginia, and he goin' to England to see some of his partners.

I thinks, Damn, but what these white massas can do when they puts their minds to it. They needs a town in such and such a place, they go and build it. They wants land on th'other side of the Alleghenies, they start a company, and the company git a piece of paper from the king, and the king say they has the right to settle a quarter million acres of land they never even seen.

And the Injuns who live there . . . well, fuck 'em. Tha's the plain talk for it, jess like when the fathers of these white massas decide they needs hands to work their farms. They's black folks over in Africa, folks we never even seen, folks mindin' their own beeswax? Well . . . fuck 'em. Bring 'em here.

That summer, Colonel Fairfax git Massa George named surveyor of Culpeper County, so we's on the move plenty. And usually we go back to Mount Vernon, not Ferry Farm, so I can see Alice and rub her belly, and feel that little baby kick inside her.

One time we come back to Mount Vernon from one of our trips, and Miz Nancy call me to come to her sittin' room right away. She got this terrible sad look on her face. She say, in this real soft voice, "Jake, your Alice wants to see you at Belvoir. Ask your master if you may go . . . right away."

Well, if Alice want me, and Miz Nancy been cryin' . . . I can only think somethin' bad happen.

Massa George let me go, and I gallop over to Belvoir.

My belly clench like a fist, my hands shake, but when I throw open the cabin door, there's Alice, sittin' up in bed, holdin' a little bundle. She smile at me, and she say, "Jake, you's a papa. You has a little girl."

And I take that baby in my arms and I tell you I never seen nothin' so beautiful. I jess start to cry. I'se so proud, I put her in a cart and go ridin' up to Mount Vernon. The house slaves come out and git all oogly and googly. And then Massa George come out, not even smilin'.

I say, "Look, Massa, I'se a papa."

He say, "Well done, Jake."

I say, "We's namin' her Narcissa, after my mama."

And Massa don't even smile. He say, "The sound of a healthy baby is not what Miss Nancy wants to be hearing under her window right now, what with her own baby Mildred just dead."

Birth and death. Happy and sad. The world keep turnin' for the white folks and the black.

C.D.—*In setting down these stories, it was becoming clear to me that when a man tells you a tale from his life, he makes himself the main character. It would fall to me to keep the stories advancing in step with the life of the man who was meant to be the center of them all, a man just beginning to make his way in the world.*

*Washington had opened a surveyor's office in Winchester, but for most of the next two years he was in the field, living in camps, "amongst a parcel of barbarians and uncouth people," competing with them for the sleeping berths by campfires, and staying in his clothes for weeks on end, as he said, "like a Negro."*

*He pined for a certain lowland beauty, perhaps*

*Fanny Alexander, and he relished his visits to Belvoir and Sally Fairfax, who quickly became his ideal of femininity.*

*But femininity occupied less of his attention than land. While surveyors might be paid in tobacco certificates, he preferred hard money—"A doubloon is my constant gain every day that the weather will permit me going out"—with which he bought his first Shenandoah land: 1,459 acres on Bullskin Creek. He was only eighteen, but he had learned well from his half brother.*

*As for Lawrence, he had been made president of the Ohio Company. The king had promised that if they began to settle the Ohio Valley, he would expand their grant by 300,000 acres. They were building a rough road northwest from Virginia, and they had sent agents to placate the Indians. Placating the French, who eyed this territory from the north, would be more difficult.*

## Jacob, Mount Vernon Slave:

Doctors don't know nothin'. They has their medicines and their bleedin' tools. They has their opinions and their fancy airs. And mebbe if you break a bone they can set it for you. But mostly they don't know nothin'.

They for certain know nothin' when my mama take sick. She start passin' blood when she . . . when she do her business. The overseer give her some medicine. And the local slave doctor—he know some African cures and spells, too—give her some herbs. And finely the doctor from Fredericksburg come by and bleed her. But she jess keep passin' that blood.

In six months that big, happy woman go down to skin and bones. Then jess bones. Then jess dust in the Rappahannock ground. She never see no more than a chunk of land 'bout sixty mile from one end to th'other.

But the fall she die, 1751, I git to go on a ship all the way to Barbados. 'T'ain't a happy trip 'cause, like I say, doctors don't know nothin', and for certain, they don't know how to make Massa Lawrence stop coughin'.

With winter comin', he decide to git out of the Virginny damp and cold. Colonel Fairfax, he know a doctor in Barbados. So tha's where Massa Lawrence go. But Miz Nancy, she jess have another baby, and she ain't up to travel. So Massa George go 'stead. This mean he don't git those good fall months for surveyin', but he never say a word. His brother need him. And Massa George need his slave, to lay out his clothes and help with the trunks and such like.

When that schooner clear the Virginny Capes and commence to rockin' and rollin', all's I'se thinkin' is, What do my granddaddy think when his slave ship move like that? Do he git seasick? I'se sure seasick. I'se scairt, too, and I *know* why I'se on this ship, not like my granddaddy, chained down below, not knowin' nothin'. . . .

In Barbados, Massa Lawrence go see this Dr. Hilary. Folks say he know more 'bout coughin' sickness than any doctor in England. He listen to Lawrence's chest. He tap it here and there, front and back. He look at Lawrence's spit, which I guess is somethin' you don't mind doin' if you's a doctor. Then he tell

Lawrence he gonna be fine. All he need's a little rest and a few months of warm weather.

Well, tha's good news for Lawrence, and for us, 'cause we gits to stay all winter on a island that be greener 'n anythin' you ever seen in Virginny even in the summer. And the house we stay in have this fine view of the ocean and all the ships comin' in and out.

Massa George go all over the island. He see how folks live. He take notes. He visit the English gents who wants to buy him drinks and hear 'bout Virginny.

But Lawrence keep to the house and keep coughin'.

Massa George say, "Lawrence, ride with me. A ride would do you good."

Lawrence say, "I can go about at night or ride at the first dawn of the day, George. But by the time the sun's a half an hour high, the heat's too hard."

"So we'll ride at dawn." Massa George say this real gentle, see. He talk more gentle to his brother than to anyone else, 'fore or since. "You'll be ravished by the beautiful views . . . fields of cane, corn, fruit trees . . . a green so delightful it'll make you forget everything but itself."

But whenever they ride, Lawrence break out in a cold sweat and have to come back. And when they go out at night, for dinner or to someone's house, where mebbe they's a little dancin', Lawrence say he can't dance, 'cause a doctor tell him dancin' give you yellow fever. Truth is, he can't dance 'cause it start him coughin'. He even too sick to go to the theater.

But Massa George see a play called *George Barn-well*. And he talk about it for days. He love the fine clothes and the way the actors move, and sometime, out on the lawn, when he think nobody lookin', he practice somethin' some actor done—a bow or a movin' of the hands or the way one of 'em draw his sword. Only natural for a boy with no father to learn from the men he see, from Massa Lawrence and Colonel Fairfax, and from actors puttin' on shows.

Best thing that happen while we's in Barbados—best and worst, both—be the smallpox. Massa come down with it after he visit a house where it's been.

It's bad 'cause half who gits it die. And I worry the whole time 'bout gittin' it, too. But it's good, 'cause Massa don't die, so he can't never git it agin. And I don't git it neither, which is good too, 'cause I don't want it.

Massa start feelin' better when them little poxes crust over and start itchin' like burrs. But scratchin' bring on scars. So him and Lawrence sit on the veranda and look out at the sea, one tryin' not to cough, one tryin' not to scratch, till one day, Massa Lawrence say, "You've survived, George. Now you may go anywhere that there's pox, and go without fear."

Lawrence sittin' in a shirt and linen waistcoat. His skin's as red as a berry even though he never spend more 'n an hour in the sun. He have that high forehead, and the hair backin' off it like a field goin' fallow, which give him the look of a skull. He stare out at the ocean and say, "George, our bodies are too relaxed here. We need winter to brace us up."

And Massa George say, "You don't think this climate has helped you?"

"Do you?"

George jess look out, like he know the truth.

Lawrence know it, too. "I miss my Nancy, George.

And our new baby. And this island wears on me. Time to move on."

"To where?"

"I'm for Bermuda. A more temperate clime may agree with me. You're back to Virginia as soon as the doctor ends your quarantine."

Massa George try to say somethin', but Lawrence keep talkin'. "You must get in your surveying before the trees leaf out. You must get on with your life."

Massa George put his hand on his brother's arm, which you don't see much; he don't touch folks much. He say, " 'Tis your life that's important now, Lawrence. Important to your family . . . to the Ohio Company."

"There's the true order of things." Lawrence give that smile I 'member from the first day I seen him at Mount Vernon. He's only in his thirties, but to me he's a old man, I been lookin' up to him so long. He say, "I feel like a criminal condemned, though not without hope of reprieve."

Massa George say, "I'll stay with you."

Lawrence shake his head. "Get home. I'll have Nancy meet me in Bermuda. There's a doctor there who claims to have conquered consumption. His patients forswear meat and strong drink in favor of regular riding and . . . milk."

"Milk?" George can't believe that; me neither.

"If milk is my cure, then milk it shall be. If I grow worse, I . . . I"—he stop, like he startin' in to coughin' agin, but his eyes fill up with tears—"I shall hurry home to my grave."

I can't say for sure, 'cause I never seen it afore, but it sure look to me like Massa George wipe away a few tears of his own.

* * *

'Twas a sad trip back. Massa George know his brother be dyin'. But he know life got to go on, too.

We put in at Yorktown in late January and go straight to Wil'lumsburg. Massa George need to see the gov'nor. He have letters from his brother. And he have a plan. I don't 'spect he tell me, 'cept he don't have no one else to tell. He say, "My brother won't be able to hold the adjutancy of Virginia much longer. He's too sick. The governor should know that. So I'll tell him in all honesty . . . and then I'm going to ask for the post myself."

"Th' adjutancy?" I shouldn't be sayin' nothin'. But sometimes I say too much. "Massa, you don't know nothin' 'bout soldierin', do you?"

And he jess look at me, with the same look his mama have. Kind of steady and flat. Like to say, don't git in my way and don't ax questions.

Now, I gits to visit Wil'lumsburg with Massa a few times. And that Duke of Gloucester Street jess about the handsomest street I ever see. At one end, they's the House of Burgesses, all fine red brick. And at th'other end, they's the college named after King Wil'lum and his wife.

The gov'nor have a palace at the end of what's called the Palace Green. And the entry hall be the finest room I ever seen. High ceilin', fancy carvin'. . . . but that ain't the half of it. Up on the ceilin' they's muskets, see, a big wheel of brown Besses with shiny bayonets all pointin' in. Sixty-four of 'em. I count 'em all. And above all the doors they's pistols, and ever'place else they's shiny swords.

Imagine you's a Frenchman or a Injun or a Marylander come to complain 'bout somethin'. You look up and see all them guns and swords, and you know they's jess *decoration*, and they's a powder house loaded with muskets and pistols enough to outfit a whole army. Well, suh, you git friendly right quick.

Massa George, he jess look at it all with his mouth wide open, like he seein' the power of the Crown itself, right there on the ceiling.

Now, this Gov'nor Dinwiddie, he got a hand in the Ohio Company, see, and he doin' his damnedest to see that they build their road and get treaties with the Injuns, so the company can git on with business.

Massa say Dinwiddie be good to have for a friend, and I reckon Massa make a friend up in the gov'nor's chamber that day, 'cause Dinwiddie come down to see him out.

Dinwiddie dress fine, but he ain't too tall, and he got this big mouth and this flat-across nose and this stumpy neck that make him look like a frog, see, a frog in a fancy white wig. He say, "Your brother's a fine man, George. I can see his reflection in you. I shall tell him so when I see him next."


But next time anybody see Lawrence is when he come home to die, like he promise. He shrinkin' down to nothin', not eatin', coughin' his lungs up. And for all his money and polish and fine friends, they's nothin' to help him—no medicine, no milk diet, and for certain no doctor, 'cause doctors don't know nothin'.

I watch Massa George the day they put Lawrence in the Mount Vernon tomb, a hot, steamy July day. He standin' apart from his other brothers and sister, like he's the loneliest man on earth, and he keep his hands clasped behind him and his head bowed, and I swear he bite his lip like to draw blood.

He lose his best friend, and the man who teach him everything.

But life go on. After six months, that friendship he strike up with the gov'nor, it pay off. He git swore in as adjutant of Virginny jess like he plan. He git a red uniform jess like what his brother wore. He put it on once a month, and he look good in it, too.

But looks is all he got. He ain't no soldier, 'less readin' a couple of books on soldierin' make you one. He's only twenty-one, and he wouldn't be adjutant 'less his brother been adjutant afore him. And folks know it. So how he gonna give orders to officers who know more 'n he does?

Well, he find out that next year, but I ain't with him. He send me to work at Mount Vernon, see. He say the best slave be a happy slave, and he know I'se happy if I can go nightwalkin' to Belvoir. I'se glad to go. I miss some famous things, but I don't mind missin' no wars.

## Hesperus Draper:

'Twas a small world, and up there on that top rung 'twas as cozy as a quilt.

The king had given patents to the Ohio Company to claim the land on the far side of the Alleghenies. But the French built forts south of Lake Erie. And they went in canoes down the Monongahela and Allegheny Rivers, drivin' out the English traders and buryin' lead plates wherever they went. The plates told whoever dug them up that the land had been claimed by the French king.

Goddamned French sneaks, if you ask me, afraid that if they put up good, honest stone tablets, some Englishman would come along and knock them all down.

Now, the pivot point of all this maneuvering, the leg bone in the joint of the broad-hipped Ohio River, was the place where the Monongahela and the Allegheny come together, where Pittsburgh stands today. From there, traders could travel all the way to the Mississippi, and from the Mississippi all the way to the sea. The king told Dinwiddie to warn the French away from the Forks of the Ohio, and if the French would not leave, Dinwiddie was to threaten them with war.

And who got to deliver Dinwiddie's warnin' letter? The Fairfax favorite, that's who. Colonel Fairfax was on the governor's council, and he knew that here was a chance for a boy to polish his reputation. So he plumped for George, and when a Fairfax plumped, folks listened.

I'll admit it. Washington had a few qualifications. He was adjutant of Virginia, so he *seemed* like a military man, even if he'd never fought a battle in his life. And he didn't say much, which is a good way to get men to trust you, especially married men who spend most of their time listenin' to women chatter. And after four years as a frontier surveyor, he was as tough as any pelt-trappin' backcountry French frog-eater he'd run into.

'Twas good that he was tough, because he had to cross four hundred miles of winter wilderness—by horse, by canoe, and on foot—all the way to Fort Le Boeuf, up near Lake Erie, before he could find a French officer who'd accept the letter.

Along the way, he got his first look at the Forks of the Ohio. Met the local Injuns. And he drank with all the French officers he saw. He could drink more than most men, on account of he was so big. Even if he was matchin' those French drink for drink, he probably stayed sober while they got drunk. And when they were done drinkin', he knew all about the French plans to take the whole Ohio Valley. . . .

C.D.—*My uncle said the best person to speak with about that trip would be an Indian who lived near Pittsburgh. He wrote a letter of introduction, which he assured me the Indian would be able to read. He gave me his bodyguard, the sullen and silent Mr. Stitch, as a guide. And we set off northwest for the frontier, like Washington and Hesperus Draper in their youth.*

*To quote Washington on his first visit to the wilderness, "nothing remarkable happened" until Stitch and I went beyond the muddy streets and smoky chimneys of little Pittsburgh to a farm on the far bank of the Allegheny, where the Indian John Britain lived with a white woman named Mary.*

*Their home was a dirt-floored hovel that reminded me of one of my uncle's more apt descriptions—"a miserable shack with a push-away chimney, settin' in the middle of those dark, wet woods"—except that here the woods had been cleared back and small fruit trees were stretching their limbs toward the taller trees around them like children reaching toward their parents.*

*Mary wore conventional garb—white mobcap, shirt and shawl, woolen skirt and apron.*

*John Britain wore a woolen hunting shirt, mocca-
sins, and buckskin leggings. He kept a feathered tricorne on his head, so that I could not see what Indian
wonders he might have worked with his hair. He was
lighter-skinned and taller than I expected, and he spoke
English as if he had learned it from a lawyer, so careful was he in his selection of words.*

*But he had savage blood. That was plain. A ring
pierced the septum of his nose. Shiny copper wire
hemmed his ears. And though his laugh was as guileless
as a child's, there was a darkness in his gaze that reflected, at worst, the violence he might have seen, and
at best, the dark, wet woods that formed his world.*

## The Narrative of John
## Britain, known as Silverheels:

Washington? We named him Caunotaucarius.
We named him in the winter before the war
between the English and the French.

We were the Iroquois nation, six tribes bound as
one: Mohawks, Oneidas, Onondagas, Cayugas, Senecas, Tuscaroras. You cannot know of our greatness in
those days. For hundreds of winters we had been bound,
since before the whites.

I was of the Mingo people. We had been made by
the marrying of Senecas and Cayugas. Our sachem
was a Seneca, Tanacharison, called by the English the
Half-King. He was strong and fierce, and even when
I had seen only seventeen summers, I could see that he
wrapped strength and fierceness in a blanket of wis-

dom. That was why the Great Council of the Iroquois League made him their speaker with the whites.

When Washington brought his letter, he went first to see Tanacharison at Logstown.

There we had built the longhouse in which our councils met. There, two summers before, we had signed a paper with the English. It said they could make settlements in our Ohio Valley. It said they would help us protect our lands from the French. It said we would live with them as one people.

We did not want to live as one with any whites. But the fathers of the Great Council were not fools. They knew we had to choose between the French and the English. The French had made allies of our northern enemies, the Algonquin peoples—Hurons, Ottawas, Abenakis. So we chose the English. But English or French, both were bad choices.

In the summer before Washington came, the French had gathered to the north. Their numbers were greater than we had ever seen. So Tanacharison went to them and asked if they were coming with raised hatchets or good hearts.

They laughed. They said they would come as they wished and take what they wanted, and no Indian or Englishman would stop them.

Washington told us he carried a letter that would order these French to leave. He asked Tanacharison to help him deliver it. He did not say that this letter claimed our land for his king. He said only that we were allies. So, as allies, we went back to see the French again.

The journey was to the north, in winter. The going was hard. But we did not stop until we reached Fort Le Boeuf.

There was a new French captain there, named Saint-Pierre. He did not laugh at us. He said the French wished to be friends with all the tribes. He treated Tanacharison like a guest. He flattered Washington's red Virginia soldier's suit. He took Washington's letter and promised he would send it north to Quebec.

Washington asked why his men were building so many canoes along the creek bank. Were they coming south?

Saint-Pierre said only that he had to keep his men busy, so he had them build. Then he poured brandy.

My first taste was like drinking fire. But a fire that burns can warm, too, and the brandy fire warmed enough that I wanted another drink. The second did not burn so much and warmed more. The third was like a warm summer night.

For days, the French poured us brandy and promised us gifts. Washington watched and warned and made mad faces. We did not care.

On the third day, Washington changed from his soldier's suit to his buckskins. He came to the great fire we had built on the creek bank. It was cold. Big snowflakes were falling, but the French brandy still warmed our bellies.

Washington told Tanacharison, "Do not let French brandy or fine French speeches pry you from your treaty. We are your true friends." Then he ordered us to go.

But we did not want to go. And he could not order us. Each time we made to leave, the French reminded us of the gifts that were coming. Then they brought out more brandy. My head hurt very much.

But Washington was stubborn. He told Tanacharison that he had come to Fort Le Boeuf with his Mingo allies and he would not leave without them.

Tanacharison said he liked the French brandy.

From the gate of the fort, Captain Saint-Pierre watched and smiled.

Washington whispered to Tanacharison, "Every scheme the fruitful French brain may invent is being practiced here to entice you from your friendship with the English. You do not even see the deceit."

Tanacharison looked up at Saint-Pierre and smiled, the way the dog smiles at the master he is thinking of biting; then he whispered to Washington, "French brandy is good, and if they give us muskets for gifts, we will have more muskets to shoot at them."

"They offer these things only to make you stay," said Washington. "And if you stay, you will be swayed from your English fathers."

Tanacharison said he was not one to be swayed. Then he took a drink.

Washington put out his hand for the brandy pot, and Tanacharison gave it. I think he was glad that Washington would drink with him.

But instead of putting the pot to his lips, Washington threw it into the creek. Then he stepped back and by some magic, he pulled himself up so that he seemed even taller than he was. He clasped his hands behind his back. He said in a loud voice, "I accuse Captain Saint-Pierre of breaching military etiquette. He is keeping my escort here by devious means. I order him to deliver the presents he promises to my Mingo allies, and I order Tanacharison and his warriors into their canoes."

These words were turned into Iroquois and French by the word changers, who took big gulps of air and whispered the words hard and sounded scared as they spoke them. That was because these words were an outrage. No man gave orders to Tanacharison. And no man threw away his brandy.

I was standing behind Washington. I put my hand on my tomahawk and waited for Tanacharison's order to strike him. The French soldiers cocked their muskets and waited for Saint-Pierre's order to shoot.

I heard the water trickling along the ice that edged the creek bank. I imagined Washington's scalp hanging from my belt. I was not afraid.

But then . . . Tanacharison laughed. And he slapped Washington on the arms, like an old friend. He said, "The Virginian speaks the truth. It is time to go. If the French have presents for us, let them be brought now."

From where I stood, I could see Washington's hands, still clasped behind him. One hand held the other tight as if, together, they could keep from shaking.


That night we made camp downstream. And Tanacharison gave Washington his name: Caunotaucarius. He said that it meant Town-Taker.

"I thank you," said the new Caunotaucarius, "but I have taken no towns."

"Your great-grandfather took them," said Tanacharison. "He took many towns in the war, in the year you call 1676. We have kept his name alive, and now we give it to you."

You cannot know how great were the Iroquois people, that we could remember such things for so long. But we knew our history as you know yours, and in all our words with Washington after that, we called him Caunotaucarius.

The next morning he left us to go home with news of what he had seen among the French. We told him to wait and we would go with him, but he was in a great hurry. He built a raft. He fell into a river and almost drowned. He spent a night in frozen buckskins. A weaker man would have died. But Caunotaucarius was strong.

## Hesperus Draper:

The news Washington brought back scared Governor Dinwiddie right out of his peruke. Sent him runnin' to the King's Council, cryin' that they needed a Virginia regiment to stop the French from takin' the Ohio Valley.

Dinwiddie even had Washington's journal printed to show that the French were buildin' canoes and makin' plans. Some in the council said it was all a ruse to protect the interests of the Ohio Company, and they were half right. Others read Washington's journal and said that if we did nothin', we'd have French rats comin' through our back doors afore we knew it, and they were only half wrong.

So Adjutant Washington was ordered to raise a company up in Alexandria. Come March he set up headquarters and put out the word. But there wasn't many who wanted to risk their necks, especially for the Ohio Company.

I was in Alexandria, still workin' for my uncle, still payin' back the money I'd lost, keepin' his books, stokin' his fire, sweepin' out his office. Had no more interest in soldierin' than in wearin' a skirt.

Then Dinwiddie sent out a proclamation titled, "Encouragement to the People to Enlist with Spirit." 'Twas put up in broadsides all around town. Dinwiddie was offerin' a bounty, a share of 200,000 acres of good bottomland on the east bank of Ohio River just below the Forks, "to such persons who by their voluntary engagement and good behavior in the said service shall deserve the same."

All we needed to do was to show up with powder and musket, do our duty, and the land would be ours. And the longer we served, the more land we'd get.

Next mornin' I was at the sign-up desk at Market Square. Lined up ahead of me was some sorry-lookin' fellers—drifters, tavern dregs, troublemakers. But there were a few like me—office boys and countin' house hackers who knew there'd never be a chance like this again, a chance to own land in the great Ohio Valley. And my friend Eli Stitch was there, too.

Now, if you want to know why I never had any love for Washington, remember who Dinwiddie wrote that proclamation for—*enlistees*. Not officers.

The snow was sprinklin' down, and Washington was standin' aside his sergeant and his drummer boy, watchin' with that flat, steady gaze of his, watchin' every man who signed up as if he could look right into their bellies and know if they'd be good soldiers.

With the gals at the dances, that gaze made him seem as interestin' as a fireplace brick. But in a recruitin' line, his face was like confidence itself. Think of Rule Number Nineteen: "Let your countenance be pleasant but, in serious matters, somewhat grave." 'Twas the face of a man that nothin' could fluster, no matter how flustered he might really be in his belly.

He was just twenty-two, still had all his teeth, reddish brown hair, and he stood taller than anyone in sight. Six feet and three. His tricorne added another three inches to that. And his red uniform—red coat, red waistcoat, red breeches—fit him like bark fits a tree.

He give me a nod after I signed, and he said, "I was hoping to attract men with frontier experience, Draper."

" 'Twas the land bounty that attracted me," I answered.

"You knew how to charm Indians with a mantel-piece clock back in '48. Are your frontier instincts still good?"

I thought a lie might get me a better position, but it might also get me some trouble. So I said, "I haven't been on the frontier since that trip, George . . . sir."

"You'll be there soon enough."

'Twas early spring. Sap was runnin' in the trees. Runnin' in the recruits, too. But for all the talk at Williamsburg 'bout raisin' a regiment and payin' 'em right, nobody'd paid us a penny. Most of the boys didn't have the money to go up to that house on the north edge of town where an old hag named Chastity Dibble kept three girls in her upstairs rooms and two loaded pistols in her skirt.

She also kept two nigras in the parlor. One played the fiddle, the other played the flute. Always had 'em playin' quick little jaunty tunes. Think she done it to speed up the beat of things in the rooms. 'Twas for certain the music done nothin' to cover up the thumpin' and the gruntin' and the other sounds in that house.

And while waitin' your turn, not only did you have to listen to the music, you had to *look* at Chastity.

And *talk* to her. She talked like the whore she was, about the ways the girls could pleasure us, with—how'd she put it?—"quims as soft as beaver pelts, as warm and juicy as melons in the sun." Guess she figured if she talked like that, we'd be primed and ready when we got to the girls. She didn't know that if you looked at her too long, you'd lose the urge altogether.

She'd floated so far down the river of time 'twas a wonder she hadn't been swept under years ago. Even *looked* waterlogged. Body saggin', face all pruned up. Filled her wrinkles with flour and painted her lips bright red. But when she made that smile and said, "Dearie, your wench is waitin'," most men decided she was the beautifullest thing they'd ever seen, so long's they had the money to pay.

That's where I come in.

Even workin' off my debt to my uncle, I'd been savin' a few coins, so I was in a position to lend the lads what they needed. So I started doin' what the London Stock Exchange calls futures tradin'. I'd advance a lad some janglin' money, but he had to sign over a share of his bounty on the Ohio. 'Twas like stealin', but there's some things a man'll pay just about anything to get, and 'tis always easier to make him pay with currency he ain't holdin' in his hand.

Soon enough I had three more full shares. So long's I kept my face to the enemy when the fightin' started, I'd have me a fine estate on a fine big river when that war was over.

Had a few coins left to spend at Chastity's, too. Went up there one night when there wasn't much business. The nigras were playin' somethin' slow and soft—"Greensleeves," I think—and the girls was just sittin' there, listenin'. Looked kind of homey, kind of sad.

But at the sight of me, Chastity pulled her red lips into a smile and give me an "Evenin', soldier." Then she told me I could have my pick of the girls—Nancy, Diana, or the new girl, named Bee.

Well, Nancy looked like a young Chastity, with even more face paint.

Diana I'd had before. Called herself fashionable. Wore a corset that pushed her breasts up so high you could see her nipples. Wore her hair like women in Europe. Stuffed it under a foot-high wig that was supposed to make her look elegant, which maybe it done for fashionable European ladies. But when you spend your time on your back in a corset that shows your titties, a tall wig won't give you any elegance at all, especially when it looks like there's things nestin' in it.

But this Bee had a fresh look, like the newcomer she was. And for some reason, 'twas a familiar look, too. She had nice yeller hair that she didn't do much more than comb. She was a full-bodied woman. Looked like she might have some strength in her. And when she smiled, she showed real good teeth. Always liked good teeth.

Up in her room we got right down to business. She slipped off her skirt and shirt but left on her corset and stockin's, which was black. Always like that milk-white skin 'tween the top of the stockin's and the bottom of the corset.

Down in the parlor the nigras started playin' somethin' quick, with a jaunty beat, like the music was tryin' to poke holes in the air, a marchin' tune called "The World Turned Upside Down."

We didn't turn the world upside down. She wasn't near so experienced as Diana, but I liked her more. Liked her enough that I wanted to talk to her while

I was pullin' up my breeches. Asked her where she was from.

She just said, "Here and there. What about you?"

I said, "I'm a poor honest Chotank boy. Joined the Virginia Regiment to get me some of that land out on the Ohio."

"Pretty country out that way," she said, "but hard, hard as a Dutchman's heart."

"You been out there?"

"Lived out there some. Finished with that now."

I took a shillin' from my pocket and put it on the little table beside the bed. Then I saw the hat hangin' on a peg on the wall, the fine red-feathered hat I'd bartered to find a river crossin' some four years before. And I knew where she'd lived, and who the hard-hearted Dutchman was.

I looked at her and said, "Mrs. Beverly Mensing. I reckon you like the hat."

There was no more than a candle lightin' the room, but 'twas enough for me to see how wide her eyes went.

"How do . . . *You*. The peddler . . . I thought you drowned."

"No. Just my slaves."

"That hat was the only nice thing that ol' Dutchman ever give me. Most of the time, all he give me was the back of his hand."

"You'd never know," I lied. Looked like her husband hit her more than once. Had a crook in her nose like the bend of a dog's hind leg.

She flashed them nice teeth; then her smile guttered like the candle in the corner. "I run away. Couldn't take it no more. You ever see him, you won't tell him what I'm doin', will you?"

"Hell, no. Thought he was an old son of a bitch."

"Me too." She threw back the covers. "Climb in here and I'll pay you back good and proper for that hat."

'Twas the best tumble of my life. And as soon as I could, I went back. And when I wasn't with her, I was thinkin' about her.

*C.D.—While transcribing my uncle's narrative, I received the first answer to one of my letters. It had only a short distance to travel, from Dr. James Craik in Alexandria.*

*Craik had known Washington from their young manhood until he closed Washington's eyes the last time. He said he would speak with me, if only to offer an antidote to my uncle's bilious opinions. We met at Gadsby's, and over several tankards of ale, this heavyset and prosperous-looking physician recalled a youth in which "we were all much trimmer around the middle and much lighter in the purse." He proved an invaluable resource, especially on Washington's life before the Revolution.*

## The Narrative of Dr. James Craik:

I was born near Dumfries, Scotland, in 1730 and educated at the University of Edinburgh. Nae having been born to the gentry, I determined to raise myself in the world by becoming a man of medicine, doctors holding the same standing in society as ministers and barristers. But there was a sufficiency of doctors in Edinburgh. So in the year of our Lord 1750, I migrated to the colony of Virginia, arriving in good time for the war about to start betwixt England and France. And wars, as anyone knows, make good opportunities for young physicians.

I was proud to sign my name and become the surgeon for George Washington's Virginia Regiment. His bravery and resource was the talk in all the taverns. Imagine a young laddie marchin' eight hundred miles in the middle of winter, just to look the French in the eye and give them the king's warning.

From the beginning, there was about him a reserved cordiality that he seldom shed. But I do not flatter myself to say that we became close colleagues who shared Madeira and conversation on many a night.

"The men seem a healthy lot, sir," said I after a day spent examining them. "Considering that, in the generality, they be nae the most clean-living sorts, I found rather few venereal diseases and skin rashes, rather more teeth—"

"Doctor," he said, "our best efforts have produced a force made up mostly of loose, idle men, destitute of home, many without clothes. I've written to the governor of our need for uniforms, but Williamsburg will give us no money."

I said, in my professional opinion, "Uniforms are of less importance, sir, than simple clothes and shoes. Some of these men be all but barefoot."

"We need uniforms, Doctor. 'Tis the nature of Indians to be taken by show. A uniformed force will give the Indians a much higher conception of our power when we march out among 'em."

But uniforms were nae forthcoming. When Washington suggested that the soldiers might receive an advance on their pay, with which to buy uniforms, he was rebuffed on that, too.

He blamed his troubles on his rank, which was a

festering boil to such a proud and sensitive young man. He hoped that by serving well in the colony, he would receive a king's commission. But a mere colonial major could never hope for royal advancement. So he wanted a promotion.

Indeed he complained so constantly to Williamsburg that he was finally raised from major to lieutenant colonel. But the letter that brought the commission also brought news that drove him toward the kind of cold fury he displayed whenever he thought he had been wronged. Dinwiddie told him that none of the colonial officers would receive the pay promised, the same pay as they would have received had they been in the British army.

"We *are* in the British army," George said. "We are in the service of the king."

"An outrage, sir," said I. "With one hand they give you your just due, and with the other they take it away."

"This cannot be Dinwiddie's work," said Washington, his face flushing as if from fever. "It must be the council."

"Indeed, sir," said I. "Small men of small mind."

Washington looked out at the Potomac. One of his companies was drilling on the riverbank—fifty amateur soldiers trying vainly to keep in step, like a line of goslings trying to keep in step with their mother. Then he said, "There's one on the council who's no small man. We'll go and see him. We'll see Colonel Fairfax. A visit from a physician might be just the thing for him."

Belvoir was a magnificent brick manor, as fine as anything you might see in Scotland, and the master was most busy in a large office on the first floor.

George introduced me as a physician in whom he placed high trust. I think he was worried about Colonel Fairfax. What sickness could have affected his mentor so extremely that he had declined the command of the Virginia Regiment?

"I need no doctor, gentlemen," said his honor, in an accent as fine as any ever heard at the Court of Saint James. "I'm simply too old to go riding into the wilderness to fight Indians or French."

But we prevailed upon the colonel to unbutton his waistcoat so that I might listen to his chest.

"You flatter me, George." Fairfax held his eyes on Washington while I placed an ear to his bony chest. "A war threatens . . . nay, it beckons . . . and you come here to see after my health."

"I must tell you," said George, "that I'm thinking about resigning."

I raised my head so quick that I bumped it on Colonel Fairfax's chin. I'm nae sure which hurt more. Head or chin. I said, "Resign?"

Colonel Fairfax waved me away. "What is all this about, George?"

"The council would cut my pay below that of regular British officers."

"But you're not a regular British officer, George."

"A man must value himself, sir. You've taught me that yourself."

"You're a proud one," said Fairfax. "Proud . . . but a bit too touchy."

"Many agree with me over the matter of pay, sir. My own officers—"

"Oh, yes, sir," said I, believing a united front was always best for military men to display, though I had only been a military man for two weeks.

"—and many in the House of Burgesses. If they cannot see to it that we are paid according to our service, I shall have to resign."

Fairfax hardened his voice. "Many years ago, George, we sought a midshipman's appointment for you because we knew what military glory could do to enhance a young man's reputation. Did we not?"

"Yes, sir."

"Do you still wish for glory?"

"Of course, sir."

"The first step to glory is service. So how can you speak of resignation?"

One of Washington's strengths was stubbornness. 'Twas also a weakness. "Because . . . because I believe myself to be in the right, sir."

Fairfax took the Dinwiddie letter and scanned it until he reached a passage which caused him to read aloud: "Our knowledge that the French are moving in force makes it necessary for you to march what soldiers you have immediately to the Ohio." He looked Washington in the eye. "The enemy approaches and you're worried over the punctilios of rank."

George kept his chin at a firm angle, but 'twas clear that the words of his mentor struck hard. "Without the punctilios of rank, our system will totter, sir."

At that moment a young lass came into the room, a long-necked beauty with black hair flowing halfway down her back and a straightforward gaze that belied the coquetry one expects from women so gifted by nature. This, I knew, was Sally Fairfax.

"Why, George!" she cried. "How dare you come to Belvoir and not announce yourself to me immediately?"

Doctors are observant people, observation being the most important of the diagnostic arts, and I observed young Washington leap to his feet, shift his weight from one foot to the other, and stammer—a sure sign of nerves—"It . . . it . . . it is your father-in-law who deserves our first attention, ma'am."

"But not your last at Belvoir, I hope."

"It may be his last," said Colonel Fairfax angrily, "if he ignores his good sense and follows his wounded pride. He wants to resign."

"Resign?" Sally furrowed her dark brow. "And leave our frontier exposed to the French?"

"That is his plan, but he does not reckon with my power in the governor's council." The colonel turned his attention to George. "Go back to your troops. Stand by them. Earn your reputation and military glory. I shall stand by *you* in the matter of pay and rank. You have my word."

"And you have *my* word," said Sally, "that if you resign, I shan't welcome you to Belvoir ever again." This was said with a small smile, suggesting she was not serious, and I could see now that she was a co-quette after all.

George gave her an exaggerated bow. "That, dear madam, would be a fate worse than . . . than waging war for a foot soldier's pay."

Colonel Fairfax cleared his throat, as if such inno-cent flirtation between his son's closest friend and his daughter-in-law was nae something of which he ap-proved or wished to witness. He said, "You should be ready to serve, George, though you receive not a brass farthing. 'Tis expected of a gentleman."

"Yes, sir. You're right, sir."

"And consider the responsibility placed in your hands." The colonel read the rest of the letter: "You are to act on the defensive, but if attempts are made to interrupt our settlements, you are to restrain the offenders, and in the case of resistance make prisoners of or kill them all. You are to conduct yourself as you find best for the furtherance of His Majesty's goals and the good of his dominion."

"Oh, George." Sally clasped her hands to her breast and all but swooned.

And there was no doubt but that these was stirring words. Here was a call to the defense of the Crown. We were soldiers of the king.

Soon after, with his face turned bravely to the west, his left hand holding the reins, his right hand pressed to his hip, his fractious mare prancing beneath him, Lieutenant Colonel George Washington, all of twenty-two years old, led one hundred and twenty men toward the Blue Ridge.

The race for the Forks of the Ohio had begun. On the one side was a small regiment of amateur soldiers. On the other, the army of France.

## John Britain,
## known as Silverheels:

In the first warm days, our scouts brought word: the French were coming in their canoes. Tanacharison went to the Forks of the Ohio to warn the British who had gone there to build a fort. But the British major said not to worry, because Washington—Caunotaucarius—was coming north with a great army.

Tanacharison said they should hurry their work so the fort would be ready if the French arrived first. He said his Mingoes would help. And so we did. And so we worked like women, or dogs. We worked until our muscles burned and knives of pain pierced our legs. We worked, but Caunotaucarius did not come.

By the fourth day we had raised the stockade all around. We were hanging the gate on greased hinges. We were almost done.

I had worked hard beside Tanacharison, so I was bold, and I asked him, "Why is it that we take the muskets that the French give, but still we are better friends to the English?"

"The English have been better friends to us. They are as foolish as the French, but our fathers smoked pipes with them in the past, and so do we."

I looked around at the sharpened logs of the stockade. They pierced the air like spears. "Is it good, sachem, to have a white man's fort in our land?"

"Once the fort is built, we will have a place to trade. We will bring pelts, and the English will trade muskets, blankets, brandy. What we cannot stop, we must welcome, so that we make it our own."

I looked out at the place where two rivers joined to make a third. The Ohio was big and brown in the sunlight. It carried the dirt of many mountains. It carried the cold of many snows. I wished to be like the river and flow away from this place.

But the next day the French came in four-man canoes. At first a few, then many, then many more. Three hundred canoes came—more than one thousand French. And behind the soldiers came heavy rafts with great cannon. They ran their canoes onto the bank. They formed on the meadow grass around the fort. They pointed their cannon at us.

The officer who ran the fort—his name was Ward—he

asked Tanacharison what they should do. I did not think this was a good sign. It was like Tanacharison asking an Englishman what we should do in the middle of the forest.

Tanacharison said, "Tell the French captain you are of no importance. Tell him he must take his message farther south. This will buy you time."

Ward did this.

And the French sent a message back: "Surrender in one hour or die."

Tanacharison began to shout, "They are dogs! I will cut their captain's throat. Then I will boil him and eat him, as they did to my father."

All the Mingoes made war cries. I looked at my friend, whose name, in English, was Slow Bird. I whispered, "Did the French eat Tanacharison's father?"

Slow Bird shrugged.

Tanacharison said he would salt the French flesh and pass it out among his tribes so that they could all eat it and gain strength. He said this with much anger and wild waving of arms.

Ward said, "Does this mean you do not wish to surrender?"

Tanacharison lowered his arms and whispered, "Only a fool would not surrender now. These things that I promise . . . I . . . I will do them later."

So we surrendered, but the French were merciful. They gave us brandy and told the English to go back to their lands in Virginia.

I was glad to be out of the fort. I was gladder to be alive.

Tanacharison sent me ahead with Ward to take a message to Caunotaucarius. Tanacharison said I was the fleetest of his warriors, like one with silver heels. That is how I was given my name.

We went hard down the trails and deer paths, hard through the greening woods. We went sixty miles or more, to the camp of Caunotaucarius at a place called Wills Creek. And my heart was saddened by what I saw.

This was no great army. There were maybe a hundred and twenty-five soldiers. And no colored suits, except on the officers. The rest wore dull clothes. Their cook fires made small smoke. Their tents looked flimsy, even in the spring sun. In front of the largest tent was the English flag. Inside was Caunotaucarius.

## Hesperus Draper:

I was guardin' Washington's tent when Ward and this Injun named Silverheels come into camp. I made the Injun wait outside. He held up this wampum belt, like 'twas supposed to mean somethin', but I just shook my head. He was no chief, and so far's I'd been told, only officers and chiefs got into Washington's tent. Didn't like playin' doorkeep, but I was followin' orders.

While I listened to Ward passin' the bad news, I eyed this Injun. Didn't get too close, 'cause he was pretty smelly. Smeared bear fat all over himself. Kept the bugs away. Most white men, too.

Injuns are strange creatures altogether. Strange to us, strange to each other. These Iroquois tribes wore their hair different from the Delawares I'd known, painted themselves different, too. This one had red paint goin' from his forehead down his cheek, around his chin, and up the other side, just like a big circle of blood. Scare the hell out of you, if you was given to such things.

But along about then we were more mad than scared.

You'd be mad, too, if you marched all the way from Alexandria to Winchester, expectin' wagons and supplies, and found nothin' but a few farmers pickin' their teeth and holdin' out their palms. From Winchester we'd pushed on to Wills Creek, where we were supposed to find pack animals and more supplies. If you call a squirrel a pack animal, we found 'em. And considerin' what was there for supplies, we didn't need more than squirrels to carry 'em.

And now came bad news from the Forks of the Ohio.

Washington called the Injun into the tent. Took the wampum belt from the Injun and read the Half-King's letter, written out by one of the interpreters.

"The Half-King says, 'Have good courage, and come as soon as possible. You will find us as ready to fight them as you are yourselves. We have sent this young man to see if you will come. If so, he is to return to us, that we may await you. If you do not come now, we are undone, and we shall never meet again.' "

For a minute or two, nobody said nothin'.

Then one of the officers—Captain Stephen, I think— he whispered, "By God, there's an ally."

Washington called me into his tent. "Draper, you heard that, and you've shown an instinctive understanding of the savage in the past. Any instincts now?"

That surprised me. Officers don't often ask privates

to speak their minds, especially in front of other officers. I couldn't tell if Washington was just stallin' or if he really wanted to hear what I had to say.

Decided I better sound smart. If officers think you're smart, they'll be less likely to sacrifice you when somebody has to be sacrificed. I give it all a bit of thought and fixed on one part of that letter. "This Half-King says he's as ready to fight as we are ourselves."

Washington nodded, grave as a priest.

So I kept talkin', feelin' more certain of myself, "If we don't show some backbone now, he'll just disappear into the woods."

"Yes." Washington looked at the others. "If we desert the Half-King, the Iroquois will desert us. But we're not strong enough to fight the French without reinforcements."

"So what do we do?" asked Lieutenant Van Braam, his translator.

I don't think Washington knew. So he did what he would later do hundreds of times: have a council of war, ask the opinions of his officers.

Now, we may have been short on supplies but if opinions were beefsteaks, we'd've et like kings.

Washington's officers were all older than he was, and more experienced. Captain Adam Stephen was a big-drinkin' Scots blusterer who'd been a surgeon on a British ship. Captain Hogg had fought at the Battle of Culloden. Van Braam had been in the Dutch army. And all of them had somethin' to say.

Washington listened. Cocked his head. Asked questions. Let them argue. And got them all to agree on a plan that wouldn't get us all killed or scalped but would still keep us in the field.

We'd push on to the place where Redstone Creek

meets the Monongahela, 'bout thirty miles upstream from the Forks. There was a storehouse there, built by the Ohio Company. He said it would make a good place to strike from, and we could run like hell if the French came after us.

Then he wrote a letter to the Half-King. 'Twas full of compliments, to keep the Injuns happy, and full of lies, to keep 'em loyal. It thanked them "from hearts glowing with great affection." It said the French had caused only a small bump in our plans, 'cause we were "a small part of the army advancing toward you, clearing the road for a great number of our warriors that are immediately to follow with our great guns, our ammunition, and our provisions."

We said "great" a lot, but there was no great army comin' after us, no great nothin', just enough reinforcements so that eventually we'd have to fight or dishonor ourselves.

Washington gave Silverheels another belt of wampum, like a safe conduct, and we watched him go runnin' off into the dark, wet woods.

Van Braam said, "They are strange-looking creatures."

"Strange-looking and strange-acting," said Washington. "Human only in their form."

I said nothin'. Wasn't my place. But I didn't like it that Washington thought so little of the Injuns. Not human? There's nothin' more murderous than a human, and no human can be more murderous than an Injun. Best respect him.


Now, let me tell you about buildin' roads. 'T'ain't near so much fun as soldierin'. And considerin' that soldierin' is about as pleasant as havin' dysentery on a cake of ice, imagine what it's like to be a soldier buildin' a road.

Cuttin' trees, pullin' stumps, smoothin' grades . . . made two miles most days. Best we ever done was four. Absolute hell. Followed an Injun trail over Great Savage Mountain, more than two thousand feet high, then down into a forest called the Shades of Death, maybe the darkest, wettest woods we saw in a spring that men said was the wettest they could remember. Then we went over Negro Mountain. And every step of the way, we fought black flies and mosquitoes that bit so bad both my eyes closed up, and I couldn't see to walk, never mind chop down trees.

And every day we met more scared trappers, haulin' their pelts and their goods, bringin' stories of the French. First eight hundred was comin' . . . then nine . . . then a thousand . . .

Finally we reached a place called the Great Meadows, 'bout fifteen miles from Redstone Creek. Remember stories about the deserts in Araby, about how men felt when they finally come to an oasis? Well, the Great Meadows was like an oasis to us.

After a month in the woods, we looked out on grass, tall grass wavin' in the breeze of a day as bright as a gold guinea coin, two miles of grass, with wooded hills on both sides and two streams joinin' right in the middle. The ground was a little wet, but the streams meant good water, and the grass meant good forage.

Washington set us to work clearin' bushes from the meadow, givin' clear paths for musket fire. 'Twas like pickin' flowers after a month of cuttin' trees, and by nightfall, we were done.

Things were quiet. Most of the men were eatin'. I

moved out for picket duty. I was leanin' on my musket, watchin' a bird swoopin' and dartin' over the meadow. Washington come up beside me, hatless, coatless, fingers inkstained from writin' letters to Dinwiddie. And for a few minutes, we just stood there, listenin' to the soft evenin' sounds.

Washington was lookin' out across the meadows toward the hills, like he could see the future. Then he muttered something.

I didn't know if I was supposed to hear it, so I said, "Sir?"

He looked at me, "I said, 'A charming field for an encounter.' "

"Encounter?" said I. "You mean a battle?"

"It's why we're here, isn't it, Draper? To fight for king and country?"

Wasn't why I was there. And if there was a battle, I was plannin' on fightin' from behind one of the wagons. But I just said, "Yes, sir."

"A charming field for an encounter," he said again. Then he went walkin' through the tall grass like he was seein' a battle take shape, fightin' it in his head.

I knew right then that we were in for trouble. Our leader was just another boy soldier lookin' for glory.

Washington's slave was fetchin' a bucket of water. Name was Jester. Little scrawny feller, nothin' like that big Jacob back at Mount Vernon. I wondered what Jester made of his master's musin's. So I said, "Charmin', ain't it?"

And he said, "Oh, yassuh, charmin' night. Make you glad you's alive."

Poor bastard, he had no idea. . . .

\* \* \*

Next evenin', just after dark, that Silverheels come stumblin' into camp with a message from the Half-King for Washington: "We find French raiding party. Thirty-five, maybe forty. Six mile. Come quick."

Washington didn't even call an officers' council. He just said, "We must strike them before they strike us."

An hour later we set off in a light rain with Silverheels in the lead, Washington close behind, and about forty of us followin', Injun style, one after the next, so we wouldn't get lost in the dark. Like a march of blind men.

If ever the woods was dark and wet, 'twas that night. Dark to black and waterfall-wet. Rained so hard the water filled up the brim of my hat and started pourin' down over all three corners at once. We kept our powder horns covered and our flints in our cartouche boxes, but there wasn't a one of us thought that our muskets would fire when the time come.

I was followin' the big arse of Eli Stitch, and Henry Dundee was bumpin' along behind me, and he never shut up. 'Twas "Bejesus this" and "Mother of Christ that" and "God damn it all to hell" every minute. But mostly I couldn't hear him over the roar of the rain. Felt him plenty, though. Kept steppin' on my heels and walkin' into me when I stopped.

We finally come to the camp of Tanacharison, the Half-King, just about the time we could see shapes brightenin' around us, and all we found was seven Injuns. And two of them was no more than boys.

As for the Half-King, he was just another savage. Plucked his hair into a little ridge at the top of his head. Used bear grease to make it stand up. Wore a long scalp lock down his back, like most Iroquois.

Had little lines tattooed across his forehead, a streak of yellow paint across his eyes, and a ratty red blanket over his shoulders. Pretty sorry king.

Leastways, the rain had stopped.

## John Britain,
## known as Silverheels:

I was glad to come to Tanacharison's camp in the first graying of the sky.

I was glad, because Caunotaucarius was very mad. He thought I was a bad scout. Once, I walked into a tree, and he called me a foolish savage. I did not like him.

Tanacharison said, "We have found the French. They are the ones that boiled and ate my father."

I do not think Caunotaucarius believed this. But I knew it was true, even if it never happened.

Tanacharison said that we should attack right away, before the day went further, before the French could attack us and boil and eat Caunotaucarius.

"I would be hard to swallow," said Caunotaucarius. "But we will attack."

## Hesperus Draper:

We smelled the French cook fires 'fore we saw the smoke. 'Course, with the air so heavy and gray after the rain, everything looked a little smoky.

I remember comin' down, down through tall trees,

down toward a rocky outcrop that dropped away to nothin'. One of the scouts said the French were camped below, in a little glen, a little horseshoe of rock open to the forest at the far end. We had 'em right where we wanted 'em.

But I kept askin' myself the same questions. Was the powder dry? Would the flint spark? Could I kill a man? Then I'd think of that land at the Forks and my courage'd come right back.

I wasn't much of a soldier, but it looked like this French raidin' party was even worse. No pickets. Didn't hide themselves. Went clatterin' pans and chatterin' and singin' some silly song down below. But nobody had declared a war so far as we knew. Washington was just actin' on his own hook.

He took off his hat and snuck to the edge of the rocks, so he could peer down. Then he started makin' hand signals. Don't recall that his hand shook. Don't think he had a second thought about the ambush he was about to spring.

Stephen moved off to the right. The Half-King and his Injuns slithered away as silent as snakes, to cut off escape through the woods below. And the rest of us slipped out, keepin' low, holdin' our cover, waitin' for the word.

And who do you think spoiled the surprise? The boy soldier himself. 'Fore we were in position, he let the French see his red uniform. And they started screamin', "Les Anglais! Les Anglais!"

Now I got a clear look at 'em—men just wakin' up, some wearin' nothin' but shirts and boots, a few pullin' on their breeches, others bare-assed and ballocky and stumblin' for their pants and their muskets at the same time.

But for all that, one of *them* got off the first shot. A bullet hit the boulder right beside Washington's ear and went whinin' away. He didn't even duck. He just give a little twitch at the sound so close to him. He stood up straight, right on the lip of the rocks, all but darin' the French to shoot at him again, and he screamed, "Fire!"

But we were all weak-kneed amateurs more used to shootin' at ducks than men. Our first volley was just a lot of little pops and loud bangs, pan flashes and muzzle blasts, and smoke comin' out in clouds all around, clouds billowin' up above us and clouds fillin' that little glen, too.

I know my musket went off. I don't know that I hit anyone. Saw some Frenchmen go down, though. They tried to answer our fire, so we gave them another volley. 'Twas better than the first, and it convinced them 'twas time to run.

So they went scurryin' toward the woods at the open end of the horseshoe. That's when they got the ugliest surprise of their French lives, and I heard somethin' that made my blood go colder than a January wagon wheel. 'Twas the screamin' of the Injuns.

I'd never heard it before, and I hoped never to hear it again.

The French run right into them, right into a volley from the muskets they'd given those Injuns as presents. And the next thing you knew, the French was runnin' back toward us, and one of them, he was wavin' a white handkerchief and screamin' in French.

Washington jumped to the edge of the rocks, and called for us to hold our fire. But the bad part was only just beginning.

# John Britain,
# known as Silverheels:

Our blood was up. Our anger at the French was great. They had invaded our land. They had boiled and eaten our fathers.

Tanacharison gave a war cry and ran into the glen.

Seeing his bravery made me brave. I gave a war cry and followed him. I told myself that the first Frenchman I found I would scalp.

I saw one on the ground. His shirt was bunched up at his waist. He wore no breeches so his balls hung like a toy between his legs. He had been shot in the hip and was crying out. I went to finish him and take his scalp, but Slow Bird reached him first. The man put up his hands, but Slow Bird was quick with his club. He brought it down hard on the Frenchman's skull. So I ran on.

All was confusion.

The English were coming down from the rocks. The French were throwing down their weapons and running toward their white brothers. And we were running to get ourselves between the English and the French, so that we could take prisoners, which was our right as warriors.

A bird flew overhead. He fluttered, as if he did not know the place where he came each morning. Then he flew away. I thought he was a wise bird.

Caunotaucarius was shouting, pointing this way and that, and the word changer Van Braam was telling him what the French were saying. Some French were shouting. Other were moaning like women.

Caunotaucarius looked from one face to another,

as if he was not certain where to look. I told you, all was confusion.

And now Tanacharison said to Caunotaucarius, "I demand my prisoners."

Caunotaucarius said, "I demand that you stop killing the wounded."

Tanacharison said, "They are our prisoners. And I want others."

This was the way of Iroquois war.

"They are *my* prisoners," said Caunotaucarius, and he turned his back on Tanacharison.

He was insulting Tanacharison in front of his warriors. Again our sachem would not let this insult anger him. A warrior must fight with fury but not anger. Tanacharison would not strike Caunotaucarius, but he would take what was his. So he turned to the French leader, who was pouring out a river of French words.

## Hesperus Draper:

I was guardin' the head Frenchman. Watchin' his mouth, listenin' close, figurin' if I did, I could understand his jabber. Concentratin' so hard I didn't even see the Half-King come up behind me.

He pushed me out of the way. Then he shoved his face right up to this Frenchman and he said, "You French?"

And the Frenchman just looked at him. Acted like this Injun was vermin, which I suppose he was. Wrinkled his nose, like the Injun stunk, which I know he did. Then looked over at where Washington was givin' orders and started shoutin' again, all in French, like the Injun wasn't even there, which he surely was.

The Half-King didn't like this at all. He knew this

was the head Frenchman, and he hated Frenchmen. So, 'fore I had any inklin' of what he was doin', he pulled out his tomahawk, planted his feet, and stove in that Frenchman's skull like he was bustin' in a barrel.

The Frenchman went down like a poleaxed horse, and the Half-King—half man, half beast, if you ask me—dropped right down on top of him.

His warriors closed tight in around him, made a wall to protect him while he slammed that tomahawk down again. Blood splattered everywhere. Then that damn savage shoved his hands right into the Frenchman's skull! Right into his head! Come out with two fistfuls of brain, all gray and red and, I swear, still pulsin' with that Frenchman's thoughts.

And his warriors all screamed and hooted. This was how they expected their chief to treat his enemies, especially the ones who'd boiled and eaten his father.

Then the Half-King pulled out his knife and sliced off the Frenchman's scalp, neat as you please. I almost puked. But he wasn't finished. He saw another French prisoner, a dark, squat feller, and he ran at him.

This time Washington stepped in front of him, actin' like he didn't even see the blood and the brains still drippin' from the Half-King's hands, like he wasn't surprised by anything that the heart of a savage could invent. Looked hard at this Injun and said, "No more killing."

And the Half-King's bloodthirst must have been slaked, because he backed off, but he held that scalp up and waved it at the other Frenchman. Then he waved it at Washington for good measure.

The Frenchman spat. Washington turned away, chewin' on his cheek, tryin' to keep from cursin', or maybe from pukin'.

* * *

The last I saw of that little glen, the Injuns was plunderin' the French baggage, and the head of some dead Frenchman—had a fine mustache and a black chin beard—was lookin' down on everything from the top of a sharpened pole.

There was ten dead Frenchmen and one dead Virginian. I didn't think on how stupid 'twas to give up your life in a little forest fight. I was just glad to be marchin' back to the Great Meadows. And so was the survivin' French.

But once we were on the trail, the French officer—the dark, squat one—he started askin' questions. And he spoke good English, so Van Braam didn't have to translate. "Are we being treated as prisoners or emissaries?"

Washington said, "You are prisoners, of course."

"But the one who lost his brains, Coulon de Jumonville, he was sent as an emissary, sent from Governor DuQuesne."

That stopped Washington right in his tracks.

The Frenchman almost grinned. "Yes . . . the papers you took from his body, they were his orders to meet with you and tell you peaceably to leave."

Washington took the papers out of his pocket and glanced at them. But they were all in French, so I knew he couldn't read them.

The Frenchman knew it, too, so he just kept talkin'. "We should be treated as you were treated last winter. With respect."

'Twas plain that Washington was surprised. I could see the wheels turnin' inside his head. If this was a French emissary and his escort, the boy soldier had blundered, and his Indian ally had committed one heinous murder.

Washington told the Frenchman, "Last winter I traveled in the open. I did not hide in obscure places surrounded by rocks. You came to spy on us and attack us."

Then he had Van Braam translate the papers, and sure enough, they carrried diplomatic intructions. They also carried orders for the French "emissary" to set down how many of us there were and what we were doin'. That made them all spies.

Still, no matter how close you shaved it, our attack was an act of war. 'Twas as if that little rock-walled glen was a powder keg and Washington walked up and set a match to it. And one blast would set off another, because those French at the Ohio Forks, they'd hit us hard now.

Back at the Great Meadows, Washington told his officers, "If we do not get reinforcements, we must either retreat or fight very unequal numbers. But that's what I'll do before I give up one inch of what we've gained."

The officers looked at each other and shook their heads. A few rolled their eyes.

The boy soldier looked out at the meadow again, at that charmin' field for an encounter. Then he ordered the men to build a fort right in the middle of it.

# John Britain,
# known as Silverheels:

I brought my woman to the Great Meadows. Her name was Bright Leaf. She was big with child. I thought that at the Great Meadows she would be safe. That was before I saw the fort they were building.

It was weaker than what they had built at the Forks, which the French took in ten minutes.

Tanacharison told Caunotaucarius, "This fort will not stand against the wind that soon will blow."

Caunotaucarius answered, "It will withstand an army of five hundred men."

"What if six hundred come to fight you?"

Caunotaucarius spoke with great certainty, "The French will engage us in line of battle, out in the meadow. After we've volleyed and weakened them, we'll fall back to our entrenchments and rake them with our four-pounders."

Later Tanacharison came to my wigwam. He said that he liked to see my wife's belly filling with life. He asked if he could touch it. I was very proud.

Tanacharison said that the child would be a brave boy. Then he looked out across the meadow to the puny English fort. He said, "Caunotaucarius is a good-natured man, but he has no experience. He will not win the fight that is coming."

# Dr. James Craik:

It has been said that George Washington had nae sense of humor. The same has been said of the Scots. But on the day I arrived at the Great Meadows, as part of the first reinforcing column, I would have laughed like a fool at what Washington had built there, except that he planned to fight there.

He had raised a circle of pointed logs, forty feet in diameter, with a wee shed in the middle. Trenches surrounded the stockade, and the wigwams of our Indian allies spread out beyond the trenches. To my medical eye, it gave the impression of some kind of concentric fungus—ringworm, perhaps—growing on the green meadow grass. The name that Washington had given to this place, with nae sense of irony, was Fort Necessity.

The necessity most pressing was for more reinforcements. They arrived a few days later, heralded by the sound of fife and drums in the wilderness: the independent company from North Carolina. They were easy to sight even before they emerged from the woods—a hundred men in scarlet coats, led by a mounted officer in a white wig. They brought great rejoicing to the camp, as they were driving some sixty head of cattle.

Everyone went out to greet them—the men, the officers, and our Indian allies, too, though the Indians were happier to see the cattle than the soldiers. The Half-King had brought about a hundred of his people to the Great Meadows, and they had all brought their appetites.

Now, this independent company had a special distinction. They were colonials, but their commissions came direct from the king. So they were considered superior to provincial soldiers like ourselves and were better paid because of it. Their demeanor made it plain that such knowledge was nae lost upon them.

In a letter, Dinwiddie had warned Washington to treat them with respect: "As the officers of the independent company are gentlemen of experience in the art military, are jealous of their honor, and come well recommended, I hope you will conduct yourselves toward them with prudence and receive their advice with candor, as the most probable means of promoting His Majesty's service and the success of the expedition."

"Does this mean you give orders to them, or they to us?" I asked.

"That," Washington answered, "is a delicate question."

And no one was more delicate about such matters than himself. Washington had threatened to resign once again, a week before the fight with the French, so misused did he feel by the powers in Williamsburg.

He had read to me a part of his letter to Dinwiddie: "I could enumerate a thousand difficulties we have met with, more than other officers who receive double our pay. Giving up my commission is contrary to my intention. But let me serve voluntarily and I will devote my services to the expedition without any other reward than the satisfaction of serving my country; but to be slaving dangerously for a shadow of pay, through woods, rocks, mountains—I would prefer the toil of a daily laborer."

Rank and pay, pay and rank. It played like a reel in all our heads.

Of these North Carolinians he said, "I expect that their officers will have more sense than to insist upon unreasonable distinctions. I'll make it clear to them that though they have king's commissions, we have the same spirit to serve."

However clear Washington made it, their commanding officer dinna see it. From the first, James Mackay treated Washington correctly but nae subserviently, though his rank was two levels lower. He gave our little palisade a disdainful look and said he and his men would choose their own campsite.

Washington bowed graciously.

Around dusk, with the cook fires rising and the smell of fresh beef bringing juices to every mouth on the meadow, Washington sent Hesperus Draper—he wasn't a carbuncle then, merely a wee pimple—over to Mackay's tent with the parole and countersign, the nightly password in the camp.

A few minutes later, Draper returned: "Captain Mackay rejects the passwords . . . respectfully. Says he ain't required to accept orders of any kind, on any matter, from a colonial of any rank . . . sir."

I remember a smile crossing Draper's skinny face, as though he thought this was just silliness. Of course, it wasn't.

Washington's face reddened, and he snapped, "Who is to give the passwords if not myself?"

## Hesperus Draper:

Some people thought the business with Mackay was silliness, just a pair of jealous officers pissin' on their turf like he-dogs. But 'twas more than that.

Why should troops commissioned by the king get

better pay for less work than good, honest colonials? What made them so special? Think about where that line of reasonin' can lead, and you'll see what it could grow into.

Next mornin' I was guardin' Washington's tent when Mackay come by.

Beneath the white wig and the banty-rooster strut, this Mackay was a good soldier, but stubborn. He said, "Colonel, a colonial governor cannot issue a commission to supersede mine."

Washington said, "Nor does your commission supersede *mine*, sir."

Mackay answered, "I am sure you know, sir, that a royal commission supersedes *any* colonial commission."

"I am a colonel, sir," answered Washington. "With all due respect, a captain cannot supersede a colonel."

"With equally due respect, sir, your governor cannot give commissions that command me, sir."

Even with all the *sirrin'*, 'twas plain they were gettin' nowhere fast. Finally Washington said, "But you will join us in road building, will you not?"

"My men are soldiers, sir, not laborers," answered Mackay. "If they are to build roads, they will have need of another shilling of pay per day."

Washington's voice got a little higher, the way it did when he was tryin' to control himself. "My men are paid nothing extra for building the road."

"Blame that on their commissions, or lack thereof."

Washington stood. He was gettin' red, gettin' mad, and gettin' Mackay out of his tent. "I think, sir, that it would be best if we operate our commands as allied but independent."

"That, sir, is why we are called an independent company."

'Twas all very correct, all very precise, and much more serious than silly.

What *was* silly was Washington's decision to keep buildin' the road toward Redstone Creek. We had our reinforcements, and the French still outnumbered us. The road would just bring them down our throats that much faster.

But the next day Washington had the wagons loaded with shovels and supplies, and the regiment was mustered. If he couldn't stay in his own camp and give the orders, he'd leave the camp to the North Carolinians and take to the road.

# John Britain,
# known as Silverheels:

Tanacharison said the forest was like a lake. The white men were swimmers. And we were fish. The fish know the currents and the sandbars and the places where the springs come into the lake. The swimmer must make friends with the fish or drown. So Caunotaucarius asked Tanacharison to call the tribes to a council.

Mostly Delawares and Shawnees came. Some of the Six Nations. Even some Mingoes came who did not like the English.

We met at a plantation on the road between Fort Necessity and Redstone Creek. We drank brandy. We heard speeches.

Caunotaucarius even let the unfriendly Mingoes speak. Their leader was called Hardhand in your language. He was of the clan of the Eel. But he looked more like a porcupine, his hair all bristles, his weapons all sharp. He said, "We have heard that the English will attack every village that will not march with them."

Caunotaucarius said, "That is not true."

"We have also heard that the French are going to drive the English back over the eastern mountains."

Caunotaucarius said, "That is not true."

"You say these things are not true, but we believe the truth we see. You are weak, and the French are strong. They have built a great fort at the Ohio Forks. You have built a little circle of logs at the Great Meadows."

Caunotaucarius stood and did the magic that made him taller than he was. "I am the vanguard of an army coming to maintain your rights to put you in possession of your lands, to make the whole country yours."

He looked into the eyes of every Indian, to convince them of his truth. But Tanacharison would not meet his gaze. Tanacharison put his eyes on the ground because he had brought the tribes together to hear this lie. And he was sorry for it.

Caunotaucarius kept lying. "It is for the safety of your wives and children that we fight. This is our only motive. Join us to oppose the common enemy."

These fish knew that the swimmers would do what they always do after they swim. They would grow hungry. Then they would try to eat the fish.

After three days, a runner came with a wampum belt from the Great Council of the Iroquois at Onondaga. They decreed that the Iroquois and their vassals, the Shawnees and Delawares, should do nothing in the fight between the English and French, "nothing but what was reasonable."

To the Delawares, this meant to stay out. To the Shawnees, it meant to join the French. To our mixed band of Mingoes and Senecas, it meant we should look out for ourselves. So Tanacharison led us back to the Great Meadows.

I heard Caunotaucarius say to the doctor named Craik, "If I had gifts to give them, I could have brought them all to our side."

*Gifts.* That was all he thought we would need. I was beginning to think that Caunotaucarius was a great fool.

## Hesperus Draper:

Our Injun allies had decided to sit back and watch. Our North Carolina allies wouldn't lift a finger, except to drill and look pretty in their red suits. And then we got the news we'd been expectin': the French were comin' in force.

At first Washington wanted to dig in and fight where he was. Then he changed his mind, which he could do as often as a woman with her monthlies comin' on, and he fell back to the Great Meadows.

That retreat was the longest thirteen miles of my life. Imagine pullin' cannon over a rutted, stump-filled road in the kind of damp heat that gives you a prickly rash 'tween your legs even when you're someplace civilized and can change your breeches every week. And worse than the heat, there wasn't an ounce of food waitin' for us at the Great Meadows. Washington might have kept runnin', but he knew we were too damn tired and weak. Better to meet the French there on that charmin' field than on some forest road.

So he set us to diggin' in the four-pounders. The

guns wouldn't be much good for knockin' down troops at a distance, but if we loaded 'em with grapeshot and the French got close, we could do some fine damage. Even the independents lent a hand, which I took as a sign of how bad things was gettin'.

Me and a few of the boys were diggin' in a gun when I sensed someone lookin' at me. 'Twas the Half-King, suckin' on a little dip of tobacco, spittin' every now and then, watchin' us with the snake eyes you see on an Injun sometimes, when he's lookin' at you like he's tryin' to figure out how to swallow you whole. Then he just shook his head and went off.

Later I heard him advisin' Washington to leave.

Washington said, "I told you. This fort will withstand an army of five hundred."

The Half-King just laughed. 'Twas the first time I'd heard that, and it scared me more than seein' the independents swingin' shovels.

Then Washington said, "Send out your scouts."

The Half-King said, "You will not order us to fight in a bad place." And he started pointin' here and there, goin' on like a preacher, tellin' Washington his sins. "You have not cleared the woods beyond musket shot. Your trenches are dug by a stream, so they will fill with water if it rains. Your men are starving. And you think the French will fight standing out in the field, as if they are stupid."

"I'll say it again"—Washington raised his chin— "send out your scouts."

Well, the Half-King didn't send out scouts. Didn't do much of anything the rest of the day but sit in front of his wigwam and spit tobacco. Then, around dusk, his people packed up and disappeared into the forest.

That scared me more than anything.

*  *  *

And the savage was right—about the French, the rain, the whole damn fight.

Come the mornin' of July 3. Cloudy and hot. Been rainin' like hell and looked like 'twas fixin' to rain again. In between downpours, a scout come in with news: the French and Injuns were just over the ridge, and they were *all naked!*

Well, the Injuns were mostly naked, but the French were dressed like regulars, in powder-blue coats, or like trappers, in the same kind of buckskins and huntin' shirts we wore. They come into the meadow, knee-deep in the grass, and made a long, lazy skirmish line, with the Injuns movin' slow and easy on either side. I couldn't quite tell how many there was, 'cept there was a hell of a lot more of them than of us and a hell of a lot more than five hundred.

Washington was standin' out in front of our trenches, and he said to his captains, very calmly, "Bring the men into the field."

At the same time, Mackay called out to the independents, "Form line."

Now, *that* was silly. With the French comin', those two was still worried over who was givin' the orders. We formed up. Dressed our lines three deep. Stood ready to volley and fall back, then volley again and drop to the trenches.

Yes, sir, in the middle of the North American wilderness, the boy soldier had found the one place where he thought he could fight like a European.

The French fired a volley from about six hundred yards away, which made me feel better. Only fools fired from that far out. Then they came closer. We stood our ground, scared to death, knowin' we'd never knock them all down with one volley. But the French weren't fixin' to charge. Before they come into range, they stopped and loped off into the trees on either side of us, like they were goin' off to a picnic.

That was when I knew why the Half-King had been laughin'.

These French weren't fools. They'd learned their lessons from their Injun allies, and they knew good cover when they saw it. For a month we'd been settin' in that damn meadow, and nobody'd thought to cut the trees back on the hillsides. Now the French and Injuns had better cover than we did, and they could look down into our fort like we'd left up a ladder for them.

All we could do was hunker back in our trenches and wait. For a while, the Injuns whooped at us from the woods, like they were tryin' to beat us just by curdlin' our blood. When that didn't work, the bullets started flyin'. Never a big volley, mind you. Just a steady splatterin', like hailstones hittin' the sides of a house.

They killed our horses and the few stringy cows we still had. Even killed two or three of the camp dogs. And they killed plenty of us, too. The independents— had to hand it to them—they took the most exposed position and did most of the dyin'.

We tried to fight back. We kept our muskets poppin' and bangin', even after the rain started. Filled those trees with lead. Filled that little valley with smoke. And kept those four-pounders barkin' like beagles. Judgin' by noise alone, we were winnin'.

The bodies told another story.

Washington kept runnin' from one place to another, movin' quick and only crouchin' a little. One minute he was in the trenches, then over with Cap'n Stephen, then in the stockade. And every stop he made, he had more dead to count.

His slave, Jester, ran around behind him, doin' his biddin', and scared to death about it, too, considerin' the size of those white eyeballs in his black face. He was smart to be scared, because along about four o'clock, a musket ball took him in the stomach and he went down with a big bellow.

But there was no time for Washington to be worryin' about a gut-shot nigra. He called two men to get Jester into the stockade, and he kept right on movin', always movin', always lettin' his men see him. He'd gotten us into a hell of a spot, but he was actin' like he'd get us right out of it again.

"He's either the bravest boy soldier in the backwoods or too damn dumb to know they're shootin' at him," said Henry Dundee. That made me laugh.

Laughed more at the fix we were in than the joke. 'Twas late afternoon and rainin' harder. Water was ankle deep in our trench. Sides were all mud. We were all mud. Funny as hell.

But while I was laughin', a musket ball hit Henry at the base of the skull and come out his throat. He died gurglin' in the water at the bottom of the trench.

You'd have thought that after the fight in the glen, I wouldn't be shocked by the sight of blood. But this struck me hard. I liked Henry, even if he talked too much. I just slid down into the trench and damn near started cryin'.

Then it commenced to rainin' as hard as it had that whole miserable, foot-rottin', mushroom-makin', brain-soakin' spring. 'Twas the kind of rain that roared. Roared so loud, it drowned out the sound of the musket fire. Then it drowned out the musket fire 'cause all the powder got wet and nobody could get off a shot. Then it came damn near to drownin' all of us in the trenches. 'Fore long, we were waist-deep, with the water risin'.

And that was when we were most frightened, because if the French couldn't shoot at us, they knew we couldn't shoot back. Might decide to rush us with bayonets and tomahawks.

## Dr. James Craik:

Cutting off a limb is ugly business. The screaming is truly the wail of the banshee. The blood and the mess would sicken a vulture. And the sight of living bone, white and pure in the midst of bleeding meat, speaks volumes on the fragility of life itself.

All day, the men were brought to me, and I practiced the craft for which I was trained. Those I could help received the benefits of all I had learned. Those I could not received what laudanum I could spare. When the laudanum was gone, I opened one of the rum pipes stored in my hut, and I saw that each dying man received a dram or a draft, whichever he wished.

About an hour before dark, Washington came to see me. The rain was pounding so hard on the roof that I felt as if I were inside a drum. Water was leaking in. Sweat was pouring from my forehead and mixing with the water, and both were flowing down to mingle with the blood at my feet. And by now a hundred men, a third of our force, had been killed or wounded.

Washington still tried to wear a mask of calm, but

'twas hard with the sounds of suffering as loud as the rain and his own slave lying in a drunken stupor, quietly bleeding to death.

I told him there was naught I could do to save Jester.

"And what about these others? Are any of them fit to fight?"

There were twenty men crowded into the hut. Of the few who might have returned to the fight, none would even cast their eyes in his direction.

"Doctor"—Washington gestured for me to step outside, into the rain, where the wounded men would nae hear—"we are determined not to ask for quarter. We'll screw our bayonets tight and sell our lives as dearly as possible."

I'd had no time to consider the possibility of defeat . . . or death in this miserable wilderness. I swallowed the sick fear that rose in my throat like suet, and I told Washington that I would do all that I could to rally the wounded.

When I went back inside, I noticed that one of the rum pipes was missing. And a few moments later, after two soldiers had carried in a wounded man, I noticed that another was gone. Our soldiers had determined that they would nae sell their lives dearly at all. They preferred dying drunk to dying honorably.

## Hesperus Draper:

Men do strange things in the face of death. I admit that I did. Some of the boys got into the rum supply, and they was passin' a hogshead along the trench. I took a good long swaller, and the next time it come by, I took an even longer one, and when it come by a third time, I took the longest swaller yet. Eli Stitch had his share, too. In stomachs so empty as ours, this rum done its business like a match does business to a wick.

I don't recall which of us come up with the idea of givin' Henry Dundee a swaller to speed him to his reward. But we dragged him to a place in the trench where the water wasn't quite so deep. Then we sat him up like he was still alive. Put his musket in his hands, poured a bit of brandy onto his lips. Then we both toasted him and had a few more good swallers of our own.

'Twas gettin' near dark. Rain was lettin' up some. Washington was comin' along the trenches, tellin' us to bear up and be ready for whatever come next. Whether he could see that we were drunk or not, I don't know. In the half-light, I don't think he could even see that Henry was dead. But he must have seen how hopeless things were. I sure did.

Then the damnedest thing happened. Over the patter of the rain we heard a Frenchman shout, "*Voulez-vous parler?*"

Somebody said, "I think it means they want to talk."

"'Talk?'" That made me laugh.

## Dr. James Craik:

The French terms were so generous as to make us suspicious.

We learned later that they believed we were about to be reinforced, and so they wanted to end this quickly. We would be allowed to march out with the honors of war, under the British flag, and in possession of our arms, so long as our officers agreed not to invade land that belonged to the king of France for one year. Since none of us accepted that this land belonged to the king of France at all, 'twas a parole we could honorably accept.

Near midnight, negotiations was completed between the French and Jacob Van Braam, the only one of our number who could speak French.

In our wee hut, Van Braam tried to read to us the blotted, rain-splattered sheets he had translated, but we had only a single guttering candle for light, and his own writing was all but illegible, so he gave up and told us in his own words: "The first part says the French did not want to trouble the peace between England and France, but only to revenge the killing of Colon de Jumonville and his party, and to stop any English settlement on land claimed by their king."

Washington said, "I am to admit that we attacked the party in the glen?"

"The French insist," said Van Braam. "Jumonville, the one the Half-King killed, he was brother to the commander of the force surrounding us."

"Jumonville was leading a war party," said Washington. "He was a casualty of war, killed in the confusion of the fight."

"Then admit the truth," said Captain Mackay, "and take the terms."

Washington looked into the haggard faces of the officers around him, as if trying to discern their thoughts or gauge their endurance. Then he said, " 'Tis plain. I have no other choice."

The next day was July 4, a date that no man in our regiment could ever have seen himself celebrating. The British flag came down in the bright sunlight, and the French flag went up. What baggage we could nae carry was piled up and would, the French promised, be protected. So would the wounded, who would be staying under my care.

I worried much about them, and myself, because the Indian allies of the French had come into camp and were demanding prisoners. The French were refusing them the human spoils of war, but they could nae stop the Indians from breaking into our baggage, nor from stealing the mahogany medicine chest my father had given me when I left Scotland.

The one who did the stealing must have been practiced at it, as he had at some point stolen a mantelpiece clock. His breastplate was the clockface, and his earrings were the brass finials that once decorated the clock case.

The other Indians closed around him and began grabbing at the medicine chest, as a dog pack will when the bravest of them steals a piece of food. I took some pleasure in knowing that those savages would soon be consuming the contents of my medicine bottles and soon after that, some would be vomiting uncontrollably; others would be shitting as they never shat before, and still others would be in a stupor . . . all of which would serve them right.

## Hesperus Draper:

Yes, sir, my fine mantelpiece clock was now just decoration, and that Injun was just another plunderin' scavenger. Once I'd been awed by these savages. Now I was just disgusted. The sooner we swept 'em aside, the sooner we could make somethin' out of all that wilderness.

## John Britain, known as Silverheels:

We were not there when the English marched out. We had moved off into the woods. So Hardhand came to us and told us what had happened and said that we should all go over to the French.

He told of some who took the things that the English carried, which was their right as warriors. He told of taunting Caunotaucarius: "I called him brother. I asked him how he did on a day that he surrendered to the French."

But Hardhand said that Caunotaucarius did not lose his dignity. He kept his eyes ahead and did not answer Hardhand's taunts.

So Hardhand had spoke to Caunotaucarius the words that Caunotaucarius had once spoke to us: "The things I do, I do for the safety of our wives and children . . . *brother*."

Still, Caunotaucarius would not even look at Hardhand, which angered him.

Tanacharison was angry too. He said he would not go back to the English: "If Caunotaucarius is the best leader they have, they cannot win. He treated us like slaves when he should have treated us like brothers."

"They will both treat us like slaves," I said, "the French and the English both." I was no longer afraid to speak before my elders. My baby had been born. I had been in a fight. These things had made me a man.

"They are both no good," said Tanacharison. "The French acted as great cowards and the English as great fools in the fight."

"So who will we fight for?" I asked.

"We will do as the council says," Tanacharison answered. "We will watch out for ourselves. And we will watch out for your little boy."

Tanacharison was very wise.

But soon he drifted away. They say he went to the Mingo villages far to the west, on the banks of Lake Erie.

Later I heard that a sickness came upon him. He was not old, but his strength left him fast. They say it flowed out like water from a leaky gourd. He lost his heart. He lost his hope. I was very sad when I heard. But it was only a small sadness compared to those that would come to us all.

## Hesperus Draper:

In French, the word for "assassin" is "*l'assassin.*"
Now, I don't know how in hell a man could see
that word in a surrender and not get the idea it meant
somethin' other than honorable action on the battlefield. But that's what Van Braam did. He translated
the world *l'assassin* as "death."

When Washington signed the surrender, he didn't
know that he was admittin' that he had *assassinated*
a French diplomat named Jumonville. Never mind that
the Half-King done the assassinatin', and never mind
that Jumonville was up to no good when we jumped
him. After that translation made the rounds, the French
had a fine time goin' on about English treachery in the
backwoods of America.

One lord in the English government called the surrender "the most infamous a British subject ever put
his hand to."

But by then Washington was pointin' a finger at
somebody else: his translator. The last we'd seen of
poor Van Braam, he'd been wavin' good-bye when
we marched out of the Great Meadows. He'd volunteered to be a hostage till we exchanged the French
prisoners we took in the first fight.

You'd think Washington would stick up for Van
Braam. But when Washington heard what that translation meant, he took a sharp breath like a woman
learnin' her husband's been visitin' the whorehouse.
"How could Van Braam be so stupid?"

Cap'n Stephen said, "You can't be blamed for sign-
ing this."

"You can't," said Cap'n Mackay, "nor can I."

Mackay'd put his name to the surrender too. As jealous over surrenderin' as he was over commandin'. Damn fool even put his name *above* Washington's. But Washington had ordered the attack in the glen. Everybody knew that. The blame'd be on his head. Unless he could shift it.

And Stephen said, "Maybe Van Braam wasn't so stupid." And from there they spun the story that Van Braam must have been in the pay of the French.

'Twas a fine tall tale. And Washington let it grow. 'Twas better to have folks sayin' that the worst thing he did was trust a Dutchman. And the second worst was to trust the government. It would take time for the bad opinions in London to reach him.


As for the troops, we straggled back to Alexandria, all beaten, dirty, damn sad, and dressed in rags. It cheered us considerable to see Washington ride in with a bag of three hundred pistoles, the governor's reward for the men who'd marched out. 'Twasn't much next to the land we'd been promised, but better than nothin'.

Some of the boys bought clothes with the money. I spent mine on two things: extra gunpowder and Bee Mensing.

Word was the governor was plannin' to send a bigger expedition against the Forks before the snow flew. Struck me as damn foolery, considerin' what we'd just been through. But so long as there was a chance for me to get that Ohio bonus land, I was goin'. So I spent my days practicin' with my musket and spent my nights in Alexandria with Bee's legs wrapped around me.

'Fore long I could hit a standin'-still target at seventy-five yards, a movin' target at fifty. No better musket-shootin' than that. Thought about gettin' me one of them Pennsylvania rifles, but they was too expensive and took too long to load.

And Bee . . . well, she was pretty expensive too, but it didn't take me no time at all to load . . . *or* to fire. 'Twas more than the old in-and-out, though. 'Fore I went to the Great Meadows, I was glad to do my business and pull up my breeches. But after you've looked death in the face, couplin' with a woman is like feelin' the beat of life, and couplin' with one who likes you is like a glimpse of life after death, even if you have to pay to see it.

Bee had her faults. Most women do. A quick temper. A powerful thirst. That crooked nose. But that skinny Dutchman, he never hit her in the mouth. Didn't want to spoil them good teeth. Always liked good teeth.

What's more, she was good company. And gettin' better the longer she stayed at Chastity's. Learned how to make you laugh, how to tell you something good about yourself, how to take your mind off whatever was botherin' you. I wasn't so dumb as to think she done this just for me. But I always thought she done it a little more for me.

The last night I visited her I could smell her vanilla-extract perfume as soon as I stepped into the room. There was just one candle flickerin'. But I could see that straw-colored hair on the pillow and those fine teeth glistenin' from all the way across the room. She was wearin' more paint. Her cheeks were rouged and her lips were red. But I didn't mind. And the bedbugs didn't matter a bit. Our main business went fast, like always. Then we talked, like always.

I asked her if she'd been busy.

"What do you think, with all you soldier boys comin' through?"

"Well, that's over. We're headin' back."

She sat up in the bed and looked into my eyes. She looked so worried, she could've been my mother. "Back to the Forks?"

"Back the Forks, aye. But don't let it worry you."

"I ain't worried, but . . . you boys leave, us girls won't have nothin' to do."

I pulled her close. Didn't hear the mercenary meanin' of what she just said. I was thinkin' about that kindhearted look she'd just given me. And the kindhearted gifts she'd given me in that bed. "I have things for you to do, honey."

"Not if you ain't here. Why don't you stay?"

"I can't desert." Then I got serious. "What I'm doin' is for the future, for me and the woman who comes with me to the Ohio country someday."

"You got a woman in mind?"

I leaned into her a little more, "I was thinkin' about you, darlin'."

That was wider than I'd ever opened my door to anyone. Expected her to walk right through and give me a kiss. Instead, that painted face of hers looked like 'twas dryin' up and fallin' off. "Hesperus Draper, what would I want to go back to the wilderness for?"

"To . . . to be with me. That's what I was thinkin'."

She looked into my eyes like she was searchin' for somethin'. And then she give out a laugh. Like 'twas all a big joke.

And I hate to be laughed at. Last thing my father did, before he left for good, was laugh at me for how scrawny I was. Hurt me plenty. So did she. I swung my legs out of the bed, pulled up my breeches, and said, "What else should I expect from a painted whore?"

Right then Chastity came bangin' on the door. "Time's up. Another shillin', son, or be off with you."

And I reckon Bee must've seen I was serious about what I'd said, because right then she grabbed for my arm. I pulled it away, so she grabbed for my shirttail. I shoved it into my breeches, so she grabbed for my leg. I pulled it hard and dragged her out of the bed. When I slammed the door behind me, she was cryin'.

They say a mad soldier's a good soldier, and I was good and mad after that. Washington led us back to Wills Creek. Set us to drillin'. And whatever I did, I did hard. And did right.

One day Washington called me to his tent. "I'm making you a sergeant."

"Thank you, sir."

"You've shown leadership . . . of late. 'Tis something we'll need if we're asked to retake the Forks."

"Yes, sir." I always agreed, even to the stupid things, like tryin' to retake the Forks . . . with what little we had.

He said, "I expect a royal commission for my leadership. Your leadership is rewarded in advance."

Royal commissions didn't grow on trees. You needed friends in England, and even if you had them, you still had to pay for whatever rank you got. But I didn't question Washington, not with the friends he had.

He made a wave to dismiss me, then said, "One more thing, Draper. If you ever pass a rum pipe during battle again, I'll flog you to the backbone."

\* \* \*

By August, Dinwiddie had come to his senses. Decided only a fool would attack the French with what little force we had, which was just what Washington had been tellin' him ever since we got back.

But nobody give Washington credit, leastways nobody in power. The British ministers had heard the stories of assassination in a forest glen and flimsy forts on marshy ground, and they'd decided to step to this little gavotte themselves. Too much at stake to be lettin' boy soldiers make bad decisions in the backwoods.

The Virginia Regiment was broke down, broke into companies, with no better than a captain commandin' each company. And the only royal commission went to the governor of Maryland. So Washington did what any self-respectin', headstrong, touchy, arrogant young man should do. He quit.

*c.d.—The British ministers had heard one other story that I am compelled to include.*

*After his attack on Jumonville, Washington wrote to his brother, "I have heard the bullets whistle, and believe me, there is something charming in the sound."*

*These words were reprinted in a British gazette, and even the king was amused, saying, "He would not think so, had he heard many."*

## Dr. James Craik:

Upon learning of Washington's decision to resign, I hurried to his tent, bringing with me my last bottle of Madeira. I poured two glasses and told him of my disappointment.

His voice mixed equal portions of anger and resignation. "If they thought me capable of holding a commission that had neither rank nor emolument, they must have held a very low opinion of me."

"But the men of the regiment hold you in high esteem," I said.

"And every half-pay officer bearing the king's signature now ranks me."

"But, sir—"

He raised his hand. "Doctor, you know my inclinations are strongly bent to arms. I've said as much to Dinwiddie, but I won't brook a demotion."

"It might only be temporary, sir."

"I've earned better. At least I know we stood against a superior army. We stood the heat and brunt of the day. I have the thanks of my countrymen for the services I've rendered."

I'll nae deny it. He could eulogize himself like a professional mourner, particularly when he was young and uncertain.

So I said, "The thanks would be even greater if you stayed."

"Doctor, my mind's made up. Now pour me another glass of Madeira."

'Twas nae the first time that I poured him a dram. Nor would it be the last. But 'twas the first time he had ever disappointed me. Of course, as I saw it later, he was right. He understood the principle of a thing as well as any man I ever met.

## Jacob, Mount Vernon Slave:

In all them months that I work for the Mount Vernon overseer, Alice and Narcissa and me, we live together. And I feel like I finely belongs to somethin', to a real fam'ly, see.

'Course, what I belongs to is the Washin'tons, and when the Mount Vernon overseer don't need me no more, I'se shipped back to Ferry Farm. I miss my second baby bein' born. A boy which Alice name Matchuko. Leastways I ain't killed like po' Jester.

Then one day, comin' on to Christmas, Ball-and-Chain call me in. She still the queen bee of Ferry Farm, and she got no plans to leave her partic'lar hive. Now that he's past twenty-one, the place belong to Massa George, but he ain't the kind to put his mother out. And if'n he don't have to, he ain't the kind to live anywhere near her, neither.

Most of the time, when he be at the Tidewater, he be at Belvoir. Colonel Fairfax still treat him like a son, even if he quit soldierin'. And now that they's both older, him and George Wil'lum be like brothers. And Miz Sally, she have the sweetest smile. . . .

So what do Ball-and-Chain want with me? She settin' by the fireplace, rockin' in her chair, spittin' tobacco. Growin' old done nothin' to soften her. She still have that strong look. Strong and leathery. She jess say, "Pack yer things."

And I thinks, They're sellin' me. And I thinks, Oh, Lord, don't let 'em be sellin' me south, further from my family.

But the news turn out good, even if she take the roundaboutest way to git to it. She say, "You know baby Sarah's died, don't you?"

"Yes'm." I felt awful bad 'bout that. See, po' Miz Nancy Fairfax, she lose Massa Lawrence, and she lose all her chilluns, too.

"Baby Sarah was Lawrence Washington's last heir. She would have inherited Mount Vernon."

"Yes'm."

"Now that she's passed and Miz Nancy's remarried, your master has rented Mount Vernon." She spit in the fire and it make a little sizzle. "Why he needs another plantation when he has Ferry Farm, I don't know."

"Me neither, ma'am."

She give me a look, to make sure I ain't bein' fresh. I'se lyin' to her, but I ain't never fresh to her. Then she say, "And why he wants to take a good slave like you away from me I don't know, either."

I jess say, "Me neither, ma'am."

"Leastways, he only wants you. He could've taken the lot of you, and left me with no help at all."

"Well, ma'am," I say, "Massa George be a good son."

She jess spit in the fireplace agin and say, "Git goin'. Be at Mount Vernon by sundown tomorrow."


Comin' up the road to Mount Vernon, I'se thinkin' I'se the luckiest slave in Virginny . . . if there be such a thing.

Mansion house be smaller then. But strange how empty it feel . . . no furniture in it . . . no Massa Lawrence or Miz Nancy, no babies, all of 'em dead and buried. No wonder Massa George don't look too happy when I come in the parlor. He never one to go about smilin' like a fool, but he look mighty serious that day. He ain't never lost at nothin' afore, but he lost at war, and he lost his rank, too.

He say to me, "You heard about Jester?"

I say, "Yassuh. Mighty sad."

"I need a personal servant. Your nightwalking . . . I won't forbid it, but I rise before dawn. I expect my water to be hot and my razor to be sharpened."

I say, "Over to Belvoir they has the noisiest rooster you ever did hear. He commence to crowin' soon's the sky git light."

He warn me, if it don't work out, I'll go to the fields and he'll find another servant.

I say, "Fair 'nough, suh, fair 'nough."

That night, when I come walkin' in the cabin where Alice and my babies live, her eyes pop out of her head. Her first words is "Jake, you ain't run away again, is you?"

I don't say nothin'. I jess throw my new livery coat on the table. And little Narcissa come runnin'. We's a fam'ly agin.

Come spring, Massa's mood improve some. I don't know why. I reckon 'tis jess the comin' of the light.

And one April afternoon, George Wil'lum and Miz Sally Fairfax come by for tea. She bring some pictures of furniture, things she say Massa George should order for Mount Vernon. He's standin' aside her, lookin' over her shoulder at the pictures, and all the talk's 'bout Chippendale-this and mahogany-that and yellow damask and red silk.

George Wil'lum git so bored, he go outside and look out at the river.

I brings in some tea, but Massa George don't even look up. He too busy hangin' over Sally. He listenin' hard, and from where he standin', I guess he have him a fine view down her dress. If I thought I wouldn't git whupped for doin' it, I might've tooken a peek myself. Fine-lookin' woman.

Then George Wil'lum come runnin' in the house, eyes popped wide. "There are ships in the river—transports, carrying troops."

Massa George look up like Jesus Christ and the twelve apostles be sailin' past. He grab his spyin' glass and go runnin' out to where he see the river through the trees. And he say, "By God, they've arrived."

Miz Sally say, "Who?"

Massa say, "General Braddock and the British army."

Now, slaves ain't s'posed to ax questions, but I can't help it. I say, "What . . . what this British army plannin' to do, suh?"

"March to the Forks of the Ohio. Take Fort Duquesne. Do it the proper way." Massa put the glass to his eye and sweep it up and down the river. "By God, look at those transports—supplies . . . soldiers . . . officers . . . artillery . . ."

George Wil'lum say, "You should be going with them, George."

And Massa get this smile on his face. "I wrote to Braddock when he reached Yorktown. I offered him my services, and he has invited me to join his family."

So there's the reason he been brightenin'.

"Family?" say Miz Sally. "Are you related?"

"A military term," he tell her. "The general calls his staff his family. Like we call our plantation people family."

"You're going to accept, aren't you?" say George Wil'lum. "My father would be quite disappointed if you turned down a proper offer."

Massa George close his spyglass, and the excitement go out of him some. "Until I meet General Braddock and hear his proposal, I can make no decision."

"But, George," say Miz Sally, "you know you want to be a soldier."

He say, "A *proper* offer." When it come to what he call his honor, my massa be stubborn as a stump.

Massa George bring me with him when he go up to Alexandria to meet the general. He want Braddock to see that he be important enough to have a slave followin' him 'round all day.

Braddock set up at the house of Massa Carlyle, another son-in-law of Colonel Fairfax. Officers keep comin' and goin', all buzzin' 'round, like they's the flies and Braddock's the prize bull at Red Coat Farm. He ain't no big man. But he have a solid look. And he wear a wig so white it make his skin look boiled, like he always mad.

When Massa George come in, Braddock don't even look up. He ain't the most mannerly sort, see, and he signin' the papers his men keep puttin' in front of him. His quill flutter so fast I reckon it still attached to some bird. Finely he say, "Mr. Washington . . . I hear you know Indian country."

"I . . , I . . . I do, sir." Massa George be mighty impressed with what he see around him. This the first time he ever meet a real general, and he put on his best coat and lace trimmin's, and satin waistcoat, too, and he stand so straight you think he have a ramrod up his ass.

Braddock say, "I hear that you also believe that you are as good as any British officer."

Massa George swallow. "I . . . I . . . believe, sir, that none who achieve rank and respect should be asked to surrender it when they've served with honor."

"Honor . . . What about patriotism?"

"I believe that without one, sir, we cannot have the other, sir."

Braddock give a grunt. "Well put. Sit down and tell me what you know about the country we plan to march across."

And they talk a long while. Massa tell plenty about the lay of the land out where he done his ambushes and took his beatin'.

And you has to say this—Massa have somethin' about him that make men trust him. After all them years of readin' the Rules, he know how to seem sure of hisself while seemin' polite, too, and he have that straight-up look that men like. Why else this mad-faced old general go and offer him a job?

Braddock say he can't give him no rank. But if Massa George serve as a volunteer, maybe when it's all over, he git the royal commission he want worse than a drunken field hand want another swaller of rum.

Still, he spend about a week tryin' to decide what to do. He talk plenty with Colonel Fairfax 'bout whether this be a honorable offer. Then come the April mornin' he plan to give his answer. He tell me to saddle up his horse.

But 'fore he leave, a carriage pull up. And who be in it but old Ball-and-Chain herself. I don't recollect she been here in years. She step out and look around . . . kick at a little pebble in the path . . . and march up to the door.

I answer it 'fore she git a chance to knock. "Mornin', Miz Washin'ton."

She say, "Is my son here?"

"Oh, yes, ma'am." I let her in and tell her to please wait in the passage. I like makin' her wait, see, after all the orderin' 'round she done to me.

She jess say, "Tell him to hurry."

In the parlor, Massa George whisper, "My mother? Here? Today?"

I say, "Yassuh."

He have on his waistcoat. But he don't let me bring her in till he put on his topcoat, like she some stranger.

"Mother," he say, "what a surprise."

You know from his tone it ain't no good surprise. Jess a surprise. He tell me to fetch tea. I tell Beatrice, the kitchen slave, to do it, so's I can stay in the passage and listen to what's goin' on 'twixt Massa George and his mama.

Well, suh, Ball-and-Chain git right to it. She say, "George, what's this I hear about you marchin' off with General Braddock?"

He say, "Word travels."

"It travels to Ferry Farm."

"Then you know more than I've known myself, at least until this morning. I'm bound for Alexandria today, to confer with the general."

She plunk herself down in the big chair by the fireplace, plunk herself down like she plannin' to stay. "A son who goes ridin' off to Alexandria when his mother come all the way from Fredericksburg ain't been raised right, I'd say."

"Would you like tea?" Massa George ax, like he can't think of nothin' else to say. "A son who serves his mother tea has been raised right, hasn't he?"

"What about a son who goes against his mother's wishes?"

"What wishes?"

"That you don't go off and get yourself killed."

"Mother, I have no intention of getting myself killed."

"Then you *are* goin'?"

"Serving as volunteer will serve my honor well, and if I serve the general well, a royal commission may follow."

She give a snort. "Honor . . . royal commissions. They're no good if you're dead. And you come damn near to bein' dead at the Great Meadows."

He git up and walk to the windows. He do that sometime when he tryin' to control hisself, see. He say, "I was serving the colony."

She get up and stand aside him. She reach out to stroke his hair, but she don't quite do it. Don't think I ever see her touch him. She say, "I sure would hate for that chestnut-colored hair to end up hangin' from some Injun belt."

George step away. "No Indian'll scalp me. They call me Caunotaucarius, the Town-Taker. They fear me."

"They're savages . . . George, if you're killed, who'll manage Ferry Farm? Or Mount Vernon? You're too valuable to your family to be endangerin' yourself."

'Twas the same ol' story. Like when he want to go to sea. Who gonna take care of the spread? Who gonna take care of the family? Who gonna take care of her? She only got fifteen slaves to do the job. Reckon that ain't enough.

Massa George say, "I'm taking this offer. I may never have a chance to enhance my reputation at arms again."

She say, "What about your reputation as a son?"

They go back and forth an hour or more. Massa
George keep lookin' at the clock, jess dyin' to git to
Alexandria. But she keep gnawin' at him, like a pig
on a corncob, till finely he quit arguin'. Then she start
axin' when she gittin' a tour of the spread, 'cause, like
she say, Lawrence never invite her in the whole time
he live there . . . and, oh, yeah, she want to know what's
for supper.

Massa George know he can't go ridin' off when his
mama come to visit, or there be hell to pay. So he write
a note to General Braddock, sayin' he sorry for missin'
the meetin' and sayin' he'll serve, if the offer still stands.
I know, 'cause he tell me tha's what's in the note, and he
want a fast rider to git the note to Braddock right away.

'Bout four hours later, jess 'fore Massa and his mama
set down to supper, the rider come back with a letter
from the general.

Massa George tear it open, and I can see by the
smile on his face, the general say yes. So Massa eat a
nice dinner with his mama and don't tell her none of
it. Far as she know, he stayin' home, jess like she tell
him to.

Yassuh, he have him some woman troubles in them
days. Have 'em with that hard-shelled old crab of
mama, and with Miz Sally, too.

Jess 'fore he leave with Braddock, he ride over to
Belvoir to see her.

My Alice, she a house slave, and she keep her feather
duster whooshin' while she listen. Massa George and
Miz Sally set on the veranda, talkin' soft.

Miz Sally say, "A pleasant surprise, George. I'm
sorry George William's not here."

"So am I. But I've come to see you. To tell you of my intent."

"Intent? Intent to what?" Miz Sally sound surprised.

And he stammer some: "To . . . to engage your correspondence. I would like to write to you while I'm in the field."

Miz Sally giggle some, which Alice say she done when she tryin' to make a man rise to her bait. "Why, George, what'll General Braddock think if he hears you're writin' to a married woman?"

He say, "Corresponding with friends is the greatest satisfaction I can expect to enjoy on this campaign."

"Oh, George, you do go on so in the presence of a lady. Drivin' the French from Fort Duquesne would be the greatest pleasure any man could enjoy . . . especially a man so soundly beaten by them so recently."

He act like he don't even feel that little tweak. He jess say, "Please write."

"Well . . . maybe just one letter . . . or two." She make her voice sound all singsongy and sweet—another a little trick of hers when she playin' with a man.

But he actin' serious as a overseer findin' mealy bugs on the tobacco leaf. He say, "None of my friends are able to convey to me more delight than you can."

"Oh, George . . ."

"Please write. And please give my compliments to Miss Hannah, Miss Dent, and any others you think worthy of my inquiries."

Well, Alice say what Miz Sally say: Massa do go on in the presence of a lady. She reckon he's sweet on Miz Sally, which ain't too good, on account of her bein' married and all. She think that deep inside, my massa jess a lonely man, rattlin' 'round his big house, wishin' he have somebody who love him. Tha's why he want Miz Sally to 'member him to all them other women, see, in case one of them want some courtin' from one of General Braddock's aides.

Now, Massa George decide to take a white servant with him on the march. Don't ax me why. I jess see it as a blessin', 'cause I gits to sleep later. His brother Jack, who come to run the plantation, he don't git up so early or make me work near so hard. And tha's jess the way I like it.

## Hesperus Draper:

Well, let me tell you about the great British army as I witnessed it in the spring of 1755.

Take ignorant bog hoppers and tavern dregs, dress 'em up in red uniforms and white breeches. Then flog 'em. Flog 'em till they can't have a thought without you thinkin' it for 'em. Flog 'em till they fear you more than they could ever fear the enemy. Flog 'em if they make a face. Flog 'em if they drink. And flog 'em if they gamble. Flog 'em if they're late from the whorehouse, too.

Hang 'em if they desert. Shoot 'em if they run. And drill 'em till their dicks fall off. Drill 'em to fire as one and charge as one and march into a wall of cannonballs and hellfire any time you tell 'em to. Then set 'em on the road with their drums thrummin' and their fifes tootlin' and their red coats lookin' like fresh blood. Then they'll strike fear into anyone, and like as not, fear'll win the fight.

And don't forget the officers. All with bought commissions. Most with contempt for the poor flogged, ignorant fools they're commandin'. Some good men.

Some silly twits. And all of 'em think they know more than you, just 'cause they're from England and you're not, even if they're crossin' a wilderness where you've spent years and they've never been before.

And they have women taggin' along too—washerwomen and hospital servants at sixpence a day. And some of the men march with their wives and mistresses, and some of the wives get to be mothers for whole companies of men, and some of the mistresses get to be somethin' else. The women go with the baggage trains by day and sleep with their soldiers at night, and the soldiers that get slept with, at least, they're happy on the march.

We got our first look at this great British army in early May.

My company'd been out at Wills Creek buildin' Fort Cumberland. 'Twas a monstrous thing, that fort. Big rectangle of logs, ten feet high, four hundred feet long, two hundred wide. Set up on a hill. Woods cleared well back on all sides. Even had a trench runnin' from the fort down to the creek, so we'd have water if we was attacked. But who would attack us, with the strength we had now?

The Forty-fourth Regiment of Foot come up first, followed a few days later by the Forty-eighth, all of 'em marchin' to "The British Grenadiers," and "Lillibullero," bayonets glitterin', flags flutterin', ground thuddin' under hundreds of feet.

Braddock came in a chariot—the four-wheeled kind—with his officers canterin' alongside. And damn my eyes but who should one of those officers be, dressed in the new blue-and-red uniform of the Virginia Regiment, but the boy soldier himself? There'd been talk of him joinin' the general's family, but I was only half-expectin' to see him. Hadn't learned yet about his luck. In the fall, he'd gone home like a young girl insulted at a tea party, and here he was back and bold.

The commander of the Forty-fourth, Sir Peter Halkett, ordered a seventeen-gun salute. Cannon banged. Big smoke rings rolled down the creek and disappeared into the trees. And out of that chariot stepped a short, heavy, droopin' man with a scowl that could bend the tines on a pitchfork.

We all come to attention, Virginians and the king's troops, both, while Braddock's officers dismounted around him.

Halkett said, "Did you have a pleasant journey, sir?"

"No," Braddock said. "There's no describin' the badness of the roads."

Sir John St. Clair, an aide, looked around and announced, "Just as I said, General. A ridiculous place to build a fort. It covers no country, nor do we have communication open behind, either by land or by sea."

"What's behind us doesn't matter." Braddock snorted like he had some snuff caught in his nose that he couldn't sneeze out. "We're pushing ahead, once we get the wagons and livestock to do it. Any sign of them?"

"They haven't arrived yet, sir," said Halkett.

"Bloody country. Bloody provincials. Bloody ministers who sent us here."

I don't believe the common soldiers were supposed to hear this. Or maybe 'twas assumed we wouldn't listen. But Braddock seemed like a bad-tempered son of a bitch. This made him a man after my own heart.

Followin' him, however, was a man not after anything, it seemed to me, but reputation, recognition, and a British commission. What I wanted to know was how in hell the boy soldier had managed to kiss Braddock's ass . . . and how I could do the same thing.

Washington looked at me as he passed. "I hope you're avoiding the rum."

"Oh, yes, sir," said I, "avoidin' the rum and loose women, too."

If I couldn't kiss the general's ass, I'd kiss the ass of him who had.

Now, once the Forty-eighth come in, there was twenty-four hundred men campin' around that stockade. Women, too. And about fifty Injuns with their families. Even though we dug new necessaries every other day, that's a lot of shit to get rid of, and just 'cause we dug the necessaries downstream, that didn't mean downwind.

One day I made my visit, held my nose, did my business, moved off right quick. Comin' back up, 'twas only natural to sneak a peek at the women's pit. 'Twas surrounded by pine boughs for privacy, but damn if I didn't see a fine red-feathered hat stickin' up. And sure enough, there was Bee Mensing, comin' out, straightenin' her skirt.

I decided to follow her.

The tents were all pitched in long straight lines that ran up the hill, like spokes on a wheel, with the fort at the hub. For a woman, goin' by them tents was like runnin' an Iroquois gauntlet. Boys called out, hooted at her like loons. But Bee kept her eyes straight ahead. No laughin', no banterin' . . . as if she belonged to somebody and didn't need customers.

Then a red-faced Irish corporal come past her and

give her a slap on the ass, a big *thwack*, and he shouted, "There's the sound I likes to hear. A wench with no corset . . . flesh as firm as a horse's flank. Music to me ears, it is."

And without a word, Bee Mensing pulled a sock from her skirt—a sock loaded with bird shot. Skulled that big redcoat right in front of all his mates. Set him down like a drunk with straw legs.

Then she marched on, but she only went a few steps 'fore that Irish mountain was fallin' right on her, grabbin' her by the arm . . . twistin' her . . . screamin' that no one strikes a soldier of the king. So she swung the sock again. Swung it with one hand while tryin' to hold on to her red-feathered hat with the other. Swung the sock so hard all the darnin' come out of it and the bird shot went flyin'. Sock went as limp as an old man's prick, and all the other soldiers roared.

Don't forget, soldierin's damn borin' business, and here was some entertainment.

That big corporal had a look on his face . . . I swear, if I was a woman, it would've made me hate men forever. His teeth were drawn back, eyes all lidded down like a snake's, features all sharp . . . a look of hate and lust that made you think he might take a bite out of her.

That's when I decided to step in. The Irishman was twice my size. So I give him a boot right in the balls. Followed that with both fists doubled up and swung like an ax. Chopped him right down. But he popped right back up. One tough Irish tree. I chopped him again, right in the nose, but he kept comin' and caught me by the throat.

So I grabbed a piece of his cheek and tried to gouge at his eye.

He roared and shook his head like a big bull. I kicked at his balls, and he roared again and squeezed his hand harder around my throat.

That was when I saw two blue sleeves reachin' into the little space between us. And two strong arms pushin' us apart.

Now, that corporal had me so tight I couldn't have pried his hand loose with an iron bar, but the strength in the arms inside them blue sleeves was somethin' amazin'. I don't think the Irishman knew who was wearin' the blue coat that the sleeves was attached to: the only Virginian on the general's staff, with arms like a pair of ax handles, long and thin and strong as hickory wood.

'Twas Washington, shoutin', "Stand down!"

And I done it, right quick. But the Irishman kept pokin' at me. There was a mistake. Washington's face went red, and them little pockmarks went purple. He turned both arms on that Irishman, grabbed him by his red coat, and lifted him, absolutely lifted him, right off the ground.

While the Irishman was still in the air, Washington got these strangled words out: "I said, 'Stand down.'" Then he didn't so much drop him as throw him, right onto his ass.

Twitched his hands at his waistcoat, ran 'em down both sleeves, straightened himself, and said, "I should have you both flogged." Then he dug those small eyes into me and asked the meanin' of this.

I tilted my head toward Bee, still standin' there in her dirty skirt and fine red-feathered hat. "She's my sister."

"Sister?" said the Irish redcoat. "*Sister?*"

Washington looked at me like I was tryin' to sell

him a lame horse. Maybe he knew I didn't have a sister. Maybe not.

Then Bee picked up the lie. "My brother didn't know that Corporal Kenney's an old friend. Corporal give me a small gesture of . . . of friendship, which my brother thought were somethin' else."

"I . . . I misinterpreted it, sir," I said.

Kenney flicked his eyes and give me a little nod, as if to thank me.

" 'Twas a disagreement over a misunderstandin'," I went on.

"Aren't all disagreements that?" said Washington.

"It won't happen again, sir," said Kenney. "Now that it's cleared up."

Washington was not the most merciful of men. He could use the lash better than most. But that day he just said, "If this happens again, you'll all be flogged, all three." Then he stalked off.

I looked at the Irishman and, before any harsh words could be muttered, offered my hand and an apology for kickin' him.

Fortunately for me, Corporal James Kenney was not the vengeful sort. And he was gullible. "I'm sorry for slappin' your sister in the arse."

Hands were shaken. And then 'twas time for private explanations, which I didn't get till I escorted Bee down to a big tent near the creek, where a dozen women was workin' over washtubs, under the eye of a big, heavy old harridan with a craggy face and scraggly hair.

As soon as she saw me, this woman said, "No favors, son. 'Less you've brung somethin' to be washed for pay, be on your way."

By the sound of the voice and the refrain of money

in her talk—and only by those—did I recognize old Chastity Dibble, takin' on another job for the troops.

"He's my brother," said Bee.

"Your brother?" Chastity eyed me as if it was no more likely that I was her *sister*. Then she picked up two buckets and shoved them into my hands. "If you're this girl's brother, help her do some work."

And together, Bee and I went down to fetch water. When we were alone I asked, "Why are you wearin' the hat?"

"So nobody'll steal it." Then she tugged on a little cord around her neck and pulled a purse from out of her shirt. "They'd steal this, too, if they could. All the girls wear their goods on their bodies. Nobody trusts nobody."

By the time we reached the creek, I'd learned that Chastity'd gotten her girls attached to the army as general help. So long as they were subtle about it, they could offer their more personal services, too.

"How are you making your money?" I asked.

"Sixpence a day washin' clothes. Better than makin' money on my back."

"You shouldn't be wearin' that hat, then. It announces you."

"It got your eye. . . . That's why I come out here."

And I felt better than I had in a long time.

## Jacob, Mount Vernon Slave:

Bad drought that spring. By the end of May, things brownin' off, livestock gittin' weak, and one damn hot summer layin' ahead. Then Massa George come ridin' back, with a big dust cloud followin' his horse up the road. First thing I thinks, he's up and quit again.

But he jump off the horse and say, "Jacob, I need another mount. I've broken down three horses between here and Fort Cumberland."

"I don't know where you'll git a mount, Massa. Men from the army been takin' horses and wagons and shippin' 'em to General Braddock all month. Even took Massa Fairfax's best team and his slave Simpson to drive it."

"General Braddock needs wagons and teams. And I need to get to Williamsburg on the general's business."

That make me feel better, knowin' he ain't quit the army again. Braddock trust him enough, he send him to Wil'lumsburg to get cash money for to pay the troops. But Massa need a horse. Hard to believe they ain't no good ridin' horses to borrow or buy on the Tidewater.

'Course, they's quicker ways to git to Wil'lumsburg from Fort Cumberland, so I reckon he want to see how his brother runnin' the plantation, and I know he want to do a little visitin', too.

Him and his brother Jack go to Belvoir for dinner that night. Colonel Fairfax been called away to Wil'lumsburg. So it's jess George and George Wil'lum and Jack and, 'course, Miz Sally.

My Alice serve that night. I stand by the door. And George Wil'lum go on and on 'bout how they come and take one of his teams.

Massa George say, "We must help Braddock. He's already formed a low opinion of what he calls the provincials, lost all patience with us because of the frequent breaches of contract he's encountered among our people in the backwoods. Instead of blaming the individuals who fail him, he sees the whole country as void of honor. He and I have had our disputes on this matter."

Miz Sally's eyes go wide. "You argue with General Braddock?"

Massa George lean back a bit in his chair and sound kind of proud, almost cocky. "Our talks are quite heated on both sides. I'll tell you honestly, the general is incapable of arguing without temper. And he never gives up any point."

"So," say George Wil'lum, "what about my team and slave?"

And Massa George, he get a little temper of his own. He say, "I'll see what I can do, but I'm rather busy at the moment."

"We can see that," say Sally, smoothin' things some. "Bein' General Braddock's aide must be a heavy responsibility."

"Heavy indeed. But I have a good opportunity of forming acquaintances who may be helpful if I choose to push my fortune in the military way."

George Wil'lum give a laugh—a hoot is how Alice put it. He know what we all know: that Massa George want to be a British officer with a commission from the king. He want that more 'n anything.

But he don't like to be hooted at. He jess give his

friend one of them looks, and George Wil'lum, he change his hoot to a cough, to cover it up. And I feel a passin' right there. George Wil'lum always been on top, always called *Mister* Fairfax, but now Massa George be the one settin' the tone of the table talk. Him . . . or Miz Sally.

She say, "We're all proud of you, George."

"I would be warmed if you spoke of your pride in a letter." Then he look at George Wil'lum, and he git friendly agin, like he tryin' to smooth a little bump in the road. "She promised to send me a letter."

George Wil'lum say, "I don't recall that she's written to me more than a dozen times in seven years of marriage."

And Miz Sally give a giggle. "Now, you two, stop goin' on. There's more important things to be worried about than how regular I write letters. How, for example, is George going to get to Williamsburg, so he can get the money to bring back to General Braddock, so that the general's troops don't mutiny and the locals don't stop sellin' him food."

"We need to find him a horse," say George Wil'lum.

And after this long pause, Miz Sally bring her napkin to her mouth, dab a bit, and say, "There is a horse that I can think of."

George Wil'lum say, "You're not talking about Black Pepper, are you?"

Miz Sally bat her eyes at her husband, then bat 'em at Massa George. Alice say that gal have the battin'est eyes in Virginny. "I should be a very poor neighbor were I to deny him help. George, you may take my horse. She's the sweetest filly on the Tidewater."

"Well, there you have it," George Wil'lum slap the

table. "Braddock may complain about the provincials, but he can't say the Fairfaxes aren't patriots."

Massa George don't even look at George Wil'lum. He have his eyes on Miz Sally, and he give her this smile, like a sweet candy meltin' in his mouth. "One more thing for which I'll be forever indebted to the Fairfaxes."

She say, "I'm happy to do it, but I must be informed of your safe arrival back at Fort Cumberland, along with the charge that I entrust to your care."

"I shall write to you as soon as I get there."

Miz Sally say, "Include a message to me when you write to Miss Hannah Fairfax or to your brother. That would be better."

Massa Jack say, "Oh, yes. I'd be glad to bring a message over."

But Massa George's smile crack like a piece of glass and fall off. "Are you forbidding my correspondence?"

She flutter her hands and say, "Oh, George, save your time for more important things than writing to me."

Massa George seem a little sad after that, but I declare, Miz Sally know how to play men like they's harps.

## Hesperus Draper:

They say an army marches on its stomach. It also marches on a pocketbook, and once Washington come back with hard money, we got ready to move.

But before we did, the British drillmasters tried to turn Virginia troops into a parade-ground army. Considerin' that our best skill was in woodland fightin', I thought the whole exercise was a waste of talent, like tryin' to turn deer into packhorses.

One day, while we were drillin', Braddock come out to watch us stumble through our paces.

And right in front of us, his aide, Robert Orme, said, "I'm sorry for you to see this, sir. These Virginians are languid, spiritless, and unsoldierlike in appearance. Add to that the lowness and ignorance of most of their officers, and I have little hope of their future good behavior."

Right in front of us. They were an arrogant bunch. But before it was over, they'd change their tune.

## John Britain, known as Silverheels:

O ur Mingo band had become like children. We followed the white traders wherever they set up their posts. We gave good pelts for trinkets, better pelts for liquor. I did not see it, but it was the beginning of our end.

The British wanted us to scout, to be their eyes in the forest. So they called us to their camp. I did not want to go, but Bright Leaf said that the British were now more powerful than the French, so I should go, for the good of us all.

The Shawnee chief Monacatootha was there. He was a friend of Tanacharison, and so he was my friend, too.

But Tanacharison had been like a wind, one day blowing hard, the next day a wisp of breeze, the next day a gale, and the day after that, nothing at all.

Monacatootha was like a tree. Whatever wind blew, he only bent a bit. He was a faithful friend of the British, even when Braddock told him the Indians would take orders, not give advice. Monacatootha asked me to march with him because I knew the British hearts better than most.

I told him, "You are a Shawnee. I am a Mingo. The Shawnees are going to the French. Most of the Mingoes are going home. Besides, I do not like this Braddock. I like him less than Caunotaucarius."

Monacatootha wore tattoos: a tomahawk on his chest, bows and arrows on his cheek. They were good marks. He said, "Braddock is a bad man. He treats us like dogs and will not listen. But the French are no better."

It was true. Braddock did treat us like dogs. But he and the French were dogs too, bigger dogs. And they were fighting over our country. So, like all small dogs, we had to choose the pack we thought would win.

## Hesperus Draper:

I was with Bee Mensing the night before we marched. Was with her down by the river, against a tree. Didn't have much time. She raised her skirts. I heard a mournin' dove cooin'. It only cooed four or five times and I was done. But I was young and in a hurry.

'Twas a warm dark night. No moon. Air so thick you could drink it. Told Bee, "The memory of this will get me all the way to Fort Duquesne."

And she whispered, "I'm goin' with you."

"On the march?"

And her smile just sparkled in the dark. "There's wives marchin', and the officers, they said they need a washerwoman. Washington spoke up for me. Said I had a brother in the company, to watch out for my honor."

Next mornin', I was goin' with my company to our place in the line. Washington was standin' in front of Braddock's marquee.

We weren't yet in formation, so I said, "I thank you, sir. Sister thanks you, too. She knows there's good money to be made washin' officers' shirts."

"The brighter the shirts," said Washington, "the brighter the reputation."

I don't know if he put a little extra meanin' in those words. He wasn't the kind to mean more than one thing at a time. I think he just liked how she washed his shirts.

That day the tents come down, the drums beat, the fifes tootled, and Braddock's army stepped off. 'Twas all grand and glorious. Some of us had been given uniforms by then, new blue uniforms of the Virginia troops. Looked like blue sugar sprinkles in a long, twistin' red pastry.

## Dr. James Craik:

The bloody flux began shortly after we left Fort Cumberland. Twelve days later it infected almost every company.

It first presents with a feverish headache. Then it moves to the nether regions, and there be neither necessary, shit pit, nor hole in the ground close enough for the afflicted. Betimes they pass their blood and guts away and die. But usually they survive, weak and wobbly, more like babes than men.

On the thirteenth day of the march, Washington appeared at my tent. He was flushed with fever and had already made his first run to the pit. He was even sicker the next morning, but when General Braddock sent for him, he went, sickness or not. Afterward he related to me the following dialogue:

Braddock began by saying, "Washington, you look terrible."

Washington answered, "I'm at your service, sir."

"Good. Because I need your advice."

I imagine that Washington puffed up like a peacock. Any of us would have.

Braddock said, "We've barely made two miles a day from advance to rear guard. Our maps show that it only gets worse from here. What do you say?"

"I would say the maps are right, sir."

"What about reports of French reinforcements descending from Canada?"

"The present drought is our ally. The rivers north of Duquesne are much susceptible to it. The French canoes will be badly hampered until it rains."

"You would urge all possible speed, then?"

"I would suggest that we pick a detachment of light infantry equipped with only a few artillery pieces and supplies for thirty days. Let them press ahead, and leave the main baggage train to move at their own pace."

Washington told me, as proudly as the young nephew whose uncle has taken him into the family business, that Braddock took his advice. "A wise man always listens to advice."

"I'm afraid," I said, "that he took mine, too. I told him you're nae in condition to march."

Washington staggered, leaned against a tent pole, and almost collapsed. "Craik, how could you?"

"You haven't the strength to push on."

"But, Craik, this is the chance of—" Just then his body was racked by cramps and he went running off.

But Braddock sent him a note, promising that Washington would be brought to the front before the fort was finally reduced. He also suggested a dose of Dr. James's Powder for the young patient.

I had found this to be a fine medicine—a phosphate of lime and oxide of antimony known to drop a fever and restore a man to health—and I gladly prescribed it.

Generals dinna ordinarily worry about the health of their aides. Generals dinna ordinarily divide their command in enemy territory on the advice of an aide. It was plain that Braddock held a high opinion of young Washington.

## Hesperus Draper:

Our company was one of the units movin' ahead. Glad of that. Nobody wanted to be draggin' along with the supply train.

On the day we left, Washington came out of the surgeon's tent to watch us, lookin' as pale as the canvas.

"Don't think we'll be seein' him no more," said Eli Stitch, clompin' along beside me, as usual. "Wouldn't mind gettin' a touch of the flux myself."

"You don't want the flux," I said. "You want to be there when we take Duquesne. If you ain't, it could cost you acres when they give out the land."

He said, "I told you, I'm sellin' my land to you."

"All the more reason to get as many acres as you can."

I remember lookin' back, just 'fore we 'rounded the bend. Washington was still standin' there, watchin' us through the dust, like a little boy watchin' his pa leave home. Then he doubled over and went runnin' off.

But he wasn't my worry, because Bee and her fine red-feathered hat were bouncin' along in one of our supply wagons. Eight women were movin' out with the advance unit. The officers really liked how Bee done their shirts.

# John Britain,
# known as Silverheels:

They made their army smaller to move it faster. But still they took ten wagons, and still they stopped to build bridges over small streams and cut trees and level small hills. They would not swim in our great lake of trees. Instead, they tried to smooth its waves. But only the Great Spirit can do that.

We marched past the Great Meadows. The burned circle of Fort Necessity and the bleached bones of dead soldiers lay there together.

Soon some of the fish in this lake became bold. They were Ottawa fish, and Huron, some Delaware and Mingo, too. They killed and scalped drivers who hunted horses that strayed in the night. They captured Monacatootha and tied him to a tree. They would have killed him, but one who captured him was of his tribe. So they asked him if it was true that many British were coming with cannon to take the fort. He said it was. So they went running back to tell the French.

I do not think that Braddock cared. He did not think he could be defeated.

We Indians were the eyes of the army. We moved ahead. We camped without fires and slept in trees. One night I was in a tree. I heard the sound of two people coming through the woods below me, coming from the camp.

There was a good moon. I saw the woman's red-feathered hat and the man's blue uniform. They looked around like they were stealing something. They had come outside of the picket line to do their fucking. They were very stupid. We were under twenty miles from Duquesne. We were too close to the enemy for men to be fucking women outside the picket lines.

But they slipped into the bushes. Soon the bushes were shaking. An ass was going up and down like the head of a white bird pecking for food in the moonlight. The man made grunts. The woman made little squeaks, not like an Iroquois woman, who squalls like a cat and lets her man know she likes what he does.

I thought of my woman. And I thought that it was good she was far away, with the other squaws, because there were two Hurons creeping through the woods.

## Hesperus Draper:

We weren't supposed to be sneakin' off through the picket lines, considerin' all the lads who'd been scalped. But a man ain't supposed to make the two-backed beast with his own sister, neither. So I needed some privacy, 'cause I wanted Bee somethin' terrible.

And that was how I damn near got her. Right in the middle of my fun, I caught sight of a pair of moccasins. I jumped up with my breeches 'round my ankles and my dick . . . well . . . A tomahawk hit me off the side of the head and I stumbled on the breeches.

Nothin' makes a Injun look better than gettin' to the enemy's women. And I had delivered Bee right into their hands. One Huron grabbed her. The other came to finish me. What a way to die, with your breeches down and your dick still wet, and some savage draggin' your woman off.

But like an angel with a tomahawk, a Mingo dropped from the trees, straight down, straight into the middle of us. You never saw two Injuns more surprised than them Hurons, so surprised that he brained them both in a single motion. Down and *thunk*, then up and *splat*. Those Huron heads sounded like melons.

Now, this Mingo could've asked for a bit of what I was gettin'. Could've just taken it, considerin' that I was unarmed, groggy, and bare-assed. He knew I was lookin' at a thousand lashes for sneakin' out of camp, a thousand more to be doin' what I was doin' . . . especially with my . . . sister.

I remembered him from Fort Necessity. I said his name—Silverheels—and shook his hand and hoped he remembered me.

But his eyes were on Bee. And she showed how smart she was. She took that fine red-feathered hat off her head and plucked a feather out of it, and by God, that satisfied him just fine. . . . Oh, and he scalped the two dead Hurons, too.

## Dr. James Craik:

We were confident on the march. Our scouts had gone as far as Fort Duquesne itself. They counted only three hundred French. There was no doubt that within days we would avenge our defeat at Fort Necessity.

My only regret was that Washington had nae joined us. But when the chance for glory and honor presented itself, so did he. His wagon thumped into camp the night before our final advance, and he came to the physician's tent looking unsteady and skinny, weak and well worn, from his fluxing and from the bone-jarring wagon ride he had taken to catch up with us.

I said, "I dinna expect to see you, George."

"I wouldn't miss this for five hundred pounds."

His eyes flickered with excitement, but I was a physician. It was my job to see more in his gaze than the hot reflection of a campfire flame. In truth, beneath the excitement, he looked as weak as second-brewed tea. So I asked him, "Do you think you can sit a horse tomorrow? Ride up and down the column delivering the general's orders? Do the job of an aide-de-camp?"

"With a bit of help . . . yes."

"Help? How can someone help you to sit a horse?"

## Hesperus Draper:

*T*he *son of a bitch made it.* That's what I thought when I saw him that night. Couldn't miss a chance for glory, even if he was half dead.

Strange thing was, when I seen him, he was tyin' a pillow onto his saddle.

I said, "Welcome to the advance column, sir."

"Good to be here, Draper."

"Tomorrow's a day we'll tell our grandchildren about." I could make idle chitchat with the best of 'em.

Just then Craik come out of his tent carryin' two more pillows. I asked what they were doin'. Washington told me to be about my business. Fact was, they were paddin' Washington's saddle so he could take the jarrin' of horseback. He was that weak. That sore from the bloody flux. That stubborn, too.

I didn't much care 'bout him, though. I was lookin' for Bee. Found her doin' what she done best—makin' money, stirrin' a pot for a bunch of soldiers. They were payin' her to make squirrel stew. Famous for her stew, she was. Made it with fresh-killed squirrel and whatever she found in the woods—dandelions, Jerusalem artichokes, oniongrass, wild thyme, bay leaves—and, by damn, 'twas delicious.

She give me a big smile that lit up in the firelight. "Have a seat, brother, and listen to our boys tell about the Injuns."

"Yes, *brother*." Eli Stitch pointed to a grizzled old teamster in buckskins. "This here's Heman Dillaway. He's tellin' the lads what the Injuns'll do to them if they catch 'em."

There were half a dozen from the companies we were marchin' with. There was that big Irish red-coat Jamie Kenney and some of his friends, and every one of them was slack-jawed at what they were hearin'.

"Yes, sir," old Dillaway was sayin', "if the Injuns takes you alive, you'll be wishin' you was dead afore long. They'll strip you. Then they'll skin you. Then, if you're lucky, they'll tie you to a stake and burn you to a crisp. If you ain't so lucky, they'll give you to their women, who'll cut off your balls, then . . ."

Those soldiers were like little kids who wanted to hear a story over and over, just for the bloody parts. And right in the middle of it, a real Injun walked into camp, that Silverheels, wearin' the red feather in his hair.

Jamie Kenney grabbed his musket, like he was expectin' to git skinned alive and lose his balls right then.

I jumped in front of Silverheels. "He's a friendly one, James."

"Friendly?" said Jamie, settlin' down some. "So what's he want?"

The Injun made a motion to his stomach and said, "Hungry."

"So let him eat with his own kind," said Kenney. "Bloody savages."

But Bee flashed them beautiful white teeth and give Silverheels a mug of stew. She'd made a friend for life. 'Twas good to know some of the good Injuns. Made the bad ones seem less like devils.

Later, in the shadows of the washerwomen's tent, Bee give me a kiss and said it, said it for the first time: "I love you, Hess Draper."

"I love you, darlin'," I said, and I wasn't lyin'. "When this is over, we'll build us a fine home right here near the Forks, on the bounty land."

Then, like she'd been thinkin' on it a long time, she reached into her shirt and pulled out her purse, with all the coins she'd made on the whole march. She put it into my hand and said, "Take care of this . . . for us."

And I give her somethin'—a pistol. To take care of herself.

All the next mornin' the main body marched through those dark woods, which was not too wet in the drought year of 1755. Then, about midmornin', a cheer come runnin' along the column. The van, a company of light horse, had come to the Monongahela River crossin', and our company of engineers was finishin' the grade on the far bank. We were almost there.

Soldiers started slappin' each other on the back, throwin' their arms 'round each other, and cheerin'. For all the bloody stories from the teamsters, here we were, not five miles from Duquesne, without a breath of an Injun around and the one place where we'd be vulnerable—the river crossin'—now firmly in our hands.

Braddock held the main body on the bank until the

engineers finished the grade. Then he said somethin'
to Washington, who come gallopin' along the ranks,
ridin' his pillows, bringin' the general's orders. The
band struck up the grenadiers' march, the regimental
colors come out of their cases, columns formed up,
and into the river we went.

Us Virginia boys was marchin' near the rear, marchin'
with Sir Peter Halkett's regular unit. From where we
were, we could see down the whole line of wagons, and
ridin' in the sixth, wearin' her fine red-feathered hat,
minus a feather, was my Bee. Thought, How excitin' all
this must've been for her. How many women ever seen
anything like this? Hell, how many men?

I was caught up in the show of war. 'Twas like I'd
never heard of Fort Necessity, never been there, never
poured rum onto the cold dead lips of Henry Dundee.
Didn't even notice how wet my feet got marchin'
across that river.

## Dr. James Craik:

The surgeon's wagon was third in the line. So from
where I was sitting, I could keep a sharp eye on
Washington.

He dinna sit his horse with the usual confidence.
And betimes he doubled up on the pommel as if he
had nae the strength to stay in the saddle. But they
were small waves of weakness washing over him, for
he would always straighten up after a time and get on
with his business.

And what glorious business it was—music playing,
sun glittering off musket barrels and flagstaff finials, feet

tramping, wagons rumbling through the shallow water. In jig time we were across and up the embankment. The land rose, and we moved away from the river, in under a fine, high hardwood canopy. As the underbrush was light, our engineers had little difficulty in making way. Now and again, above the music, we might hear the sound of a trunk cracking as a tree was felled, but in the main 'twas easy going.

With the summer leaves fluttering above and the coolness of their shading a most welcome sensation, I could feel a new sense of purpose in the men all around me. Braddock had put out proper flanking parties and sent scouts ahead, but we were firm in the conviction that at the riverbank the French had missed their best chance to strike.

## John Britain,
## known as Silverheels:

The forest is a silent place.

The white man does not know this. He will say that there are birds singing . . . breezes blowing . . . the rush of a river over rocks. But the heart of the forest is silence. Seek the silence with your ears, and other sounds will go. Then the breaking of a twig will echo like a gunshot. The fall of a moccasin on the forest floor will be like the fall of a tree.

But on that day I could not find the silence. I could not hear the hundreds of moccasins moving through the trees before me. I could hear only the stupid tramping of British boots and silly flutes playing silly music.

And so, like a white man, I was amazed to see a huge party of enemies—eight or nine hundred—appear in the woods ahead. There were French and Ottawas and Hurons, too. I even saw some Mingoes who had joined the French.

Before they saw me, I turned and ran toward our column. The first officer I came to was marking trees to chop down. I tried to speak. But a white scout came running in, shouting, "The Indians are upon us. The Indians are upon us."

That is how the white men always thought in a fight. It was Indians upon them. Not Hurons. Not Ottawas. Not enemies. Just Indians.

The officer fired a warning shot. Then he turned and ran, shouting it again: the Indians were upon them.

I thought the next few minutes would be a bad time to be an Indian.

The soldiers from the advance guard ran forward. They were grenadiers. They wore tall hats that looked heavy and hot. Some said the hats made the soldiers look bigger. I thought the hats made them look stupid.

The French and Hurons and Ottawas came running from the other direction. But the sight of red coats made them stop fast, like galloping horses digging in their hooves.

The British captain was shouting, "Make ready!" And the grenadiers were forming their lines. Only white men try to make straight lines in a crooked forest. The French captain was shouting and pointing. The Hurons and Ottawas were running right and left, around the ends of the straight lines.

I dropped to my belly. I tried to make myself a snake and slither away.

## Hesperus Draper:

The rear guard had just come up from the river-bank. Meant the whole column was across. Must have been about one o'clock. Sun was dapplin' down. Trail dust wasn't too thick. We'd slaked our thirst in the river. Everything was goin' fine.

Then we heard a shot up near the head of the column. A minute or two later we heard a volley and ragged fire answerin' it. We was stretched out for near a mile, don't forget, so the firin' sounded puny, and the echoes were swallowed up in the trees. Didn't think 'twas much. Still and all, 'twas enough to stop the column.

Bee give a look back toward me, and I give her a grin so she wouldn't worry, 'cause I wasn't. Not yet anyway.

We stood there waitin' for orders, listenin' hard. Then we heard another volley. And the answerin' fire got more general. And mixin' with the fire was the sound of somethin' worse—that blood-freezin' war whoop . . . Injuns out for scalps.

Now I was worried.

## Dr. James Craik:

Washington's back stiffened at the first shot, as if he was trying to will the strength into his body. He would need it, because there followed a volley, then the sounds of a full engagement some distance up the road.

Braddock ordered one of his aides to ride up and

see what was happening. Then he ordered Colonel Burton to take six companies forward.

I watched the men go by and hoped I would not need my medical kit.

# John Britain,
# known as Silverheels:

The grenadiers wore stupid hats, but they were good soldiers. They moved forward fast, presented, and fired fast. They filled the woods with smoke and sound. And one of their shots struck down the French leader.

But the Hurons and Ottawas did not need French officers: They were already hiding behind trees on the rising ground to the right and along the edge of a deep ravine to the left. They were fighting on Indian ground, in the Indian way.

Another volley from the grenadiers struck nothing but air. Then the musket balls began to fall on them like rain. And the splatter of the bullets traveled down the length of the advance column, like a summer storm that comes on, comes over, and delivers its rain, all too quickly for us to escape.

Soon the grenadiers were falling back upon the engineers, and the flanking parties were running back from the woods, and confusion came upon the British, who had always seemed so sure of themselves.

The captains tried to rally the men, and some of the men tried to do as they were told. But there was no room on that twelve-foot-wide road to do the things they had been taught on the parade grounds. Nor was there a heart for it. Too many were gripped by fear and struck dumb by terror.

The Hurons and Ottawas knew what to do first—kill the officers.

They shot at any man on a horse. Those they missed they shot at again. The soldiers were clumped like dumb cows in the road, and like dumb cows, they would die.

But there was scalping at the start. Only warriors who think the battle may go against them scalp at the start. I decided that no one would get my scalp.

I was a Mingo. I wore my hair like a Mingo. I painted my face like a Mingo. I knew that the Hurons and Ottawas would not fire at a Mingo they saw moving from tree to tree. So I crawled on my belly. I crawled up the hill toward the Mingoes I had seen running through the woods.

## Dr. James Craik:

Braddock, flanked by Washington and Orme, sat nervously on his horse, squinting into the trees ahead, as if he might see what was happening up where the firing and the war whooping were growing louder by the minute.

I was glad to see that Washington had mastered himself. His head swiveled right and left, the picture of vigilance in his Virginia blue uniform. He had mastered his horse, too, a black mare that shied at the sound of gunfire, but with a few steady tugs on the reins, he kept her firmly in her place.

Finally Braddock told Washington, all very calmly, "Take my compliments to Sir Peter. Tell him to leave a rear guard at the wagons and come forward with the rest of his men. Then follow me forward."

"Yes, sir." Washington wheeled his horse and pounded down the column.

Braddock and Orme spurred on toward the fighting.

I reached into the wagon and pulled out my medical kit.

## Hesperus Draper:

When I saw Washington's face, I knew things was gettin' worse. He had on the hard look he'd worn at Fort Necessity, a look that tries to show nothin' and, in the tryin', shows all. He rode up to Sir Peter Halkett and said, "General's compliments, sir. He orders you forward, all but the rear guard."

And we was off at a dogtrot, runnin' past the wagons and all the nervous drivers. They weren't soldiers, and 'twas plain that with the sounds of the firin' and whoopin', they were gettin' mighty scared.

Runnin' past Bee's wagon, I said to the driver, old Heman Dillaway, "You take good care of my sister."

Dillaway pulled a musket out of the wagon and laid it across his knees. "Your sister's the prettiest gal in the army, son. Don't you worry a bit about her."

But I was plenty worried. And the deeper we went into them dark, deadly woods, the more worried I was. After about a half mile, we run right into the bloody rear of Burton's men, who'd run right into the two or three hundred men in the advance guard, who were retreatin' from where they'd first bumped into the French and Injuns. Some were fallin' back in good order, volleyin' as they came. But most were just runnin', as wide-eyed and disorganized as flushed deer.

The officers—what officers was still mounted—were screamin' at their men and beatin' 'em back into formation with the flats of their swords. But what did they expect from an army of flogged tavern dregs and ignorant bog hoppers who didn't have a notion of how to handle a forest fight like this? Bullets were thumpin' into men from every direction. The war whoops were more frightenin' than the bullets. And volley fire was pointless, because no one could see a target. But every time somebody shot into the trees, everybody else shot in the same direction.

And right in the middle of it, Braddock was wavin' his sword, bellowin' for his captains to pull their men into platoons, and sendin' Washington and Orme up and down the line with orders.

Didn't take long before Orme was blown off his horse. 'Twouldn't be much longer before Washington went down, too. That's what I thought, anyway. At least, he'd gotten what he dreamed of—a big battle, on another charmin' field for an encounter.

But us Virginians didn't think 'twas too charmin', and we wasn't so stupid as to stand out there makin' targets of ourselves. Without orders, we made for the trees along the edges of the road and got ourselves down.

Some damn-fool British officer ridin' a horse that looked about as wide-eyed scared as he was, screamed at us to get back in line, but we ignored him. So he screamed even louder. "I issued you an order! I demand—"

Right then a bullet hit him in the mouth. He made

a funny gurglin' sound and dropped out of the saddle, deader than salted cod. Served him right.

Air was so thick with lead you could almost see it . . . slammin' into tree trunks . . . ricochetin' off rocks . . . thumpin' into flesh . . . 'Twas plain to some of us that if we didn't get control of the risin' ground to our right, we'd all die right where we were. Braddock didn't see it, though. Not yet.

But Cap'n Waggener—he commanded our company—he wasn't waitin' for Braddock's order. Called to us: "Virginians! Up that hillside! Make for that big felled tree 'bout halfway up. We'll fight our way from there."

Fifty men jumped up and give a yell, loud as an Injun war whoop. It felt good, that yell. Felt good to get some of that fear out of us, almost like a good puke after a bad meal.

Then we heard an officer—'twas probably Braddock—shoutin' behind us, "You men! Stop! Form line! Stop!"

Didn't matter. We was goin' up that hill. The Injuns started firin' at us, but we didn't slow-march with our pieces at our hips like a bunch of regulars. We ran from tree to tree, took good shots, hit a few targets, and made it all the way to the felled tree without losin' a man. Then what do you think happened?

We got hit in the *back* by a volley! Those damn-fool British troops down on the road fired up at us! Maybe they thought we were French. Maybe some officers thought we were runnin'. I don't know.

We went up that damn hill with fifty men, and I'll bet there wasn't but twenty come down in one piece. And as soon as we were down, the Injuns come out and started scalpin' our dead on the hill . . . scalpin' our wounded, too . . . And if you want somethin' to make your blood go colder than the sound of an Injun war whoop, just add the screamin' of a man havin' his hair skinned off with a knife.

I stopped at the edge of the road, raised my musket, and blew one red scalpin' bastard right to hell. Then I was hit on the head with the flat of a saber.

'Twas Braddock, glarin' down at me, face as red as raw beefsteak. "Wait for orders before advancing again . . . or firing. Platoon firing is the order. There'll be no firing from behind trees!"

"General," I said, "you are a damn fool! And if you ever hit me again, I'll shoot you!" And I was mad enough that I would have, too.

Now Braddock spied Washington. "Put this man on report."

"Yes, sir." Washington wobbled in his saddle a bit, like he was still weak from the flux. The bullets were flyin' so thick around him, they were like flies followin' a bull. But instead of flinchin', Washington ignored them, like they wouldn't dare hit him. Had to admire such brainless courage. Had to admire his good sense, too. Puttin' me on report mattered a lot less than winnin' the battle.

So he said to Braddock, "Sir, let me collect the provincials and fight the Indians in their own way. We'll move up and flush them."

But that stupid bastard Braddock refused.

"Sir"—Washington kept at it—"please, before the confusion becomes too general for us to do anything—"

Braddock said, "No! These savages will melt away when confronted by the king's disciplined troops. We'll restore discipline and fight our way out of this."

Then Braddock's horse screamed and bowled over. Slammed right to the ground. For a second I thought Braddock had been shot. Hoped so, too. But 'twas just the horse. Braddock come up kickin' and shoutin' and ragin'. "Find Halkett!"

"Halkett is dead, sir," said Washington.

"Dead? Damn . . . Find his captain, then. Order him to set the colors of the Forty-eighth at the rear of this line. Then ride forward and advance the colors of the Forty-fourth. We'll bring order to this mob if it's the last thing we do. *Then* we'll take that hill."

Braddock wasn't much of a general. But he was a stickler for goin' by the book.

Washington wheeled his horse, and the big mare took a shot in the head. If Washington'd been a fraction slower or faster, the bullet would have hit him square in the chest. The horse went down, kicked once, and just plain died, with Washington pinned under him.

Braddock shouted, "Get up, George, and do your duty." Then he grabbed a riderless mount by the bridle and went off in another direction.

'Twas left to me to help Washington get up while more bullets thumped into the horse and tore up the ground all around us.

I said, "We should be takin' that hill, George."

He give me a quick look—I couldn't see any meanin' in it, which was always the way with his looks—and then he started huntin' for another horse.

# Dr. James Craik:

We set up our wagon as an infirmary. And very quickly we could see the progress of the battle in the number of wounded we treated.

The captain of the rear guard positioned his men well behind trees, so that each time the Indians approached, our men fought them off. 'Twas a great comfort to me and the other physicians. The job of closing bullet holes and extracting arrows is made easier when one is nae ducking bullets and arrows oneself.

We were some half mile from the fighting. 'Twas difficult for officers and men to move from the battlefront back to us. Many accomplished the task, but only the officers chose to go back after they were stitched or bandaged. The foot soldiers found it much more safer to hide under wagons and feign exhaustion or slip toward the rear and sneak back across the river.

All through the fight, I expected to see the tall figure of Washington, but he dinna appear. This I took as either the best of signs or the worst, and each wounded officer who came to me was quizzed: Did Washington live? Some filled me with hope, others could nae answer, and so it was left to me to do my job and put the fate of my friend out of my mind.

We were assisted in our labors by women still with the baggage train. While some of the females was struck motionless with fear, others made bandages, fetched water, and did what they could to ease the suffering of the wounded.

There was a washerwoman in a broad-brimmed red hat who stayed by our wagon much of the afternoon, doing our bidding and bringing water to the men of the rear guard, even when they came under fire. I asked her why. She said that her brother was fighting at the front, and she was sure that he was thirsty, too.

## Hesperus Draper:

Every so often I could hear the gunfire from the direction of the wagon train. Told Eli, "I'm worried about Bee. But if I try to get back to her, I'll be shot for certain, most likely by some British officer."

"Maybe not," said Eli. "Maybe they wouldn't even notice."

"All right, then. Come on." 'Twas time to get out of there.

We made it to the engineers' wagons, where there was maybe a hundred men hidin' and duckin'. Then we slipped past the colors of the Forty-eighth keepin' in the shadows of the trees, movin' away from the main fight.

Then Washington come poundin' up behind us. He was ridin' a chestnut geldin' now, and he wheeled in front of us. "Get back there. I won't have any provincials runnin' away."

"But, sir," I said, "my sister, sir. I'm . . . I'm—"

"Don't fear for your sister. She's safe with the rear guard. Join your unit."

"George, I have no unit. They're all dead, 'cept for me and Eli and a few others."

"Then get yourself behind a tree. Kill a few of these savages." He leaned down closer to me. "Act like a man and die like a soldier."

Now, when somebody says somethin' that stupid to you, best laugh in his face. I *was* actin' like a man, worryin' about my woman. And by damn, I'd behaved like a better soldier than most of those redcoats.

But when Washington said it, I couldn't laugh. He wasn't askin' us to do anything he wasn't doin' himself. Eli and I knew that if we ran, we'd never hold our heads up again back home. Maybe that was why Washington sat up so straight on that horse, even though every Injun seemed to be shootin' at him. Like I said, reputation means everything. So Eli and I, we went back and hunkered down behind a fallen log and got back to the business of fightin'.

You may not believe it when I tell you that we stayed there for damn close to three hours. You couldn't exactly say that we *held* the ground, 'less you'd say that a big tom gobbler holds his ground in a turkey shoot.

We Virginians did what we could, but the great British army, they just stood there dyin'. Or retreatin' till they was rallied by their officers so they could die some more.

You may also not believe that Braddock and Washington were still mounted at the end of it. Washington had a bullet hole in his hat and two or three more in his coat. And between the two of them, he and Braddock must've had half a dozen mounts shot out from under them. But there were plenty of riderless horses, considerin' that most of the other officers were dead.

Washington was plain brave and lucky. He may have been the luckiest son of a bitch that ever pissed against a tree, and I'll take a lucky man with a good head on his shoulders over a bad-luck genius any day of the week.

Toward the end, Braddock reined in his horse right near where I was crouched. He could hear what I heard—war whoops and musket fire, gettin' closer to the wagons at the rear. If the Injuns took those wagons, 'twould be the end of all of us.

So Braddock called to Washington, "Inform the company commanders that we will withdraw to the wagon train, take off our supplies, and recross the river."

"Yes, sir." And Washington went gallopin' off.

Braddock was turnin' to shout an order, and that's when his luck went bad. No matter the myths you've heard, no Virginia soldier shot him. I saw British soldiers shoot their own officers that day, especially them that took sabers to cowards. But the ball that hit Braddock come from the trees.

So there we were—general shot, most of the senior officers down, about two hundred British troops still fightin' with discipline, and the rest clotted up like blood, shootin' at shadows and dyin' in bunches. *Now* was the time for some good old-fashioned panic. First in little groups, then in whole platoons, the troops finally did somethin' organized—they ran.

Washington come gallopin' back, tryin' to stem the tide, screamed at them, beat them back with his sword, but the men on that narrow road through those dark, deadly woods, they were like a redcoat torrent rushin' down a sluiceway. And nobody paid Washington any mind at all, no matter how many times he shouted, "Stop, men! You must save the artillery! The baggage!"

Finally I heard him shout to Braddock's orderly, "We might as well try to stop the wild bears in the mountains." Then he commandeered the only covered cart that still had a horse attached to it, loaded Braddock on, and led the cart down the road, in the midst of the torrent.

And all the while the Injuns was shootin' and whoopin', runnin' along through the woods on either side of us, makin' one bloody gauntlet of that road. Men were fallin' left and right. Some were just exhausted and givin' up. Others were wounded so bad they had to give up.

We come to that big Irishman, Jamie Kenney. He was covered in sweat and dust, sittin' on a rock, holdin' his belly, beggin' for help.

I stopped and said, "Jamie, c'mon."

He looked up, through these big tears and said, "Shoot me, lads."

"Shoot you? Why?"

Then he took his hands from his belly and showed us the hole. "Gutshot I am. Finished I am. And too big to carry. But I don't want them Injuns to skin me alive, like that old scout said, so—"

"Ah, they ain't gonna skin you, Jamie," I said. "And we ain't shootin' you."

And whilst I was sayin' it, a musket went off practically in my ear, and Kenney's brains was splattered all over a tree trunk. 'Twas Eli killed him. "They would've skun him, Hess. You know it, too. Scalped him and skun him."

"I reckon."

'Twas a sorry thing though. Some Irish boy, a year ago diggin' potatoes and shearin' sheep, and now he's dead in those damn dark woods, all 'cause he took the king's shillin'.

We tried to put Jamie out of our minds, 'cause there

was still Bee to worry about. But we didn't worry so much when we come up on the wagon train and saw that all the horses were gone, probably ridden off by their drivers. This made me feel good, because I figured the women must have crossed the river too.

I told Eli, "We'll check her wagon. If she ain't there, we'll keep runnin'."

'Twas the last thing I said for a time, because a bullet ricocheted from somewhere and struck my hat. Felt like an ax handle. Knocked me cold. . . .

Next I knew, I was wakin' up on the far bank, and Eli was splashin' water in my face. He'd thrown me over his shoulder and carried me across the river, with the Injun bullets chasin' us all the way.

First thing I asked was, "Where's Bee?"

Eli said, "She warn't in her wagon. Must've made it across."

Well, that riverbank was swarmin' with riderless horses, stampeded cattle, stunned men. A line of soldiers was still fleein' through the water. Injuns was firin' from the trees along the high bank. And worse than that, they was plungin' into the river to kill stragglers—tomahawkin' 'em and scalpin' 'em and screamin' like 'twas all a fine bloodsport.

Washington led Braddock's cart up onto the bank, and soon's the general was safe, he tried to rally the rest of those stunned, scared redcoats. Had to admit it. There was leadership in him even then. He shouted, "The Indians are into the baggage train! Into the rum. They're not pursuing. We'll fall back into the woods, to the nearest hill. We'll plant the colors there. Defend the high ground until reinforcements arrive."

He wasn't payin' much mind to the stragglers still tryin' to get across the river. But I was, 'cause all of a sudden I heard Bee callin' my name.

First, I looked around, figurin' she was on our side of the river. Then I saw that red-feathered hat and that yellow hair. She was just comin' out of the woods on the other side, up at the top of the bank. Her and Chastity and three or four other women. Left behind somehow. Never figured out why. Never wanted to.

## Dr. James Craik:

Those who failed to retreat in good order could nae be helped. 'Twas more important to get the general to safety.

But for some reason several women dinna get across when the troops retreated. Some had been bringing water to the rear guard. Some had been waiting for their husbands to appear. It looked to me as if the one in the red hat had rallied them, because five of them appeared together on the far bank.

I was examining Braddock at the time. The ball had traveled through his arm and into his side, and I was probing the wound with my finger. He clenched his teeth and bore the pain silently, while I ascertained that the bullet was too deep to be extracted. I was attempting to determine if the wound was mortal when I heard the women screaming. . . .

## Hesperus Draper:

Bee was wearin' a bright pink dress and a white apron. The other women were dressed in yellows and light blues. Female colors . . . soft colors.

"Hess!" she screamed. "Hess."

"Run, Bee! Run, darlin'."

The women were in the water now, and a passel of Injuns—big strong-lookin' copper-bodied bastards—come streakin' down the bank after 'em.

I grabbed a musket from a soldier, grabbed another one from the ground, and started to run, with Eli right behind me.

Bee was screamin' for me, and I was screamin' for her. But I couldn't shoot from this distance. I'd be as likely to hit her as the red devils chasin' her.

Now, you ever had one of those dreams where you're tryin' to get away from somebody and you feel like your feet are stuck to the ground and you can't move? That's how I felt runnin' back across that river. But the Injuns, they seemed to be flyin', liftin' their legs high and splashin' hard. They caught up to Chastity first. Skulled her with one swipe of a stone tomahawk.

Then one of them caught Bee by the hair. But—damn, she was brave—she pulled out the pistol I'd give her and pushed it into the Injun's belly. Blasted a hole right through him.

Now we were close enough, I thought we might save her. I stopped and fired. Dropped one Injun, not three feet behind her. Eli dropped another.

And still there were four on her tail. They'd taken the other women down like dogs on deer, so there was screamin' and flailin' and scalpin' goin' on in the water all behind Bee, but they wanted that yeller-haired woman the most.

I fired the second musket on the run. Shot went wide. But Eli's didn't. That left three Injuns after Bee. One caught her, caught her by the hair. But from somewhere up on the bank, a shot took that Injun right in the back. Couldn't tell who fired it, but it give me time to get out my knife.

Now there was just two Injuns. Even odds for Eli and me.

But the Injuns were closer. And faster. And one of them caught her by the collar, and right in stride he drove his tomahawk through the brim of that fine red-feathered hat . . . right into the side of her head.

I just screamed . . . didn't scream a word. Just screamed. Screamed out all the rage that was in me and threw myself at them Injuns.

The one who skulled her was too busy finishin' her to see me comin'. Drove his knee into her back, pulled out his scalpin' knife, and commenced to slicin' off that yeller hair. The other one turned on us.

Eli come at him, swingin' his musket like a club. Eli was quick for a big man, but that Injun was bigger and quicker. Ducked Eli's musket, then swung hard with his war club and took Eli right in the side of the head. Knocked him senseless.

Then that Injun turned his club on me, but I'd never been filled with so much fury before. I ducked the club, come up underneath it, and drove my knife right into his gut. He took a whack at me, so I drove up even harder, drove up till I could feel him twitchin' on the end of my knife.

I said, "Die, you red fuck. Die." And I tell you, my heart still beats fast to think about it. I am ashamed to say it, but it felt good. Felt good to kill an enemy with my bare hands.

But you know what that Injun done? He spit. Spit his own blood in my face.

Then his friend come at me, with Bee's bloody scalp in one hand and his knife in the other.

I tried to free my knife, but I couldn't. The blade was stuck. Thought I was finished. Then that scalpin' Injun was hit by another shot from the far bank. Dropped like a sack of rocks. For a long time afterwards I cursed whoever done it 'cause I wanted to kill that Injun myself . . . or die tryin'.

## John Britain,
## known as Silverheels:

I made two good shots. I killed two Hurons in the river. None saw me do it. But the white woman in the red hat, she had been kind to me. So I tried to save her. I felt bad for deserting the British in the middle of the fight. And for deserting Monacatootha, who stayed and fought bravely.

After I killed the second Huron, I watched the skinny white man drop to his knees. He cradled the head of his woman in his hands. The head was bloody. The woman was dead. I knew he was crying. So I fired another shot, made it splash near him, to remind him there was killing all around him.

The shot scared him. He stood up and threw his

big friend over his back. He left his dead woman and made for the other bank.

A minute later an Ottawa came into the river and saw the red hat floating. He picked it up and put it on. It looked very stupid on him.

## Dr. James Craik:

That night Hesperus Draper was plunged into black despair. His woman—she was nae his sister, as we all knew—was dead. His best friend lay insensate. At least he summoned enough spirit to move back to the high ground, to await the attack that still we feared.

I had nae even a dram of rum to give him, all of it having been left in the baggage train.

Then, with dark coming on, Washington told him to find a horse.

"What for?" asked Draper.

Washington said, "The general has ordered me to ride back to Colonel Dunbar with the main body. I'm taking a few men with me, men who know the woods. Find a horse."

Draper somehow managed to laugh. "Dunbar's forty miles away. And you look like you're ready to fall over, George."

Draper was right on both counts. They would be riding all night and part of the next morning. And Washington was already at the brink of collapse. But there was iron in Washington's constitution. Did that iron infuse his character? Or was it the iron in his character that infused his constitution? No one yet knew. The character of a twenty-three-year-old man is still forming. I suspect that iron in each strengthened the other, giving him an almost supernatural power of endurance that, in the worst of times, was his greatest quality.

## Hesperus Draper:

They say Washington never forgot that ride back to Dunbar's camp.

'Twas for certain that I didn't.

What he never forgot, so he said, was "the dead, the dying, the groans, lamentations, and cries along the road of the wounded for help." Over and over that night, he said, "'Twould pierce a heart of stone ... but we must keep riding."

What I never forgot was my own despair. 'Twas black as the night.

But blackness meant no one could see me cryin'. Meant we didn't have to look at the faces of misery around us, either. Some of the wounded soldiers had dragged themselves as far as ten miles. But deep in the woods they lost their strength. Fell by the roadside. Cried out like lost babes when they heard us go past.

I suppose 'twas also good that the darkness shielded our faces from them. Because they cursed as we went. But if we'd stopped to help the ones who'd run, we'd've betrayed the ones who stayed behind to hold the high ground. Like Washington said, we had to keep ridin'.

## John Britain,
## known as Silverheels:

That night I stayed in the woods near Fort Duquesne. I saw the white prisoners brought in. They were stripped naked and daubed with soot. They were tied to stakes before the fort. Wood was piled around them. The flames rose. The warriors whooped and danced. The white men screamed like women. The wind brought the smell of burning flesh to my nose.

But torture had to be done.

The British knew about torture. They feared that they were fighting devils. This made them fight hard, but it made them fight stupidly. They fought from fear, from fear of torture. Fear of torture mattered more than torture itself. And fear weakened an enemy's heart. If the torture was not done afterward, the enemy would no longer fear it. So it had to be done.

## Hesperus Draper:

We reached Dunbar the next day. He was camped where we'd struck Jumonville the year before. The British called the place the Rock Fort.

I hate to say it, but our news did not inspire the vengeful spirit of men whose mates had been slaughtered. Inspired panic instead. Soldiers started pickin' up and leavin', like this was a picnic and the food was gone. Dunbar had all he could do to collect a few companies and some supplies to send forward.

Washington collapsed in exhaustion. But I couldn't sleep. Found a rum pot and had a drink. Thanked Washington for bringin' me with him, for forcin' me to act when I wanted to curl up into a ball and die. Then I rode back to make sure that Eli, at least, got out alive.

## Dr. James Craik:

The next day our ruined column reached Rock Fort. Though in great pain, Braddock was still in command. He ordered all of the supplies and wagons to be burned. Then he ordered a retreat to Fort Cumberland.

We'd been mauled. With the twelve hundred in Dunbar's main body, this was still the most potent force in North America, but all resolve was gone, and there were few officers left to rally the men.

Despite his wound, Braddock tried to give orders as we retreated. His breathing grew more labored—a sure sign that the ball had lodged in his lung—but there was little blood in his sputum, and it was my hope that he might survive until we reached Fort Cumberland.

At one point he said to Washington, "We'll know better how to deal with them next time." But there was to be no next time for Braddock. The bad-tempered but courageous general died on the night of July 13.

The next morning, Washington saw to his burial, in the middle of the road between Rock Fort and the Great Meadows. There would nae be a marker for the commander of the most powerful army ever to have appeared in North America. Instead, the remnants of that army would trample dirt on his grave as they retreated, so that no Indians would discover the body and defile it.

I could only guess at Washington's emotions as he read a psalm over the body. Braddock was nae a man to inspire love. But he had taken Washington into his family, had given him trust, confidence, and the promise of a British commission. Now Braddock's patronage was gone.

Colonel Dunbar reached Fort Cumberland, a stronghold that twelve hundred men might command against all comers. But he dinna stop there for more than a few days. He kept on running, all the way to Philadelphia, where he announced that he would go into winter quarters . . . in early August!

## Jacob, Mount Vernon Slave:

Some bleak days 'round Mount Vernon that summer.

Bad news make ever'body worry. Word come that all the officers with Braddock been slaughtered, includin' Massa George.

So, on the day that a rider bring a letter up to the house and Massa Jack go in the parlor to read it, we all crowd close to the door and listen hard. It don't take long 'fore we hears a big laugh . . . first one we has in that house in some time.

Then Massa Jack come out and read to us: "'Dear Brother, As I have heard, since my arrival at Fort Cumberland, a circumstantial account of my death and dying speech, I take this early opportunity of contradicting both, and of assuring you that I am of the living, by the miraculous care of Providence, that protected me beyond all human expectation. . . .'"

And while he read it, we was laughin' and cheerin' and thankin' the Lord.

End of July, Massa come home. And he look a sight. Wore out, skinny, eyes sunk. But we's sure glad to see him. Like seein' someone come up out the grave. Soon's word git out that he's back, they's notes comin' over from Belvoir.

Colonel Fairfax send one. And Miz Sally, she write, "I must accuse you of great unkindness in refusing us the pleasure of seeing you this night." She say that if he don't come over to Belvoir to visit the next mornin', she comin' to Mount Vernon at noon. And she thank the Lord he's alive.

That make the massa smile. Miz Sally always make the massa smile.

C.D.—*Of the twelve hundred British and Virginians engaged in the Battle of the Monongahela, nine hundred were killed, wounded, or went missing. Of six hundred Indians and three hundred French Canadians, there were fewer than a hundred casualties. It was left to Benjamin Franklin to put the punctuation on this defeat. Years later he would write, "This whole transaction gave us Americans the first suspicion that our exalted ideas of the prowess of British Regulars had not been well founded." As my uncle said, Dr. Franklin was a philosopher and a master of understatement too.*

## Jacob, Mount Vernon Slave:

Massa George talk with his brother Jack after he come home. They's lookin' out at the river. Massa still ain't feelin' too good. You know, that fluxin' sickness drain a man.

Brother Jack say, "Your reputation's grown, George. They're callin' you the Hero of the Monongahela. That'll lead to something more, even with Braddock gone."

Massa George say, "I don't know that I can afford something more."

Brother Jack say he don't understand.

Massa George git mad, see, like his brother missin' somethin' simple. "Look at all I've endured since my service began. I was employed to go on a journey in winter, when few would have undertaken it, and what did I get? Expenses borne!"

"And the respect of Governor Dinwiddie," Brother Jack say.

Massa George grunt. "I was appointed with trifling pay to take a handful of men to the Ohio. And what did I get? After spending my own money to equip the campaign, I went out, was soundly beaten, lost everything, came back, and had my commission taken away."

"At least General Braddock restored you to—"

But Massa George keep talkin', "Braddock promised me a royal commission. And what did I get? I lost all my horses and one of Sally's and most of my gear."

I'se thinkin', Lots of fellers lose their *life* with Braddock.

But Massa keep complainin': "I've been upon the losing order ever since I entered the service, Jack. Two years."

His brother try to cheer him. "With Dunbar burrowed in like a rabbit in Philadelphia, the defense of Virginia will fall upon Virginians again, and that means upon your head."

Massa pick up a stone and fling it out at the river. "Mother's already worrying about that. She's written, begging me not to go back."

"As usual," say Jack.

"I told her, if I'm able to avoid going to the Ohio again, I will. But if command is pressed on me, on terms I can accept, 'twould be dishonorable to refuse it. I told her my dishonor should give her more uneasiness than my endangerment."

Well, sir, command come pressin' from the colony of Virginia not a month later, and I reckon the terms be good enough, 'cause he take the job . . . agin.

## Hesperus Draper:

War does terrible things to a man. It turned plenty of men into cowards on the Monongahela. It made Washington a hero, but it showed what an arrogant, rank-hungry young fool he was, too. And it turned me into a drunk.

Now, a man prone to drink can find any excuse to swallow. But you have to understand . . . the French were still holdin' the land I thought would be mine, my best friend was back in Chotank and didn't even know his own name, and the woman I loved, I imagined her floatin' down the Monongahela, catchin' the current where it run into the Ohio, ridin' the waters all the way to the Mississippi. Somehow that made me feel better. But to see her like that—golden-haired and floatin' toward heaven—I had to get drunk.

Now, there were rules against drunkenness at Fort Cumberland, and Washington had always warned me that he'd flog me if he caught me drunk again. But he wasn't at Cumberland to do the floggin'. He kept his headquarters back at Winchester and spent most of his time down in Williamsburg, makin' a pest of himself. He made all kinds of demands for supplies—shoes, weapons, food, pack-horses. But the main reason he was a pest was the first reason he'd been a pest—rank.

And what was botherin' him most was the rank of a Maryland captain named Dagworthy, a tall, skinny feller with a face like the blade of a rusty hatchet. He'd marched into Fort Cumberland with thirty Marylanders and taken command of our three hundred Virginians, all because he'd once held a royal commission. He started treatin' Adam Stephen, our captain, like a wooly-headed pickaninny. And there wasn't a damn thing we could do about it. 'Twas the Mackay business all over again.

I expected fur to fly when Washington finally got there. Except he never came but once. And when he did, Dagworthy was out on patrol. Washington didn't even wait to see him. Delivered his orders, told Stephen to do what Dagworthy told him, and skedaddled 'fore lookin' Dagworthy in the eye.

Looked *me* in the eye, though. Said, "You've just been broken to private. Get sober, or I'll flog you when I come back."

I was too drunk to care about demotions or threats. I said, "Where you goin', George?"

"Matters of rank demand my attention, if it's any business of yours. And the proper form of address, Private, is *Colonel Washington.*"

## Dr. James Craik:

I was puzzled by Washington's avoidance of Cumberland during the fall and winter after the Braddock massacre. But the rank-bred infection was deep, and it had been festering since the beginning of the war. He meant to cut it out at the root before the fighting began again. So he stayed in Winchester, demonstrating his dignity in avoiding direct conflict with Dagworthy, and he deluged the authorities in Williamsburg with letters to bring Dagworthy down.

C.D.—*In answer to Craik's comment, my uncle said that dignity mattered less to Washington than rank. And he was nothing if not persistent in pursuit of it. When the snows were deep enough that there would be no more fighting on the frontier, Washington went north, visiting for the first time America's great cities— Philadelphia, New York, and, finally, Boston. There he presented his case to Governor Shirley, the new commander of British forces in America.*

*Shirley treated the young Hero of the Monongahela with great respect, but he rendered a decision worthy of a colonial Solomon. He said Dagworthy's royal commission did not permit him to command provincial officers of higher rank—a victory for Washington. But he offered Washington no royal commission, nor would the Virginia Regiment be taken into the regular army. Whatever promises Braddock may have made to Washington, they now lay with him in an unmarked Pennsylvania grave.*

*So Washington bought three new suits and a fine hat. Then he went home, intent again upon resigning after what he considered yet another outrage. But it was spring, and far greater outrages had begun on the frontier. If he quit, his reputation would never recover, and as my uncle said so often, reputation mattered.*

## Hesperus Draper:

I hated bein' a soldier. Hated the drill. Hated the discipline. Hated the boredom. Hated knowin' that after two years I was further away from that bonus land than when I signed up. Hated the horror, too, whenever it happened.

Month after month we'd go after some band of red murderers, most times findin' nothin' but scalped bodies, burnin' farms, dead livestock. Injuns would hit, then run. Never got close to 'em. 'Cept when they'd try to ambush us. Then we'd have real standup fights. Virginia Regiment lost a third of its men in the bloody year of 1756.

Small wonder I stayed drunk till November, when Washington finally come to stay at Fort Cumberland. Even after he won his pissin' contest with Dagworthy, he'd stayed away. Tryin' to make a point with

Dinwiddie. Wanted us to quit Cumberland altogether. Said 'twas too far away from the line of forts he was buildin'.

If you need proof of how little Washington knew about warfare, just look at those forts. He built them along the frontier, each a day's march from another, maybe a fort every fifteen miles. No room there for Injuns to slip through, no, sir. Those forts were so effective that by the end of the year there was talk that we'd lost control of the whole Shenandoah Valley and we ought to be fallin' back to the Blue Ridge.

With everything goin' from bad to worse on the frontier, and the regimental officers threatenin' mutiny over all the criticism they was gettin' from Williamsburg, Dinwiddie finally *ordered* Washington to go to the fort.

The day Washington rode in, I was on guard duty. But I couldn't even present arms. I was too numb, but 'twas a nice numb, 'cause I was thinkin' about my floatin' Bee and her golden hair. Washington just looked at me and shook his head.

He had a little puppy with him, little foxhound cradled in his arm, and the damn thing was so cute . . . I just reached out and petted him.

Well, sir, you don't touch an officer, and you don't pet his little dog.

Few hours later, Washington posted his orders. Started with the next day's parole, the password "Massachusetts." Then there was orders for a train of horses to go back to Winchester to bring up supplies, then orders for a court-martial for "one Private Draper, suspected of drunkenness on guard duty."

No surprise I was found guilty. A hundred lashes. Felt like nails bein' driven right into the little spaces between the bones in my back. I decided right then, if I ever had slaves, they'd never be whipped.

But you know what? Even though my thirst stayed powerful, 'twas like that pain snapped me out of feelin' sorry for myself. Give me a reason to hate Washington. 'Course, next day he looked at me like nothin' had happened. Had me drillin' with my mates and doin' my jobs. Even-handed. I'll give him that.

And I did my damnedest to keep away from the rum. Knew if Washington ever got it into his head to flog me again, 'twould kill me, or I'd kill him.

But I liked the talk I heard when Washington and Craik were together and I was guardin' the door. They'd go on about how to fight the Injuns, and Washington would always say, "The only way to beat them is to take Fort Duquesne."

"Aye," Craik would say. "Cut off the French head and the Injun beast will die."

And I'd think about the bonus land. Even if I didn't have anyone to share it with, 'twas where my Bee was, at least in my mind, so I still wanted it.

And Washington come up with a new plan to get a march on Duquesne, and to get that rank he lusted after. He'd kissed Braddock's ass, and it done him some good—leastways till they crossed the Monongahela. He'd gone all the way to Boston to kiss Shirley's. Now there was two new buttocks to smooch.

Come January of 1757 he left Cumberland to see Lord Loudoun, the new British commander, at the governors' conference in Philadelphia.

## Jacob, Mount Vernon Slave:

T'was gittin' to be a reg'lar thing, travelin' to some big city to complain about rank ever' winter. This time 'twas Philadelphie. Got there in February and set around for two weeks, waitin' to meet this Lord Loudoun.

Massa go to plays. Drink in taverns. And one night he spy Dinwiddie in a gentlemen's club. I'se standin' by the door, like I'se s'posed to, in my white coat and white wig, so I git to watch.

Massa and Dinwiddie ain't too friendly no more. They been arguin' a long time over how to fight the Injuns, and where to fight 'em, and who to fight 'em with—you know, reg'lar troops? Militia? Both?

Dinwiddie lookin' older. That frog look he have, well, it look even froggier. He move like he have hatpins stuck in his joints, and if he move too fast, they dig too deep. And he act like he jess sick and tired of all what he have to go through runnin' the colony.

Massa go over to him and ax if he can sit with him.

Dinwiddie don't say yes. Instead, like he been thinkin' on it, he say, "I can't conceive what service you could offer to the colony by coming here, George, when there's business to be attended to on the frontier."

Massa say, "I must press my case, sir."

"Have I not pressed it for you in the past?" Dinwiddie sound hurt. "Though I must say, there's no better advocate for his own interests than Colonel Washington."

Massa give a little tug at his waistcoat, and he say,

"I am an advocate for the regiment, sir. And w-w-we hope for a soldier's reward."

"Royal commissions?"

"Commissions for the whole regiment, sir."

Dinwiddie start whisperin', low and hard. "Royal commissions cost money and require preferment . . . familial connections. You lack the money, your connections are tenuous, and you're only twenty-five, George. Be thankful for what you have. Be thankful for your Virginia Regiment."

Now Massa George speak real slow, and his voice have some steel in it: "I can't conceive that being Americans should deprive us of the benefits of British subjects. We have a right to expect more for three years' hard and bloody service on the frontier than we would for ten years spent at the Court of Saint James."

"Don't speak to me of rights. Service to the king is a privilege. And an honor. You've advanced yourself further than any American of your age could hope to go." Dinwiddie swallow down a glass of port, but it don't settle him much. "You've defended your homes, as men should."

Massa say, "We've fought and died for the king's dominions, too. That makes us worthy to be called king's regulars, with king's commissions and the respect they bring."

"And half-pay for the rest of your life. They bring that, too."

And Massa git all uppity and a little too loud. "Sir, you deny my honor."

Dinwiddie jess make a sigh, like he plain tired out from all this. He pick up the newspaper, give it a shake to straighten it, then start to read. And tha's that.

You know what I thinks? I sure would like to be able to read a newspaper like that, so's I could make a big feller look small.

Well, Massa have Dinwiddie mad at him, and I reckon Dinwiddie git to Lord Loudoun, 'cause on the day that Loudoun finely see Massa George, it go like this:

Loudoun don't even close the door to his office, which show he don't think no more of Massa than he do of any low soldier. It also mean I peek in and listen. Loudoun remind me of Braddock, see, same age, same red coat and white wig, same bad temper.

Massa wearin' his best officer's coat, with the silver lace trim, and he have his best hat tucked nice and neat under his arm. He say, "Good afternoon, sir, and may I thank you for d-d-doing me the honor of seeing me. I bring a memorial from my officers, a petition that we hope will inspire Your Lordship to—"

"Leave it on the desk," say Loudoun.

So Massa take the paper out of his pocket and put it down.

Then Loudoun say, "Your reports have been quite thorough."

Massa like hearin' that. "Thank you, sir. May I say—"

And Loudoun jump right on him, snappin' like a bulldog. "You are ordered, Colonel, to return to your regiment immediately."

Massa get a funny little catch in his throat. "Yes, sir . . . but—"

"You are ordered then to remove your headquarters

from Fort Cumberland back to Winchester. Maryland troops will henceforth garrison Cumberland."

"Thank you sir. May I say that it has been my opinion all along that—"

"Your opinion is of no concern to me, *Colonel*." And he say "colonel" the way some massas, when they's talkin' to a slave with one of them Greek names, say it like a joke. You know, "Tha's a good idea, *Socrates*."

Seein' how Loudoun treat him, Massa should be hunchin' down. But he stand up straighter, put his head higher in the air, like he can take whatever bein' dished out. I'se proud of him for that.

Loudoun keep bitin' his words: "You are ordered to follow all of Governor Dinwiddie's prescriptions regarding the defense of the colony, as those orders are my own."

"But, sir—"

"Is that understood, *Colonel*." He say it again with that funny ring.

"Yes, sir. Th-th-thank you, sir. Now, may I ask about your plans for retaking Fort Duquesne?"

"No, you may not." And Lord Loudoun, biggest muckety-muck in the British army, he turn his back on Massa Colonel George Washington and look out the window.

Massa start to stammer. "Sir, G-G-General Braddock . . ." But he don't say more. He know it's over.

The lord's aide say, real polite, "I'll show you out, sir."

But Massa pull himself up again and say, "I'll find my own way." The door slam behind him and all but hit him in the ass.

Outside, 'tis a warm winter day. But the massa's face say cold, cold as ice. We start walkin', and after a time he jess stop in the middle of the sidewalk and say, not barely loud enough to hear: "I had the promise of General Braddock . . . a promise."

Leastways, he don't say he be quittin' again. 'Tis plain he ain't done with his job, but he done with the British army.

## Dr. James Craik:

What I write now may sound strange to one who dinna make the study of sickness his life, as it has puzzled many a man who does: I believe that a person in distress, a victim of loss, or one of sensitive nature, uncertain of how others perceive him, is more vulnerable than most to sickness.

In the fall of 1757, Washington fell for a second time to the bloody flux, followed by violent pleuritic pains, which were the sure sign of a pulmonary complaint.

Now, why did he suffer these? Consider the troubles descending upon him:

First were the frustrations endured over three years of trying to secure the borders of Virginia. And his treatment at the hands of Lord Loudoun had destroyed any hope that he would ever look upon a British commission. Then, in early September, he received news at Winchester that his true patron, a second father in all but blood, Colonel William Fairfax, had passed away.

And while he prepared to attend Fairfax's funeral, his troubles with Dinwiddie came finally to a head. In Williamsburg people were saying George had lied about the strength of the Indians in order to gain more support for his regiment. He blamed Dinwiddie for spreading this falsehood and wrote him angrily: "I may have made military mistakes, but I would think it more generous to charge me with my faults, and let me stand or fall according to the evidence, than to stigmatize me behind my back."

Dinwiddie was blunt: "My conduct to you from the beginning was always friendly, but you know I had great reason to suspect you of ingratitude, which I'm convinced your own conscience and reflection must allow."

The issue that fomented the argument faded, but angry words grew angrier.

Washington wrote: "I do not know that I ever gave Your Honor cause to suspect me of ingratitude, a crime I detest." And he begged leave to come to Williamsburg and explain himself.

But Dinwiddie coldly refused. "Surely the commanding officer should not be absent when daily alarmed with the enemy's intent to invade our frontiers. You have no accounts I know of to settle with me."

So . . . one close patron dead, the other grown distant. And all the hands of favor and influence that he had played so assiduously come to naught.

Down he went to a bed of desperate sickness.

It began that summer as a mild dysentery. But by October, he had grown weak and wobbly. Then came the pleuritic pains which indicated a general worsening of his condition. Twice in a week I attempted to bring him some relief through bleeding. But he dinna improve. It was my diagnosis that the whole mass of blood was corrupted, and nothing but rest and clean air, away from the stenches of Winchester, would cure him.

He at first refused, saying that he was as strong as an ox and he had a duty to acquit to the people of Virginia.

I told him that if he was an ox, he was a very sick ox, an ox soon to drop in its traces, an ox that then would be good for nothing but oxtail soup. So, with great reluctance, he went home.

## Jacob, Mount Vernon Slave:

Member how Massa Lawrence git that skull look when he dyin'? Well, Massa George have it now. He coughin' real bad. And when he ain't coughin, he dumpin' out the other end faster 'n a grass-eatin' dog.

One day I'se over to Belvoir, in the kitchen. Little Match—he three—he settin' near the hearth, tied up so's he don't burn hisself. Narcissa, she four, and Alice learnin' her how to make soup—duck soup with cabbage leaves.

Alice say, "Honey, you learn this good, 'cause they's no better way to live good than to know how to cook. Always keep you out of the sun, so you never end up no common hoe nigger."

She sound jess like my mama. She take Narcissa's li'l hands and hold 'em whilst together they holds the knife, and they chops up some cabbage together, and I thinks, if'n we gits broke up 'cause Colonel Fairfax be dead . . . broke up and spread 'round like we's no more 'n a litter of kittens . . . well . . . I don't know what I'se gonna do.

But Alice ain't thinkin' on such things. She's a

woman. She jess think on what all's in front of her nose—duck soup with cabbage—and who she makin' it for. She say, "From what I seen, Jake, I don't think your massa live till spring."

"Don't say that," I tell her. "That be bad news for all of us."

And Miz Sally come in the kitchen: "I'll have your master up and about by New Year's Day. Now, have you put the duck into the soup yet?"

"Well, yes'm," say Alice.

"Take it out. Quick." She say it like this the most important thing she ever tell anyone. "Doc Green has forbidden him to eat meat. He prescribes jellies and other such smooth foods. Now, do we have any hartshorn?"

"Yes'm."

"Fetch it. A jelly of hartshorn. The best potion he can have. And hyssop tea and"—she glance down at the note from Massa George—"some Canary Islands wine, if we have it . . . to mix with water and gum arabic, to be drunk twice a day."

"That'll bind him up for certain, ma'am," I say.

"We need to do more than bind him. We need to heal him, Jacob."

And my, oh, my, but Miz Sally set out to do that.

Massa George Wil'lum Fairfax, he be off to England, see, to do some business now that his father be dead. So Miz Sally come to Mount Vernon plenty, bringin' them jellies and soups and special wines. Most times she come with one of her sisters or in-laws . . . you know, the ladies of Belvoir, the ones Massa George always tell her to 'member him to.

She know it don't look right for her to be goin' to Mount Vernon alone. But sometime she do, and her and Massa, they sit and talk. Or play cards. And them's the only times he smile or laugh. And she laugh, too—deep, throaty laughs, not them tinkly little laughs she give when she playin' with a man.

And sometime they talk real serious, real soft, which is somethin' I never hear before when the massa talkin' to a woman.

One day he tell her 'bout the day with Lord Loudoun, like he lettin' her see somethin' he don't show nobody else: "General Braddock promised me, Sally. He promised me . . ."

And she say, "Don't worry, George. Good things will come your way."

I keep the fire stoked in the parlor. I brings tea. And one time I come in and Sally standin' over him. He sittin' in a chair, see, pulled up close to the fire, and she have her hands on his shoulders, kneadin' 'em like he be a big piece of dough.

When she hear me, she pull back, and the massa, his face git all red. He say, "Just leave the tea, Jacob." Then he stand up and say, "And pull this chair back from the fireplace. My face is burnin'."

After that, Miz Sally don't come for a while, and never again without she have one of the Belvoir ladies with her. And they never talk that soft again, or laugh quite so much.

But Alice and me, we talk 'bout them. Tha's one thing slaves is good at—talkin'. White folks stay up at night readin', mostly, 'cause they can. We can't, so we talk . . . after we do th'other nighttime things.

"I think your massa gettin' lonelier and lonelier," Alice say. "Now that Brother Jack marry Hannah Bushrod, they be some squeakin' beds at Mount

Vernon. Hard for a man with red blood to hear squeakin' beds and not want to be squeakin' one his-self."

I say, "I think he want to squeak the bed with Miz Sally."

"I think she like him, too," say Alice, "but they know what's what. . . . So do Massa George Wil'lum. . . ."

"What make you say that?"

" 'Fore he go to England, he tell Miz Sally to act with . . . with dis . . . discretion . . . while he gone. Miz Sally get good and mad. She don't throw nothin', but she tell him to git out the room. Massa George Wil'lum, he run like a rabbit."

That make me chuckle. Massa George Wil'lum be all bark and no bite. And sometimes he ain't even got the bark.

Alice say, "Your massa, he need to git hisself a wife of his own."

But my massa jess keep goin' downhill all winter, fluxin' after he eat, coughin' all day, lookin' out the window, watchin' the cold drizzle come down. Still, he try to look ahead. One day he talk with his brother Jack. First off, they go over the plans for spring plan-tin'. And talk like that git him talkin' 'bout his plans for expandin' his house. "I'd like to put up a second story, a full story with proper headroom."

Jack say, "An expandin' house wants an expandin' family, George."

"Your family?"

"Yours. There must be some beauty out there wil-lin' to share this fine view with you. You know . . . there's a rich young widow down on the Pamunkey."

Massa say, "The Custis woman? Martha Custis?"

Brother Jack—you know how brothers is, they likes to josh—he say, "So it *is* her that's got you actin' like a lovesick pup!"

"I've met the woman once or twice. I hardly know her."

"Don't matter. Not if she's rich. Get to know her. A rich widow needs a husband. If you're not sweet on her, be sweet on her seventeen thousand acres."

And Massa git mad. I know 'cause his voice git real cold, see, and he say somethin' I ain't sure Jack quite git. He say, "The world has no right to know the object of my affections. . . . Nor do you."

Plain to me this widow Custis ain't who he's talkin' about.

Then Massa say, "I'm sorry, Jack. It's been a hard winter."

Jack say, "We'll make it a better spring."

Massa jess keep talkin'. "More than a hard winter, a hard three years. I have no wife. No hope for a royal commission. I'm too sick to do what a commander must. I've been a failure in every pursuit, public and private. I've been thinking of quitting my command and retiring from all public business, once and for all."

And I thinks, *Agin?* But this time he got good reason. If he dyin', best spend what time he have right there at home.


Well, he don't die that winter, and when he smell that warmin' earth in March, he decide to find out if he gonna be smellin' flowers come April. So we head for Wil'lumsburg, to see a doctor. Sometime, he make the trip in two days. But this time we takes ten. We even stop at Ferry Farm and he visit his mother for three whole days. Tha's how weak he be.

The doc in Wil'lumsburg, he's s'posed to know 'bout the bloody flux. I try to picture what a man have to do to learn 'bout such things. But it ain't pretty, so I leaves it behind.

The massa go in his office lookin' like he ain't never comin' out. But when he do, he smilin'. He say, "Let's go, Jake. 'Tis a fine spring day. King Street never looks better than in the spring."

And I know right then the doctor tell him good news.

Few days later he head north to a place called White House, lookin' for the kind of medicine that's better than the best day of springtime—a rich widow.

*Part Three*

❧

# THE PLANTER
# AND THE REBEL

c.d.—*I tried to conjure up the Washington growing before me.*

*He did not seem a young man destined for greatness, simply one of apparent self-possession seeking to possess more. But apparent self-possession may mask something quite the opposite. And the man with the least true self-possession is sometimes the most acquisitive.*

*A royal commission—providing pay, rank, respect, and, upon retirement, half pay for the rest of his life—must have seemed irresistible to the semi-educated third son of a middling Virginia planter. However, rank and property were merely the rewards that flowed to a man who had, by his deeds, earned the respect of his peers, and a man who had made a reputation.*

*Washington had not yet learned that the best reputation was built through steadiness. So the loyal officer defending the Virginia frontier could quickly become a petulant rank-seeker, ready to resign at the drop of a pay grade. He had not grown the thick skin that an ambitious man should have. He had not found the balance that an acquisitive man needs if he is ever to do more than merely accumulate.*

*So how did he become what he did?*

*That was a question far more interesting to me than any about his letters to a wealthy young widow. And that widow, aged now and widowed again, had decided to see me, after all.*

*Her note informed me that I was to appear on January 12, at which time, she would be happy to speak about her "dear departed husband," with the son of a good Federalist like the late Joshua Draper of Boston.*

*Once more I traveled to Mount Vernon on a bright winter day. Once more I was ushered into the passage. Once more, as I awaited Tobias Lear, I tried to absorb the atmosphere of the house. The very air seemed thin and deflated, as if an elemental gas had been burned away. This sensation grew even stronger as Lear ushered me into the west parlor, where a small woman was perched on a buff-colored sofa.*

*She was all but overshadowed by a billow of white hair, kept in place by a mobcap large enough to serve as a sail on a river-running sloop. And the combination of hair and cap made everything else about her seem even smaller. Her face, features, hands, and feet all seemed to have been rendered in miniature. Even her plumpness was made to seem smaller by the color of her dress—a light pastel blue overpowered by the darker blue walls and woodwork around her.*

*She looked like an aged bird—something small, of course, perhaps a squab—fattened by a cook who had come to like her so much that he had made her into a pet instead of a casserole.*

*When she saw me, her small mouth curved invol-*

untarily into a smile, as if grief could not keep her from expressing the pleasure she took in personal contact. The smile forced her small eyes to brighten. And she said, in a small voice, "Welcome to Mount Vernon, Mr. Draper."

I answered with the most courtly bow I could muster, and my eyes drifted to the portrait on the wall behind her: George Washington, wearing the uniform of the Virginia Regiment, sword at his side, musket in the crook of his arm.

"My dear departed husband at the age of forty," said Mrs. Washington, "painted by our good friend Charles Willson Peale."

And I saw for the first time the Washington I had been writing about, rather than the old man immortalized in so many mezzotints and engravings. Here was one in whom vigorous youth still resided, who had swum icy rivers, ambushed French in the forests, endured dysentery, survived massacre.

He was not built to inspire classical sculptors. His shoulders were narrow, his chest rather sunken, his belly widening beneath his red waistcoat. But there was formidability in his bulk, grace in the long limbs, ambition in the cock of the head.

He seemed to be gazing at the pair of portraits on the adjoining wall. One was of a young woman with almond-shaped eyes set in an almond-shaped face, tender breasts displayed in a low-cut dress of blue and yellow satin, brown hair combed simply and held in place by a strand of pearls, and of course, a kindly smile. This was Martha in youth, her natural warm-heartedness as apparent when glimpsed through the mists of pigmented time as when seen through the prism of widowed grief.

Beside her, rendered by the same artist, were two small children—a boy of perhaps four, in a blue suit, his arm extended to serve as a perch to a red bird, and a girl of about two, in a white satin dress. Both children had the same almond-shaped eyes and the same delicacy as the woman. Beyond that, all that could be discerned was their innocence.

Mrs. Washington gestured for me to sit at the tea table by the fireplace. And as smoothly as she poured tea, she poured forth small talk about the weather, politics, and the world from which she seemed so well insulated. The entertaining of guests, over tea and chitchat, was something she knew well.

And thus it began. For the rest of that January day, Martha Washington told her story. Tobias Lear joined us now and again, just to remind me that he was on the watch. But the business of running the plantation had fallen to him, and even in winter he had many responsibilities.

So I had her to myself. I did not, however, broach the subject of the letters, as she was lost in her reminiscence of courtship, and I was loath to bring her out of such reflected happiness. Besides, as the inspiration for such fond memories, I hoped to rise in her estimation.

And I must have, as I was invited to stay the night. I dined with Mrs. Washington. I walked the grounds. I met a few more slaves. But Miss Delilah Smoot studiously avoided me. And Tobias Lear watched me as if I had come to steal ideas and silverware both.

The next day, Mrs. Washington and I continued our conversation. But our morning and afternoon sessions both ended with tragedies so unspeakable that she determined she could not go on.

*"You must forgive me, Mr. Draper, but I shall need a few days to recover."*

I gave her a week, then returned to Mount Vernon, but Mr. Lear met me at the door and informed me that Mrs. Washington could not see me again. He said that in my presence, she had recalled so much that was so painful that her grief was growing more acute.

And I had not yet asked the most important questions. I stood for a moment, staring at the implacable visage of Mr. Lear. Then I said I would call again after more time had passed. Lear did not encourage me.

## The Narrative of Martha Washington:

I always considered myself a happy woman. Homey, happy, cheerful as a cricket, and busy as a bee. But the death of my husband, Daniel Parke Custis, had left me a widow at the age of twenty-seven.

Although much older than I, Mr. Custis had been in fine fettle until the moment he collapsed. He died intestate, and some criticized him for not preparing for death, as any man of property must out of mere practicality, as any man of life should out of expectation of the final reward. But why should he have expected to die when not a sign of sickness was upon him? The Lord, as they say, works in strange ways.

After his death, I was determined to manage his huge estate well. And the first step was not to marry until I had found a man in whom I could allow my trust to repose, as by Virginia law, a wife cannot hold property in her own name. She must place it in her husband's control, which is all for the best, considering the extent of a woman's other responsibilities and the breadth of knowledge that men have in matters of property.

But to be a well-off widow of marrying age is most disconcerting, as you can never be certain of a man's true intentions. Does he call on you because he has interest in a partnership of love and trust, or because of your money?

I put aside these questions when Colonel Washington came to visit at White House, on the Pamunkey, in March of 1758. I knew him to be an honorable gentleman. I was also flattered that one so recently rumored to be at death's door, and more than once rumored to have passed its portals, would wish to visit me.

I had, of course, met him several times before, had dined with him, had even danced with him, but all while my husband was still alive.

Don't forget, our society might have been widespread, from Alexandria to Williamsburg, but it was still quite small. And the Hero of the Monongahela was one of its shining lights—a noble soldier, a fine figure in his blue-and-red uniform, and a man who could dance minuets and country reels with equal grace. Add to this the fine property he held on the Potomac, and Colonel Washington was what some called a prize catch.

Still, when he called upon me in my widowhood, I treated him with the formality I offered all my suitors. We took tea in the parlor. We talked of the weather and the war, and I noted, though I was not so forward as to mention, that he seemed quite haggard from his recent sickness. I did, however, offer him a second tea cake, then a third.

When I urged a fourth, he laughed—he had a very comforting and gentle laugh—and said, "You'll fill me until I bust, ma'am."

I said, "Colonel Washington, I don't think there are enough tea cakes in all of Virginia to fill you up just now."

"In my present state, I suppose you're right. I'll have another."

We made more chitchat, at which he was most uncomfortable. Then our talk turned to planting, which put him at his ease. He asked me questions of the kind I had only learned to answer when I took over the running of the plantation: How soon after Christmas did we plant the tobacco seeds? What kind of mulch did we use to protect them? When did we thin them? Transplant them?

So I offered to show him the fruits of our labor, and we strolled for what seemed like hours through fields of greening tobacco shoots. And I began to think how . . . how blessed a woman could be when a man of substance and repute came to her door.

## Jacob, Mount Vernon Slave:

I watch the massa walkin' with Miz Martha, and I thinks, This here could be the one make him fergit Miz Sally. This here could be the one he marry. I see it in how he laugh and how she turn her head to him, and how he offer his arm and she take it when they come to a big muddy spot in the path. I see it in all that, and in her seventeen thousand acres, too.

# Martha Washington:

As I felt quite easy with him and knew also that he faced a long ride back to Williamsburg, I invited him to dine with me and my children and stay the night. I ordered another place to be set for dinner and linens to be put upon the bed in the guest room. Then I sent for my children.

My Jacky was four and little Martha, whom we called Patsy, was two, and, oh, but they were marvelous little treasures. Bright-eyed and curious and as full of mischief as the fairies of fable.

Mr. Washington stood as they came into the room. 'Twas his natural inclination to stand when he met anyone, even children. He studied manners as a boy, you know. He may not have known, however, the impact that his great height and handsome uniform would make upon a little boy more used to lookin' up at his mother. I am, as you can see, barely five feet tall.

He extended his hand, and Jacky, dear boy, just looked upon it as he would a strange dog.

I said, "The colonel is a great hero, Jacky."

Mr. Washington, putting on a voice of grave seriousness, said, "No little boy will lose his scalp when I'm in charge of the Virginia Regiment."

'Twas a rather grisly image for such a sensitive little boy, and Jacky took a step back rather than a step forward.

But dear little Patsy reached out and touched the brass buttons on the colonel's coat. He looked down at her for a moment. Then he smiled and swept her up into his arms. And my thoughts grew warmer.

His must have matched mine, because ten days

later, as he returned to Winchester from Williamsburg, he stopped once more at White House.

The details of that visit I prefer to leave untold.

Suffice to say that within a few days each of us placed orders in London. I sent for a "genteel suit of clothes for myself, to be grave but not extravagant, and not to be mourning." I also had my favorite nightgown dyed a pastel blue. Mr. Washington wrote to London, for "as much of the best superfine blue cotton velvet as will make a coat, wasitcoat, and breeches for a tall man, with a fine silk button to suit it." We had ordered our wedding clothes.

But the wedding, we had decided, would not take place until he had fulfilled his duties to the colony, by which he meant the taking of Fort Duquesne.

## Hesperus Draper:

In the summer of '58, John Forbes, the new British general, did two things that should have made Washington a happy man: he said that British officers wouldn't command colonial officers of higher rank, and he made Duquesne his goal for the year.

But it was hard to make Washington happy, and when Forbes said he would strike from Pennsylvania, instead of taking Braddock's Road from Virginia, our boy soldier got downright gloomy. Didn't matter that the Pennsylvania route was forty miles shorter. Washington owned land along Braddock's Road. And he'd been elected as burgess from Frederick County. His land, and the land of all his voters, would rise in value if the march went by Braddock's Road.

When Forbes decided for certain on the Pennsylvania route, I heard Washington cry to Craik, "Oh, poor Virginia! Stabbed in the back!"

Craik said it sounded like treachery. I thought it sounded like Washington had been seein' too many plays. Poor Virginia, my ass.

Forbes should've demoted him for insubordination. But Washington had a martial dignity about him, even when he was whinin'. Forbes just ordered him to stop complainin', then gave him command of the forward units. It was November when we stepped off for Duquesne.

## John Britain,
## known as Silverheels:

After the Braddock fight, I took my family to a Mingo village upstream of Fort Duquesne. We let the French run us. We took their gifts. We did their bidding. And I will not lie. I went on raids. I scalped and burned.

But I knew the French dog would lose the fight. I knew when the British took Fort Niagara and food and powder stopped coming downstream to Duquesne. I knew when the British promised the Great Council of the Iroquois that the land beyond the Alleghenies would be ours forever. White men are good at saying you can keep what is already yours. And I knew when I heard that Caunotaucarius was coming.

I told Bright Leaf that the French would run before he came. I said we should run, too.

She was big again with child. She said the baby would not come until the snows were deep. But she was bleeding. And as the days went on, she bled more.

One day I went into the woods to find two strong poles to make a pallet, so I could drag her when we went. And I saw smoke rising above the trees. The French were burning the fort. They were running. I hurried back to Bright Leaf.

Many Mingo families were already gone. They took their babies and their blankets and went toward Lake Erie. Others went to the fort, to be there when Caunotaucarius came in, to sniff the balls of the dog who won the fight.

An old Mingo mother had stayed with Bright Leaf. She said we should leave. But Bright Leaf was losing the color in her face and the light in her eyes. Her blood was coming faster. She held her legs together, but the blood would not stop. She lay with her bottom higher than her head, but still it would not stop.

The old mother was of the Clan of the Turtle, Bright Leaf's clan, so she said she would be a real mother to Bright Leaf and stay as long as we stayed. But she said she was afraid of Caunotaucarius.

I told her I knew him. And he might bring one who could help Bright Leaf.

The old woman said, "Only the medicine man can help. And he has gone."


Caunotaucarius came in the last light. He wore a blue-and-red uniform. He rode a big horse. He led many men. They carried the British flag, but they were Virginians. Some wore blue suits. Most wore hunting shirts and buckskins. They did not tramp like fools. And there was no silly music. These men were warriors, and Caunotaucarius was their chief.

There was nothing left of the fort but tall chimneys and burned timbers. There would be no spoils for Caunotaucarius. There would be no torture. Only a cold place at the forks of a cold river. The British flag fluttered up the flagpole and hung above the ashes.

The light was gray. Soon it would be black.

I came out of the woods. But I came with a strong step. I did not come like the other Mingoes and Shawnees, who stood in a clump and waited for permission to come forward.

Two Cherokees saw me. They had fought for the British, for money. They were dogs, too. One of them spit on me. But I kept walking. I did not even look at them. I would show them that I did not care about them, even when they began to hoot.

This drew the eye of Caunotaucarius. He rode toward me, and the Cherokee dogs made way. He stopped his horse in front of me. He looked hard at my face. Then he said my English name. "Silverheels?"

I knew some English now, so I thanked him for driving off the French.

He said, "I thought you were dead."

I told him it was my wife who was dying.

So Caunotaucarius sent Dr. Craik with me. But he sent four soldiers, too. He thought I was setting a trap. But I was only a man worried for his woman. One of the soldiers was the skinny one whose yellow-haired woman was killed in the river. He remembered me, too. So I had two friends.

I led them back to our village. Nothing was left but two longhouses, some dying fires, and the sound of an old woman's death song.

## Dr. James Craik:

The young squaw had miscarried and hemorrhaged to death. It was nae within my power to bring the dead back to life, but the quiet bravery of her husband could not be denied. He knelt beside her and held her in his arms. He closed her eyes. Then he began to rock back and forth.

Hesperus Draper knelt beside them. He touched the shoulder of the Indian. Then he ran his hand through the hair of the dead woman, as if caressing her. Then he did it again, and his hand came to rest on a red feather in her hair.

Silverheels slipped the feather from the hair of his wife and gave it to him. Hesperus went outside, and I am certain that I saw his shoulders shake with a sob.

## Hesperus Draper:

'Tis a true fact that only a man who's lost his woman can know the pain of a man who loses his. I looked at that sad Injun and saw myself, holdin' my Bee in the river. I also figured this ignorant savage might think we'd brought the angel of death, 'less we showed him we were sorry.

But he was a rare Injun. Remembered me. Remembered Bee. Remembered enough that he give me Bee's red feather. I didn't know what to do with it. So I went outside and stuck it in my hat.

Sun was goin' down; 'twas gettin' colder. I looked

at his two sad little Injun boys, and a shiver come over me.

C.D.—*Washington might not have gotten British rank, but he had gained the respect of the colony and achieved his military goal—to protect Virginia from attack by taking Fort Duquesne. The war was moving to the provinces of Canada, the bloody fields of Europe, the mysterious landscapes of far-off India. But it was Washington who had started it all.*

*As the essayist Horace Walpole would write of the attack in Jumonville Glen, "The volley fired by a young Virginian in the backwoods of America set the world on fire."*

## Jacob, Mount Vernon Slave:

Somethin' seem funny to me. 'Stead of comin' back to Mount Vernon from Fort Duquesne, Massa George go straight to Belvoir. Why do you suppose he do that? Why don't he go straight down to see Miz Martha?

Well, Alice tell the story:

When Massa George come ridin' up to Belvoir, Massa George Wil'lum be standin' on the veranda, waitin' for a slave to bring 'round his horse. He give a big wave and shout. "George! By God, you've done it."

Massa say, "Thank you. Thank you."

"A fine year it's been for you, George. Conquering Duquesne . . . and, even better, betrothal to the Custis woman."

But Massa George ain't come to talk to George Wil'lum. It's Miz Sally he want to see. And when she come out of the house and shake his hand, real formal like, Massa George can't keep his face from flarin' up with a big smile.

Massa George Wil'lum say, "I'm needed at my overseer's house. You'll allow Sally to entertain you, and of course you'll stay for dinner?"

And tha's what Massa George been lookin' for all along, I think. A chance to set with Miz Sally.

My Alice, after all she hear 'bout discretion and whatnot, she don't think George Wil'lum ever plan to leave his wife alone with Massa George again, not till Massa George marry someone else. But betrothed is good enough, I reckon.

So Massa George and Miz Sally go in the parlor. They sits in chairs on one side of the fireplace and th'other. But tha's as close as they git.

My Alice find a way to be flutterin' 'bout, bringin' in tea but fergettin' to bring the tea trimmin's, so she git to come back, and back again.

Massa George say to Miz Sally, "I've missed you."

"And we've all missed you on the Potomac, George," say Miz Sally.

He say, "I've missed *you* particularly."

And Miz Sally say, "Alice, what do you expect me to stir my tea with? A finger?"

Alice go scurryin' into the dinin' room to git two spoons from the sideboard. When she go back, she go real quiet, like a water bug on a puddle. Tha's how she learn to go when she's a little girl, see, when she don't want the massa knowin' she's 'round.

Miz Sally sayin', "I thought my last letter made my feelings clear, George."

And he say, "I thought my last letter made *my* feelings clear."

Miz Sally say, "George, you're to be married soon. Martha Custis is a fine woman. And you should consider yourself most fortunate."

"Most fortunate. I do. But not so fortunate as I've dreamed of becoming."

Miz Sally say, "Alice, you bring spoons, but nothin' to spoon. You know Colonel Washington likes to sugar his tea."

"Yes'm," say Alice, and she go scurryin' for sugar. She know exac'ly where she left it, right on the sideboard. She dip her finger in the bowl, like always, and take a taste, then go water-buggin' back into the parlor.

Miz Sally be standin' with her hands folded in front of her.

Massa George lookin' up at her, sayin', "Is that your answer?"

And she say, "What other answer can there be, George?"

Alice come in and put down the sugar bowl.

"Leave it, Alice," say Miz Sally.

"Yes'm." And, real slow, Alice start for the door.

Then Miz Sally say, "But what is this? You know Colonel Washington loves cakes with his tea."

"Yes'm."

"So bring us tea cakes." And she bat her eyes at Massa George. "Sweets for the sweet, George."

Battin' her eyes . . . singsongin' her voice . . . playin' with him agin. She know that "sweet" ain't a word we use too much when it come to Massa George.

Alice come back a minute later with the dish of cakes, and the massa jess finishin' up his talk. He standin' too, and he say, "I've spoken as plain as I could, ma'am. I'll not trouble you on the matter again."

She say, "You're never any trouble, George. You know that."

And Massa give a little bow. "You are most kind. You have always been most kind. But 'twill be for the best."

Miz Sally say, "It could . . . it could not be otherwise."

"I'm now fixed with an agreeable consort for life. I hope to find more happiness in retirement than I've ever experienced in a wide and bustling world."

"Tea cake, sir?" say Alice.

But Massa keep his eyes on Miz Sally and say, "I'll always remember your kindness. And if the role were ever offered, I would gladly play Juba to your Marcia . . . Romeo to your Juliet."

Miz Sally start blinkin' real fast, like she got somethin' in her eyes, or maybe she gittin' teary. Then she look at Alice and say, "Alice! Leave the tea cakes. Leave them on the table and don't bother us again."

## Martha Washington:

Our wedding came on a bitter morning in January, but the warmth of spirit that filled White House still warms my heart.

I shall always remember our dear friends, George William Fairfax and his Sarah, whom we all knew as Sally. They were like brother and sister to my husband. Brother Jack and his wife, Hannah, came. Brother Charles and sister Betty. George's mother found the distance too great in winter, which was something of a disappointment. But there was so many others, so many friendly faces wishing us joy.

My dress was yellow grosgrain silk, not nearly so grave as I had first ordered, but 'twas surely no day for mourning. My husband had dressed most fashionable in a blue velvet suit. When he saw me appear in the entrance to the parlor, the expression on his face, which had been grave and rather nervous, brightened like a candle.

And that night we danced. Oh, how we danced! Oh, how Mr. Washington loved to dance! There were minuets and marches, gavottes, even a jig. The cold January wind blew, but the warmth of forty dancers steamed every pane of glass as though a giant kettle had been left on to boil. And the champagne flowed and the Madeira and a rich hot wine punch, too. . . .

After the dancing, after the last guest had gone to his bedchamber, I retired with my husband. And . . . and . . . I remember the gentleness with which he . . . I remember the taste of Madeira. . . . Oh, my . . . Mr. Draper, you must think me . . .

C.D.—*I stopped making notes, realizing how acute was her embarrassment. . . . Then she regained herself and leaped all the way to their arrival at Mount Vernon:*

It was on a bright spring day that our carriage, followed by several wagons full of belongings and servants, came up the road to this house. Of course, Mount Vernon was smaller then. A second story had been raised in the year since our engagement, so there were four full bedrooms upstairs. But the outbuildings had fallen into much disrepair, having been neglected over the years that Mr. Washington had been on the frontier.

All that could be got ready for us was done. My husband had written ahead and ordered his servants to set up extra beds for the children, to bring out furniture and see that it was polished and the like. But there was much work ahead, both inside and out.

Jacky took one look around and said, "Mother, can't we please go home?"

I tousled his lovely hair and tried to explain that this was home.

He said, quite understandably, "I want my old home, Mother. I want to go home to White House, please."

You must remember that, in losing their father, my poor little children had suffered perhaps more greatly than I, for I had found another husband. No matter how carefully I smoothed the path, it would take time for them to accept Mr. Washington as their new father.

## Jacob, Mount Vernon Slave:

We work like whupped dogs for two days 'fore Massa George bring his new family home. He want them new upstairs rooms all spit-shined and ready, so us house slaves does it, and . . . all the while we's wonderin' which of us gonna get sent outside when the massa's new wife bring her own servants.

Me and th'other house slaves, we's standin' in a line

in the carriage turnaround, so we see all their faces when they step out of the carriage and see the house for the first time.

Massa George look as proud as if he jess build the place hisself. He say, "Welcome to Mount Vernon." Then he reach in the carriage.

And I see that smilin' face of Miz Washington. It squinch up for a second, 'cause she can't be too happy at what all she see at such a half-done place. But she do a fine job of not showin' it, makin' her face go all smiley again. Then she stick out her little foot, reachin' for the carriage step.

Then her little boy try to scramble past and all but knock her down.

Massa George stick out his arm, like a gate, to keep the boy in the carriage. And he say, "Jacky, ladies before gentlemen."

I swear, that kid look at him like he want to hit him.

Miz Washington step out, and the boy try to duck under Massa's arm, to git ahead of his sister, see. And Massa say it agin, "Ladies before gentlemen."

And the boy say, "But she's my sister!"

And Massa say, real soft, "All the more reason. Do as you're told."

Jacky say, "You're not my father."

Then the sister come scramblin' down behind her mother, squeezin' her way out 'tween Massa George and little Jacky.

And the mama, like she ain't heard or seen none of this, she say, sweet as honey, "Climb down now, Jacky dear, and see your new home."

And Jacky dear, he git out, sayin', "I don't want a new home. I don't like this place. Take me back to White House."

Massa George's face don't show nothin'. He jess turn his back on the boy, let the mother chatter at him a bit, stroke him, make him feel like she love him.

Ain't no doubt this be tough on a little feller, and on the big feller, too. The massa got hisself a whole fam'ly, not jess a wife. And that boy, he got hisself a hard new father to go with his sweet-talkin' mama.

That boy jess turn up his nose like he smell shit. He got a little round face and a fancy little suit, and he already know how to give you one of them looks, with his eyes all hooded like a sleepy snake, the kind of look that say he know jess where you sit on the ladder, and jess where he sit, too.

But his mama, she look at you like you's real folks. She come down the line of slaves and ax each of us our name—five of us back then—and she tell us we's all stayin' right where we is and her servants'll help with the extry load.

And I thinks, I like this lady.


## Martha Washington:

The day after I arrived, Sally Fairfax visited, bearing a neighborly basket of jellies and teas. She had been to my husband like a big sister who provided encouragement in matters of the heart. I've always secretly wondered what she might have said to him in regard to our union, though I'm certain that whatever it was, it was nothing but generous.

I suffered her to sit with me that day and take tea . . . in this very room.

We were not well matched, at least to the eye. She

was tall and slender. I was . . . I was not. But we struck a fine friendship, a borrowing-neighbor kind of friendship, you might say.

Our talk covered many things . . . my dear children, my plans for decorating the house. I'd been studying the wallpapers that Mr. Washington had ordered from England and settled upon a color scheme of blue and white to complement them.

But what I remember most vividly is going through her basket of sundries and commenting upon each of them. I was especially interested in a small jar of hartshorn jelly. 'Twas the color of amber, sealed with wax.

I said, "I've heard of the beneficial effects of hartshorn."

She said, " 'Twas certainly most beneficial for your husband in his sickness a year past. I ordered the hartshorn powder from England. A fine strong hart brought down after a long chase, or so they promised. Whenever Mr. Washington's strength lags, dose him with this jelly and see him revive."

I must admit to you that the small laugh she added suggested much in the way of personal knowledge, and I felt a tinge of jealousy, not that Mr. Washington ever gave me cause to submit to such base emotion.

Besides how could I be jealous of such a good neighbor and faithful friend?

C.D.—*While men like my uncle remained in the army until the war ended, so that they could accumulate more credit toward the bonus lands, Washington threw himself into the life of a Tidewater planter. He told friends, "I have many memories from the war that I must strive to forget." And strive he did. With his own ambition to drive him, and Martha's money behind him, he raised himself in the next four years to ever greater prominence in Virginia society. Men like my uncle went back to their jobs and waited for their bonus lands.*

## Hesperus Draper:

L et me tell you about the Proclamation of 1763. After all our fightin' and dyin' to drive the French from North America, the king proclaimed that no colonist could own land on the far side of the Alleghenies, and only handpicked traders could do business there. 'Twas supposed to keep peace with the Injuns. Truth was, the British were just tryin' to bunch us up at the coast so nobody got any land that the Crown might want later on.

And the bonus lands? What they decided in London mattered more than what old dead Dinwiddie had promised a handful of enlistees ten years before.

But what right did British ministers on the other side of the Atlantic have to be tellin' me where I could own land and who I could trade with? That proclamation started a lot of colonists askin' questions, includin' Washington.

And now that he was a tobacco planter he had plenty of questions, because colonial planters were playin' against marked cards. If you were a planter, the only place the British let you sell your tobacco was England. And your only pay was English credit. So if you wanted to buy anything, you had to buy in England. 'Twas the classic two-step of colony and mother country:

send us your raw goods; buy our finished goods; work hard; enrich us.

And the funny thing about this credit business, it always worked in favor of the creditors. I didn't know a single planter who wasn't in debt to some London factor. To keep it that way, the British controlled the flow of cash in the colonies. And they were tight with it, too, as tight as an asshole in icy water, so credit and barter were the only real forms of exchange between colonists, along with some paper money the colonies printed on their own.

Now, most of Washington's business went with Cary and Company in London. He sold tobacco through them, and he placed his orders with them for everything from plow blades to port wine. Sometimes his orders came all on one ship that went right to Mount Vernon, but sometimes a small shipment would come to Alexandria, to be stored for him at the warehouse of a local importer. That was what brought him to my uncle's office one summer afternoon in 1763.

Uncle Jonathan was in his sixties by then. Could still eat half a pony if you made a nice sauce for it, but the work of haulin' his belly around had worn him out. The sight of Washington cheered him, though, because Washington lived as well as any planter on the Tidewater, and that meant business for us.

Planters were supposed to enjoy fine and fancy things, so folks could see how successful they were. If they weren't eatin' off the best china, drinkin' the best wines, sniffin' the best snuff, and sittin' their asses on the best mahogany chairs when they ate the fancy tinned foods they imported . . . well, if they weren't doin' all that, they might not be so successful as they let on.

And don't forget the clothes. Washington dressed his part, like an actor in a play—always just so, always just right, whether he was dancin' or ridin' to hounds. He ordered suits made special—linen suits for summer, wool suits for winter, fancy velvet suits with lace collars and cuffs for best—good boots, good shoes, silver buckles for the shoes, kid gloves, feathers . . .

My uncle bustled Washington into his office and started butterin' straightaway: " 'Tis a true honor to have you here, sir."

"An honor to sit with you, gentlemen." Washington nodded, as if agreeing with himself. Whatever he'd been workin' on in his twenties, he'd perfected by his thirties. Held your attention just by bein' in the room. Moved well, stood straight, sat straight, always wore a polite face, but never got too friendly, never laughed too loud. 'Twas as if he was still livin' by what he'd read in *The Rules of Civility*. Acted like his whole self was a team of four horses, who'd pull strong and steady, so long as he held the reins tight.

My uncle kept butterin', sayin' how beautiful Washington's two little children were.

But Washington didn't smile. Never smiled much, and he'd already lost a tooth, which made him smile even less. He just said, "Thank you, Mr. Draper, but they are my *step*children."

"Well," said my uncle, "they're fine-lookin' little'ns just the same. And think of how handsome your *own*'ll be."

From the way Washington stiffened, I could see he

didn't like this talk at all. Had to rankle him that he didn't have kids of his own after four years of marriage.

I could see the stepkids through the office door. The girl was clutchin' the hand of that slave named Jake. The boy was on his knees, shootin' glass agates with another slave. Imagine, havin' the money to buy your boy a servant who'd polish his shoe buckles and shoot aggies with him, whatever he wanted.

Washington may have started on the same rung as me, but he'd climbed a lot faster. Good marriages hadn't hurt—his own to Martha and his late half-brother's to Nancy Fairfax, who had since passed away herself. Washington had married the richest widow in Virginia, and he'd used the money to double the size of his plantation, which he wasn't rentin' anymore, because at Nancy Fairfax's death, the property had passed to him, free and clear.

He'd been as lucky buildin' an estate as he'd been survivin' in battle. And remember what I said about luck. Most men can smell a lucky man a mile off. That's why my uncle was all over Washington like flies on cow flop.

"Now, sir," he said, clappin' his chubby hands together, "is there anything I can do for you before you pick up your goods?"

"Not immediately"—Washington took a sip of the port placed in front of him by a slave—"but you should know I'm selling wheat to Carlyle and Adams."

"The grain brokers?" said my uncle.

"They assure me they'll handle it all, but I may need storage."

Grain was one product that didn't have to go

through England. It could be sold in the colonies for credit, bills of exchange, local money, or barter.

"My warehouse is at your service, sir," said my uncle.

"I'll expect the usual rates, then," said Washington.

"For the Hero of the Monongahela," answered my uncle, "a special rate."

Washington nodded, as if the compliment was no more than his due. Annoyed me, 'cause I guarantee you, I did more killin' than him on the Monongahela. And I lost more, too. But nobody'd ever called me a hero.

So I tweaked him. Shouldn't have done it. Couldn't resist it. "Growin' more food, George?" I said. "Must mean the tobacco's not comin' in so good."

Washington turned his big head in my direction. "It means my wheat is coming in very well."

"So maybe you should grow more wheat and less tobacco," I said.

"Are you suggesting my tobacco is not quality leaf?" If he wanted to take offense, he could twist a remark like a prissy young girl.

But the truth was that there was two things his luck hadn't touched—fatherin' children, as I said, and growin' tobacco.

Oh, he grew a lot. One year 150,000 pounds. But as a rule he got lower prices than most. Blamed his factors in England. His factors blamed his poor-quality tobacco. He blamed the weather for the poor quality. And none of it could do his reputation any good, because a planter who grew second-rate tobacco just might be second-rate himself.

Fact was, the Mount Vernon fields weren't much better than cobblestone for growin'—light topsoil, clay a few feet down, hardpan under that. And a crop like tobacco needs prime dirt, which ain't prime once tobacco's been grown in it. So Washington was growin' more wheat, more corn, too.

"You know, sir," said my uncle, "I have some fine outlets in New England and the Indies. If you grow grain for market, I'd be happy to handle whatever Carlyle and Adams can't. You'll find my credit rates are most competitive."

"Glad to do business with you," answered Washington, "but not for credit."

Now, a planter turnin' down credit was like a hound turnin' down a proud bitch. I asked him why he was doin' it.

"Because credit is no more than a leash to control those who put it on."

"If Washington wears a leash," I said, "it must have a silver collar."

"I'll wear no leash of credit." Washington finished his port, gathered up his hat, and made to leave. "Because the converse of credit is debt."

My uncle saw business goin' right out the door, so he said, "Damn me, Mr. Washington, but there's truth in what you say. I prefer barter myself. Rather trade a few cones of sugar for a side of pork than a whole pig for credit."

Washington stopped in the doorway, about as smug as a man could get: "We produced six thousand pounds of pork at Mount Vernon last year. It would take a mountain of sugar to barter for it, if we didn't eat it all ourselves."

*There* was something to warm a fat man's heart— three tons of ham, bacon, and pork loin. My uncle just whispered, "Bravo." Silly old fool.

I said, "You must need a lot of grain to feed that many hogs, George. You plannin' to buy more land to grow it on?"

"To move ahead in the world," he said, "a man must have an eye for land."

"But the king's proclamation blinds the eye," I answered.

He stepped back into the room. He'd step back into a burnin' house if there was land to be talked about. "Well said, Draper, but too strongly."

"So what did we fight for, George, if not for bonus land beyond the mountains?"

"We fought for king and country."

That was a laugh. Washington fought for rank, and he didn't get it. I fought for land, and I'd be *damned* if I didn't get it.

He said, "Someday we'll get the bonus lands, Draper. Shorten your gaze, buy local lands, and bide your time."

Easier said than done if you're an office clerk livin' in a colony where the well-chosen men own all the good land already.

But Washington was done talkin'. "Gentlemen, my stepchildren have waited patiently for their presents from London. Take me to my goods."

This was the part of a visit that my uncle avoided. Not all planters were happy when they saw how their orders were filled in London. Shoddy goods, the wrong goods, not enough of somethin', or too much of somethin' else—'twould make any man mad. So he left the job of delivery to me. Said he was too old.

I led Washington and his stepkids downstairs, to where we held shipments. His wasn't large—tins of food, tea, clothes, a mahogany table in six pieces.

"Where are the soldiers for Master Jacky?" he asked.

"They're on the inventory," I said. And quickly we found a box of lead soldiers, painted in the green uniforms of Rogers's Rangers.

Washington cut the wrappin' with a penknife. At the sight of the soldiers, his face brightened. "Excellent, Master Jack. A fine-looking platoon."

"Can I have them, sir?" asked Jacky.

"*May* I have them," Washington corrected. And after the boy had repeated the correction, Washington extended the package. The boy grabbed, and Washington withdrew, like he was playin', or testin' the boy's discipline.

"Please, sir?" said the boy.

"Don't grab, son." He gave the boy the box. Jacky went scurryin' off.

And Washington turned to the little girl, who had been clingin' the whole time to the leg of that slave. The smile he gave her was about the most genuine I'd ever seen on his face. "And what do we have for you?"

"A . . . a doll baby, sir."

"Yes," he said, "a fine doll baby, with a china face and silk clothes."

He offered the girl his big hand, and she reached out like 'twas a trusted old dog. 'Twas plain she liked him, liked him more than the boy did, and he liked her, too. How could he not? With her big eyes and round face and downturned little mouth, she looked like a little doll baby herself.

But I wasn't thinkin' on how pretty she was. I was searchin' the inventory for "one doll baby." And I could not find it.

She said, "Papa, I want my doll baby. You promised."

And I started sweatin', flippin' the pages of the ledger.

And Washington put his big head right over my shoulder and looked at the ledger, sayin', "It must be here. I sent specific instructions to Robert Cary."

And I got fresh. I said, "Maybe Cary can't read."

And the little girl said, "Papa! My doll baby. You promised."

Washington took off his hat and wiped the sweat from his forehead. Gave the girl a few *there-there*'s, then said to me, "Draper, if you don't find that doll, I'll have your job."

"You can have my job, George, any time you want. Don't blame me because they forgot to load the doll baby on the ship in England, or *you* forgot to order it!"

Right then the little girl's chin started to quiver, and she give out with a wail you could hear all the way over in Georgetown.

So Washington set his slave to openin' all the crates. But every time another one come up empty, she wailed all the louder. I swear she bawled like her mother just died. And if the cryin' and the creakin' crates and the cursin' slave weren't enough, the brother was off in a corner, fightin' a battle with his toy soldiers. Every time he shouted "Bang!" like a musket, she'd wail all the louder.

Washington's face turned red. The veins bulged out on his temples, and he said, "You see why we must look to ourselves, Draper? If we count on London, we'll not even be able to amuse our children."

'Twas then that my uncle appeared from a corner of the warehouse, carryin' a big box. "Will you look at what I found, stored by accident with another order."

He opened the box, and there was a beautiful doll baby with a china face, blond tresses, and the nicest little silk taffeta dress you ever saw.

Well, once she stopped screamin', that little girl lit up the whole warehouse with her pretty upside-down grin. Mighty happy myself, though I was forgettin' that there'd soon be another little girl who'd find no doll baby in her shipment from England.

After they left, I said, " 'Twas very kind of you, Uncle, very kind indeed."

"I have kindess in my bones," he answered. "And Washington's a man on the make. 'Tis good to earn his friendship."

A sentimental old fool, my uncle.


## Martha Washington:

My children came to admire their stepfather, and he stood as father to them in all but blood. Sadly, 'twas the will of the Divine Being that I was not to conceive again, so we would have no natural children of our own. I hesitate to discuss this. 'Tis a deeply private matter. I will say only that he bore his unhappiness without ever communicating it to me, though every man would wish for a son of his own.

Outside of that sadness, they were good years, though there were small storms that foretold the great hurricane that was to come.

I can still recall his cold fury at a letter from Robert Cary and Company—sometime in '64—reminding him that he must pay down a debt of two thousand pounds because our tobacco had failed to fulfill expectations that season.

"They cannot distinguish between misconduct and the mischances of weather and soil," he said. Then he loosed an angry letter, offering to find a method by which to discharge his debt and find a new factor, because, as he wrote, "it is an irksome thing to a free mind to be always hampered in debt."

And he began to apply frugalities that would lead to our economic freedom. I saw no frugality in a fine carriage or good Irish linen ordered from London. And he was always prepared to buy strong slaves. But he applied many economies, and slowly and steadily, our debt decreased.

Just as steadily, his public responsibilities increased, not surprising for a man with such a sense of duty. He was elected vestryman of our parish. He served as executor on many wills because of the trust that people placed in him. And he served each year at the House of Burgesses, where debates grew warmer as the first new taxes were levied to pay for the late war.

In '65 he was called home before the end of the session, so he was not there when news arrived of a stamp tax on legal documents, nor did he hear the oratory of a new burgess, Patrick Henry. But when he read Mr. Henry's speech in the *Virginia Gazette*, he responded with nods of approbation, words of approval.

We were sitting by the fire of a quiet spring evening. He smoothed the paper on the table and said, "Patsy"—he always called me Patsy—"listen to this: 'The General Assembly of this colony have the only and exclusive right and power to lay taxes and impositions upon the inhabitants, and every attempt to vest such power in any person or persons whatsoever, other than the General Assembly, has a manifest tendency to destroy British as well as American freedom.'"

This sounded like a great lot of inflammatory verbiage to me, and I said so.

My husband disagreed. "Mr. Henry is right. Last year the sugar tax. Now this. All to pay for the war we helped win. And we have no say in any of it. 'Tis un . . . unconstitutional."

'Twas the first time that I heard that word. Remember, we claimed the rights of Englishmen, and among these was the right to elect those who levied taxes on us.

"Mark me," he said. "The expectations of the mother country will fall far short in this. Taxes will lessen our imports, which must hurt their manufacture."

"You mean, they bite off their nose to spite their face?"

"Their nose, yes, while the eyes of our people are opened. They'll soon see what we've seen already at Mount Vernon: the luxuries we lavish on ourselves from Great Britain can be dispensed with. The necessaries of life can be had right here in our own colonies."

And he practiced what he preached. By the following year we had stopped growing tobacco. Wheat and corn would be our crops thenceforward. Purchases would go through local factors, men he could hold directly accountable if he was unhappy with what they sold. Our rebellion had begun before anyone else's.

## Jacob, Mount Vernon Slave:

Used to be I know every slave at Mount Vernon. But that spread git so big and need so many hands, I jess lose count. Leastways I'se a house slave in livery, and every night I go back to Belvoir, to that little one-room cabin, where me and Alice and the two little ones live. So we live pretty good. 'Course, the little ones ain't so little no more.

Narcissa gittin' pretty as her mother. Match growin' up strong and straight.

One evenin', Match and me go fishin'. Fishin' time's good time for a papa to tell things to his son, see, so I tell Match, "Now that you's thirteen, working the fields, remember: be a yassuh-nosuh nigger. Work that hoe. Do what you's tol'. And mebbe someday Massa Washin'ton buy up our whole fam'ly."

Now, most boys gits feisty when they git hair 'tween their legs. They think they know more 'n their papas. My boy be no dif'rent. Tha's why he use a piece of wadded-up bread for bait, 'stead of a nice fat worm, and why he say, "Hoein' tobacco for the Fairfaxes or corn for the Washin'tons, all the same to me."

I say, "If these Fairfaxes git it in their head to sell some slaves, and you's sold south, you'll strum a dif'rent tune. Do what you's tol', and mebbe I can brag on you some, and mebbe Massa George buy you."

"If he buy me, I work for him for the rest of my life, jess like you."

That hurt me, see. I say, "You don't see another slave livin' as good as me, do you? What other slave gits to go home to his wife ever' night, like a white man . . . and raise his kids, like a white man?"

"But ever' day's the same as before, no matter who you workin' for."

"Boy, you's too young to know nothin'."

"I knows what I knows. And I knows I got a bite."

The fish take our minds for a bit. Match wrassle in this big carp. Biggest one I ever seen. Haul it up on the dock, pull out the hook, and say, "See, Pa. I tol' you these carp like bread."

I say, "That fish make us one fine supper tonight."

"Mama say they's bony."

"They is. But they's good. You be good, too, son. You don't want to be sold, 'cept to Massa George."

And my boy say, "I hear he once sell a bad-tempered slave for a barrel of limes. Why do I want to work for a massa who sell a slave for a barrel of limes?"

And I say, " 'Cause he treat a good slave like he worth a barrel of *money*. You wants to be treated good, don't you?"

"Sure, till I run away." Then he laugh. That boy be a trickster, tha's what I think, and he like scarin' his old papa.

Speakin' of scary, things was gittin' scary in the mansion house. Somethin' wrong with little Patsy, and none of us slaves wants to be left alone with her.

## Martha Washington:

During their childhood, we had our children tutored at home, and for as long as I could, I postponed the inevitable—sending my son away to school. But in the summer of '68, my husband prevailed and arrangements were completed to send Jacky to Reverend Jonathan Boucher's school for boys in Caroline County.

He was fourteen and had hardly been out of my sight since the day he was born. Now I'd be without him for months on end, with only a few thoughts scrawled on a sheet of paper to bring me close to him.

I would have been heartbroken, except that a few weeks before Jacky left, our Patsy, then twelve, was fearfully stricken.

'Twas a Sunday afternoon. We had been to a gay barbecue at Belvoir. The talk of the ladies had been about food and fashion and the growing cost of English goods. The talk of the men had been about taxes called the Townshend Acts. Then we had all eaten our fill of pork, slow-cooked and sauced for hours.

Upon returning home, my husband went to his study. I went upstairs to loosen my corset, to make room for all the pork I'd eaten. And suddenly I heard a strange, strangled cry from downstairs.

The house slave, Jacob, shouted in a voice of the utmost horror, "Massa! Massa! Come quick! They's somethin' wrong with Miss Patsy!"

I rushed, half dressed, to the top of the stairs and looked down to see my daughter stretched out on the floor, her body as stiff as a washboard.

I cried her name and scrambled down to her. As I drew closer I saw spittle at the corners of her mouth. Her eyes were unfixed, her face turning a fierce shade of red, as though an invisible hand had taken her by the throat.

My husband rushed in and knelt beside her, calling her name ever more frantically. But she seemed unable to hear or comprehend.

"George, what's happenin'?" I cried.

"A fit," he said, and several more times he called her name.

But even if she had been able to hear, she could not have answered, for her jaws were clenched tight, as if they'd been locked in place.

My husband took her by her shoulders and tried to shake her out of her trance. In the trying, his hair came loose from its tie and fell around his face like a shroud. I thought, for a fleeting instant, that we'd all be wearing shrouds unless something was done.

I moved my husband aside and attempted to cradle Patsy in my arms, but her body was so stiff that she would not mold herself to my embrace. I called her name and rocked her while my husband snatched up a leather riding crop and forced it between her teeth.

After what seemed an eternity, her body relaxed. The clarity came back to her eyes. Her breathing grew normal. And, God's mercy, she seemed to remember nothing of what had happened.

I, however, could not forget it. And I would see it many times more. Our home, our daughter, had been invaded by an invisible enemy.

## Dr. James Craik:

People sometimes ask when I knew we were headed for rebellion, and I say Anno Domini 1769. Inevitably they are surprised by my foresight, which they believe is a result of my skill as a diagnostician. But it was Washington who had the foresight.

Parliament had taxed us to pay for the late war,

and now they were taxing us to pay the salaries of the customs commissioners who collected the taxes, thereby adding insult to injury. The Townshend Acts taxed tea, paper, glass, lead, and pigments for paint. In Boston, New York, and Philadelphia, men were organizing to resist by refusing to import taxed goods, and Washington approved.

"Will nonimportation hurt the business of our Alexandria merchants?" I asked one evening, on a visit to his home.

"Nonimportation is like medicine," he said, "hard to swallow but good in the long run. The less we import from England, the less will be our indebtedness."

I sipped my port and considered what he said. I considered also what I saw before me. He was nae the rash young man that once he had been. His years as a planter and family man had settled him, as a soothing dram settles an addled mind. I also considered what I saw in the bookcases that surrounded us in the little parlor. He kept works on agriculture, history, and political theory; Seneca's *Morals,* well thumbed and dog-eared; and a copy of Addison's play, the *Tragedy of Cato*, about a Roman republican who stood against Julius Caesar. I mused to myself that if Washington had read half of these, no matter that he had nae attended university, he was an educated man, and one whose words deserved heeding.

"Mark me, Craik," he said, "at a time when our lordly masters in Britain will be satisfied with no less than the depreciation of our freedom, we must do what we can to maintain the liberty our ancestors have left us."

I asked him, "What if nonimportation fails?"

"If nonimportation fails"—Washington leaned

across the table—"no man should hesitate for a moment to use arms in the defense of liberty."

"Arms?" I would have thought it were a joke, but it was easy to tell when he was joking. I would have thought it were the port, but he could drink a hogshead and never show it. I said, "You're serious about this, George?"

"I'm as loyal to the king as you are. But yes. *Arms.* The last resort."

I was shocked at his words and at the calm conviction with which he spoke them. What I said next I said as much to comfort myself as to learn his thoughts: "You would prefer, however, to make nonimportation work?"

"The more I consider it, the better I like it. But we must take care to explain it, and those who violate it should be stigmatized, cut out of the business and social life of the county."

Was this the Washington who had worked so hard to become a soldier of the king? Never before had I heard a man say he would take up arms against taxes, or stigmatize his neighbors. But Washington was showing foresight of the rarest kind.

A few months later I was in Williamsburg when the royal governor dissolved the burgesses over their opposition to the Townshend Acts. En masse, the body marched to Raleigh tavern, and amidst cries for the governor's head and countercries of loyalty to the king and counter-countercries for ale and adjournment, I heard Washington propose adoption of nonimportation resolves, like those in the North.

He spoke softly in the noisy taproom, and by the very calmness of his manner, he set himself apart from the sharp-voiced Patrick Henry and the other angry solons. That day he became a leader of the movement that would, at length, bring independence. The first flush of fever was coming upon us.


## Hesperus Draper:

Treaties with Injuns are made to be broken . . . or ignored . . . or rewritten, dependin' on their value to the white man. Been that way since white men arrived, and I suspect 'twill be that way even if this country reaches right to the Pacific.

In late '68, the Crown had rewritten the treaties bottlin' us up and erased the proclamation line. Decided they'd draw off some of those tax-hatin' colonists crowdin' the coast, like a good bleedin' draws off an inflammation.

News about the proclamation repeal couldn't have come at a better time. I was in love again, and fixin' to marry the fine-lookin' woman in the portrait on the wall in my office, Charlotte Spencer of Annapolis.

'Twas mercantile business that built Annapolis, so a young man representin' his uncle's mercantile interests was always welcome there. I spent many a happy night enjoyin' what the Annapolitans called the genteel pleasures of their town—fancy dinners, card parties, balls. I may have been born on one of the bottom rungs, but now that I had some money, I bought nice velvet suits, had silver buckles on my shoes, even took to powderin' my hair in the evenin's.

I met Charlotte on a September night in '68, durin' the Annapolis racin' season. 'Twas at the fine big home of Jedediah Stafford. Fifty dancers—includin' the famous Tidewater horseman, George Washington—were swirlin' in the music room. Sixteen feet of food covered the fifteen-foot table in the dining room. And in the upstairs parlor there was a game of whist, and a seat was openin' up just for me. Better yet, 'twas between two ladies.

The woman to my left wore a weddin' band and a losin'-hand scowl, but to my right was a vision glitterin' in the candlelight. She wore a beautiful yellow satin dress, just enough rouge to redden her cheeks, a little white face powder. Pulled her hair back and fixed it with a strand of pearls, simple and elegant. I knew her to be the daughter of a barrister by the name Spencer. I also knew her to be single.

She said, "You have taken a very unlucky seat, Mister . . . ?"

"Draper. Hesperus Draper . . . and considerin' the beautiful ladies beside me, I can't see anything but good luck here." I was gettin' smoother at these things.

Miss Spencer gave me a devilish little smile. "We'll decide how lucky you are after you've played a few hands."

I have to admit I paid more attention to her than to the cards, and before long, she'd won so much of my money, she said she felt like dancin'. If a man said that, I might shoot him. With her, I decided to dance instead. Wasn't lettin' her out of my sight. Fine to look at. Smart, too . . . nasty-smart, with a taste for sarcasm that made me look like a young preacher in a roomful of country ladies.

Down in the music room, we watched Washington pirouette and bow his way through a minuet, and one of the ladies said that no man could fill a room like the Virginia colonel.

Charlotte muttered, " 'Tis his big ass fills the room. He just comes in ahead of it."

After that, I'd ride the thirty-five miles to Annapolis at the drop of a hat. We'd go to the theater. Find quiet corners in the gardens behind the big houses. Laugh and whisper and hold hands in the shadows. Go to dances. And you know, she was right. Washington had one big ass.

Come spring of '69, I decided to ask her father for her hand.

Peter Spencer, Esquire, took one look at me and said he'd sooner have needles poked in his eyes. 'Twasn't the age difference, though I was in my thirties and she was only twenty-four. He said I couldn't have much vision if I'd gone that far in life with no land, estate, or weight in the world, "Except for what comes from that fat warthog of an uncle of yours."

I knew then where Charlotte got her taste for sarcasm. And wherever she got her backbone, I was glad she had it, because she insisted on comin' with me to see her father. Wasn't exactly common practice, but if she wanted somethin', she got it. Told her father I'd given so much of my youth to the defense of the colonies, I deserved extra time to gain somethin' for myself, and I deserved a good wife at my side while I did it.

Lord, I loved her.

Didn't have much use for her father, though. He had a pinched face that made me think of a close-bred terrier. But he loved her. So he listened to her. Then he looked me over again, like a terrier fixin' to piss on a post, and said, "I'll give you a year to make somethin' of yourself. If you do, you can marry her."

Well, by then I'd heard the news about the proclamation. Figured, 'twas only a matter of collectin' my bonus lands and settlin' on my own estate.

But the pathway to that land went through Washington, who had an appetite for land the way my uncle had an appetite for anything with gravy. That was both a good thing and a bad thing. 'Twas good, because Washington had petitioned Governor Botetourt, askin' that the bonus lands be distributed. 'Twas bad because of what Dr. Craik told me. . . .

Went to him for a case of runny eye. Didn't want to be showin' my face in Annapolis with my eyes all crusted over. So he dabbed some salve on my lids, and told me that the governor had heard Washington's petition, just before he got mad at the burgesses and sent them all home.

That made me forget the sting of the salve. "Does this mean I get my land?"

"It means we'll have to petition again, when the House reconvenes," Craik said, "but in time, we'll all be gettin' our land."

And I said, "What do you mean, 'we'?"

"You, me, Washington, Adam Stephen, Eli Stitch—"

"Hey, Doc," I said, "you and Washington and Stephen were *officers*. That 1754 proclamation from Dinwiddie was for *enlistees*."

Craik looked at me like the salve was softenin' my brain. Then he got mad. His Scots burr got so damn thick I could barely understand it. "We all served, Hesperus. We all deserve a piece of that land. All of us from '54."

## Dr. James Craik:

I went to see Washington about the bonus lands, but another matter vexed him: Patsy was still suffering fits, known since Roman times as the falling sickness.

She was growing into a lovely young lady. She had the same friendly eyes as her mother, the same tight upper lip that came from controlling a natural instinct to smile. But her face was longer, more graceful. A beauty in the making, she was. Who knew where insidious sickness came from to besmirch such beauty?

I asked him, "Did you apply an iron cramp ring to her finger?" The ring was said to help those subject to fits, perhaps by a kind of magnetism.

He said, "The ring cost one pound six and did her no good at all."

"Has Dr. Rumney prescribed mercurial tablets? Valerian?"

"Yes and yes," answered Washington.

"Then Berkeley Springs are worth consideration."

We were talking in the passage of the house, where the breeze was freshest. We were watching Martha and Patsy walk up from the river. Both wore straw sun hats and carried baskets of wildflowers, and together they formed a picture of tender devotion that a painter would have been inspired to put on canvas.

"If you think we should go to Berkeley, I'll consider it," said George. "I'll consider anything that eases Patsy's pain, and Mrs. Washington's mind."

Such a trip would ease her mind, but I had come

hoping to ease my own of a conversation with Hesperus Draper. I told Washington of the sticking point—that officers dinna deserve the bonus lands.

"Doesn't surprise me that he'd come up with something like this," said Washington.

"I told him he was crazy."

"More greedy than crazy," said Washington. "He knows that the fewer the number of people involved in the land grant, the more land available for him."

"George," I said, "I dinna enlist for land. I dinna recall that it was offered."

"You enlisted," he said, "to serve your colony. 'Twould be gross injustice if those of us who led the first resistance to French expansion were not to reap the rewards of service. That's my position. And I believe 'twas Dinwiddie's, too."

The logic was incontrovertible. So I agreed that while he was at Berkeley Springs, I would contact the officers who might wish to join a petition and press for a claim. We would also ask enlistees, as they were the backbone of the fighting force and should be the backbone of our petition, even Hesperus Draper.

## Hesperus Draper:

I signed the petition. Still didn't think the officers deserved any of the original bonus lands. But they were banded together, and the enlisted men weren't. . . .

And come fall, it seemed like a good idea. The British ministry was in a conciliatin' mood, liftin' the Townshend Acts. Governor and assembly were in the same mood, endorsin' our petition for the bonus lands.

I could almost feel that rich Ohio Valley bottom between my fingers. And I could almost feel Charlotte Spencer wrappin' her arms around me. Could wait for the land, but not for Charlotte.

So I rode down to see Washington one January afternoon. Hated goin' to anyone with my hat in my hand, but I had a favor to ask him.

About two miles from the mansion, I heard hounds bayin'. Then they came snufflin' and smellin' along the road, lookin' for a fox. And there was the master, wearin' a brown coat and buckskin breeches, ridin' a black mare, with his stepson ridin' alongside him. A fine picture of family harmony.

At the sight of me, Washington reined in his horse.

I tipped my hat. "Good afternoon, Mr. Washington."

"What can I do for you?" asked Washington, with all the warmth of a tree trunk in a blizzard.

And Jacky, he just looked annoyed that I was spoilin' his fun. He was about sixteen. Had one of those faces where the baby fat hadn't quite gone away, just settled into his cheeks and chin, givin' him a look of someone who didn't give a fig for anything or anybody but himself. They say you can't tell a book by its cover, but with Jacky Custis, you could.

Seein' as they was itchy to ride on, I was quick about why I'd come.

"You want a *letter*?" said Washington. "To your future father-in-law?"

"A letter sayin' I'm close to receivin' my Ohio lands."

"But we have many difficulties and uncertainties to struggle through before our rights to these lands are recognized," he said.

"Then . . . then you won't write the letter?" I hated this more than he did.

"I'll write a letter to the effect that, as one of the privates—"

"I made sergeant, George."

"*After* the Great Meadows. And how many times were you broken back to private? You're entitled to a *private's* share, once all the details have been attended. But it could be two or three years."

"Two or three years? I'd appreciate it if you didn't add that part."

"You love this woman?"

"I wouldn't be marryin' her if I didn't."

His eyes were driftin' down the road, to where the lead dogs were startin' to raise a ruckus in the underbrush. "Remember, love is a confection, Draper. You'll need strong porridge to hold together."

I think he was tryin' to be friendly. But 'twas none of his business whether I liked confections, gray gruel, or carp boiled in its own blood. "Will you write me the letter, George? Yes or no? I won't be able to marry this woman without it."

"Papa," said Jacky, "the dogs . . ."

"Yes, Jack. I see." Washington's horse was gettin' fractious. "Draper, I'll write the truth, that you're to receive land in the West . . . sometime."

Cold comfort. But if that was the best I could hope for, I'd take it.

Then Washington said, "Would you care to join the hunt?"

Me? Even my horse was shocked that Washington would invite us.

Just then Jacky shouted, "Bitch fox comin' out!"

And a red vixen darted across the road and down into the underbrush.

The lead dogs had flushed her and now the whole pack—must've been fifteen or twenty—all picked up the scent, and before I could say yes, no, or maybe, Washington and Jacky Custis were off, dogs bayin' and horseshit splatterin' in the road.

I was no foxhunter. But my uncle always said there was nothin' like a fox hunt to make a customer a friend, so I spurred my horse, and she leaped like she'd been waitin' all her life for this.

In half a second, the woods were sweepin' past me faster than I'd ever seen 'em go. Winter woods they were, mostly leafless tree-skeletons. The branches scratched and grabbed at me as I went gallopin', holdin' on to the reins and lettin' the horse run where she wanted.

We leaped fences and crossed meadows and galloped along deer paths, from Dogue Run to Muddy Hole and halfway back to Alexandria, or so it seemed, and I longed for an ass as well padded as Washington's. Finally when I was about to vomit from the bouncin', I saw that scared little fox scramble over a fallen log, then try to scratch her way straight up a tree.

But those dogs were bred to run all day, and they were quicker to the fox than Jack, who was just raisin' his musket for a shot. The strongest of the dogs took a big jump and caught that little fox right by the tail. Dragged her down into the pack, and the rest of 'em just tore her to pieces 'fore Washington could do a thing to stop 'em . . . not that he wanted to.

I never did like foxhuntin'.

But 'twas Washington's favorite thing to do. And it *was* exhilaratin', what with the noise and the speed and that smart red quarry out ahead of you. He said to his stepson, "Master Jack, you're first to the fox. The tail is yours."

The boy was practiced at this, well taught by his stepfather. He spurred his horse in to break up the dogs, then he climbed down and kicked the last of them aside so he could claim his prize from what was left of the little vixen.

Washington turned to me, and never had I ever seen such a look on his face. His skin was red. He was pantin'. There was a strange light in his eyes—blissful, you might say, like he'd just been in a saddle far softer than one made of leather . . . if you get my meanin'.

"Well rid, Draper. I'll tell your future father-in-law that you're coming into an estate in the West, and you'll hunt many a fine fox across the acreage."

Right then I was glad I went foxhuntin'.

## Martha Washington:

Reverend Boucher, who ran Jacky's school, had always been welcome at Mount Vernon, even though he had moved the school to Annapolis and taken my son that much farther away.

I should never speak so of a man of the cloth, but I found him to be a most self-satisfied individual, most indulgent of his own tastes, round of belly and of face, but with all that, a fine dinner companion. So a fine dinner was set out on the day of his visit.

The table talk, at first, was of weather and work, of the new mill we were building, and of course, of politics.

"Your Virginia gentlemen have formed a new non-importation association," said Reverend Boucher.

"Formed much upon the old plan," said my husband, "but more relaxed."

"Wise to relax, as Parliament wisely relaxes the Townshend duties."

My husband refilled the minister's glass. " 'Twas as much the failure of stricter measures as it was Parliament's softening that led to the new plan."

"Yes," said Jacky. "Virginians can't seem to live without sugar and cheap trinkets and leather saddles imported from England."

My husband gave Jacky a glance in which I saw no small degree of pride that the boy was taking interest in such things. "Jack, the new agreement was the best that friends of the cause could obtain. 'Tis too relaxed, but at least 'twill become general."

"So you still consider nonimportation a good thing?" asked our guest.

"We must make a stand," said my husband.

We did not know it, but the Reverend Mr. Boucher was deeply opposed to the measures my husband supported. He later returned to England and published strong words against our revolution and my husband. But that night he had come to talk of Jacky.

Once the boy had gone off, my husband said, "In all honesty, how is Master Jack doing? A lad of good genius like him—untainted in his morals and innocent in his manners—he should be thriving."

"In all honesty?" Mr. Boucher seemed at a loss for words. So he drained his glass again and took another, which he drained in turn. He could drain a glass very quickly. Then he said, "I'm afraid I've seldom known a youth so exceedingly indolent or so surprisingly voluptuous."

"Voluptuous?" I said. This was a word I did not normally hear in my house.

"Forgive me, ma'am, but he has a propensity for the opposite sex which I am at a loss how to judge, much less describe."

"Then how am I to envision it?" I said, and I looked at my husband, who sat on the other side of the table, all but expressionless.

"Well . . . given his attitude at school," Mr. Boucher went on, "one would suppose nature had intended him for some Asiatic prince."

"Asiatic prince?" I remember feeling as if a hand were closing around my throat in anger or shock, I know not which.

My husband made a small gesture, as if to quiet me, but I would not be quiet. I said, "Jacky may not have been made to be a scholar. But a more companionable young man you'll never find."

"Absolutely." Mr. Boucher surprised me with his sudden shift of opinion. "Companionable, but in need of broadening. Time away should free him of his unhealthier interests. That's why I would like to accompany him on a European tour, to broaden his horizons."

"Like an Asiatic prince?" said my husband.

"Like the young Virginian prince that he is," answered Reverend Boucher.

"How much will it cost?" asked Mr. Washington.

Reverend Boucher seemed unnerved by the sharpness in my husband's voice. "A . . . a . . . thousand pounds. But I hope you know, sir, that I do this for Master Custis, not for myself."

"I hope you know, Reverend Boucher, that as trustee for Master Custis, I'm answerable to the court. While the boy has a good estate, it is not a profitable one. I can't be spending his money freely, even though you and he might be inclined to."

"Indeed not," said the good minister.

"So we defer this decision until the boy matures."

Wise counsel was something that my husband could always dispense.


He was father to my son. And I tried to be daughter to his mother.

She lived, independent as a frontier trapper, at Ferry Farm. We visited her at the end of July, 1770, as my husband had called a Fredericksburg meeting of officers petitioning for bonus lands. There, on Friday afternoon, while my daughter and I were having a cup of tea with Mother Mary, as I called her, Patsy dropped from her chair, limbs stiff, eyes rolled back.

Her fits were happening so often now that I should have been prepared for them, but I never was.

Mother Mary, however, took one look at my daughter and said, "Had a slave once who threw fits."

"Can you send for the doctor?" I said, kneeling next to the girl.

"Never got a doctor for the slave."

"Well, my daughter is not a slave. Can you get a doctor?"

"I'll get Doc Mercer. He's a good one. But he charges plenty."

"I don't care. Just get him. And hurry."

"Don't order me around my own house, dearie."

"Please!" I said, which seemed to soften her.

After that, she moved quickly. She called orders to her slaves and was back in a moment with a wooden spoon to work between Patsy's teeth. Then she tenderly stroked Patsy's forehead, whispered calming words to her, and said to me, "Don't fear. My nigger always come out of his fits. The girl will, too."

She could exasperate you, but she could show the kindness of a mother, too, and so I forgave her.

We did not, however, stay with her but one night. After that, we stayed with my husband's sister Betty and her husband, Colonel Fielding Lewis, in their brick house, the finest in Fredericksburg. My husband found such surroundings more conducive to concentrating on the business before him: the officers' meeting.

## Hesperus Draper:

Charlotte and I took a honeymoon trip to England. Her father sent us there. Wanted me to see the glory of Saint Paul's and Westminster. Hoped that after I did, I'd be convinced of the British ministry's goodwill. Didn't work out that way, but we sure had a fine time.

Then we come home and I heard about that officers' meetin' in Fredericksburg, enlisted men not invited. Seems the officers of '54 got together and decided who'd get how much land and where; they named Washington to go west and scout for the best lands; and they put up money to pay for surveys. And remember this little truth: those who pay get their way.

# Dr. James Craik:

'Twas my privilege to scout the bonus lands with Washington. We went in the autumn of 1770, after the leaves had begun to fall and the sightlines through the woods had lengthened.

We headed for Fort Pitt, which stood on the site of old Duquesne. From there we would canoe down the Ohio to the Great Kanawha and visit the ten parcels of land from which the Governor's Council told us to take our patents, marking the plots and making our judgments on the quality of the lands.

They were wondrous days. We rode through the Great Meadows. We slept at the farms of old friends and in rude Indian villages, and many a night the stars were our roof. We wore buckskins and high boots and basked in the golden days of October. Our faces were stung by the first winter snows. We felt the power of the Ohio current as we dipped our paddles and skimmed downstream.

The fur-trading town that had been born at the Forks of the Ohio was now expanding across the triangle of land between the rivers, and the trees were in retreat. Washington said the whole Ohio Valley would one day see trees retreating, farmers coming in, commerce opening, and we would be part of it.

We found good bottoms and useless hillsides of rock. We looked for watercourses and wide meadows where a plow would cut clean. And at length we came to an Indian village called Mingo Town.

# John Britain,
# known as Silverheels:

M any winters had passed since I last saw them. Caunotaucarius was still tall and straight. Craik still had a kind face, but his belly was growing bigger. White men's bellies always grow bigger when they get older. The bellies of Mingo men do not.

I had gone to the shores of Lake Erie, but I did not stay long. I knew that moving west to escape the white men was like moving north to escape mosquitoes in summer. No matter how far you go, they will always catch up.

So I had come home to my river, where my boys grew. And I took a second woman. Her name, in your tongue, was Smiling Sister. She had a big belly. Her hips were big, too. All of her was big, even her laugh. I liked a big woman. I liked a happy woman.

Mingo Town was a happy place. There was no other village between us and Pittsburgh, a distance of seventy-five miles. That was why we were happy. We grew our corn. We caught fish. We hunted buffalo where they still ran. But when King George rubbed out the line that kept settlers on the other side of the mountains, I knew the white men would come. When I saw Caunotaucarius, I said, "I knew you would come."

He thanked me. He thought I meant that I *hoped* he would come. I meant only that I *knew* he would come, in the way that winter comes. It is not a welcome thing. But it is a thing that we must face.

Caunotaucarius and Craik were looking for land. I said I would guide them. I took them downstream, away from our village, to a place where the buffalo no longer ran, a place on the warriors' path to Cherokee country. The sun was bright on the meadows and trees. The leaves of the swamp maples had turned red, like beads in a belt of green.

Caunotaucarius walked the land in one direction, then the other. He told Dr. Craik it was good earth. He pointed to a fallen sycamore. "We can run a line, three or four miles east from that tree, then north until it strikes the river."

"A huge tract," said the doctor.

"Three or four thousand acres," said Caunotaucarius.

A Mingo beats a path though a thicket to go from one place to another. But he owns nothing along the path. A white man with a compass on three legs draws a line over a mountain, and the line makes the mountain his. That was why we called the compass the land-stealer.

"The most valuable land we've seen," the doctor said. "So who would receive it among the petitioners? An enlisted man or an officer?"

"Officers," answered Caunotaucarius. "And perhaps those who have worked the hardest."

"Us?" asked Dr. Craik. "Is it fair for us to take this land for ourselves?"

"Is it fair," asked Caunotaucarius, "that you and I are here, spending money for expenses, while others sit in Virginia, waiting for us to return with land for them, land they've done next to nothing to obtain? We'll make our distributions scrupulously, Craik. But we'll remember this parcel."

# Hesperus Draper:

Let me give you the figures on the bonus land: fifteen thousand acres, nine thousand acres, and four *hundred* acres.

Who got what? *Who do you think?*

In 1771 the Governor's Council made the recommendations on the distribution. But who made the recommendations to them? *Who do you think?*

Field officers like Washington got fifteen thousand acres apiece. Captains and doctors got nine thousand. And privates got four hundred. *Four hundred.*

Charlotte said, "So our big stake in the West turns out to be a pea patch on a hillside. Let's go to Annapolis and tell the good news to my father."

"Tell your father nothin'," I answered.

"But he'll be so pleased."

I'd made enough money workin' for my uncle that I could buy Charlotte a decent house in Alexandria. But 'twas nothin' compared to the house she come from in Annapolis.

And whenever I went to Annapolis, her father would ask me, usually at the dinner table, "So . . . when does your indenture to your uncle come to an end?"

I wasn't indentured. He knew that. I was bidin' my time. Two of my cousins had gone down in a leaky merchantman, so my share of my uncle's pie was gettin' bigger. And the more cousins I outlived, the more money I'd get. And nothin' wrong with a good inheritance. Washington was livin' proof of that.

Now, Charlotte and I weren't at our happiest just then. She'd miscarried twice since the weddin'. We both wanted kids. Not havin' them hurt us more than you can imagine. And in bad times folks fall back on the things that make them comfortable. Charlotte fell back on her sarcasm. I fell back on the bottle.

I was no puke-on-my-waistcoat drunk. I just knew that if I kept myself shrouded in the fog, 'twould be harder for Charlotte to hit me when she fired words at me like bullets.

Still, that "pea patch" remark hit me right between the eyes. So I decided to do somethin' about it. I'd go to the next officers' meetin' in Fredericksburg.

Considerin' the personal fog I was in, 'twas a wonder I found my way the whole thirty-five miles. Walked in, shook the rain off my hat, and took a seat in the back of the taproom, where the meetin' was beginnin'.

There was about a dozen officers there . . . plenty of familiar faces, includin' Craik and Adam Stephen. Time had been good to some of them, and some of them looked like they was payin' for their sins before they died. But the man who held the center of the room had never looked more complacent.

I listened all mornin' while Washington explained the methods for the surveys and the distribution. Every so often he'd shoot his eyes toward me, as if he was expectin' me to start some trouble.

But I kept a dumb smile on my face. Even clapped when Washington said he'd recommended to the Governor's Council that enlisted men be given their land forthwith, while officers waited.

"I see we have an enlisted man at the back," said Washington.

"And proud of it!" I shouted. "Proud of those four hundred acres I earned, too. Though not near so proud as you must be of your *fifteen thousand*."

Washington ignored me and said that we should all come forward and examine the plats laid out on the tables, to see where we'd be gettin' our land. Needed a lookin' glass to find mine. 'Twas just like Charlotte said, a pea patch on a hillside. Maybe five hundred decent acres in the five shares I'd accumulated.

I looked at it and shouted, "Swindle!"

The buzzin' in that room stopped like I'd dropped a rock on a bunch of flies swarmin' around a meadow muffin.

Washington shot me one of those looks that could freeze a stone.

Adam Stephen was standin' next to me, big and burly as ever. He said, "This be an officers' meetin', Draper. You're lucky we let you in the door."

"You were officers twenty years ago," I said. "Now you're just men lookin' to get your own while others are cheated."

The crowd parted, and Washington came at me, big and mad. A lot of him to get mad, too. But I was determined to stand my ground.

He looked me in the eye, "Do you feel that you've been wronged here?"

"Wronged?" I answered. "I've been bent over a cannon and caned. Me and all the enlisted men."

Craik said, "Draper, you're drunk."

I said, "How much bottomland did *you* get, Doc?"

"The good and the bad were distributed fairly," said Washington.

"Don't believe it."

"Then make your protest," snapped Washington.

"Protest? To who?"

"The Governor's Council." Washington looked around the room and raised his voice. "There's a provision in the bill. I requested it myself, because I'll not allow m-m-my honor to be impugned like this."

Even in my amber ale fog, I realized that Washington was about to make himself look good at my expense.

He said, "If any man has a question as to the equitability of this distribution, he may protest to the Governor's Council. If any complaint is judged to have cause, I will give up all interest under my patent and submit to the will of the council." Then he walked away.

Like a martyr. Like a hero in a poem. Like a man who knew someone wanted to shoot him, so he turned his back to make a better target.

I'd just met the best actor I'd ever see on any stage. Room was buzzin' again. The flies had come out from under the rock.

But I wasn't backin' down. I said, "I'll bet that none of the land on any of these plats is so good as yours or Craik's."

Washington turned again and struck a pose in the middle of the room. "Be cautious what you say, Draper, or you'll feel the marks of my resentment."

What was he going to do? Flog me?

He said, "Drunkenness is no excuse for rudeness. If not for your stupidity and sottishness, you'd know that you've been treated as fair as any man."

"We've all been treated fair," shouted Craik.

And the officers started cheerin', more like sheep than flies.

I knew when I was beat. Picked up my hat and backed out. Had a foot in the stirrup when I heard someone shout, "Hear! Hear! A proposition! A resolve! That the Governor's Council relieve Colonel

Washington of the promise to surrender his own lands, should a complaint be justified against him!"

"Second!" shouted someone else. Then came a roar of *ayes!*

I rode off with the rain poundin' hard into my face, but I could see one thing clear: the Governor's Council would never hear a complaint from me. So I took the land I was given. And when I sobered up enough to see everything clear, I printed an apology to Washington in the *Virginia Gazette*.

I might have been a hypocrite, but I was no fool. You didn't insult the reputation of a man who'd spent his life buildin' one, especially if the man was George Washington. He never mentioned my letter. Always treated me cold anyway. So I don't know if he ever forgave me. But I know I sure didn't forgive him for that paltry two thousand acres.


## Dr. James Craik:

There was good arable land given to every man who lived long enough to take possession after the Revolution. And without Washington, none of us would have gotten a thing. The distributions were finally made because of his money, his reputation, his persistence, and his firm belief, oft stated, that land is the most permanent estate and the most likely to increase in value.

## Martha Washington:

Life advances, all in step with the plans of the Divine Being. Of that I have no doubt. Though sometimes his ways are hard.

Jacky never took a grand tour, but in the spring of 1773 he was admitted to King's College in New York, the city that Reverend Boucher described as "the most fashionable and polite place on the continent." Jacky also announced his engagement to Miss Nelly Calvert of Maryland.

We did not try to stop the marriage, but my husband sent the girl's father a cordial and carefully worded letter, explaining that a young man of nineteen should have an education before a wife. Mr. Calvert agreed entirely. The parents joined forces, the families joined hands, and the wedding was postponed.

However, I was quietly pleased that my son, with his so-called propensity for the opposite sex, had selected a young woman in whom virtue could so plainly be seen.

We sought to bring Miss Nelly into our world, as we did not want postponement to seem like rejection. And so she was there on a June Sunday when the Divine Being surpassed my understanding and very nearly my endurance.

George's brother Jack and his family had come for a visit, so the gathering at our table was large and cheerful. The children chattered; we ladies passed our remarks on the things that interested us; and of course, the gentlemen discussed politics.

I especially enjoyed observing the giggling intimacies passed between Patsy and Nelly. Because of her affliction, Patsy had enjoyed few friendships with girls her own age, and no young men had come to court her, which was a source of deep sadness to a pretty girl of seventeen.

But after the meal, as we watched Patsy and Nelly go off, my husband said, "I don't believe I've seen Patsy look so happy since before her first fit."

Around five o'clock I was in the smokehouse when a wide-eyed slave burst in, screaming that Master Washington wanted me to come quick.

I'd been summoned like this many times, always to be greeted by the sight of frantic action around the prostrate figure of my daughter. But as soon as I entered the little parlor this time, I knew that something was different and something was—this memory is still so painful—something was terribly wrong.

Nelly Calvert was sobbing. One of the slaves was running out of the room. The body on the floor—I could glimpse only the legs and feet because of the people surrounding it—lay motionless. My husband was kneeling beside her, his big back to me. But at my approach he turned and came quickly toward me.

I don't remember his expression, only his arms enveloping me.

I pushed out of his grasp and ran to her side, and . . . Oh, Lord . . .

Her hand was still warm, her cheek still rose-red, the sound of her voice still ringing in my ears. But no breath escaped her lips. I raised her to my breast and called her name and began to rock her, as if I could rock my baby back to life. But my Patsy was dead.

Then I heard my husband's voice, " 'Twas merciful,

dear. She expired quickly, without a word. I don't think she knew what happened."

I admit that at that moment, I lost control of my emotions. . . .

## Jacob, Mount Vernon Slave:

You ain't never heard such wailin' as they be in that house that day. One of the sorriest things any of us ever live through, 'cause we all love Miss Patsy.

Miz Washington kneel down and take the girl in her arms, and I thinks Patsy look jess like one of them little doll babies she always love when she's little. And then Massa George kneel down next to his wife and he whisper in her ear.

And she scream, "Mercy? What mercy? Where's God's mercy in this?"

And for days you hear her weepin' in her room, goin' on like they's nothin' on earth to save her. For days she don't even come out of that room.

Now, over the years I hear folks say my massa ain't a man with much in the way of softness or warmth. And he don't show his feelin's too much. But that don't mean he ain't happy sometimes and sad some other times.

He walk 'round for weeks, lookin' like he jess finish cryin' or jess be fixin' to cry. Sometime, I see him settin' alone, lookin' out at the river. Sometime, when he should be ridin' his rounds, he jess walk in the woods, walk with his hands behind his back and his head down.

One day, Billy—tha's Billy Lee, Massa's personal

servant, a mulatto boy he buy when he finely git tired of me nightwalkin'—Billy tell me the massa want to go for a ride.

So I brings 'round the chariot. It be smaller and lighter than the carriage he bring from London a few years afore, the one he take when he want to go to Wil'lumsburg in style.

Then Massa come out the house with Miz Washington. He wearin' a black armband. She have on mostly black clothes and don't say nothin'. I helps Miz Washington into the carriage and I say to Massa, "I'se drivin' today, suh."

"What? Oh . . . yes. Mrs. Washington would like to get out. We'll just be taking a little ride."

I thinks, Jess a little ride? With nowhere to be goin'? 'Tain't like the massa a'tall. But, we jess ride, ride for hours, and all the while there ain't a word from 'em, 'cept, "Go a little further, Jake, a little further."

For three weeks Massa hardly leave his wife's side. And they take more of them long rides than they ever done afore or since. He be her rock, see, her plain, hard rock.

## Dr. James Craik:

I sought to comfort Mrs. Washington with nerve drops—a compound of sugar water and laudanum to bring on a mild state of relaxation.

She offered a wan smile. "I need no nerve drops. They did no good for Patsy." Then she excused herself and went off, distracted and sorrowful, a miniature of her daughter clutched in her hand.

"Healing the body is child's work when compared with healing the heart," I said to Washington as we walked later along the river.

"She's at the lowest ebb of misery. I wish we had the consolation of Sally and George Fairfax. Gone to England for doctoring. Stomach complaints."

I said, "Stomach ailments are near as difficult to heal as broken hearts . . . even for English doctors."

Washington looked downstream, toward Belvoir. "We miss them both."

After the first blankets of bereavement were cast off, George and Martha began to travel—to Williamsburg, to Fredericksburg, to Annapolis for the fall races. Their house filled once more with visitors. And Jacky begged permission to leave school and marry. 'Twas against Washington's better judgment, but permission he gave. Jacky, after all, had proven as indifferent to his studies at King's College as he had at Reverend Boucher's.

Such were the things that occupied Washington's mind that fall. I doubt that, at first, he paid much attention to the Tea Act, which brought a new tax and a monopoly for the London East India Company.

Parliament was seeking to prop up the company, whose imminent bankruptcy would take hundreds of smaller firms with it. The irony was that taxed East India tea, sold in monopoly, would be cheaper than untaxed tea passing through merchant middlemen. It would even be cheaper than untaxed tea smuggled in by American shippers.

But if a monopoly and tax could be granted on tea, what else might Parliament choose to control?

Then, just before Christmas, I brought momentous news to Mount Vernon: a band of Boston rowdies, dressed as Indians, had boarded three merchantmen and dumped a fortune of East India Company tea into Boston Harbor.

Washington heard this with an impassive face.

"What think you?" I asked.

"I condemn it."

"Condemn it?" I was shocked. "'Twas a demonstration of political will."

"I condemn the destruction of private property."

And of course he was right. He was the most orderly revolutionary any nation could ever have had, and in the long run, that was for the best.

## Hesperus Draper:

In May of '74 the British closed the port of Boston. Till Boston paid for the tea steepin' in the harbor, the charter of the colony, the guarantee of every man's rights, would be suspended. Virginians didn't much care what happened in Boston. Still don't, except when folks in Boston try to tell folks in Virginia what to do. But whatever the British did in Boston, they might decide to do in other places. So our burgesses decreed a day of fastin' and prayers for the guidance of the king and Parliament.

The new royal governor, a bad-tempered son of a bitch by the name of Dunmore, didn't think the king and Parliament needed any prayers. So he dissolved the session.

But you didn't just tell men like Patrick Henry and

Tom Jefferson and George Washington to go home and keep their mouths shut. Once he got back to Fairfax County, Washington was elected to help draft a response to all this. 'Twas called the Fairfax Resolves.

I was there that hot July afternoon at the Alexandria Court House, at the meetin' for gentlemen and freeholders, to hear the readin' of the Resolves.

Yes, sir, I was now considered a gentleman. I was climbin' the ladder. I was a respected merchant, mostly because my uncle was. I had a little land—damn little, but I didn't spread that around. And I was the son-in-law of a rich Maryland barrister who called all of this agitation a prelude to treason. Didn't spread that around, either.

Hadn't crossed paths with Washington in a while. He'd done his business elsewhere since that day in Fredericksburg. Gave me a curt nod when he sat down. Wasn't bein' polite. 'Twas just to let me know he'd be keepin' his eye on me.

I was no revolutionary. I just wanted to be rid of these nonimportation rules so we could get back to business. But I'd always been a rebellious bastard. It comes with bein' born on one of the low rungs when you know you're smart enough to be higher.

And that's what I had in common with Washington.

Think of how he'd rebelled, first against that domineerin' mother of his. Then against all those half-pay officers like Mackay and Dagworthy, who thought they could order him around like rich uncles, just because their commissions came from the king and his came from hard experience. And now he was turnin' against a domineerin' mother country, too.

He didn't read the Fairfax Resolves. 'Twas his

neighbor George Mason who read them. A lot of it I'd heard before, about how 'twas "the laws of nature and nations," not Parliament, that guaranteed our rights. But I cheered out loud when Mason came to the nub of the matter. "It is our greatest wish and inclination to continue our connection with the British government; but though we are its subjects, we will use every means which heaven hath given us to prevent becoming its slaves."

I kept cheerin', and my eye caught Washington's, and some kind of understandin' passed between us. In this fight, anyway, we were on the same side.

That meetin' approved the toughest nonimportation rules I'd ever heard. And I cheered again, even though 'twould cost my uncle money. Then the Resolves called for delegates from all the colonies to meet in somethin' called a Continental Congress, in Philadelphia. I cheered that, too.

## Martha Washington:

We missed George William and Sally Fairfax deeply. But by the summer of '74, they had decided to stay in England and asked my husband if he would oversee the auction of the furnishings and slaves at Belvoir.

A few weeks before my husband left for the first Continental Congress, we went to Belvoir and met with Bryan Fairfax, the youngest son of Colonel Fairfax. Our mutually unhappy task was to secure items that Sally and George William wished to have shipped to England, and approve the prices at which the auctioneer would start the bidding on the other items.

My husband was near as close with Bryan as with George William. But where George William had been warmly disposed to my husband's political positions, Bryan was cool.

The house was filled with memories that made us all deeply melancholy, knowing as we did that our happiest days there had passed. We moved from room to room, making our judgments on the furniture, searching through drawers and escritoires for papers that George William had requested, and all the while, as if to distract themselves, my husband and Bryan kept up a political dialogue.

In the front parlor, chairs, settee, and tables were all covered with sheets, like corpses. There was nothing here that the Fairfaxes wanted. So the auctioneer set opening bids on each of the items, and we agreed to all.

Bryan said, "I'm glad we agree on something. But I do not agree that it's time for nonimportation. A simple petition to the king should be made instead."

"Haven't we tried that already?" said my husband. "Haven't we addressed the Lords and remonstrated with the Commons? It should be as plain as the sun in the sky that there's a plan forming to fix taxation on us without our consent."

Bryan, who was bigger and sturdier than his brother, could still muster the Fairfax look of offended disappointment when you disagreed with him.

My husband answered it by leading us into the dining room where so many wonderful meals had been enjoyed. He examined the sideboard and asked the auctioneer what he would set as the opening bid.

"I would say twenty pounds, sir."

My husband said to me, "A fair price. Perhaps we should buy it. We could use a sideboard."

Bryan Fairfax said, "We could use calm heads. Everyone is so swept up in the assertion of their rights that we forget the simple truth: we're all Englishmen."

"The simple truth," answered my husband, "is that the Parliament of Great Britain has no more right to put their hands into my pocket for money than I have to put mine into yours."

Then my husband led the auctioneer upstairs to the bedrooms, where the slaves were working, removing the protective sheets, dusting, polishing.

We went quickly from room to room, assenting to every price the auctioneer suggested, until we reached the bedroom of Sally Fairfax. There, lace curtains fluttered at the window, and the afternoon sunlight danced in the fabric. We entered quietly, as if not to awaken the woman who had once slept there.

My husband looked around, then touched the coverlet, his hand drifting across the pillows. Would it seem strange if I said I felt a twinge of jealousy?

But it fled as quickly as it had come. My husband was a hardheaded businessman, even in the matter of bedding. He gave the pillow an appraising fluff. "Yes, yes, fine down in these, Martha. I think we should buy them."

"Of course," said I.

Then he said, "Why don't we buy all the bedding? The coverlet and bolster match the pillows so well."

Bryan Fairfax said, "What about the Negroes?"

"The Negroes? The slaves?" said my husband. "If we do not assert our rights against an abusive Parliament, we'll become like the slaves over which we rule with such arbitrary sway."

"I was not speaking metaphorically. I was asking

about . . ." Bryan gestured with his eyes to the female slave who was dusting the chest of drawers in the corner of the room.

"Oh . . . Oh . . . They will be sold, according to the orders of Mr. Fairfax."

The Negress looked up with a start. Then quickly she lowered her head and went back to her work.

## Jacob, Mount Vernon Slave:

When I come home to Belvoir, I see a face on Alice like the mask of death.

She say, "We's bein' sold, Jake."

"Sold? When?"

"At the auction next week. What we gonna do?"

"I don't know." This hit me like a hay bale dropped off the barn roof.

That night I tell my family I'se findin' a way to keep us all together, and Match jess spit on the floor. . . . Now, I build us a cabin with a real wood floor, and he spit on it. Make me mad, see. I tell him to git the hell outside if he want to spit.

Well, suh, he go stalkin' off and don't come back that night.

Next mornin' the roosters don't wake me up. I'se awake already, sick with worry. I pulls on my pants, and tha's when I sees that Match's bed be empty.

I goes out to look 'round for him, figgerin' maybe he gone night-walkin'—he the age for it—and maybe now he comin' home. Then it hit me: he run away.

"What we gonna do?" I ax Alice.

"I don't know. . . . I jess don't know."

Whilst I'se ridin' over to Mount Vernon, things don't come no clearer.

And the massa be waitin' when I ride up, lookin' at his watch. "We can't have slaves comin' late, Jake. Too much to be done."

He buildin' a new wing for his mansion house, see. Gittin' hisself a new bedroom upstair and a fine office down. And he have plans to build another wing on th'other end, a big fancy room for dancin' and such.

Everything on the south side all framed, and the rough wood sides is on. All 'round, they's sawhorses and planks and ladders. And the air's got that sweet smell of fresh-cut wood, see. And I can hear the work gang comin' up from the slaves' quarters. They's talkin' and laughin' and some even singin'.

Massa look at his watch agin. "I hate to be going off to Philadelphia, Jake. The work here goes on much better whilst I'm present."

"Well, suh, I don't know about that."

"But you know about carpentry."

"Yassuh." I made money over the years makin' tables and chairs and such, first for the fam'ly, then for to sell at Alexandria on market days. And then I build them nice slave huts over to Belvoir. Not many slave huts in Virginny with real wood floors.

Massa say, "I'm giving you a new job. Overseer of a second carpenter's gang. I'm bringing your son over from Belvoir to work for you." He smile, 'cause it make him happy to give me a present. "I'm buying your whole family, Jake."

I don't know to laugh or cry. Two nights later, Alice and Narcissa and me, we moves our stuff to a new hut at Mount Vernon. Narcissa, she be twenty-one, but old Matchuko tell me 'fore he die, "Don't you make that little gal a breedin' wench 'fore her time." And I protect her pretty good. They's jess the three of us, but we's happy to be there. And happy that Massa buy Match, too, buy him at a special low price, seein' as how he ain't there to be bought.

Then Massa put a notice in the gazette, showin' a picture of a barefoot slave carryin' a bag on a stick. Tha's what they always show for a runaway. And he paint a word picture of Matchuko—"Negro boy, in age about nineteen, standing six feet high, well-muscled, broad forehead, features even and distinct, speaks English with no African dialect, attitude hostile"—and he offer a reward of five pounds to the man who bring the boy back.

Soon enough it come clear. Match ain't gone and hid under no dock. He gone west, or north, where they can't get him. I wonder if I ever see him agin.

# John Britain,
## known as Silverheels:

The white men on the east side of the mountains worried about taxes on tea. We worried about the white men. They came, as I knew they would, in great numbers. Then a war came. Whether we started it or they, it did not matter. It was bound to come, once the whites came.

First, they destroyed the villages and farmlands of the Shawnees. The Shawnees fought hard, and we fought by their side. But the whites fought as if to make an end of all wars by making an end of us. Streams ran red with blood, and the sky went black with smoke.

My first son and I killed many whites. I do not count

how many because it was bad business, and by then I had seen enough of the whites to know that however many we killed, we could never kill enough. Besides, there was no need to count because there were no French to buy their scalps.

And there were no French to help us when the whites moved on Mingo Town. They moved hard and fast when we were still downstream with the Shawnees.

My son and I hurried upstream, but we knew we would be too late.

We saw the smoke over our town, and the blood left my heart. We went through our own burned cornfields, toward our burning lodges, and the life wanted to leave my body.

I found my wife shot in the back, dead on the riverbank. I never found my second boy.

Sometimes I pictured him floating on the great river, floating down to the Mississippi, to a place where there were no white men. Sometimes I saw my wife floating with him. Sometimes I saw all the Mingo people, floating to a better place. But the Mingoes were now blown to the four winds.

They called this Governor Dunmore's War. I wondered if Caunotaucarius had fought. His name meant "Taker of Towns," and our towns had been taken.

## Martha Washington:

On the August afternoon that my husband left for the First Continental Congress, I tried to put on a face as brave as his.

Sober Edmund Pendleton and vociferous Patrick

Henry had come to Mount Vernon as delegates to accompany him, and I bade a final good-bye to them all in the bright sunshine before the house. They impressed me as noble warriors, off to do battle.

I wanted to encourage them, so I said, "Stand firm, gentlemen. I know George will."

And my husband chuckled. "My wife is an inspiration, gentlemen."

Patrick Henry leaned down from his horse. Adding force to his intellect was his piercing dark eyes. He said, "I can assure you, madam, the Crown may call our Continental Congress an illegal assembly in Philadelphia elected by illegal assemblies in every colony, but we will all stand firm."

"And if we do," said my husband, "our firmness will prove our resolve, and the king will force his ministers to their senses."

And then they were off, their horses' hooves crunching on the pebbled drive before the house.

I watched them until they had rid into the trees at the edge of the road. Then I went back into the house, into the cool recesses of the passage. 'Twas midday and the heat was coming on.

The carpenters, as yet, had not broken through from the new wing, so the sound of their hammering was muffled. The house slaves were all off at their tasks. There was quiet in the house. 'Twas the quiet of emptiness, of pleasant voices now no more than echoes. I thought that the loneliness would overwhelm me.

And for just a moment, I thought I saw my Patsy walking past the east door, which looks out toward the river. I fancied that she was wearing her straw sunbonnet and carrying the wicker basket we had so often filled with wildflowers.

But 'twas only a shadow of a passing cloud.

Patsy was gone to her grave and would be with me now only in memory. Jacky had gone across the river to Maryland to begin his life with Nelly. Sally and George William Fairfax had left us. And who could tell when my husband would return, and with what new and heavy responsibilities?

I hurried to the west doorway, hoping to hail him back, if only for a few moments more. But all I could see was trail dust rising above the trees, marking the path that he and his companions had taken.

# Part Four

## Amateur General, Born Leader

C.D.—*Like Washington, I was riding to Philadelphia. But I was in company with my uncle rather than Patrick Henry, and I was not on horseback but in my uncle's coach, a capacious and comfortable brougham with heavy springs, fine leather seats, and little side pockets containing flasks of brandy.*

*The route to Philadelphia would be long and circuitous, but the reason for the journey was as cold and direct as a bayonet.*

*"Damned Alien and Sedition Acts." My uncle muttered the words under his breath whenever he ran out of things to say. The editor of his* Philadelphia Witness, *John Hereford, had printed strong Republican sentiments and now stood accused under the "Federalist sham." So my uncle was off to fight for freedom of the press.*

*I was off, with some trepidation, to meet the president. My uncle's advice: "Look the little Boston bastard in the eye. Ask him about Washington. Whatever he says, we'll use against him in the caucuses come fall."*

*If the government would prosecute John Hereford, a well-respected writer, what would stop them from prosecuting an anonymity like me? I did not think I was quite as courageous as Mr. Hereford, nor was I quite so naive as to think that Adams would welcome probing questions, even from the son of one of his staunchest political allies.*

*After four days of travel over the icy ruts that passed for roads between Washington and Philadelphia, we arrived at our destination, taking residence in a suite of rooms three blocks from the Delaware River. My uncle rented them year-round, he said, so that he would always have lodging in the capital, even in fall, when the yellow fever left and the Congress arrived.*

*He spent his week attending to Mr. Hereford. I prepared to visit John Adams. On Tuesday afternoons the presidential mansion was opened, and any gentleman, suitably dressed, might pay a visit of compliment to the president. On Friday evenings ladies and gentlemen might attend a public tea. Using the time to summon my courage and collect my thoughts, I waited until Friday.*

*I put on a lace stock, gray breeches, stockings as white as any that George William Fairfax may ever have worn, dark blue coat, and—my only true finery— a silk waistcoat of cerulean blue, which would have added a touch of elegance had I been wearing nothing better than buckskins.*

*It was warm for late February, so I went without benefit of greatcoat through what I considered to be the greatest city in America. Nowhere else on the continent could you stroll such wide, well-paved avenues or tread upon brick sidewalks wherever you went. Tall elms shaded you by day. Whale-oil lanterns lit your way by night. Two theaters and a public library enriched the meanest of residents. Ten newspapers, including my uncle's, vied for readers' pennies and opinions. And the finest hospital in America awaited the sick.*

*Why the federal government would depart Philadelphia for the mosquito-infested miseries of the Potomac marshland was a question that only politics could answer, so I simply enjoyed my stroll past the state house, where independence had been debated and affirmed in 1776, past the courthouse at Chestnut and Sixth, which now served as the federal capital, and on to the fine Market Street town house, where the president resided.*

*When the British occupied Philadelphia in the Revolution, General Howe had lived in this house. When Washington became president, he rented it from its owner, Robert Morris, for the enormous sum of $225. And now John Adams had taken up the lease on the house and the headaches of the office.*

*One of those was the business of meeting the public twice a week. Washington had begun the tradition. His levees were meant to seem democratic and yet dignified, though critics said they smacked too much of monarchy, like audiences at court. It was said that even an aging Washington had dominated them by his simple, quiet presence.*

*John Adams, by his simply garrulous presence, all but disappeared into the crowd. He wore a handsome green velvet suit. His reputation and achievement surpassed those of anyone around him. And yet, like most men, Adams in a crowd was simply another duck in the flock, afloat on the pond of his surroundings.*

*That, I suppose, was the difference between most men and George Washington.*

*While I planned my approach to Adams, I took tea and let my eye explore the female sights in the receiving room. Here a long, lithe neck, a head thrown back in alluring laughter. There a dress cut low, a powdered bosom, a beauty mark adorning a breast. Here a flirtatious smile. There the touch of a delicate hand upon a gentleman's forearm. Here a curious gaze toward the president. There a whispered comment, one lady passing opinions to another from behind an artfully held teacup.*

*It was an amazement to me that in that roomful of such feminine wonders, a lady of fifty-five, in fragile health, should hold the center of masculine attention. But Abigail Adams was an amazing woman.*

*When she noticed me, she excused herself from those around her and came to greet me. "Young Christopher Draper . . . What a surprise!"*

*I had not seen her in several years, and then only in large gatherings like this, but like a loving aunt, she took my hands in both of hers and made me feel that I was the only person in the room.*

*After a moment's pleasure at her attention, I noticed how much she had aged. Her limpid brown eyes, offset by high arching brows, seemed to be growing larger as time chiseled angles into her cheeks. Her mouth had tightened around several missing teeth, and a filigree of lines had tightened around her mouth. To soften this severe aspect, she wore a loose-fitting headdress that left a rim of brown curls girlishly framing her face. But any trace of girlishness that Abigail Adams ever possessed had long since left her.*

*"What brings you to Philadelphia, Christopher?"*

*"I'm here because I'm writing a book . . . a book about George Washington."*

"*Splendid,*" she said. "*No better man ever lived. He never misused his power, he never acted for private gain, and he suffered the barbs of men like your uncle with a silence that was the soul of dignity itself.*"

This opinion was a breath of fresh air after some of the fumes given off by my uncle.

"*What can I do for you?*" she asked.

"*Give me a bit of your time, and perhaps a bit of the president's. After all . . .*"

"*Yes, yes.*" She took me by the arm. With a deft move and a few cheerful words, she thrust me toward her husband and drew his others guests away, so that I might have a private moment with John Adams.

In his early days as vice president, when he had sought to establish a tone of majesty for the new government, Adams had presided over the Senate wearing a white wig and a ceremonial sword that heightened his already pompous demeanor and caused his many detractors to nickname him "His Rotundity."

After three years as president, rotundity remained in round paunch and pie-round face—a pie with jowls— but he no longer wore the wig. His own natural hair, long gone from the top of his head, was fluffed out like a gray cumulus that covered his ears and drifted down along the sides of his face. Most appropriate, I thought, for our famously bad-tempered president, that he should spend his time walking around under his own private cloud.

"*A book about Washington?*" he asked. "*To be printed by . . . ?*"

I could not dissemble. "*My uncle, sir. Hesperus Draper.*"

Adams sucked in his cheek, worked it ruminatively through a space where he, too, had lost a few teeth.

*"You are a bold one, coming to me as an emissary from your uncle."*

*"May I interview you, sir, about General Washington?"*

*"He was a great man. That's all you need to know."*

*"His greatness was entwined with your own, sir."*

*"I have no time for long talks with flattering scribblers, Christopher."*

*"But, sir, my uncle hopes for me to find the flaws in Washington."*

*"Not surprising, considering the flaws in your uncle. But a good biographer balances a man's flaws against his fine points."*

*"Just the reason I would talk with you, sir . . . Washington's fine points."*

*Adams's eyes were shifting to others in the room. "I nominated him to command the Continental army. I was his vice president. He did the rest."*

*"But sir," I said, surprised by my own persistence, "your opinions are—"*

*And my persistence finally piqued that famous temper. Adams lowered his voice to an angry whisper. "My opinion, Draper, is that if you're under your uncle's influence, you'll excoriate Washington, as your uncle does regularly just before he excoriates me. If a brighter influence sways you, the best I can hope for is that you're better than most historians of the Revolution."*

*I stupidly admitted, "I've not yet read any historians of the Revolution."*

*"Excellent." Adams drained those three syllables of every sarcastic drop that was in them. "Forming opinions without reading, and most likely without thinking. You are your uncle's nephew."*

"*Sir, you do me no justice.*"

"*Most historians do the Revolution no justice.*" *Adams put a hand on his hip and struck a lawyerly pose, though he continued to speak* sotto voce. "*They would have it that Dr. Franklin's electric rod smote the earth and out sprang General Washington. Then Franklin electrized Washington with the rod, and henceforward those two conducted all policy, negotiations, legislatures, and war. Ignore those historians, Christopher, and ignore your uncle. Read deeply, and think.*"

"*I will, sir, but—*"

*And without another word Adams was moving away, leaving his envy of Washington hanging in the air like smoke after a pistol shot.*

*I was left standing there, wondering if I should make for the door with my coattails between my legs.*

*And once more Abigail Adams materialized beside me.* "*I heard him mention Dr. Franklin's rod.*"

"*Yes, ma'am.*"

"*A favorite theme of his, though usually expressed in private. Put your questions in writing, Christopher. I'll see that he answers them.*"

"*I would hope that you might answer a few, also. Your woman's intuition—*"

*She gave a laugh and arched her brows a bit higher.* "*This project of yours, does it have a theme?*"

"*It best could be called 'The Making of the Man.' But I'm also driven to discover what may be a rather intimate secret.*"

"*Intimate?*" *She gave a conspiratorial look around and leaned closer.* "*How intimate?*"

"*It's said that Mrs. Washington burned her husband's letters at his death.*"

*This revelation caused Abigail Adams to stagger, quite literally. It was as if she physically shrank from such an act. "Burn her husband's letters?"*

*"Aye, ma'am. The question is Why?"*

*Abigail thought for a moment. "Some women think little of their own letters, as they are poorer-educated souls. But their husband's letters? I have no explanation for this, except perhaps that it's something southern women do."*

*Not exactly what I had been hoping for, but it convinced me, if I needed convincing, that much the better course was simply to seek Washington and let the secrets reveal themselves along the way.*

*If only Sally Fairfax would answer my letter, and give me her opinion of the grown man who had bought the pillow and bolster from her bed.*

*A few days later my uncle and I parted company. He was returning to Alexandria. I was bound north to continue my quest.*

*True to her word, Abigail had delivered narratives from herself and her husband. Those would occupy me on my journey. I also hoped to meet Alexander Hamilton in New York. I planned a stop in Boston. Then I was bound for France, because a fast mail packet had brought me a letter from the Marquis de Lafayette. When I returned from France, promised my uncle, Thomas Jefferson would meet with me.*

*My horizons were expanding as Washington's life grew more complicated.*

# The Narrative of John Adams:

The first I heard of George Washington was a story that raced ahead of him to Philadelphia in the late summer of 1774.

In a speech before the House of Burgesses, he was supposed to have said, "I will raise one thousand men, subsist them at my own expense, and march myself at their head for the relief of Boston."

Here was a statement of support more electrifying than any I had heard since the beginning of the crisis. 'Twas sublime, pathetic, beautiful. I considered it the most beautiful speech that had ever been made in Virginia or anywhere else.

That no one has been able to prove that Washington actually said it matters not. He never denied it, and he left the impression, all through the First Continental Congress, that he would do it if called upon.

Of course, most of what he did in that First Continental Congress was to leave impressions. From the beginning, men commented upon his "hard countenance," and they were taken by his manner of speaking, described by one congressman as "modest, but in cool and determined style and accent."

The truth was that Washington spoke little. Some thought this was because he had little to say. Others thought it was because he believed that actions spoke louder than words. In time I came to believe in the validity of both opinions.

## Hesperus Draper:

The men at that First Continental Congress were good at makin' toasts. In the fall of 1774 they made plenty. There was this: "To the best of kings." And later in a hard-drinkin' night, there would be this: "May the sword of the parent never be stained with the blood of her children."

I liked that second toast. Best keep our swords sheathed. Still, we should be ready if reason, or the best of kings, failed. So, by the spring of 1775, Fairfax County had one of the finest militias in the colonies. And I was part of it.

"Why are you joinin' up?" Charlotte demanded on the night that I told her.

"I'm hopin' your father will finally respect me."

"You don't give two damns about what my father thinks."

I laughed. She could see right through me.

We were gettin' ready for bed. I was under the covers. She was brushin' out her hair. Always liked to watch her. Always forgot whatever was botherin' me. And when she blew out the candles and climbed in next to me, I'd try to make her forget everything, too.

For a woman so small and slender, she was mighty soft in all the right places, but she had that fifty-caliber tongue, and deadly aim, too, even in the dark.

"Don't be pawin' me," she said, "till you tell me whether you're in this for patriotism, personal gain, or more poor-man's plantation beyond the Blue Ridge."

"I guess I'm doin' it for . . . for our children."

"Hesperus"—she had a way of hissin' my name

when she was mad—"there aren't going to *be* any children."

I looked up at the moonlight shinin' in the window. "You've conceived four times, darlin'."

"And not carried once. Find another reason."

Didn't think the business about bein' a natural rebel would sway her. So I said, "We have a warehouse of goods, all in violation of the nonimportation act. We can try to sell them, and we'll be tarred and feathered. Or we can stand with the leaders of the colony, and gain the everlastin' thanks of the folks who matter most, the ones who line our pockets."

"That's better," she said. "Just make sure that this time, you're an officer."

Now *there* was good advice.

Militia units elected their own officers. Best way to get elected was to trumpet your military experience, of which I had a share, and stand all the boys to drinks after a muster, which I did on a regular basis. Come April of '75, I got myself elected captain.

Washington didn't have to stand, of course. He'd been named commander in chief of the Fairfax companies by acclamation. Hell, he'd been asked to command half the militia companies in Virginia, as if he was the only man in the colony who knew anything about organizin' a group of men into a fightin' unit.

All the officers were sworn in at the City Tavern. Washington shook hands with each of us, and the lads who'd elected us set up a great ruckus of clappin' and foot-stompin'.

Washington was wearin' a new uniform he'd designed himself, in the colors of our Fairfax company: a blue coat with buff-colored facings, buff waistcoat and breeches. He looked about as martial as a man could. Posture straight, face steady, movements careful. Remember Rule Number Twenty: "The gestures of the body must be suited to the discourse you are upon." And the discourse was command.

He shook my hand and said coldly, "I'll expect you to control your tongue and your thirst."

"Here to do my duty, George. Don't even expect any bonus land."

The muscles in his jaw flexed. But he was gettin' better at hidin' his temper. Just said, "Do it well and stay sober."

"As sober as a preacher." Then I shouted, "Drinks all around." The lads let out with a cheer, and I give Washington a wink. "They like their new captain."

"You'll need more than their affection, Draper. 'Tis my intention to devote life and fortune to this cause. Serve well or answer to me. . . . Now I'll have an ale."

*Life and fortune.* Sounded like Washington was playin' a role again. The uniformed savior of Fairfax County. So I just laughed and ordered him an ale. Ordered one for myself, too . . . but only one.

Week later, British regulars in Boston marched out to Concord to seize gunpowder and rebel leaders. They got themselves into a day-long runnin' fight with the Massachusetts militia, and by the end of the day they were holed up in Boston with thousands of colonists comin' from all over New England to keep them there.

The sword of the parent had been bloodied. The swords of the children, too.

C.D.—*During my short stay at Mount Vernon, I had met a moonfaced old Negro named Billy Lee. Trained as a valet and known for his horsemanship, Billy had been purchased by Washington in 1768 to replace Jacob as a personal servant. Jacob admitted no resentment over this. Indeed, it was he who introduced me to Billy.*

*Though Washington's will had freed him, Billy had remained at Mount Vernon, cobbling shoes and recounting his life, through a sweet haze of rum, for any traveler who would listen. I left aside the early part of his narrative, a period covered well by Jacob, and picked up his story in the spring of 1775.*

## The Narrative of Billy Lee:

I knew things would be different when we went to that Second Continental Congress. You know how?

'Twasn't when the news come about the fightin' around Boston. 'Twas when Master told me the clothes to pack for the trip—waiscoats, breeches, shirts with lace, and such. Then he said, "And, Billy, pack my uniform."

I asked, "Sir, you mean your Fairfax militia uniform? The blue-and-buff?"

And he said, "Yes. See that it's clean."

That's when I knew. This Second Continental Congress, 'twould be more than just table-poundin' talk.

He didn't wear his uniform till they made him head of a committee to tell the folks in New England about gettin' supplies. Come the first meetin', he had me set out the blue-and-buff.

"The other congressmen wearin' uniforms too, sir?" I asked him.

"I don't know. But I'll put mine on. Perhaps it will increase confidence."

Confidence of Congress in him, or him in himself? I wondered about things like that. I tried to think hard about the things I saw around me.

But when Master stood in front of the mirror and held out his arms and I slipped that fine blue coat onto him and he smoothed back his hair, which he didn't always powder durin' the day, so 'twas still reddish brown with hardly any gray, and he stood back and looked at himself, I had such confidence in him, I'd've followed him into battle myself.

## John Adams:

The vital question for the Second Continental Congress was put in early June. It came from the provisional congress of Massachusetts: "As the army now at Boston is for the general defense of the rights of America, we would beg Congress to consider taking the regulation and general direction of same. . . ."

For three weeks we had skirted this issue, three long weeks during which I was afflicted with headaches, bellyaches, and low spirits . . . all the fidgets, piddlings, and irritabilities a man would expect, were he attempting to rouse the supine body of the Continental Congress. While most understood that the work before us was as great and important as any ever entrusted to a body of men, nibbling and quibbling were the norm in that congress, as in most congresses.

There is no greater mortification than to sit with a

dozen wits, deliberating upon a petition, address, or memorial. These great minds, these subtle critics, these refined geniuses, these learned lawyers, these wise statesmen, are so fond of showing their parts and powers as to make their consultation very tedious indeed.

There was a faction that shuddered at the prospect of blood, even though blood had already been spilled. They were abetted by a faction that recoiled at the prospect of breaking from the mother country, even though the mother country had sought to punish her child as a vindictive jailer punishes a felon.

Instead of producing a resounding call for arms, this Congress produced something called the Olive Branch Petition, an appeal to the king, over the heads of his royal ministers. Instead of issuing a call of support for the men who had taken Fort Ticonderoga, they appointed a committee. Instead of proclaiming a general for the army that had materialized around Boston and might just as quickly evaporate, they nibbled and quibbled.

But it was plain, from the day that George Washington entered the hall in his blue-and-buff uniform, that he was neither nibbler nor quibbler.

He never spoke at length in open session. But by his experience and abilities in military matters, he was a great help in committee. And in that uniform, he had a galvanizing presence.

Out of doors, out of session, away from the nibbling and quibbling, I began to discuss Washington among the delegates. It was my firm opinion that for our army to be truly continental, the leader should come from somewhere other than New England.

I stopped Dr. Franklin as he was coming into the

statehouse one morning. He looked fresh and pink-faced, despite a night that had ended far earlier for me than for him. I asked him his opinion of Washington.

He studied me over his spectacles, as clear-eyed as a tea tippler, and said, "John, I can't take my eyes off the man. There's an air about him. He moves easily, sits easily. Why, he may be the most graceful big man I've ever seen."

I said, "Physical grace is not everything, Franklin. His speech is—"

"Yes, yes . . . faulting, ill at ease. But I get the feeling that he has such a fine sense of his own inner life that he bears not the least embarrassment at speaking poorly. And from what I've heard, he's as brave as a stag in rut." Then he jabbed his walking stick at me like a rapier. "Mark this, John: he's our man."

Armed with that opinion, I canvassed the southern delegations, finding that most would support an army, if Washington was at its head.

So I went to the Virginians, who knew him best.

I approached Patrick Henry one afternoon after the other delegates had left. Henry was working at the Virginia desk, in the back row on the right side of our deliberative semicircle.

He said, "Colonel Washington may have no pretensions to eloquence, but he is a man of more solid judgment and information than any on the floor."

In the statehouse garden, I spoke with Virginian Edmund Pendleton; he said Washington would not be a good choice. He preferred Artemas Ward of Massachusetts, already commanding at Boston. But Ward could not bring the South into the fight, and though in his forties, he looked to be in his sixties; Washington, at forty-three, looked like a man in his prime.

I asked Pendleton why he was so clear and full against the appointment of his friend.

He said, "New England soldiers may not fight for a Virginian. Different regions. Different countries. If you relieve Ward, your militia may go home."

Did Pendleton speak his own firm belief, or was he speaking the true feelings of Washington, so that Washington would not have to speak them himself?

I decided to seek out the object of my pursuit.

Like most members of Congress, Washington frequented the City Tavern, where much important business was completed, many firm alliances were formed, many troublesome quibbles were smoothed with the lubrication contained in a mug or a glass.

One evening, I spied Washington there in the company of several friends who kept a regular table. I begged a private word. He excused himself and followed me to a table in the corner. The taproom was close and crowded, a closeness made all the more oppressive by the humidity that lay upon Philadelphia like a damp wool carpet, but Washington looked almost cool beneath the film of perspiration covering his forehead.

It could not be said that we were friends. I had few friends in Philadelphia. Though I was respected for my beliefs and the ardor with which I advanced them, I was considered obnoxious and overbearing. As for Washington, he showed a polite cordiality to all, but he seemed not to have the habit of intimacy with any.

"Now, then, Colonel," I said, "I'll be direct. You've heard talk of making you commander in chief?"

"I have."

I had hoped for a glimmer of pleasure, or perhaps a scowl. Even indifference would have been an answer. But his face was completely neutral, as if he would give me no indication of how he really felt.

I said, "Your excellent universal character, sir, and your skill and experience as an officer make you the best candidate. And you *are* in uniform."

" 'Tis time for uniforms."

"Does that mean you'll accept the position?"

"If 'tis offered, I shall have to consider it. But I do not solicit it."

"But you will consider it?"

"Honor will bind me. But 'twill be done through no desire or insinuation of mine. There may be others more qualified."

"What others?"

"Horatio Gates. Charles Lee. Men who held royal commissions in the late war. Men of experience who have shown the vision to embrace our cause."

"But foreign-born." I said, " 'Tis most honorable of you, sir, not to solicit something of such value. You're too modest. Thank you, and good night."

Washington did not seem pleased by my conclusion, nor at the prospect of leading an army. This in itself made plain to me the wisdom of my selection, for it demonstrated his understanding of the challenges that lay ahead. What man, in his right mind, would actually wish to shoulder such a burden?

The next morning, full of anxieties and apprehending daily that we should hear very distressing news from Boston, I walked with my cousin Samuel in the statehouse yard, taking a little exercise and fresh air before the hour of Congress. There I told him that the time had come. I was determined to take a step that would force this Congress to declare themselves for or against something . . . anything.

In the hall, flies buzzed. Delegates dozed. Someone groaned when I rose to speak. Someone else remarked on "Massachusetts magpies." But I was inured to such reactions.

I launched directly into a depiction of the troubles that faced us: the distresses of the army, the danger of its dissolution, the difficulty of collecting another. Then I introduced my motion: "That Congress would adopt the army at Boston and appoint a general."

Everyone in the hall had by then given me their attention. I said, "I have but one gentleman in mind for the important command, a gentleman from Virginia whose skill and experience as an officer, independent fortune, great talents, and excellent universal character would command the approbation of all Americans and unite the colonies better than any person on the continent."

Mr. Washington, who happened to sit near the door, darted into the library room.

John Hancock, my countryman from Massachusetts, and president of the Congress, heard me with visible pleasure, expecting that I would nominate him. When I came to describe Washington, I never remarked a more sudden change of countenance. Mortification and resentment were expressed as forcibly as Hancock's face could exhibit them.

But I could not worry about Hancock. Washington was my concern. Perhaps he had left us to express his desire that this cup should pass from his hands.

Perhaps he left because of natural modesty, a sense of propriety that led him instinctively to understand that we would feel more comfortable debating his fate if he were not present.

## Billy Lee:

I was in the library that mornin', tryin' to read a pamphlet, pickin' out the words I recognized. The door flew open and in came the master, movin' fast, like he was tryin' to outrun that squeakin'-hinge voice of John Adams.

He wiped sweat from his forehead. Then he began to look at the books, like he wanted to take his mind off somethin'. But nothin' seemed to catch his eye. So he stepped out by another door, without even a word to me.

## John Adams:

The following day we had a new general. He appeared before Congress bearing a speech, which he read with his head down, in a soft and almost monotonous voice that implied none of the drama in the words: "Though I am truly sensible of this high honor, I feel great distress from a consciousness that my military experience may not be equal to its important trust. However, as Congress desires, I will enter upon this momentous duty and exert every power I possess in support of the glorious cause."

Then he couched his main point most starkly. "Lest some unlucky event should happen unfavorable to my reputation, I beg it may be remembered that I this day declare, with the utmost sincerity, I do not think myself equal to the command I am honored with."

That this was not a rousing speech disappointed some. But its tone was properly sobering. It was also to Washington's great credit—and my great comfort—that he was no demagogue. History is filled with stories of men whose ability to stir the baser emotions of their followers leads them all to disaster.

And his next remark stirred us only in its sincerity: "As to pay, I beg leave to assure the Congress that, as no pecuniary consideration could have tempted me to accept this employment, I do not wish to make any profit from it." He would accept nothing but his expenses.

I found something charming in the conduct of the man. A gentleman of one of the first fortunes upon the continent, leaving his delicious retirement, his family and friends, sacrificing his ease, and hazarding all in the cause of his country . . . for nothing. Here was a man we could trust.

## Billy Lee:

I don't think nothin' ever scare me so much as seein' the master with tears in his eyes. But I saw it, the night after he was made general.

'Twas at the tavern called Burns's in the Fields that Mr. Patrick Henry said, "Congratulations, George. Our hopes are with you."

My master took Mr. Henry's hand in both of his and said, "Remember, Mr. Henry, what I now tell you: from the day I enter upon the command of the American armies, I date my fall and the ruin of my reputation."

That's when I saw the tears shinin' in the candle-light. I knew I had to think with a more serious mind about all the things happenin' around us.

That Saturday night, after a busy week, the master set alone in his room.

I asked him if he was goin' out.

"Not tonight, Billy. I've a letter to write to Mrs. Washington, and . . . and—"

He just went silent and stared at the lantern flicker-in' beside him. Some people glaze over right quick starin' at a flame, but he was never one to do that, not until then. He just glazed over and sat, still as a rock, starin'.

I think he was thinkin' hard about what he'd got himself into.

So I brought him his writin' case and said, "You wanted to write a letter, sir?"

For the rest of the night I could hear the pen scratchin'.

## Dr. James Craik:

I endeavored to visit Mount Vernon often in my friend's absence.

On a June day I was ushered into the parlor, where Mrs. Washington was to be found. I thought at first glance that she was ill, her face was so drawn and gray.

It was afternoon, by which time she was usually dressed for visitors. But she still wore a shift more appropriate for morning, and a shapeless brown bedgown of the sort that common women wear for comfort around the house.

"What's wrong, ma'am?" I asked her.

She waved a letter. "They've made him the general."

"Of what?" I asked.

"The whole army." Then she handed me the letter, saying, "There is nothing so personal here that you should not read it, Doctor."

And I felt Washington's deep anxiety in every word, his deep love in every line: "Believe, my dear Patsy, that, so far from seeking this appointment, I have used every endeavor to avoid it, not only from an unwillingness to part with you and the family, but from a consciousness of its being a trust too great for my capacity. I should enjoy more happiness in one month with you at home than I have the most distant prospect of finding abroad, if I stay there seven times seven years."

There was greater intimacy here than Martha normally revealed, more poetry than I had heard in all my years of friendship with Washington. Whoever doubted that he loved his wife would think differently, had he read those lines.

He said that, putting his faith in Providence, he would return in the fall.

I said that she should take heart from this promise.

Martha smiled, though there were tears in her eyes. Then, busying herself to keep her emotions from overflowing, she poured two cups of tea, and we made a toast: "To a safe return in the fall."

# John Adams:

Before the week was out, we had elected those who would surround Washington. Charles Lee, Artemas Ward, Philip Schuyler, and Israel Putnam were made major generals; Joseph Reed and Thomas Mifflin, well-spoken young Philadelphians, would serve as secretaries; Horatio Gates, still in Virginia, was named adjutant general. Washington had campaigned hard for the appointments of Lee and Gates, Reed and Mifflin. Congress had squabbled over the rest, as it squabbled over everything.

All squabbling stopped, however, at word of another battle, on Bunker Hill. Washington left at dawn the next day. To see him off, we brought out several militia units, a fife and drum band, and a group of leaders from Congress. Hands were shaken. Godspeed was wished. And Charles Lee made a point to speak with me.

Lee, a former king's officer, knew I had fought a major scuffle on the floor to have him appointed. Despite the bugbears and objections of the timid and the cunning, who did not trust him or preferred to advance their own friends over him, the great necessity for officers of skill and experience had prevailed.

He now looked into my eyes. As his face was unnaturally bony, with a receding chin and a nose that preceded it like a lowered lance, a look from him could be as unsettling as a conversation with him. And his uniform was no uniform at all, but a self-styled officer's coat of light blue, stained here and there by old meals. Yet his words, for all their profanity, were pointed and apt: "Don't worry, Adams. With fifteen thousand militia, we'll sweep Boston of all the king's troops, God damn them all to hell."

Lee was probably the only man in Philadelphia who had read more military history than I. So I asked him, "Do you think, sir, that mere militia can do the job?"

"*Mere* militia, sir?" He stuffed a pinch of snuff into a nostril large enough to hold a musket ball. "We're going to build a new army, dispensing with the tinsel and show of war. Our men are lovers of liberty while the British army are merely whores to kingship. And which would you prefer, sir, lover or whore?"

I assumed it was a rhetorical question, particularly as Lee was often seen in the company of strumpets. And if I had attempted to answer, my response would have been drowned out by Lee's snuff-induced sneeze.

He was a queer creature altogether. To love him, you had to love the dogs that traveled with him like a pack and you had to forgive a thousand whims for the sake of the soldier and the scholar.

With Lee's sneeze echoing, Washington mounted his horse and gave a galloping inspection to the men of the Philadelphia Light Horse. As he passed, the riders pulled themselves to attention in their saddles. Their pennants snapped. Their horses pranced. And in the half-light of dawn, I could see the sparks struck by Washington's horseshoes upon the cobblestones.

The band struck a jaunty air, appropriately entitled "The Road to Boston." The captain of the Light Horse gave a call, and the rest of us hurried for our carriages so that we could accompany Washington to the outskirts of the city.

It was a stirring scene in the red glow of sunrise. I thought that perhaps we were looking at the sunrise of our new republic. And yet I felt a wave of melancholy roll over me.

Washington was riding off to glory. I, poor creature, worn out with scribbling for my bread and liberty, low in spirits and weak in health, would leave others to wear the laurels I had sown, others to eat the bread which I had earned. For it was through my efforts that this war had been made a common cause.

The rest of the day, my hopes and my fears were alternately very strong.

## Hesperus Draper:

I was goin' to war. Or at least to Boston.

One of our best customers was a former British officer with squinty eyes and a little potbelly by the name of Horatio Gates. They say he was the bastard son of the Duke of Leeds. I don't know. I do know that he was able to rise just so high in the British army and no higher. So he retired and moved to Virginia.

But with some men, once a soldier, always a soldier. And when Gates smelled a war, he was ready.

Offered me a job as his aide—a glorified errand boy, message runner, and personal secretary. I took it, because Gates said he'd speak for me when the time came to name the quartermaster, the one who supplied the troops, selected the vendors, made interest off the army's money, and took a three percent commission on every purchase. Profiteerin' for a quartermaster was as time-honored as pillagin' for a foot soldier. And mixin' patriotism with profit was a lot better way to spend a war than bein' a captain in a little militia unit.

As for the fact that I'd never been anybody's aide, well, remember my motto. Learn by doin'.

But when the time came for me to ride off, Charlotte cried. 'Twas the only time, other than when she miscarried, that I ever saw her cry. She said, "What if the British come out and crush your little army and destroy you all?"

"They tried to do that at Bunker Hill, darlin', and they failed. Besides, 'tisn't a little army at all. There's twenty thousand men at Boston."

Charlotte said nothin' to that, nothin' for a long time. All I could hear was the tall case clock in the stairwell, tickin' out our last minutes together.

So I took her in my arms. "Washington says it should be over by autumn."

And she give me one of those looks, the kind you get when your wife sees a lie growin' like a big carbuncle on the tip of your nose. "That's the first time you've ever believed Washington about anything."

"He wouldn't stick his neck out if he thought the British could slip a noose around it. If he says we'll be home by autumn, we'll be home in August, lookin' like heroes in the bargain."

"I don't believe it," she said.

I shrugged. "I don't either."

"That's more like it." She wiped away her tears and straightened herself. "You should know that one honest word gets you further with me than five artful lies. Go to Boston. Come back in one piece. And tell that uncle of yours that I'm comin' to work for him while you're gone."

What a woman. A mountain of trouble, but worth a mountain of gold.

c.d.—*A letter reached me in Philadelphia from the wife of one of those to whom I had written, Joseph Reed: "My husband went to his reward in 1785. He did, however, leave a description of his time with Washington, which I forward herewith." My uncle's files would need annotation. But Reed's voice echoed eloquently from the grave.*

## The Narrative of Joseph Reed:

My story with Washington had begun during the First Continental Congress, while I was a member of the Philadelphia Committee of Correspondence. I had been communicating with Lord Dartmouth, so my knowledge of English political matters was in demand among Congressmen, including Washington, with whom I dined often.

When time came for him to form a military family, he asked if I would join as secretary. "I'm sorry, but there is no other post that I can offer you," he explained. "And you are well known for the letters you write."

I was reluctant. I told him of my fragile wife, Esther, and three small children, in addition to a law practice only then beginning to thrive.

He answered that the struggle might last only a few months, during which time he would bear an enormous weight of correspondence. As an attorney, I could be counted on to execute his orders, even to anticipate his thoughts. And as Boston would be a land of strangers, he should enjoy the company of a few good friends.

I said that I would ride north with his entourage and give my answer in New York. But I did not encourage him.

'Twas plain that the men in Washington's headquarters would be the first to suffer ministerial wrath should our army meet with disaster rather than autumnal success. And it took no great imagination to envision the sea of troubles that awaited the commander who took over the militia in Boston.

Those who made Washington their general chose him for his vigor, his Virginia roots, and his military experience. But never had he commanded more than a few hundred troops. Never had he used artillery or built large fortifications. And most of his field experience had come in defeat. When he said he was not ready for such a large undertaking, he was telling the truth.

I carried these thoughts with me to New York, and there we heard the details of Bunker Hill—that the British had overwhelmed the Americans, though at a staggering cost of a thousand casualties. It was plain that this would be a war in earnest, not merely a demonstration of arms. So I determined to go to Boston.

I suppose I had no inclination for half-treason. When a subject draws his sword against his prince, he must be prepared to cut his way through, if he means ever to sit down in safety. I had taken too active a role in what might be called the civil part of our opposition to renounce, without disgrace, the public course when that course led to danger. I had the most sovereign contempt for a man who could plan measures but had not the spirit to execute them.

Before we left New York, Washington appeared at their provincial congress to receive congratulations on his appointment. But the final sentence of their tribute was something to make a proud man bristle: "We have the most flattering hopes of success in the glorious struggle for American liberty and the fullest assurance that whenever this contest shall be decided, by that fondest wish of each American—an accommodation with the mother country—that you will cheerfully resign the important post committed into your hands and reassume the character of our worthiest citizen."

A copy of these remarks was given to us a few hours before the ceremony, so that we might frame a response. I watched Washington read, watched him redden, and for a moment, thought he might tear the sheet into pieces. Instead, he shoved it into my hands and said, "Why on earth do they think I took this job? To keep it? I didn't even want it. We must answer politely but firmly."

I composed an answer for him. But the most important sentence was his: "When we assumed the soldier, we did not lay aside the citizen."

As events proved, it could have been his epitaph.

## Hesperus Draper:

Let me tell you about the great Continental army as we saw it in the early summer of 1775:

Take about twenty thousand Yankee farmers and shopkeeps, a fair share of 'em rascals and rapscallions, with a scatterin' of Injuns and freed nigras, too. Bring 'em together at a college called Harvard, on the banks of a twisty little brown river called the Charles. Make sure most of 'em haven't been twenty miles from home in their whole lives, so some of 'em have a case of killin' homesickness, and the rest are after the most serious hell-raisin' they can find.

Then let 'em do whatever the hell they please. But don't discipline 'em. Don't flog 'em when they fight. Don't flog 'em when they talk back. Don't flog 'em when they decide to go home. Let 'em live wherever they want, from Harvard rooms to fine tents to mud huts, and don't even tell 'em where to shit. Because if you start givin' 'em orders, the *lot* of 'em might decide to go home.

That's because these New Englanders believe all that talk about one man bein' equal to another, no matter what rung he was born on. They don't like anybody put over them, and for certain not the friends and neighbors they've elected as officers. Hell, in that camp, if a company captain was a barber, his men expected a shave twice a week.

Now, instead of drillin' 'em, give these boys shovels and set 'em to buildin' earth forts on every damn hill around Boston. Leastways you'll be takin' advantage of somethin' a Yankee farmer knows how to do, which is dig. And it's good that you've got shovels, because half of 'em don't have muskets, and half the muskets they do have are older than that Harvard College, which has been settin' there for damn near a hundred and forty years.

By the time I got to Cambridge, Washington had begun the business of puttin' everyone in their place. Almost nobody had any uniforms, so he ordered them to wear insignia—red cockades for field officers, yellow or buff for captains, red cloth shoulder stripes for sergeants, and so forth. And he'd started floggin' a few of the hard cases, too. But 'twas only the beginnin'.

He was set up in a big yellow house that some Tory had abandoned. Had a fine view of the river and a fair breeze blowin' in from the west. Always found the best place in town to hang his hat and write his dispatches, but I reckon that was part of showin' who was boss.

He greeted Horatio Gates like a long-lost brother. Give him a big smile, a handshake. Peppered him with questions. Seemed as happy as if Gates had brought ten battalions trailin' after him. But the only man Gates had brought was me.

Before he saw my face, Washington saw my Virginia uniform. Hadn't worn it on the trip, except in Philadelphia, so it still looked sharp and clean. But any uniform would have looked good to Washington. Then he saw who was wearin' it.

I took off my hat and bowed my best bow. "A privilege to serve you, sir."

Gates said, "General, my new aide. I believe you are acquainted."

I'd told Gates what he needed to know about Washington and me.

With his usual coldness, Washington said, "'Tis good to see you wearing your new uniform so proudly, Draper. Bear in mind that men will watch you closely in it."

"That's why I wore it, sir," I said.

Washington had Gates take a seat in his office while his secretary, Joseph Reed, showed me where I'd be workin'.

Reed looked somethin' like Washington—same kind of broad forehead and wide-apart eyes—except he smiled more. But then, my saddle smiled more. Reed led me through a door in the back of Washington's office, into another room about the same size. There was six tables crowded in and six young men writin' dispatches.

Reed said, "We fight this war with paper, ink, and sealing wax."

"I used bullets and powder in the last one," I said.

"This army moves on daily orders posted across a fourteen-mile front, on regimental instructions, on requisitions, on reports to the Continental Congress and the Massachusetts Provisional Congress, too. A thousand details, almost beyond human capacity. But now much of it will be dropped on the adjutant general."

"And me?"

"You'll have blue fingers soon enough."

"Blue fingers?"

Reed held up his ink-stained forefinger and thumb. Better, I supposed, than a bullet.

That evenin' I rode to a place called Fort Hill, a height that commanded Roxbury Crossing, where the two main roads to Boston met.

From there I could see the whole lay of the land. Boston was a town well suited for a siege. Well suited for defense, too. By land there was only one access, a natural causeway called the Neck. Looked more like a thin wrist, with the town reachin' out in the shape of a mittened hand. To the left was the Back Bay, the estuary of the river Charles. To the right was South Bay, separatin' the city from Dorchester Heights.

'Twas a peaceful sight—hills and fields, marsh meadows and calm water, Boston steeples and British works. But somewhere behind those works, livin' in tents on Boston Common, marchin' and drillin' and takin' their ease, were some of the best troops in the world.

'Twas just a matter of time before they decided to break out. And maybe those Yankee boys on all those hillsides might stand and fight, like they did at Bunker Hill, and maybe they might decide to run.

## The Narrative of Abigail Adams:

I went to Cambridge in mid-July so that I could report to my husband on what I saw there, and to satisfy my own curiosity about General Washington.

Approaching the bridge over the Charles to Cambridge, I believed that I could almost smell the army before I saw it. Indeed, I believed that I could almost see the smell, hanging like a miasmic fog in the smoke of the thousands of campfires above Harvard College.

And then my eyes were struck by the most shocking sight that ever I had seen. All about the bridge, there were men, cavorting in the water, diving, laughing, splashing, and most, if not all, were naked! Yes, as naked as the day they were born, though not nearly so innocent. And as I went by, not a one of them took the least shame in appearing so before a woman.

If this was the Continental army, what sort of man could their general be? 'Twas the grimmest of times, remember, and anything that caused us to lose confidence in our leaders, or in the troops they led, was deeply disheartening.

My fears were quickly allayed at headquarters. My husband had prepared me to be impressed with Washington. But the half of it was not told to me.

He greeted me as cordially as if I were visiting his seat upon the Potomac.

With equal cordiality, I welcomed him to Massachusetts.

The gentleman and the soldier seemed agreeably blended in him. I determined immediately that here was a man who combined dignity with ease and a complacency in his post that must inspire confidence in all around him.

Then Charles Lee ambled in, preceded by five dogs whose nails set up a great scratching on the wood floor. Here was a careless hardy veteran, but certainly not a face to launch a thousand ships. Indeed, his nose was so prominent that behind his back, some people called him Naso.

However, he seemed unbothered by his impression, affecting instead an air of noblesse oblige, as if all the rest of the world were somehow out of step with him. After shaking my hand, he introduced his Pomeranian, a bright-eyed and intelligent beast that he made to sit before me.

Washington folded his arms and a bemused expression crossed his face, as if this small distraction were most welcome amidst the demands of office.

"Now, then, Spada," Lee said to his dog, "shake hands with Mrs. Adams."

The dog did not seem to comprehend, so Lee simplified: "Spada shake."

And the dog raised his paw. Not wishing to insult such an intelligent beast, I took the paw and shook it, which caused Lee to nod approvingly, although I realized 'twas I who was earning Lee's approval, not the dog.

"General Lee is a lover of good canines," explained Washington.

Lee offered a disconcerting smile. "When my quadruped friends, madam, are equaled by the bipeds in fidelity, gratitude, and good sense, I shall become a philanthropist of the first order. But to say the truth, I think the strongest proof of a good heart is to love dogs and dislike mankind."

My husband had warned me that Lee was "a queer creature altogether." Once more, I had not been told the half of it.

Our talk then turned to as much military discussion as gentlemen thought they should permit with a lady. When I spoke of the scene I had passed on the bridge, Washington's fine manly features flushed red with anger.

"Were these men unclothed, Mrs. Adams?"

"You could say that they were all Adams, sir, of a fashion."

He offered not a flicker of a smile, but called to his secretary, and in a voice that displayed the tightest control, he said, "They're at it again. Issue an order."

Shortly, Joseph Reed returned and read his composition: "The general does not mean to discourage the practice of bathing while the weather is warm, but he forbids it at or near the bridge in Cambridge, where it has been complained of that many men, lost to all sense of decency and common modesty, are running about naked, whilst passengers, and even ladies of the first fashion, are passing over it, as if they meant to glory in their shame."

My honor had been protected and a bit more order brought to the army.

As I said, the half of it had not been told to me.

But I told all to my husband, John, in a letter. And in recounting my meeting with the General, I found myself longing for more masculine company. I begged my husband to write to me with warmth, with sentimental effusion, so that I would think on him rather than on our noble General.

## Joseph Reed:

Overflowing necessaries ... Filthy campsites amidst the fine buildings of Harvard ... Naked men waving their privates at ladies of quality ... Sentries grown accustomed to sleeping on duty ... Officers, who had ignominiously run at Bunker Hill, still strutting proudly around the camp ...

After a day spent cleaning these Augean stables, Washington would sometimes take off his coat; send his slave, Billy Lee, for Madeira; and seek to lighten his load through quiet talk. I do not flatter myself to say that in these evening talks the General treated me more as friend than secretary.

"I've made a pretty good slam among these New England officers," he said one hot July night. "Breaking a few of them has worked wonders on the rest."

"Eliminate the bad and bring on the good," I answered. "I'm most impressed by young Mr. Knox and by Nathanael Greene of Rhode Island."

"Such officers may help to bring good order among the men."

"The floggings have also had good effect, as has the requirement that troops attend divine services."

"All the preaching in the world won't help, should the regulars come out." He slapped at a mosquito on his cheek and waved two more away.

For a time we sat in silence, mosquitoes buzzing, walls vibrating with the snores of an exhausted staff. 'Twas well past midnight, and he seemed to be sinking into a world of dejected thought where I was not invited to go.

To cheer him I said, "If the British loss was so great when they tried to force Bunker Hill—entrenchments thrown up in a single night—what must it cost them to attack the works we've been constructing since we arrived, works supported with cannon?"

" 'Twould cost dearly, so long as our men could be counted on to fight." Washington refilled our glasses. "And they would fight well if properly officered, although, in general, these New Englanders are an exceedingly dirty and nasty people."

That he offered such a strong opinion shocked me, but at the same time, it made our friendship even more intimate. So I offered advice: "I would not allow remarks like that to be put about, sir."

"No. You're right. I simply must live with the truth

and hope the enemy stay put. But we must try to be ready for them. We must appeal to the Massachusetts authorities for the powder they've promised."

"They believe they can supply some three hundred barrels."

"We'll need every grain."

Late the next afternoon, the General received a kind of news he was growing used to: bad. A letter arrived from the Massachusetts Provisional Congress, responding to our request for powder. It said we were mistaken in expecting three hundred barrels. Their store amounted to no more than thirty-six.

After reading the letter, Washington simply sat back with a blank expression on his face.

"Is there a response, sir?" I asked.

"Close the doors." His voice was as blank as his face.

"Sir?"

"The doors. Close them both. And leave me."

I did as I was told, and for a half an hour, there was silence from the General's room. It was the silence of shock, almost the silence of the grave.

When finally it was broken, we poured out dispatches to the surrounding colonies, requesting powder and lead, but doing it with care so as not to reveal the extremity of our situation: that we had powder for no more than nine cartridges per man. Should the British obtain this intelligence, we might be crushed.

For weeks, reading the word "powder" in a letter set us all a-tiptoe.

But the word was often followed by good news. Powder was coming from Pennsylvania, raised by the Continental Congress. Powder was coming from New York, powder from Rhode Island, and from New Hampshire as well.

This is not to say that things improved so much that we could relax. We were in the situation of a man with little money in his pocket who will do twenty mean things to prevent breaking in upon his stock.

We were obliged to bear with the British rascals in their works atop Bunker Hill, when a few shots now and then would have given them alarms and kept our men vigilant. We were also obliged to keep the riflemen from their entertainment.

The riflemen were the first units to arrive from outside New England, tough backwoodsmen from Virginia and Pennsylvania. They wore tow-cloth hunting shirts and buckskin leggings and carried scalping knives near as long as their rifles. One company had come all the way from Winchester, Virginia, to Boston, in three weeks . . . on foot.

For entertainment, the riflemen would sneak out and pick off British officers, until our economy of powder forced them to find their fun elsewhere. Then they turned to brawling with New England troops.

## Dr. James Craik:

In August, Washington wrote to his cousin, Lund Washington, who had taken over the management of Mount Vernon in his absence. Lund showed the letter to me.

'Twas full of instructions on spinning and milling and planting and finishing the house. But his main concern was nae for business. 'Twas for his wife, who had moved to her ancestral home in New Kent County so as to be safe from river-borne attack, should the vengeful Governor Dunmore decide to make her a hostage.

"She will be out of his reach for two or three months," he wrote, "in which time matters probably will take such a turn as to render her removal either absolutely necessary or quite useless."

This meant he still expected a resolution by autumn.

I was hoping to offer my services. But he anticipated me: "Tell Dr. Craik that I should be very glad to see him if there was anything worth his acceptance, but the Massachusetts people suffer nothing to go by them that they can get for themselves."

In Massachusetts they wanted doctors from their own country, and at that time, believe me, we were thirteen separate countries. The General's hands were tied by politics. His army was nae Continental as yet. It was still as provincial as those New England farmers or those backwoods Virginians.

## Billy Lee:

Every day, the master rid out from headquarters, and I went with him. He give me a good mount to ride and a good coat to wear, too. He wanted his servant to look good, because he always did. Never a man rode a horse better. Or sat one better. And never a man could strike a better pose. He'd hold the reins in his left hand, put his right hand on his hip, and look jess like a fine statue.

One day we come ridin' across the Cambridge Common, headin' for that Harvard Yard—a wide greensward with all fine brick buildings 'round it. And right in the middle we had our camp—tents and lean-tos and shacks, even a big barracks the General designed hisself. Some officers drilled their men in the Yard, but it didn't always work too good. And for certain not that mornin'.

We figgered as much when we heard shoutin'. Master reined in his horse, listened a bit, give me a funny look, then went gallopin' toward the noise.

We come around the corner of the building called Harvard Hall, and I swear there was hundreds of men in the Yard, fightin' the biggest brawl you ever seen. A punchin', kickin', eye-gougin', ear-bitin' mess, and right in the middle was a bunch of Virginia riflemen, maybe two hundred, fightin' as many Yankees.

Nobody knew what started it. All's I knew was that the General jumped off his horse and marched into those men like a farmer goin' into a wheat field. Only he wasn't swingin' a scythe. He was swingin' his fists and kickin' and shoutin' for all this to stop.

He went right for the two biggest fellers on the field, grabbed 'em both, and shook 'em and shouted at 'em and shook 'em some more. And all while he was doin' that, the rest of that mob was scatterin' like a bunch of carrion bugs when somebody kicks the carcass.

I tried to see some of the faces, so I could tell the General who was who, in case he wanted to flog any of 'em. I always tried to do what I could to help him.

Most of the Yankees was from the Marblehead regiment. I knew because there was a dozen or so Negro freedmen in the regiment. And one of them run right past me. And by damn but he looked familiar.

I shouted, "Hey!" and he give me a funny look. We both knew we knew each other from somewhere, but he was movin' fast. Besides, I couldn't run him down and leave the General with such a handful.

He had him a feller from Virginia and a feller from Marblehead and he was shakin' 'em like two puppies pissin' on the rug. But everybody else was gone. Just plain gone. Scared to hell by the General.

And he was shoutin', "What caused this fight?"

Both of 'em was answerin' at once, about "Damn arrogant Virginians" and "suck-egg Yankees, who wouldn't never come to help us drive the British out of Winchester" and the Yankee callin' the Virginian a thief and the Virginian callin' the Yankee a nigger-lover and so on.

And he shook 'em again and shouted, "You're soldiers in the same army! You're *Americans*, God damn you both. Act it. And take your punishment. Forty lashes apiece."

By now Daniel Morgan of Virginia and John Glover of Marblehead had come ridin' up. The General give over these brawlers to their commanders; then he come stompin' back to his horse, grabbed the reins, and rode off so fast I had to kick my mount to catch up with him.

Like I said, I was tryin' to think hard about things in them days. And I thought there was wiseness in what he said about everyone bein' Americans, even if he did think the New Englanders wasn't as good as Virginians.

# Hesperus Draper:

If the walls of Washington's office could talk, what a tale they'd tell.

'Twas in that room that Washington first met a Connecticut officer named Benedict Arnold, who brought a plan for taking Canada. The less said about him the better. 'Twas in that room that Washington talked strategy with Charles Lee and Horatio Gates, the two men who proved the greatest threat to his command. And 'twas in that room, in November, that he devised a plan with Henry Knox that made the difference in the siege of Boston.

Knox was the biggest, fattest man I ever set eyes on. Stood six foot three and weighed two hundred and fifty pounds. Made my uncle look like Jack Sprat.

He was all of twenty-four, self-taught in the business of fortification and artillery, and one of the few Massachusetts officers Washington liked. So he was given command of all our artillery. He told Washington that this was a high honor, even if we didn't have enough artillery to wake up the old maids in Boston, even if we fired every gun at once. Then he volunteered to go all the way to Fort Ticonderoga, some two hundred and fifty miles, collect all the cannon there, and drag them back across the snow to Boston.

I was sick of headquarters by then. Sick of the jealous officers and the squabblin' army, sick of writin' dispatches, and certain that Charlotte would never let me touch her with my ink-stained fingers. So I was tempted to volunteer.

Like most fat men, Knox brought a blustery kind of cheer to everything he did, but I thought he was an apple-polisher in addition to an apple-eater, always showin' up with another book on artillery, always makin' sure the General saw him readin' it, always makin' jokes, tryin' to get Washington to smile. . . . That kind of feller can wear you right down. And the weather had turned as ugly as the asshole on a high-tailed dog. All things considered, drudgery at a desk in Cambridge looked better than freezin' to death in the wilderness with a jolly fat man.

But drudgery does have its drawbacks, especially when you're layin' siege to a city and the enemy in the city is better off than you are. Fact was, we seemed to go from one crisis to another in Cambridge. Camp fever began to spread in November. December brought the end of enlistments for thousands of men. And before all that, Joseph Reed, Washington's right hand, decided to go home.

## Joseph Reed:

I will not attempt to justify leaving. I stayed until late October, when the entreaties of my family and the demands of my legal practice drew me home. I left, however, with the intention of returning and with the certainty of acting on the General's behalf in Philadelphia, a place where he needed friends.

'Tis no small irony that, in leaving, my intimacy with the General seemed only to increase, as he revealed his innermost thoughts to me in writing.

His heaviest burden was in the end of so many enlistments, as replacements bargained like horse traders when the recruiting officers came around.

"Such a dearth of public spirit and want of virtue," he wrote, "such stock-jobbing in all the low arts to obtain advantages, I never saw before and pray God I may never be witness to again. What will be the ultimate end of these maneuvers is beyond my scan. I tremble at the prospect. Could I have forseen what I have and am likely to experience, no consideration upon earth should have induced me to accept this command."

## Martha Washington:

I cannot say I was happy when the General wrote in October that I should come to Cambridge. 'Twas his way of telling me that hopes for an early resolution had been dashed, and he expected the war to last at least through the winter. So I prepared, however reluctantly, for the longest journey of my life.

My Jacky could sense my fears. Don't forget that I had never traveled outside of Virginia before. So he insisted that he and Nelly accompany me. Their presence was like a sweet balm to me, as perhaps mine was to them, in that they had suffered the death of an infant child only a month before.

And so we ventured together into the unknown land of a northern winter.

On the outskirts of Philadelphia we were met with great pomp, and I first heard myself called Lady Washington, and, for my whole time there, I was treated as if I were a great somebody.

A light snow was falling when, two weeks later, we arrived at the Cambridge headquarters. The General was standing on the veranda, a heavy cape across his shoulders and his hat piled up with snow, as if he had been waiting for days.

He remained on the upper step and greeted us in the dignified manner of a commander in chief, with a handshake for Jacky, polite bows to me and Nelly. But I could not deny that when I felt his hand touch my back, to guide me up the stairs, 'twas as if he was touching me for the first time. And when he took me to his chamber, directly above his office, we had a moment of privacy. But 'twasn't a day for us to take our leisure.

"The British are busy," he said. "My opposite, General Howe, seems to be moving troops from Bunker Hill back into Boston, and we don't know why."

Naturally, my heart leaped into my throat. "Are they planning an attack?"

"I pray not. But they may know of the disaffection in our ranks, especially amongst the Connecticut men. Their enlistments are up, and they're leaving, conscience and loyalty be damned."

To me that never seen anything of war, word of such things was terrible indeed, and my husband must have seen the fear on my face, for he took me gently by the shoulders and said, "Don't worry, Patsy. 'Tisn't the first time they've moved troops about, but I'd best be on the lines today. The men must see me."

I watched him ride off, wondering if he would be in battle within a few miles. Then I decided to unpack and do my best to keep my fears at bay.

British intelligence could not have been good, for they did not come out that day, nor the next, nor the day after that, even though our troops were soon going home by the hundreds.

You can imagine that none of us looked to a happy Yuletide.

## Billy Lee:

Snow started 'round dusk on Christmas Eve and went on all night. Next mornin', sun come up in a sky as clear blue as heaven. 'Twas the brightest Christmas Day ever. I took it as a good sign for 1776. So I went over to the camp, to see how that dirty place looked with clean snow all over, and how did the men keep Christmas.

Some of them was roastin' a goat on a spit. Another was playin' the fiddle. The happiest was the ones who'd made up their minds to sign for another year. The grouchiest was them who couldn't go home for another week. And the saddest was the militia, short-run replacements brought in for six weeks, so sad that the others called them the Long-Faces.

Now, like I said, I'd tooken some interest in the Marbleheaders, 'cause they had Negro freedmen, and freedom was a thing I liked to think hard about. And there was that boy who'd been on my mind since I'd seen him in the brawl.

I'd asked about him some. The Negro boys in the regiment always said they didn't know nothin'. But the boy must've knowed I was lookin' for him, 'cause he always managed to make himself scarce when I rode through with the General.

Now, most of the Marbleheaders had gone to sail in Colonel Glover's little privateer navy. There was just one company of 'em still in Cambridge, and they was fixin' to leave soon, too. So I paid 'em a visit Christmas mornin'.

And by damn, but there was that boy, comin' up from the necessary. All but walked into me before he saw me.

"Mornin', son," I said.

He stopped right in his tracks. His eyes went wide. He pulled his little sailor's hat down and kept on goin'.

"Son," I said, "I know who you are."

He stopped again and turned back to me. "You ain't gonna tell, is you?"

He was about twenty, stood near six feet high, had a broad forehead, straight features, skin about three shades darker than mine ('course, my pa was white, or so my mama told me), and a voice that said if I did tell, he'd come and find me and fix me good.

He didn't know I was bluffin'. I couldn't place him. I wouldn't know who to tell or what to tell, even after one of the other Negroes in the regiment told me the boy's name: Matt Jacobs.

## Martha Washington:

On Christmas night the generals gathered at headquarters, and wine punch brought cheer, despite our predicament.

Even the New Englanders, who are not known to keep Christmas, proved warm and friendly, all except Artemas Ward, whom my husband had replaced. He remained at his Roxbury headquarters, begging illness.

Connecticut's Israel Putnam, however, was an old tavernkeeper who never missed a chance for a swallow or a story.

I said, " 'Tis a pleasure to meet one of the heroes of Bunker Hill, sir."

Putnam, who had a face like a pillow and a body like a big soft feather bed, gave me a hearty laugh. "I was no hero, madam, simply a soldier who saw his duty and done it."

My husband had not prepared me for Putnam's great size, or for his lisp. But I suppose that a man who had been saved from burning at an Indian stake when a miraculous thunderstorm put out the fire— or a man who could invent such a story—had the right to lisp . . . or stutter, or sit mute, whichever he choosed.

Nathanael Greene of Rhode Island walked with a limp and did not seem a martial man, which was not surprising for a Quaker. But his Rhode Island troops had the best discipline in the Continental army, and for that reason my husband had made him a brigadier general. His wife, Kitty, a dark-haired and vivacious child of twenty-one, was there also and, as they say, eating for two.

John Sullivan of New Hampshire, son of Irish indentured servants, was dark-haired and dashingly handsome. "I'm proud to serve your husband, ma'am. He'd have made a fine Irishman, for he has a fine, healthy dislike of the British."

I said, "I think, sir, 'tis British injustice that my husband dislikes."

"When the word 'injustice' follows the word 'British,' 'tis redundancy, madam."

My, but these men were witty.

Charles Lee arrived late from his headquarters in Medford town. Though many considered him strange in the extreme, he always saw to my flattery. He took my hand and brought it to his lips, "Madam, there could be no one else in America who would bring me these four miles on a winter's night, unless your husband called."

I told Lee that my husband considered him a trusted counselor.

This brought a gentlemanly bow from Lee. "'Good counselors lack no clients'—*Measure for Measure*. But I am loyal to only one."

Charles Lee was the most experienced general in the room, and an educated man, too. Small wonder that my husband leaned so heavily upon him.

One of the servants brought a glass, which was raised by Lee: "To Lady Washington and her consorts. And to the king, God save him."

"Hear, hear," said Henry Knox.

"May God save the king," added my husband.

Then a sly smile crossed Lee's face, as if his toast was only half done. "May God save the pop-eyed Hanoverian son of a b———, because we won't."

Nathanael Greene cried, "Such language, before ladies!"

And Lee immediately bowed in apology.

You see, we still toasted the king's health and condemned the ministers, whom we blamed for our trouble.

My husband remained quietly angry at Lee's outburst for the rest of the evening. But I was not about to let him spoil our Christmas celebration.

# Hesperus Draper:

There was four bedrooms on the second floor. The ink-stained aides, all six of us, slept in the room that backed up to Washington's. The others fell asleep quick. But I couldn't. Feelin' too envious, seein' the generals' wives. Missed my own.

Missed her even more when I heard a creak in the next room, then a thump, then a creak-thump-creak-thump-creak-thump, then . . . well, you get the idea. In some things, at least, Washington moved fast.

'Twas hard enough to sleep, with the snorin' and the bed-fartin' and the strange smell of India ink. Now a soft little female giggle—'twas Martha—give me a case of hot-coal envy that could've burned a hole in my shirt.

I tried to conjure up Charlotte in my mind's eye, and maybe the thinkin' of her might lead to the feelin' of her, and . . . 'Tisn't natural for a man to be alone for so long. But when I thought of her, 'twasn't her body that came to mind but her last letter, her latest scheme to make money and help the cause, too.

She'd been pokin' in my uncle's warehouse and found a printin' press we'd imported for a feller who wanted to put out a Tory paper. But before he took possession, he changed his mind. Sold off everything he had and headed back to England. Left us holdin' the press, the type cases, and five hundred pounds of printer's ink.

Charlotte, bein' an enterprisin' and opinionated woman, decided to start printin' pamphlets and such. She wrote to me about the fine things she'd read in the *Pennsylvania Magazine*. And couldn't the Drapers publish something like it?

*Pennsylvania Magazine* was edited by an Englishman who'd come over a few years earlier. His name didn't mean much to me then—who'd ever heard of Tom Paine? I was driftin' off, wonderin' about publishin' somethin' when I heard another creak, then another thump, then another creak-thump, creak-thump, creak-thump and . . . well, the Washingtons were havin' a fine Christmas.

But no one had a fine New Year's Day, because men were goin' home by the thousands, but they were only bein' recruited by the hundreds. Lines were so threadbare, if General Howe moved his arms quick, he could've poked his elbows through just about any-place.

To show you how bad things were, Washington was even lettin' us sign free nigras. He'd stopped that business when he first come to Cambridge back in June. Hadn't wanted to upset the southerners strea-min' into camp. But now, he'd sign clowns and court jesters if he thought they could shoulder muskets.

And on a day as bleak as that New Year's, he de-cided to put on a show. He was always good at knowin' just when to put on a show.

Had his whole staff ride out in a windy day, over icy ruts and holes, all the way to Prospect Hill, the highest spot on the American left. He gathered us all around the flagpole. Let the British on Bunker Hill see us plain through their spyglasses. Then he called to the drummer for a roll, and his slave pulled a red-and-white bundle from his coat.

What the British saw runnin' up the flagpole was thirteen stripes of red and white, with a Union Jack in the canton. They thought 'twas some kind of surrender flag.

But there was no surrender about it. 'Twas the Grand Union—thirteen stripes for the thirteen United Colonies, banded together to protect their rights. The Union Jack in the canton was to show that we were still loyal to "the best of kings."

Well, I prided myself on bein' a man who didn't care about symbols. I was only in this to be quartermaster. Only in it for the money, you might say. But I felt somethin' stir in me when I saw that flag begin to flutter and dance.

But a few days later, people said we should find somethin' else to put in the canton, because we got word that the best of kings had gone to Parliament and promised to put a speedy end to our rebellion. Said he'd hire European mercenaries to grind their heels on our heads, and only grant pardons when he "received the submission of any province or colony disposed to return to its allegiance."

In short, kiss the king's ass and he wouldn't fart in your face.

There'd been some talk about independence from the beginnin', especially among the New England radicals. Now everybody was talkin' about it. At headquarters, we even stopped toastin' the king's health. This was no longer a fight against faceless royal ministers. Now 'twas personal.

And soon enough everybody was talkin' about a pamphlet that went right to the heart of the matter. 'Twas called *Common Sense*, by that Tom Paine. He had it printed in Philadelphia and sold cheap—two shillin's apiece. But he struck gold, in his ideas and in his sales.

I remember readin' it, readin' faster and faster, noddin', laughin', readin' on. He could write, and he used words that made sense to any man, common or not.

Try this, on the colonial system: "To be always running three or four thousand miles with a tale or a petition, waiting four or five months for an answer, which, when obtained, requires five or six more to explain it in, will in a few years be looked upon as folly and childishness. There was a time when it was proper, and there is a time for it to cease."

Try this, on the so-called best of kings: "Of more worth is one honest man to society, and in the sight of God, than all the crowned ruffians that ever lived."

In the next post, I sent *Common Sense* off to Charlotte with a little note. "This may be a thing to run on that printing press. And a thing to sell. Sell cheap—two shillin's—and sell plenty."

A new flag, the words of Tom Paine inspirin' new recruits, and a chance to make some money—I was beginnin' to like this idea of independence. But it would be hell to get it, and I didn't think I could last in such a fight, missin' Charlotte the way I did.

# John Adams:

I had not expected to return home at the end of 1775, but my wife's loneliness, and her grief at the recent death of her mother, had drawn me across the face of winter, thirteen days' ride, so that I could hold her hand and raise her melancholy spirits, while the presence of my little ones served to raise my own.

But of course, there was business to be done. I spent near a week at the Massachusetts Provisional Congress in Watertown, and several evenings with General Washington in Cambridge. I found him in decent spirits, like a man whose execution had been stayed but might not be permanently avoided.

"Recruiting goes slowly?" I asked.

"Yes, but Howe won't attack us. Not now. Not in winter."

"Can you attack Howe?" I asked, remembering the talk at Philadelphia of our army sitting idle, consuming resources and spending money. Congress wanted action. They had even sent Washington a resolution stating that if an attack were made on Boston, he could proceed however he thought expedient, notwithstanding that the town might be destroyed.

"I'd attack in an instant, if I had the means," he answered. "But, Mr. Adams, consider all that we stand in need of."

"The list is long," I said, "but the goal is clear: drive Howe from Boston."

He leaned across the table and fixed me with his small, hard gray eyes. 'Twas not the fierce look of an angry man, but a level gaze, far more assuring. "Congress may look upon this as the season for action, sir, but if Congress cannot furnish the means, I cannot attack. I need more powder, more men, more cannon."

"Colonel Knox is bringing the cannon, is he not?"

"He promises artillery before the month is out."

"With cannon, you *can* drive Howe from Boston. You must."

"I must?" Anger could not be discerned in facial expression or voice, but in the movement of his powerful frame. He stood, he stalked, he swooped back upon me. But I held my position, neither frightened nor chastened by his display.

He said, "Sir, you may search the vast volumes of history through, and I question whether a case similar to ours is to be found."

Having read most of the vast volumes of history through, I was in a position to agree, which placated him somewhat.

He sat again, calmed himself, and said, "We've maintained this post against the flower of the British army for six months, without powder. We've disbanded one army, and we're recruiting another within musket shot of the enemy. Since I've come here, I've scarcely emerged from one difficulty before plunging into another. But if Boston can be taken, sir, I'll take it."

I agreed again.

"In the meantime," he said, "we have other worries."

"The burning of Falmouth and Norfolk?" I asked.

He shook his head. "The enemy can attack every coastal town from here to Georgia, and I can't stop them. But our spies tell us Howe is mounting an expedition for New York. I believe we must occupy and fortify New York first."

"Yes. General Lee has been in communication with me on the matter."

"With you?" A frown crossed Washington's face, like a little williwaw passing over a fallow field. A major general should communicate with his commander in chief, not his congressional supporters.

I explained, "General Lee has many correspondents, sir."

"Since you are one of them," he said with a touch

of sarcasm, "you know that I wish to send Lee to New York, unless such a step may be looked upon in Congress as . . . as beyond my line."

And I saw the shrewdness of the man. Congress had appointed the major generals. Congress had mandated that Washington entertain councils of war with them. Congress had sought to look over his shoulder. So he would seek congressional approval for his actions. He had traveled this way before, with Dinwiddie and the Governor's Council. He knew more about the quicksand of politics than the hard reality of war.

So did I. I said, "Your commission constitutes you as commander of all forces. You may act as you think fit for the good of the service. You don't need congressional approval for every decision."

"Then Lee shall go to New York," he said. "That should please his many correspondents in Philadelphia, as his letters will reach them that much faster."

Our general was shrewd, and he already had a tender spot or two.

## Hesperus Draper:

If Joseph Reed could go home, so could I, especially since the quartermaster's job I coveted had finally been given to Thomas Mifflin, and it looked like he meant to keep it.

One January mornin' I was at my desk writin' out a resignation. Nobody else in the office. 'Twas quiet, except for Martha chatterin' to her daughter-in-law upstairs, and the daughter-in-law pukin' into a bucket. Sickly girl, or so I thought.

All of a sudden, there was a dog snufflin' around at my feet.

I kicked him away and someone said, "That's a flogging offense, sir." Only one man in that army used dogs as an honor guard: Charles Lee, big nose as red as a berry, the rest of his face a frozen gray. He went over to the fire and warmed his hands. "As cold as a witch's tit out there, Draper."

"Been so long, sir," I said, "even a witch's tit would look good to me."

Lee's bony face formed a smile, which showed a line of the teeth as yellow as watery piss.

I said, "The General and adjutant general are out, sir."

Lee warmed his bottom by the fire. "I'm not here to see them, Draper. I've heard that you have some knowledge of fortification."

"I spent some time at Fort Cumberland, sir."

"And your opinion?"

"If the world has an asshole, sir, that's where it is."

Lee cackled. "Well spoken. Gates said you were a man of wit. He also said you helped to build Fort Necessity."

"We dug entrenchments and raised a little stockade. 'Twas a joke compared to the British works in Boston."

"But," said Lee, "you have experience. And in the land of the blind, sir, a man with one eye is king."

I hated men who talked in riddles. "What are you sayin', sir?"

"I need an aide, Draper, and Gates has graciously released you. We're bound for New York, you and I. We'll take hold of the city before the British and fortify it, like the Romans building a wall around Londinium."

I just looked at him. Wasn't impressed in the least by the Roman chatter. "I was plannin' to go home and see my wife."

Lee came over to me and put his hands on my desk. "''Tis ever common that men are merriest when they are away from home' *Henry the Fifth*."

"I miss my wife."

"But, Captain—I call you captain, as I've requested the commission and the General has forwarded it to Mr. Adams. . . . Of course, if you don't wish to accept—"

Now he had my attention. I asked, "Who's your quartermaster?"

"Why, I don't have one." Lee smiled. "But if Congress should provide for one, I'll say Captain Draper is my choice. Then shall it be up to them."

That 'twas better than waitin' around for Mifflin to drop in his traces. And New York was halfway home. So I took the job. Two days later I rode out with one of the most slovenly, bad-tempered, brilliant damn fools in the Revolution, and I left the comin' Battle of Boston behind.

# Joseph Reed:

In the depths of January, Washington wrote me his bleakest letter. Benedict Arnold had assaulted Quebec and come to grief. Recruiting continued badly. There was still not enough powder. The nights were long and cold.

"The reflection on our situation," he wrote, "produces many an unhappy hour when all around me are wrapped in sleep. Few know the predicament we are in. I have often thought how much happier I should have been if, instead of accepting this command, I had taken my musket on my shoulder and entered the ranks or, if I could have justified it to posterity and my conscience, retired to the back-country and lived in a wigwam."

There were times when he could sound quite sorry for himself. But even in his despair, he was planning to strike. His effectives were down to a mere 5,582 men, but he was levying more short-term militia and hoping to have enough men to attack before the British were finally reinforced, as seemed inevitable.

"When the attack can be attempted," he wrote, "I will not undertake to say; but no opportunity can present itself earlier than my wishes."

There was resolve in his words, but desperation, too.

I wrote back: "Your sleep may not be sound, sir, but an attack at the wrong moment, with too few troops, all too green, must leave our cause in a sleep from which it would never awaken."

## Martha Washington:

These were parlous times, but I found that every person seemed to be cheerful and happy at headquarters, even on days when we had numbers of cannon shells fired at us from Boston. These never seemed to surprise anyone but me. I confess I shuddered every time I heard the sound of a gun.

On some days Jacky rode out with the General, and I worried a bit more.

One afternoon they returned, and Jacky bounded up the stairs ahead of his stepfather, his cheeks red from the cold, his eyes wide with excitement, like the little boy he once had been. "We saw a British cannonade, Mother."

Nelly Custis came into the upstairs hallway. "Were you in danger?"

"None," said his stepfather, coming up after him. "We were never in range."

"Still, 'twas more excitin' than a foxhunt," said Jacky. "Papa must be a sorcerer, to make it seem that our paltry troops occupy twice the space they should. Perhaps 'tis done all with mirrors."

" 'Tisn't done with cheap tricks," said the General, "or cheap jokes."

Jacky took this as a challenge. He said, "I told you, Papa, I'll shoulder a musket."

This caused Nelly to break into tears and hurry off.

The General said, "See to your wife, Jack."

"I can do it," said Jacky most truculently. "I can soldier."

"Jacky dear," I said. "Go to Nelly. She's been sick all mornin'."

I waited until Jacky left the hallway; then I said to my husband, "He's not meant to be a soldier, George. Don't let him think on it."

"I've not asked him. His heart wouldn't be in it."

"And my heart is dead against it, for many reasons."

I sought to enumerate those reasons that night when we sat by the fire in our private chamber, as was our habit before retiring.

He was reading, but he spoke first: "Patsy, this pamphlet, this *Common Sense*, 'tis something you should read."

I said, "George—"

"Listen to his peroration: 'O ye that love mankind, ye that dare oppose not only tyranny but the tyrant, stand forth! Every spot in the Old World is overrun with oppression. Freedom hath been hunted round the globe. . . . O! Receive the fugitive and prepare in time an asylum for mankind.' He's talking about America."

"Yes, George. That's very good." My mind was not on politics or Thomas Paine, but I could not distract my husband from either.

"By God, Patsy, a few more flaming arguments like Falmouth and Norfolk, joined to the sound reasoning in this *Common Sense,* and no one will question the propriety of separation."

"Separation?" I said. "Independency?"

"Yes. I've been convinced since we heard of the king's speech."

How cold that upper chamber suddenly felt. I knew that my husband had been turning slowly toward independency. Now he spoke it plain. And yet there he sat, placidly reading by the fire, as if, in speaking the word, he made it his own.

"Now," he said innocently, "what is it you wanted to tell me?"

I had almost forgotten. "George, you should not let Jacky come so close to the British cannonade. You see, he's to be a father, and—"

"Nelly's with child?"

"She has the morning sickness, the languor, the . . . other things."

His face, at that moment, became like a mirror

reflecting the glow of the fire. 'Twas as if I had given him this joyous news about ourselves. He threw his arms around me, and his warmth lessened all my fears.

Then he looked me in the eye. "We should send her home."

"In winter?"

"Winter will grow very warm if I see my plan through."

*C.D.—In late January the man my uncle called an apple-polisher achieved the impossible. Henry Knox crossed the frozen New England wilderness from Ticonderoga, bringing with him "a most noble train of artillery"—sixty pieces, some no more than a foot long, others great siege guns to batter the British defenses. "We dragged those cannon over mountains from which we could almost have seen all the kingdoms of the earth," he proclaimed, and he was hardly exaggerating. Now Washington might put his plan into action.*

## Billy Lee:

I can't say that in all the years I served him, I ever saw the General do anything quite so strange as what he done one mornin' in the middle of February.

He rose at sunrise, like always, come down to his office, where I'd set out soap, a bowl of warm water, a towel, and a new-stropped razor, like always. I asked him did he want his hair powdered. But that day, he was in too much of a hurry. He just shaved quick and asked the temperature.

'Twas one of my jobs to check the mercury glass each mornin.' "Three degrees, sir. 'Bout as cold as I ever seen it. Colder even than yesterday."

And do you know what he said? He said, "Good."

I said, "Master, we's southerners. What so good about cold? I damn near froze just goin' to the necessary."

He didn't explain. He didn't have to. Just told me to get his horse.

'Twas a bright, sunny day along the river, but so cold 'twasn't long before I couldn't feel my toes or the tips of my ears. And that northwest wind, it made you think you was about to snap in half. We rode a few miles, till we come to Lechmere's farm, a big spread right across the river from Boston. Water was frozen all the way across, as hard and shiny as silver.

The General got down and walked out on the ice. I was a little worried, 'cause the British could see him, and if they wanted, they could have fired at him.

But he just went about his business—a big man in a black cape, takin' little baby steps so he wouldn't slip. After he'd gone some distance, he stopped and jumped up and down. Some picture, ain't it? A general playin' like a little boy on the ice. Then he come hurryin' back up the bank.

# Martha Washington:

"Patsy," my husband announced, "the time has arrived."

"Time for what?"

"Action. I've called an officers' council."

He snapped off his gloves, threw his hat and cape at Billy Lee, and began to stalk about his office. "Our manpower crisis is near an end. We have over eight thousand United Colonies troops, seven thousand militia here or on the way. We have artillery, too. As for the British, they number near five thousand but must be reinforced before long."

"You're planning to attack, then?"

"The Back Bay is frozen. The time is ripe for an assault across the ice. A stroke, well aimed at this juncture, might put an end to the war."

I was excited and terrified and could not contain my concerns. I must admit that, back in my room, I went straight to the fireplace, which shared a common flue with my husband's office below. Though the day was bitterly cold, I let the fire die down, then I listened as the officers' council began.

I heard my husband make his presentation. Then there was a moment of silence. Then I heard the London accent of Horatio Gates; he said that even experienced troops would be hard-pressed to dislodge the British and their artillery from the entrenchments around Boston, never mind untested militia.

There was a rumble of agreement.

Gates and Artemas Ward suggested fortification of Dorchester Heights, instead, using guns that Knox had brought from Ticonderoga.

Israel Putnam, another veteran of Bunker Hill, agreed: "I said it in June, before we went on Bunker Hill, and I'll say it again: A Yankee soldier is more afraid of his legs than of his head. Just give him somethin' to stand behind and he'll fight all day."

There was another rumble of agreement.

My husband was not a man accustomed to opposition, so I am sure that his anger was boiling inside him, but all I heard in his voice was calm control: "Very well, gentlemen. The question being put, your opinions expressed, a vote should be taken. An assault across the ice, or the fortification of Dorchester Heights?"

And the officers voted for Dorchester Heights. But they supported my husband's suggestion that if such an action drew the British into a frontal assault, as at Bunker Hill, we would launch a secondary attack from Cambridge, across the ice, or by boat across the Back Bay to Boston.

A short time later, I went to tend Jacky and Nelly, as both were ill. The fire in their room had died down and there was no slave nearby to tend it. So I went to throw on a log, and as I did, I heard voices rising through the flue from the room below, which was the office of Horatio Gates. He was speaking to an anonymous listener: "An attack across the ice . . . an amateur plan from an amateur general. We have saved him from himself."

I did not tell my husband, though I never again trusted Horatio Gates.

# Billy Lee:

'Twas a tense time 'round the house. And not only 'cause of the battle we all thought was comin'.

Upstairs, Nelly Custis was throwin' up every morning, bein' with child and all. And Master Jacky was down sick with the fever, so they couldn't leave for a safer place. Naturally, this made the mistress a little jumpy.

And there was a seamstress in the house now, by the name of Margaret Thomas, and she made me a little jumpy. She were just about the finest-lookin' mulatto woman I'd ever seen. She sewed things for the family, mended things for the staff, even made one of those Grand Union flags.

I've heard wise men say that opposites attract, and I s'pose that's what we was. We was both mulattoes, but she was free, so she thought of herself as half white; I was a slave, so I thought of myself as half black. But the more time we spent together, the more we thought we was made for each other.

Early one mornin', 'fore sunup, I met her in the barn. 'Twas the only place where we could get any quiet, what with the other slaves and servants and all. And just as we's about to git down to business, down in the hay in one of the empty stalls, I heard this "Mmmghhmm."

Margaret popped up and said, "What's that?"

I said, "I don't know. One of the horses or somethin'."

Then I heard that familiar high voice say, "I'm no horse."

I looked up, and there was the General, standin' in

the next stall. He was lookin' away, very polite, but talkin' to us. "I called for you, Billy."

I popped up, pullin' up my breeches at the same time. "Sorry, sir."

"What are you doing when you should be making my breakfast?"

I couldn't think of a thing to say. "I'm . . . I'm . . ."

But Margaret was whip-smart and smart-girl sassy. She said, "He's spendin' time with his wife."

The General looked down at her and said, "Wife?"

And I looked down at her and moved my lips to whisper, "Wife?"

"Yes, sir. Wife. And you know somethin'?" Now she jumped up, madder than hell. "You should give a man and his wife their privatcy."

The General shifted his eyes to me. "When did you marry?"

She said, "Last night."

The General looked around and saw a broom leanin' against the door.

"So," said Margaret, "we'd like some privatcy, George Washington."

"You'll address me as *General* Washington. As for your *privacy*, 'tis less important than my need to see what General Howe is up to. I'll expect my horse in five minutes."

Well, sir, as soon as he went out, we put that broom on the ground and stepped over it. She said that by and by we could find a minister. I don't think the General liked Margaret too much before. After that, he didn't like her at all.

## Abigail Adams:

The lengthening days of early March had done little to warm the bitter nights, or my bed, which was as cold and lonely as a country road.

On the night of March 2, I sat in the kitchen of our farmhouse and wrote to my husband, in faraway Philadelphia. The children were asleep. The candle was guttering. My shawl was drawn tight around my shoulders, for the supply of seasoned firewood was running low.

"I have been kept in a continual state of anxiety ever since you left," I wrote. "The battle is soon to begin. It has been said, 'tomorrow' and 'tomorrow' for this whole month, but when the dreadful tomorrow will be, I know not."

And 'twas as if Mars chose that moment to enlighten me. I heard a distant thump, and the very air felt as if it had been struck with a hammer. 'Twas the sound of a cannon shot, echoing to my lonely little Braintree farm.

I went to the door and listened. I felt the air shudder again and perceived faint flashes in the night sky. I knew there would be no sleep for me that night. And if I could not sleep, who had no guilt upon my soul with regard to this cause, how could the miserable wretches who had been the procurers of this dreadful scene lie down with their load of guilt? How could those who were actors?

C.D.—*On the night of March 2 the Americans fired a salvo from the battery on Lechmere Point, beginning the battle for Boston. For three nights they kept it up, as though they had all the powder in the world. Bombs burst in the air, cannon thundered, and with every flash the church steeples of the city appeared, as one witness told my uncle, "like holy spirits praying in the night." It is said that the shaking of the earth dried up Boston wells and sent Boston dogs into distemper.*

*This barrage from the north was done to mask the actions of the army to the south, where two thousand men and three hundred teams of oxen ascended Dorchester Heights in the moonlight of March 5. First they dragged great wooden chandelier frames, then fascines, gabions, and bundles of twisted hay to put into the frames for fortification. Then they dragged cannon and barrels full of rocks to roll down on the British.*

*At dawn, General Howe looked up at the Heights and cried, "Good God! They have done more work in a single night than my army would do in a month!"*

## Billy Lee:

I was with the General that mornin' on Dorchester Heights. The ground fog had burned off. The Grand Union flag was snappin' in the breeze. And the rooftops of Boston was covered in folks who'd come out to see another fight like Bunker Hill.

" 'Tis a fine day, sir," said a young lieutenant.

"A fine day after a fine night," answered the General, in a big voice, so all the men around him could hear. "I've never seen spirits higher. It looks to me like you're all impatient for a fight."

That brought a cheer from the boys, but a British shot cut the cheerin' off at the knees. We all watched the puff of smoke, then the ball hit halfway up the hill and went bouncin' along the frozen ground.

Somebody shouted, "They'll never shoot us off this hill!"

"No!" shouted the General. "They'll have to assault us. But we'll be ready for them!"

He'd made an order that if any man run in the comin' fight, he'd be shot on the spot. But from the cheerin' I heard, not a man on that hill had any thoughts of runnin'. 'Twas a stirrin' sound, that cheerin'.

Stirred me so much I rode over to the General and said, "'Scuse me, sir. But when the British come, I'd like to shoulder a musket."

He didn't even give it a thought. He just said, "Billy, you stay by me. There'll be plenty for you to do."

I wanted to tell him there was black men shoulderin' muskets all along the lines, men he'd enlisted when it looked like he wouldn't have enough white men to hold with, men fightin' for freedom.

But I didn't. I just looked away, so he wouldn't see how I felt. I looked away, looked up at the flag. And that's when I saw that the wind had backed some. 'Twas comin' out of the south-southeast. In that country, the sight of the wind backin' toward the east was a bad omen.

Well, all mornin' the British set up a ruckus, but they couldn't hit us, even when they dug in their cannon wheels to raise the angle of their barrels. By eleven-thirty, they'd quit firin'. Noon tide was comin'. Time for the British assault.

The General rode along the works, shoutin' "Remember the date! March the fifth. Anniversary of the

Boston Massacre. Remember, men, and return the favor."

And the men were ready. The guns were ready. Soon as the British attacked us, pennants would go up on Dorchester Heights. Lookouts at the Roxbury Meeting House would see the pennants and raise theirs, which would be seen at Prospect Hill on the Cambridge side. Then our men in Cambridge would take to their boats and attack Boston. Then there'd be hell to pay for the British, and maybe for us.

But the tide rose and then fell, and the British didn't come. 'Twasn't till late afternoon that they loaded up their flatboats and moved their men down the harbor to a fort that would make a good jumpin'-off point. But were they plannin' a night attack? With the way the clouds were comin' in and the wind was blowin' up?

## Abigail Adams:

That night we were visited by a storm the like of which I had never seen before or since. Torrential rain, sheets of rain, rain so heavy it was denser than fog, all driven by a wind so fierce that it forced water right through the clapboards of our house and caused it to shake as violently as the trees outside. When one of the windows blew in, several frightened children snuggled into my bed beside me.

Had we lived in ancient times, I would have said that the gods were sending us a message. Of what, I was not certain.

## Martha Washington:

My husband slept in our bed that night, so convinced was he that the weather would not permit of a British assault on Dorchester Heights. But 'twas a fitful sleep, comprised more of tossings and turnings than of deep breathing, more of eyes wide open than of peaceful dreams. In the middle of the night, a shutter broke loose and began to slam against the house. After that, we slept not at all.

I thought of our men, hunkered down behind fortifications, drenched by the copious rain. Never could they have been more miserable. Compared to the roar of that storm, the cannonade of the previous night was like a song played upon a lute.

Toward dawn the rain slackened, but the wind kept up, and in this, the resolve of the wind surpasseth that of the British.

While preparing to ride the four miles back to Dorchester, my husband received a dispatch from General Ward. As he read, his face fell. At first I thought the British had forced our works. But no. They were returning to Boston. There was to be no assault.

My husband, who was not one to curse, said, "Damn," and tossed Ward's letter on the table.

C.D.—*There would be no Battle of Boston. For a few days the enemy remained in the city. Then Howe made an offer: if he was allowed to leave in his ships unmolested, he would not destroy the city. It was not learned until later that he had already been ordered to quit Boston. He had seen the entrenchments on*

*Dorchester Heights as a challenge to British honor, but the storm had given him time to reconsider, and he had decided that British honor might better be served in some way other than discarding the lives of thousands of men.*

*While Howe might have broken the back of his army on Dorchester Heights, Washington would surely have ruined his by sending green troops in an assault across the Back Bay, for Howe held thirty-eight hundred regulars to defend Boston. Howe was a professional. Washington was not. Washington should have been satisfied with a bloodless victory, but he was not.*

## Martha Washington:

Even news that American mothers had begun naming their newborn sons George, in honor of the successful siege of Boston, did not amuse my husband. He told me, "We could have ended the war right here but for that storm. Providence must have sent it for some wise purpose, though for the life of me, I can't see what it was."

We were alone in the room where we had spent so much of our private time during the siege. The British had sailed off to Canada, and my husband was convinced that when they appeared again, 'twould be in New York.

He looked out the window at a line of troops beginning the long walk south. "Howe will be reinforced. More regulars, mercenaries . . ."

I told him he would succeed again, as he had in Boston.

He smiled. "We beat them in a most shameful manner, didn't we?"

"Yes."

"Beat them out of the place that might be the strongest to defend on the whole continent."

"Yes."

"Fortified in the best manner, at enormous expense."

I said yes again, emphatically. When a man's spirit falters, 'tis the role of a good wife to restore him. "So go to New York. I shall follow once Nelly and Jacky are safely on the road to Virginia."

"Yes," he said. "Nelly must have a good birth. At home."


## Billy Lee:

On our last day in Cambridge I figured somethin' out.

The General was doin' some last-minute business, when in runs Matt Jacobs, that colored boy from the Marblehead Regiment. He come with a dispatch from Colonel Glover 'bout a ship they'd captured.

Well, I took one look at the wide eyes on him, and I remembered. And when I remembered, I all but fell over.

I'd seen them eyes dozens of times on a little boy runnin' into the Belvoir kitchen, callin' for his mama 'cause he'd catched a nice fish. His real name was Matchuko, son of Jacob of Mount Vernon. Why didn't I see it sooner?

But before I could say a word, he was runnin' out

again, like a field hand stealin' food from the master's table.

Well, sir, I tol' my Margaret all about it that afternoon.

And she said, "You're not plannin' to tell the General, are you?"

"I don't rightly know. The boy's a runaway. Master owns him now, and—"

"If you want me to stay your wife, you'll say nothin'. I been a slave and I been free, and I'll tell you right now, there ain't nothin' better than bein' free. That boy's fightin' for freedom. You let him do it."

'Twas hard for me to keep somethin' from the General. He'd always treated me like more than a common hoe nigger. But like I've been tellin' you, I was thinkin' hard about things in them days, and I thought that my Margaret was right.

I decided to keep my mouth shut and pack for New York.

## Hesperus Draper:

From Boston to New York. From the fryin' pan to the fire.

New York was the key to the continent—the deepest harbor, the best location, and that Hudson River, like a runnin'-water moat between New England and the rest of the colonies. Whoever controlled New York controlled the Hudson. Whoever controlled the Hudson controlled America.

So how did we defend a piece of land thirteen miles long, two miles wide, and surrounded by water, against an enemy with the greatest navy in the world?

When Charles Lee arrived in February, he saw the problem from his usual angle—canine. He said, "Trying to defend New York makes me feel like a dog in a dancing school. I know not which way to turn."

But he said he'd make the city itself a battlefield "so advantageous that, if our people behave with even common spirit, it'll cost the enemy thousands of men." He'd dig earthworks to defend the roads, plant batteries to enfilade the intersections, and emplace big guns in Brooklyn to cover the harbor and the East River. Bragged that he'd make New York "a square mile of hell for any invader."

I said, "With all due respect, sir, I think we should burn the place and run."

"Draper, you may be right." Then he gave me one of his cacklin' laughs. The man did have a strange sense of humor.

And his biggest joke came a few weeks later: he was ordered south to defend Charleston, so he named me as engineer in charge of entrenchin', and he put a Jerseyite windbag who called himself Lord Stirling in charge of the troops.

Stirling's real name was William Alexander, but he claimed royal blood, as if we'd be impressed. He was built like a barrel and had a face the color of medium rare beef, at least in the morning. But the more he drank, the rarer he looked. By suppertime he usually looked damn near raw. But he was a good soldier, so everyone went along with the "Lord" business.

I got my men about the business of diggin'. Dug all across the top of the town. Dug at the end of every street. Dug sixteen little forts. Then we dug on Brooklyn Heights. Felt more like moles than soldiers. And I knew I wasn't doin' the best job. Wasn't surprised, later on, that a British engineer called our works "more designed for amusement than use."

And I'll tell you, no one was happier to see our army than me. They arrived in mid-April, and all the New York Tories went quiet at the sight of ten thousand Americans marchin' down the Broad Way. I don't know what surprised them more—how many there were or how scrofulous they looked.

Most everyone in New England wanted to throw the British out from the beginning. But in New York, as many folks called themselves Tories as patriots. And why not? Business was good. Folks were fat. Even with all the taxes, Americans ate better and lived better than folks in Europe. Why fight the Crown?

Hell . . . all while we'd been diggin', the royal governor'd been sittin' on a British ship in the lower harbor, waitin' for his chance to come back. And the Tories in the town, they'd watched us the way cats watch canaries build nests. And every day, on the Bowlin' Green, I'd had to look up at a big lead statue of King George, all gilded like a god, ridin' a fiery steed to nowhere.

One thing you shouldn't forget about the Revolution: so long as there was money to be made, there were Americans ready to do business . . . with anybody. I don't guess more than a third of the country supported us, a third wanted to see us drawn and quartered, and a third had their asses planted right on the fence rail, with a cheek on each side, waitin' to see which way they should fall.

C.D.—*That spring, as my uncle might say, things went from worse to worser. Bad news came from Canada, where difficulty was piled upon calamity and compounded by disaster. General Howe was in Halifax awaiting reinforcements with which to destroy Washington—thirty thousand regulars and Hessian mercenaries.*

*Some of Washington's best troops, the ruffian riflemen from Virginia and Pennsylvania, were leaving when their enlistments expired on July 1. So Washington went to Congress in June to seek help. But in Congress, nibbling and quibbling were the order of the day, despite the efforts of Massachusetts and Virginia to drag everyone else toward independence.*

*Small wonder that Congress turned a deaf ear to Washington's requests for an enlargement of the Continental army, for money to pay enlistment bounties, and for an extension of enlistments for the duration of the war. And if Congress was not ready to face these commitments, they were certainly not ready to confront independence.*

## Joseph Reed:

During his visit to Philadelphia, I dined with Washington, and our talk went straight to the important issue before us.

"Independency. As soon as possible." Washington put it that starkly. "No man who hopes this dispute can be settled by a board of commissioners will run the same risks as one who believes we must conquer or submit to unconditional terms."

"Unconditional terms . . . such as the confiscations, trials, and hangings that will come if we lose?"

"The threat of such things concentrates the mind." He pushed a plate of stew away. He had been chewing all night on one side, as if a tooth was bothering him. Now he turned entirely to the mug of ale before him. "I'm expecting a very bloody summer, Reed, but I'm sorry to say we're not ready for it, either in men or in arms."

"And concentration may help?"

"Concentration, and the help of the best men." He looked into my eyes. "When will you be back with me, Joseph?"

I temporized. I had my reasons, my this and that, my here and there.

He said, "Joseph, you have diplomatic skills. You have the ability to phrase things to the Tories we would draw to our side. You can help me to cement a union among the colonies. Union is the only way we can survive. After a year, I see it plain."

Still I resisted. I told him there was much in Philadelphia to keep me—my work, politics, my wife and family.

And then he said, "Would you rejoin me if you were more than a secretary? If you were to fill the position left by General Gates, now that he has been appointed to command in Canada?"

"You mean adjutant general?" I was shocked. "But, sir, I have no experience as an adjutant general."

"A year ago I had none as a general. Now I am the hero of Boston. I need you, Reed. Your country needs you. I intend to recommend you."

\* \* \*

"We need you, Joseph." My wife was in no way pleased when she heard the news. "Your family needs you."

But I convinced her that this was a great revolution in my prospect. Washington was raising me higher than I could have hoped, higher than I had any right to expect. Besides, an adjutant general's pay, seven hundred pounds a year, could support us until this calamity was at an end.

So the next day I accepted a job for which I did not think myself qualified, just as my friend had done the year before. And Washington *was* my friend. Who but a friend would put such trust in another man? What lay ahead, however, would sorely test our friendship.

## Hesperus Draper:

I'll never forget a certain June mornin'.

Felt bad, mostly because of the night before. I'd had too much to drink. Then went to the Holy Ground. 'Twas a cemetery, and at night there were so many painted strumpets there they scared all the ghosts away and . . . Well, I missed my Charlotte, you understand, and . . .

Hadn't seen her in a year. I'd written to her to come join me. She wrote back about the printin' business. We'd sold twenty-five thousand copies of *Common Sense*. And she was puttin' out a newspaper in Alexandria, so she wanted me to write her long letters filled with things to print. Instead of herself, she sent me a locket with a miniature of her smilin' face.

Well, that's why there were strumpets at the Holy

Ground, and why cathouses like Katie Crow's did such a fine business. But in the mornin' I felt bad, bad in my head from all I'd drunk, bad in my heart for doin' what I'd done. Had a poundin' in my head and a burnin' in my breeches. So I was upstairs in an outhouse, hopin' to piss away the burn and be done with my mornin' strainin' at the same time.

And while waitin' for my discharge, I peered out at the harbor and saw somethin' that would've made me shit, even if I wasn't sittin' where I was. 'Twas like a giant movin' forest of sails and spars comin' through the Narrows.

By midmornin' there was fifty ships in the lower harbor. By afternoon, there was a hundred or more, all anchored near Staten Island, unloadin' thousands of troops the way a fat female frog unloads thousands of eggs.

I went down to the Grand Battery—the brick parapet wall that ran around the whole tip of New York Island like a sheep-gut condom on the tip of a proud prick. Went down to get a better look at the ships. And when I did, I just wondered what in hell we had got ourselves into.

I almost asked Washington, because he was standin' there with Henry Knox. And he was wearin' his face from the Braddock Massacre, the face that tries to show nothin', and in the tryin' shows all.

Captains are supposed to speak only when spoken to. But I said, "A damn lot of ships out there, General."

"A damn lot." Washington put his glass to his eye and studied the harbor. "We count on your works, Captain. And on Colonel Knox's cannon. And on Congress to reinforce us before Howe attacks."

Knox let out a blusterin' laugh. Made him puff up

like a pig bladder. "You can count on the cannon, sir. If Howe comes up like a man and brings his ships before our batteries, there'll be the finest fight that ever was seen. We'll bring a hundred cannon to bear on him at once."

A pig bladder, I thought, or a windbag.

Knox give me a glance. "I'm sure we can count on your works, too."

"That leaves Congress," I said. "Them I'm not so sure about."

"Be that as it may"—Washington closed his glass; he'd seen enough—"we'll give Howe a proper reception when he comes."

"And trust in Providence," added Henry Knox.

I thought Providence had already sent a message. 'Twas written plain in them ships: burn the city and run like hell.

## Martha Washington:

Our farewell was hurried, though heartfelt.

"All of the wives are leaving," he said. "You must go. Back to Mount Vernon. Back to help Nelly with her baby. This second child must survive."

I hesitated, and so he took me to the window of our headquarters house on Richmond Hill. He gave me his glass and said, "Look toward the Narrows, Patsy. Count the ships."

Being the dutiful wife, I put the glass to my eye. I tried to peer through the smoke and dust that seemed always to hang above New York. Then I began to count aloud: "One, two . . ."

He snatched the glass away. " 'Tis fruitless, Patsy." Then he drew me over to his desk, to the mountain of papers, and told me to look at it all—requests and requisitions, entreaties to him, entreaties to Congress, letters from Gates in Canada, inquiries from our infant navy as to the disposition of prizes . . . a thousand niggling details to drive a man crazy, were he *not* facing the might of Great Britain.

He said, "Please don't add your safety to my worries, Patsy."

I said I wished I could go through all the papers for him.

He laughed at that and said, "I'd gladly give them to you."

Then I told Billy Lee to start packing my trunk.

We were becoming skilled farewellers. But the next day, as I looked from the Paulus Hook ferry toward the mighty fleet now gathered to destroy him, I wondered if we had bidden our last farewell.

## Joseph Reed:

For days we waited, but the enemy seemed in no way disposed to attack. The tension grew as unbearable as the sulfurous summer heat. Fevers and dysentery wafted through the streets and settled upon our troops like the humidity. Boredom battled nerves, and both fought fear.

Then a document arrived from Congress that I likened to a cool breeze—the Declaration of Independence. We'd been hearing rumors for days. Now we held hard evidence in our hands. The die had been cast. The General smiled for the first time since the British fleet had arrived.

He ordered that all the troops be gathered at six o'clock that sultry evening, so that the declaration could be read to them, along with a few words from himself: "The General hopes this important event will serve as a fresh incentive to every officer and soldier to act with fidelity and courage, as he is now in the service of a state possessed of sufficient power to reward his merit and advance him the highest honors of a free country."

I wrote out Washington's remarks, refined them a bit, as was my wont and his desire, and said, "So now it's nooses or glory, sir?"

"Nooses or glory, Reed, victory or death. The only course."

Later there was a riot in the town, a joyous riot in which the statue of King George was pulled over and beheaded. Better than its destruction was the use they put it to. They melted the king down into 40,000 musket balls, enough to kill every British soldier coming to fight us, and some of them twice over.

## Abigail Adams:

The grand news of independency arrived in early July.

My husband wrote: "I am well aware of the toil and blood and treasure it will cost us to maintain this declaration. Yet through all the gloom I see the rays of ravishing light and glory. This is our day of deliverance."

Then he turned his mind to more practical things—the army that would have to effect our deliverance, the army that had taken Boston by entrenchment and was endeavoring to protect New York in the same way: "The practice we have hitherto been in, of ditching round about our enemies, will not always do. We must learn to use other weapons than the pick and spade. Our armies must be disciplined and learn to fight."

## Hesperus Draper:

Two days after we pulled down King George, I was workin' at the Grand Battery. Fat-Ass Henry had set his biggest guns there—thirty-two-pounders and twenty-fours—some under the direction of a New York artillery captain even younger than he was, a nineteen-year-old with the crispest blue uniform and the cutest little leather cocked hat you ever did see—Alexander Hamilton.

I was inspectin' the places where we needed to repair some brickwork when a signal shot come echoin' on the wind from Governors Island.

Two British frigates—the *Phoenix*, carryin' forty-four guns, and the *Rose*, a twenty-eight—were ridin' the incomin' tide, and for just a minute I thought how pretty they looked, with their sails all stretched in the bright summer sun.

In front of Fat-Ass Henry's house the drummers were beatin' the call to arms, which was bringin' out more townsfolk than fightin' men. And most of the soldiers who did show their faces looked like they could use a few more hours abed.

"Too damn much drinkin' and whorin' in this army," said the sponger at Gun Number One, near where I was standin'.

"Be quiet and prepare to fire!" cried Hamilton. Then he gave orders to all the guns. "Make ready! And fire!"

White smoke and thunder jetted out from the battery. The water around the ships splashed with skippin' cannonballs. And the noise of those guns echoed from Brooklyn Heights to the Jersey Palisades.

But the ships were movin' fast, and not a single shot hit either of them. New York, on the other hand, was a lot bigger, and 'twasn't movin'.

So the *Phoenix* let go with a broadside. Then the *Rose*. Cannonballs came screamin' and skitterin' and twackin' against the walls of the Grand Battery, sendin' up big gouts of brick and mortar and sendin' half the gunners scramblin' for their lives.

Above us, on the parapet of Fort George, Fat-Ass Henry was bellowin' at his crew to hurry, hurry and load, hurry and fire, hurry and sponge, too. He must've been thinkin' about his promise to the General, that this was goin' to be the finest fight that ever was seen. Some fight.

Those British ships weren't even interested. They were out to prove somethin', so they swung to the west, like a pair of quick Chesapeake skipjacks, and scooted up the Hudson, firin' broadsides for target practice and thumbin' their noses at every little gun emplacement we'd built all the way up to the Harlem River. So much for controllin' the Hudson. So much for holdin' New York.

## Joseph Reed:

The following day, we were informed that General Howe wished a letter to be delivered to Washington. So Colonel Knox and I were rowed out to meet the barge bearing the missive, under strict orders not to receive it unless it were properly addressed.

It was a fine, sunny afternoon, with a southwesterly breeze setting up a decent chop on the harbor. At our approach, the British officer, dressed in the dark blue of the Royal Navy, stood and bowed with great ceremony. We were obliged, out of politeness, to do the same, however difficult in our rocking cutter.

The British officer then informed us of a letter for *Mr.* Washington.

"Sir," I said, "we have no person in our army with that address."

"But, sir," answered the officer, "will you look at the address?" He then withdrew the letter from his pocket and held it for the both of us to inspect: "To George Washington, Esq., Etc., Etc., New York."

I put on my most lawyerly air and said, "I cannot receive that letter, sir."

"I'm sorry, sir," said the officer, "and so will General Howe be, that any error should prevent its being received by General Washington."

I told him, "I must obey orders."

"May I ask by what title Mr. Washington wishes to be addressed?"

"You are sensible, sir, of the rank of General Washington in our army?"

"Yes, sir, we are. And I'm sure that General Howe and his brother, my Lord Howe, will lament exceedingly of this affair, as the letter is quite of a civil nature. They also lament that they were not here a little sooner."

We bowed and parted on the most genteel terms imaginable.

As the British officer was rowed away, I said to Knox, "A little sooner, I suppose, to have stopped our Declaration of Independence."

A few days later the British requested that "His Excellency General Washington" meet with their adjutant general to discuss the letter. When their request was put in such terms, Washington could not but accommodate them.

The meeting was set for the next day, at the house occupied by Henry Knox in lower Broad Way. The General arrived wearing his best uniform. His hair was freshly powdered. His manner was as calmly composed as if he were instructing his slaves on the planting of a line of trees. He stationed his guard in front of the house, in two ranks, so that they might greet our guest with a crisp "present-arms."

British Colonel James Paterson seemed a gentleman in all things, his manners polished, his red uniform impeccable. He presented himself to the General with a bow and an apology almost too exorbitant: "General Howe in no way wishes to derogate from the respect and rank of yourself, sir, but conceives the address on the letter to be consistent with what has always been used by ambassadors wherever difficulties of rank have arisen. You see, Excellency, 'Et cetera, et cetera' implies everything."

"And nothing," answered Washington, very coolly.

Colonel Paterson then produced the same letter that had been offered to us in the middle of New York Harbor.

The General spied the inscription, the "Etc., Etc." and firmly declined it, saying, "A letter directed to a person acting in a public character should have some inscription, sir. Otherwise, it must appear to be merely private business."

Paterson looked at the letter and, with an expression of disappointment, put it back into his pocket, saying he would try to touch upon the most important points found therein.

"Touch delicately," said Washington, "and I will listen."

I glanced at Colonel Knox, who was attempting to restrain a smile at Washington's performance. I almost smiled myself.

Paterson said, "The Howes have been specially nominated peace commissioners by the king. They would take great pleasure, Excellency, in effecting an accommodation."

"From what I've heard," the General responded, "they are empowered only to grant pardons. Those who have committed no fault need no pardons."

Paterson feigned some confusion at this.

So Washington clarified his position. "We are only defending what we deem our indisputable rights, sir."

Paterson managed a weak laugh. "That, Excellency, is a matter which would open a very wide field."

"Very wide indeed," said Washington.

So wide, in truth, that the meeting had no further to go, and Paterson excused himself, declining our polite invitation to a cold collation, or even to a glass of wine, saying that the Howes would wish to hear his report immediately.

After Washington had put him in his place with all the skill of a joiner fitting a piece of wood, Paterson stopped in the doorway and asked, "Has Your Excellency no particular commands with which you would please to honor me to Lord and General Howe?"

Washington replied, with a slight inclination of the head, "Nothing, sir, but my particular compliments to both."

Washington understood the importance of ceremony as well as any man. The Howe brothers had to be made to know that they were negotiating with the representative of a sovereign government, and he would be respected, even if he could not stop their frigates from peppering his city with cannonballs.

He had played his role in this scene most ably, in his wardrobe and his appearance, and in the polite implacability of his demeanor.

Afterward Henry Knox said to me, "Paterson appeared awestruck, as if he were before something supernatural. Indeed, I don't wonder at it. He was before a very great man indeed."

I think Knox himself was awestruck. I was most impressed.

## Hesperus Draper:

Good news raised our spirits in late July—Charles Lee had turned back a British invasion of Charleston, South Carolina. Withstood a barrage for twelve hours. Rallied his men. Won a battle. Everybody drank a toast to Lee.

In his general orders, Washington ladled on the inspiration like gravy. "The dying heroes of Charleston conjured their brethren never to abandon the standard of liberty, and even those who had lost their limbs continued at their posts."

I heard a few snickers when that was read. Nobody in our army was plannin' on losin' their limbs, and 'twas for certain that nobody was plannin' to keep their posts if they did, unless they lost a leg and couldn't run away.

And dimmin' the good news of July was bad news in August. That's when the mercenaries arrived—eight thousand Germans, mostly Hessian—tall, hard-disciplined fightin' men, wearin' dark blue uniforms, brass-fronted hats that added another foot to each of them, and twirled-up, boot-blacked mustaches that made them look even fiercer than they were.

A few days later the Howes made the opening move in the great chess match to be played out around New York.

Washington had tried to cover all the squares—a regiment on Long Island under Nathanael Greene; another at King's Bridge, holdin' the northern approach to New York Island; and three in the city itself. But the British didn't come straight at New York, as Washington expected. Instead, they started ferryin' men across the Narrows to Long Island. At first, Washington thought 'twas all a feint.

But the Howes wanted to take the hundred-foot cliff of Brooklyn Heights and the little popgun batteries we put there to stop the British fleet from comin' up the East River.

Then, at just the wrong time, Nathanael Greene came down with the camp fever, so Washington replaced him with John Sullivan. But once the British had landed twenty thousand troops, Washington realized that this was no feint, so he gave the command to Israel Putnam. Truth was, Sullivan and Putnam together didn't equal one Nathanael Greene on the battlefield.

Hell, the whole command structure was enough to depress a gigglin' lunatic. There was Big-Ass Henry, all of twenty-five years old, directin' our cannon with a slow match in one hand and a textbook in the other. Adjutant General Now-and-Then Joseph Reed, who might go back to Pennsylvania the minute the courts reopened. And Old Put—a fine fighter, but no oil paintin' of a general, wearin' the sleeveless white waistcoat that he called his summer uniform, with his hanger belted to his shoulder so his sword wouldn't get in his way when he got on his horse. The only one who looked the part was Washington.

I asked myself again what in hell we had gotten ourselves into.

Now, whenever I needed to understand a battlefield, I tried to see it like a bird. Helped me when I was engineerin' and when I took command of troops and whenever I had to retreat, which was damn near as often as when I advanced.

So imagine 'tis about eight o'clock on the mornin' of August 27, 1776. You fly out over the East River, followin' the wake of a boat headin' for the Brooklyn landin'. Swoop low and you'll see that Washington is aboard that boat, on his way to leadin' his first real battle. Joseph Reed is with him. And the slave Billy Lee is holdin' their horses.

The rays of the sun are still low from the east, and there's a fine gold tint to the green landscape up ahead. Fixin' to be a fine day.

Fly over the ferry landin' and follow the road. It bends some, rises a bit, then runs right through the village of Brooklyn. You see church spires, brown rooftops, and cook-fire smoke curlin' from brick chimneys. The cliffs of Brooklyn Heights are to your right. And there's Fort Stirling, one of three earthworks built to command the East River, not that there's much that's commandin' about any of these dirt piles.

Fly east, about half a mile from the town, and there's more dirt, a big brown scar of it a mile long, runnin' right to left across the green farmlands. 'Tis a line of trenches connectin' four earthen forts. Stretches from Gowanus Marsh on the right to Wallabout Bay on the left, so both flanks are anchored in impassable mud.

Out beyond the American lines are two more miles of wheatfields and cornfields and orchards cut by four roads, all as neat as the buttons on Washington's waistcoat. And beyond the fields is a stretch of hills called the Heights of Guan, which are maybe a hundred feet high, covered in woods. And there's only four passes through them.

One is to your far right, near the coast—the Gowanus Road. There's smoke risin' there, because two thousand Americans, under Lord Stirling, face seven thousand redcoats demonstratin' before them. That's military talk for doin' some marchin' and some noise-makin', just to keep an enemy off balance.

About two miles to their left, in the center of the Heights of Guan, are the passes formed by the Flatbush

Road and the Bedford Road. There's smoke risin' from the woods down there, too. Sullivan's men are defendin' those passes across a mile-long front, while the Hessians demonstrate.

Now, Sullivan's right and Stirling's left support each other, but Sullivan's left is, as they say, in the air. That's because the pass formed by the Jamaica Road, about three miles farther along the heights, is undefended.

The day before, Washington and Putnam had ridden the ground and decided that the British would never take the Jamaica Pass. Too circuitous, too slow, too wooded, too this, too that. And they'd have to march an extra ten miles to get to it.

Now, fly higher, up and over the woody Heights of Guan, so that you can see beyond, onto the great plain of Long Island.

You've just flown over a rabble of nine or ten thousand men, tryin' to defend a triangle of land sixteen miles around, with twenty-nine cannon and damn few bayonets. Now, you're lookin' down on a real army, enormous and well made. It's said that there's twenty thousand of them, and their tents seem to stretch to the horizon. But between the Hessians below you and the British off to your right, you can see only about ten thousand men. Where are the other ten?

*There.* Over on your left, movin' in column, comin' across the tops of the Heights, followin' the pass that Washington thought they'd never take. They look like a two-mile-long blood vessel—dragoons, foot soldiers, grenadiers, and artillerists draggin' forty cannon. They've been marchin' all night, led by three Tories who know the shortcuts. They've moved without music, without shouted orders, with their bayonets sheathed to keep 'em from reflectin' the sun. And in the places where they've had to take down trees, they've used two-handed saws. No ringin' axes allowed.

It don't take long for that redcoat vein to start pumpin' men down out of the woods, down along a road that cuts on a diagonal from the Heights of Guan through the village of Bedford and on toward Brooklyn. Dragoons and flankin' parties are fannin' out toward the woods. They trample wheat and knock down cornstalks as they go. Meanwhile the regulars keep up a quick march, stretchin' their column as far as they can toward the Gowanus Road, all to cut off the thirty-five hundred Americans on the Heights of Guan.

Then you see smoke jet from two cannons near Bedford Village. 'Tis the signal. The flankin' force is in position. Time to stop the demonstratin' and attack.

The Hessians below you give out with a roar and go chargin' up the hill against Sullivan. Off to your right, British bayonets glint, and the redcoat mass moves forward against Lord Stirling. The Americans on the Heights of Guan have been trapped between an anvil and two hammers.

I watched all of this from the earthworks, not from the sky. I'd come over from New York to strengthen our defenses on the far left, between Fort Putnam and the Wallabout Marshes. This section was held mostly by New York militia. I had 'em throwin' up big piles of dirt, settin' abatis in the ground, diggin' rifle pits for sharpshooters . . . and ignorin' the sounds of battle out in front of us.

But when they heard those signal cannons, where

there should've been nothin' but cows and corn, they all stopped. Hell, they all but froze.

So I ran through the sally port at the rear of Fort Putnam—an acre-square dirt pile—and scrambled up the rampart for a look. Through my glass, I saw the British regulars flowin' through the village of Bedford, flowin' through the orchards and cornfields, flowin' between us and the Heights of Guan.

In the center, where the battle smoke was the thickest, our boys were pourin' out of the woods like birds flushed from cover. Runnin' so fast, with their coats and knapsacks flappin' in the breeze, they looked like they just might take wing. Some of them ran into British dragoons. Others were run down by Hessians or shot by regulars. But some managed to pick their way through the grass and orchards and fields, and make a run for our works.

The scary thing was that they were our best troops, our Continentals. Washington had ordered Putnam to put them out there, where there might be some real fightin' to be done. Said he'd hold the skittish militia behind the earthworks.

And Putnam had agreed. "That's right, sir. Remember their legs."

Well, our New York militiamen were worried about their heads, too, because they were crowdin' fast into the fort. And they were a lot more than skittish. You could smell the fear on them, as sharp as the smell of the fresh-turned dirt.

I figured a little labor might settle them, so I jumped down from the rampart and shouted the name of one of the militia captains: "Bangs's company! Outside! Strengthen the trenches. Sharpen the stakes. Collect as much brush as you can to cover the approaches."

Bangs wore a red cockade on his hat to show he was a captain. Otherwise, he looked like what he was, a skinny shopkeep with a lazy eye. He spit some tobacco and said, "Well, boys, you heard the officer."

But nobody moved.

I took a few steps toward them and said, "I issued an order, Captain. If you can't make these men obey, I will."

"We ain't here to do no more diggin'," said one of the big farm boys.

"You're here to do what your officers tell you." I puffed myself up, but when you're as skinny as me, that's a hard trick.

The farm boy snapped right back, "If I want to dig holes, I can do it at home, without nobody shootin' at me."

Then, from behind me, came a familiar, high voice, cuttin' through the fear like a knife: "All of you take your posts. Now!" Washington kicked his horse into that frightened mob and shouted. "If I see any man disobey orders or turn his back today, I'll shoot him through. I have two pistols loaded to do it. But I'll not ask any man to go further than I do. I'll fight as long as I have a leg or an arm."

He may have gotten us into this mess, but he was actin' like he'd get us out of it, too. Militiamen must've believed him 'cause they started back to their posts.

"Obey the orders of Captain Draper!" cried Washington after them. "Whether he tells you to dig a ditch or charge the enemy."

He jumped down from his horse and leaned a little closer to me. "I may need new field officers before this day is out. Experienced leaders for inexperienced men."

I thought somethin' I didn't say: from what we'd

just seen, the experienced leaders were all wearin' red coats.

In three quick steps, Washington bounded up onto the rampart to where Israel Putnam was standin'.

Putnam said, "They've used the Jamaica Pass, sir. A damnable surprise. But if they get close enough, we'll give them another Bunker Hill." All with a lisp sprayin' spit everywhere.

"So long as these men remember what they're fighting for," answered Washington, "we'll prevail."

He could say the right words, and say 'em loud, but it didn't change things. Before long, all four dirt-pile forts were filled with frightened men who'd found their way back from the front, some spewin' stories about Yankee boys pinned to trees by Hessian bayonets, some spewin' lies about how brave they'd been in the face of a British charge, and some just spewin' blood.

## Joseph Reed:

Washington was everywhere, galloping up and down the line, going in and out of each fort, and encouraging every man he saw. "Quit yourself like soldiers," he would cry. "Remember, all that's worth living for is at stake!"

He was made for leadership on the field. But no man was made for the decisions he faced. His hardest came at Fort Box, on the far right. We'd climbed to the top of the rampart so that he could see the fighting beyond the Gowanus Marsh. And what we saw was the work of heroes.

Out by a big mill, Lord Stirling and a Maryland regiment—two hundred and fifty of the best-uniformed, best-armed men we had—were standing off thousands of British troops. They did not do it because they wanted to, but because the enemy had cut the Gowanus Road, leaving the marsh as the only avenue of retreat for Stirling's men, who now were floundering through it.

A messenger hurried up to Washington to beg help for the Marylanders.

Washington looked at me. He looked out toward the battle. He looked along the line toward the far left, as if some answer might be offered in that direction. Finally he fixed his stoniest expression on his face and told the messenger, "They're fighting a rearguard action. They're to retreat in good order. I cannot reinforce them."

Once the messenger went off, Washington looked again to the scene on the far side of the marsh. "Good God, Reed, but what brave men I must lose today."

## Hesperus Draper:

Just after noon the first units of British regulars came across the fields toward the earthworks. They were a good mile off, but they were aimed right at my shaky spot, like a pack of wolves pickin' out the weakest deer in the herd.

Keepin' my eyes on them, I said, as cool as I could, "Captain Bangs, best get your men into the trenches."

But Bangs didn't say anything.

"Captain!" I snapped. "They'll be in our laps in a bit."

I just heard a whimper behind me and turned. Bangs was standin' there, holdin' his musket, with a yellow puddle formin' at his feet. Lucky for him most of his men hadn't seen this. They were all watchin' the redcoats comin'.

I stepped closer to him and said, real low, "Sing out, mister, or you'll never hold up your head in Poughkeepsie again."

Bangs looked at me with tears in his eyes. "I . . . I . . . I can't."

So I shouted, "Yes, Captain Bangs, you're right! All the men into the trenches! Grab your muskets, take your posts, and prepare to fire in two ranks."

The men just looked at me. So I pulled a pistol. "Remember what the General said about shootin' any man who runs! It goes double for me."

"How can it go double," said the big farm boy, "when you've only got one pistol, and Washington has two? That's goin' half."

He had me there, so I aimed the pistol right at his goddamn head. "I'll shoot you first, then reload."

Nothin' like a little flintlock point-makin'. In jig time, I had my New Yorkers hidden in the trenches, but for their muskets and the crowns of their hats. I was standin' up on a dirt pile, showin' 'em I wasn't afraid, which was a plain lie.

When our boys fired a cannon on the rampart above me, I thought I'd wet myself. And what was worse, the British didn't even flinch at the shot. Just kept comin'. And farther to the right, I could see somethin' glintin' out in the cornfields. 'Twas the sun shinin' off the brass fronts of those tall Hessian hats.

They were headin' toward our center, marchin' in big blue squares, like they were on a parade ground. Soon enough the whole mile-long line of trenches and dirt forts would be under attack.

I said, "Captain Bangs, make ready!"

And from up on the ramparts, Washington shouted: "Remember what you're fighting for, men!"

Israel Putnam cried, "Don't fire till you see the whites of their eyes." He'd said that on Bunker Hill. I s'pose he thought it might work here, too.

But Washington corrected him. "Don't fire till they're thirty yards away."

I tried to gauge which was closer—thirty yards or the whites of their eyes.

These British regulars were yellin' as they came. Some were even runnin', which smart soldiers never did. I reckoned we'd get in one good volley and then they'd come with bayonets, and my New Yorkers would *all* piss their breeches.

But when they were about two hundred yards out, the damnedest thing happened. Their officers wheeled their horses in front of the men and began ridin' back and forth, swinging swords and shoutin'. And, by God, but those red ranks slowed down.

All along the front, enemy units were marchin' into view, comin' up the roads, fannin' out into all the cornfields and wheatfields. Fifes were tootlin', drums thrummin', flags flutterin', brass and steel glitterin' in the sun. The ground was thuddin' so hard that clumps of dirt were rollin' down from the walls of the fort. I swear, before long, there were twenty thousand men marchin' toward us.

And then it *all* stopped. Music stopped. Thuddin' stopped. Everything stopped. And it got deathly silent.

Loudest noise was the snappin' of those flags in the northeast wind.

Up on the rampart, Washington was swivelin' his head about, tryin' to take in everything across the whole front. I don't imagine he'd ever seen so many men in one place before. I sure hadn't. He'd even stopped yellin' to the troops, as if he couldn't think of anything else encouragin' to say.

We'd been backed into a triangle of land, not much more than a mile on each side. When they came at us, which shouldn't be more than a few minutes, there'd be no steep slope like Bunker Hill for them to climb. Just a gentle grade.

I took my new locket from around my neck and flipped it open and asked Charlotte's little face: "Darlin', what in hell have we gotten ourselves into?"

## Billy Lee:

I was glad I'd sent Margaret off with the other women. This was lookin' bad. Inside Fort Putnam there was mud everywhere—reg'lar brown mud, and red mud from the blood of wounded men. I tried not to look at that. Made me feel sick.

So did the view out in them cornfields. 'Twas as if all the armies of Europe was drawn up right in front of us. Figured 'twas almost over.

The General had on his show-nothin' face, but I declare, his jaw dropped wide open when all them soldiers started wheelin' like they was on parade grounds. The officers was shoutin', the fifes and drums started up, and that mighty army that could've rolled us over

like we were chilluns, fell back and started pitchin'
camp. 'Twas as if they couldn't quite bring theirselves
to kill us.

Israel Putnam said, "I'll be damned."

"But not today," said the General.

Colonel Reed said, "There's always tonight."

"Tonight," said the General. "See that the men are
kept at their posts. And get me the returns from the
advanced units." Then he come marchin' off the rampart like there was nothin' more to see and he had
business someplace else.

I give him his reins and whispered, "What's happenin', sir?"

He didn't say nothin' till we was outside the fort
and ridin' along the left side of the line, covered
by that New York militia. He said, "Billy, I can't
always be answerin' your questions on the battlefield."

"I'm sorry, sir."

"Listen and you'll know what's happening." Then
he called over that Virginian, Captain Draper. He said,
"Good work with these men. I want brush and abatis
before all our forward trenches, all the way to the
Wallabout Marsh."

"I'll do my damnedest, sir," said Draper.

Then the General leaned down and spoke softer,
"Howe may attack tonight, once he's brought up cannon, axes for cutting our abatis, and ladders to scale
the walls. This is the best ground for an attack. Will
you hold them?"

"I'll do my damnedest, George."

"I'll get you some help," said the General. Then he
straightened up and shouted, "Keep your hearts, men.
Remember what you're fighting for."

None of those boys cheered, but I'd have to say he bucked them up some.

As he rode away, Colonel Reed caught up and said, "Sir, you can't get them help. There's no help to be had in Brooklyn."

The General said, "I know."

He was in the saddle most of the night, ridin' from post to post, givin' orders, talkin' with Reed and Putnam in the torchlight, sendin' his aides here and there. Waitin'. Just waitin'. But Howe didn't attack.

So the General tried to sleep 'round two o'clock. Slept in a chair in a farmhouse he was usin' as his headquarters, mebbe a half a mile from our lines.

I told him I'd stay awake so he wouldn't have to.

But 'long about four-thirty 'twas his voice that woke me. Him and Reed was talkin' again. Talkin' low. Talkin' fast. Talkin' scared, if you ask me.

"You're bringing more men to Brooklyn?" Reed was sayin'. "But once the wind shifts, the Royal Navy will own the East River. We'll be surrounded."

The General answered like he'd made up his mind. "We need more men here, whether Howe attacks or attempts to take us by regular approaches."

"Regular approaches? A siege? All the more reason not to trap more men."

Most officers who used Reed's tone with the General, they'd get the cold eye. But the General got kind of shifty-eyed, didn't look hard at Reed, just said, " 'Tis the best I can think of at the moment. Write out the order."

Reed stood there a minute, like he was after more arguin'. Then he just said, "What units do you want?"

"Shee's Pennsylvania Third, Magaw's Fifth, and Colonel Glover's Marbleheaders." Then the General told me to bring him his horse.

I said, "Yes, sir." Sky was brightenin', but there was clouds comin' in, too.

C.D.—*My last stop, before I left for France, was the packet landing in Boston, and a boat captained by a Negro named Matt Jacobs. He greeted me warmly and introduced his crew—his fourteen-year-old son and a skinny white man with a squint eye named Willard Walt. After ascertaining my good intentions, he talked.*

## The Narrative of Matt Jacobs:

After I run away from Belvoir, I slipped onto a Massachusetts ship in Alexandria. I'd heard 'bout Marblehead bein' a fishin' port, and I liked to fish, so I went to a captain there and offered to fish for nothin' for one trip. I done the job as good as a white man, and after that, I was treated near as good as a white man. And nobody ever axed where I come from.

So when the time come to fight for freedom, I figured nobody knew better than me what it meant. I joined up, and I fit in, with most of the lads, anyways, seein' as how there was eight or nine Negroes in the Marblehead Regiment. Never thought that by joinin' I'd end up lookin' Washington in the eye.

On the day after the big battle on Long Island, we

was ferried from New York to Brooklyn, marched through the town and into the trenches on the far left. The New Yorkers in the line cheered us as if they thought we was the lads who might do somethin'. And I have to say, we looked like better soldiers than most, in our sailor-suit uniforms—little black hats, blue neckerchiefs, short blue jackets, smart white breeches. Some us wore tarred breeches—a old sailor's trick for keepin' his ass dry—and by the end of that day, we all wished we was wearin' 'em.

The General had sent some Virginia riflemen into the woods beyond our trenches, and all day they kept a-pop-pop-poppin', just to give those redcoats somethin' to think about. But the left was where the redcoats had plans. Late afternoon they drove our riflemen back. Then they come at us.

We'd done our damnedest to keep our powder dry—'twas rainin' by then—but our first volley was as ragged as the tail of a field hand's shirt. Misfires and pan flashes, and not enough lead to bring down a single duck in a flyin' flock.

In no time, thirty redcoats was on us, comin' in with bayonets slashin'. None of us had bayonets. And clubbed muskets ain't no match for a blade. So we all started scramblin' for the trench behind us.

One feller turned to fire his piece, and he was stuck right in the chest. Then the feller on my right, little Willard Walt, who never had much to say to me, 'cept that he didn't like niggers, he slipped in the mud, and two redcoats come at him.

I could've left him, but 'twasn't the right thing to do. Instead, I took my musket and started swingin' . . . caught one redcoat in the side of the head. Stunned him, like he didn't expect a Negro to do such a thing.

So I hit him again, and crunched his skull just like lobster shell. Awful. Just awful.

His mate turned on me, but Walt was on his feet by then. He could've left me, but he didn't. He hamstrung that redcoat with his knife, and when the redcoat turned to stick him, Willard drove the knife right into the poor feller's chest, right above where his cross belts met. Feller looked down at the blade like he couldn't believe it. Then he looked at us and shook his head and fell over.

Willard Walt looked at me and said, "I guess niggers ain't so bad after all." Then we ran.

Lord, but war is an ugly thing. And that fight? All for a trench that the redcoats left once they'd driven us out, 'cause they knew they couldn't hold it.

## Hesperus Draper:

That night was one of the miserablest I ever spent. The rain came hard and cold and never let up. Rain down my neck. Rain under my collar. Rain soakin' me right the way through. Had no tents to cover us, not like the British troops a mile across the fields. Had no campfires, either, so we et our pickled pork raw. Leastways the rain softened up the hardtack biscuit that went with the pork.

Off to our left, the redcoats and the Marbleheaders skirmished some durin' the night. 'Twas good that Howe only sent skirmishers. If he'd come in force, with nothin' but bayonets, he would've made pincushions of ten thousand cold, hungry, half-drowned amateur soldiers and one amateur general who kept ridin' the lines, tellin' everyone to be brave and all would be well.

'Twas said, later in the war, that any general but Howe would have beaten Washington, and any general but Washington would have beaten Howe. 'Twas never truer than on Long Island. But Howe was out to win this fight by the book.

At dawn, when the black rain turned gray, we saw why they'd been skirmishin' on the left. About six hundred yards from Fort Putnam the British had raised a redoubt. From there they'd dig a slip trench, then a parallel, then another and another, all angled so we couldn't fire into them. Once they were close enough, they'd bring up their heavy guns. Then we'd have to surrender or be pounded to pieces. And if Howe did it all by the book, he might not lose a man.

I looked up at the rampart of Fort Putnam. Washington was standin' there, silhouetted against the gray clouds, him and the clouds both drippin' rain. Then I looked at my men, standin' in a trench, knee-deep in water. And do you know what I thought of? Fort Necessity.

## Joseph Reed:

I was terribly fatigued, having been riding for most of two days and obliged to lie each night in my clothes.

The heavy rain had had a most unfortunate effect on our men, on their minds, bodies, and arms. However, we hoped to make a good stand, as our lines were pretty strong. But our situation was truly critical.

Washington had committed one of the cardinal sins of warfare—dividing his army before a superior force, leaving seven thousand men on New York Island and putting nine thousand on Long Island, along with his adjutant general, a major general, and several brigadiers, two of whom—Sullivan and Stirling—were now prisoners. He had failed to fortify a vital road. His army had been trapped. And then, as if he could think of nothing else to do, he'd brought another fifteen hundred men into the trap.

The rain had slacked off into a dense, drizzling fog. Everywhere I rode, I saw despairing faces, bodies shivering beneath soaked blankets, men standing in trenches half filled with water. And from the battery on Red Hook I peered through curtains of fog at the Royal Navy maneuvering against the wind.

We were running out of time. So I hurried back to headquarters and found the General at a small writing desk, quill, ink, and paper before him.

"Sir," I said, leaning over the table, "the wind is shifting. Once the fog lifts, the Royal Navy will be in the East River. Neither our guns nor the hulks we've sunk are sufficient to the purpose of stopping them."

"What do you propose?" the General asked.

"The men are so dispirited, I propose evacuation, sir . . . as soon as possible." I then stepped back, like a schoolboy who had just confronted the instructor over some perceived injustice, and awaited an answer.

Washington said, "I'm glad you agree with me." He then produced an order, written by his own hand, for the collection of every boat from Brooklyn Heights to the Harlem River. "We're leaving tonight."

## Matt Jacobs:

Come dark we was ordered out of the line. Rain was still comin' down, sometimes heavy, sometimes not, and we was glad to get out of them wet trenches.

But we wasn't moved to a new place in the line. We was marched back to the ferry, which was like bringin' field hands back to the barn. But when I saw all the flatboats and rowboats and sailboats, too, and Washington and Reed sittin' there on their horses, that's when I knew what was happenin'.

I heard Washington tell Colonel Glover that he'd kept the maneuver secret, so there wouldn't be deserters sneakin' off to give news to the British. Then he said, "I've heard that your men are hardy and adroit . . . weatherproof lads. Can they ferry us to safety?"

Glover said, "If anybody can do it, sir, 'twill be my boys!"

"Good," said the General. "Get them to work. We've a long night ahead."

And right quick we was into the boats. Our officers knew who could sail, who could row, who could pilot. And I'll tell you, nothin' could make me feel better than havin' an oar in my hand.

## Hesperus Draper:

Think like the bird again. You're flyin' back over the British lines toward New York. 'Tis near dawn. But there's fog rollin' over the scene. In some places you can't see more than a dozen yards. In other places the fog's light and misty, puttin' a kind of dreamy feelin' to what you see.

The British and their Hessian mercenaries are camped in a sea of tents. The canvas rooves are just brightenin' in the gloom.

Over on the British right, the torches are burnin' holes in the fog. That's where British engineers and sappers are diggin' trenches. You can hear their shovels scrape and scratch. Won't be long before you'll hear their cannon.

British pickets are watchin' in their forward positions, and all seems right on the other side. American campfires are burnin'. American pickets are in place . . . or are they? A party of British guards is creepin' out from their lines to spy.

Swoop down and follow them. At first they go very cautious, their red coats bright in the gray mist. But gettin' closer, they get bolder. Then they start to run. They reach the American forward trenches and peer in. The fires are dyin'. The trenches are empty. The British fire their pieces into the air and scream the alarm.

Fly a little further across the wet fields, but be careful, because it's gettin' foggier as you move toward the river. Up ahead, the buildin's of Brooklyn loom out of the gray. And there are the last units of Americans, the rear guard, quick-marchin' for the ferry. When they hear musket shots, they break into a run.

Fly on into the thicker fog lyin' like a blanket over the last Americans. Swoop down through it, down close to the ferry landin'.

And there, by the last boats, you see a man sittin' on a bay mare. No question who he is. He sits up straight and tall, as if he's had a good night's sleep though he's barely closed his eyes in forty-eight hours.

The ground all around him is trampled with footprints. And you think of what's gone on there since nightfall, with one unit after another pushin' down the steps to the landin' . . . frightened men seein' those boats and feelin' the kick of hope, knowin' they're about to dodge a bad fate . . . and maybe some of those men push a little too hard, afraid that the enemy might swoop down on 'em before they can get their personal asses out of the way. But always there's the man on the bay mare, barkin' orders, steadyin' scared boys, seein' that they keep their discipline.

Once the rear guard has taken to a boat, the General gives a final look over his shoulder, then leads his horse aboard. 'Tis the first time that he does what he'll do better than anything else in the war—retreat.

## Billy Lee:

I was sure glad to get back to New York, and mighty proud of the General for what he done to get us out of that fix. But I was mighty worried about him, too. He hadn't had but a few hours' sleep in three days. I swear he nodded off twice in the saddle whilst we was ridin' up to Richmond Hill. He walked into that house and turned to go into his office, and I knew, if he went in there, he wouldn't get no sleep at all. His aides, Harrison and Tench Tilghman, they'd start shovin' papers at him, and . . .

I couldn't order him to bed. But I'd been thinkin' hard whilst we was ridin' up from the city. You know, if you want to help someone sometimes you has to think harder than them, and he wasn't thinkin' too much at all. So I said, "General, I reckon you'll want to shave and change your clothes, bein' in them for so many days and all. Why don't you go on upstairs and I'll bring up some hot water?"

He rubbed a hand over the stubble on his chin—'twas already gray even though his hair was still that chestnut color—and he said that was a good idea.

In his room, I helped him out of his coat and waistcoat, helped him peel off the shirt, too. 'Twas soaked with sweat—strong-smellin' nerve sweat.

He said, "Bring me the hot water."

"First, I'll turn down the bed, sir, in case you want to take little sleep."

And that did it. He saw them pillows and just dropped down, all but dead.

## Joseph Reed:

Washington did not return to his duties until the next morning, so exhausted was he. He deserved to sleep, for what he accomplished—moving ten thousand men out of the line, before a powerful enemy, and past the prows of the Royal Navy, all in a night—is rightly regarded as one of the great military maneuvers of modern times, no matter the blunders that put us there.

In his report to Congress, he was brutally honest: "Our situation is truly distressing. I am obliged to confess my want of confidence in the generality of the troops. Till of late, I had no doubt in my mind of defending this place, nor should I have yet, if the men would do their duty. But this I despair of."

And I said frankly that I despaired of confidence in the Congress, whose councils seemed dark and intricate and very badly calculated to assist us.

The General did not dispute me. He finished dictating and said, "We must get on with things, Reed. We must reorganize. We must determine if we are to leave New York or, if Congress wants us to stay, how to defend it."

I sometimes thought my mind a very peculiar one; it rose when the spirits of others fell. I had made it up for whatever might happen, and I felt no other concern than what arose from thoughts of my wife and our dear little folks. And even those thoughts I got rid of as soon as possible, for they could only unfit me for duty without doing my family any service.

Observing Washington at the time, I felt that his mind was like mine, made for crisis.

## John Adams:

The news arrived on the third of September.

Of the battle on Long Island it could be said that, in general, our generals were out-generaled.

# Hesperus Draper:

Our escape from Brooklyn slowed the slide from bad to worse, but you could say that after Long Island, we were all of us Long-Faces. Of the eight thousand Connecticut militia we had, six thousand of them just up and left. They'd finally figured out that in a war, *you could get hurt!*

Washington didn't even try to bring 'em back. He was losin' faith in his men. The men were losin' faith in their officers. And the officers were losin' faith in their General.

Washington issued an order expressin' "amazement and concern" at the breakdown of discipline. More depressin' than amazin', if you ask me. All over New York, soldiers wandered about, vacant-eyed, exhausted, drunk. Some deserted. Others took to thievin'. Stole from the homes of rich Tories. Stole from each other. Even picked over the gear of poor Lord Stirling, now an unwillin' guest of His Majesty.

Washington fell back on threats and floggin'. But floggin' wouldn't change the truth: these were not the men to stop the Howes from makin' their next move. And Washington was not the man to anticipate it.

A few nights after the retreat, I had a tankard with a colonel from Delaware, name of Haslet, handsome feller with a fine-lookin' regiment all dressed in new brown uniform coats. He admired the way I'd held those New York militia in position. I liked how his troops held their discipline. So we patted each other's backs a bit; then the talk turned to Washington.

Haslet said, "I revere the General. His character, his disinterestedness, his patience and fortitude . . . They'll be an everlasting remembrance. . . ."

"But?" I asked. I always asked for the *buts*.

"The burden seems too much his own. Beardless youth and regimented inexperience are all around him."

"Like Knox?"

"I slander no one in particular. Knox was in New York during the fighting. Only"—he drained his ale—"would to heaven that General Lee were here."

Charles Lee. Still in the South but rumored to be comin' north, with an honor guard of barkin' dogs.

Would Lee have known where to move his pawn to block Howe's knight? Would he have looked the Long Island field over and seen it like Caesar? Would he have done what I'd told him? Would he have burned the city and run like hell?

Washington began his next officers' meetin' by readin' the answer of Congress to the matter of the burnin' of New York: "'We would have especial care taken, in case the General should find it necessary to quit New York, that no damage be done to said city by his troops on their leaving it, Congress having no doubt of recovering the city, though the enemy should, for a time, obtain possession of it.'"

'Twas my first officers' meetin', so I didn't open my mouth, and for a time neither did anyone else.

Finally Joseph Reed said, "They're giving us permission to leave."

Nathanael Greene, Israel Putnam, and Henry Knox agreed.

But Washington said, "Congress would prefer that we stay."

"I agree," said General Mifflin. "It's implicit in the order. They wish the city to be maintained."

"Even if Howe attacks with all his force?" asked Nathanael Greene.

"Howe." Israel Putnam gave a snort. "I've been thinkin' about the way Howe fights us. I've decided he's either our friend, or no general."

That brought a chuckle from a few in the room, and when Washington cracked a bleak smile, everybody felt free to laugh.

Then Washington spoke about the way *we* had to fight *Howe*. Seemed he'd been up late, thinkin' hard. "History, our own experience, and the advice of our friends in Europe demonstrate that on our side this war should be defensive, a war of posts. We should avoid general action, and never put our young troops to risk in the field, unless we're compelled by necessity."

It made sense. A war of posts: fight from behind fortifications and fences; fall back when you have to; protect the army; keep it alive.

But if Washington couldn't burn the city, he wouldn't leave it, either. He was too proud, too stubborn, too worried. Worried about Congress, worried about the fence-sitters watchin' to see if this stumblin' army could hold the most important spot on the continent, and always worried about "the other hand," the second choice, the option that sapped a man's decision.

He reminded me of a he-dog chasin' a pack of pissin' bitches, not knowin' which puddle to piss on.

He even said it: "On the other hand"—and he kept talkin'—"to abandon a city which some people deem defensible, and on whose works we've bestowed so much labor, it could dispirit the troops and enfeeble the cause."

So they came up with a compromise, and in warfare compromise is first cousin to confusion, and confusion is a close relation of disaster. They spread that scared little army up and down the length of New York Island. Put five thousand in the city; nine thousand diggin' like damn fools at Harlem Heights; and five thousand more, mostly militia, spread thin along the East River.

I was beginnin' to long for Charles Lee myself.

For weeks, Howe just waited, like he wanted us to wear ourselves out tryin' to entrench the whole island. Finally, one sunny Sunday in September, I was in Harlem, a neat little village with a single church steeple. Washington had come to ask me how I planned to fortify it.

"Well, sir," I was sayin' to him, "the best thing to do—"

Just then I felt a funny pressure in my ears and heard the low boom-Boom-BOOM of about a hundred cannon firin' off at once, someplace to the south.

Washington looked at his aides, kind of puzzled, and without a word, he turned his horse and galloped for the sound of the guns.

I rode with them. Figured whatever was happenin', I should see how my earthworks held up against Royal Navy broadsides, though most of the works on the East River were no more than ditches dug along the bank.

We rode hard down the Post Road, and all the while that roar kept gettin' louder, and big billows of gray smoke went puffin' into the September sky like clouds. Then the noise stopped all at once, stopped the way the drummin' stops when the drummer boy takes a bullet.

Washington reined in his horse, and his aides all jumbled up around him in a dusty circle.

"Sounds like the barrage is over, sir," said Tench Tilghman. "They must be landing troops. I can't believe they'd interpose their army between our forces in New York and Harlem."

Washington didn't say anything. I don't suppose he could believe it either. Howe was aimin' to cut the chessboard right in half.

And while we were thinkin' on that, do you know what we heard? Singin'. That's right. *Singin'*. It carried all the way from the riverbank. German singin'. Hymn singin'. Washington give us a funny look; then he squared his shoulders and spurred his horse toward the smoke and the sound of that singin'.

'Twas the Hessians singin' hymns on the flatboats whilst they was comin' ashore. And the good Lord must've liked their voices, because he sent them up against Connecticut militia, the greenest men in our army. Those boys didn't fire a single shot before decidin' 'twas time to get their asses out of the trenches and start runnin' hellbent for Harlem.

We hadn't gone but half a mile more down the Post Road when we saw them . . . flyin' like birds, runnin' like rats, and nothin' behind them but dusty road.

I heard Washington mutter, "God damn them." Then he went gallopin' in amongst them, swingin' his ridin' crop, shoutin', "Stop! Stop, men! Stop and turn! Stand and fight! Fight like men!"

The aides commenced to do the same, so I was obliged to do as much. Pulled out my pistol and began wavin' it and shoutin'. Told those boys they was runnin' from nothin'. Leastways nothin' we could see. The Germans was all still down at the riverbank, still singin', and the General was so damn mad *he* was the one they should be worryin' about.

But one look at the faces of them Connecticut boys told me we'd lost this day. Most of them never had a musket fired at them before, and here the British had just pounded them for close to an hour with naval broadsides. And then they'd sent out boatloads of giant singin' Germans.

Those boys passed over us the way a cloud passes over a cow patch, and they went scramblin' up the road, with Washington screamin' after them, cursin' them for a lot of damned cowards.

Then he wheeled his horse so hard, I thought he'd throw her over. A few hundred yards south, down near a crossroad that ran over to the Bloomingdale Road, there were two regiments movin' toward us in good order—Massachusetts militia and Connecticut Continentals. Maybe *they'd* fight.

Washington took a quick conference with the officers of these two regiments and figured out exactly where the enemy had landed—a place called Kips Bay. That meant the British and Hessians were fannin' out in a wide semicircle not too far to our south. Couldn't see them yet, the land bein' depressed some down by Kips Bay. But they were comin'. We knew that.

Washington said to his aides, "We'll make a stand here at the crossroads. Stone walls for defense. Cleared fields for fire." Then he told the regimental officers, "Bring up your men."

The orders were shouted from the captains to the lieutenants to the men in the column. And the column kicked ahead. Made me proud, after what I'd just seen. Then the column stopped. Then it sprang apart like some cheap watch. Those troops just plain lost their nerve. In a second, all order was gone, and we were in the middle of another runnin' riot. We all tried to help, gallopin' this way and that, swingin' our ridin' crops, and shoutin' threats and bloody murder.

If Washington was mad before, 'twas nothin' compared to this. He was in an absolute rage, screamin', "Hear me, men! Take the walls. Take the cornfields! Stand and fight!" And all the while his face was gettin' so red I thought his head might burst.

Maybe a hundred boys were more afraid of him than they were of the enemy, so they did what he told them. The rest ran like this was a race and that Connecticut militia had a head start.

Then a party of British—no more than fifty or sixty, popped up at the lip of the little grade about a quarter mile south. They moved slow and cautious—advance units, feelin' their way up from the river and across the farmland.

Washington rode out for a better look. Then he glanced back over his shoulder to say somethin', and what he saw made him bellow, "God damn you!"

The troops who'd obeyed him were all up and gettin' into that race to the rear. Washington went gallopin' after them, cursin', swingin' his ridin' crop, the veins bulgin' in his neck, the neck even redder than the face, and the whole army runnin' lickety-split for cover, throwin' down muskets, powder horns, hats, and pride as they went.

Finally, Washington tore off his hat, threw it on the ground, and screamed, "Good God! Have I got such troops as these? God damn you all to hell!"

And his voice echoed off into the trees, right behind the last of those runnin' soldiers. Then he looked at me and his aides—we were all spread around, after tryin' to stem that second tide—and I heard him say, a little softer, "Are these the men with whom I am to defend America?"

The British were movin' up the hill now, movin' a bit faster. No reason for them to know the big man on the horse, but he sure looked to be a prize catch.

And Washington? He just watched them, as if to say, let them come, let them shoot. His horse even took a few steps toward them, and he didn't even pull up on his reins.

That's when I spurred my way over to him. Grabbed the bridle, and I swear, Washington looked at me like a man just wakin' up. The sweat was pourin' down his cheeks, carryin' long streaks of flour from his powdered hair. His eyes were small and squinted in the sun. His face was so red his pockmarks looked infected.

Tench Tilghman came up on the other side of him and said, very gentle, "General . . . General . . ."

Washington raised his hand to his head, "My hat. Get—"

But I yanked at the bridle and pulled him away. British were gettin' too close to be worryin' about hats.

## Billy Lee:

I missed the scene at Kips Bay, bein' busy settlin' the new headquarters at Morris House in Harlem. But I heard the aides talkin' afterward, usin' words like "towerin' rage" and "volcanic temper."

I'd seen it plenty, that volcanic temper. And I'd seen him hold it down plenty, too. Folks called him cold, icy. Fact was, he was always pourin' cold water on himself, just to keep that temper tamped down.

That night he rode the lines at Harlem, seein' that the men was in their places. But he was low, as low as I'd ever seen him. He didn't shout no fine words to the men, didn't have much to say at all.

The only compliment he give was to some New York Artillery. Their captain was that skinny Alexander Hamilton. But mostly I think he was disgusted with his soldiers. And they was disgusted with him, too.

We come on some Connecticut men settin' in the torchlight. They was the ones who run first. The General stood in the shadows and listened to their chaplain go on, in a whisperin' voice: "Washington blames the men for retreating, but the fault was in the officers. They couldn't anticipate the attack. The men showed good sense in running when they had possibility of surviving."

The General just rode on into the shadows.

## Joseph Reed:

That night, I wrote my Esther. She wanted me to come to home. I wanted to go, but I told her, as heaven was my witness, that so strong was my affection, and so powerful my wishes, that were I to give way to them, all other considerations would vanish. Such a step would affect not only myself but the public as well.

I yearned for her. I saw her face as I wrote in the candlelight. I heard her step in the footfalls that awakened me from a doze. But the steps were Washington's, pacing in his own chamber deep into the night, as well he should.

Had General Howe pressed straight across the island he might have bagged half the army, along with Israel Putnam, Henry Knox, and an artillery officer by the name of Alexander Hamilton. But Howe had determined to wait for reinforcements, and so had bided his time at tea in the home of the Widow Murray, may Providence shine upon her. Meanwhile Putnam and his men had made good their escape up the west side to join our main force at Harlem.

The city that Howe took was nearly deserted. Of the twenty-two thousand who had lived there, all had fled but about five hundred Tories, who, it is said, greeted the British with untrammeled joy. That evening, those loyal folk painted red R's on the doors of known rebels—as a service to the king, of course. They thought our revolution was all but crushed.

Many of the men on Harlem Heights might have agreed. And the next morning the British showed by their contempt that they felt the same way. Advance British units skirmished with an American scouting party. After driving our men back, the British came within sight of our lines and on a bugle played the derisive two-note "whoo-whoop," the call that ends a successful foxhunt.

I never felt such a sensation before. It seemed to crown our disgrace. As the General was an old fox-hunter, no one could have felt the insult as acutely as he. But we struck back. The General sent seasoned units from Virginia and Massachusetts against this contemptuous group of redcoats, and before the day was done, we had finally put the enemy on the run.

I will admit that the fight was inconclusive, but you cannot conceive of the change it made in our army. The men recovered their spirits and fought with new-found confidence. I could only hope and pray that the spirit would remain.

While Howe was pondering his next move against us, disaster befell New York. I stood with Washington on the night of September 20, and we gazed from Harlem toward the southern horizon, where great sheets of orange and red danced in the sky, as if fire were a manifestation of some celestial purpose.

Handsome mansions, ancient Dutch cottages, or the mighty Trinity Church—it made no matter. Fully a quarter of the city, five hundred buildings or more, collapsed in a giant conflagration.

"Well, Reed," said the General, "Providence, or some good honest fellow, has done more for us than we were disposed to do for ourselves."

The next morning I gave him the report, "Had the wind not changed, sir, the whole city might have been destroyed."

Washington said nothing, his mood being much darker than the morning.

I said, "Sir, this is good news. It shows, as you say, that good honest fellows are on our side everywhere. I wouldn't want to be in Howe's shoes today."

"Howe's shoes are still quite comfortable," said the General, "while, were I to wish the bitterest curse to an enemy on this side of the grave, I'd put him in my shoes, with my feelings."

"But, sir, the men have proven themselves, and Congress has finally accepted your proposal for enlistments to last the duration of the war."

"We have lost New York," he said. "And the new enlistees are no more than imaginings. And the men we presently have must prove more than what they have."

He was right, of course. The skirmish on Harlem Heights offered only a momentary upswing in morale. The scenes at Kips Bay seemed much the more likely to be repeated, as a spirit of desertion, cowardice, plunder, and shrinking from duty prevailed generally throughout the army. Washington knew it, and sometimes his knowledge was too much for him to bear.

He drew a long, deep breath. "Fifty thousand pounds would not induce me to undergo what I've done this last year, Reed, or what lies ahead."

It was the first day of autumn. If his spirits sank further, it would be a long, cold winter. I should have reckoned with his ability to pull himself out of the deepest pits, whether on the battlefield or in his own mind. I should also have reckoned with a sad truth: the pits were nowhere near as deep as they would become.

C.D.—*For two months the chess match continued. Howe kept three brigades before Washington while he sought to put the rest of his army at Washington's rear. There were British landings and fights at Throgs Neck and Pells Point. But before Howe could outflank him, Washington retreated north. At White Plains another battle was fought, highlighted by Washington's blunders and Howe's inability to convert advantage into conquest.*

*Washington gave ground again, to New Castle, above White Plains, and once more it became a war of posts. Washington waited for Howe to attack, but winter attacked first. The colder the weather grew, the faster the Continental army melted away. Each dawn revealed new desertions until, one morning, almost miraculously, the graying of the sky revealed that the British were leaving, too.*

*Washington concluded that they would now attempt to take his rooks—Fort Washington, on the northern tip of New York Island, and Fort Constitution, on the opposite bank of the Hudson. But where else might Howe strike? New England? Philadelphia? The Hudson Highlands? The season was late but the choices many.*

*Like the he-dog of Hesperus Draper's description, Washington did not seem to know which way to turn his attention, so he divided it and his army.*

*Four thousand men, under Nathanael Greene, garrisoned the Hudson forts. Four thousand were sent to the Highlands, to keep open the route to Canada. Washington took units raised west of the Hudson— some two thousand men—and led them back to that side of the river, to oppose a thrust at Philadelphia. And Charles Lee took command of the five thousand New Englanders at New Castle, blocking the invasion route to their home states.*

*Enlistments were ending in November and December. Within six weeks the fragments would themselves be fragmented.*

## Hesperus Draper:

S o Charles Lee had returned.

In October he had stopped at Philadelphia. Congress had cheered him, patted him on the back, probably patted his dogs, too, and voted him thirty thousand dollars to pay off his debts. Then they'd sent him north to the scene of the real troubles.

Some in our camp had waited on him as if he was leadin' a thousand archangels all dressed in blue-and-buff. Washington had been so happy to see him that he changed the name of Fort Constitution to Fort Lee.

Now, let me tell you about those forts. They were star-shaped dirt piles loaded with cannon and men, sittin' like portals on the lower Hudson. The gate between them was a line of hulks, chains, nets, spiked barrels, and other junk, all sunk in the river. The idea was that British ships comin' upstream would be slowed by the junk—"obstructions" was the fancy word—and the artillery in the forts could pound them.

Well, on November 7, two British ships sailed right up, blasted broadsides in both directions, and sailed on without so much as a "By your leave."

"Hah!" said Charles Lee when he heard the news at his headquarters. "This proves that those forts are as useless as teats on a bull, Draper."

I'd been made Lee's adjutant. 'Twas a step down for a captain, but Lee promised me a promotion and a regiment of my own at the end of the campaign. Besides, servin' on Lee's staff had side benefits, too: Lee had an eye for willin' women, if not good-lookin' ones, and sometimes you might catch one goin' by. And when you dined with him, you'd be treated to a show by his dogs.

But if you sat with him for even a few minutes, there was a chance that one of them might try to mount your leg. Never went to Lee's office but I kept my ridin' crop handy, just to protect my boots.

"Fort Washington should be evacuated," said Lee, over a meal of greasy duck. "I've written the General my opinion. I cannot conceive what circumstances give to Fort Washington so great a value as to counterbalance the probability of losing two thousand of our best troops when it falls."

"Answer's simple, sir," I said, "Congress wants it held."

"Congress." Lee took a slab of duck skin and threw it on the floor, sendin' up a splatterin' of grease and startin' a riot amongst the dogs. "Fools."

"Fools? But some congressmen have shown you great favor, sir."

Lee wiped a sleeve across his face. I wasn't sure if this was to take the duck grease from his cheeks or the crumbs from his sleeve. In any case, grease and crumbs spread out about equal on both. "They're fools. And I do not mean one or two of the cattle, but the whole stable. I told Washington that if they continued to fail him, he should threaten to resign."

"But, sir," I said, "if he resigns, won't you be the one to replace him?"

"That would be the chain of command, yes." Lee poured me more wine. "Do you not find it telling that he has given me much the largest part of his army? He understands what a professional man may do with such a force."

"That depends on whether the boys feel like fightin' for you or not."

Lee tore into a duck leg. "I understand the men,

Draper. Washington wants a regular army, all discipline and direction, on the European model. I believe that Americans make up a radical new army. They fight best as partisans. And they'll fight better than British regulars with the proper leadership."

By which he meant himself.

## Joseph Reed:

I believed that the Hudson forts should be abandoned, as did General Lee.

And Washington dictated a letter to General Greene: "If we cannot prevent vessels from passing up, and the enemy are possessed of the surrounding country, what purpose can it answer to attempt to hold a post from which the expected benefit cannot be had?"

I suggested that Greene be ordered to abandon the fort. But Washington said, "No. I must give him the right to make the decision. Say this to him: 'As you are on the spot, I leave it to you to give such orders, as to the evacuating of the fort, as you think best.'"

Indecision. Compromise. Division of force before a superior enemy. The one sin he had not committed was to overrule a trusted officer in the field, and in this case, it was the one sin for which he would have been forgiven.

At length we went to Fort Lee, where Greene kept his headquarters. It was November 14, a sunny and surprisingly warm afternoon that turned bleak when Greene informed us that, far from evacuating Fort Washington, he felt so confident that he had begun to reinforce it!

The General glanced at me, then quickly turned his gaze toward the fort on the other side of the river, as if to deny me the opportunity to voice my opinions. I knew that he was at war with himself. He did not chew his lip, however, or grasp his neck or fall victim to any of the other twitches that afflict a man in the midst of crisis. The more uncertain he was, the more impassive his expression became.

Then Greene said something that swayed him mightily: "We cannot continue to abandon posts, sir. We cannot continue to discourage the country."

"The war of posts," said Washington, echoing himself.

"Yes, sir," said Greene. " 'Tis why Congress resolved that we hold the forts."

"Yes . . . yes," said Washington. " 'With every art and at whatever expense.' They made themselves clear."

Greene was a good officer. But he gave no good advice that day.

And Washington seemed to hesitate more than I had ever known him on any other occasion, more than I thought the public service permitted.

Of one thing, however, he was certain: Howe would not move faster against Fort Washington than he had against any other position. In that certainty, Washington was more wrong than ever he had been, because Fort Washington fell two days later, while he watched in quiet agony from the opposite bank. We lost guns, supplies, and some twenty-eight hundred men. They were marched to British prison ships in New York Harbor, mercilessly crammed belowdecks, and left to rot. It was the worst disaster yet.

## Hesperus Draper:

"Fools!" That's what Charles Lee screamed when he read the dispatch on Fort Washington. "God damnable fools!"

Lee was workin' himself into more of a lather than I'd ever seen, not that a little lather would have hurt him any. "I predicted it. Foresaw it all!"

"You certainly did, sir," I knew that ass-kissin' had an honorable place at any headquarters, even a decrepit dog-smellin' farmhouse above White Plains.

"If they'd moved for Fort Lee, oh, you'd have seen it evacuated soon enough. But Washington couldn't let his namesake be surrendered without a fight. Oh, no, Draper. Vanity, all is vanity."

Vanity, for certain. And no one had more of it than Lee.

But he was right. Four days after Fort Washington fell, the British attacked Fort Lee. This time Washington didn't even blink. Ordered the whole garrison out. Too bad the boys weren't fast enough to save anything but their gunpowder and themselves. They left breakfast on the fires, along with a thousand barrels of flour, three hundred tents, and thousands of picks and shovels, which was maybe the worst loss of all, considerin' that we fought more by diggin' than by shootin'.

'Twas bad news for us, way up above White Plains, and worse news for Washington. Because now Lord Cornwallis was on the Jersey side of the Hudson with seven thousand men. And Washington was just six miles away from him, on the other side of the tricklin' little Hackensack River. And the November rains were fallin', and the October provisions were gone, and the summer shoes were wore out. So Washington did the only thing he could: he ran. He began tradin' miles and miles of flat Jersey farmland for whatever time he could get.

Two days later, Lee called me into his office. Weather had turned colder and 'twas rainin' harder, but somethin' made him as cheerful as one of his dogs at dinnertime. He said, "Well, Draper, Washington's the quarry now. He's fallen back upon the Passaic with Cornwallis hot on his heels. Good soldier, Cornwallis."

I couldn't see anything cheerin' in this, but Lee had all he could do to keep his tail from waggin'. He read from Washington's letter: "'This country is almost dead flat, and we have not an entrenching tool, and not above three thousand men, very much broken and dispirited.'"

Lee skimmed his finger down the page and kept readin': "'Unless, therefore, some new event should occur, or some more cogent reason present itself, I would have you move across the river and join my command.'"

So that was the reason Lee was cheerful. We were movin'. Straight off, I started thinkin' like a good adjutant should. I said, "I'll make the plans, sir."

"Not yet." Lee raised a bony finger. "The General has not *ordered* us, Draper, but merely requested. This throws me into the greatest dilemma."

"Commander in chief asks for help, sir, we should give it." Seemed plain enough to me.

"But the cogent reasons, Draper." Lee tapped his

finger on the letter. "Our troops are so ill-furnished with shoes, stockings, and blankets, they'll perish in this wretched weather. More are to be dismissed on Saturday, New Englanders all. If we turn them away from home now, they may simply choose to quit."

There was no doubt that this sloppy scarecrow was a good soldier. He'd won at Charleston. He'd commanded the units that protected Washington's flank on the retreat to White Plains. He'd seen the trap at Fort Washington. But he was as vain and ambitious as any man in America, and he was provin' it now. He was also provin' that he wasn't too smart, because he was puttin' his proof in writin'.

That afternoon, the letters flew from his headquarters. 'Twas the first time since I'd worked for Horatio Gates that I had writer's cramp.

First Lee dictated a letter to be delivered to Washington: "Withdrawing our troops from hence would be attended with some very serious consequences which at present would be too tedious to enumerate."

Pretty high-handed. Said he'd recommend that our units at the Hudson Highlands move down, seein' as they was already on the west side of the river. Then he spun off a letter to the governor of Massachusetts about sendin' troops to him instead of to Washington. Then he had me copy a letter he'd written to Benjamin Rush, doctor, congressman, no friend of Washington.

"You're writin' to one of the cattle?" I said.

"One of the *intelligent* cattle."

He wrote: "The affair at Fort Washington cannot surprise you more than it amazed and stunned me. I must entreat that you will keep what I say to yourself, but I predicted all that happened. My last words to the General were, 'Draw off the garrison or they will be lost.'"

Lee was a seasoned infighter. Pattin' his own back while stabbin' somebody else's was as easy for him as pickin' his nose. But he was after more.

He went on, "I could say many things. But let me talk vainly: I could do this nation much good were I to dictate affairs for just one week. But I am sure you will never give any man necessary power. Did none of you in Congress ever read Roman history?"

Lee had treated me better than just about anyone in the army, but I felt damned uncomfortable, readin' that. Make a man a dictator for a week and he just might get to likin' the job. And I *had* read some Roman history.

Then I noticed another letter on Lee's desk, this one from Joseph Reed.

"Ah, Draper, your eyes are sharp," said Lee. "If you think *I'm* critical of our General, you should read what his closest confidant has written."

Lee thrust the letter at me. "This was delivered under the cover of Washington's request for aid."

Well, bein' around Lee had started me quotin' Shakespeare too. My first thought after readin' that letter was *"Et tu, Brute?"* I couldn't believe that Washington's closest aide would put his hand to such a thing.

Reed had written to Lee: "I do not mean to flatter or praise you at the expense of any other, but I confess I think it is entirely owing to you that this army is not totally cut off. You have decision, a quality often wanted in minds otherwise valuable. Oh, General, the indecisive mind is one of the greatest misfortunes that can befall an army; how often I have lamented it in this campaign."

With friends like Joseph Reed and a second-in-command like Charles Lee, Washington didn't need the British. He had enemies enough.

## Billy Lee:

Express rider from General Lee reached us at Brunswick the mornin' after we stopped there. Thirtieth of November.

I know the date, 'cause some Pennsylvania militia up and left, even though they was signed for another month. General wanted to send men after 'em, but he didn't have enough. So he just shook his head and let 'em go.

We been retreatin' a long week by then. And the General looked grimmer every day. Weather was cold and rainy. Roads was rutted, slick, hell to move on. Rivers was hell to cross. But we never felt safe till we put some runnin' water 'tween us and the British.

We burned the bridges on the Passaic and the Rahway. Then we crossed the Raritan and pulled up for a time in Brunswick.

The General had give me one of the most important jobs in the army: I carried his papers—letter books, general orders, everything. I protected 'em in two big leather saddlebags. I carried 'em when we moved. I seen that they was put on the table when we stopped and made headquarters in a farmhouse or tavern. And seein' as he needed me, I got to sleep where he slept, and seein' as he needed a roof over his head to do his generalin', I got one too.

But a lot of that army was sleepin' in the open, without tents, without beds, shiverin', complainin', coughin'. There was men on that march who didn't have shoes, and men whose breeches showed more butt-bottom than they covered. And most of 'em had beards. I declare there was so many beards, 'twas like a scene from the Bible . . . long, scraggly, greasy beards. And them boys, they'd come to look as pasty as the pickled port they et for supper, when they had any supper.

And that month of November, it don't just bring down the cold rain. It brings the dark, too. 'Tis a month when a man don't need no British army to make him sad. November can make a man sad just by bein' what it is.

No surprise that every mornin' the sergeants counted heads to see who deserted and who was dead.

Now, like I say, on the last day of November, this rider come in, all drippin' wet and covered in mud. He said, "I've orders to place this dispatch in Colonel Reed's hands."

'Twas my job to take such papers and give 'em out where they was s'posed to go. I said, "If you want Colonel Reed, you have to go all the way to Burlington. General sent him on business."

That confused the rider some. He said, "I reckon if Colonel Reed ain't here, I should maybe put it in the General's hands."

When I told the General that this rider was carryin' a dispatch letter from General Lee, he all but flew out the chair. Few days before, he'd wrote Lee a pretty mad letter, sayin' he didn't want the men from the Hudson Highlands comin' to help him, "It is *your* division that I want to have over."

The General looked at the address on the outside

of the letter: "To Joseph Reed, at Headquarters, from Gen'l Lee, White Plains."

"White Plains?" The General flexed his jaw, threw some of that cold water on his temper. "Why is he still at White Plains?"

The rider just shrugged. The General sent him off, then tore open the letter and commenced to readin'. 'Twas like somebody died. His face got longer and whiter. Color drained out of him. He read this letter right to the bottom, then just dropped into a chair, brought his hand to his mouth, and stared into space.

I waited a minute; then I had to say somethin'. "Sir? Sir? What is it, sir?"

He just shook his head and said, "Even Reed."

After a little bit, I asked him, "Is there anything I can bring you, sir?"

"My writing case."

## Joseph Reed:

Burlington would always be a place of joy for me. That was what I believed as I arrived on a night in late November, wet, cold, and exhausted. I had come to confer with the governor of New Jersey, in hopes that he could find troops for our shrinking army. But I had another reason: I had urged my wife to bring our family out of Philadelphia, as that seemed the ultimate objective of the enemy, and so she had come to my mother's house, in that little town on the Delaware.

You cannot conceive of the joy of such a reunion as when I came into that house, just after sundown, to find my little ones in play by the hearth and their grandmother sitting close by. And then to see my Esther rushing to my arms.

I shall never forget that night and the warmth I felt in the bosom of my family. Those few hours of bliss, both familial and connubial, were almost enough to make me understand the militia who longed always for home and fled the army at the first opportunity.

But the next morning I was met with mortification. It came in the form of two letters—one from General Washington enclosing another from General Lee.

Washington's letter was coldly polite: "The enclosed was put into my hands by an express from White Plains this evening. Having no idea of its being a private letter, much less suspecting the tendency of the correspondence, I opened it, as I have done all other letters to you upon the business of your office. This, as it is the truth, must be my excuse for seeing the contents of a letter which neither inclination nor intention would have prompted me to."

Esther said, "Joseph, what's wrong. You look as if someone's died."

I laid Washington's letter aside and turned to Lee's. I had grown used to feeling the bottom drop from my stomach in those months, but nothing in my life could ever equal what I felt as I began to read.

These were Lee's incriminating words to me: "I received your most obliging letter and lament with you the fatal indecision of mind which in war is a much greater disqualification than stupidity or want of personal courage. Accident may put a decisive blunderer in the right, but eternal defeat and miscarriage must attend the man of the best parts if cursed with indecision. I will soon be there, for to confess a truth,

I really think our Chief will do better with me than without me."

Washington knew my thinking. He could only believe I had betrayed him.

C.D.—*I had passed through New York on my way to Boston, expressly to see Alexander Hamilton. There was much to be said about Hamilton, mostly controversial. This much could be said safely—he was brilliant, he was tireless in the service of his ideas and his country, and he was the most Federalist of Federalists; however, he hated the Federalist Adams as much as he hated Jefferson. These men seemed as generous in their pettiness as in the grandeur of their vision.*

*His house, however, reflected only the grandeur. It was a fine estate, on the high west side of New York Island. The view was commanding, but the host was not to be seen. He had been called away. He had, however, left me a detailed recollection of his days with Washington, and I decided that I liked him even without meeting him.*

## The Narrative of Alexander Hamilton:

Washington was to be an aegis very essential to me, so my opinions of him, while varied, are brightly colored.

He believed, as I do, that the sacred rights of mankind are not to be rummaged for among old parchments or musty records. They are written, as with a sunbeam, in the whole volume of human nature, by the hand of divinity itself; and can never be erased or obscured by mortal power. That belief carried him, as it did me, through the darkest days of our retreat through the Jerseys.

I first laid eyes upon him in June, during an inspection of the Grand Battery at New York. One could not help but be impressed by his height and bearing, by the regality with which he moved. To have had a general of such presence was an absolute necessity, as there was very little of presence anywhere else in our army. I, however, took pride in the appearance of our New York provincial artillery, and Washington took note of us that warm morning.

He spoke to me for the first time on the September night that we retreated to Harlem Heights. But it was not until the first of December that I engaged in a real conversation with him.

On that morning, at Brunswick, elements of the Maryland and New Jersey militia were preparing to leave. I had my guns dug in on a hilltop above the Raritan, protecting the bridge that was the only crossing for many miles in either direction, and with disgust, I watched the militiamen striking camp in the field below.

A Maryland captain came to me to offer his hand.

I said, "I'll take your hand only if you stay."

"No, sir," he said. "I've done my share, and so have these boys. Winter's comin'. We're wore out. We have farms and businesses. We have little ones."

"You have the British troops coming hard." I pointed across the river, to the crest of a hill like the one we were on. Both were treeless, covered in brown grass rimmed with hoarfrost. "They'll be coming over that hill before the day is out."

"All the more reason to run." The captain put his hand behind his back. "Time for somebody else to shoulder the burden. We done our share."

And there was the end of any respect I had for militia.

Around one in the afternoon, the General rode onto the hill, his slave Billy Lee close behind, to watch the last of those cowardly detachments fold their tents. He sat the horse with a majestic stillness that expressed, simultaneously, both his disappointment in those militia and his own commitment to persevere.

Then suddenly all attention was turned to the opposite hilltop, where our rear guard was appearing, bringing the alarm: the enemy had been sighted.

Washington was suddenly animated. He galloped down to the bridge, calling out, "How many? How many are coming?"

"Cornwallis and his whole damn army, sir! Not five miles back."

Washington wheeled his horse toward me. "Cover the bridge, Captain. Cover it until you're told to retreat!"

Then he galloped off toward the camp, the sound of commotion following him as if it were cheering. The drums began to beat the long-roll, the sergeants began to bellow, and the men came tumbling from their tents, whilst the last of the craven militiamen fled for their lives. In short order the sergeants had our troops paraded in lines pointed south toward the Delaware River.

Meanwhile, our engineers rushed onto the bridge

to tear it up. But from the woods on the sides of the hill came the rifle fire of the Hessian jaegers, fire so accurate that it drove our men off, the job of destruction only half done.

But the British could not advance because our own riflemen did their business as well, and we worked our battery with as much speed, accuracy, and steadiness as could be mustered. That bridge was the choke point, and I resolved to keep it closed with cannonballs for as long as necessary.

On the opposite hilltop, the British unlimbered two guns and began sending balls toward us. For two hours the bang and echo of the cannon fire leaped across the river, one side doing so little damage to the other that the excitement of the duel soon faded into no more than a noisy day of work. But we did the job we were emplaced to do: we kept the advance units of Cornwallis's army on the other side of the bridge, until finally we were called off, leaving only our own riflemen to guard the rear.

That night we stopped our retreat just north of Princeton, and the General sent for me. I tucked my hat under my arm and stepped into his tent. He seemed tired, but he sat behind his camp table as tall and erect as he sat his horse.

He said, "You handled your guns with great courage and skill today, Captain. A very smart cannonade."

I thanked him and told him that I was proud of my men.

At this, he smiled, tight lipped. "How old are you, Captain Hamilton?"

"Nineteen, sir."

"Nineteen? So young, and yet so talented."

"Thank you, sir."

"Keep up your discipline and your spirits."

"I will, sir," I said. "The liberties of America are an infinite stake."

"They are that." He smiled again, a bit more warmly, though he kept his mouth tightly closed. Even then, his natural teeth had been darkened by port, and he did not always wear the artificial teeth that closed the gaps where he had lost real ones. "You'll now excuse me, Captain, but I have letters to write."

I had no premonition that, soon enough, I would be engaged in writing more of his letters than he was.

## Joseph Reed:

I sent my resignation to Congress. How could I ever have Washington's trust again, though I might explain myself with perfect logic?

But the next night I was sleeping in the arms of my wife when I was awakened by a pounding at the door. 'Twas an express rider from Washington's camp north of Princeton.

The General was urging me to rescind my resignation. The plans of the enemy were coming clear, he said. The British were intent on driving through to the Delaware River, and he needed his adjutant general. It was as if all the unpleasantness of the previous day had been forgotten.

The next morning, I bade good-bye to Esther, who made not the least complaint. She knew how deeply

I was moved by Washington's midnight letter, a cry for help from a friend.

The next night I reached Trenton. I had grown up there and remembered a fine little town, but now that our army had arrived, it seemed as despairing as any square of ground I had ever stood upon. Hulking shadows surrounded the campfires in the fields. Soldiers huddled against the houses to stay out of the wind. The men of Washington's guard presented arms crisply, but their eyes were as hollow as rotted stumps, and there was not a clean-shaven man among them.

Stepping into the General's headquarters—a farmhouse—I rehearsed my speech again. It was as well polished as my first argument before the Pennsylvania court. "General—"

"Colonel Reed." His voice betrayed neither pleasure nor anger.

"I . . . I would like to thank you for the note that you sent me last night."

"Thank you for returning." He looked at me now, his expression flat and direct. "We need you where you can do the most good."

I fumbled to unbutton the clasp of my cape. "I'd like to say that I'm—"

"We can't hold Trenton, Colonel. We have to cross the river. We'll be safe on the other side, at least until the river freezes. Then we'll have to find other answers."

"Yes, sir. I'd like to say—"

"If we retreat to the back parts of Pennsylvania, do you think the people will support us?"

"If the eastern counties are subdued, the back counties will surrender, sir."

Washington brought a hand to his throat. "My neck was not made for a halter. We must plan for the long range, to retire to Augusta County in Virginia and carry on a predatory war. If overpowered, we must cross the Allegheny Mountains and keep the men together."

"Yes, sir." I was still hoping to clear the air of our other matter.

But he was moving on to the logistics of our crossing. "I want you to see to the collecting of every boat on the Delaware, every boat for sixty miles."

"Sixty miles?"

"'Tis the only way to be certain that Cornwallis will have no means of crossing after us."

Just then Tench Tilghman came in with a letter. "Excuse me, sir. I've drafted your latest message to Charles Lee."

"Perhaps Colonel Reed might go over it with you." The General spoke without sarcasm, but implicit in that remark was a comment on my connection with Lee. It would have been the moment for me to bring the matter up, except now for the presence of Tilghman.

The General took the sheet and read aloud, "'General Lee, I cannot but request—and this comes by the advice of all the general officers with me—that you march to join me with your whole force with all possible expedition.'"

He glanced at me, as if for approval.

I said, "It can't be better stated than that, sir."

He signed the letter and gave it back to Tilghman, who hurried out.

And I was left standing before him. I could have wished for an hour of private conversation, that I might explain myself. I could have wished to obtain the letter I'd written to Lee, that I might show it to the General and defend it, point by point.

But the General said, in a most direct and uninflected manner, "Best get about your business, Joseph. There are many boats in sixty miles of river."

I know that he was deeply hurt. He admitted as much to me in a letter the following summer: "hurt, not because I thought myself wronged by the expressions contained in a certain letter, but because the sentiments were not communicated immediately to myself."

Our friendship was repaired by the letters passed in the succeeding eighteen months, but it might have returned to its former strength, had our misunderstanding been melted by warm conversation, rather than frozen, as it was that night.

But in those times, there were far greater worries than our petty feelings. Would Philadelphia survive? Would our army? Would we?

## Hesperus Draper:

"Good God! Have I come from gathering laurels in other parts of the world only to lose them here?" That's what Lee shouted at Washington's latest letter.

But he finally took to movin' because he realized that there'd be no glory on the east side of the Hudson. He drafted out the sickest of his men and the ones who couldn't march because they were lame or had frostbit feet or no shoes. Left himself about twenty-seven hundred Continentals and a militia force that we estimated around four thousand. But estimatin' militia was like estimatin' how many crows was pickin' over a plowed-in cornfield. One minute there'd be a thousand, the next minute there'd be a dozen.

Our best soldiers were the boys from Marblehead. But just lookin' at them would make a drunk go sober. 'Twasn't because of their tarred breeches or that rollin' sailor's gait or even that they marched so many nigras. The soberin' thing was that in three weeks their enlistments would end. And most of them were plannin' to go back to sea. Makin' money as a privateer seemed a lot better than the empty-bellied mud march that *we* were settin' out on.

But Lee wasn't thinkin' about them. He was thinkin' about Lee, and his reputation. At the Hudson crossin', he said, "Draper, mark this. I am going into the Jerseys for the salvation of America."

We hurried over the river, then hurried inland, to take a route that the British didn't control. 'Course, by then, they controlled most of New Jersey. Howe had offered pardons to anyone who'd swear loyalty to the king, and plenty of folks were takin' him up on it, some because they wanted to and some because they feared the plunderin' that Howe's troops brought. To the Hessians, stealin' everything in sight was all in a day's work, and it didn't matter a damn that the people they were stealin' from might be friends.

I remember ridin' alongside Lee on a miserable sleetin' afternoon, crossin' a range of hills west of Newark, headin' for the village of Chatham. 'Twas so cold that the spit froze in the fifes, but the drums beat a steady rhythm, to keep the men puttin' one foot ahead of the other.

Lee was payin' more attention to the trees his dogs was pissin' on than he was to the men. 'Twas as if he didn't want to look at that column behind him. Maybe that was because the four thousand militia had already dropped down to two thousand, and there were fewer of them by the day.

I said, "Sir, from Chatham we should be able to reach the Delaware in three more days."

"Reaching the Delaware is of secondary importance, Draper. We're here to reconquer the Jerseys, which were in the hands of the enemy before our arrival."

Most of it still was, I thought. "But, sir—"

"No *buts*. I have a plan we must follow if we're to save America." Lee stopped his horse and looked at me. "'There is a tide in the affairs of men, which, taken at the flood, leads on to fortune.' *Julius Caesar.*"

In that army, you couldn't argue with Shakespeare. Only Washington was foolish enough to try. In his next letter, he ordered Lee to come, and come fast.

Lee answered: "It will be difficult, I am afraid, to join you. I believe that we can make a better impression by hanging on the enemy's rear. Howe will not move on Philadelphia if he knows we're in the hills, waiting to pounce. Nevertheless, I shall look around tomorrow and inform you further."

It took a lot to make me feel sorry for Washington, but I did now. Imagine, havin' to beg this vainglorious popinjay in a dirty shirt. It even seemed like Washington was losin' his nerve, proof of which was his next letter to Lee: "Were it not for the feeble state of the force I have, I should highly approve of your hanging on the rear of the enemy and establishing the post you mention. But I must entreat you to march with your whole force, with all possible expedition."

*Entreat.* It never did a general any good to entreat anybody over anything.

## Martha Washington:

I spent my days at Mount Vernon, doing what I could, with the devoted help of Cousin Lund Washington, to see that the plantation ran smoothly.

My joy was that Nelly had been delivered of a baby girl in August, and the child was as vibrant as the days were despairing. In all my letters to my husband, I wrote of baby Eliza. His letters spoke of many things, from the hard realities of the war to the much happier tasks of running a plantation.

"O Patsy, I wish to heaven it was in my power to give you a more favorable account of our situation. Our numbers are quite inadequate to opposing General Howe, yet I have hope of delivering a strike that will be to our benefit."

Then he might speak of instructions he had sent to Cousin Lund, regarding the planting of holly trees at Mount Vernon. He expressed concern that the Negroes not suffer for want of clothes that winter, despite the enormous cost of them. And in one letter, he informed me that my carriage must make do with two old gray mares, as he did not have the time to send me the horses that he promised.

As if such a thing mattered to me.

What mattered far more was how deeply I felt his pain, and how I wished that by sharing it, I might relieve him of it.

Sometimes he spoke directly to me of his fear. I remember his words on the enlistment of a new army: "If this fails, I think the game will be pretty well up." With what consequences, he did not tell me.

At other times, he sought, through circumspection, to protect my feelings.

I awoke before dawn one rainy morning to the sound of someone rummaging in the General's study, which was directly below our bedroom. What could this be?

I slipped out of bed, and barefoot, I tiptoed across the cold floor and down the stairs. These led from our bedchamber to a narrow hallway, which led to the study.

I heard male voices, furtive voices, and lanternlight glowed from the study, brightening the gray gloom.

I slipped into the room, and there were Cousin Lund and Jacob, the oldest of the General's bondsmen, rifling the General's desk and bookcases.

"What are you doing?" I demanded.

At the sound of my voice, Lund jumped, and a sheaf of papers skittered across the floor. I saw that they included letters, financial records, diary entries.

"Good Lord, ma'am," said Lund, "but you scared the devil out of us."

"Those are private!" I said. "What are you about? Lund? Jacob?"

"I'se jess doin' what I'se told, ma'am," said Jacob. "I can't even read."

I turned my eyes to Lund.

"Well, ma'am," he began, "you see, unh . . . we . . ."

"Lund," I said angrily, "why are you here at this hour . . . doing this?"

"Well, ma'am . . . ah, hell . . . the General wants us to collect his papers, have 'em ready to move, should the British come up the river."

I all but collapsed in relief, knowing my trust in Lund was still secure. "Why didn't you tell me? I would've helped you."

"Well, ma'am," said Lund, "the General wrote that he didn't want us to give alarm or suspicion to no one. I reckoned by that, he meant you."

Very seldom did I cry for my husband. But my emotions were very strong, when I saw the care that he was taking to spare my feelings. I could only excuse myself quickly and return to my bed. I did not emerge until almost eight.


## Hesperus Draper:

Charles Lee had some new friends, a pair of French officers who'd showed up at his headquarters in White Plains. Names was Boisbertrand and Virnejoux, a species that would become all too familiar in the Revolution—the European officer who comes to America and expects Americans to bow down, just because he's seen a little shootin' someplace else.

I always let these fellers know I'd been with Braddock, so I'd seen the way a European army acted when things went bad. And when you think about it, they couldn't have been much as soldiers, considerin' that this was the army they chose to join, and this was the time they chose to join it.

Well, in the second week of December, Lee decided he and his friends needed a little rest. We were camped at a place called Vealtown, takin' our own sweet time gettin' to the Delaware. Our numbers were down to twenty-seven hundred. If we waited long enough, we'd have nothin' left when we got to Washington. Maybe that was Lee's plan.

He knew of a widow by the name of White, an Irish lady, who kept a tavern about four miles away, at Basking Ridge. Said there'd be soft beds there, and if they were lucky, soft girls in the soft beds . . . for a price, of course.

He rode off that afternoon with the Frenchmen, his aide Will Bradford, and a guard of fifteen men.

'Tisn't hard to imagine what went on that night. All I know is that the next mornin' I went to get Lee movin'. The day had come up sunny but cold enough that the road wasn't turnin' to mud, so the army had already marched.

Two of Lee's guard were stationed at the front door of the tavern. Four more were around back. The rest of the boys was in a barn nearby, sleepin' off their rum. And of course, there were dogs here and there, snufflin' and snoozin' and humpin' each other like old-dog friends.

Mrs. White, a grinnin' old harpy with breath like the bottom of an ale cask, greeted me in the entry, took one look at my uniform coat, and said, "You'll find the general in the taproom."

And there he was, still in bed slippers and blanket robe, wearin' a shirt so dirty you'd think he was one of his own bedraggled soldiers. He was sippin' a cup of tea and dictatin' a letter to Bradford.

"Ah, Draper, good morning," he said. "Did you sleep well?"

"Not so good as yourself, sir," I said, "from the looks of things."

'Twas a dark room, with a smoky fire on the hearth, but once my eyes cooled down from the bright snow, I saw the two Frenchmen, pawin' a pair of jills in a corner. Leanin' against the bar was a lieutenant I recognized as Jamie Wilkinson, an aide to Horatio Gates. And another jill was lollin', half asleep and half drunk, in a snug on the other side of the room. She had one foot upon the table and her big toe stickin' out from a hole in her stockin'. And Lee's dog, Spada, was under the table, sniffin' up her leg.

"I slept very well," said Lee. "I had angels to sing me to my rest."

"Well, sir," I said, "time for them to be singin' you to your horse."

"Worry not. I'll finish this letter for General Gates and be along presently." Then he turned to his aide, "Now, where was I? Oh, yes. '*Entre nous*' "—he gave his French friends a little wink—" 'a certain great man is most damnably deficient. He has thrown me into a situation where I have my choice of difficulties. If I stay in the province, I risk myself and my army, and if I do not, the province is lost forever. In short, unless something which I do not expect turns up, we are lost.' "

"*Entre nous*"? I knew what that meant. "A certain great man"? Had to mean Washington. And if he wanted to keep his opinion private, why did he speak it for all of us in that taproom to hear? I turned to the window and looked out at the snow. Thought it might do me some good to look at somethin' clean.

That was when I saw them. At first they were no more than a few glints of brass and a few flashes of color on the snow. Within seconds they were a whole company of British dragoons in their short green coats, gallopin' up the lane to the tavern.

"General," I said, "best write your farewells. We have guests."

At that, the two Frenchmen jumped up, all but droppin' the jills on the floor. Lee scuttled to the window. And those dragoons came poundin' right into the dooryard, sabers swingin'. Our two sentries did what you'd expect smart soldiers to do—they ran. But for all their brains they were ridden right down and skewered like slow pigs.

Then I got a look at the British commander. Thought he was a girl, he had such a soft face and such thick red lips. But he turned out to be maybe the most hated man in the Revolution, a cruel little rat by the name of Banastre Tarleton. He shouted to his men, "Fire into the house!" And before you could draw another breath, glass and bullets was flyin' everywhere.

The two jills on the floor screamed and dove under a table.

I fired through the broken window. Bradford and Wilkinson did the same. And one of the Frenchmen went scuttlin' into the foyer with Spada barkin' behind him. I cursed him, figurin' he was runnin', but he showed more spine than most Frenchmen I'd known and started firin' out the front door.

'Twas Lee whose spine was wobblin'. He shouted, "For God's sake, where is the guard? Damn them, why don't they fire?"

And 'twas like Tarleton could hear him outside, because he shouted, "Run down the guard. Cut up as many of them as you can!"

The jill in the snug was up on her feet, shoutin', "General! General! We have to hide you, General!"

Lee looked at her, then turned to me. "Draper, do go and see what has become of the guard."

Well, sir, I thought, thank you for the privilege of saving your sad ass. Then I went runnin' down the hall to the back door, while Lee scrambled upstairs after the girl, and old Mrs. White put her hands to her head and went shoutin' "Oh-dear-Oh-God-Oh-Jesus-Christ-Almighty!" from one room to another, with the bullets flyin' in the windows and the stupid dog chasin' her now, nippin' at her heels like this was some kind of game.

At the rear door I found four muskets, but no guards attached to them. The guards were runnin' across the field. And then one of the Frenchmen came from somewhere in the house, almost knocked me down, and went runnin' after them. Before you could say "God damn the king," the guards were shot down and a dragoon laid open the Frenchman's skull like a watermelon.

Decided I'd take my chances in the house. So I ran upstairs.

Spada by now had figured out this was no game, so he was runnin' from room to room, barkin' for his master, and the bullets were comin' through the windows so fast 'twas a wonder—and a pity—that he wasn't filled with holes.

I found Lee before the dog did, in the end chamber, lookin' down at the slats on a bed, while his half-drunk whore held back the mattress and said, "Lie on the slats and I'll cover you. They'll never—"

"'Tis an embarrassment," said Lee, wrinklin' his nose.

"No more of an embarrassment than bein' caught here," I shouted.

Lee peered out the window and down the road. "Reinforcements, Draper? Could there be reinforcements?"

"I told you, General, your army's marched."

Just then we heard the front door slam open, and old Mrs. White went screamin' outside and threw herself on her knees in front of Tarleton. "Oh-dear-oh-God-oh-Jesus-Christ-Almighty!"

"Yes, ma'am. I'm here," said Tarleton. "What is it?"

"Don't kill me. Please. And don't kill General Lee. He's in the house."

"So we've heard." Tarleton stood in his stirrups and shouted up at the windows. "If General Lee does not surrender in five minutes, I'll set fire to the house and put everyone in it to the sword!"

Lee said, "For God's sake, Draper, what shall I do?"

"General, you've got us in a very tight spot. There's no way out."

When I put it to him that way, Lee took his fate like a man. Told the girl to put the mattress back where it belonged. Sent me down to surrender.

Soon's I stepped out the door, Tarleton pointed his sword at my chest. "General Lee once commanded our unit. You, sir, are not General Lee."

"Nor do I hope to be him, sir. But you shall have him presently."

Then Lee appeared behind me, still in his slippers and blanket robe. Straightaway he was thrown onto his horse. Then they dragged the Frenchman out, along with two other guards they found hidin' under a tub.

But what about Wilkinson and Bradford?

Lee said to Tarleton, "Could I have my clothes, and my dogs?"

"Of course, General," answered Tarleton with the elaborate politeness that a British officer shows to a captive officer. Then Tarleton looked down at me. "You there, be a good valet and bring out your commander's uniform."

I went back into the house, past the door to the taproom, up the stairs to Lee's room, all the while tryin' to figure out how in the hell I'd get out of this. And where were the others? Got the clothes, went back down, and noticed, in the taproom, that Will Bradford was wearin' the long leather vest of a tavernkeeper and wieldin' a broom on all the broken glass.

He made a little motion with his head, pointin' to a hook on the wall, where the shirt and waistcoat of a tavern servant was hangin'. Well, nothin' ventured, nothin' gained. I shed my hat and coat and turned myself into a servant. Then I went outside and handed the clothes up to Tarleton.

He wrinkled his nose, whether at the smell or the stains, I don't know. Then he looked down at Mrs. White and said, "Thank you, madam. You have rendered us up the only man in America who might do us any harm."

And by God but he was so intent on gettin' away with Lee, and so damn glad he'd captured him, he forgot about the officer he'd sent after the clothes.

I went back into the taproom and watched from a window as they rode away, with Spada and three other dogs barkin' after them. Then I asked Bradford, "Why is it so damn smoky in here?"

As if to answer, Wilkinson dropped from the chimney, took a drink of ale, grabbed the *entre nous* letter, and rode off to rejoin General Gates, who was supposed to be hurrying to Washington's side.

And that, or so I thought, would be the last we'd see of Charles Lee.

## Martha Washington:

Christmas came on, racing winter to see which would arrive first.

And my husband sent me the bad news about General Lee. "Taken by his own imprudence, going three or four miles from his own camp and within twenty of the enemy."

'Twas melancholy intelligence, but there was little he could do about it, so he turned attention to his troubles: "Patsy, I tremble for Philadelphia. It is next to impossible to guard a shore for sixty miles, as we have endeavored to do. In truth, we may have to continue our retreat. Should it come time to fall back to the Alleghenies, I will want you with me. But I shall not quit or resign, no matter what. I cannot entertain an idea that our cause will finally sink, though it may remain for some time under a cloud."

I trembled for my husband.

## Matt Jacobs:

Once Charles Lee was gone and General Sullivan took command, we set to marchin' hard and fast. No more of that three-miles-a-day business. 'Twas ten, then fifteen. Hard-poundin' miles. My feet hurt, my legs . . . spine, too.

And the worst part was, the nice boots I started out with in the summer, there was holes wore through both. Plugged 'em with tree bark. Second worst thing was that we was marchin' to join Washington. And I always worried he might reco'nize me. Third worst was Willard Walt, my new friend. Lord, did he complain, steady as the beatin' of the drum that kept us walkin'. His shoes was wore out altogether. So he wrapped his feet—imagine this—in the skin of a steer slaughtered the day before.

On top of that, 'twas usually snowin' or rainin'. And when the sun come out, it brung on the thaw, and that brung on the mud.

Willard would say, "We're sailormen, Matt. What's the reason for us to be marchin' like this? And all with cow flesh squishin' 'tween our toes?"

"A war," I'd say. "And buy better boots."

"Hell and damnation but there's a war at sea, too, a privateerin' war where a man can make some money. Our enlistments is up in what? Twelve days? December 31. So why are we goin' south, when we'll be turnin' home so soon?"

"A war," I'd say.

"Hell and damnation," he'd say.

By the time we reached the Delaware, just afore Christmas, Washington had crossed to the Pennsylvania side and spread his army up and down the bank like rancid butter. The British had gone back to New York till fightin' season started again, leavin' the Hessians hunkered down in posts all across Jersey, includin' them fine warm barracks at Trenton.

When we come into camp, Washington was sittin' his horse, watchin' us, and I heard him say to Sullivan, "You've only brought two thousand? Two thousand? General Lee promised five."

"I came as quick as I could, sir," said Sullivan, "before we lost more."

I shouldn't have been lookin' at him as I went by, 'cause the General noticed me. He give me a glance. Then he looked back like he knew me from somewhere. At least that's what I thought. Then he said somethin' to Billy Lee.

I just put my head down and went on walkin'.

## Billy Lee:

The General said, "Billy, who was that black boy who just went by?"

I admit it. I lied: "I don't know, sir. Never saw him before in my life."

Some other time the General would've sent me ridin' after him. But not that cold afternoon. He had too much on his mind. He was already turnin' to Sullivan. "You've done a job we appreciate, sir. We'll wait upon General Gates and the Ticonderoga regiments. Fifteen hundred more."

# Hesperus Draper:

S ix hundred men. That's all Horatio Gates brought.
He then beat a personal retreat to the town of Bristol, claimin' he had the dysentery, leavin' Washington
in the lurch, right when he could use some help. Always thought the men called him Granny because of
his round shoulders and his spectacles. I was beginnin' to think it had more to do with his backbone.

A few days later I visited Washington in his little
farmhouse headquarters. Two smoky candles were
burnin' on the table, a smoky fire sputtered on the
hearth. He looked up from his writin' and looked me
over with eyes as red as a bloodhound's.

Figured 'twas the smoke . . . or cryin'. Wouldn't
have blamed him. Any man would cry who'd watched
his army starve, freeze, and all but dissolve on a month-
long retreat. Any man would cry whose two closest
generals were down, one for dysentery and the other
because he was billygoat-randy. And any man would
cry if he knew that those generals had been writin'
*entre nous* letters and that both thought they'd make
a better commander in chief than him.

His voice seemed as bloodshot and tired as his
eyes. "What do you want?"

No sense in beatin' 'round the bush. "A command,
sir . . . I . . . I hear that you're reorganizin' the troops."

"You've heard wrong. I can't reorganize what'll disappear in eight days." He went back to his writin'. "I'll
be down to fourteen hundred effectives soon, most of
them sick, dirty, so thinly clad as to be entirely unfit. . . .
The Hessian commander calls us country clowns."

"But the new Virginia units, sir . . . I'd rather be

marchin' with them than ridin' with General Lee or retreatin'—"

"Retreating?" He looked up like I'd prodded him with the tip of my sword. "I'm sick of retreating, Draper, of being pushed from place to place, of acting with fear, with . . . with a fatal supineness that will destroy us as surely as defeat in battle. Sick of it."

All I wanted was to put some distance 'twixt myself and Lee. And here he was, showin' me the face behind his mask, the face of a man who'd been gettin' beat for most of the last five months, a face as sad as a freezin' mud puddle.

I took a step closer to the table and noticed that he wasn't really writin'. He was playin' with his pen on little strips of paper, like an idle-minded shop clerk. After a bit, he said, "We must defend Philadelphia, Draper, or we lose the loyalty of Pennsylvania, just as we've lost New Jersey. Do you know that Jerseymen tie red rags to their doors to show that they've signed Howe's pledge of loyalty?"

"I saw such on the march, sir."

He dipped his pen again and went on with his little scratchings. "We must use what strength we have, what faith is left in us. There's still hope for a stroke against the enemy."

"That's why I'd like a command, sir."

"There may be something. You'll know soon."

"Thank you, sir." I turned to leave, and as I did, I swept a slip of paper onto the floor. Naturally, I picked it up, and snuck a look at what he'd written. 'Twas the words "Victory or death."

He saw me do it and said, " Yes, Draper. 'Victory or death.' Password and countersign for an attack upon the Hessian post at Trenton."

I was shocked at the boldness of the plan, and shocked that he'd trust me.

"'Victory or death.' Reveal it under *pain* of death."

He'd been beat, but not beaten. Backed into a corner, all but alone, blinkin' bloodshot eyes in a dank little farmhouse, but not beaten. Never thought he was.

## Joseph Reed:

I knew the country up and down the Delaware as well as any, and so the General had dispatched me to scout, to observe, and to act as his representative with General Cadwalader, who had brought out the Philadelphia militia.

After several days, I wrote to the General: "Our affairs are hastening fast to ruin if we do not retrieve them by some happy event. Delay with us now is equal to total defeat."

His response, delivered to me at Bristol, sent a chill down my spine: "Christmas night is the time we have fixed for an attempt on Trenton. For heaven's sake, keep this to yourself, as the discovery of it may prove fatal to us; our numbers, sorry am I to say, being less than I had any conception of; but necessity, dire necessity will, nay *must*, justify my attack."

Immediately, I rode to Trenton to give him my advice on the terrain around the town. I hoped as well that I would be given an assignment in the assault.

## John Adams:

A correspondent of mine was Benjamin Rush, congressman and physician. In December he went out as a volunteer surgeon for Cadwalader's militia, and he described for me a journey he took with Colonel Reed to Washington's headquarters on the Delaware, nearly opposite to Trenton.

Rush said that along the way, Reed recited instances of Washington's want of military skill and ascribed most of the calamities of the campaign to it. Reed concluded by saying, "Doctor, I fear that Washington is only fit to command a regiment."

This, from Washington's closest aide, was no encouragement.

## Joseph Reed:

After listening most politely, though rather coolly, to my advice, Washington dispatched me back to Bristol and Cadwalader, saying my services could best be rendered there. Our job, in the coming attack, would be to cross the Delaware well downstream and move against the Hessian outpost at Mount Holly, which was commanded by Count von Donop. The attack was merely a diversion. I left disappointed, knowing that Washington's trust in me was shaken, but resolved to do my duty.

## Hesperus Draper:

The boys sensed somethin' was up when they were assembled in small groups so that we could read Tom Paine's latest to them. 'Twas called *The American Crisis*: "These are the times that try men's souls. The summer soldier and the sunshine patriot will, in this crisis, shrink from the service of their country; but he that stands it now, deserves the love and thanks of man and woman."

I watched the faces of the men. Didn't see them brighten. 'Twas too cold, and there was eight inches of fresh snow on everything. And for most of those boys, the time for shakin' fists at fancy words was gone. But a few were noddin'. And there were others who usually stood with their eyes on the ground, and they were lookin' right at me, listenin' hard, takin' it all in, and takin' it back to their tents with them.

Next mornin', Christmas Day, the orders come down. We were to parade our men behind the hills approachin' McKonkey's Ferry, startin' at four in the afternoon.

Washington had ordered me to the Fifth Virginia Regiment under Adam Stephen. That's right, Stephen from the French and Indian War, still a big Scots blusterer with a bad taste for barleycorn and a boomin' temper, drunk or sober. Washington had given Stephen's men the honor of crossin' the Delaware first.

The boys thought he did it because he was partial to Virginians. But he'd been doin' his damnedest to show that he wasn't partial to anybody. Fact was, those boys hadn't been in the field as long as most, so most officers still had uniforms; most men still had shoes and blanket coats. I reckoned Washington knew the first units across would be waitin' the longest in the weather, so he picked the ones who might stand the cold the best.

'Twas a bad evenin', fixin' to get worse. Clouds were so low, if a mounted man stood in his stirrups, I swear, his head would disappear in the mist. There was a raw wind blowin' out of the northeast, and blowin' harder as we come down to the ferry landin'. And if the weather wasn't enough to make you cold, all you had to do was look at that river. 'Twas the color of liquid lead, flowin' fast, carrying cakes of dirty ice, some so big they looked like white steers in a stampede.

And the boats that would take us across, they was called Durham boats. Big, strange-lookin' things. But Colonel Glover and his Marblehead lads were swarmin' about the landin', and I reckoned they'd get us through.

## Matt Jacobs:

We never seen nothin' like them Durham boats. They was built for the Delaware River trade . . . carryin' pig iron downstream, haulin' goods back up. Forty or fifty feet long, with eight-foot beams that made 'em ride steady and flat. They didn't draw more than two feet loaded, which was the beauty of 'em. Meant they could carry fifteen tons, or a damn lot of men, in shallow water. And they was curved, bow and stern, like big black canoes, so you never had to turn 'em 'round, which made 'em good for ferry-boats.

But you didn't row 'em. You poled 'em, from narrow platforms runnin' along the gunwales. Polin' was the best way to move upstream in a river with a strong current and a shallow bottom. But we wasn't rivermen. We was seamen. We knew sails and oars, not poles. I said as much to Willard Walt.

He said, "Hell and damnation, when you're a cocksman and you come upon a woman, you don't ask, Is she fat or skinny? You ask, How do I fuck her? Well, we be boatsmen, and these be boats. So how do we pilot 'em?"

Then he hopped aboard a boat and grabbed a pole, and before long, we was movin' the Fifth Virginia across the river. We was boatsmen, sure 'nough.

## Hesperus Draper:

Even after we reached the far bank, you could hear Henry Knox shoutin' to hurry up the loadin'. Big belly. Big voice. He was directin' the loadin' and pushin' hard, but he had to. Not only were we plannin' to move two thousand four hundred men. We were bringin' all eighteen of our field pieces, because there was snow in the wind and a musket is not the most reliable weapon when wet.

Washington's plan—almost as ambitious as the one at Boston—called for us to cross the river nine miles upstream of Trenton, then to march into position and attack from three directions at once before daybreak. Too complicated by half, but timing was the genius of it. A man who's filled his belly with Yuletide cheer in the night is never at his best in the dark before dawn.


## Matt Jacobs:

By seven o'clock we was already behind schedule, and that Henry Knox was bellerin' louder than ever. It had took us that long to get Stephen's regiment across. And things was gettin' worse. That northeast wind was blowin' snow. Ice was gettin' thicker. And my hands felt like they was froze permanent to my pole.

I pulled my hat low to keep out the wind. Didn't do much good, but it made it harder for Washington to see me, whenever our boat come to the landin' and we come into the torchlight.

But I couldn't be worried 'bout Washington, not when I had that current to fight. I lost one pole to a chunk of ice that snapped it right in half. 'Nother time, a chunk hit the boat in the middle of the river and I thought we'd tip over. Made a thund'rous crunch, and all the soldiers in the middle of the boat, they let out with big shouts.

"Hell and damnation!" cried Willard Walt. " 'Stead of bawlin' like babes, grab sticks and start fendin'. Make yourselves useful."

## Billy Lee:

I was a little behind the General, just to his right, ready to do what needed to be done. He was sittin' his horse, watchin' the lads come down to the ferry, and some sad, sorry sights there was to be seen. Sick men, coughin' men, frostbit fingers, and every regiment that went by left bloody footprints on the snow. Yes, sir, red blood on white snow. I swear it, I seen it.

'Bout the time the last of Stephen's men was boardin', a messenger come ridin' up with a letter.

"Letters?" said the General. "What a time to be handin' me letters."

"Sir, General Gates sent me."

"General Gates? Where is he?"

"I left him in Philadelphia this morning."

"What was he doing there?"

"On his way to Congress, sir."

"On his way to Congress?" Then the General looked at Henry Knox and said it again, "On his way to Congress." That was all. Didn't sound mad or disappointed or nothin', but you knew that was how he felt.

Granny Gates was too sick to help, but he felt good enough to go tell some tale to Congress. I got a bad smell from him. And I have a good nose.

Just after that, the General decided to cross the river, like he was too mad to sit still. 'Twas hell wrasslin' our horses aboard the boat, because that snow was comin' steadier now, and it warn't meltin'. Wherever it landed, it left an ice glaze so slick the *men* went slippin', never mind the horses. And the worst part was that you could barely see, 'cause we was only usin' a few lanterns, all masked, in case there was spies on the other side of the river.

I stood at the stern, on the planks laid across the boat for the horses. The General stepped over to a seat just forward of me, and he looked down at the water, which was damn near sloppin' over the sides.

"Don't worry, General," said a skinny little feller workin' a pole on that side. "These boats is so steady, we can load 'em almost to the gunwales."

"Then load 'em, Mr.—"

"Walt. Willard Walt, and that Negro feller standin' right beside you there, that's Matt Jacobs. He saved my life on Long Island, sir."


## Matt Jacobs:

Willard was tellin' the General my life story, and tellin' him my *name*, too!

"Yes, sir," he said, "Matt Jacobs . . . Never liked Negroes till I met him."

Washington give me a squint, but that was all.

He was too busy actin' like the wind and snow wasn't botherin' him, like the weather hadn't been made yet that could bother him. But when he set down by the lantern, I saw that his nose was red, just like any white man's nose who's been out in the cold. And the snow was collectin' on his brows, just like it collects on any man's face, black or white.

We got the order and the boat kicked out from the landin'. One of the horses whinnied and shied some, and I done some shyin' of my own, tryin' to keep out of the General's view. 'Twasn't easy, seein' as my job was to dig in my pole amidships and walk back along that little platform till I reached the stern, pushin' the boat for'ard as I went. Meant I had to walk past Washington twice every minute or so, all the way across the damn river.

There was four of us workin' the poles, and eight or nine fellers fendin' off the ice cakes. Problem was that now there was more ice cakes than clear black water. You'd get hold of one cake, and whilst you was tryin' to lever it away, another would hit it from behind and knock it loose. Then you'd have two cakes comin' at you, and the polemen would pull their poles out of the water to hold the ice off, and when they done that, the boat could swing into the current, and before you knew it, you could be ridin' the nine miles downstream to Trenton, which for certain would spoil the surprise.

We was halfway across with the General, and things was goin' good. I was thinkin' nothin' but good thoughts. Thinkin' about summer. Thinkin' about stew.

Then I heard Willard shout, "See the ice. Matt! See the—"

And *wham!* A chunk of ice hit us amidships. Just like that. I lost my step on that skinny little platform. I slipped. I felt the pole diggin' into the mud and tryin' to lever me off the boat.

"Leave go of the pole!" shouted Willard Walt.

And I did, but I was fallin' still. Figured I was headin' for that slick black water, or right between two cakes of ice, headin' for a drownin' or a crushin' or maybe both. But then a strong hand grabbed me by the collar and pulled me back and held me till I had my balance.

'Twas Washington his very self, sayin', "Stand steady, boy. Stand steady."

I looked him in the face, and even though 'twas dark and the snow was makin' my face look as white as his, I could see it in them small, hard eyes. He knew me. He knew where I come from.

But what he said was, "Well, Matt Jacobs . . . is it victory?"

I didn't know what he meant, so I just started yammerin'.

So he said, "Victory or . . . ?"

"Death, sir?"

"Victory or death. Let's make it victory, Matt Jacobs. Stay in the boat."

## Billy Lee:

'Twas a blowin' blizzard now, but I was sweatin', you can bet.

Finally somebody shoved a pole into Matt's hands, and the boy got hisself back to work. None too quick if you asked me. And we got to the other side of the river, none too quick neither.

There was torches burnin' around the ferry-house, like you'd expect. But no campfires. General said campfires would throw a glow into the sky and give us away. So the men stood or crouched where they could, keepin' out of the wind.

The General watched our boat pull away as another came slippin' in.

And I said, "You want your horse, sir?"

"No. And Billy, the Negro, the one I asked about, I found out his name."

"Sir?"

"Matt Jacobs . . . from Marblehead."

Well, you know how he don't show nothin'? 'Tis easier to do in the snow and cold. He didn't show me nothin' about his thinkin' right then. But he knew who that boy was. And he knew that I knew and that I'd probably knew all along.

## Alexander Hamilton:

Time grew short, and the storm grew sharper. The floating ice in the river made the labor almost impossible. But it was as if the men on those boats took their perseverance from the General.

By two o'clock in the morning, the troops were all on the Jersey side; in another hour, the last of our field pieces and Henry Knox reached the landing.

By then we were four hours behind schedule and the snow was turning to a bitter sleet.

The General called to Knox. "Is that it, Colonel?"

"Yes, sir." Knox pointed to his watch. "But we'll never reach Trenton before daybreak."

"Henry," he said, "we can't retreat without being discovered. Having the Hessians attack us while we're recrossing the river would be more dangerous than striking them now. We're pushing on at all events."

Those words were like hot tea in my frozen belly. I wanted no retreating after all we had gone through.

None of us had ever seen Washington so determined. In the most calm and collected fashion, he delivered orders to Generals Greene and Sullivan to prepare their divisions.

The cry of "Shoulder firelocks!" was heard up and down the line.

I called to my men to prepare their limbers, and our frozen army stepped off into the howling storm.

## Hesperus Draper:

That night was as dark as the inside of a hat. Washington ordered that there be no flames, except in masked lanterns. No talkin' in the ranks. And no steppin' out of the line of march.

Every man added a few rules of his own: Don't raise your head into the sleet; instead, follow the tracks right in front of you. No sittin' if the column stopped, because those who sat might freeze in place. No closin' your eyes and tryin' to sleep on your feet, because it couldn't be done. No complainin' at the lad who stepped on your heels, because he was just keepin' close enough to you to block the wind, and you were doin' the same to the lad in front of you. And no despair, because that could kill you as quick as the weather.

And you know, for how miserable it was, for how wet and heavy that damnable snow was, for how tired those boys were, they kept on, through the darkest, wettest, snowiest woods that ever I'd seen.

And the whole time, Washington went ridin' back and forth, urgin' the men along and, when they straggled, tellin' 'em, "For God's sake, stay together. Stay with your officers."

The column split at Bear Tavern. Sullivan's unit went right, Greene's unit, with Washington and the Virginians, went left. Washington liked his complicated plans. If they worked, they made a general look like a genius. But most of the time, in battle, nothin' works the way it's planned, particularly if the plan calls for officers to work from watches all set to the same time. And at Bear Tavern, we all set our watches to six o'clock.

A bit more than an hour till light. But it would be a grim, gray dawn when it came. All the better for us. And that boomin' wind and blowin' sleet, they was allies, too, no matter how miserable. They muffled the sound of our limber wheels. And they lulled sleepin' Hessians into sleepin' on.

Mean bastard fighters, those Hessians, but fighters for pay. They couldn't understand what would bring men out into a storm like this. They couldn't understand that some men fought for ideas, or that some ideas were grand, like freedom, and some were personal, like keepin' a good reputation or rescuin' one about to sink under the weight of five weeks of runnin'.

Around six-thirty, a rider come from Sullivan's column with a message. He said, "Sir, General Sullivan sends his compliments."

"What is it?" snapped Washington. There was nothin' in *The Rules of Civility* on how to act durin' a forced night march through a sleet storm.

"General Sullivan says his men have wet flints and flashpans. He doesn't think their muskets will fire."

"Then tell him to use the bayonet," said Washington. "Tell him to advance and charge. I'm determined to take Trenton."

And even though we didn't attack till after eight o'clock, full daylight, the surprise was complete.

The Fifth Virginia drove in the Hessian pickets. Then we heard the beatin' of drums and the blast of a bugle at the west end of town. That was followed by the low thumpin' boom of a field piece—the signal that Sullivan's men were in position.

Washington's face lit up brighter than a box of candles in a house fire.

And now the wisdom of bringin' all eighteen cannon came clear.

Brave men on a bright summer day can lose their nerve before a cannonade. Imagine a Hessian with a rum-drunk headache, hearin' the boomin' of big guns and the screamin' of his sergeant at dawn. He comes tumblin' into a sleet storm, half dressed and half asleep. The muzzle flash of the cannon clears his mind. So he tries to form up and fight. But the iron balls start comin' at him like he's a ninepin on a rich man's lawn, while the grapeshot tears up the half-dressed men in his half-dressed ranks.

And all around him, at the head of every street, on his flanks, inside the houses, and runnin' from door to door, are dark masses of men . . . rebels in rabble who've appeared from the storm, not like soldiers at all, but like feral dogs come to tear him apart, or maybe like dark angels come to send him to hell.

'Twas more than enough to convince twelve hundred Hessians to ground their arms.

When it was over, Henry Knox shouted, "What a glorious morn! The hurry, fright, and confusion of those poor fellows, 'tis what I expect to see when the last trump shall sound." He talked that way, big and blustery and full of holy blasphemy, but his cannon had earned him the right to talk any way he wanted.

Within a few days, Hessians were withdrawin' from their posts all along the Delaware.

And Jerseyites—good patriots and smart weather-cocks all—started pullin' the red rags from their doors, like they'd never meant to put them up in the first place.

C.D.—*Washington had made the stroke he hoped for. He had given Americans a victory, however small. He had given them hope. Then he recrossed the Delaware, to give his men rest, rum, and a fair accounting of all they had seized from the Hessians.*

*Congress gave him, for a term of six months, "full, ample, and complete" powers to organize and supply his army. It was like making him dictator.*

*But he wrote to Congress: "Instead of thinking myself freed from civil obligations by this confidence, I shall bear in mind that as the sword was the last resort for the preservation of our liberties, so it ought to be the first to be laid aside."*

*But his victory had done little to stem the tide rising to destroy his army.*

*On January 1, hundreds of enlistments were to end. And though the victory at Trenton had brought local militia flocking to the cause, his military concoction needed the gluten of veteran troops. So once more he crossed the Delaware.*

## Joseph Reed:

Students of warfare are sometimes befuddled by Washington's decision to bring his army back to Trenton.

I admit that I urged him to do it. In reconnoitering the Jersey side, I had found the Hessians had all but deserted the state. And there was, as yet, no indication of retaliation from the British. It seemed that we were throwing away an opportunity to regain all the territory we had surrendered.

I was most gratified at Washington's response: he had already made the decision. The regiments were on the way. He would try to retake the Jerseys. And he hoped that in returning to the scene of their victory, his men would be moved when he entreated them to stay past their enlistments.

## Matt Jacobs:

I waited for the General to send someone to arrest me, someone to come and take me back to Mount Vernon. But I didn't run. I was through runnin'. 'Sides, where would I run to? I figured, if the General sent me back, I'd get to see my mama and papa, then run away again.

But the way things was headed, I don't reckon the General was plannin' on arrestin' anyone who could shoulder a musket.

A few days before New Year's, he brought us back to Trenton. Then he ordered two New England regiments—maybe eight hundred men—into the orchard on the east side of town.

We knew what this was about. 'Twas mostly New Englanders whose enlistments was endin'. Colonel Glover already told the General we was leavin', and nothin' would change our minds. We was damn-near wore out from marchin', and we wanted some of that privateerin' money, too.

Washington sat on his horse and watched us march in. He had his staff with him, a line of drummer boys, too. He barely moved his head as we went past, but I looked right at him. Wasn't hidin' my face no more. No, sir.

I tried to find a place to stand where the snow was trampled, so it wouldn't get in the holes in my boots. 'Twas all I was worried about, 'cause my mind was made up, like everybody else's. I was goin' back to Marblehead.

After we was in position, Washington come forward on that big horse, so's he could look out over us. You didn't see him give speeches much. And he wasn't one to mix with his men. There was generals, and they rode horses, and there was soldiers, and they walked. Simple as that.

But he sat there, and with a voice that maybe half the men could hear, he told us what a fine job we done in the battle, and how he 'preciated it, and if we'd stay just six more weeks, we'd all get a bounty of ten dollars.

Willard Walt whispered, "Is that Continental paper or gold?"

I said, "Paper, I reckon."

"Then I don't want it. They keep printin' that money, pretty soon it won't be good for nothin' but cartridge rollin'."

Washington said, "Now, men, step out and show your patriotism."

"I'd step out," Willard whispered, "but my feet is killin' me." He'd gotten rid of the beef skins. Now he was wearin' boots that was too small. Pulled 'em off a dead Hessian.

The drummers made a roll that went echoin' off the buildings of the town. But not a man of any company stepped out. 'Twas so silent I thought we was standin' in a graveyard, 'stead of an orchard.

But Washington's face didn't change a bit. Only thing I noticed was that the steam from his breath seemed to come a little faster.

Then a wind blew over. First it rattled in the trees; then it fluttered the scarves of them lucky enough to have scarves. The lad to my right shivered. Somebody else coughed. Those boys was plain done in.

Willard Walt whispered, "I'm goin' home, Matt. I miss my wife."

"We all miss our wives," whispered another of the Negro boys, Sam Brisby.

Washington's horse give a big snort, and Washington turned him toward the town. I figured, that was the end of that.

But all of a sudden he reined the horse and come back and started ridin' back and forth in front of the ranks, like this was too important to quit on. And he shouted, so everyone could hear, "My brave fellows! You've done all I asked you to do, more than could be expected."

Willard whispered, "That's the truth."

"But your country is at stake—your wives, your houses, all that you hold dear." At that last part, he stopped in front of me and looked down. Didn't look long, but 'twas as if he was pinnin' me to the ground with them words. 'Twas freedom I held dear.

Then he kicked the horse again and shouted out, so they could hear him in the back ranks, "You've worn yourselves out with fatigue and hardship, but we know not how to spare you."

'Twas like he was tryin' to look into the hollow eyes of every hungry man on that field. "If you'll stay only one month longer, you'll render a service to the cause of liberty, and to your country, that will be invaluable."

And he finished, in a pleadin' voice, "Men, we're living the crisis that will decide our destiny. We need you."

He stopped, like he was tryin' to think of more to say. Then he backed his horse up again and give the drummers another nod.

## Hesperus Draper:

He was no man to beg. But he'd just finished as plain a beggin' speech as any man ever made. He didn't climb down from his horse, though. His horse was like his stage, and a good actor stayed on the stage. But this actor knew, on pure instinct, how to play to the groundlings. So he played the father in need of help from his sons.

And then the drums rolled again.

And we waited, with the wind blowin' little funnels of snow across the orchard. Finally a feller stepped forward, a Rhode Islander. Then one of his mates did the same. And I heard a man in another company say,

"I'll do it if they will." And another one said, "We come this far, I reckon we can go a little farther." And before long, up and down the line, men were steppin' out, standin' straight in the snow, all except the sickest and the weakest.

The only men who weren't comin' out were the ones that I was watchin' closest—the Marbleheaders.

## Matt Jacobs:

Not a one of us moved till that Negro boy, Sam Brisby, he went and done it.

Willard muttered, "Damn fool."

"I don't know," I said. My eyes was on Washington. He was noddin', like he was glad of what he was seein', and proud, too.

"What do you mean, you don't know?" asked Willard.

Right then my throat tightened up. But I done it. I said, "I'm stayin' too." And I stepped forward.

"Well, damn you, Matt Jacobs," Willard whispered about as loud as a man could. "They always said niggers was dumb. We can be on the deck of a ship in two weeks, and rakin' in prize money a week later. Step back into line here. Nobody seen you."

I looked over my shoulder. "I'm stayin', Willard. And I ain't dumb."

"Hell and damnation, Matt. If you stay, I have to stay."

"No you don't."

"But you saved my life."

"You saved mine, too. Go home."

"Ah, hell and damnation." And Willard Walt stepped forward.

Sergeant asked the General, "Should I get 'em all to sign, sir?"

"No. Men who show such spirit can be taken at their word."

Out of four hundred in our regiment, maybe forty stayed. We formed up with Colonel Shepard. And I fought for what I held dear.


## Joseph Reed:

In the end his speech and the entreaties of other officers persuaded some twelve hundred New Englanders to stay. And in the days to come we would need every one, as we needed the twelve hundred New Englanders who went home, and the hundreds from other units who did the same.

For on December 31, while on a reconnaissance trip with six members of the Philadelphia Light Horse, I came upon a farmhouse just south of Princeton. A party of British dragoons had stopped there and were, at that moment, about the business of capturing a savory mince pie from a New Jersey mother.

We moved against this enemy, surrounding them even as they surrounded the pie. Twelve British dragoons, well armed, their pieces loaded, having the advantage of the house, surrendered to seven horsemen, six of whom had never seen the enemy before.

I said to my men, "When you tell this story, don't say what heroes you are. Say that one Philadelphia Light Horse can take two British dragoons any day."

The men liked that. But Washington did not like what we learned from those dragoons: a large British force under Cornwallis was driving south. They would be in Princeton the next day, Trenton the day after that.

"Cornwallis moves faster than General Howe, sir," I said.

"Too fast," answered Washington.

We might have fled back across the Delaware, but our boats had been dispersed up and down the river, as Washington had been making plans for moving farther into New Jersey. He had ordered unit officers to "hold themselves in readiness to advance at a moment's warning." Now, he sent parties north to harass Cornwallis, while issuing orders to strengthen our position on the high ground south of Trenton, with the Delaware at our back and the Assunpink Creek before us.

The next day, light rain and a January thaw turned the Post Road to mud. Add to this the fine harassing work of Colonel Hand's riflemen, and it took the fast-flying Cornwallis most of another day to cover that last eleven miles to Trenton.

There was sharp fighting in the town. Washington had ordered Hand to slow the enemy until dark, so his riflemen fired from buildings and from behind fences, falling back steadily but just slowly enough to keep the enemy from attacking our positions that day. It was not until four o'clock that the riflemen reached the stone bridge across the Assunpink.

And Washington rode out to urge them to safety. He took a position on the Trenton side of the bridge and sat his horse resolutely, like a caped beacon in the gathering gloom. Enemy bullets were flying around him and Knox's artillery was thundering from behind, but he never flinched. Neither, according to reliable reports, did his horse.

Only when all the riflemen were safely within our lines did Washington come back across the bridge and leave its defense to our cannon.

## Hesperus Draper:

E ven after turnin' the worm at Trenton, Washington was still a blunderer. There were now eight thousand enemy troops at our front, with nothin' but a little six-foot creek keepin' 'em where they was. At our rear was the Delaware—too frozen to row across, but not frozen enough to run across. And even if Knox's cannon kept the British from crossin' that bridge, there were fords on that creek and, come dawn, Cornwallis would find them.

Then we'd have British in our front, and British on our flank. And the two thousand or so Continentals we had left, and the three thousand militia from Pennsylvania and New Jersey, they'd be trapped.

"A worse spot than Long Island," I said to John Haslet. He and I were lookin' out at the British torches and campfires lightin' up Trenton.

"From one bad spot to another," said Haslet, grim as a pallbearer. "And me with not a man to command." His fine unit of Delawares had all refused the bounty and gone home. He just shook his head. "I'll say it again: Would to heaven that General Lee were here."

"You wouldn't say that if you'd been with him in the Jerseys," I told him.

The day had been warm. Now the wind was kickin' up from the northwest. Haslet buttoned his coat across his neck. "Lee or not, tomorrow will be very hard."

"If I was Cornwallis, I'd come tonight."

Over on the other side of the Assunpink, some British officers were tellin' Cornwallis the same thing, so the story goes. But Cornwallis wouldn't move. His troops were exhausted. 'Twas dark. And they had Washington right where they wanted him. He told his officers, "We'll go over and bag the fox in the morning."

To which a British officer is supposed to have answered, "If Washington is half the general I think him to be, he won't be there in the morning."

## Joseph Reed:

Others have taken credit for proposing our escape route that night. Some have even tried to give it to me. I would be proud to take it, considering that I have been blamed for much. But I only provided tactical information.

It was Washington who made the proposal that saved the army and demonstrated, once and for all, what a bold leader he could be.

That night we gathered for a conference in a cold farmhouse. The faces were long, the lamps hung low, the shadows dark. We were trapped.

Henry Knox spoke first. "I have forty cannon facing the enemy. You saw their work today. If Cornwallis sends columns across that bridge, you'll see their work tomorrow."

"A spirited opinion, General," said Washington.

"I believe our right flank is too vulnerable to make a stand, sir," said Nathanael Greene. "I propose a retreat, back along the riverbank."

"We'll simply be running again," answered Washington. "At length, we'll be forced to turn and fight, most likely on ground not of our choosing." He looked at me, "You grew up here, Colonel Reed. You attended the college at Princeton."

"Yes, sir."

"Is there not a secondary road to Princeton, one that runs parallel to the Post Road? One by which we might slip around the British left?"

I could sense a stirring in the smoky little room. Washington may have blundered, but remember the mind that rose when the spirits of others fell, the mind made for crisis.

"There's a new road, sir," I said, "called the Quaker Road. It runs through woodlands and the Barrens and reaches the Post Road a mile south of Princeton."

"Good," said Washington.

And now Greene said, "Instead of standing or running, sir, perhaps we might take this new road and get in the enemy's rear by a march upon Princeton."

"First Princeton," said Washington, "then the British supplies at Brunswick."

"But the road, sir," said Henry Knox. "I've heard 'tis mostly mud and stumps. How will we move the artillery?"

"Henry," said Washington, "you've dragged those guns all over America. Find a way to pull them eleven miles to Princeton."

And then Billy Lee spoke up. "Sir, I just been outside. And the wind's comin' up good. Puddles is icin' up'. Ground'll be froze solid 'fore long."

Washington looked at us and said, "There you have it, gentlemen. Providence is with us."

## Hesperus Draper:

We kept the fires burnin'. We kept a small rear guard scrapin' shovels through the night. We muffled the wheels of our cannon and their limbers and wrapped the hooves of the horses, too. Officers unhitched their hangers so they wouldn't rattle. And for the second time in six months, we snuck away, leavin' the British with an empty bag.

Only problem was that we were marchin' deeper into enemy-held territory. Retreatin' in the wrong direction, you might say. We were also pit-belly hungry and dog-ass tired. I actually saw men walkin' while they was sound asleep. Hell, I fell asleep myself on my horse, so I got down and walked. Felt better once the sky got light, but I still thought this was Washington's wildest roll of the dice yet.

The sun come up as bright as we'd seen in a month. 'Twas bitter cold, but dry and calm. No wind at all. And the hoarfrost trimmed rail fences and trees and everything else.

We came to a fork in this road, and Washington sent General Mercer and three hundred men off to the left to destroy a bridge about a half mile away on the Post Road.

My Virginians moved toward Princeton as part of Sullivan's division, one of the most mixed-up brigades in the history of warfare. We had Virginia Continentals; Colonel Hand's Pennsylvania riflemen; Shepard's regiment, includin' a little remnant of Marblehead men; and New Englanders from Rhode Island, New Hampshire, and Massachusetts. And behind us by about a thousand yards were Cadwalader's Pennsylvania militia. What we had was truly Continental, also truly tired, cold, and hungry.

A low run of hills screened us from the Post Road, and up ahead, across the fields, we could see the rooves of the Princeton College. Then we heard the sound of musket fire, followed quick by the bangin' of several field pieces, all comin' from the direction of Mercer and the bridge.

Straight off, Washington had half of us turned and movin' back toward the noise—volleys, cannon blasts, screamin' horses, shoutin' men. It all sounded like a . . . a bad dream on such a bright calm morning.

Comin' over a low ridge, we saw two American cannon, dug in near a farmhouse, holdin' off a slew of redcoats in an orchard below them.

Mercer had run into two regiments of British, four or five hundred men, hurryin' down the Post Road to Trenton.

The British were as surprised to see him as he was to see them. But they rallied quick. They drove in Mercer with a volley and a bayonet charge. Then they turned on Cadwalader's Pennsylvanians, who did what militia always did when bayonets flashed—lost their nerve and ran.

Now, 'twas just the two cannon keepin' the British at bay in the orchard, whilst John Haslet tried to order up the men from Mercer's unit, because Mercer was down on the field, and from the way the British were workin' him over, we'd find more bayonet holes than buttonholes in his coat.

I arrived just in time to see Haslet take a musket ball in the head. Hadn't seen anyone I cared about shot down on a battlefield in a long time. Damn hard puttin' it out of my head, but I had to. Because this was bad. If the British pushed through at that farmhouse, they'd split our whole column in half.

But Washington was takin' command, shoutin' to me and Colonel Hand: "Form up on the right of the cannon. Wait for my order. I'll bring up the Pennsylvanians."

Then he went gallopin' along the crest of the rise, past the farmhouse, and into the stand of trees where those Pennsylvanians were huddled.

I don't know what magic he worked on them, bein' so busy pullin' my own men into line and duckin' the musket balls that was blowin' past my ears.

They say he shouted, "Parade with us, boys! There's but a handful of the enemy over there, and we'll have them presently."

And this time he didn't need a ridin' crop to make them obey, because they believed him. They'd never done more than practice on their town greens, but they came marchin' out of the woods like regulars, with the big man on the bay horse leadin' 'em.

And I thought, What a target. Decided to dismount and lead my men on foot.

Washington stretched a line of men all the way across that low hill—militia on the left and Continental veterans on the right, with a force of tough, blooded British regulars holdin' their red formations in the orchard and field before us, darin' us to attack and hopin' to keep us on this field till reinforcements arrived.

And now came the moment when George Washington proved what kind of man he was. No matter what I've said, or what I'll say, I'll always admire him for that day at Princeton.

He pulled off his hat, waved it, and shouted, "Forward!"

And all of us kicked on his order, a big, lurchin', ragged line of soldiers comin' down the rise, crunchin' over the snow.

But we didn't scare the British, not one damn bit. They could see our rags and tatters. Figured we'd fight like rags and tatters, too. Their sergeants, all as confident as cocks, were shoutin', "Make ready! Prepare to fire by volley!"

But Washington didn't stop us until the two lines were thirty yards apart, prime range for a musket. Then he shouted, "Halt!"

I'd been in some big fights before, but I'd never been in somethin' like this. 'Twas like a giant duel, a long brown line of men countin' off the steps and closin' with the line of redcoats slashed across the snow. And the officers were bellowin' orders, and the bravest—or the most frightened—of the men were shoutin' across those thirty yards at each other, and I was callin', "Make ready!" to my men. And the muskets were all rattlin' into place. And . . .

Just before the British commander shouted it, Washington screamed, "Fire!"

## Billy Lee:

I was settin' on the little rise by the farmhouse.

The second I heard the first primin' powder pop, I yanked off my hat and put it over my face. I couldn't watch my master shot down, and I didn't see how nothin' else could happen. He was in between them two armies, a big man on a white horse, with hundreds of muskets pointin' at him from both sides.

Them muskets went off all at once, and the sound hit me so hard in my stomach, I almost puked in my hat.

Then I heard men screamin' and shoutin', and I just had to take the hat from my eyes. I thought I'd see British bayonets comin' up the rise through the smoke, but what I saw was our boys, runnin' lickety-split after the tail-turned redcoats.

And the General? Why, he was still there on the horse, wavin' his hat, and shoutin', "It's a fine fox chase my boys! Run them to ground."

## Hesperus Draper:

'Twas the bravest damn thing I'd ever seen, or the dumbest. But Washington himself carried the day. There was no question about it.

And by God, but he couldn't stop himself.

When those British turned and ran, he ran right after them, his army hootin' and hollerin' behind him.

His aides looked mighty nervous, because he was out of sight for quite some time. But the man that

Cornwallis had called a fox the night before went out and bagged about a hundred British prisoners that mornin'.

Meanwhile Sullivan moved against the regiment in front of him. He forced the British back into Nassau Hall at King's College, and Alexander Hamilton set up his artillery outside. Fired two shots. One hit the buildin'. Another one, so the story goes, went through an open window and took off the head of King George in the portrait on the wall. The British must've seen that as a bad sign, because they come surrenderin' out in short order.

## Alexander Hamilton:

The stories of beheading King George in Nassau Hall are true. I'm afraid that other stories are also true. Once the British troops had surrendered to us and were properly subdued, our men ate the British breakfasts and collected the British stores. Then they looted the town.

They believed it a Tory stronghold, so they took it upon themselves to liberate what they would from the houses of patriotic Americans who had already been oppressed by Hessians and British. The looting was so widespread that no punishment could be fairly administered, and the enemy were moving toward us so quickly that there was not time to make amends.

But that outbreak of negative passion could not besmirch the achievement of George Washington during that miraculous ten days. Looking back upon it all now, I see that the enterprises of Trenton and Princeton were the dawning of that bright day which afterward broke forth with such resplendent luster.

*c.d.—All those I interviewed agreed that a push to Brunswick and the British supply depot might have changed the course of the war even more dramatically than those two victories. But Washington's men were exhausted, and Cornwallis, furious at being outwitted, was hurrying from Trenton. So Washington retreated to the hills around Morristown, which were virtually impregnable. Winter descended, the British withdrew all but a token force from the Jerseys, and Washington was a greater hero than ever.*

## Hesperus Draper:

I wanted to go home. Wasn't supposed to, but I had to. Went to Adam Stephen and told him I was sick. 'Twas no lie. I was sick in the heart at havin' been away from my wife for eighteen months. Begged Stephen to give me a pass.

"How am I to be certain that you'll come back?" he asked.

"I give you my word."

Stephen looked over my request. "You know, the lads you led at Princeton, they startin' to call themselves Draper's Regiment. What do I tell them? What do I tell the General?"

"Tell them the truth. Tell them I'm sick. Tell the General I'm happy to keep fightin', so long's I can go home to check on the printin' business now and then. Tell him there's two things made of lead that matter in this fight—musket balls and movable type."

A week later I came up to the offices of what was now called Draper Importin' and Printin'. But there wasn't much importin' goin' on. The British were try-in' to blockade the coast, and one place where they'd had some luck was at the mouth of the Chesapeake. But that couldn't be the reason that the door was draped in black crepe.

I had an inklin' on what it might be. Leastways I hoped it was my uncle and not . . . not somebody else.

Instead of the old men who'd once been hunched over ledgers in the downstairs office, there were young men hunched over type cases. They looked at me, in my officer's coat and dirty breeches, like I was an Injun or somethin'.

I hurried through that room and went up the stairs to my uncle's office. Eli was sittin' at the door, sound asleep.

I pushed open the door, and sittin' behind the desk . . . was my Charlotte.

She didn't glance up as the door swung open. She was too engrossed in the young man sittin' in the chair on the other side of her desk. He was holdin' a newspaper, and I was almost jealous at the attention she was giving him.

He said, "Here's the *Pennsylvania Journal* on Washington: 'If there are spots on his character, they are like spots on the sun, only discernible by the magnifying powers of the telescope. Had he lived in the days of idolatry, he had been worshiped as a god.' "

Charlotte asked the young man, "Do you think we should print that?"

"It's what people are thinking."

"It's a mite strong," she said. "I wonder what my husband would say."

And I sent a loud voice from the doorway: "He'd say, 'Washington is a god and will remain so until things go wrong. Then they'll damn him again.'"

And the smile she gave me erased any jealousy and all the pain.

She told the young man, who turned out to be John Hereford, to print whatever he wanted. Then the two of us rushed arm in arm through the streets of Alexandria to the little house where we'd lived for so long. I will tell you honestly that I can hardly remember any grief that day. My uncle was gone, but he had been goin' slowly for many years. And he'd left everything to me.

What I still tingle at is the joy of that reunion. Keep your Chinese potions and your oysters. Absence is the best aphrodisiac known to man. And a hot bath. Long talk with your wife works, too. So I had the bath, then we tumbled, then talked, then tumbled, then talked, then . . . talked some more. Don't forget I was forty-four by then. When I finally went to sleep, she was readin' somethin' I'd brought her—my copy of *The American Crisis*.

Fifteen minutes later she was nudgin' me awake the way she used to. Nothin' had ever felt better in my life than bein' in that bed, with her cold feet against mine and that elbow in my ribs.

"Hess . . . Hess . . . we should print this. We should print everything he writes from now on. Listen: 'Tyranny, like hell, is not easily conquered; yet the harder the conflict, the more glorious the triumph. What we obtain too cheap, we esteem too lightly. Heaven knows how to put a proper price upon its goods; and it would be strange indeed if so celestial an article as freedom should not be highly rated.' "

C.D.—*By May 1800, I had made my way to France, to a château called La Grange, some thirty miles southeast of Paris. There I was privileged to talk for the better part of a week with my next narrator, who spoke excellent English.*

# The Narrative of the Marquis de Lafayette:

I first came into the presence of General Washington in July of 1777 in the City Tavern in Philadelphia. I picked him out immediately by the majesty of his face and figure. I could not know then how close our bond would become, but it is safe to say that we became as father and son.

I never knew my real father. He was a colonel in the French army, killed when I was only two. I inherited his titles and wealth, but at the age of eleven I lost my mother and grandfather also. I was sixteen and my beloved Adrienne fourteen when a marriage was arranged for us.

So you see, I had lived much life in a very short time when Silas Deane, America's commissioner in Paris, began recruiting French officers to his country's cause. He promised high rank and high pay to those who would bring European training to the battlefields of America, and such service was something that my own country smiled upon.

I did not deceive myself, however. My captaincy in the French army had come not because of experience but because of the influence of my family. Deane knew of this influence, and he did not deceive himself either. A happy Lafayette would be a strong ally at the Court of Versailles. And so it was that I was made a major general in the American army at the age of twenty.

From the first moment that I arrived in America, I was in love with the land and the people. In them were simplicity of manners, willingness to oblige, love of country and liberty, and an easy equality. People ask me often, was I a believer in republicanism at this time? I do not say yes and I do not say no. I say only that America opened my eyes.

General Washington greeted me with cool politeness. I knew he was measuring me, as he must have measured all the many men who sought to impress him, and his eyes, of course, fell upon the major general's sash which now I was wearing.

He had been told that my rank was to be ceremonial. This I did not know.

I was hoping to be given a division. This he did not know.

He thanked me for coming. He complimented my zeal and invited me to reside in his house as a member of his military family in the coming campaign.

This offer was accepted with the same frankness with which it was made.

"Of course," he went on, "this is a republican army.

Poor in material comforts and military trappings. We should be embarrassed to show ourselves before an officer who has just left French troops."

I answered in the best way, with the truth: "Mon Général, I have come to learn and not to teach."

And that modest tone, which was not common in most of the Europeans who came to him, produced a very good effect. I could tell, because he smiled.

## Alexander Hamilton:

I had become an aide to His Excellency in the winter. Joseph Reed had resigned. Though Washington had sought to obtain for him the position of brigadier of cavalry, and the two men had expressed their friendship in letters, they were moving apart. At least, Reed had left the army for Congress, where it was hoped he would serve our purposes.

So the General needed more hands for the great volume of papers that demanded his attention. He told me, "My time is so taken up at my desk that I am obliged to neglect many essential parts of my duty; it is absolutely necessary for me to have persons who can think for me, as well as execute my orders."

I always sought to keep my happiness independent of the caprices of others. But I could not deny the General's great personal power. He had put on the face of fortitude and resolution, even while our affairs were at the lowest ebb and the continent almost in a state of despair.

So I took the position, and soon enough I was learning to write in Washington's hand as well as his voice, so that he could simply sign his name to a letter or an order and it would appear that he had written the whole of it.

That summer we spent much time and energy trying to ascertain the intentions of the enemy. General Howe had left New York and taken to his ships. His evident target was Philadelphia, but we could not be certain. So back and forth we marched, hoping to meet him wherever he came ashore. At such a time it was of little merit for Washington to be placating European officers like Lafayette, who was then arrogantly pressing to be given a field command.

The General expressed his irritation over Lafayette to Congress: "What the designs of Congress respecting this gentleman are, and what line of conduct I am to pursue, I know no more than a child unborn, and beg to be instructed. If Congress meant that this rank should be unaccompanied by command, I wish it had been sufficiently explained to the Marquis."

The answer: "Depend on it that Congress never meant he should have a command, nor will it countenance him in his applications."

There then arrived several letters from France, from Silas Deane and, more importantly, from our emissary, Benjamin Franklin.

Deane spoke directly of the value of the Marquis to America. "A generous reception of him will do us infinite service."

Franklin agreed with that but found a way to make personal the relations of self-interested states: "I have met his beautiful young wife, who is big with child. For her sake particularly, we hope his bravery and ardent desire to distinguish himself will be restrained by the General's prudence. As there are a number of very worthy persons here who interest themselves in the welfare of that amiable young nobleman, advise him with a friendly affection."

"I'll take Dr. Franklin's advice," the General told me. "Of all the Europeans, the young Marquis seems the most worthy of friendship despite his pretensions as to rank."

Soon thereafter, Lafayette came to the General's office. For all I had heard, I like him immediately.

The General delivered him the bad news: "Marquis, I must tell you that your commission, in the eyes of Congress, is considered entirely ceremonial."

Though Lafayette made some sounds of protest, the General quieted him quickly and gently. "Nevertheless, you can rely on me, my dear Marquis, that I will continue to treat you as a father and a friend."

It was my impression that the Marquis took the General's words far more seriously than the General may have meant them. A father and a friend were powerful pronouncements for a fatherless boy so far from home.

I, on the other hand, had from the beginning determined that if the General offered friendship to me, I would accept it in a manner which showed that I had no inclination to court it and that I wished to stand rather on a footing of military confidence than private attachment.

This, perhaps, is why my friendship with Lafayette endured. We were as brothers in the General's family, but not rivals for his affections.

## The Marquis de Lafayette:

"Father and friend." He said this to me on a day that I now look back upon as one of the most important in my life.

And all during that summer's campaign in Pennsylvania, and all during the years that followed, he never wavered from that promise. I never wavered in my affection for him or in my loyalty.

C.D.—*Late that summer, Howe finally satisfied everyone's curiosity by moving on Philadelphia. Washington tried to stop him at Brandywine Creek and failed, though Lafayette distinguished himself and sustained a bloody leg wound.*

*None other than Dr. James Craik, now assistant director general of the hospital department, tended the Marquis and commented to me on both the "warmth of the young man" and "the deep, personal concern of the General."*

*Of greater concern were the British. In October, Washington attacked at Germantown and was driven back, leaving Philadelphia firmly in the hands of Lord Howe. But then transcendent news arrived: at Saratoga the Army of the Northern Department, under Horatio Gates, had defeated a British army invading from Canada, thereby dashing British hopes of driving a wedge down the Hudson.*

*Though the victory was due in greater part to the battlefield diligence of Benedict Arnold than to the strategic caution of Gates, the latter ignored Arnold in his dispatch. He ignored Washington, too, sending the dispatch directly to Congress, suggesting that they, and not the commander in chief, were his superiors.*

*Washington wrote to Gates, with controlled fury: "I cannot but regret that a matter of such magnitude should have reached me by report only or through letters not bearing that authenticity which it would have received by a line under your signature."*

*Gates issued a tepid apology.*

*As winter came on, Washington lingered in the hills west of Philadelphia, trying to hold his army together and hold Howe in check, but lacking the strength to dislodge him. There were some who began to suggest that it was skill Washington lacked. Soon the name of Gates was being whispered as a replacement for him, in Congress and in the shadowy corners of cold canvas tents, where conspiracy and cabal grew like mushrooms.*

## Abigail Adams:

December 18 was decreed by Congress to be a day of thanksgiving for the victory in Saratoga, which had caused my husband to rejoice for many reasons.

He wrote me that he was happy that the victory was "not immediately due to the commander in chief, nor to the southern troops. If it had been, idolatry and adulation would have been unbounded; so excessive as to endanger our liberties. Now at least we can allow a certain citizen to be wise, virtuous, and good, without thinking him a deity or savior."

That "certain citizen" was Washington.

My husband's great fear, since Trenton and Princeton, had been that Washington would become more important than the Revolution. Having taken the measure of the man, I was not concerned about this.

But I was concerned for my husband's health. He came home a few days before the thanksgiving, worn down and exhausted by his work in Congress, and especially by his service on the Board of War, which saw to recruiting, supply, prisoner exchange, and the keeping of records. My husband was leaving Congress, the Board of War was to be reorganized, and so, I thought, was our life.

Then came news from Congress: John Adams had been selected to replace Silas Deane in Paris. Not only would he be leaving me but he would be at six weeks' distance, on the other side of a stormy sea, rather than two weeks away, in the center of a stormy Congress.

Of course the storms of Congress were less glorious than once they had been. All but two of the original delegates had gone on to other things—the army, state politics, private life. New congressmen bogged themselves down, even more than their predecessors, in the piddlings and triflings of governing thirteen disparate political bodies as one. And as the faces in Congress changed, the question became more obvious. Who was the one constant in the Revolution? Washington? Or would Horatio Gates, hero of Saratoga, surpass him?

In November we learned that Gates had been named president of the Board of War. This, in essence, made him Washington's superior, though in reality I did not believe there could be any to function in that role.

## Hesperus Draper:

Thanksgivin': It means a day of prayer. It can also mean a day with a feast. Well, a lad from a Connecticut regiment put it best: "We feasted upon a leg of nothin' and no turnips."

We were marchin' west to winter quarters, some twenty miles outside Philadelphia. The name of the place had a nice ring to it. Made you think of a valley down out of the wind, a blacksmith's forge with a fine warm furnace goin' night and day. But when you're an army of ten thousand hungry men, and there's fifteen thousand full-bellied British regulars twenty miles away, you better not be puttin' yourselves into a valley.

No, Valley Forge was no valley. And thanksgivin' was no banquet. And don't ask me why this place was called winter quarters, either. Hardly a shelter anywhere, nothin' but bare woods and a barren plateau, two miles long and a mile and a half wide, 'tween the Schuylkill River and Valley Creek.

But there were roads. Even in the snow, you could tell where they were by trackin' the bloody footprints. I saw lads marchin' with rags around their feet. Saw bare soles sliced open on the ice-shard edges of frozen footprints left by men lucky enough to have boots. Saw men limpin' along in moccasins made from untanned hides, with edges so stiff they gave you bloody ankles instead of bloody soles.

Sometimes I wondered what made those boys keep goin'. I'd stopped tryin' to answer the question for myself. Hell, I'd stopped askin' it.

I'd kept with the Virginians, though the Virginians

hadn't kept so much with me. The first nine regiments would soon be gone home. And old Adam Stephen was gone already. Dismissed for drunkenness at Germantown.

To replace him, we'd been given a man—or should I say boy?—with a head shaped like an egg. That was what I thought when I first laid eyes on Lafayette. An egg fringed with reddish blond hair, and arched brows that made him look like he was always surprised. My second thought was, If he's only twenty and I'm forty-five, how is it that he's a major general and I'm just a colonel?

Well, there were political answers to that. And he wasn't given a command till he proved himself at Brandywine. But after he was wounded there, Washington took to him with more warmth than I'd ever seen him show to anybody, except for his little dead stepdaughter, Patsy. I think if Lafayette asked for a doll baby from London, George would've moved heaven and earth to get it.

So did George need a son? Had a stepson already. But most of the men he trusted were younger, some by ten years, like Greene, most by twenty or more. What other army ever had a general of artillery the age of Henry Knox? What general ever put as much trust in an aide like Hamilton? Or gave a whole division to somebody as young as Lafayette?

Washington liked men who admired him, who flattered him somehow, who proved their loyalty before they proved they could think for themselves. That wasn't to say he didn't like the men around him to be smart. They could even be smarter than he was, so long as they knew their place or, like Hamilton, let him think they did.

That explained why I'd been promoted to colonel but no higher. I'd said things he might have forgiven, but he never forgot. So he always treated me cold and correct. After two and a half years of that damn war, I'd proven my loyalty to the cause, if not to him, but I'd never be a general.

Lafayette, on the other hand, wasn't one to treat anyone cold. Always correct, but always warm.

By the time we got to Valley Forge, he'd been our division commander for a bit more than two weeks. Called his officers to his tent for a conference. Like Washington, he said he'd live in a tent for as long as it took the men to build shelters. In the middle of December, that was the depth of misery.

But in a funny kind of way, I think Lafayette liked it. Acted like 'twas all some kind of adventure, a huntin' trip away from the castle.

"Gentlemens," he said, "I see the soldiers without shoes—"

"Hell," said General Woodfort, one of the brigadiers, "I see soldiers without breeches."

"And I've seen officers without the itch," I said. "But not many." Then I give myself a scratch in the armpit.

So Lafayette gave his head an elaborate scratchin'. And 'twas like a signal for all those officers to scratch here, rub there, and relax some in the presence of their new commanding officer.

The itch came from never havin' a chance to get clean. Some had it bad, with crusty pustules between their fingers, creepin' up their necks, festerin' in their crotches. Others had just light cases. 'Twas called impetigo. And lads who didn't have it might be favored by fleas and lice and other vermin. But everybody had some kind of an itch, you can be sure.

"Gentlemens," said Lafayette, when he was done scratching, "we must help the men. I will buy clothing for the troops, from my own funds."

Now, we all knew he came from money. First thing he did when he got to America was contribute 60,000 pounds to the cause. Put himself into everyone's good graces. But I had to ask him, "Where are these clothes, sir?"

"This I do not know. If Quartermaster General Mifflin cannot say, we must ask the Board of War, or the new inspector general."

I'd gotten a letter from the inspector general. Name was Conway. Wrote to me because I'd been Gates's secretary and Lee's adjutant. And Conway had been puttin' it about that Gates—or Lee, if he was exchanged— might be better medicine for this army than Washington. And he wasn't the only one sayin' it.

But that was a pissin' contest with skunks everywhere. I was stayin' out. Besides, wouldn't matter a damn who led the army if the troops starved or froze.

So I said to Lafayette, "General, if you can find clothes for the troops, and pay for them, I think you'll be known evermore as the soldiers' friend."

Lafayette beamed. Seemed like an easy one to flatter. But you know, he did what he said. Sent parties out, found what clothes he could, paid for them, too. And that's just what our Virginians took to callin' him—the Soldiers' Friend.

Well, after we talked about clothes, Lafayette turned to the buildin' of the shelters, as Washington had prescribed: "Dimensions are to be 14 by 16 feet; sides, ends, and roof made of logs; roof made light with split slabs; sides made tight with clay; fireplaces made of wood and secured with clay in the inside, eighteen inches thick; fireplace to be in the rear, the door to be in the end next to the street."

I said, "And the lads are supposed to do this work without anything to eat?"

"They must do what they can," answered Lafayette.

And so the men did. Ever seen a family of beavers in autumn? Then you know what those early days were like at Valley Forge. Axes rang, trees fell, mallets thumped, teams of men trudged in like oxen bearin' logs, and those huts rose, rough and mean but better than tents.

## Joseph Reed:

Some men have assailed me for my political ambition when military matters were yet to be decided. But no republican war can be fought and won without close cooperation between a nation's civil and military parts. So I had determined that it would be better to stand for Congress and serve from there than to hope for a return to my former friendship with the General.

But soon I was at Valley Forge, part of the congressional committee Washington had requested to help in reorganizing the army.

My first private meeting came with him in his marquee, where he had chosen to live until the shelters were completed. I admit that though I wore a fine black coat and waistcoat, I felt naked before his uniform and military demeanor, even in a cold tent, in a hungry place.

I said, "Your privation is a scandal, sir, in a country which has had such a fine harvest."

" 'Tis a hard fact, Congressman Reed. There are only twenty-five barrels of flour in this camp. And not a single hoof to slaughter. And you know the reason as well as any man. Pennsylvania demanded that we take residence here, to protect their countryside and their capital. And yet we daily see speculations, peculations, engrossing, forestalling—all affording proof of the decay of public virtue."

"You should coerce these farmers, sir."

"Confiscation never produces enough and inevitably turns people against us. Leave it to the enemy. They seem well practiced at it."

A cold wind buffeted the canvas walls of the tent, and Washington said, "We've demanded half the grain from all farmers within seventy-five miles. We will issue certificates to be redeemed for Continental dollars. But what we cannot pay for, we will not take."

"You know that the farmers prefer British gold to our paper."

The wind blew, and the tent poles stood a little straighter.

And anger came into his voice. "Don't blame the farmers. Congress and the quartermaster general should have seen to our needs long before the farmers. You complain that I won't confiscate food, but you won't write the law authorizing me to do it. You'd rather that I simply do it and suffer the consequences. You reconstitute the Board of War to put Gates in charge—"

"I am on the board, too, sir. You can count on me."

"Then tell the others to stop clamoring for an attack on Philadelphia. I cannot do it, and I cannot say why, or I would reveal our weakness, and in war, the next best thing to being strong is to be thought to be strong."

A gust of wind all but lifted the tent.

He looked up at the roof, then went on, " 'Tis much easier to make criticisms in a comfortable room by a good fire than it is to occupy a cold, bleak hill and sleep under frost and snow, without clothes or blankets or—"

His speech was interrupted by a strange, derisive sound: "Caw! Caw! Caw!"

He listened a moment, then went to the flap of his tent and looked out. The cawing grew louder. All around the campfires and empty commissary wagons, there were little flocks of soldiers, cawing like crows at their predicament and at their leaders.

The General grappled down his anger and said he'd show himself to the men. "And so should a member of Congress, so the men will know they have not been deserted." He then called for his guard, and as soon as he appeared, the crows fell silent, as if preparing to take flight before the entourage Washington now led across the camp.

It seems that he had offered a reward of twelve dollars—a dollar a man—to the first group that finished their hut. Some of Woodfort's Virginians had won the prize, so he marched to their little village and had the twelve winners fall in.

The General gave twelve Continentals to their colonel. As he did, we heard something new. It began softly, among a few workers, almost in rhythm with their hammers and saws. "No pay! No clothes! No provisions! No rum!" Soon the chant was rolling across the whole plateau.

Washington turned to me and said, "Be sure you tell Congress what you've heard."

I promised that I would, though in truth, I could do little.

## Hesperus Draper:

Washington gave me the twelve dollars. Then he stepped back and watched like I was givin' out twelve sides of bacon.

And he heard those strange, muffled cries, "No this, no that," gettin' louder and louder. He cocked his head, but he didn't turn around to see where the noise was comin' from. 'Twas as if he was tryin' to keep his dignity by ignorin' the noise. Always kept his dignity.

Then he turned on his heel and went stridin' back to his marquee, with Joseph Reed—who'd been smart enough to quit this mess—hurryin' along after him, and that strange chant chasin' him like a low, moanin' wind.

One of our lads looked at his dollar and said to a mate, "How do we know this ain't counterfeit?"

"Because counterfeits is printed better."

And all the boys in the line had a laugh.

Soldiers laughin' at money . . . didn't speak well for the currency. Soldiers cryin' for meat . . . spoke even worse for the commissary. And soldiers showin' their insubordination so bold . . . spoke terrible for the General himself.

## The Marquis de Lafayette:

In late December, into our misery strode an old acquaintance and new enemy, Thomas Conway. He had been in York, behind the Susquehanna, speaking before Congress, like a man sent by heaven for the liberty and happiness of America. He told them so, and they were fools enough to believe it. So they had made him inspector general, and they promised to make him a major general, too, jumping him over many an American brigadier general. What injustice!

## Alexander Hamilton:

Washington knew of Conway's machinations. He knew that Conway had written to Horatio Gates, "Heaven has been determined to save your country, or a weak general and bad councilors would have ruined it." And he knew that this was an opinion shared by others.

I warned Washington that the group of schemers coalescing against him were vermin. And the worst was Conway. There was no more villainous calumniator or incendiary in the American camp.

## Hesperus Draper:

Thomas Conway: Irish by birth, French by adoption. The Irish part made him think he could charm the angels off the altar. The French part made him arrogant enough to think the angels might want to come down, just for the pleasure of sittin' with him.

I was livin' in one of those miserable log cabins, and one miserable night, the canvas door blew back, the snow blew in, and right behind it came Conway. He was a big man, but none too impressive. Had pop eyes and a tucked-under chin, but he had that superior European attitude I told you about. Didn't matter what those officers looked like. They all looked down on us.

Now, my cabin mates had gone off to play cards. I was tryin' to read, through eyes waterin' from the woodsmoke. When I think of Valley Forge, I think first of that damn smoke. Every cabin had a wattle-and-daub chimney, and every chimney puffed more smoke down than up, so you woke every mornin' covered in soot, rubbin' red eyes, and coughin' up phlegm the color of lampblack.

But Conway didn't seem bothered. He sat on a stool and pulled out a bottle of brandy, then a long thick sausage that may have been the most beautiful thing I'd seen since Alexandria. But new-minted inspector generals didn't come callin' on colonels just for society. He was after somethin'.

So I congratulated him on his promotion, ate the sausage, and let him do the talkin'.

"Better than fire cake, eh, Draper?"

"For certain." Fire cake formed the main part of our diet—a miserable, unsalted mess of flour mixed with water and baked on a hot stone.

"Do the men blame Washington for the fire cake?" he asked.

"They blame the quartermaster and the commissary and all the cutpurse contractors," I said. "Why, we had twenty barrels of pickled pork delivered the other day, all rotted, 'cause the teamsters drained the brine preservin' the pork, just to lighten their loads. That's the kind of trimmin' we're up against."

I took a swallow of brandy to calm me. It tasted like sunshine, playin' on a field of French grapes. "So whoever blames Washington knows nothin'."

"Believe me, Draper, no man is more a gentleman than Washington, but as to his talents for the command of an army"—Conway give one of those elaborate French shrugs, even though he was Irish—"they're miserable indeed. The more I see of his army, the less I think it fit for general actions."

"I reckon some folks agree."

"Indeed," he answered. "Numerous congressman, Benjamin Rush, the Adamses of Massachusetts . . . Samuel, anyway . . . So what say you?"

"To what?"

"A movement of officers to put Gates over Washington."

"You mean a mutiny? Troops haven't mutinied. Why should officers?"

"You exaggerate. Not a mutiny. A small push here. A gentle nudge there. A simple expression of opinion."

As I said, this was a pissin' contest, and one of the skunks was right in front of me, and he had the brain of a skunk, to think that a gentle nudge would knock

Washington over. So I ate his sausage and drank his brandy and didn't make any fast moves, so he wouldn't spray.

# Billy Lee:

"Inspector General Conway? In camp?" Just like that the General said it—loud and mad. Conway was comin' with power, from the Board of War.

We was alone in the General's office, in a little stone farmhouse, and when we was alone, I was a little bolder. So I said, "This 'spector general, what does he do?"

"He inspects, Billy. What do you think?" The General was still fumin'.

I could see that, so I should have kept my mouth shut. But I'd spent time with my Margaret in Philadelphia, and she was a girl who didn't care what she said to who, and I was pickin' it up from her. So I said, "Inspect what, sir?"

And he calmed down some. "Inspector general is supposed to train the troops, pursue deserters, and see that soldiers steal no public property."

"Ain't much public property here to steal."

General didn't say nothin' to that, like the sayin' would make him madder.

Just then Mr. Tilghman come in and announced Conway. And you never felt such a cold wind as blew through that room. 'Twas like the General just called it down from the sky, so it frosted ice all over his face and put his fire right out. Amazin' how that man could get control of himself.

Conway come in dressed in his best, not a patch in sight. He didn't powder his hair, but he sprinkled himself with some kind of fine-smellin' rosewater. 'Twas like a puff of flowers come in ahead of him. Kind of nice.

"Good day, sir," he said, very polite.

"Good day." The General barely moved his lips.

"I have come to present my credentials, sir, from the Board of War." He pulled these papers from his coat.

I went to pick them up. 'Twas my job.

But the General put out his hand for me to stay where I was. He kept his cold eye on Conway. "Is there anything else?"

"I have plans for the service, sir. I would like to share them."

"As Mr. Hamilton is away from camp, share them with Mr. Tilghman."

And then they stood there, the General just fixin' this feller with his coldest stare. Time went slow and the room went colder.

Finally Conway said, "Am I dismissed?"

The General just nodded.

Conway turned, but he stopped in the doorway. "If my appointment is in any way disagreeable to Your Excellency, as I neither applied nor solicited for it, I am very ready to return to France. I will be more useful to the cause there than here."

"As you wish, sir," said the General. And that was that.

## Hesperus Draper:

I saw Conway that afternoon, and mad as a hatter he was.

"Draper, I have never met with such treatment before from any general during the course of thirty years in a respectable army."

"General," I said, "this ain't exactly what you'd call a respectable army."

"Good leadership would make it one. He thinks by his attitude to send me packing back to France. But I'm going back to the Board of War."

## The Marquis de Lafayette:

I went to the General that night. He was buried in papers, but he welcomed me, as always.

"Excellency," I said, "it is important that you know my position on Conway. Simply because he is French, this means nothing."

"Your coming is proof of your friendship, Marquis."

"He calls himself my soldier, as if he were my friend. He is not. I have inquired in his character, and I find that he is ambitious and dangerous."

"Calm yourself," he said. "The danger of disunion over this business is very great. As I've told any officer who expresses dissatisfaction over Conway's new rank be cool and dispassionate."

"Excellency, I leave coolness to you. I shall be hot in my support of you. For I am now fixed to your fate. I shall follow it. I shall sustain it as well by my sword if called upon."

The General smiled. He was a very great man, in size and spirit both. "We mustn't expect always to meet with sunshine, my dear Marquis. I have no doubt that everything happens for the best. We'll triumph over our misfortunes, and when that day comes, you'll come to Virginia, and we'll laugh at our troubles and the folly of others."

## Billy Lee:

I don't recollect ever hearin' the General invite Henry Knox or Alexander Hamilton down to Mount Vernon. But there was somethin' about that Marquis. He could get through the ice when it froze, and he could put out the fire when it flashed. I don't guess anyone ever liked the General as much, and that may be why the General liked him. But I don't know. I was just a slave.

## Dr. James Craik:

I was nae as close to him as once I had been, only because of the heavy responsibilities that both of us bore. I took leave in December, but the morning I left camp, I was informed by a certain officer that a strong faction was forming against the General in the new Board of War. I resolved, however, to say nothing until I reached home, as perhaps I might make further discoveries on my way.

At my arrival in Bethlehem, I was told of it there.

At York, I visited Dr. Benjamin Rush. I wished to discuss the typhus cases I had seen, and our talk was professional enough, but after our business, I said, "Sir, I've been hearing most disconcerting remarks against the General. Have you heard of any movement to replace him?"

Rush was a man of high forehead, intelligent feature, and large, dark eyes. At my question, his eyes seemed to grow even larger, as if he were trying to see into my brain, and he said, "I have great regard for the General, as you know."

This, I learned, was a lie served up to a firm ally of the General. To others, Rush had been heard to say, "The northern army has shown us what Americans can do with a general at their head. The spirit of the southern army is in no way inferior. A Gates, a Lee, or a Conway would in a few weeks render them an irresistible body of men."

There were adherents to such opinion all the way down to Virginia. I believed the conspiracy to be pretty general over the country.

And their method was always the same: to hold Gates up to the people while criticizing Washington's generalship. It was said that they dared nae appear openly as his enemies, but that the new Board of War was composed of such leading men as would throw such obstacles and difficulties in his way as to force him to resign.

I put all of my information into a letter to him, as a good friend. But I was forced to add that my wife was in an extremely low and weak condition. I would miss much of the next year of campaigning, as I could not think of leaving her in such a state with such a large family, and my large-hearted friend understood.

## Hesperus Draper:

For the next month, life went on. You could say that death went on, too. Men starved and froze and died of disease. They stopped complainin', stopped chantin', stopped cawin'. They were too tired and too hungry. Instead, they whispered the rumors. Who'd be in charge when spring came?

Gates was at York, with the Board of War. Conway was there, lookin' for ways to insinuate himself with men in power. Reed was there, too, and you could never be sure about him.

Me? I just missed my wife. A lot of officers had resigned or slipped off for a while. But I wanted to do things right. Like Washington, I'd joined a Masonic lodge when I was younger, and I always believed what they said: "Meet on the level and part on the square."

Woodfort was my brigadier general. Told me I'd need higher permission. Seein' as how Lafayette wasn't in the camp just then, I went to the man himself.

"You want a furlough?" Washington looked at me with a disappointed face. "Draper, I need good unit officers in the camp."

"Sir, if I don't go, she'll die."

"Women don't die for such trifles."

"Then *I'll* die," I told him.

"You've survived British bullets. You won't die."

"So what do I do?"

"Write to her to add another leaf to her book of sufferings."

Maybe he thought he was bein' funny. But I wasn't laughin'. I stepped toward his desk and said, "George

Washington, we've known each other since we were boys, and I'm tellin' you, I can't take this much longer."

"We all have to take it, Draper. For as long as we can."

"Well," I said, "I don't know what I'm gonna do." I started for the door.

And he said, "Draper . . . my wife is coming at the end of January. There may be a seat in her chariot for a woman who's been printing Mr. Paine's thoughts. . . ."

Right then I was glad I'd given Conway no brief. On the way out the door, I even said, "General, watch your back. There's men who—"

"Thank you, Draper. Your loyalty is noted."

Always correct, always cold.

## Martha Washington:

My husband's summons came in January. I set out soon thereafter for Alexandria, where I picked up Mrs. Charlotte Draper, who proved a woman of grace and geniality, two qualities I do not recollect experiencing in the presence of her husband.

However, the journey did not start auspiciously, as she kept me waiting more than a half hour while her trunk was loaded and she finished business at the office of Draper Importing and Printing. Even after seating herself, she was giving instructions out the window to a young man who noted down all her words. Then, as the chariot lurched into the street, she brought her handkerchief to her eyes

"My dear," I said, fearing a tearful trip, "what is it?"

"I've received sad news. My . . . my father has died

in London." And the tears she was holding back burst forth. "Forgive me. It is not my way to appear so . . . before a—"

"Don't say 'stranger,' dear." I touched her hand. "We won't be strangers after this trip."

"No . . . no, we won't." She drew back her tears. "He was a barrister. He fled with the Annapolitan Tories in '76. Left everything he loved behind because he didn't hold with our revolution. Mother writes that he died of a broken heart."

And I was filled with pity for her, and sadness for all the pain that this struggle between parents and children had caused. I told her, "I've recently lost a loved one, as well. My sister."

"'Tis a terrible thing to know that we'll never again see people we—"

"My dear," I said, "those who go before us make a happy exchange. And they're only gone a little while before we rejoin them, never to part."

"I hope you're right, Mrs. Washington."

And I said what I believe even more firmly today: "My dear, if to meet our departed friends and to know them was certain, we could have very little reason to stay in this world, where, if we're at ease for an hour, we're in affliction for days . . . and call me Martha."

Such honest talk brought us close and made us friends.

We reached Valley Forge in early February. And my heart bled for the poor soldiers I saw. They were in a cart. And they were dead. Yes, a dozen emaciated, cold-blackened bodies, mostly naked, riding the death cart to a miserable mass grave hacked from the frozen earth.

As for my own husband, he seemed much worn with anxiety and with the desperate sadness of those death carts. His apartment in Mr. Potts's farmhouse was very small, but large enough for me. That night I said I would brighten Valley Forge.

"Brighten as much as you will, we'll have no dancing, no cards, none of the usual enjoyments of winter headquarters. The men suffer too much."

"I shall make our pleasures simple, then," I said.

And the greatest pleasure, for both of us, was to be in each other's company again, after so many months apart.

But on subsequent evenings I gathered together the generals' ladies—Henry Knox's ebullient wife, Lucy, Nathanael Greene's vivacious Kitty, Lady Stirling and her daughter—to lighten the cares of our menfolk. There was some friction. Lucy Knox thought Kitty an incurable flirt, and Kitty disliked Lucy in turn. But we did our best to rise above our petty differences, providing nightly conversation over a dish of coffee or tea, and singing, which was always a great pleasure.

My husband was not known for his singing. He preferred to listen, though he always enjoyed chatter with the ladies. And I was happy to do anything to bring him a bit of joy, so much else weighed upon him and so bleak was that world.

I did make one suggestion that he took wholeheartedly: the men should put on a play. Yes, a play.

"There's only one play to be done," he said. "Addison's *Cato*. It could be very instructive to the men."

# Hesperus Draper:

"A play?" I laughed when I heard. But the lads liked the idea.

And I have to admit, it took the men's minds off the misery around them. Took the officer's minds off the backstabbin' that was goin' on with Conway, too.

Soldiers took to their roles as if feedin' words into their brains was better than feedin' beefsteaks into their bellies, and they put on the show in a big barn, with the wind howlin' outside and torches burnin' all around and the General and his lady sittin' right down front.

And it worked some magic. Noble Cato was called from his plow to defend the republic against Julius Caesar, and when it looked like he'd be defeated or forced to submit, he killed himself, true to his ideals. The feller who played Cato fell on his wooden sword and twitched like a mackerel. Mighty dramatic. You could hear sniffles all around.

We were sittin' near Washington, and I think I even saw tears in his eyes.

Charlotte whispered, "Don't you cry, Hess. One cryin' officer is enough."

I laughed. "Don't worry, darlin'. I only cry for you, when you're gone."

I can't rightly say that *Cato* changed anything for us. But in a place like Valley Forge, 'twas a good lesson to see men facin' up to somethin' as bad as dictatorship, even if it finally beat them.

## Martha Washington:

*C*ato was a pleasant distraction for us all. But nothing could keep my husband from lying awake in the dark hours before dawn, talking about all the shoes and blankets sitting in warehouses as far away as Boston, or about the unscrupulous contractors, or most bitterly about the enemies trying to remove him from his position.

"I did not want this job," he whispered early one morning, not long after he had seen the play.

"No one knows how hard it is, George," I said.

"I'd rather be at Mount Vernon, at my own plow, like Cato. But I'm here"—he threw himself out of bed and pulled on the breeches Billy Lee had laid out by the fireplace—"so I'll see the job through, but not by falling on my sword."

"Where are you going now?" I asked.

"To write a letter to Horatio Gates."

## Alexander Hamilton:

*T*he pen was truly mightier than the sword that winter. Mightier also than the machinations of all the cabalist vultures on the Board of War.

In early February, Washington attacked Gates by attacking Conway: "Many instances might be adduced, to manifest that he is capable of all the malignity of detraction and all the meanness of intrigue, so as to gratify his disappointed vanity, to answer the purposes of personal aggrandizement, and to promote the interests of faction."

And Gates began his retreat, solemnly declaring that he was of no faction, and hoping the General would not spend another moment on the subject. Soon Gates's supporters began to withdraw, rightly sensing that his resolve to stand against Washington was no greater than his battlefield resolve. And men of importance advanced with support for Washington, men as varied as Daniel Morgan, the Virginia rifleman; Henry Laurens, president of Congress; and Thomas Paine.

It was plain, by the last week of February, that the cabal had unmasked its batteries too soon. Now its leaders were hiding their heads, and Congress was accepting the resignation of Conway. Washington had acted with resolve and the steady hand that was the hallmark of his leadership. But all true friends of their country, and, of course, of a certain great man, had to be on the watch to counterplot the secret machinations of his enemies.

## Joseph Reed:

In all of the history of warfare, there may have been no better letter-writer than Washington. I had seen his skill. I had helped him to hone it. At the Board of War, I stood in awe before it.

As for the so-called Conway Cabal, I will only say that war produces many passions and opinions. I never supported Gates. After Trenton and Princeton, I knew that Washington was the only man with the personal gravity to hold that army together.

But after a trip to camp in February, I doubted if the Lord himself could have done it. Half of the eight thousand men left were unfit for duty. Typhus and camp fever ran wild. And in the third week of the month, there was not a steer to slaughter nor a slab of salt pork to give out nor a pound of flour to make fire cake. It was the darkest time of all at Valley Forge.

Washington told me to warn Congress that there was a prospect of "absolute want, such as will make it impossible to keep the army much longer from dissolution."

Then it would be over. I knew that better than any man. I left Valley Forge in a sleet storm, intent upon helping Washington as best I could, and more certain than ever that the best help I could give would be in Congress, for I was far more skilled as a debater than as a warrior.

I would not again see him in the war, though we would correspond on many matters, sometimes to our mutual satisfaction, sometimes not. I think we parted as friends.

c.d.—*Correspondence . . . letters . . . missives . . . notes . . . they flew like musket balls from a cold Pennsylvania farmhouse. In truth, it was not one letter but a chain of them that unmasked the Conway batteries. And it took dozens of letters to secure support for anything from Congress. It seemed that Reed's remark in Cambridge was still accurate: "We fight this war with paper, ink, and sealing wax." But no secrets had been revealed to me in the few letters I'd seen from Washington to his wife. Perhaps there were no secrets.*

## Hesperus Draper:

Best thing about quietin' Conway was that Washington could turn to what really mattered. He finally resorted to confiscation in late February. 'Twas the only way to save that army. And he had to save the army. At all costs, he had to save the army.

He made Nathanael Greene his quartermaster—a job I no longer coveted, not with money losin' value faster than a peach rots in the sun—and Greene led us into the Pennsylvania countryside with the order, "Harden your hearts. We are in a damn nest of Tories." Meanwhile, Anthony Wayne swept into Jersey and rounded up all the cattle he could find. And while the food wasn't enough to put weight on anybody, it sure raised men's spirits.

So did a stocky, beetle-browed German who called himself Baron Friedrich Wilhelm von Steuben. He was one of the few European officers I liked. Oh, he was as pretentious as most of them, struttin' around wearin' the Order of Fidelity—a medal as big as a horseshoe—on his chest. And he wasn't a real baron, either. He was a drillmaster, but he was the best damn drillmaster I ever saw.

Under him, our boys started marchin', drillin', and piece by piece, learnin' how to become a battlefield army. And the best part was, he didn't have any whinin' militia at Valley Forge. These men were all Continental line troops, men from New England to North Carolina, some signed for three years, others for the duration, so whatever they learned, they'd remember, and maybe they'd put it into practice when the time came.

Steuben picked a hundred men, and he started trainin' 'em. You'd see him scurryin' from place to place on that snowy plain, always with an American aide behind him, translatin' while Steuben barked and shouted and cursed at the men. Fact was, he didn't speak a word of English, till he learned the words *goddamn, fuck, bitch-bastard-whore,* and *lazy prick.*

Once, he lost his temper with a group of men who couldn't get a simple drill step right. Cursed at them in German, then in French, then he turned to Hamilton and said, "Now swear at them in English."

My Charlotte laughed like hell at that story.

She and I had moved to the attic of the farmhouse, where Lafayette was stayin', but we were the old farmer's only guests, seein' as Lafayette had gone off for a silly march on Canada, the brainchild of Gates and the Board of War. And I'll tell you, Charlotte made them some happy months for me.

In general, Washington didn't approve of women in camp. Thought they distracted the enlisted men. But the officers had their ladies. So he couldn't stop the enlisted wives from comin'. Instead, he dreamed up jobs for them. Had them serve in the hospital, where there was plenty to do, or in the laundry hut, where there wasn't much. And he looked the other way when the jills and hags come around. And when the lads designated a cabin to be the whorehouse for a night, I made sure the subalterns looked the other way, too.

Charlotte worried me, though, because she insisted on takin' Martha's example and visitin' the hospitals. I told her 'twould be better for her to run one of the sewin' circles that Martha had started—sit around and darn socks all day. But you didn't tell her such things. She said she'd had the smallpox, so she'd help where she could, bandagin' sores and bathin' frostbit limbs in warm water, and pretendin' like the stench of the hospital was no more than a nosegay of roses.

"If old Cato can fall on his sword," she said, "'tis the least I can do."

She was an angel, and I told her so one night as we lay together. "I don't see how I can be without you another year, darlin'."

"You have to be, Hess. We're in this as deep as Washington."

"They hang the generals, darlin', not the colonels."

"After they hang the generals, they'll hang the printers."

## Billy Lee:

I was proud as hell one March night when my Margaret rode in carryin' three crates of salt. She said she'd stole 'em from the British commissary, who'd moved into the house where she was workin' in Philadelphia.

After I'd had two or three good tumbles with her, I took her to the General to tell him what she done. I figured 'twould make him like her more.

And he thanked her all very grave and serious.

"Billy says salt is as good as gold in this army," she told the General.

"With salt, we can preserve food," he said.

"When you get some," she said.

I give a little chuckle to that, so it might sound like a joke.

But the General didn't smile. He just give her a receipt for pay.

"Ten dollars, Continental?" she said. "That ain't worth its weight in paper."

The General sat back and give her a hard look, and I eased her out.

That gal was too sassy by half, and I told her so. Made her so mad she wouldn't even kiss me good-bye. She just went ridin' off.

## Matt Jacobs:

Those days under von Steuben was worse than slavery. Drill by day. Starve by night. Freeze or choke in smoke all the time. But we was still there, the foot soldiers, doin' what we was told, jokin' when we could, and laughin' like hell whenever ol' Steuben tried to swear at us. Man couldn't swear worth a shit.

But he taught us how to wheel and charge, how to load that musket in fast steps and fire it fast, too. When he was done with us, we'd go back to that miserable cabin all tired out and as hungry as bears in spring.

Now, we had us a cabin with twelve men. And seein' as Massachusetts Negroes marched with white soldiers, our cabin was a mix—six of each.

One night Sammy Brisby started in about Marblehead and fishin', and then he started talkin' about goin' home.

"You can't do that," said Willard, "you're signed for the rest of the war."

And Sammy—he was a big feller, but mighty skinny after that miserable winter—he said, "I can't read, so how'd I know what I'se signin'? I wants to go home and go fishin'. And I wants to eat fish. And smell fish . . . and, ah, hell."

And just like that, he got up and started packin' his things into a little sack—his pipe, his tobacco pouch, some rope he used for a belt.

So we axed him where he was goin', and he said, "I'se goin' home."

We all laughed, but he went 'round the cabin, all real solemn, and he shook everybody's hand. And I said, "Sammy, you desert, they'll hang you."

And he said, "I needs to go fishin'." Then he picked up his musket, which warn't his property, and he headed off.

Me and Willard, we just looked at each other. We couldn't let this happen. So we stepped out after him.

'Twas a full moon, so we had to do some good sneakin', but we slipped the pickets and caught up to Sammy down at the riverbank.

'Twas early spring. Ice was out. River was runnin' cold and clear.

"Sammy!" I called. "We ain't lettin' you run away."

"I has to fish, Matt. I has to do what I was put here for."

"You was put here to drill and fight," I said.

And then Willard Walt told us to be quiet.

"What?" I said.

"Listen."

And I heard it—a splatterin' sound in the water, and I saw Willard grinnin' in the moonlight. He knew what it was. Then I saw the little silver waves, all across the river. And I knew. 'Twas nature takin' her course.

And I said to Sammy, "I reckon you can go fishin' right here, boy."

And Sammy knew what it was, 'cause he let out with a "Wahoo!" to wake the whole camp. Then he jumped into the water, right into all them beautiful, fat, fast-swimmin' shad. He dipped his hat and come up with half a dozen skitterin' and splashin' in the crown, and he shouted, "I'se fishin'!"

"And we's eatin' fish tonight." I fired my musket into the air.

The British could no more stop the shad from swimmin' up the Schuylkill than they could stop the greenin' of the grass. By mornin' there was shad cookin', shad fillin' bellies, shad on every man's mind. Now, we knew, the worst was over.

## Hesperus Draper:

When Lafayette came back, we said we'd move out of his farmhouse, but he insisted that we stay. "If I could be lucky enough to have my Adrienne by my side," he said, "I would thank God. It does me warmth to see a woman in this house." Then he took Charlotte's hand and kissed it.

Now, Charlotte was not impressed by such things, but that young Marquis melted her heart like a big plop of suet on a hot stone. For the rest of her time there, 'twas "Marquis this" and "Monsoor that," and when he told her about the bullet he'd taken at Brandywine and how he described it for his wife, she thought 'twas the most romantic thing she'd ever heard: "My wound is perfectly healed, but my heart is sore with loneliness."

Sometimes I thought she was sweet on him. Sometimes I thought she was motherin' him. And he always acted like he loved it.

And when he learned from France that his little daughter had died of fever, 'twas Charlotte comforted him and helped him write his letter to his wife.

Then, in May, there came news that comforted us all.

## The Marquis de Lafayette:

I remember well the glorious day. I still carried a deep wound of grief, but I had resolved to stay and serve America, in my daughter's memory. On that day the General stood in the officers' meeting, and upon his face was written an expression of absolute joy. What could this be?

He said, "Gentlemen, I must beg you to withhold this information until there is official notice from Congress, but it would seem that the court of France has recognized us as free and independent states and is entering into an alliance."

Happiness filled me for the first time in weeks. I leaped up, feeling the tears welling in my eyes and the joy overflowing in my heart. I ran around the table, seizing our general by the shoulders and kissing him on the cheeks.

He looked at me with a face so startled, it was as if I had struck him.

"Excellency," I laughed, "you are not used to our French ways."

"No. But . . . but thanks to this news," he said, "I believe I must learn."

## Hesperus Draper:

In all the days that I ever saw Washington take a glass or two or five or ten, I never saw him drunk. And only one day did I ever see him half lit. 'Twas May 6, 1778, the day we celebrated the French alliance.

It started with prayer services. Had to thank God for this miracle. Then there was a march of brigades, wheelin' to the right by platoons. Thousands of men, Steuben-trained, fish-fed, and healthy, dressed in clean, Martha-mended clothes, lookin' hard and stringy, not gaunt and dyin', like a few months before. Then a *feu de joie*—French for joyful fire. Every man in the army, lined in two ranks, firin' one after another. Then the roarin' cheers: "Huzzah! To the king of France. Huzzah! To the American States!" Huzzah! Huzzah! Huzzah!

Every soldier got a gill of rum. And the officers and their ladies gathered beneath a great canopy stitched together from half a dozen marquees.

Charlotte looked grand, eyes bright and skin flushed from the heat and the excitement and too many sips of strong wine under that hot canvas. She was wearin' a blue dress she'd decked out with white and red trim, and she puffed up when all the ladies told her how fine she looked. Didn't have a sarcastic word for any of them.

But of Washington she said, "That man could use some loosening up."

Truth was, I'd never seen him so happy. He and Martha were receivin' officers, thirteen at a time, offerin' each of them a smile, a bow, a kind word.

And the drinks flowed, and the toasts rolled, and a cold collation of meats filled our bellies. The band played marches and light airs, though no one in the tent was dancin'. 'Twasn't part of the plan. But toes were tappin' everywhere.

I was talkin' to Lafayette, and Charlotte was chatterin' away with Lucy Flucker Knox, who was even fatter than her husband.

Now, Lucy didn't chitchat with just anyone, seein' as she came from what had been one of the first Tory families of Massachusetts. But she'd learned about Charlotte's Tory family, how they'd gone back to England, like her own, so she figured that the Fluckers and the Spencers had a common bond.

I noticed that the two of them was pointin' toward the General and chucklin'. What they were pointin' at was his foot, which was tappin' to the music, to the tune "Banish Misfortune."

Lafayette noticed, too, and said, "The General would like to dance."

"Last winter quarters, at Morristown," said Lucy Knox, "he danced with all the ladies."

"Is he a good dancer?" asked Charlotte.

"So I've heard," said Lafayette.

Lucy Knox scanned the crowd, then said to Charlotte, "I'd wager you're the only woman in the room who's never danced with him."

"But a lady doesn't ask a gentleman," said Charlotte, "nor a general."

So, in the same jig time as the tune, Lafayette bounced over to Washington's side and whispered in his ear.

Washington brightened, gave a glance toward Charlotte, and excused himself from Martha, who must've been used to her husband goin' off to dance with longer-legged gals, because she didn't even make a face.

The crowd parted, and he give Charlotte a graceful bow. "I would beg one dance with a lady patriot before I return to my duties."

Charlotte dipped a polite curtsy. Washington bowed and called for "Tom Jones," a hearty little country dance. Then their hands touched. Their eyes locked. Their feet flew. And for a few moments 'twas just the two of them in the center of the tent, as if all the rest of us were pinwheelin' around them. A strange effect that man had when he moved. Strange and strong.

Before the music was done, everybody was cheerin', as much because there was dancin' again as for the dance itself. Charlotte dipped another curtsy, and Washington announced that after such a dance, there was nothin' for him but to go back to his work, so that he might forget the beautiful Mrs. Draper.

The days when even the sight of a woman could tie his tongue were long gone.

Lafayette shouted, *"Vive le Général!"* And the hats flew into the air, includin' my own. Charlotte almost threw her bonnet.

The pipers picked up another tune, and Washington and his family were played out, with the crowd followin' them into the afternoon sun. Martha took to the chariot, and the General mounted his horse. Then he turned, pumped his fist into the air, and shouted, "Huzzah!"

He was answered with a roar of cheers from all the officers.

He went a little distance more, turned again, and give out again. "Huzzah!"

I couldn't believe it. 'Twas the most demonstration I ever saw from the man.

Charlotte said, "I guess I loosened him up."

I said, " 'Twas you or the wine."

"Huzzah!" he cried again. Now there was no doubt. 'Twas the wine. The man had a glow on, and who wouldn't on such a day as that?

## Martha Washington:

The lines had deepened around my husband's eyes, and his hair had begun to gray. These things are to be expected in a man of forty-six who has spent three years living from trunks, sleeping in tents, and carrying such heavy burdens of work. But the news from France had reinvigorated him.

"Will the French assistance mean that much to us?" I asked after the party.

"Whether we've played the game well or poorly, Patsy, I cannot say. But 'tis now verging fast toward a favorable issue."

"You mean we're going to win?"

"I'm afraid to say it quite so plain."

His secretaries had all turned to sleep. I suggested that he do the same.

"I have just one more letter to write," he said. "To Jacky."

This intrigued and pleased me. I was always happy

for communication between my husband and his stepson. "What are you telling him?"

"I'm advising him to hold on to all his inherited lands, for things are going to get better." And he read: "'Lands are permanent, rising fast in value, and will be very dear when our independency is established.'"

My husband was ever a practical man.

## Hesperus Draper:

Charles Lee was exchanged in May. And Washington greeted the news like a long-lost brother was comin' home or, better yet, a long-lost general, because none of Washington's brothers could lead a division.

I figured Washington had a lot more to worry about with Lee than he had with Horatio Gates, who'd never do anythin' so darin' that he'd destroy himself, either in battle or on the Board of War. Lee spoke his mind, did what he pleased, and was still considered a military genius by some congressmen.

Seein' as I'd been Lee's adjutant, Washington invited me to join the welcomin' party. We went to a place about four miles down the road—Washington, Lafayette, Greene, Knox, and a whole gaggle of aides. Band was waitin' already, and soldiers lined the road all the way back to the camp.

And there he came, as arrogant, self-important, and flea-bitten as ever, ridin' alone, except for four of his dogs.

And Washington did what I'd never seen him do before. He dismounted and let Lee ride up to him.

Then he offered his hand and said, "Welcome back, General."

"I return at your service," said Lee. Only then did he dismount.

And then Washington did somethin' even more amazin'. He threw his arms around Lee and said, "Your counsel has been missed, sir."

I thought Washington had been spendin' too much time with Lafayette. He was startin' to act so giddy, thought he might even kiss Lee on the cheeks.

After that little scene, we paraded back to camp, with our men presentin' arms all the way along the road. 'Twas a mighty stirrin' thing.

But Lee didn't seem impressed. When we dismounted at headquarters, he took my arm and whispered, "What say you of the great General now?"

Well, time spent dodgin' Conway had taught me a few things. "What say *you?*"

"I say Washington is too enamored of Steuben's little tricks. Steuben can teach this army to dress lines, dress themselves, and present arms from here to Boston, but the simple fact is that he should be dispersing them into the population, creating a partisan army that appears, strikes the enemy, and disappears as it will."

"Some do disappear," I answered. "We call it desertion."

"I'm bringing Congress a plan for reforming the army. I tell you, I understand what we're about better than any man living." And he was more arrogant, too.

Besides, Washington already had a plan. He'd stumbled onto what was called a Fabian strategy, after a Roman general called Fabius the Delayer. A lot of people tried to take credit, but 'twas Washington who put it into action: Do what you must to keep the army together. Fight when you're strong. Run when you have to. But keep the army together. 'Twasn't always pretty, but 'twas workin'.

And Washington had endurance, which gave him a stubborn courage. He had middle-of-the-battle courage, middle-of-the-night courage, too. He'd learned that when the enemy was shootin' at him, he had to make a decision. And when those dark shadows of doubt and criticism come creepin', he'd light a candle and write another dispatch. But he never quit.

Don't ask me where all this came from. How a man gets to be what he is can be a true mystery. We're not talkin' about some Papist saint. And Washington was truly like an actor. He knew people was always watchin' him, some hopin' to see him stumble, others to see how to act themselves. So he acted as best he could. Inspired some. Confounded others.

And, not to get too fancy about it, he made that army the symbol of resistance. Congressmen came and congressmen went, but one man had stayed in place, doin' his job through thick and thin, and endurin'. And that's the last I'll say on Washington's so-called greatness.

Now, Charles Lee was not one for endurin'. Unless folks were endurin' him. 'Twas somethin' of a disappointment to me that, just before we went into headquarters for a banquet to welcome Lee, Hamilton come up to me and said, "The General orders that you rejoin the staff of General Lee."

# Martha Washington

I saw to the best meal I could invent as a welcome to Charles Lee.

My husband told me that, no matter his faults, we needed his fine battlefield judgment.

And he was at his most voluble and spirited on the night of his return.

He told us of the comforts of his captivity in New York. He showed us the new tricks he had taught his dogs. He recited for us all a speech from Shakespeare, something from *Julius Caesar*, I believe.

And then we retired.

General Lee had been given the room directly behind my sitting room. As entertainment always left me too exhausted to sleep, I had remained awake for a time, knitting booties for our newest grandchild. It seemed the middle of the night when I heard a back door open. Then I distinctly heard Lee's voice and female giggling and then . . . other sounds, all no more than a few feet away.

I dropped a stitch I was so embarrassed! I put away my needles and hurried off to bed and my own snoring General.

The next morning, Lee appeared at breakfast, which was taken in the communal dining room. He looked as unkempt as if he'd been in the street all night.

And that is hardly an exaggeration, for later that morning, I saw a young woman slip from Lee's door, a miserable gutter hussy, to say it plain, who, it turned out, was the wife of a British sergeant he had met in New York.

I said to my husband, "General Lee must be brilliant indeed, for he is a very dirty man to be tolerated by one as fastidious as yourself."

"He is more than insolent," answered my husband. "But he is a soldier."

Not long after, our spies reported that the British were preparing to leave Philadelphia and return to New York. The great questions now became: Would they go by land or sea? And what would my husband do?

On a bright June day, with summer's winds rustling the leaves of the trees which had survived the cuttings of winter, my husband and I bade each other good-bye. We did it quick and in private. As I've told you, we were practiced at farewells.

'Twas far more painful for Charlotte and Hesperus Draper. They held each other close, broke away, drew back together again and held each other tight.

Finally, Charles Lee came out on the veranda of the headquarters and called, "Draper! Parting is sweet sorrow, but the sooner we get to finishing this war, the sooner you can go home to your wife."

A moment later, Charlotte Draper climbed into the chariot beside me, and just as upon our first meeting, she was dabbing back tears. This time, so was I.

"Don't let your husband see you cry, dear," I whispered.

"Farewell, ladies!" Charles Lee was shouting. "Good luck, Godspeed, and get going before these green leaves start to turn."

"Damn that Charles Lee," said Charlotte.

"Don't let *him* see you cry, either. None of it will

make your husband feel any better. Just give him a last wave and fix your eyes on the horizon."

As our chariot rumbled away, I heard Charles Lee declaiming to Draper, "Your wife is better off at home. She'll just worry if she stays here. Remember the bard: 'A woman mov'd is like a fountain troubled, Muddy, ill-seeming, thick, bereft of beauty.'"

## Hesperus Draper:

Lee liked me for some damn reason, and nothin' I could say would insult him. For a time, all he could do was talk about how well he'd lived with the British, how he'd even had his own Italian valet to take care of him. "And now I'm back with the rabble."

I said, "If it's too hard for you, General, go back to the British."

"No. There are too many men in this army that I like too much. I can't leave them under a general who's more fit to command a sergeant's guard."

"A strong opinion, sir."

Lee give me that death's-head grin, all nose and yellow teeth. "You are a man who likes strong opinions, Draper. I urge you to speak them."

"That's my way, sir."

"Which is why you serve me rather than the General. He has surrounded himself with toadies and lapdogs—Knoxes and Hamiltons. I have no toadies, and my dogs are as like to bite you as lap you. A man such as yourself is no toady. So he remains outside the charmed circle. But well within mine."

Why did I attract these fellers? First Gates, then Lee, then Conway, and now Lee again. If Washington had ever had any suspicions about me, they had to be gettin' worse. I sure was glad he'd danced with my wife.

## Billy Lee:

Twas the middle of June that Margaret snuck out of Philadelphia with what she said was big news.

"What is it?" I asked.

"Take me to Washington."

I put my arms around her and tried to lead her toward the barn instead. It'd been months since the last time, and rollin' in the hay was on my mind.

"No barn, Billy," she said. "No barn, till you're free."

"What?"

"If this army is fightin' for freedom," she said, " 'Tis about time that everybody in it was free."

Women can be a whole lot of trouble.

Just then, the General come out the back, callin' my name.

"Yes, sir," I said, "right with you, sir, but my wife, she's come with news."

"News of what?" The General come down off the little veranda.

Margaret said, "I'll tell you if you give Billy his freedom. Right now."

The General looked at her like she was plain crazy. Then he looked at me. "Is that what you want, Billy? Freedom? Aren't you treated well enough?"

"Yes, sir," I said. "I rightly am."

"Do you want your freedom?" he asked.

I was torn. The General looked calm and steady. She looked fierce and angry, like if I didn't demand my freedom right then, she'd leave me.

But I couldn't leave the General. 'Twasn't like I was a slave at all. I was a *valet de chambre*. That's what Lafayette called me. And damn me, but I liked it. I liked carryin' the General's papers. And ridin' at his side. I wouldn't have none of that if I was free. So I said, "Sir, what I want to do is work for you."

Margaret made a mad sound, like a hiss—*ssss*. Just like that.

The General just give her the flat look and said, "You have intelligence?"

"More than my husband."

So the General said, "If you know something that might help us—"

"All right . . . I do laundry for British officers in Philadelphia. And last night they ordered their laundry returned to them, finished or unfinished."

"Finished or unfinished . . . Have other washerwomen heard this?" he asked.

"All that I talked to."

The General give this some thought. Then he muttered, almost to himself, "They're leaving Philadelphia. They're . . . Mr. Tilghman! Mr. Hamilton!"

Two of his aides were at the door in a flash.

"Summon an officers' council. The British move has begun."

Those aides went runnin' like the house was on fire, and the General went to follow. Then he stopped and pulled out a piece of silver—one of those Spanish-milled dollars—from his pocket and give it to Margaret. "A good spy deserves hard money. You've done the cause of freedom a great service."

She took the money, but she wouldn't stay. Hell, she wouldn't even speak to me. She just went ridin' off, and I didn't rightly know if I'd ever see her again.

'Twas the first time since the General bought me that I felt like a real slave, 'stead of someone who mattered. So I went out to where I'd hid a wine bottle filled with rum—dribs and drabs scrounged here and there, mostly from what little might be left in a mug after a meal. I'd saved it to drink when I was feelin' bad. Now was the time. Got myself good and drunk.

## Alexander Hamilton:

News that the British were on the move brought us all to a high pitch of excitement. Within hours we had sent twelve regiments out to shadow them on the right flank, and by the next morning the rest of the army was marching back through Philadelphia and onto their trail.

General Henry Clinton had replaced Howe, and he had been ordered back to New York, by far the best stronghold on the continent. For a week we moved behind him, waiting to see which way he'd turn, always maintaining a defensive posture, even though we were now a well-trained, well-fed, and reasonably well-clothed force that had grown to eleven thousand.

At first we feared Clinton might be trying to draw us into an action, as he made a mere thirty-four miles in six days, and he kept his best troops at the rear. But there were good reasons for his rate of march. We had destroyed every bridge in his path, and those June days were an alternating hell of heavy thunderstorms that turned roads to mud, followed by a festering hot sun that turned puddles to steam.

## Matt Jacobs:

Sometimes I wondered about Willard Walt. I was beginnin' to think the heat was gettin' to him. On maybe the fourth or fifth day into our march, he started takin' off his hat every so often, sweepin' it through the air, and plunkin' it back onto his head.

Now, we was supposed to be marchin' in step, eight to a row. 'Twas damn hard for me and the other lads to keep up with him when he was busy wavin' his arms around, and finally I said, "God damn it, Willard, what is you doin'?"

"Collectin' heat."

"You're what?"

"Collectin' heat. In my hat. Keepin' it for next winter."

"You're a damn fool."

Willard laughed. "If somebody thought of collectin' the heat last summer, we could've used it at Valley Forge. I'm just thinkin' about the winter ahead."

He should've been thinkin' 'bout the enemy ahead. 'Tis a true fact that foot soldiers is generally the last to know anything, but we knew that we was just about steppin' on the British tail.

'Twas easy to tell, on account of the destruction. Jersey in June was green country, fat country, but not after the British army went through.

They'd kill cattle for sport and leave 'em lyin' dead in the fields, or maybe just cut the steaks out of their haunches and go on. They'd tear through a farmhouse and wreck it, break all the windows, scatter the furniture outside, and leave some poor farm wife sittin' in her dooryard, starin' at the mess.

But the saddest sight I ever seen come in a cherry orchard. Our column was movin' up the road, and Washington was up on a little rise, sittin' on his horse, amidst dozens of fallen trees, whilst a farmer told his tale.

"Them redcoat bastards come through here and seen my cherries ripe on the trees. So they dumb up and took what they could. And I said, fine, let 'em eat their fill and be gone. But 'twasn't enough. They wanted 'em all. So they . . . they commenced to cuttin' trees just to get the cherries high up and . . . My pa planted them trees twenty-five year ago . . . and now . . ." And that farmer started blubberin' like a baby.

Must've been a hundred cherry trees in that orchard, and every one was cut down, so the leaves was all squashed against the ground like a dead man's face.

General just shook his head. Then he looked down and said to that farmer, "We'll make them pay, my good man. Rely on it."

"Send 'em to hell, General."

## Alexander Hamilton:

On June 24, just after we had crossed the Delaware River at Coryell's Ferry, the General unluckily called a council of war. Present were Charles Lee, Nathanael Greene, Lafayette, Henry Knox, Steuben, Stirling, the aggressive young Pennsylvanian Anthony Wayne, and half a dozen other brigadiers.

It was held in a farmhouse along the route of march, in Hopewell Township.

Washington began by inviting his officers to remove their coats, as the temperature was near a hundred degrees. But as the General did not remove his, all kept their coats on.

"Considering the situation," he began, "and the probable prospects of the enemy, I wish your opinion on hazarding an action."

"I say no," proclaimed Charles Lee. "American troops cannot stand against the British. I have seen both armies and I am firm in that opinion. The British are in superb condition."

"The British have spent a winter in Philadelphia, seeing plays and sniffing ladies," said Lafayette. "We have spent a winter growing hard."

"Not so hard as you think," said Lee. "And those lady-sniffing British are in their kind of country—rolling country, open fields. They'll be impossible to defeat on such ground, sir."

"But once they reach the high ground at Middletown, they are safe," responded Lafayette. "They make the ships at Sandy Hook in a day."

"Let them go," answered Lee, "while we repair to White Plains."

Henry Knox wiped the sweat from his forehead. This was, considering the great heat and his great size, a task almost as Sisyphean as arguing with Lee. "I disagree with the general's assessment of our troops. But if he means to suggest—"

"What I mean to suggest," said Lee, fanning himself with his hat, "is that instead of attacking Clinton, we build a golden bridge to spirit him to New York."

Washington furrowed his brow. "You'll have to explain yourself, sir."

"Do not fight useless battles," said Lee, in a tone one would use on a child. "Let Clinton reach New York whilst we wait for the French. Their entry into the war guarantees victory."

"The French appreciate your confidence," said Lafayette, "but the enemy shows a long tail. Could we not cut it off?"

"Clinton may cut off our nose in the process," answered Lee. "'Tis is a meaningless attack. I would venture to say a criminal attack."

I was taking notes, leaving great blotches of ink on the page in my anger at what I was hearing.

Steuben, who was sitting next to me, asked me to translate what had just been said, and his response was to grunt.

Washington looked at him, "The general has some opinion?"

Though he was learning English, Steuben spoke in French and I translated: "'To strike an enemy who is on the move, his line strung out over many miles'"—here I interjected that the British baggage train alone consisted of fifteen hundred wagons—"'to strike such a blow is the dream of every general.'"

"Every general with an experienced army," said Lee.

"Attack," said Brigadier General Anthony Wayne suddenly.

Washington turned to him.

"Attack," repeated Wayne. They came to call him Mad Anthony for his aggressiveness, but his advice that day was correct, though unheeded.

"I agree with Lee," said Knox, "in that it would be criminal to hazard a general action at this time. But perhaps a piecemeal action. Perhaps . . ."

And so it went. That council would have done honor to the most honorable society of midwives, and to them only. The vote was that we should keep at a comfortable distance and keep up a vain parade of annoying the enemy with a detachment of perhaps fifteen hundred. General Lee was the primum mobile of this sage plan.

But Washington was disappointed. His instinct was for action, despite the Fabian tactics he had always employed. That night, Nathanael Greene and I went to him.

He stood as we entered his office, letting us feel the force of his height. "Gentlemen . . . you wish me to fight?"

It was hot enough that he wore neither coat nor waistcoat, only his shirt, open at the throat. His hair, which he did not powder in the heat, would soon need no powder, as he was graying at the temples and strands of gray were showing on the crown. But appearing coatless seemed only to enhance his presence.

"Sir," I said, "I've ridden out ahead. I've seen the country. I've spoken with our spies. The enemy is dispirited by desertion, broken by fatigue, retiring through woods, defiles, morasses. I urge you to something stronger."

Nathanael Greene supported me and added this: "The people expect something from us, General, and our strength demands it."

That position was one to which the General was always sensitive. To maintain the support of the American people was a vital necessity. He studied us for a moment, motionless despite the mosquitoes buzzing around him. Then he said, "I agree. We must use these men. We must take this opportunity."

Upon mature consideration, the General determined to pursue a new line of conduct at all hazards. We would strike the British rear guard with a corps of five thousand men, followed closely by the main body. If a more general action could thus be brought about, we might have a signal victory, like Saratoga, and such a victory might end the war.

The question now was, who should command the advance corps?

General Lee's conduct in the matter was truly childish.

## Hesperus Draper:

'T was said that Washington lacked decision. But before Monmouth, Charles Lee would have made a flighty woman in a dress shop look implacable.

He didn't want the command when it was a mere fifteen hundred men. So it went to Lafayette. Then word came that Washington had changed the plan, so

Lee changed his tune and went to see Washington. Brought me with him.

Headquarters was another farmhouse. Sometimes I think that war was harder on farmers and their wives than anybody else. Weather was hot as hell. And the thunderstorms blowin' through didn't do a thing but make the heat wet. 'Twas miserable marchin'. Damned hard thinkin', too. So I just stood there, quiet as Washington's slave, Billy Lee, and let General Lee do all the talkin'.

"Sir, a thousand apologies for the trouble my rash decisions may have caused you"—Lee could play courtesy and condescension with equal skill, almost at the same time—"but if this detachment does march farther, I entreat you to allow me to have command of it, though, to speak as an officer, sir, I do not think that this detachment ought to march at all."

Right then I would have thrown Lee out. But Washington deferred more to Lee that to anybody else in that army. Did he really like Lee? He never liked men who were his rivals. Did he believe in the old saw, "Keep your friends close but your enemies closer"? Aside from Lafayette, I'd never seen him actually embrace any other officer. He hated Horatio Gates, who was no more devious and self-servin' than most people; but he always worried about what Lee thought.

Shows you the power of reputation. Lee had come to the Continental army with a reputation as a great soldier. And it had stuck.

"You put me in a difficult situation, sir," said Washington. "The honor of the Marquis is at stake."

"So is my own," said Lee.

"But you did refuse the command," said Washington.

"Of a small detachment," he answered. " 'Twould be dishonorable of me to refuse command of five thousand men."

Certain words worked miracles on Washington. "Honor," in all its forms, was one of them. He would not dishonor his second-in-command. And Lafayette, graceful as ever, said it would be an honor to serve under General Lee.

A few days later the British camped around Monmouth Court House, so sunburnt, thirsty, rain-soaked, mosquito-bit, and wore out that they had to rest, not fifteen miles from the coast.

Lee had joined Lafayette, and we were camped about six miles behind the British, with Washington three miles back of us. Washington had ordered Lee to bring the advance corps into action the next mornin', and he would follow on with the main body.

Our boys were sunburnt, thirsty, rain-soaked, and bug-bit, too. The cold of Valley Forge was a fond memory. But where the enemy was wearin' heavy wool uniforms, our boys were mostly in huntin' shirts and light breeches. 'Twas one of the benefits of bein' poor that we couldn't afford uniforms.

Lee called a council of war—Lafayette, Anthony Wayne, a few others. First off, he told them Washington expected that they would all put aside their jealousies over rank and take his orders, which seemed reasonable.

Then Wayne asked Lee a simple question. "What are your plans, sir?"

And Lee answered, "I'm not certain."

"You mean," said Lafayette, "you have not formed them?"

"I mean that we do not know the numbers of the enemy nor the terrain nor much else about the situation. It therefore seems much the better course to let events dictate themselves."

"You mean you have no plan at all?" asked Wayne, a persistent son of a gun, big and strong, with a wild look in his eye and a willingness to fight anyone.

"I have just given you my plan," answered Lee. "I plan to react to events. I expect all of you to do the same." And he said it with such confidence that it almost seemed he knew what he was talkin' about.

Now, there's nothin' worse than tryin' to sleep the night before a battle. First I tried outside. But in mosquito season in the Jerseys, sleepin' outside is like plasterin' sugar syrup all over yourself and lyin' down on an anthill. So I went inside, closed the windows, half-suffocated myself, and slept on the floor.

By four, I was up, watchin' the eastern sky, tryin' to read the weather.

Usually, even on hot summer days, the sun comes up golden in a cool blue sky. When the sky at dawn is hot red and the sun looks like nothin' so much as a bloodshot eye, you know you're in for hell by noon, even if you're doin' no more than sittin' under a tree.

Well, on that June 28, dawn come up as red and ugly as I ever saw.

By five o'clock we got word that Clinton was on the move. By eight o'clock our whole advanced column was after him with Lee in command, Lafayette directin' the troops on the left, Wayne on the right. And I remember thinkin' how calm and cool Lee looked. Gave me a good feelin'. I should've known better.

The lay of the land, west to east, was all undulatin' platcau, like a bedsheet blowin' in a gentle breeze. 'Twas farmland—woods, cornfields, orchards, hedgerows— peaceful land, land where nobody in their right mind would fight a battle. But that's the beauty and the horror of war. It forces you over and over again to do things you don't want to do.

There were streams cuttin' across this ground, mostly east to west, but at just enough of an angle that two of them cut the main road. The streams made ravines, and the ravines were bottomed with morasses of spongy, wet, weedy ground sure to slow down a marchin' army.

The main choke point was a bridge over the West Ravine. By ten o'clock we'd crossed it, covered two miles more, and were comin' into action in the fields just east of the Monmouth Court House. And the calm collected Lee of earlier . . . well, remember what I said about that woman in the dress shop?

We had five thousand men attackin' two thousand. With a plan, we'd have cut them to pieces and done it quick, even if they were some of the best light infantry, dragoons, and rangers in the British army.

Afterward, Lee said he'd been in complete control when the battle began. Don't believe it. Moment to moment, he led that corps like the woman goin' from gingham to lace and back again.

Seein' the British rear guard, he shouted to Lafayette, "My dear Marquis, I think those men are ours!"

Things began well—"By God, I will take them

all!"—but he didn't give his commanders any direction. 'Twas called reactin' to events.

Washington sent up a messenger to find out what was goin' on, and Lee just said, "Tell the General I'm doing well enough." Sounded annoyed to be interrupted.

But we couldn't turn the enemy's flank. And Clinton was comin' back with four or five thousand men more. Suddenly we had a British column tryin' to turn our right, and another comin' from the center. Things started to waver, includin' Lee. "We must retreat!" he shouted.

I told him we were still on good ground and Clinton was throwin' his men at us one unit at a time. Told him not to panic.

But he was spooked. "You do not know the British soldiers, Draper. We cannot stand against them. We shall be driven back. We must be cautious."

Then he started spewin' orders to units spread over a half-mile front: "Retreat! Stand and fight! Take to the trees! Fall back and take defensive positions on the high ground." And everything started to break down, like always. And Lee put on the punctuation, shoutin', "They're all in confusion, Draper! Confusion!"

That was the word. Not only was Lee mighty confused. Seemed like half the General's family was gallopin' around. Big-Ass Henry came up to watch his artillery, then went ridin' back on a poor lathered horse that didn't look like it could last the mornin' with two hundred and eighty pounds of blubber on its back. Lafayette kept ridin' between Lee and the right wing, askin' for orders and givin' advice, with those arched eyebrows dancin' like drunken caterpillars. And Hamilton was everywhere, like always, tryin' to tell everyone their business, like always.

But there was no confusion in one fact: Americans still knew how to make a retrograde maneuver better than any army on the face of the earth. That's what Lee called it. A retrograde maneuver. 'Twas also known as a retreat.

## Matt Jacobs:

Like I told you, foot soldiers is the last to know anything. They's jess s'posed to do what they's told. So when the word come for us to retreat, I didn't ask no questions. But I didn't run. Neither did Willard. We was part of one of the "picked battalions," New Englanders, mostly, sent out to hit the British that mornin'. And we retreated the way we went forward, like soldiers, in step.

But we was damn mad that we'd barely been brought into the action 'fore turnin', and we was cursin' our commanders and cursin' the heat. I was so damn dry I couldn't spit. Hell, if I'd tried, I don't reckon I could've pissed.

## Hesperus Draper:

Remember the bird . . . imagine flyin' over that battlefield about eleven thirty in the mornin'.

You're comin' from the west, comin' up on the main body of the American army. They're marchin' east, past a Presbyterian Meetin' House, toward a cloud of smoke about three miles away.

And at the head of the column is the man himself, ridin' a fine white charger, just like a general in an English oil paintin'. He's leadin' his men down a hill to the planked bridge at the West Ravine. From there, the land rises gentle, maybe five hundred yards, to a hedged fence. Then, it slopes into the second ravine and rises gentle again. Beyond are fields of Indian corn, some thick woods, and the Monmouth Road, so sandy it looks like a ribbon of yellow, cuttin' through the fields and disappearin' into the woods.

And stumblin' along the road, headin' in the wrong direction, is a little fifer boy. A lone, little fifer boy.

You fly farther and see men comin' toward you. At first a few, then a few dozen, then a few hundred, hurryin' along the road, tramplin' through the cornfield, streamin' through the woods. Some are leaderless, movin' in bunches. But most are in formation—five battalions, maneuverin' backwards, like Steuben trained them.

And ridin' with them, as proud as a crow struttin' in the gutter, is General Charles Lee.

## Billy Lee:

'Twas the hottest day of history, yes, sir.

Henry Knox had just rid up, all sweaty and red, sayin', "General, it looks like a Sunday battle."

"I don't feel much like fighting on the Sabbath, Henry. But we must yield to the good of the country."

'Twas then that we all spied a little fifer boy comin' up the road from Monmouth, movin' on the quick-step.

Seein' us, he shouted, "They're comin', Your Honors. They're all comin' this way."

Knox asked, "Who's coming, my little man?"

"Why, our boys, Your Honor, our boys and the British right after them."

The General said, "Impossible." Then, he cocked his head to listen, but all we could hear was the marchin' beat of our own drums. So he leaned down and whispered to the fifer boy, "Son, if you say another word of this falsehood, I'll have you put over a cannon and caned. Do you understand?"

"Caned, sir? But—"

"I'll make it easier for you." And he put the lad under guard.

Then he rode ahead, crossin' the bridge, passin' a hedged fence, and comin' down a slopin' grade to a spring where a dozen soldiers was stoppin' for a drink. He said, "What's going on here?"

"A retreat, sir." Their young officer gave a spit. "We're flying from a shadow."

"Who ordered this retreat?"

"General Lee, sir."

"Why, that—" But the General caught his anger in front of the men.

More and more troops were comin' out of the trees on the left, more and more comin' down into the little ravine where we'd stopped.

And then Colonel Hamilton come gallopin' hard, shoutin', "General! General! We're betrayed! General Lee has betrayed you and the entire army."

The General snapped, "Colonel, calm yourself, sir."

Whatever was happenin', wasn't goin' to be no panic on the General's staff.

"Sorry, sir," answered Hamilton, "but Lee may have brought us to disaster."

And the General spurred his horse up the rise from the water hole, onto the plateau of cornfields and wheatfields and woods that led the last mile to Monmouth. And there was our army. Retreatin'. Again.

## Hesperus Draper:

We were ridin' through the cornfield. Lee was sayin', "I was against this maneuver all along, Draper. And once more my military prophecy proved correct."

"You're a regular Isaiah, General. They should put you in the Bible."

"The history books will be enough."

'Twas then that I saw somethin' risin' from the ravine up ahead that caused me to say, "General, if you don't have a page yet, you're about to get one." 'Twas a cloud-white horse bearin' the biggest, maddest, reddest-faced Washington I'd ever seen.

Lee reined up and started to say somethin', like "Ah, good morning—"

And Washington boomed, "My God, General Lee, what are you doing?"

"Sir? Sir?" Lee pretended he didn't hear him, or didn't understand.

"What is the reason for this disorder and confusion?"

"Reason, sir? Why . . . why, there are reasons aplenty, and they are obvious."

"They're not obvious to me, sir!"

"Why . . . why"—Lee seemed shocked, but he rallied his wits better than he'd rallied his men—"contradictory intelligence, sir, officers abandoning favorable positions in the midst of battle, and you know right well what I've thought of this operation from the beginning."

And Washington just blew. "God damn you, sir! Whatever your opinions are, I expected my orders to be obeyed. The British at Monmouth are no more than a covering party!"

He was wrong about that. But not about anything else.

He give Lee a few more *God damns* while I backed my horse up a bit, tryin' to get out of the way of his temper.

"Sir," said Lee when he could force a word in, "these troops are not able to meet British grenadiers."

"You haven't tried them, sir!" thundered Washington. "They can, and by God, they will."

"Then . . . then . . . I must protest—"

"No, you will not protest, you son of a—" Washington caught himself. "You're a damned ignorant poltroon, sir. Nothin' more."

He looked at Lee and me as if we were both useless. Then he kicked his horse into the mass of men retreatin' through the corn stalks and steam.

Lee looked at me with an expression of dead shock on his face, and he started to sputter about how willin' he was to do his duty. Then he fell silent because he could hear our men cheerin'.

## Matt Jacobs:

George Washington might have kept my father a slave for all of his life, but I cheered him when I saw him come gallopin' along our lines. He'd stop this, if anybody would.

He was shoutin', swingin' his arms, givin' orders. And Varnum's boys was spreadin' out across that field, wheelin' into line to cover our retreat. Old Steuben, he sure would've been proud of how those boys looked, even if some of them was keelin' over as they went, keelin' over in the brutal heat.

## Alexander Hamilton:

I fell in with the General as he rode through the cornfield and rallied the retreating men. As yet, the only evidence of the enemy came from cannonballs plowing up the ground. These the General regarded as no more than gnats. But the words of Colonel Harrison, who now came galloping back from the rear guard, struck him like a blow:

"Sir! Sir!" Harrison shouted. "The British are pushing forward! Sixteenth Light Dragoons in the van. They'll be on us in fifteen minutes."

One could not say that the color left the General's face. In that heat, under that sun, every man's face was broiled red. But his eyes narrowed, his jaw clenched, and a simple truth assailed him: if the British caught us in full flight, we could be cut to pieces.

As he looked about to get the lay of the land,

Tench Tilghman came galloping up with a Jerseyite colonel.

"Sir!" cried Tilghman. "If you mean to make a stand—"

"I have to make a stand," answered Washington.

"Colonel Rhea knows the ground, sir," said Tilghman.

Washington turned to Rhea and said, "Well, then?"

And he took in every detail of Rhea's description of the terrain. As soon as the Jerseyman was done, the General had a plan fixed and ready to put into motion. Some have questioned the celerity of his mind. But none who saw him on the field at Monmouth ever would.

He rode forward and positioned units commanded by Colonels Stewart and Ramsay in a point of woods, from whence they could fire into the British flank. As they were part of Anthony Wayne's division, General Wayne now came up to take command.

Washington ordered him, "Dispute the ground as long as possible!"

"Yes, sir," said Wayne. "Inch by inch."

"Minute by minute will do. Just give me time to form the main body beyond the bridge."

Then Washington wheeled his horse and galloped back to Varnum's men. He ordered them up to a hedged fence on a hill some four hundred yards behind us. Once the enemy had run the gauntlet of our men in the point of woods, they would have to assail this position. By then, the main body would be properly positioned.

## Hesperus Draper:

Lee was still sittin' on his horse, where Washington had left him, still tryin' to read the ground and make a decision. Didn't take a genius to see that the best place for us to form up would be at the hedged fence on the rise to the west. Lee hadn't come to that yet, but Washington had.

Now Hamilton rode up demandin' to know what dispositions Lee had made.

Lee seemed stunned, like a duck knocked down by bird shot but still alive.

I said, "General Lee is gettin' the lay of the land."

"If he's confused—"

And Lee snapped to, jumpin' on Hamilton. "Do I appear to you to have lost my senses, sir? Do I not possess myself?"

"You're in possession of yourself," answered Hamilton. "But we seek to possess the enemy, sir."

Now Washington came gallopin' back on that lathered white charger that looked as wobbly as a three-legged table. 'Twas plain that the heat would bring that horse down before too long. 'Twas likely to bring us all down.

"General," cried Lee, lookin' past Hamilton, "are you taking command here, or shall I?"

Washington had his temper under control again. Maybe he saw the gravity of the situation that had caused Lee to retreat. Five thousand British troops were more than a rear guard. He said, "If you wish to take it, I'll return to the main body and arrange them on the heights at the rear."

"I will take command here, Your Excellency. And

I will check the enemy. And I will be the last to leave the field." Lee was gettin' windy, blowin' a big voice so all the men would hear. I was hopin' it might give him a little of his old spirit. 'Twould be better than havin' a stunned duck for a superior officer.

Then Hamilton pulled out his sword and give it a flourish over his head, like he was drunk with the heat or the excitement. What he was drunk with was sarcasm. He said, "Stay here, my dear General Lee, and I'll stay with you. And we'll both die on this spot."

Lee looked at him like he was a dog in need of shootin'. "One of us has lost his senses, sir. But when I've put the men in readiness, I will die here with you. Right on this spot, if you like."

Lee might as well have died. He thought he'd made the right decision, retreatin'. And Washington was doin' exactly what Lee had planned to do—rally on good ground, hold, volley, and fall back to the main body. But after his retreat from the courthouse, I don't think Lee could have rallied those men for a night in a tavern.

You see, there's many kinds of leadership. Lee led by complaint, blame, sarcasm, and self-importance. Washington led the same way sometimes, but on the battlefield, he rode a white horse, and Lee just kept on bein' Lee.

Still, Washington had no choice but to leave Lee in command. Then he galloped back to the main body. But that presumptuous little Hamilton decided to stay with us, and he started urgin' Lee to put more units along that hedged fence. Varnum's unit had gone in on the left. Hamilton wanted Colonel Livingston's brigade sent to the right.

Lee sputtered, "Sir, do not tell me my business. I am—"

"Sir!" I said, headin' off an argument for which we had no time, " 'Tis a strong position, that fence. And the artillery up there needs protection."

Henry Knox had put two field pieces on a little hillock behind the fence, two more on the slopin' ground in front of it, all to hold off the enemy attack we knew was comin'.

Lee opened his mouth as if to declaim somethin'— maybe more Shakespeare—then he just said, "Very well. Order Livingston's brigade to the fence."

So we all went gallopin' up that hill, and with a few good shouts, we had Livingston's lads wheelin' into position like old, blooded professionals, just like Steuben had trained them. 'Twas a beautiful thing.

Then I looked back at the point of woods juttin' into the cornfield. And there were the British—the Sixteenth Light Dragoons, advancin' in line through the trampled stalks way cavalry does when they're fixin' to charge, and followin' them, about two thousand grenadiers and King's Guards. Hell-on-horseback leadin' hell-on-foot.

Knox's cannon started barkin', but at six hundred yards, they did damn little damage to those fine British lines. 'Twas the boys hidden in the point of woods who'd strike the first blow. Strike hard, I thought, then run like hell.

## Matt Jacobs:

We was hidden in the trees, maybe six hundred of us, down in the shadows, down in the cool shadows, the only cool place on the field that day. Front rank was kneelin', second rank was standin', and every man's shoulder was anchored to his mate's, or pressed hard against a tree.

We let the dragoons go by with their spurs janglin' and their hangers clankin'. We didn't want them and their big horses comin' in at us.

We was waitin' on the infantry, the King's Guards and the grenadiers in them tall hats. They come by in column, all red and white, marchin' left to right, as tall and arrogant as soldiers ever was. 'Twas as if they didn't even think we'd be waitin' in them woods to ambush 'em. The tramp of their feet and the tootlin' of their fifes was so loud they couldn't hear Anthony Wayne and his officers, whisperin', "Steady, lads . . . steady . . ."

Willard whispered, "When's that crazy bastard gonna tell us to fire?"

"When the whole flank's exposed," I whispered. Then I wiped the sweat from my hands so I wouldn't wet my cartridges as I handled 'em.

I didn't like havin' Anthony Wayne commandin' us. He'd charged like a madman at Brandywine. And they say he was driven crazy by the massacre at Paoli's Tavern, when the British caught his men at night, mostly asleep, and put 'em all to the bayonet. No wonder they called him mad.

"We better shoot soon," said Sammy, "or they'll be past, and those boys on up at the hedgerow, they'll have hell to pay."

Then the whispered order of "Make ready" went down the line.

Then "Front rank, *fire!*"

I pulled my trigger, and those trees were filled with roarin' noise and smoke so chokin' that you'd think you was in the chimney instead of the oven.

Then "Second rank, *fire!*"

That column closest to us all but collapsed. Boys were down, groanin', bloody, dead. But now the rest of them turned on us, fired one blastin' volley that did more damage to the tree branches above us than it did to us. Then they came chargin', bayonets lowered.

Our lads got off one more blast 'fore they was on us—seven hundred of 'em, scramblin' over their mates, screamin', slashin', slammin' into us.

'Twas like nothin' you can imagine.

There was bodies swirlin', bloody steel flashin', redcoats comin' from every corner of your eye, and a sound that mixed together all the bad noises you ever heard—all the shrieks of pain and shouts of hate, all the thumpin' and thunkin' of bone and flesh and steel and wood, and all of it happenin' in burnin' smoke and heat so bad it was killin' men all by itself.

I tried to run—I ain't ashamed to say it—but them woods was so jammed with fightin' men and so cramped with trees that I *had* to fight, just to find room to run. A big grenadier come at me. I parried and lunged, like I'd been taught, and somehow I stuck him in the thigh and he went stumblin' off.

And all whilst I was fightin' for my life, Willard Walt was fightin' for his.

And so was Sammy Brisby . . . till he took a British

bayonet, right above his crossbelts. I heard him scream, "No! No! Oh, Goddamn, no!"

And the redcoat that stuck him, he screamed, "Die, you nigger fuck. Die!"

So, I drove my blade right into the side of that redcoat's neck. I didn't look at his face. Didn't want to see his eyes. I just screamed "*You* die, you redcoat fuck! *You* die!"

That brung a grenadier screamin' at me. But Willard's musket went off right in his face. Blew his brains up into his hat.

Then we heard the thumpin' of hooves and the screamin' of horses. The dragoons was comin' in where the trees was thin, comin' in with sabers slashin'.

'Twas time to run. We left Sammy, dyin' in the middle of all them swirlin' boots and screamin' men, with that neck-stuck redcoat gushin' blood all over him.


## Hesperus Draper:

Wayne's ambush at the point of woods was a beautiful thing to see from six hundred yards, but it must have been hell up close, and hell with bells on when the British turned on the lads who done the ambushin'.

By then, our line stretched four hundred yards along the hill. Charles Lee had gotten hold of himself and was ridin' back and forth, shoutin' orders. Hamilton was ridin' wherever Lee wasn't. Henry Knox was huffin' and puffin' and hollerin' to his cannoneers on the hillock behind us. And I was on my horse, tryin' to steady the nervous lads on the far right of our line.

But the first action was comin' on the far left, over where Wayne's lads were streamin' out of the woods, rushin' down the ravine, then up toward the safety of our hedged fence.

The dragoons who'd flushed them had those boys right where mounted troops always want infantry—out in the open and on the run. They sabered the stragglers and ran down them who turned to fight. And they used our boys like a movin' shield, ridin' right in amongst 'em, right at that fence. They figured they could gallop right up to it, and once they'd jumped it, have themselves a fine slaughter. 'Tis a basic truth of warfare that dragoons are death to infantry in line.


## Matt Jacobs:

Runnin' for my life. Runnin' with them horses thunderin' after me. Runnin' hard for that hedged fence, never even wonderin' where Willard was. But when I was maybe forty yards away, I heard someone behind the fence shoutin', "Front rank, present!"

Then I seen the worst sight of all that day. 'Twas the muskets of our own lads, pokin' through the hedge, pointin' right at us!

And I heard someone screamin', "Aim high! Aim high! Take down the dragoons!" But you know the truth. After thirty or forty yards, nobody knows where a musketball's goin'.

I run on, tryin' to decide if I should keep runnin'

and be shot by my own men, or drop and be trampled by them dragoons. When someone screamed "Fire!" I dropped, and I ain't afraid to say it—I pissed my breeches.

The volley blew out at us like a hot smoky wind. Lads all around me went down, but plenty of horses screamed and went tumblin', too, and enough dragoons was hit that the rest of them reined up. And when they heard an officer scream, "Second rank, present!" they turned and ran right away as fast as they'd chased us.

There wouldn't be no second volley. That hell was over. Lord, was I thirsty.

## Hesperus Draper:

I couldn't have given the order to fire into my own men.

But I had no time to think about it because just as the dragoons were fallin' away from Varnum's volley, guards and grenadiers were pourin' out of the point of woods. Down into the ravine, past the spring and up the rise they came, screamin', ragin', some droppin' from the heat, but none of them worried about musketballs or cannonballs or Yankee courage.

I spied a mounted British officer, ridin' over from where the dragoons had been beaten back. 'Twas General Clinton, and he was screamin', as clear as a bell, "Charge, Grenadiers! Charge! Never heed forming!"

But heed our muskets, I thought, when Livingston shouted, "Present!" and our men rammed their pieces through the hedge. Every man stood his ground, even if we were outnumbered three or four to one. It made me proud.

Then Knox screamed, "Fire!" And the two cannon on the hillock behind me sprayed grapeshot at the red wall in front of me.

An instant later, Livingston screamed, "Fire!"

Now the air was so dense and hot that the roar of cannon fire and musketry had nowhere to go, so it doubled back against your skull, and the sulfurous, chokin' smoke had nowhere to blow, so you sucked it into you like stingin' poison.

Out in front of our lines, men's arms flew out from their bodies or flew to their faces or grabbed to their guts. Hats and muskets went whirligiggin'. Men were wasted and thrown away like doll babies or lead soldiers.

But they kept comin', kept roarin'. 'Twas fury they were showin', fury at us and fury at the lads who'd ambushed them from the point of woods.

Then we saw that the dragoons had flanked us on our right. They'd ridden from one end of the line to the other and found the end of the hedgerow. Now they were poundin' hard toward our flank.

Henry Knox was already pullin' his guns off the knoll, gallopin' them across the field toward the West Ravine Bridge. 'Twasn't cowardice. 'Twas war. You saved the artillery. At all costs, you saved the artillery.

Charles Lee screamed for a retreat, and this time he was right.

The drums took up the fall-back tattoo. But do you know that those boys along the hedgerow tried to stand and fight, fight hand to hand? They were buyin'

Washington more time than he needed. Things sure had changed since Kips Bay.

The platoon commanders had to call them out, and they fell back company by company, keepin' up a steady coverin' fire as they went. Nobody threw away weapons. Nobody panicked. With the British chasin' us, and the dragoons thunderin' hard toward our flank, we fell back across a rollin' field toward the bridge, about four hundred yards to our rear. Beyond it, our own main army was now drawn up, with artillery in position, all dug in, all ready. If we could just make it across that bridge—

I wasn't but a hundred yards from it when my horse went down. Stepped in a hole, broke his front leg. And right then, a big dragoon decided he wanted me.

But a platoon of Livingston's men stopped and turned, fightin' the rear guard. They shouted at me to drop, then they presented and delivered a volley of ball and buck right over me.

The dragoon's big horse screamed and went down, with the dragoon barrel-rollin' right over him, losin' his helmet, landin' on his own right arm. It snapped as he hit, and he came to rest in a sittin' position, lookin' at his flopped arm like it belonged to someone else.

I pointed my pistol at him. Could've killed him. But with all those other grenadiers and dragoons comin' after us, runnin' seemed a better use of my time.

Up ahead, hundreds of men were squeezin' onto the planked bridge. Lee was wavin' his sword, urgin' the stragglers to safety. And Hamilton, well, he was like me, mountless and movin' hard by shank's mare.

As I come closer, I could see two batteries of six-pounders in position on the rise beyond the bridge. I could hear the gun captains callin' orders. I could see the sergeants sweepin' their long linstocks through the air, lowerin' their quickmatches to the touchholes and . . . well, I reckoned that one way or the other, from front or rear, I was about to die.

Those four cannon banged, and I swear, I saw bags of grapeshot come shootin' out into the sunshine and tear open in midair, and then I could hear hundreds of pieces of shot come whizzin' over my head, not five feet above me.

I thanked the Lord and never looked back till I was over the bridge.

By then, those cannon had fired two or three more times and turned the field before that bridge into one bloody mess. Dragoons and grenadiers were down everywhere. Horse were screamin' and stumblin' and gallopin' off, wide-eyed.

And our American positions, well, thanks to the delayin' action we'd fought, they were rock solid.

Washington had arrayed his men in three lines across a wide front on the risin' ground of Perrine's Hill. Knox's cannon were covered by Anthony Wayne. Behind them, and runnin' toward the left, Lord Stirling commanded his division. And somewhere at the top of the ridge, workin' with a reserve, was Lafayette.

As for Lee, he'd been ordered to withdraw to Englishtown, to rally the troops who were "the most exhausted and demoralized" by the retreat. 'Twas like sendin' the drunkards off to sober up with the brewmaster.

I decided to make for the center of the action, for the big man on the white horse. I was hurryin' up the hill when, all of a sudden, the big man was down.

## Billy Lee:

I seen the General go down, and I cried, "Oh, no!" There was British cannonballs plowin' up the ground around us now, and I thought . . . well, you know what I thought. But 'twasn't the General who was down. 'Twas his horse. Guess that big white charger hadn't been trained for this kind of hell. Horse just collapsed right under him.

'Twas my job to see that the General was always mounted, so right quick I brung up his favorite sorrel mare. He was back up in no time.

Men cheered all around, them who still had the voice in all that heat.

'Twas the hottest, noisiest afternoon that any man would ever go through. But I sure was glad I was there to see it. What would have happened if I'd demanded my freedom? Who would've brung the General his horse?

And I never would've seen what they call the great cannonade. British brought ten guns to the hedge fence where they'd driven our boys in. And Henry Knox had twelve guns up on Perrine's Hill. They was 'bout five hundred yards between them. And both sides kept up a roarin' hot fire for longer than ears could stand it.

## Hesperus Draper:

Those two armies went at each other until dark. Heat. Blood. More heat. Charge. Countercharge. Heat. Cotton-spittin' thirst. And only one Molly Pitcher on the whole field. And she was only haulin' water for her husband's gun crew.

I was gettin' too old for this. But somehow I stayed in the thick of it all day. Don't ask me why. I wasn't the kind who forgot himself in battle. Didn't have foolhardy courage. Every time I heard a musket, I reckoned someone was firin' at me. So you can be sure I said good-bye to Charlotte more than once on that field.

But that was a day when you couldn't duck, because nobody else was, whether they were facin' the Forty-second Highlanders in an apple orchard on the left, or fightin' hand to hand at the Parsonage Farm on the right. If you can be proud of men killin' each other, you had to be proud at Monmouth.

But battles are ugly things, especially when night comes on, and the mosquitoes start buzzin', and out in the dark, dyin' men cry for their mothers.

## Alexander Hamilton:

I never saw the General to so much advantage as at Monmouth. America owes a great deal to him for that day's work; a general rout, dismay, and disgrace would have attended the whole army in any other hands but his. By his own good sense and fortitude, he turned the day. Other officers earned great merit, but he directed the whole with the skill of a master workman. He brought order out of confusion and animated his troops and led them to success.

## The Marquis de Lafayette:

Late that night, when it was plain that the fighting and dying was done for the day, I went to visit the General. I brought a flask of brandy, a piece of sausage, a small round of hard cheese.

He thanked me and complimented me on my work that day.

"It was not so good as Wayne's or Greene's."

"You will have days as glorious." He took a long drink of my brandy and offered me that flask again.

I said, "No . . . no . . . it is all for you."

"Thank you. Brandy will help me sleep."

"Where will you sleep?"

"Here. On the ground."

He then made gesture to his military cloak, laid out beneath a tree, and he said, "There is room for two. If you promise not to snore, you can have half."

And I thought of the words he had said to me: "I will be father and friend."

It was hot, and the bugs buzzed around our ears as soon as we lay down, but the exhaustion of the day came over us. The last words that he said to me were "We shall have Clinton and all his men tomorrow."

## Hesperus Draper:

Clinton took a page from Washington's book. Left his campfires burnin' through the night and pulled his troops out. By dawn they were ten miles away and bound for Sandy Hook.

Washington claimed victory because the British left the field first. Clinton claimed victory because he held off the Americans and got to where he was goin'. But if there'd ever been a doubt as to who was runnin' the Continental army, Monmouth laid it to rest. And if there'd ever been any doubt that Americans could stand against British regulars, Monmouth proved otherwise.

Within a day or two, Lee was complainin' that he'd "been sent out of the field when victory was assured." He was even heard to say that Washington had no more to do in the victory at Monmouth than "strip the dead." Then he demanded a court-martial, to clear his tarnished name.

No surprise that he was found guilty of insubordination, among other charges, and punished with a year's removal from duty. But he kept sayin' bad and worse about Washington and his "tinsel dignity." Finally, John Laurens, one of Washington's aides, challenged him to a duel. Put a pistol ball in his side. Damn near killed him.

Lee survived, but he never returned to the army. Just went driftin', blown this way and that on the wind of his own words. When he died a few years later, only his dogs attended him. They were found lickin' his face, tryin' to wake their dead master. As Lee would have said, *Sic transit gloria!*

*c.d.—And* Sic transit *to battlefield* gloria *as well. My uncle pointed out that Washington had won three battles, lost six, and fought once to a draw. His army was maturing, but his record was hard truth for a proud, aggressive man forced to fight like Fabius the Delayer. Washington yearned for another victory, but he would not fight in battle again for three years.*

*The rest of 1778 was given over to old problems in new guises—the French and Indians. For all their protestations of alliance, the French were offering little material support, no troops, and a fleet that stayed in American waters only a short time. Meanwhile, the Tories on the frontier, in alliance with the Iroquois, had turned their fury onto the American settlements.*

## John Britain,
## known as Silverheels:

My son and I moved north to the land of the Senecas. And my son took a Seneca woman. Because it is the clan of the mother that makes a child who he is, my grandchildren would be Seneca. So I would fight if the Senecas told me to fight.

You cannot know how great were the Iroquois then, that both sides wanted us to fight for them. When it began, we told the Americans we would stay out. But the British brought gifts and promised trade. They reminded us that our fathers always fought for them. So we said we would fight for the British.

But the Oneidas and Tuscaroras sided with the Americans, and the great Iroquois union was broken.

In the summer of 1778 we marched with the Seneca chief known as Cornplanter, and the Mohawk Thayendanegea, who the British called Joseph Brant. There were five hundred of us, and many more Tories. We came from Fort Niagara. We attacked the Wyoming Valley, on the Susquehanna.

At Lackawanna, six hundred Americans came out to fight us. They thought they could beat us, so they called to us as they came. They said we were afraid. But we drew them on. We hid in the trees and grass. We surrounded them. Then we struck. Some whites jumped in the river and tried to swim to their fort. We killed them in the water. We made the river run red. We killed all but thirty-three. Then we burned their fort and scattered their wives and children, as the whites once did at Mingo Town.

Then we attacked at Cherry Valley. And the earth ran as red as the river.

The Americans cried out to Caunotaucarius. His answer, so they say, was simple: "The only sure way of preventing Indian ravages is to carry the war into their own country."

Then he sent four thousand men to do it.

I have told you many bad things already. But I will tell you more.

The American army, under Sullivan, came north. They drove our people before them. We fought when we could. We ran when there were too many. They burned our towns and destroyed our crops. They cut down our orchards.

So we fell back to the great Iroquois town of Genesee. There were more than a hundred lodges, surrounded by fine fields. But we did not think we could hold, because the army sent by Caunotaucarius was big. Our scouts watched them coming.

My son was one of those scouts. One day he saw white soldiers, twenty-four of them, coming through the woods. He let them see him, so they would chase him.

He drew them on toward his Seneca brothers, but before he came to them, the whites shot him down in a field of corn. While the blood of my son watered the cornstalks, the whites argued over who would scalp him. They were very stupid, because the Senecas fell on them and killed all but two. These Senecas brought me the terrible news with the two prisoners.

Chief Cornplanter put a knife in my hand and said, "Make the death slow." Our warriors stripped the prisoners and stretched them between poles and tied them hands and feet. But I had no heart for torture. I had no heart for anything. I gave the knife back to Cornplanter.

"Torture must be done, old man," the chief said. He wore a silver ring in his nose and a headdress of turkey feathers. He stood straight, as a chief should.

But I would never stand straight again. I said, "Let others do it. Torture cannot be done if you do not have the heart for it."

So others made stabs in both men, in places where great pain would not bring death. They skinned one, so that the white of his ribs showed, and his scream was like a knife driven into the air. Then they punched out the eyes of the other. Then they cut off the balls of them both.

I went away from their screaming. I went to a quiet place by the river.

And the captive white woman came to me. She had lived with the Senecas many years. Her man had been killed fighting Sullivan. She said, "We both have pain worse than what those whites have."

"Theirs will be over tonight," I said.

"And ours will go on." This woman was Mary Britain. And she was right.

*c.d.—Washington wrote to General Sullivan: "The commander in chief congratulates the army on its success against the Senecas and their allies. Their whole country has been overrun and laid waste and they themselves compelled to place their security in the British fortress at Fort Niagara."*

*But this was the only American success of 1779.*

*The true history of that year was best expressed in a single line from Washington: "We have reached the point where a wheelbarrow of currency will not buy a wheelbarrow of goods." A dollar in specie, worth five Continental dollars in 1778, was worth forty in 1779, and would be worth ninety in 1780.*

## The Marquis de Lafayette:

I was in France for most of 1779, acting on behalf of my American friends.

It was hard for me to leave my family the following spring, now that I had a new son, but my efforts had helped to convince the Count de Vergennes that in addition to naval support, France should send an army to America. Now I was charged with bringing the glorious news that six thousand troops under the Count de Rochambeau would soon embark.

Though I was welcomed in Boston as hero and ally and was spirited through the streets to the sound of church bells and booming cannon, the America to which I returned was not a place of happiness. Snow lay four feet deep from Boston to Pennsylvania. And Washington's winter quarters at Morristown, New Jersey, may have been the most sorriest place of all.

Upon our reunion, the General's eyes filled with tears. My return to America had been a surprise. And so was my glorious news about Rochambeau. The joy on the General's face was as unrestrained as the joy in my heart.

"We must find wine," he said. "But lately we've been contented with grog, made of New England rum and drunk out of a wooden bowl."

"That would be a fine drink with which to toast to the French army," I said.

And so the toasts were drunk, and we talked long into the night.

"With this news," he said, "we must redouble our efforts with the states to make the American army worthy."

"The states?" This puzzled me.

"My dear Marquis, the money issued by Congress has grown so worthless, they have surrendered to the states the business of paying and outfitting troops."

"Does this not make your job more complicated?"

"Impossibly. I see one head gradually changing into thirteen."

"Like the hydra-headed beast of mythology?" I said.

"The hydra replicates itself and can't be killed," answered Washington. "But when Americans no longer see Congress as the controlling power of the United States, they are killing their hopes for independency."

I took the grog pot from the table and refreshed our bowls.

"Unity must be our principle," he went on. "But the people now look to their states for everything. And each state is driven to follow its own interests. This is how we began back in Boston."

I said, "This is no way for an army to fight a war."

"No, but"—he stood—"I've become so inured to difficulties in the course of this war, that I've learned to look on them with much more tranquillity than at the start. The troubles ahead will demand all our efforts, but I'm far from despairing. And I sleep well. So I'll light you to your room and bid you good night."

His hair had grown grayer and the lines cut deeper furrows in his face, but like a father, he said words that made me forget my own worries.

C.D.—*Their optimism was not well founded. The French under Rochambeau were not nearly as cooperative as Lafayette had expected. They temporized in Rhode Island while Washington returned to the Hudson to await his chance for an attack on the British army in New York.*

*Meanwhile, Cornwallis led a second British army through the South. At Camden, he met Horatio Gates, in command of the southern department. Gates fought, was beaten, then ran, leaving his army and galloping a hundred and eighty miles in three days. Alexander Hamilton said that such a ride "does admirable credit to the activity of a man at his time of life. But it disgraces the general and the soldier."*

*Things only grew worse. The Hudson, and Washington himself, were almost lost to the perfidy of Benedict*

*Arnold. The man whom many considered the best field general on either side—frustrated by his treatment from Congress, in need of money, married to a Tory— had turned traitor. Washington was heartbroken.*

*Meanwhile, the troops continued to grumble over worthless money. Some threatened a march on Congress in protest. Others mutinied, and their ringleaders were hanged. Washington wrote, "We are at the end of our tether, and now or never our deliverance must come."*

*Some small hope arrived with the Articles of Confederation, which outlined the powers of Congress, though the beast with thirteen heads still stalked the land, or perhaps it was thirteen separate beasts.*

## Alexander Hamilton:

I might ascribe the following scene to a toothache, of which the General was suffering many; or perhaps to my frustrations over the approval of the Articles of Confederation, which created a toothless and taxless Congress; or perhaps the simpler explanation was that both of us had worked the night through on correspondence for Rochambeau.

The scene occurred at the headquarters, at New Windsor on the Hudson, one February morning in 1781.

The work of the day, as always, was heavy and pressing, with aides hurrying to and fro, making the house a great beehive of business. I passed the General on the stairs, and he informed me that he wished to speak to me.

I answered that I would wait upon him presently, then went below and delivered to Mr. Tilghman a letter. Then I passed by the Marquis de Lafayette, and we discussed some matter for perhaps a minute. Then I hurried on.

Instead of finding the General, as usual, in his room, I found him waiting for me at the top of the stairs, where he accosted me in a very angry tone: "Colonel Hamilton! You've kept me waiting here ten minutes. I must tell you, sir, you treat me with disrespect."

I replied, without petulancy, but with decision. "I am not conscious of it, sir, but since you have thought it necessary to tell me of it, we part."

"Very well, sir," he said angrily. "If it be your choice."

And by this I did not mean that we parted for a short time. I had done with such scenes. I was leaving his service. That very day.

Within a half an hour, the General sent Mr. Tilghman to tell me of his candid desire to heal the difference, blaming it upon a moment of passion. This was typical of the General's overall spirit. But my mind was made up.

I did not like the position of aide-de-camp. It had in it a kind of personal dependence. And though I held high place in the General's counsels, I had felt no friendship for him. Our dispositions were the opposite of each other, and the pride of my temper would not suffer me to profess what I did not feel.

I will tell you that the General was a very honest man. His competitors were men of slender ability and less integrity. His popularity had been essential to the safety of America. But I yearned for field command, like my friend Lafayette. And I had been subjected once too often to the temper that he showed to me on the stairs, a temper he showed more to his family than to anyone. But as we were family, he showed us as well his understanding, and by July, I had a command.

My years at his headquarters, however, had made it plain to me that it would be by introducing order into our finances—by restoring public credit—not by gaining battles, that we would finally gain our object.

## Jacob, Mount Vernon Slave:

Well, that spring the British come into Virginia. I 'member the day. A fine April mornin'. I'se workin' in the mansion house, sweepin' out the new north room, what they called the large dining room. Walls is all roughed in, fireplace is finished, jess like the General order it. . . . Do you know, even in '76, with the British tryin' to push him off Harlem Heights, he write Massa Lund 'structions about the buildin' of that room? Reckon such thinkin' relax him. . . .

Comin' onto six years since the General leave. And we has our own way of doin' things now. And I has to say it: things is nice.

Alice be in the kitchen, makin' up dinner for Massa Lund and his fam'ly, like always. And my daughter, Narcissa—she's 'bout twenty-seven—she's hangin' laundry out by the spinnin' house, like always.

And every time I sweeps my pile out to the west door, I see her there, workin' in the sun. She's a fine-lookin' gal. But I don't look so much at her. 'Tis her little Billy that catch my eye. He's only two . . . settin' on the ground nearby, babblin' to his mama . . . can't talk much, see. But he's the apple of Grandpa's eye, 'cause one of the words he *do* know is "Grandpa."

So I stand there in the doorway, sweepin' and watchin', wishin' that the boy she jump the broom with ain't such a damn fool. When he hear that they's a British army down Richmond way, he decide to run away and join up, fight for his freedom 'gainst the white massas. So little Billy got no papa, see. But tha's the way 'tis with most slave chilluns. Leastways he got a grandpa.

I give Billy a wave. He don't see me, so I give a little hoot. And tha's when the plantation bell commence to ringin'.

Down by the kitchen door, Skunky Tom be poundin' the bell. He git his name 'cause he sprayed by a skunk once and don't never smell right again. He's poundin' the bell and shoutin', "The British is comin'! The British is comin'."

I look out at the river—I can jess see it 'cause the leaves ain't filled out yet—and sure 'nough, they's a ship out there, and a boat comin' ashore under a white flag, with a dozen redcoat marines and a officer in a nice blue coat.

Massa Lund, he come runnin' out from the mansion house whilst the overseers and servants and slaves all gather 'round.

And one of the overseers shout, "Mr. Lund, the British is here to burn us out. Burn us out for certain, like they done in Maryland."

Massa Lund look scairt, but he keep calm. "We ain't certain of nothin'."

"What's certain," say the other overseer, who been

to the dock, "is that one of our cutters is headin' out to the ship now, carryin' 'bout a dozen slaves."

Massa Lund, he be tall, see, but he ain't what you call a straight-up man, not like the General. He be kind of slumped and skinny. Don't have no air about him. When he wear a simple brown coat, he don't look like a true massa dressed for comfort. He jess look like a man who got nothin' to wear but a simple brown coat. And he don't know what all to do.

I reckon 'tis a good thing Miz Washin'ton ain't there.

Massa Lund shift his eyes from the overseers to the slaves and back, and you know, funny thing, there ain't so many slaves as jess a minute ago. Seem like they's siftin' off into the woods. Disappearin', maybe.

I looks behind me, and I see Alice, but Narcissa be one of the disappearin' ones. And little Billy gone with her.

Now Massa Lund give some orders. Then he go runnin' off down the path.

Th'overseer, a bulky feller named Smoot, with a nose that look like a prune, he tell us all to git back to work.

I takes Alice by the arm and move back some, but nobody else move at all. So Smoot finger the whip he carry coiled up in his belt. Never see coiled whips when the General be about, but times change, they do.

Now, they's a slave by the name Ned, bad-tempered boy who already run off more 'n once. He say, "I hear tell 'bout how these British, they give you your freedom if'n you goes and fights for 'em."

And Smoot snort through his pruney nose, "Git back to work."

But nobody move. 'Cept me and Alice. We start backin' toward the house. This here don't look too good. I ain't thinkin' no more 'bout Narcissa and Billy. I'se wonderin' if the mansion house slaves is all fixin' to rise up.

But right then another overseer and two white servants come runnin' out the big house with muskets. That break things up right quick, and everyone go back to they business. Everyone still there, that is.

But Narcissa ain't there, nor little Billy. I look in the kitchen, over by the laundry, back in the room where she live. But she jess plain gone.

'Bout four hours later, I go on that British ship.

I'se part of the slave crew that come out in two big rowboats loaded to the gunwales with food, see. Good food—Mrs. Washin'ton's hams, salted herrin', cornmeal, cider, molasses . . . Hell, we empties the pantry and the smokehouse, too.

I hears Massa Lund standin' on the back of the ship, and the British captain talkin' with him.

"My dear sir," the captain say, "how kind of you to bring two boatloads of provisions. One would have been sufficient to save your plantation."

"Well, you see, sir"—and Massa Lund's voice shake—"I've brung the second boat to trade."

"Trade? Trade for what?"

Massa Lund point toward the front of the ship. "For them."

And there was the slaves, all clustered together, like the cap'n still tryin' to figger out where to put 'em all. They's twenty-five, mebbe. Mostly from our plantation, but I see some strange faces in there, too.

I got me a big ham over my shoulder, but I walks toward the front, tryin' to see if my daughter be there.

Then one of them redcoat marines puts his musket in front of me, and he growl, "Git back there, you."

Then I hears it, plain as day. "Grandpa!"

And I see my little Billy, in his mother's arms, and his mother's right in the middle of that crowd of Negroes.

I say, "Narcissa, what all is you doin'?"

"She runnin' away!" shout one of the other slaves. "Runnin' to freedom."

"Yes, indeed," say the British captain, and he come forward to a place where he's right in front of the slaves. "They've all asked for freedom. By the decrees we've made, I'm bound to give it."

And Massa Lund, he say, "Sir . . . sir, we're prepared to trade our second boatload of provisions for all the Mount Vernon slaves."

The captain say, "Sorry, sir, but I've given these people my word."

And them damn hoe niggers, they fall in with sayin' "Yassuh, cap'n," and "Thanks, boss," and all like that.

But I jess keep my eyes on Narcissa, and all's of a sudden, she yell, "Come on, Pa! Come and join us!"

And you know what? For a second I wants to. I wants to run away to freedom and find my boy. But what about Alice? What about Mount Vernon? I say, "Narcissa, you gots to come home. This ain't nothin' good for you, honey."

She shout, from all the way across the deck, "I gots to go. I gots to find Billy's pa."

"You ain't never gonna find that boy. He gone!"

"Mr. Lund Washington," say the captain, "remove this nigger."

And Lund tell me, real sharp. "Get off the ship."

And Narcissa yell, "I ain't goin' back, Pa. This be my only chance."

I gits to the little gangway, and I look back. Tha's when my heart feel like it might bust, 'cause Narcissa take little Billy's arm and wave it at me.

Then I hear the British captain say to Massa Lund, "I'll give you none of the slaves by the fo'c'stle. But I'll trade the second boatload of provisions for the slaves who've brought the first boatload aboard."

Then he make a big show of countin' how many of us they is. "Six. Yes. Those six slaves shall remain your property, through the goodness of His Majesty. And I shall not burn Mount Vernon."

Well, 'bout fifteen minutes later, we's rowin' away, see, and I look up at the ship and there's Narcissa, callin' to me, "Don't worry, Pa. I'se goin' to a better place. Me and Billy both."

First my boy, and now this. Jess don't seem right.


C.D.—*Washington wrote to Lund, "I am thoroughly persuaded that you acted from your desire to save my property and rescue the buildings from impending danger. But to go on board their vessels, carry them refreshments, commune with a parcel of plundering scoundrels, and request the favor of surrendering my Negroes was exceedingly ill-judged and might become a precedent for others. It would have been less painful to me to have heard that they had burnt my house and laid the plantation in ruins."*

*Washington may actually have believed his words, because, as always, he knew that his actions defined his reputation. But I think he was secretly pleased that his home had been saved. After all, he concluded the letter: "You shall never want of assistance, so long as it is in my power to afford it."*

*Meanwhile, the war raged on in Virginia. Washington sent Lafayette to provide some resistance. The young Frenchman marched with an army of about twelve hundred, mostly Virginians and men drawn from New England regiments.*

## Hesperus Draper:

We marched into Alexandria in late April.

Lafayette sent me ahead, hopin' I could prepare the Alexandrians for the bad news: we needed wagons and horses and food and shoes and . . . well, 'twas the usual predicament of the Continental army.

Lafayette guessed 'twould be better if a Virginian did the beggin' in Virginia. So he give the job to the man who owned the *Alexandria Gazette*.

But from the minute I rode into town, I knew there'd be nothin' for the army. 'Twas a market town. Lived and died off trade. And with the British blockadin' the coast, there was damn little trade goin' on, damn little hard money, and too damn much Continental paper. Grass grew between the boards on the docks. And the warehouse of Draper Importin' and Printin', 'twas plain empty. Even the mice had went elsewhere.

But still, Charlotte done her best. Even before we got there, she put an article in the paper about us comin'.

Then we printed up a handbill: "Alexandrians! A Patriot Army, come for your defense, calls to you for aid! We are in need of wagons, horses, shoes, et cetera, et cetera. For the sake of your state, for the sake of your country, help us."

We sent our apprentices out to spread the handbills. Then Charlotte and me went back to our house and slipped between the sheets.

Only did it once before we got up and had ourselves some supper with Lafayette. She loved seein' him, of course. And he played the admirin' boy, like always. He had all the tools to be one fine ladykiller—charm, flattery, and that smilin' lack of guile. Women loved him.

But Charlotte came back to bed with nobody but me. And you know what we did when we got to bed? We went to sleep. That's what happens when you get late in your forties. I wouldn't tell things so private, but the one truth you shouldn't ever forget is that life goes by faster than a long-dicked stallion chasin' a proud mare. So enjoy every minute, even the misery.

Now, once the folks of Alexandria got a look at them handbills . . . well, they did what self-respectin' patriots should do: they hid everything.

So Lafayette asked me if I'd go 'round and impress wagons and such. He explained, with that wide-eyed innocence he could play so well, "I would like a Virginian to do it. And you may use sergeants and privates, handpicked, so that we may be certain of their delicacy toward the inhabitants."

I said, "You mean you want me to go around, all nice and delicate, and say to folks, 'I need your wagon and your best horse, and here's a certificate for the value in Continental dollars.' Is that what you want?"

"It is my hope."

"General," I said, "I have to *live* here after the war."

"Ah, yes." And Lafayette raised his eyebrows, as though that fact had not yet occurred to him. "I see what you mean. I'll send someone else."

But no one could get much out of those people. Just a few wagons and a few more horses. And between Alexandria and Fredericksburg we didn't see so much as a swaybacked mare. That's how quick folks was to hide things out of fear of those damn near worthless Continentals.

So Lafayette kept the men movin' on foot, but he never wore them out in the heat. The longer the war went on, the truer that nickname was—the Soldiers' Friend. Lafayette said it best about the march: "When we are not able to do what we wish, we must do what we can."

And as I marched, I thought of how much of my life had gone by without Charlotte. And of how much money we'd lost in that damn war.

Fact was, officers had gone home by the hundreds because their families had gone to poverty. 'Twas one of the worst parts of the whole struggle. Washington fought tooth and nail for the promise of half pay for life for all officers. That was the way the British did things. 'Twas the right way, too.

Finally Congress come 'round. They made that promise. But that didn't mean anything would ever happen, because nobody believed Congress about anything.

C.D.—*My uncle rode with Lafayette all through that Virginia summer. Cornwallis had announced, "The boy cannot escape me." But for three months the boy played catch-as-catch-can with the great general. Finally, his bag empty yet again, Cornwallis was ordered back to the coast to await supply or withdrawal. He took a position between the York and James Rivers, at a place called Yorktown, and dug in.*

*That was when the French commanders saw a chance to strike a blow in Virginia. They informed Washington that Admiral de Grasse would bring his fleet north for six weeks, but he would come no farther than the Chesapeake.*

*At first, Washington resisted a move south. He believed that New York was the most strategic spot on the continent and he hoped, by retaking the city, to erase the humiliations of 1776. But as so many of my narrators had said, he was ever a practical man. He knew that the time had come for action.*

*So he ordered Lafayette to hold Cornwallis in check. Then he began a grand campaign of deception. He allowed papers to fall into enemy hands, outlining an invasion of New York. He built an encampment in New Jersey, complete with ovens for the baking of bread, and he hauled barges toward the Jersey Shore, all to convince the British that he was preparing to attack lower Manhattan.*

*Then he marched his army from above New York toward the Jersey encampments. Then he marched them right past the encampments. Then he put them on the road to Virginia. By the time the British realized what was happening, Washington and Rochambeau were halfway to Yorktown. And the French fleet was approaching the Chesapeake. The trap was closing.*

## Martha Washington:

I cannot imagine what was in my husband's mind on the September day when he rode up to Mount Vernon for the first time in six and a half years. So often, in so many cold camps, he had spoken so longingly of his fine prospect above the Potomac, and for so many years, it had seemed that defeat would prevent his ever seeing it again.

Oh, yes, my husband knew what the fruits of defeat would have been: a gallows, perhaps, or banishment, most likely. And how often the house faced the threat of destruction by the British.

But there it stood, shining before him in the dusk, larger and handsomer than he had left it. He had ridden the sixty miles from Baltimore in a day. And he was greeted that night not only by a loving wife, but also by Cousin Lund and his wife, by Jacky and Nelly, and perhaps most wondrously, by the four little children born to them in his long absence.

I shall never forget that night and the ineffable joy of having my husband beside me in our house once more, if only for a few days. The next morning, General Rochambeau and his family arrived, so there were meals to plan, sleeping arrangements to see to, but, oh, how much easier it was in our own home than in some cramped farmhouse in New Jersey.

## Jacob, Mount Vernon Slave:

I have to say the massa change some in them years. He be more than half gray, and he look real grave, but he still have that fine carriage.

And when he go in his office to talk with Massa Jacky Custis, they's no doubt he's still the man in charge.

I never like Massa Jacky. His mama coddle him somethin' terrible, see, and ever since little Miss Patsy die, she coddle him even more. And he jess don't seem a man to stick to. And for most of the Revolution, he ain't. But now there's this night in the office. He say to the massa, "I think you could use me, Papa."

"Use you, in what way?"

"In the coming campaign. As an aide, perhaps, to help you in your dealings with the French. They must be very complicated."

"The dealings or the French?"

"Both," say Jacky.

And that bring a smile to Massa's face. "You're right."

"Please, sir. I have a fine knowledge of manners, which the French take very seriously. I've done you no service till now. It would give me considerable honor to be part of a victory in Virginia."

"It would give all of us honor. . . . What does your mother say to all this?"

"Oh, sir, she approves."

"Are you prepared for the life at camp?"

"Yes, sir."

"Are you prepared to be punctual, and not to wander off when the tedium of the work no longer suits you?" Massa startin' to sound a little harsh now. He know Massa Jacky real good.

"Oh, yes, sir," say Massa Jacky.

"Then you'll serve as a civilian volunteer aide. I can always use another well-mannered gentleman."

A man and his son ... or stepson. Nothin' closer. Nothin' further apart.

Later that night he must be thinkin' on that, see, 'cause he ax me 'bout my son. I say, "Massa, I ain't never seen or heard of him since the day he run away."

He jess nod and say what a shame it be that Match run away, then my daughter and my little grandson too. "But . . . perhaps 'tis all for the best."

I say, "What?" Jess like that. 'Tain't like the massa to say that a slave runnin' away be all for any kind of good.

He don't say no more but jess take the candle and go to bed.

By and by I'se walkin' back to the slave quarters, when I hears Billy Lee come up behind me.

"How ya been, Jake?"

"Oh, jess 'bout the same," I say. "What about you?"

"Gittin' along. I'm married now. To a free mulatto gal up in Philadelphie."

I chuckle. "Bring her down. Mebbe she can show us all how to git free."

"Mebbe after the war. I don't think the General like her too much, though."

We walks along some, till after a time, I ax him, "What do you hear 'bout the slaves what run away to join the British down Williamsburg way?"

"I hears bad things," he say, real low and real sad. "They all follow the army. Every British officer have two or three servants and a woman to wash his clothes. They say Cornwallis has a bunch of runaways diggin' his trenches down there, workin' 'em damn near to death 'fore he feeds 'em."

"He wouldn't take no woman with a baby to do no diggin'."

"He'd jess cut a woman loose. Or maybe she'd fall in with some greedy officer who'd sell her to the Indies. I hear that been happenin'."

And I bring my hands to my ears and say, "Don't tell me more."

"But you asked. Why don't you ask 'bout your son?" And Billy give me a sly grin, see, like a trickster slave who jess steal a gallon of cider from the massa's stock.

Well, suh, I tell you, to this day, I can still 'member the way my stomach turn over when he say that. I say, "My son? What 'bout him?"

"He's one fine man."

"What . . . what you sayin'?"

"I seen him."

"Seen him? Where?"

"He's with the Fourth Massachusetts Infantry. Fightin' for freedom."

And I start to bawl. I brings my hand to my mouth to keep from makin' noise, and I jess start to shakin' with all the happiness and all the sadness all mixed in, like a gray porridge somebody fill with apricots.

I goes runnin' fast back to the cabin, back to Alice, to tell her the news. I throws open the door. This don't set too good with Skunky Tom and his woman

Kate, who move in with us after our daughter run off, but I don't care.

I shout, "He's alive! Match is alive!"

Billy Lee say, "Don't tell anybody, or the massa have both our hides."

I look over in the corner. The blanket is goin' up and down on top of Skunky Tom, and I say, "You hear that?"

He say, "I don't hear nothin'. I never hears nothin'."

Me and Alice go out together and walk under the stars. I don't tell her what's-all's happenin' to slaves like Narcissa. I jess talk 'bout the good thing—our boy be standin' on his own two feet. Then I wonder, what do the massa mean when he say, "Perhaps 'tis all for the best." Do he know somethin'?

## Hesperus Draper:

'Tis hard to believe that everything worked at York-town. You didn't even need to be a bird to see that battlefield.

The town was a little semicircle of buildings huggin' close to the river. Surroundin' it was a semicircle of British earthworks. Surroundin' them was a five-mile semicircle of entrenchments and encampments, with both ends anchored at the river—the product of more plannin', more hard work, and more luck than had ever been seen, up to that point, on the North American continent.

And remember what I told you about luck? Washington always had it. He might have run out of food and clothin' and money in the Revolution. Hell, he came damn close to runnin' out of men. But he never lacked for luck. He was lucky when he did dumb things, like plannin' to send green troops across the Back Bay in boats. He was lucky when he was smart enough to see what could be done at Yorktown. And he always had the fortitude to take advantage of his luck.

At Yorktown, we had sixteen thousand troops—French regulars, Continentals, and the Virginia militia, who come swarmin' as soon as they smelled a victory. There were also more than a hundred cannon, includin' some of the biggest siege guns we'd ever seen, brought by ship all the way from the French post at Newport, Rhode Island. And out there in the bay somewhere, a French fleet had already driven off the British rescue force.

As one general said, we had got Cornwallis handsomely in a pudding bag.

We started by buildin' a line of siege works at the lower end of town. 'Twas the old business of "regular approaches," just the way the British had done it to us on Long Island. But, Lord, how things had changed.

Washington turned the first shovelful of dirt, and a few days later, on a sunny October afternoon, he stood at a redoubt in the first parallel trench, some six hundred yards from the British works, while Henry Knox aimed the siege gun that would begin the bombardment.

When Knox first laid eyes on that gun, I thought he might try to mount it, he was so excited. The barrel was ten feet long, the carriage was as high as a man, and whatever it hit stayed hit.

With a big flourish, Knox handed Washington the linstock for firin'.

Washington kept that serious mask on while he raised the linstock, all very slow and graceful, like an actor, raised it in a big wide arc above his head, just like he was s'posed to. The match touched the hole, and there came the loudest roar I had ever heard from a single gun in my life.

And the ball was so big, you could almost see it shootin' toward the British works. And for certain you could see it hit and send an explosion of dirt a hundred feet into the air.

Jacky Custis, who was now makin' a nuisance of himself at headquarters, shouted somethin'—"Bravo," I think it was.

And Washington could not keep a smile from his face. He told Knox, "General, begin your cannonade."

Over the next day and night, some thirty-six hundred cannonballs and shells went flyin' into Yorktown. 'Twas the most thunderous, hellacious, beautiful bombardment I ever saw. Not a man in our army slept for the watchin' of it and the thunder of it. And 'twas for certain that not a British soldier could've slept under it. Rockets traced comet tails across the sky, shells burst, the earth shook. And it went on like that for five days more.

c.d.—My uncle called Yorktown a battle to warm the heart of any man who wrote military manuals. It was as carefully staged and directed as a play.

If battles must be fought in the Age of Reason, let them be battles like Yorktown.

The British defended two redoubts on their left, as a matter of honor. The Americans took them, as a *matter of honor. Everyone's honor was satisfied inexpensively, except for the nine who died and the thirty who were wounded. And Alexander Hamilton, who led the assault against the redoubts, gained the battlefield glory he yearned for.*

*On the morning of October 19 a drummer boy appeared atop the British works and beat the call for parley. At first, no one could hear him over the thunder of the American guns, but they could see him, and one by one, the guns fell silent. After a few minutes, all that could be heard on the wide plain around Yorktown was the beating of a single drum.*

## Hesperus Draper:

Put this bit of wisdom right next to the things I've said about luck. It doesn't matter how many battles you lose, so long as you win the last one.

The tune that the British marched to on the day of the surrender was "The World Turned Upside Down." A jaunty little somethin' that I hummed a lot.

The surrender was done in a big field about two miles from town. The Americans was all on the left side of the road, the French on the right. And the British, in their red coats and white breeches, came down the gauntlet, shamblin' more than marchin', lookin' as sullen as children on their way to church. But 'twas hard for any of us Americans to see their faces, because they wouldn't look at us. They just kept their heads to their right, to the French.

Couldn't blame them. After all, who would you rather say beat you? A line of tattered rebels, some wearin' blue coats, some wearin' brown, but most of them in dirty overalls and huntin' shirts and buckskins? Or those pretty French lads, with all their feathers and their black gaiters and their white broadcloth coats with the different-colored facin's?

After all our years of runnin', fightin', and starvin', the British wouldn't give us the satisfaction of lettin' us see the loser's scowl. So, as they came past, Lafayette called for "Yankee Doodle" from his band. 'Twas the song the British played to poke fun at us whenever they could, and now we played it for them. And the British snapped their heads around like they were bein' slapped in the face.

"Yankee Doodle, keep it up. Yankee Doodle Dandy." 'Twas a fine moment.

When the front of the British column come to where our commanders were sittin', everything stopped, includin' the music. The wind puffed and fluttered the flags—our thirteen-star banner on one side of the road, the French fleur-de-lis on the other. 'Course, the British colors were cased, by order of Washington.

British General O'Hara dismounted and tried to give his sword to Rochambeau. That Frenchman, God bless him, he just gestured across the road to Washington and said, "There is our commander in chief."

For that redcoat general, it must've been the longest walk in his life to go over and look up at that big Virginian.

Washington had his reins in his left hand and his right hand pressed against his hip, just like a statue. Didn't even incline his head. Just lowered his eyes. I don't know how good he felt right then, but I felt better than I did the first time I felt a woman. And then do you know what I thought about? Fort Necessity, and how far we'd come.

O'Hara craned his neck and said to Washington, "You'll beg the indulgence of Lord Cornwallis, sir. But he is indisposed due to illness."

Washington knew 'twas a plain lie, but he just sat his horse with that dignified air, actin' like receivin' a surrender was the naturallest thing in the world. He said, "As you are second-in-command, you'll turn your sword over to my second, General Lincoln."

That was Benjamin Lincoln, who'd been humiliated by the British when he lost Charleston.

I noticed Hamilton sittin' behind Washington, lookin' as proud as if he'd won the war himself. Or maybe now he was plannin' how he'd turn everyone into Federalists. Hamilton was a puzzle, you know. Smart and brave, likable, too, but as egotistical as old Charles Lee.

'Course, all of them were egotists—Adams, Hamilton, Jefferson . . . the lot of 'em. They had to be to do what they did. They thought they were buildin' a better future, and most of them thought they knew exactly how to do it. They were the men with all the answers, but Washington was smart enough to ask the right questions.

He acted, failed, learned, then acted again, from those wild dice rolls at Trenton and Princeton, to this fine work of art at Yorktown.

The sun was gettin' low in the sky. British soldiers were trampin' onto the field and throwin' down their weapons like the sorest losers in the world. And the air was dancin' with golden flecks. Couldn't quite figure out what the flecks were at first. Golden flecks? Of what?

Then I realized that as the British walked across the field, their boots broke up the hay stubble. The wind lifted it into the air. And the afternoon sun turned it to gold. Like golden snow, or maybe a sign from Providence.

Whenever I think of Yorktown, I remember flecks of gold dancin' in the air.

## Martha Washington:

Whenever I think of Yorktown, I remember the tragedy.

Why does the Divine Being prepare us the table as he does, with a joyous meal followed by the bitterest fruit?

My husband wrote me several times of the progress of the battle, in letters that grew increasingly optimistic.

And it sounded as though Jacky were having an excellent experience. In his only letter, he thoughtfully informed me that "the General, though in constant fatigue, looks well." He was always a boy concerned with his mother's peace of mind. He was also becoming a young man who was serious about his property.

"I have made every possible inquiry after the Negroes," he wrote, "but have not seen any belonging to Lund Washington, the General, or myself. I have heard that Ned is in Yorktown as a scout for the British; Joe is in the neighborhood, though I have not seen him. They say that Narcissa was seen by a roadside trying to suckle a small child who was dead. I fear that most of the slaves who left us are not existing. The mortality that has taken place among the wretches is really incredible. I have seen numbers lying dead in the woods, and many so exhausted that they cannot walk. Also, I should be glad to hear from Mr. Lund whether he has sold any of my horses; they are not high in price in comparison to what they sell for here."

A letter full of chatty insights and mature concerns, it was.

Then arrived the grand news of the surrender of Cornwallis and his seventy-five hundred troops. We could not know that this would be the final battle of the war, as the British were still well set in New York. Nevertheless, we rejoiced.

Then, a week after the surrender, another letter arrived, this one from Eltham, the home of my brother-in-law, Burwell Basset. Jacky had taken ill with the camp fever and had been moved there for his recovery. My daughter-in-law, Nelly, and her oldest daughter, Elizabeth, and I hastened to Jacky's bedside.

We did not send word to my husband for several days. He was still thirty miles away, at Yorktown, completing the business of the army so that he could return to Mount Vernon for a week of rest. When our news reached him, he was writing in his diary. He stopped in mid-sentence and left immediately for Eltham.

He arrived at around seven o'clock. He did not need to ask the condition of the patient when he stepped into the foyer. I am certain that it was written on the faces of Nelly, me, and everyone else in the house.

But at the sight of my husband, I remember that my hopes rose. Jacky always tried to please him, and perhaps now Jacky would respond to his presence.

I led him upstairs to the sickroom. Lamps were lit on either side of the bed, casting dim yellow light. But they could not burn away the odor. With the windows shut tight and the drapes drawn to keep out the bad airs, it was very strong. It was the odor of death, though I could not admit it.

My husband stood over him and said his name, very softly. "Jack . . . Jack . . ."

Then he looked to Dr. Craik, who had come from Yorktown, at our request. The General needed not a single word to Craik.

The doctor shook his head ever so slightly, as if I might not see it.

But I had watched every motion of Craik's eyes, every inclination of his body during my son's sickness, in the hopes that I could read in them the things he might not be saying.

And now, like a hand strangling me, I felt my own emotion, and, oh . . .

## Dr. James Craik:

Camp fever—that was what we called it, though it was in fact the typhus.

Jack Custis had been showing early symptoms on the day of the surrender, but he had insisted upon remaining to witness the grand ceremony. Then, as sometimes happens, he demonstrated a small recovery.

Dr. Rush has theorized that the camp fever is carried by lice, as we find them often in the blankets and clothing of those who succumb to the disease. When men are living well apart, this fever is uncommon. But in crowded conditions, where clothing and bedding of one and another come into contact, it becomes quite prevalent.

But I have another theory. It always seems that it is the newcomers who are struck by the illnesses of the camp. The veterans are so hardy that not only have they subsisted on meager rations and survived enemy bullets, they have also risen superior to disease.

Whatever the cause, Jack Custis came to the field hospital with a mild fever, left a few days later, feeling better, and then was struck down.

Now that the General had arrived at Eltham, Mrs. Washington and their daughter-in-law seemed to lose what little resolve had been holding them together. The merest shaking of my head had sent the mother out of the room. And the wife, Nelly, could barely enter.

Jack Custis had sunk to the last extremity. His chest and shoulders were covered in the petechiae, the purplish spots and peeling skin of the typhus. His forehead was burning. And he was all but insensate.

"Have you bled him?" asked the General.

"Several times," I answered. "Consider him a casualty of your last battle."

The General stepped close to him and put his hand on his stepson's forehead. The young man's face had drawn in upon itself and lost all of its youthful—some would say sybaritic—roundness. And the skin, normally flushed with sunshine and often with wine, had a waxy yellow pallor.

"Such an amiable young man," said the General. "Such a devoted son—"

Here words failed him. In the matter of Jack, words often failed him.

The patient's breathing grew labored. I took his pulse and found that it was all but gone. I told the General to summon his wife and daughter-in-law.

The ladies hurried in. They took Jack's hands, they touched his forehead. It was a scene the like of which I had witnessed hundreds of times. It was a part of my profession that had grown as natural as sleep. And yet it was a terrible pain, especially when the person dying was only twenty-seven.

But after all the death I had seen in the war—death from wounds, from infections, from disease—it was a small blessing that a man had died with his loved ones around him. This was nae a blessing, however, to the loved ones. Nelly Custis and her daughter descended into spasms of inconsolable grief, and Martha simply sat, holding her son's hand, in a state of utter disbelief.

It was some time before Martha could be persuaded to leave the body. The General knelt beside her and whispered to her, whispered words that I could nae hear, nae was meant to hear. Then he led her away from her son's body.

He was, I know, uncommonly affected by his stepson's death. The boy had nae met the standards that Washington had set. And though he had gone to the scene of the fighting in Cambridge in the first winter of the war, I dinna think he was ever made for a soldier. But there existed, at the time of his death, a most affectionate and manly friendship.

Once the Washingtons had left the room, I called their slaves to prepare the body. I watched and mused upon one of the more miserable ironies I had witnessed in my life. In moments of grandest glory, tragedy may still stalk us.

## Jacob, Mount Vernon Slave:

Soon's we hear the news, we bring out black crepe and set it around the doors of the mansion house. I even tear off a little piece and nail it to my cabin door, too, 'cause by then I know 'bout Narcissa and little Billy.

I hears it through the slave grapevine: they's thousands of dead slaves down there. Nobody ever gonna know how many. They go runnin' for freedom, and all they git is used and throwed away . . . jess like always.

So me and Alice be about as sad as we ever been, and as happy, knowin' the good news 'bout our son. Life sure be strange and sad, ain't it?


Few weeks later, the General set out for winter quarters.

For three or four days afore, it go like this: Miz Washin'ton say to pack her things. Then she say to unpack. Then pack agin. Then unpack. And always me and Alice do the job.

Po' woman, she don't know if she comin' or goin'. And every night you hear her cryin' behind her bedroom door. Cryin' and sobbin', gettin' quiet, then startin' in agin.

One night the General standin' out on his piazza, lookin' at the river in the moonlight. He call me outside, 'cause he know I jess done unpackin' Miz Washin'ton's things agin. He say, "You must be patient with her, Jake. She's suffered a terrible blow."

"Terrible, suh, terrible."

"I had expected to feel such joy here. But 'tis a house of mourning."

I say, "We's all sad, suh. We all like Massa Jacky."

"We all liked Narcissa, too."

"Thank you, suh."

And the General try to make me feel a little better. He say, "You know, after the surrender, we sent soldiers out to round up runaways, for reward. Narcissa may have been taken, and we just haven't heard the word."

I tell the General thanks. But I know by then, no Continental soldier findin' my daughter . . . alive, that is. I'se tryin' to look ahead, lookin' to hear from my boy. I don't tell the General that when he go back to his army headquarters, Billy Lee bringin' a message to my Match, my Matt Jacobs.

C.D.—*The war was not over. But while the British still had the strength to fight, they had lost the will. The American Revolution had ignited a world war between England and France. British troops were needed everywhere. And French ships were needed in the Caribbean. The French had also said that while Rochambeau would stay for a time, not another penny would go from their treasury to America.*

*And therein lay the last great peril of the Revolution.*

## Hesperus Draper:

October of 1782. In Paris, John Adams and Ben Franklin had been negotiatin' for eight months. But in New York City, an army of fifteen thousand British still sat and waited. And up on the Hudson, at Newburgh and New Windsor, our Continental army sat and watched them.

'Twasn't much of an army anymore. A lot of the boys had been sent home. A lot of the officers had been furloughed. I'd spent six of the last eighteen months in Alexandria, gettin' to know my wife again, and tryin' to get our business back on a payin' basis. Fact was, there was no money for investin', so we just kept printin' the gazette.

We held our share of Continental certificates, too. Charlotte had emptied all our warehouses and sold everything to the army. Then she took what hard money we had and started buyin' up Continental paper held by farmers and shopkeeps and folks who liked the feel of silver in their pocket more than they liked havin' faith in the future.

I didn't approve, but she said she was just showin' folks what she believed about her country.

I could've resigned and gone home for good, but I didn't. Believed in seein' a thing through. Learn by doin', and do by finishin'. My motto now had two parts. And don't forget, in the worst days of '81, Washington got Congress to promise that every officer who finished the war in uniform would receive half pay till the end of his life.

I'd be damned if I wasn't goin' to get my fair share. Wouldn't be like last time, with me half drunk and shoutin' that I'd been swindled.

But there was a problem. Congress had about as much power over the thirteen states as I had over the stars and the moon. And worse than that, when they learned that the states didn't want to pay us, Congress started wheedlin' their way out of their commitment, too.

This didn't set well with the officers at Newburgh. And they weren't fools. They knew the only strength in the country was right there on the banks of the Hudson. 'Twas the army and the man who commanded it.

Why, in the spring of 1782, one officer had even proposed to Washington that he make himself king. Feller's name was Lewis Nicola. Wrote to Washington that there were plenty who thought this would be a good idea.

Washington tore him up one side and down the other.

Nicola showed me the letter.

Washington wrote: "Let me conjure you, if you have any regard for your country, concern for yourself or posterity, or respect for me, to banish these thoughts from your mind, and never communicate, as from yourself or anyone else, a sentiment of like nature."

Even if he'd wanted to be king, which he didn't, he'd made a promise to Congress in 1775. And a man who reneged on a promise was not a man who deserved the respect of his peers. And remember, nothin' mattered more to George Washington than respect . . . and reputation. But the difference between the young George of Fort Necessity and the victorious general at Newburgh was that one tried to protect a reputation he didn't have by threatenin' to quit every other week, while the other built a reputation that was rock-solid by refusin' ever to think about quittin'.

What that's called, I think, is growin' up.

And part of growin' up is learnin' to see the world through other men's eyes. That's why Washington sympathized with his officers over their pay, and why he granted three of us leave to go to Philadelphia and press our case.

## Martha Washington:

After something more than a year, I was able to go on again, in the small ways that we must if we are to live in the world.

I could awaken each morning, come to consciousness, see the light falling through the bedroom window, and not be jolted into full waking by the realization that I would never look upon Jacky's smile again. I could think of his children and, in the thinking, not think of our loss but of their promise. I could think of Mount Vernon and not feel that there were rooms I would not be able to enter again.

And I thought often of Mount Vernon during those days when we were living on the Hudson, waiting for the war to wind down like an old watch.

We had planned to return for the winter just before Christmas of '82, but one cold afternoon, following a conference with Henry Knox and several of his other officers, my husband came to the small bedroom where I was knitting a sweater for our newest grandchild.

"I'm afraid we can't go to Mount Vernon, Patsy," he said. "I fear the mood of the officers. They want their pay."

"They should have it, shouldn't they?"

"That is not disputed. 'Tis the method by which they get it that concerns me. They're more irritable than at any time since the commencement of the war."

"Then . . . then you'd best stay here."

"Like a physician, preventing disorders from getting to an incurable height."

## Alexander Hamilton:

Though I was now well married to Betsy Schuyler for almost three years, and little Phil was a year old, I determined to throw away a few months more in public life and then retire a simple citizen and good paterfamilias.

I had been pretty unanimously elected to Congress, and I saw the object now to make our independence a blessing. But to do this we had to secure our union on solid foundations. Our supreme task in that direction was to satisfy the many public creditors who had taken on the debt of the Revolution, and perhaps the most important of those were the soldiers whose very service was a form of credit extended to us.

A deputation from the army arrived at Philadelphia in January of 1783—General McDougall, Adjutant General Stewart, and Colonel Draper. I was on the committee that received them one bitter night, and in hearing their argument I was made to feel a mortification that we could not fulfill their expectations.

It was most disconcerting to have General McDougall frame the question in such stark terms as these: "What if it should be proposed to unite the influence of members of Congress with that of the army and the public creditors to obtain funds for the United States?"

Without looking at the other congressmen, I said, "Any combination of force, General, would only be productive of the horrors of a civil war, might end in the ruin of the country, and would certainly end in the ruin of the army."

Colonel Draper said, "Does that mean we won't get paid?"

"It does not mean that at all," I answered.

"That's good," he responded, "because I wouldn't want to go back to New Windsor with bad news."

Congressman James Madison leaned across the table and said, "Is there a threat implicit in that remark, Colonel?"

Draper gave Madison a grin. He was a smiling fellow, altogether too smiling. "Those officers aren't in the mood for cool deliberation, sir. A disappointment now might throw them into what you'd call . . . blind extremities."

Yes, I thought, a threat. But the army was a fine tool with which to advance the business in which we were engaged—forcing the states to come to the steady and reliable support of the government in Philadelphia. Otherwise, we would be thirteen separate entities, all weak, all insignificant, conducting our petty affairs in a petty way.

After the meeting, I spoke with the officers outside and told them that their presence was much appreciated. I added: "I am your best friend in this business, gentlemen. I am trying to overcome mountains of prejudice to help you."

## Hesperus Draper:

When a man says, "I am your friend," I look for a corner to back into, so I can watch the room. When he tells me he's my "best" friend, that's when I pull a table in front of me and set out a brace of pistols.

I knew what Hamilton was up to.

He was playin' both ends against the middle. Figured he'd stir up the officers with little squibs of information about the way Congress might cheat them. Stir up Congress and the states with some worry about the mood of the army. Stir up Washington, in the hopes that he'd be the binder to hold everything together. Stir it all the way you mix pigment and oil and lead to make paint. And hope that when the stirrin' is done, you have the color you want.

I was for as much local control as I could get, for as few men as possible standin' between me and wherever I wanted in life. The more men in your way, the more rungs to the ladder. But I wanted my pay.

Galled me plenty to have to play into Hamilton's hand like this. Galled plenty of congressmen, too.

Arthur Lee was a Virginia congressman I knew. Visited him just before I left Philadelphia. He said, "Be careful in this business, Draper. Every engine is at work here to obtain permanent taxes. The terror of a mutiny in the army is played upon with considerable efficacy."

I didn't like that. But as I say, I wanted my pay. And I wanted to see that the foot soldiers got their due. They hadn't been paid in months; some of them were dressed like they'd just retreated through the Jerseys;

and that diet of pickled beef and beets was only a little better than fire cake. So I'd let Congress think the army might mutiny and march, even if I felt like a stick stirrin' Hamilton's paint.

Our committee brought the news back to Newburgh in late February. And the stirrin' began right away.

And do you know who provided an office to do the stirrin' in? Horatio Gates. Yes, sir. Two years after his embarrassment at Camden, Congress had finally put away its resolution for a court of inquiry. All was forgiven, and Gates slipped right into the second-in-command position, behind Washington.

"It's good to see you, Draper." Gates squinted at me through his spectacles.

"And you, sir," I said.

Some men aged well. But Gates wasn't one of them. He was fifty-seven and as round-shouldered as an old widow. Had a little potbelly beneath his buff waistcoat and a sag to his face that was more than age. 'Twas sadness, slicin' all the muscle away so the fat could swing free.

Think of all that had happened to him. While he was in the South, tryin' to figure out how to fight the British, his son had died. Then he lost a battle, his command, and a long measure of self-respect at Camden. Now his wife was sick and dyin' in Virginia.

I asked after her.

Gates removed his spectacles and rubbed his eyes. "I'm planning to go to her sometime this month. It all depends on events here and in Philadelphia." He put the spectacles on again. "I assume the city treated you well?"

"Philadelphia did. Congress is the problem. 'Tis always the problem."

The old man nodded. "Something must be done."

"What would you suggest, sir?" I'd learned long ago that with superior officers, when you tread marshy ground, 'tis safer to ask questions than answer them.

Gates looked out the window of his farmhouse office. "As soon as peace arrives, this force will be disbanded. Then there'll be no chance for any officer to obtain what he's earned. The army may be the best tool that any of us has to bring about fair treatment."

Rememberin' that they hang mutineers, I decided to keep my counsel. With some men, if you try to wait them out and make them talk, they'll just sit and stare, make it a contest to see who speaks first. Washington was like that.

But Gates started chatterin' again. "What say you to helping one of my aides—young Armstrong—to prepare a pamphlet on the next step we should take?"

"I'd say he's a competent young man. He can do it himself."

Gates leaned across his desk. "This would all be anonymous, of course."

"Then," I said, "you won't need my name on it, will you?"

Gates gave me a little smile that bespoke more annoyance than pleasure. "You know, Draper. I feel as poignantly for the distresses of the poor men who've been our faithful companions through the war, as if those distresses were all my own. I can live without a payment plan. Perhaps you can as well. But many of these officers cannot."

He was two-thirds right: many could not, and I probably could, thanks to my wife's brains. But I knew that Horatio Gates was up to his eyeballs in debt, and he owed most of his money to Robert Morris, the financier who'd saved the Revolution more than once with infusions of hard money. Gates owed Morris, and Morris was behind Hamilton. And . . . hell, it all gets so dizzyin' it makes you think you're lookin' into that paint bucket, watchin' the pigment swirl.

## Alexander Hamilton:

I have been accused of attempting to manipulate the army and Washington in this business so that I might advance the cause of a strong national government. But the crisis developed of its own. I simply urged Washington to take the kind of action that he had always taken—direct, incisive, and in the best interests of the nation. In short, he should, one last time, take direction of the tool that he had in his hands.

I wrote to him: "The great desideratum at present is the establishment of general funds, which alone can do justice to the creditors of the United States, of whom the army forms the most meritorious class; restore public credit; and supply the future wants of government. This is the object of all men of sense. In this, the influence of the army, properly directed, may cooperate."

## Hesperus Draper:

G ates didn't need me to write his pamphlet. His aide did a fine job, anonymously. He wrote like he was talkin' to the officers, and 'twas like throwin' a match in the magazine: "After seven long years, peace returns. But to whom? A country willing to redress your wrongs, cherish your worth, and reward your services? Or a country that tramples upon your rights, disdains your cries, and insults your distresses?"

You could almost feel the pulses startin' to throb at the temples of all the hundreds of officers readin' these words.

"Suspect the man who would advise more moderation and larger forbearance." That was a brickbat for Washington. "Let a man who can feel, as well as write, be appointed to draw up your last remonstrance. Tell Congress that the slightest mark of indignity from them must now operate like the grave and part you from that august body forever. In any political event, the army has its alternative."

And the alternative was plain: a show of force against the duly elected, though damn near incompetent, civil representatives.

The pamphlet called for a meetin' on March 11 to stir up the boys even more. But such a meetin', without authority, was itself a mutiny.

So Washington canceled it. But he knew the mood of his men. He replaced it with an official meetin' for March 15, where the officers could air their grievances and General Gates could convey them to Washington. By then, cooler heads would have prevailed. And Washington set about coolin' them.

I was summoned to his headquarters at Hasbrouk House, a fine little stone farmhouse, with a view of the Hudson that was better than the view of the Potomac at Mount Vernon. Washington's office was simple—a little desk in the corner, a little fireplace, nothing but a map on the wall.

He told me to sit, which I took as a good sign; then he came right to the point. Showed me that he still thought the worst of me, too. "You should know, Draper, that I'm issuing a general order to arrest mutinous officers on the spot."

"I have no intention to mutiny, sir, but I'll be damned if I don't get my pay."

"We'll all be damned if there's a mutiny." Then he softened his tone. "You've been in communication with General Gates?"

"Yes, sir."

He nodded, almost to himself, as if this confirmed some suspicion.

"Sir, General Gates knows what I know: these men have served for seven years to build a nation. They just want their due."

"You know that certain congressmen are trying to use the army as puppets to establish a continental funding system?"

"You mean taxes?"

"Taxes. Revenues. A central government. These things we must have. But not like this."

I sat back and said nothing. Didn't think the silence would work with him the way that it did with Gates, but he kept talkin'. Shows you how agitated he was.

"Draper, my predicament, as citizen and soldier, is as critical and delicate as you can conceive. The sufferings of this army on the one hand, the inability of

Congress and the tardiness of the states on the other, they are the forebodings of evil."

He was fifty-one, and he still looked like he could travel eight hundred miles in a bad winter, swim an ice-caked Allegheny, and show up in Williamsburg full of complaints about his rank. He had those long, strong arms, big hands, and thighs that were all muscle after a lifetime in the saddle. But age was comin' on. The color was leechin' fast from his hair, though he was still reddish brown on the top. He was growin' jowls. And if he had a false tooth to put in where that left canine was missin', he wasn't wearin' it.

But one thing was plain: he still meant what he said.

So did I. "General, I won't do anything to bring on evil. Only justice."

"Tell this to the other officers: I'll pursue the same steady line of conduct that has governed me till now. I beg them to do the same at their meeting."


## Martha Washington:

I don't think I had ever seen my husband more disturbed and distracted than the night before the officers' meeting.

I brought him tea. He was working late over a long page of paper on which he was writing in a very large hand.

"The meeting is tomorrow?"

"Yes. Gates presides."

And I expressed a small bit of intuition. "You know, I have never liked him, not since Boston."

"You're wise," he said, "for the source of these

troubles may be easily traced. The old leaven is again beginning to work, Patsy, under the mask of dissimulation and friendliness."

"Gates?"

"I have proof of nothing. But we know that the incendiary pamphlet came from his office. I don't think Gates is alone, though."

"Another cabal?"

"I don't know. There is something very mysterious in this. Alexander Hamilton warned me of agitation, which did not seem to exist. Then, as the officers returned from their meeting with Hamilton, so did the agitation. Then comes the noise from Gates's office. Then Hamilton's urgings to me . . ."

"George, you've been a doctor with an agitated patient for months."

"We've come to the crisis. Tomorrow the fever breaks or the patient dies."


## Hesperus Draper:

They were all there, the great and the small, the young and the old, all crowded into what they called the tabernacle, a big rough-hewn hall they'd thrown up so the officers would have a place for worship on Sundays and socializin' the rest of the time.

I was sittin' near the front, next to Gates's aide, Colonel Armstrong.

I had a little speech prepared, because Gates said I'd be one of the first men called. I wasn't sure Gates would like what I had to say, because Washington had certainly gotten through to me.

Up at the front, there was Gates, steppin' to the pulpit to start the business. Sittin' in chairs behind him were Israel Putnam, more of an Old Put than ever; Timothy Pickering, Washington's adjutant and one of the noisiest of the protesting officers; and Henry Knox, always loyal, but just as mad at Congress as anyone else, and fatter than ever.

'Twas a bright, sunny March day, and even though there was no heat in the big building, the two hundred officers who'd crowded in warmed the place up and steamed the windows right quick.

Young Armstrong said to me, "He didn't come."

"Who?"

"Washington. He said he wouldn't. But I was worried. Worried that he might get in the way of our deliberations."

And I thought, Deliberations? This twenty-five-year-old colonel was a boy with a pimple on his nose. He knew nothin' of deliberations.

He also knew nothin' of Washington, because just then a side door swung open at the front and a strong shaft of light dropped across the faces of Knox, Putnam, Pickering, and Gates. And the usual hum of conversation that you get in a crowded hall, it ended like a wave rollin' from the front to the back.

There he was.

I folded up my speech and put it away. Knew I wouldn't need it now.

He said a few words to Gates. Then he came to the pulpit and looked out over the crowd. He seemed agitated. He started to say somethin', then caught himself, looked behind him once or twice. Then he pulled a speech out of his coat pocket. 'Twas written on long sheets of paper in a hand so big you could see the letters from the front row. And from the way the paper was shakin', you could see that his emotion had reached out to every extremity.

This was the man who had ridden between enemy armies. And his hands were shakin' before his own officers.

As you'd expect, he began with a plea for calm and consideration: "By an anonymous summons, an attempt has been made to convene you together. How inconsistent this is with the rules of propriety, how un-military, and how subversive of all order and discipline, let the good sense of the army decide."

For fifteen minutes, he attacked the arguments of that anonymous pamphlet, written by the squirmin' little Gates-raised lackey beside me.

He promised us that "so far as may be done consistently with the great duty I owe my country, and with those powers we are bound to respect, you may freely command my services to the utmost of my abilities."

'Twas some of the best writin' I'd ever heard from him.

Gates squirmed at this line: "Express your horror and detestation of the man who wishes to overturn the liberties of our country, and who wickedly attempts to open the floodgates of civil discord and deluge our rising empire in blood."

But Washington was no spellbinder. I heard men coughin', feet shufflin', swords scrapin' on the floor as men shifted in their seats. And I didn't see many officers doin' anything but scowl. They weren't even moved by the way he finished: "You will, by the dignity of your conduct, let posterity proclaim, 'had this day been wanting, the world had never seen the last stage of perfection to which human nature is capable of attaining.'"

*Thunk*. That's what it sounded like. Fine words, but the effect in that room was as if he'd walked in and dropped a ten-pound sack of potatoes on the floor.

No cheers, no clappin', no nothin'. Just a stone wall of faces.

I felt sorry for him then. But remember about Washington—even when he looked like he was beaten, he never quit, not retreatin' across the Jerseys, and not now. So he reached into his pocket and pulled out another sheet of paper.

"Gentlemen, I hold in my hand a letter that might better inspire you. It comes from Mr. Jones, in Congress, and it describes their efforts to pay you, and it . . . unh . . . 'Dear General Washington, It . . . it . . .'"

For a second, he just stopped and looked out at us. He wet his lips with his tongue. Then he squinted at the letter again and looked out at us again, very embarrassed, as though he'd suddenly forgotten how to read.

Then, very slowly, he placed the sheet on the lectern in front of him, and from his pocket he pulled out a pair of spectacles. He kept his head down as he put them on, almost as if he was afraid to let us see him do it. When he looked up, 'twas as if the whole room had just taken a deep breath.

And he said, "Gentlemen, you'll forgive me, but not only have I grown gray in the service of my country. Now I find myself going blind."

And for a moment he stood there, lookin' out at us, just lettin' us see a man who had given everything he had.

Then Henry Knox brought his hand to his mouth, as if to stifle his emotion. I swear I heard somebody sniffle. I glanced behind me and two or three officers were lookin' up at him the way young men look up at their fathers when they finally realize that their fathers are mortal. I saw tears, actual tears.

Who knows if he planned that little gesture with the glasses? He was actor enough. But he was also smart enough to seize the moment. Smart enough to know his audience. And smart enough to get off the stage.

He folded the letter from Congress, put it back into his pocket, and said, "Gentlemen, you know my mind and my heart. Good afternoon."

And he was gone. The door closed behind him, and a moment later we heard him gallop off.

Then Henry Knox shouted, "A motion! A motion of thanks for the General's counsel."

Right then George Washington had saved the republic. You can have the tearstained scene at Fraunces Tavern six months later, when he bade good-bye to all of these men for good. You can have the ceremony at Annapolis, when he turned over his commission and his army to Congress.

That moment at the New Windsor Tabernacle was the crowning moment of his generalship.

## Matt Jacobs:

Come June, we was discharged. I got my settlement certificate, which promised me my pay someday. I sold mine for thirty cents hard money on the dollar, so's I could buy some decent clothes. Willard done the same. Then I got a message to Billy Lee to come and see me in the camp.

Billy was lookin' older. He liked to drink, and that can age a man. He told me how the General promised to pay for to bring his Margaret to Mount Vernon, now that the Revolution was over. But Billy didn't know if Margaret would go.

I said, "Can't blame her. She's free. Why she want to live like a slave?"

Billy just shrugged. "She ain't been around but a few times here. Maybe she don't love me no more. . . . You comin' back?"

I just chuckled. "No, Billy. But I'd be obliged for a favor. I'd be obliged that you tell my papa and mama I done good. Tell 'em I love 'em. Tell 'em, I'm goin' fishin', like Papa taught me."

"I surely will." I reckon there was tears in Billy's eyes. A few in mine, too.

The next day, me and Willard set out for Marblehead.

"How far you reckon?" he axed.

"About two hundred miles," I said. "Just about due east."

"Hell and damnation, but I'm sick of walkin'."


## The Marquis de Lafayette:

They would call him the father of his country, though he had no children of his own. This is a thing of great sadness. But think of all who carried his name: George Washington Craik, son of James, born in 1765; George Washington Reed, son of Joseph, born in 1780; and Georges Washington Lafayette, son of Marie Joseph Paul Yves Roch Gilbert du Motier, Marquis de Lafayette, born in 1777.

C.D.—*And George Washington Jacobs, son of Matthew, born in 1785.*

# *Part Five*

❦

## THE PRESIDENT
## AND THE PRECEDENTS

C.D. . . . *And the Marquis de Lafayette finished his story.*

To leave Washington in the bright sun at the New Windsor Tabernacle was a temptation. But there was another act to be played, a confrontation with the forces of disorder, contention, and simple self-interest that swirl after every revolution.

How would Washington—who had rejected kingship, who had opposed military dictatorship, who had assumed the soldier but never laid aside the citizen—how would he hold his countrymen to the republican principles he had fought so long to put in place?

That question was very strong with me just then, because I was in France, a place where it had not been well answered.

As I said, my quest for the truth of Washington's life had taken me all the way to the home of the Marquis de Lafayette. Though small by the standards of French châteaux, La Grange seemed to me like a dwelling from fable—a handsome composition of *five stone towers in the form of a medieval fortress, the perfect place for a man to retreat and restore himself.*

*Lafayette had been one of the early leaders of France's revolutionary movement. He had nearly lost his head when that revolution turned into the Reign of Terror, and he probably would have, but for his early commitment to the principles of the American Revolution.*

*I had sensed from the first that I would like him. For all that he had been through, he carried himself with the bearing of a man who had not been worn down by events, and his expression was one of benevolent bemusement, brows arched high above lively hazel eyes, features slightly elongated by the oval shape of his face. He was forty-three, but he had remained almost boyish in his enthusiasms, and especially in his enthusiasm for conversation.*

*We talked for a week, while strolling the grounds, while dining, while reclining in his marvelous circular library.*

*When I finally mounted my horse to leave, he took my hand and gripped it tightly. "Thank you, Christopher, for all you have done to help me bring my friend back to life."*

*"Thank you . . . Excellency . . . Marquis."*

*"I have told you, call me M'sieur or Citoyen. Citizen. After the recent fashion." And he gave a small chuckle.*

*"M'sieur," I said, and I promised that I would send him a copy of the book when it was done, though I promised no hagiography.*

*"Simply show Washington as a man," said Lafayette. "That will be best."*

*I rode under the portcullis, across the moat, and down the long, tree-lined allée. Then I turned for Paris.*

*What extraordinary beauty was to be found in that city. And what extraordinary tension.*

*On my last day there, I observed a guard of dragoons galloping down the Champs-Élysées. Each was marvelously uniformed, helmeted in brass, and armed with a lance. The man leading them, however, wore nothing more than a simple tricorne and uniform coat of dull gray. He needed no accoutrements, for one's eye was drawn involuntarily to Napoleon Bonaparte, First Consul of France.*

*And something my uncle said would echo back to me whenever I remembered that moment: "Make a man a dictator for a week, and he may get to likin' the job."*

*At least order had been returned to Paris, and the blood had stopped flowing in the streets. For two years, the heads had rolled, and those who had done the beheading in June were often the ones beheaded in January.*

*Considering all that, I determined that it would be best to join the crowd in cheering loudly for their latest hero . . . while I cheered silently for Washington.*

*I left Paris in late May, bearing many small treasures of reminiscence.*

*I reached Alexandria in July, a place and a time never to be recommended in the same breath, and certainly not in 1800, when the political fever raged and the Federalists and the Republicans contended for the soul of a nation.*

*Who would rule America?*

*The Federalists would put it thus: Do you want well-educated men of commerce to show the way, or will the great unwashed rabble be left to fix their own fate? The Republicans would ask: Must the hand of government restrain the plow, or will the simple strength of simple, self-motivated Americans be allowed to break the earth? And all Americans wondered: Would there be taxes, duties, and tariffs to support a federal structure governing from afar, or would the governed keep their government close and their money closer?*

*This dispute extended beyond the relationship of Americans to their government. It also embraced the relationship of the American government to others. The Federalists believed that, for all our past enmity, friendship with Britain was essential to America's future. The Republicans believed that France had been, and would continue to be, America's best ally.*

*The Federalists, envisioning a strong presidency, were accused of having instincts as monarchical as those of the British. The Republicans, desiring a diffusion of power, were considered as radically republican as the French, whose revolution had embraced "the rights of man." And when royal Britain and revolutionary France went to war, Federalists and Republicans took the expected sides.*

*All of these disputes had begun in Washington's presidency, like winds, at first blowing gently, some offshore, some on. But steadier and stronger they had blown until, at length, they whirled themselves into a hurricane.*

*Finally, with England and France both impressing American seamen and restraining American trade,*

*Federalist President John Adams turned against the French. No more than a few sea fights ensued, but the Federalist Congress used the Quasi-War of 1798 as leverage to pass the Alien and Sedition Acts, by which to control pro-French agitators in the United States and a Republican press they considered not merely opinionated but downright irresponsible.*

*The Republican press had not surrendered, however, and newspapers on both sides continued to fight. Upon my return to Alexandria, I read all the vitriol, in all the papers, while awaiting an audience with my uncle:*

*The Republican* Philadelphia Aurora *printed the names of editors recently charged under the Alien and Sedition Acts:* "Callender is in prison. Duane has a dozen suits against him. John Hereford of the Philadelphia Witness *is free on bail, and publisher Hesperus Draper may soon face indictment. Their persecution is proof that they have spoken the truth.*"

*The Federalist* Gazette of the United States *had proclaimed:* "The abuse offered to Mr. Adams in the Aurora and Witness *shows the base disposition of the opposition to divide and destroy all Federalists. United we stand, divided we fall prey to all the horrors which France has experienced from the bloody fangs of the Jacobins, whose guillotine inspires our American Republicans.*"

"So," *demanded my uncle, when I sat down with him,* "have you found the answers?"

"To what?"

"The secret of the Martha letters."

"There's no secret," *I said.*

*He gave me a squint.* "Have you been wastin' my money?"

"No. But from what I read, you've been courting imprisonment."

He chuckled. "Nothin' wrong with a little imprisonment, if you get to call the Federalists 'a batch of half-baked, half-British hypocrites'—like the alliteration?—'bent on nothin' so much as the creation of a government in the image of the nation that was our open enemy for eight years and our shadow enemy ever since.' I'm told that sounds treasonous."

"You're told right."

"Well, the Federalists called us French Jacobins. We're not Jacobins. But we're not monarchists, either. We want a president, not a king. We want Jefferson. And Jefferson wants to see you. So get goin'."

As I approached Monticello a few days later, my first thought was that I was gazing upon a Greek temple. That, of course, was Jefferson's intention.

My second thought was that here was a fine bit of irony. Jefferson, the man of the people, lived like a god on his mountaintop, attended by an army of slaves, some of whom had skin as light as a Frenchman's and hair the color of their master's. John Adams, the man supposed to be leading America back toward the darkness of monarchy, owned a modest farmhouse, served by hired labor.

Activity swirled around Monticello that day. Slaves wielded hammers and trowels, lugged bricks and planks, built scaffolding. And standing among them, like Pharaoh watching the Israelites build his pyramid, was the man who had written that all men were created equal.

"Welcome, citizen." Jefferson actually used that form of address with more sincerity than Lafayette.

"*I'm glad you came. In Philadelphia, I must see to my duties. Here at Monticello, there is more time for talk . . . more time for everything.*"

*Everything indeed, I thought, as I entered the house and was greeted by a magnificent coffee-colored young Negress who, given the proprietary air with which she went about her business, seemed far more than a mere slave. This, I surmised, was Sally Hemings.*

*Jefferson was fifty-eight, as tall and skinny as a French poplar, with hair more reddish than brown, and a soft Virginia accent that was as pleasant to hear as the breeze through those poplars.*

"*You know of my project?*" *I asked.*

"*And I approve, though not if you have set out to denigrate Washington. No matter what you may hear otherwise, my admiration of him remains un-dimmed.*"

"*Mine has grown,*" *I said,* "*especially since I set down a description of the scene at the New Windsor Tabernacle.*"

"*His moderation and virtue that day prevented the Revolution from ending the way most others have, by subverting the liberty it was meant to establish.*"

*Perhaps the events in France were on Jefferson's mind.*

"*And,*" *he asked,* "*how many generals have ever surrendered their commissions and their armies to a civilian Congress after winning a revolution?*"

*I said,* "*No others come to mind.*"

"*Nor will they.*"

*Jefferson himself showed me to a guest room in his amazing house. The room had, in addition to one of the first indoor privies in Virginia, an alcove bed that would be a snug and embracing place to sleep in the depths of January, but that I feared would suffocate me in July.*

*The evening breezes, however, allayed my fears. After we dined we walked in the gardens, and the cooling waves of wind seemed to dance from the top of one little mountain to the next.*

*We discussed natural history, the French countryside, and my impressions of Napoleon, however briefly made. And talk of the new French consul led Jefferson back to discussing Washington.*

*He said, "I think I knew him intimately and thoroughly."*

*"Most of your association with him came after the war?"*

*"You might say the war was not over. It had simply entered a new phase."*

*"Do you think," I asked, "that he understood his presidential struggles in that way?"*

*"I think"—Jefferson gave me the enigmatic smile for which he was famous—"that Washington's mind was great and powerful, without being of the very first order. It was slow in operation, being aided little by invention or imagination, but sure in conclusion."*

*Twilight came quickly in that hilly country, so that the sky behind Jefferson cast an ethereal glow that left his features all but indistinguishable. I think that was how he preferred it when rendering such an opinion.*

*"Do you think he arrived at the correct conclusions in his presidency?" I asked.*

*He gave me a somewhat broader smile. "We will discuss that in the morning. Right now I think we should be paying attention to the western sky. My almanac tells me that Jupiter will be visible this eve-*

*ning, just after dusk. Have you ever looked for Jupiter, Mr. Draper?"*

*I admitted that I had not.*

*"Let us look now."*

*He was a man of precise meanings and specific opinion, and yet there was about him an intellectual airiness that made it seem as if he might float away in a gentle breeze, as evanescent as the beautiful sunset behind him.*

*But opinions about Jefferson were neither gentle nor evanescent.*

*That was made clear on my next visit to Mount Vernon.*

*I had decided to go unannounced, hoping that perhaps I could find Mrs. Washington in better spirits. But Tobias Lear met me at the door, and the story was the same. She had said all that she would.*

*"I know she prefers not to speak about the death of her children. But—"*

*"She has always felt that pain. And she has always been loath to share her grief. She considers the display of it unseemly. But there's now another reason."*

*Naturally, I asked what it was.*

*"Word has reached us that you have been to Monticello to speak with Mr. Jefferson," he said. "Mrs. Washington prefers not to speak to anyone who has been speaking with Mr. Jefferson."*

*I said, "I know they did not part as friends, but—"*

*"She has called Jefferson 'one of the most detestable of mankind.'"*

*I was shocked. This was a bitterness I could not fathom. "Do you think she would tell me why?"*

*"I think she has told you enough. She grows more*

*reclusive, rather than less. She has retreated to a tiny bedroom under the eaves. She will not even go into her husband's study, let alone their bedchamber. She wishes to reveal no more of herself to the world. She repents revealing what she has, and"*—Lear peered over the spectacles balanced on the end of his nose— *"she will reveal no more of her correspondence with her husband."*

I suppose my jaw dropped at that.

"Yes," he said, "Mrs. Abigail Adams is a dauntless writer of letters. Her latest went into great depths regarding an interview that she had with you. Mrs. Washington was shocked. As for Miss Delilah Smoot, she's been dismissed."

And again, Lear left me standing in my own metaphorical puddle.

But while waiting for my horse to be brought 'round, I was approached by a young woman pushing a baby pram. My only surprise should have been that in two other visits I had not met her. She and her husband were living at Mount Vernon while they built a house on nearby property. In fact, she had lived at Mount Vernon since childhood.

She was Nelly Custis Lewis, third child of Jacky Custis, granddaughter of Martha. And she was, quite simply, beautiful. She had a delicately slender face, a small mouth, lively brown eyes, and fine height that could not have come from her grandmother. She was perhaps twenty-one, and the baby daughter in the pram looked to be six or seven months.

"You're Mr. Draper?" she said. "My grandmother has spoken of you."

"Not very well of late, it would seem."

"It's a wonder to me that she has spoken to you at

all. You know, we Virginia women are trained not to share our grief."

"She shared a great deal of joy with me as well."

Nelly invited me to walk with her as she pushed the pram down the road toward the river.

I said, "Tobias Lear might disapprove."

"Don't worry about him. He was my tutor when I was a girl. I've incurred his disapproval many times. Besides, he knows I'll not speak well of Mr. Jefferson. I've become an outrageous politician, a perfect Federalist."

And down the long sloping path we went, past the plantation bell, past the stables, past Washington's tomb, and back into the past.

## The Narrative of Nelly Custis Lewis:

My first first memory of my stepgrandfather—I always called him Grandpapa—came on Christmas Eve of 1783. He had ridden all day from Annapolis, where he had surrendered his commission to Congress, which was meeting in Maryland because a mob had driven them out of Philadelphia. Congress, as you know, was like the unwanted child of thirteen fathers.

Grandpapa swept into the house in his blue officer's coat, bringing cold fresh air and a saddlebag filled with presents for all of us—my two older sisters and my little brother. I was four. And four is a most impressionable age, sir, when a giant of a man brings you gifts at Christmas.

There were whirligigs and tops, fiddles and doll

babies and books and . . . I would not say that I loved him from that moment, for love is something that must grow. But he became, and he remained, a father to me and to my little brother, George Washington Parke Custis, known as Little Wash.

Now, why would my mother permit two of her four children—Little Wash and me—to live with their grandparents, while she moved off with a new husband and her two older girls? As she said, "What could I do? It would have been barbarous to have taken you from your Grandmama. She was so unhappy after your father's death."

In truth, I too would have been unhappy, for we younger children had grown up at Mount Vernon and felt most loved in the care of Grandmama. It was not always joyful, but think of all the wonderful things we saw.

Let me begin with the Marquis de Lafayette.

What I always remember of him is the smile that lit his whole face. I took a particular liking to him, because he said I reminded him of his own little daughter. Whenever he sat down, I insisted that he dandle me on his knee, which I know pleased the Marquis and my grandfather, too. Even now I correspond with him and call him *"mon cher papa français."*

One of the earliest memories I have is of a conversation between my grandparents shortly after the Marquis left for France. I think it buried itself in my mind because Grandpapa seemed so unhappy, and he was not the cheeriest of men to begin with.

It was a snowy night. He and Grandmama were sitting close by the fire in the little parlor. The house seemed especially quiet, especially dark, as if the brilliant candelabrum called Lafayette had been extinguished and replaced by a guttering old taper.

Grandmama said something to that very effect.

And Grandpapa said, "I rode all the way to Annapolis with him, Patsy, 'twas so hard to say good-bye. I still feel such love for him. I've been asking myself ever since he left whether that was the last sight I should have of him."

Grandmama was knitting. When she looked up at him, the firelight reflected in her spectacles. "He has promised to return."

"As likely as our visiting France," he answered.

"Oh, no, George," said Grandmama. "I could never travel so far on a ship. What if it should sink?"

He looked at her as if to say that she had made his point. "I watched him riding off and it reminded me of the days of my youth, long since fled."

"And never to return, dear," said Grandmama, her needles ticking.

I do not think that men like to be reminded of their mortality. When women consider it, they turn their noses to their knitting, or some other task of the here and now. Men stare into space.

Then Grandpapa said, "Patsy, I'm now descending the hill I've spent fifty-two years climbing. I'm blessed with a good constitution, but I come from a short-lived family. You know that."

"Yes, dear." Grandmama kept at her knitting.

"I'm serious, Patsy."

"Yes, dear. You always are."

"Most of my brothers have died. My father didn't pass fifty. I might soon be expected to be entombed in the same dreary mansions."

"You're sounding rather dreary already."

He picked up the newspaper. "These thoughts darken the shades, Patsy. They give gloom to my hopes of ever seeing the Marquis again . . . But I'll not repine."

"Read the paper instead."

"I'll not repine, nor complain," he said. "I've had my day."

"You certainly have."

## Jacob, Mount Vernon Slave:

The General be pretty sad after Lafayette leave, but he have some hard things to think about, 'cause him and Lafayette do some hard talkin'. Lafayette be one feller who ain't afraid of speakin' his mind to the General.

One night I hears them talkin' 'bout slavery. I'se putterin' 'round the dinin' room, cleanin' up, seein' that the glasses is filled and all, and listenin' all the time, too.

Lafayette sit back, hold his glass 'fore the candle, swirl the Madeira 'round some, say how fine it be. Then he say, "Now, my dear General, as I have written to you, I have a plan that might be greatly beneficial to the black part of mankind."

By that, he mean us, I reckon. Ain't exac'ly sure 'cause he put the words t'gether in a funny way, and he talk funny, too.

The massa say, "I have always sought to benefit our Negroes."

Well, if he say so. Leastways, he never gone lookin' for my son.

Lafayette say, "Let us unite in purchasing a small estate where we may try the experiment to free the Negroes . . . use them only as tenants."

I'se thinkin' this be the damnedest idea I ever hear. Massa just say, "Yes . . . yes . . . go on."

"We might render it a general practice, and if we succeed in America, I will cheerfully devote a part of my time to render it fashionable in the West Indies."

Massa jess give Lafayette a little smile and say, "I've already considered your proposal. I have received enough letters from you on the matter."

Lafayette lean across the table. "And?"

"It's evidence of the benevolence of your heart."

"And?" Lafayette press the General more 'n any man ever do.

"I don't see it as workable. To set our slaves afloat all at once would cause much inconvenience and mischief. But by degrees it might be tried."

"What if by legislative authority?" ax Lafayette.

I set out a bowl of walnuts, 'cause the General like walnuts. He grab two and start rollin' 'em in his hand. He don't even look at me. Course, I ain't there, is I?

"Marquis," he say, "no living man wishes more sincerely than I to see the abolition of slavery. Seeing the bravery of Negroes in the field . . . it changed my mind about many things."

There's words to make a slave daddy proud.

"But—"

"I am always afraid of your 'buts,' my dear General."

"But by *degrees*. We must lay a foundation to prepare the next generation for something different from that in which they were born."

"Absolutely," said the Marquis.

"It would afford some satisfaction to me"—the General shell a walnut—"and it might be pleasing to the Creator."

Well, I'se pretty excited to hear that. Mebbe it mean that someday my Matt come back to Mount Vernon. So I goes back to the quarters that night, fixin' to tell Alice all what I hear, how the massa plannin' to free us all. And who do I bump into, pickin' his way through the snow, but Billy Lee.

I say, "Evenin', Billy. What you doin' out?"

"Lookin' for somethin' to ease the pain."

"Which one, in you leg or you head?"

"Both." Billy have a bum knee by then, and a broken heart, too.

"You find somethin'?"

He pull a bottle from his coat pocket. "Madeira dregs. Drained 'em from a cask. Reckon, a few sips, I'll forget this cold. Few more, and I'll forget my knee. Few more and I'll only 'member the good times with Margaret."

"Don't be so drunk you ain't ready for the General in the mornin'."

"Depends on how fast the wine goes through me."

And I thinks, that boy be gittin' old fast. Been six months since he fall and break his knee pan, and a year since he send to Philadelphie for his wife. The General pay for her to come, 'cause Billy be so faithful to him in the Revolution. But she don't come. They send the money, and they wait and wait. Now Billy be the only one waitin'.

"You know," he say, "Margaret always call me a coward for not demandin' my freedom. Bet she don't want to be married to a coward."

I say, "Billy, can that gal read?"

Billy say she can.

"So write and say the General plannin' to free his slaves."

"Hah." Billy take a long drink. "When's he plannin' on that?"

"Soon . . . sometime. I jess hear him say so."

Well, I don't know if he ever write that letter. But the wife never come, and Billy, he jess get drunker and drunker.

## Nelly Custis Lewis:

Though none ever could make my grandfather as happy by their arrival—or as sad in their departure—as the Marquis de Lafayette, there were hundreds of visitors in those years after the Revolution. I remember one year he counted up four hundred and seventy. He was by then a very great personage. And travelers came from great distances just to gaze upon him.

There was Mr. Noah Webster, a very—*ahem*—wordy gentleman, who solicited a secretary's position. The two Jameses of Virginia, as I call them, James Monroe and James Madison, who came often to discuss the difficulties of governing under the Articles of Confederation. The two Methodist ministers who brought a petition to eliminate slavery, which my grandfather would not sign, though he promised that if the Virginia legislature took up the matter, he would take the side of the ministers. There were actors from England, new friends, old soldiers, regular visits from his friend Dr. Craik.

And there was a Mr. North, late aide to Baron

Steuben. I remember him because of the violent emotions he raised in me. I did not quite understand what he was saying, and even now his remarks are embarrassing to repeat, but they should be set down to dispel rumors about slave women at Mount Vernon.

"Will you believe it," Mr. North grumbled, whilst he and a friend walked the paths past where I was playing, "I've not humped a single mulatto since I arrived."

"Nor I," said the friend, "and there are some fine-looking specimens."

"Here we can expect three meals a day, but no dallying. The great man retires to his study after breakfast and we to our room. The wife has a certain goodness of heart, I must admit, but she is such a figure, and squeaks so damnably, I can barely stand to be in her presence."

"We should leave soon or go crazy."

I threw a rock at them and ran away. . . .

Of course, the visit I remember most, other than Lafayette's, came from another Frenchman, who arrived late one night, bearing a letter of introduction from Thomas Jefferson. His name was Jean Antoine Houdon. He was a sculptor. And two days later he gave me the greatest fright of my childhood.

I was only six, and, once again, should not have retained any recollections of the visit, had I not seen the General as I did—dead and laid out for burial.

Yes. That was what I thought.

I was passing the white servants' hall and saw his corpse. I went in and found him extended on a large table, a sheet over him, except for his face, on which Houdon was engaged in putting plaster to form a cast. Quills were in the General's nostrils, and the portions of his face not already covered in plaster were coated in shiny oil.

Houdon told me he was making a life mask, a likeness of the General, and it would not hurt him. That was all I remembered. But the bust we now have from Houdon is the best likeness one could hope for, better than all the portraits Grandpapa was forced to sit for as he became America's greatest personage. Look at the bust and see the power of the man.

## Jacob, Mount Vernon Slave:

With Billy Lee crippled up some, I go on some trips with the General.

Him and Dr. Craik make one into the backcountry one year. The General have some thirty thousand acres out there now, all good bottomland. But he have trouble with it. They's squatters to put off, and a drunk runnin' his mill, and while the land ain't worth much, they's taxes to be paid. But I jess 'member how beautiful it all be, how wild and free.

What ain't beautiful is Mary Ball Washington. Never been. Never will be.

But you can't tell no story 'bout the General without you tell a little bit more 'bout her. She always complainin' 'bout money, always writin' to him.

And one time he go down there to visit, and she start in. Now, he have her fixed up in one of the nicest little houses in Fredericksburg . . . small, but plenty big enough for an old lady and her servants, specially seein' as how her daughter Betty Lewis can come right down from her big house on the hill to visit.

So the General come in the livin' room, and he set by her.

She give me a look, more like a squint, and she say, "Jacob?"

I admit it, I likes that she 'member me. So I smile. "Yes, ma'am."

"I thought you was dead."

"No, ma'am."

"Good to have long-lived slaves, so long as they's healthy to work."

The General say, "Mother, did you receive the fifteen guineas I sent you?"

"I did. And I need fifteen more. Like I told you."

"That was all the cash I had."

She give a "Hmmph," like she don't believe it for a minute. Me, neither.

He say, "Mother, over the last few years, I've advanced you four hundred pounds, and still you paint me to the world as an unjust and undutiful son."

"Someone has to look after me, George."

He look around the house, which ain't but three rooms on the first floor. "You might hire out your servants, except for two to care for you, or break up your house and go to live on the hill with Betty."

The old lady jess look at her son and chaw her gums a few times, like she got some cud in there or something. And she say, "What if Betty don't want me? Will you take me in?"

He say, "Mother, Mount Vernon would be far too tiring for you, what with servants buzzing about, and people from so many important walks, whose presence would compel you to appear only in your best clothes, and never in nightclothes, and—"

He thinkin' of another reason, but she say it: "I know, George. I'm an old woman, like an old almanac, all out of date, and you don't want me."

And the General start to git mad. He tell her he tryin' to help her be happy. "And remember, Mother, happiness depends on the internal frame of a person's own mind, not on externals in the world."

"I s'pose so, dear," she say, sweet as cake, "seein' as you're so happy."

And tha's when the General look at me and say, "Jake, don't you have something to do outside? Go water the horses."

Well, I'se already done that, but I know he don't want me watchin' this, even if it ain't no different from what-all gone on 'tween 'em from the beginnin'.

But I tell you, the General git pretty sad when he learn she die some time later. He be president by then. He git mournin' cockades and put 'em on his hat, and all the hats that us slaves wears.

He tell his wife: "The death of a parent is awful, Patsy, more awful than I anticipated."

"She lived long, George, and with all her mind still working."

He think for a bit: then he say, "Yes. Let's hope that she's translated to a happier place. We must submit to the decrees of the Creator."

I hear Miz Washington talk like that plenty, 'cause she have plenty of reason, but the General don't. Not too often, anyways.

Now there was one other time you should know about that I took a ride with the General.

'Twas earlier than some of the stuff I jess tol' you,

but you gots to remember, I'se gittin' old, and a lot of this stuff jess git jumbled up on me.

Lots of times, in the evenin', the General go out on the piazza and whenever he do, he always look off to the south, off to where the land jut out into the river, off to where Belvoir used to be. But Belvoir be gone by then.

Late in the war, see, they come this big storm of thunder and lightnin', and the next thing we know, they's smoke risin' over the trees to the south. Yassuh, Belvoir burn right to the ground.

So this one day—'twas winter 'cause the leaves was all off the trees—the General rides over to Belvoir. I rides with him, jess to keep his horse.

They's a little bit of snow spittin' down, a raw wind blowin'.

What's left of the big house ain't but a few standin' brick walls. Most all everythin' else burn up. The floors is gone inside, and soon enough, the whole place fall in on itself. 'Tis a sad sight, like a strong man who have a stroke.

For a few minutes the General jess stand there, lookin'.

Then I say, "Sure be a lot of memories here, General."

"Our youth was here, Jake. Yours, mine . . ." And he walked up the front step, which was made of stone, like he was fixin' to go in. "Colonel Fairfax . . . my brother Lawrence . . ."

"Massa Lawrence sure be proud of you now, suh."

The General don't say nothin' to that.

He jess keep namin' the names. "George William . . . Sally . . . all the gay Fairfax ladies . . . Fanny Alexander . . . all the—"

And he can't say no mo'. He jess turn and grab his horse and go gallopin' off, like he's afraid the ghosts might come and chase him.

C.D.—*I alluded earlier to small treasures that I brought back from Paris.*

*The most important of them had come to me two days before I left.*

*Returning from my week with Lafayette, I had found an envelope awaiting me at Hotel Coislin. The letter F was pressed into the wax seal.*

*I hurried to my room and popped the seal: "Dear Mr. Draper, I am in receipt of your letter from Paris, and as I had been planning a trip thence, I will save you the bother of coming to England. You may find me at the apartment of Madame Marie Fauvel, Hotel de Langeac, 92 Avenue des Champs-Élysées, any afternoon in the week of May 20. Yours, Sarah (Sally) Cary Fairfax."*

*Two days later I met her, the woman who had captivated the youthful Washington.*

*She was now seventy. Her long and graceful neck, such an object of beauty in the eyes of early narrators, was shrouded in folds of lined flesh. Though her black hair had gone white, her eyebrows remained dramatically dark, and there was still a sparkle in her eyes, a nimbleness in her step, and a clear coquettishness in her greeting. "I declare, I shall have to come to Paris more often, if such handsome men come to visit me."*

*I answered, "You're as beautiful as I had expected."*

*"Sir, you are either a man of great charm, or in need of spectacles."*

*I suppose that we could have gone on like that, wittily gainsaying one another all afternoon. So I said directly, "About George Washington . . ."*

*"Yes, yes . . . so handsome, so serious, so devoted to his friends . . ."*

*She led me to a table by a window. On the table was a small box, sitting in a shaft of sunlight. From the look she gave it, I sensed that it contained something of great significance.*

*She said, "It's hard to believe that the people we know in our youth may grow to greatness."*

*"Do you think he grew to greatness, or was he great from the beginning?"*

*"Do you think he was great? I know the reputation of your uncle."*

*"Madam, I'm beginning to think that even my uncle saw his greatness."*

*"Good." She slid the box toward me. "These are letters from him."*

*I wanted to grab the box but she drew it back, almost as if she was teasing me.*

*"Letters interest me," I said, as calmly as I could. "I'm glad you saved these. It's been said that Martha burned George's letters at his death."*

*"All women burn a letter or two, but"—her brow furrowed down—"I think 'tis better to keep them."*

*"Indeed," I said. "How will the world know a man, if not by his letters?"*

*"A fair question." The wrinkles in her face tightened, the eyes danced. Then she opened the box. There were only three letters inside. She allowed me to copy each one, then she leaned across the table and began to talk.*

# The Narrative of Sally Fairfax:

W e could never go back to America. The beauties of Bath, England, the friends we made, the life we lived there, all were such that George William and I had no wish to leave. And though we had been very much in support of our Virginia friends in the Revolution, who would believe us?

So it seemed a divine message when lightning took Belvoir.

Then, in 1785, George wrote to us a long letter that touched upon many subjects.

Being a man who was always careful with a shilling, he described financial difficulties which, if they hurt him, must have crushed many others. "My accounts stand as I left them near ten years ago; those who owed me money, few instances excepted, availed themselves of what are called tender laws, and paid me off with a shilling and sixpence to the pound. Those to whom I owed money, I have now to pay under heavy taxes with specie, or its equivalent value."

Being ever ambitious, he told us of the Potomac Canal Company, in which he had taken a position, the goal of which was to dig a canal between the headwaters of the Potomac and the Ohio, near his western lands.

Being surprisingly sentimental, he touched us with this passage: "Of all my hopes, I would wish that the both of you once more were fixed in this country. And I beg that you would consider Mount Vernon as your home until you could build with convenience—in which Mrs. Washington joins very sincerely.

"I never look toward Belvoir without having this uppermost in my mind. But alas! Belvoir is no more. I took a ride there the other day to visit the ruins—all sinking under the depredation of time and inattention. But when I viewed them, when I considered that the happiest moments of my life had been spent there, when I could not trace a room in the house (now all rubbish) that did not bring to my mind the recollection of pleasing scenes, I was obliged to fly from them and came home with the most painful sensations."

One thing that George had not lost was his flair for the dramatic. To think that of all he had seen and done, he remembered his days at Belvoir as the happiest moments of his life . . .

## Hesperus Draper:

Land-rich and cash-poor.

You could say that about Washington in those days. Hell, you could say that about all of us.

The officers of the Continental army went home with the promise of full pay for five years, which was fine, except that the certificates they received weren't worth anything, because the limp-dicked Congress didn't have the power to raise taxes to pay a *standin'* army, let alone a disbanded one. Hell, that Congress hardly had any power at all.

Whoever called it the thirteen-headed beast wasn't far wrong.

A lot of folks were glad to pat one head and ignore the rest, but a lot of folks thought that these thirteen heads spent too damn much time snappin' at each other and no time at all pullin' in the same direction. Some states put out so damn much paper money that it became as worthless as . . . as a Continental.

Most Virginians thought the future was tied to Virginia alone. And they weren't far wrong. Soon after the war, Virginians were exportin' as much tobacco and rice as ever. Those of us who handled cargoes didn't mind payin' a small tariff to our state, because we had some control over the men who'd spend our money.

Then we heard that Alexander Hamilton and a few others were tryin' to get a convention organized at Annapolis to strengthen the Articles of Confederation. That would've been in '86.

I told Charlotte, "I don't like it."

"You don't like that the value of your money would go up with a stronger government?"

"At what cost?" I said. "You know that all of us in the South will be the ones who pay. The northern states will try to put all the duties on the things we produce for export, not the things they manufacture."

"So," she said, "there should be a gathering to discuss it."

"All they'll want to discuss is the war debt and who's to pay for it. Virginians have paid their share. The northern states are still hopin' somebody else'll do it, which means puttin' it on our shoulders."

And I wrote my first editorial against strengthening the federal government.

I won't take the credit for it, but the Annapolis convention was a gratifyin' bust. Only five states sent delegates.

But somethin' else happened in '86 that made everybody nervous. A bunch of Massachusetts farmers—sick of depreciatin' state currency and foreclosures on their farms and heavy taxes laid by the state—marched against an armory in Springfield. They set a few fires, made some threats, raised some general hell.

'Twas a small thing, a local demonstration, and no business of Virginians, which is what we tried to say in the paper. But the constitutionalists, the ones who wanted a stronger federal government, the ones already startin' to call themselves Federalists, they fanned Shays' Rebellion into another full-scale revolution.

## The Narrative of Thomas Jefferson:

I was serving as envoy to France when Mr. Shays led his rebellion, and I viewed it in a more sanguine fashion than did some in America.

What country, I wondered, can preserve its liberties if its rulers are not warned from time to time that the people preserve the spirit of resistance? What signify a few lives lost in a century or two? The tree of liberty must be refreshed from time to time with the blood of patriots and tyrants. It is the natural manure.

## Nelly Custis Lewis:

The name of Colonel Shays was heard often at Mount Vernon in those months. You know, this was called by some the Critical Period, and critical it was.

I remember Grandpapa reading aloud to Grandmama a letter from Henry Knox of Massachusetts about a political machine composed of thirteen independent sovereignties perpetually operating against each other.

Another letter came from Alexander Hamilton, warning that the next time there was an uprising, the leader might be a Cromwell or a Caesar, not an ignorant Massachusetts farmer. And with what consequences to the freedoms of the Republic? Mr. Hamilton, as you may know, was more fearful than most of what he called the masses.

"Good God!" cried Grandpapa after reading Hamilton's letter. "It is but the other day that we were shedding blood to obtain the Articles that govern us, and now we're unsheathing the sword to overturn them. This federal government is at a stand. We'd best be vigilant, Patsy. If its powers are inadequate, we must amend them or alter them. But we can't let this government sink."

## Hesperus Draper:

S o off they all went to Philadelphia, to dream up a
better constitution and form a more perfect union.
More perfect than what?

I'd become friendly with Patrick Henry because he
liked our newspaper and he liked what I'd written
about this Constitutional Convention.

One day, when he was in Alexandria, he visited me,
and I asked him why he didn't go to the convention.
"Weren't you invited?"

"Oh, I was invited," he answered. "But I smelled
a rat."

The proceedin's were meant to be secret, but I had
my spies there at Independence Hall, so I knew what
was goin' on.

Washington was elected president of the convention. He reminded them all about the secrecy. And
that was that. Except to gavel the day to a start, he
said hardly another word durin' all the deliberatin'.

With most men, if they sat in front of you for three
months as dumb as the Sphinx, you'd think they
were operatin' under the old adage that it's better to
keep your mouth shut and be thought a fool than to
open it and remove all doubt. But Washington's silence, so they say, only added gravity to the business
at hand.

And I'll admit it. By then the man carried gravity in
his pockets. Somehow people saw it as wisdom, and
sometimes it was.

After James Madison introduced the Virginia Plan,
which called for three branches of government—
judicial, legislative, and executive—old Ben Franklin

said, "Well, gentlemen, we know that the first man to be made chief executive will be a good one."

And all eyes turned to Washington. 'Twas a comfortin' remark from a man who had a fine way with comfortin' remarks.

But even Franklin was worried, considerin' what he said next: "Nobody knows what sort may come afterward. The executive will always be increasing in power, till it ends in monarchy."

I could give you a long story of how the Constitution was proposed and amended and fought over and ratified. Hell, you could write a book about the ratification fight in Virginia alone. But this much you should know:

Washington, the Virginian, came from one of the most solvent states in the Union, the state which proved that in a big country some things were best done by folks mindin' as little of anybody else's business as possible. But Washington, the general who'd led an army that was never properly supplied or supported by the Congress that authorized it, he knew better than anyone that some things could not be done without a strong central government bindin' folks together.

I'd read somewhere that this Constitution was called the Gilded Trap. And that's what I started callin' it in the papers. It was awful pretty, but in the wrong hands, it could be awful dangerous. It would be up to Washington to keep it from snappin' shut.

## Nelly Custis Lewis:

On the morning that he left to travel to his inauguration, there was great commotion in the house. The slaves who would accompany him busily packed the coach with his trunks. Grandmama, who was to follow later, gave orders. And the crisis of the day was that Billy Lee had appeared too drunk to take a horse. This was happening more often of late, ever since he had fallen a second time and damaged his good knee.

Grandpapa looked at him, shook his head, more in disappointment than anger, and said, "Stay here, Billy. Come north with Mrs. Washington and the rest of the family." Then he told Jacob to pack for a trip.

Billy stood bewildered for a time, until two house slaves led him away.

A few moments later I followed my grandfather to his study, hoping for a few moments of privacy with him. But when I was just outside the door, I heard voices within.

"George," said Grandmama, "you're supposed to be leaving. What are you writing?"

"An entry in my diary." And he read. "'About ten o'clock, I bade adieu to Mount Vernon, to private life, and to domestic felicity; and, with a mind oppressed by more anxious sensations than I have words to express, set out for New York . . . with the best disposition to render service to my country in obedience to its call, but with less hope of answering its expectations.'"

I peeked 'round the corner and saw her give him a peck on the cheek. Then she said, "You'll do fine, dear."

"I wish I wasn't going." He closed his diary and got up.

"I wish that none of us were going," said my grandmother. Her words were sincere, I knew. Often I had heard her say that she had prayed her husband's long absences were done. And she could not yet bring herself to leave with him for New York.

But I was not so certain of my grandfather's sentiments. Consider how long he had been at the center of the nation's life and how closely he had followed political developments through papers and letters. To have remained at Mount Vernon while the grand American experiment went forth would have left him like a stallion, kicking at its stall. But still, he hated to leave.

He said, "Patsy, I could not refuse this, any more than I could have refused command of the Continental army."

His words sounded mushy. He had only two or three of his natural teeth left, and in the privacy of his office, he had taken out his dentures. The plates were made of gold, the teeth carved of hippopotamus ivory or actual human teeth. Upper and lower were fastened together with springs attached to little rivets that must surely have dug into the insides of his cheeks, and the whole device was cleverly fashioned to fit around his remaining teeth.

Many people said that my grandfather looked terribly grave and seldom smiled, which was true. But because of the springs, he was compelled to keep his jaws tightly clamped, or the springs would force his mouth open. This, of course, deepened the gravity of his expression.

The first time I saw these dentures, I thought them

some torture device, and I resolved to brush my teeth with salt and pick them carefully each day.

Grandpapa forced his dentures back into his mouth, as if preparing himself to be seen by the world again. "I've spent fifty-seven years building my reputation, Patsy. All I can do now is diminish it."

"Not if you do a good job, George, and you will do a good job."

"Patsy"—he straightened his black waistcoat—"You can't realize the difficult and delicate part which a man in my situation has to act. I walk untrodden ground. There's scarcely any part of my conduct that won't be drawn into precedent."

"Then do your best. And I'll soon follow to help you."

He leaned forward and kissed her on the forehead, which must have been painful to one or the other of them, considering the protruding teeth.

And off he rode to his inauguration.

## Jacob, Mount Vernon Slave:

Goin' north. Yassuh, I'se mighty excited. Goin' north to where men breath free. And what a trip.

I never know how much folks loves the General till then. They loves him in Baltimore, in Philadelphia, in Trenton, and in all the little towns along the way.

Then they's the big day in New York, the grand reception.

The General come across from Sandy Hook on a big barge all decked out in red, white, and blue, with thirteen oars on each side, and up ahead they's hundreds of boats, all waitin'. 'Twas like everybody in New York come out in a boat to greet him, see. And when our barge pass the battery at Staten Island, they fire a thirteen-gun salute. And every boat in the harbor, like on a signal, run up a pennant or a flag or jess a bright rag of color.

I swear, the general start smilin' about as broad as you ever see from him.

They's bells clangin' and cannon firin' and music playin' all at once, and folks everywhere wavin' and shoutin' and givin' out with huzzahs and hallelujahs! And all them boats sail along 'side us, see, jostlin' for position, and as we go by, folks throw flowers and cheer.

'Twas the most joyous, excitin' thing I ever did see.

And right in the middle of it, this pretty schooner called the *Columbia* come shootin' 'longside of us. And her master doff his hat and make a fancy bow.

The General take off his hat and bow back. Then he stand bolt upright, 'cause he see somethin' funny behind the feller. I swear to you, they's a cage on the boat, and two big apes with long arms and orange fur, jumpin' around inside.

Now, I can't read, but one of th'other servants can, and he read the big signs on this boat. One say, "Dr. King from South Africa, with a collection of natural curiosities." And the sign by the apes, it say, "A male and female orangutan, remarkable for their striking similarity to the human species."

And I look agin at the General. And he's jess lookin' like he ain't never seen nothin' like this in his life, and he jess don't know what this feller's up to. I'se mighty puzzled, too. But we don't think on it for long, 'cause up ahead, they's everybody waitin' at the dock, and they's bands and cheerin'. . . .

That night, after all the parties and banquets, the General seem wore out and kind of sad, see. He set down and write in his diary whilst I lay out his clothes for the next day.

And I ax him, "Is they somethin' wrong, suh?"

He say, "You wouldn't understand, but . . . a day like today can be as painful as it is pleasing."

"How so, suh?"

"I imagine the scene if, after all my efforts, we fail. How many more will bring their apes to bid me good-bye?"

## Hesperus Draper:

The one with the orangutans? Philip Freneau—poet, publisher, anti-Federalist, Anglophobe. He spent two years on a British prison ship durin' the Revolution, which explains why he hated the British. And like a lot of us, he saw this new federal power as a dangerous thing. Few men could write a heroic couplet like he could, but I guess he thought two red-haired apes, tended by someone named King, would send the best message to Washington about the business he was on.

## John Adams:

I expressed no aspirations for the presidency, knowing that it would go first to Washington, knowing that it should. However, I stood for the vice-presidency, which I considered the second most important position in this new federal structure. Any other position, I had decided, would be beneath my station.

On the appointed April day, Washington stood on the balcony of the new Federal Hall, before the throng on Broad and Wall Streets, erect, grave, perfectly turned out in a brown suit made of Connecticut broadcloth, and he took the oath.

The chancellor of the state of New York proclaimed, "It is done! Long live George Washington, President of the United States!" The ground shook with the thunder of the great harbor guns; church bells pealed above the cheering; and Washington, after executing two deep bows, stepped inside to deliver his speech before the House of Representatives.

I would have hoped for a grander oratorical style now, but though he read softly, his words carried great weight. He spoke of the "indissoluble union between virtue and happiness, between duty and advantage, between the genuine maxims of honest policy, and the solid rewards of public prosperity." In short, we should reap what we sow, which is always the case.

And he begged "that no local prejudices or attachments, no separate views nor party animosities will misdirect our great assemblage of communities and interests." That, unfortunately, would not be the case.

But in the early days, party animosities were not yet

the order of the day. All seemed intent on a smooth start to our enterprise. All seemed to understand, as Washington said, that Providence had placed the destiny of republican government in the hands of the American people. We should all proceed carefully.

He seemed most careful in the secretaries he appointed. All were men he knew well: Alexander Hamilton as secretary of the Treasury, Henry Knox for War, Thomas Jefferson for State, and Edmund Randolph as attorney general.

And within a few days he was writing me as to what line of conduct he should pursue, not only with regard to the business of treaties, negotiations, and legislation, but in the minutiae of daily life, down to the matter of whether the President might be allowed to make private visits for tea with friends.

He may have been the best actor we will ever have in the presidency. He studied the gestures of the role as if he were preparing to play *Cato*. And I gave him the best opinions I could, opinions with which many disagreed. But that has always been a condition with my opinions.

I believed that we must appear with pomp and circumstance, thereby giving the office a royal dignity to impress Europe, and not because I bear any true affection for monarchy, although hereditary institutions may have their place, as Britain proves. Hamilton agreed, suggesting as well that the President never pay personal calls, but hold himself aloof from the masses. We both agreed that the best way for him to present himself to men and women of quality would be with an appearance at his home, twice a week, to receive visits of compliment, a practice that I have continued.

So also have I continued to avoid personal appearances before the Senate, a lesson learned by Washington.

The issue that brought him before the Senate for the first and only time was a treaty with the Creek Indians. He communicated to me, as vice president and presiding officer of the Senate, his wish that we advise and consent on the matter, and on the appointed day, August 22, he appeared in Federal Hall, in company with Henry Knox.

Our chamber was hot, dusty, and noisy, as the windows were open and the clatter of Wall Street echoed as loudly as our deliberations . . . or *their* deliberations. It was my job merely to preside, as president of the Senate. But when the President came to visit, what was I?

Washington gave me the treaty to read, which I did in my best courtroom voice, though it was plain that not all the senators were listening. Some were lolling, others whispering over separate business, some could not hear for all the noise rising from the street.

Even Washington, who was seated at a table in the middle of the room, brought a hand to his ear to try to catch the sound. After I had finished, Washington stood to request ratification for this treaty.

Instead, Senator William Maclay leaped to his feet. He came from the backwoods of Pennsylvania and paraded his distrust of all our efforts as though it were a badge of honor. "Mr. President," he cried, meaning me and not the President, "this business is no different from any other. And no matter who comes to speak for it, we should not vote until it has been referred to committee."

"Committee?" said Washington, turning his implacable face onto Maclay.

"You don't expect us to vote on something we

haven't examined more closely, do you?" said Maclay, unimpressed by the famous stare.

Washington reddened, pursed his lips, which was always a prelude to an outburst, and snapped, "This defeats every purpose in my coming here."

Nevertheless, the treaty went to committee, and Washington stalked out, with Henry Knox after him.

A few moments later, in my private chamber, he glared at me as though it were all my fault. "I'll be damned, Adams, if I ever subject myself to something like that again."

"Nor should the dignity of the presidency be subjected to such as Maclay," I said.

The President made no answer to that. Instead, he put his hat so firmly upon his head that a small cloud of hair powder puffed out from under it. Then he stalked out. And a precedent was established. Presidents would not appear before Congress or the Senate to advance their business.

Another precedent was set in Boston in October. Washington was by then recovered from a tumor that had grown on his thigh that summer. . . .

## Nelly Custis Lewis:

Oh, yes, the tumor, the great carbuncle. We had barely arrived and settled ourselves into his house on Cherry Street when it made its appearance, in accompaniment to a fever. I was not old enough to understand what a cancer was, but all who spoke this word spoke it with consuming fear.

What I remember is that the General—or should

I say, President—lay for two weeks on his side, unable to work or move, in excruciating pain, while the creature grew on his upper leg.

Being a curious child, and completely comfortable with my grandfather, I went to the room once and asked to see it, but instead he called for Tobias Lear to take me to my studies, so that I would not be thinking about such things.

After a time, the growth abscessed, and two doctors were called to lance it. I remember putting a glass to my ear and listening through the floor above the room in which the cutting was done. And I shall always remember one doctor saying to the other, "Deeper, cut deeper. Can't you see how well he bears it?"

People often speak of my grandfather's commitment to the Roman virtues, none so plain as the stoicism he displayed in the face of physical pain, personal frustration, and political opposition, all of which the presidency would provide.

## Abigail Adams:

I arrived in the late summer in New York, when the President was recovering from his tumor. I did not see him, but Martha invited me to tea.

She received me with great ease and politeness. She was plain in her dress, but the plainness was the best of every article. Her hair was white, her teeth beautiful, her person rather short. Her manners were modest and unassuming. At her levees and dinners, I found myself more deeply impressed than ever I did before Their Majesties of Britain.

But after she had admitted me into the parlor of the house on the corner of Pearl and Cherry Streets, she admitted of her loneliness.

"I lead a very dull life," she told me. "I never go to any private homes, as the President should pay no calls. Sometimes I feel so angry . . ."

"It is difficult," I said, "to know how a president and his lady should act. No one has ever been a president before."

She poured out two cups of tea and said, "Some would have him act like a monarch, others like a backwoods burgess."

Outside, horses and wagons rolled by, the rumble of their passing dulled by straw, which had been spread across the street so that the President would not be disturbed by the noise.

I said, "Your husband has more presence than George III. He will know what to do. He will know instinctively."

"You are very kind. But I would much rather be home. Younger and gayer women would be happier here."

"Yes, Martha," I said, "but you are here."

"So I am . . . so I am . . ." She sipped her tea and gave herself a little nod of the head. "And I'm determined to be cheerful and happy. For I've learned from experience that the greater part of our happiness or misery depends upon our disposition and not our circumstances."

Whoever would tell you that she was a simple woman had best mean simplicity of the best sort, because she had seen much and understood deeply.

# John Adams:

The trip to Boston in October 1789 was part of our national tour. The President was intent upon showing himself to the nation, state by state.

By then we had heard the first rumblings of trouble that would soon send France into turmoil—the uprising at the Bastille.

"I read of such things," he said, as his chariot rocked along, "and it seems as if they occur on another planet."

"You should travel," I said. "Travel brings the world together."

"The very reason that I am traveling to Boston," he said.

I asked what his French friend said about this uprising.

"The Marquis de Lafayette is most hopeful that it will lead to better times. He is in command of the National Guard, a figure trusted by both the royals and the common people. But"—he looked out of the window at the colors of fall flaming across the Connecticut landscape—"I fear that this may be no more than the first paroxysm."

"From my experience among the French," I said, "I believe you may be right."

"Yes. A revolution is of too great a magnitude to be effected in so short a space, with so little blood. To forbear running from one extreme to another is no easy matter. Rocks and shelves not visible may at present wreck the vessel."

He might easily have been speaking of the voyage upon which we ourselves were now embarked, as all the issues of local and federal control appeared in

Boston in a single day, all in a kind of symbolic political pantomime.

First, who would lead Washington into the city? The selectmen of Boston or the representatives of the state, whose capital was Boston? This argument stopped the procession right at the Neck, within sight of the ancient British fortification that once protected the city from Washington's army.

A cold wind blew across the Back Bay and chilled us all to the bone. But in Boston, cold is no argument for cooperation. There were raised voices. There was almost a brawl. And an army of little children, brought out by the selectmen to lead the procession, ran about throwing rocks, first into the water, then at us.

And all the while, Washington sat on his horse, above the fray, as if expecting such displays in his honor.

Finally, with the help of the sheriff, the business was settled and the procession went forth, led by the selectmen, followed by the state representatives, followed by various tradesmen. This parade took us down the street once called Orange, now called Washington, until we came to the statehouse, where banners and arches extolled "The Man Who Unites All Hearts" and other such sentiments.

Washington mounted the balcony and greeted the throng, but even though we were at the statehouse, there was no governor. You may remember that Governor John Hancock had been the president of the Continental Congress in 1775. Though lacking military experience, he had coveted the command that we gave to Washington. And though his executive experience was minimal, he had harbored some hope of being named the first president.

Now he thought he had a point to make. Though Massachusetts was a Federalist state, Hancock was a most reluctant Federalist. He believed that the governor was sovereign in the state and the President merely his guest. So, without paying the first call on the President, he invited Washington to his home for dinner.

Washington had taken up residence at the boarding-house of the Widow Ingersoll, in Tremont Street. He asked, "Is the governor coming to my quarters first?"

I said, "I believe not."

"Send word to him that I shall not see him unless at my own lodgings."

I told him I approved of his position.

Soon the lieutenant governor, my cousin Samuel, appeared at Ingersoll's to apologize, explaining that the governor was ill. I knew, from the way he spoke, that he believed Hancock no more than I did.

Washington, with no hint of annoyance at such an obvious performance, said, "I shall be glad to receive the governor when his health permits of it."

It was the correct position. The President is the guest in every state, and sovereign of the whole nation. He deserves the deference of every governor. So the President and I dined alone at Ingersoll's that night.

The next day, demonstrating a flair for the dramatic that outstripped Washington's, Hancock wrote to him, "The governor will hazard everything, as it respects his health, to see the president."

No proper form of address was used, neither "Mr. President" nor any of the more exalted names that I had invented for the office, such as "His High Mightiness," names for which I had been derided by the anti-Federalist elements of our government, but names that polite written discourse would demand. None of that from Governor Hancock, but merely "the president."

Washington wrote back: "The President of the United States presents his best respects to the Governor and has the honor to inform him that he shall be home till two o'clock. The President of the United States need not express the pleasure it will give him to see the Governor, but at the same time, he most earnestly begs that the Governor will not hazard his health on the occasion."

There was a sly sarcasm about Washington that people seldom saw, and perhaps by its very slyness, it had its effect.

Thus came a scene that would have played well in a cheap New York theater: the governor of Massachusetts—his feet elaborately wrapped in bandages, his person ostentatiously displayed in a carrying chair, his retainers laboriously lifting him up the stairs to the President's lodging—at last placed the call of courtesy on the President, begging that, of all things, he had the gout.

It was from such details as these that a presidential image would be formed. Protocol mattered. I had been an envoy to the courts of Europe. I had seen their relations. I knew that nothing could advance us more surely in their eyes than to show them that we knew how to do things.

But if you look for me to have some further impact on this presidency, you look in vain. For I must tell you that the vice president, though cordially treated by the

President—so cordially that dinners, visits to the theater, and horseback rides were regular occurrences—was seldom part of his inner circle.

This I attribute to several things—the machinations of Hamilton, the bastard brat of a Jamaican planter, the jealousies of Jefferson, and the jealousies of Washington himself.

To his credit, Washington sought information from all quarters and judged more independently than any man I ever knew. That was the way he had led his army, and that was the way that he governed. But we must be honest about this: he was unread and uneducated, and my presence may have discomforted him.

So my country, in its wisdom, placed me in an office, the most insignificant that ever the invention of man contrived or the imagination conceived.

## Jacob, Mount Vernon Slave:

The General—I never calls him nothin' else but Massa—he bring his new French valet with him to Boston. He like the way this French feller powder his hair and tie the queue and fix it all nice and neat in a little bag. I'se surprised he bring one of his slaves too. But I'se sure glad 'tis me, 'cause in Massachusetts I see the greatest thing in my life.

Few days after the visit with Governor Hancock, and a big banquet in a place called Faneuil Hall, we pack up everything  includin' a fancy silver tea set that they give him—and we head for New Hampshire. But first, the General want to stop to see the place where some of his best soldiers come from, Marblehead, on a little finger of land 'bout thirteen miles north of Boston.

Well, suh, that whole day I has a big fist right in my belly, thinkin' that mebbe I'll see my boy. I'se to be in the very same town with him.

'Tain't much of a town. I hear the General say later, "The houses are old, the streets are dirty, the common people are not very clean." But he treat 'em all jess fine. What he be interested in is the fishin' fleet. He say that they's eight hundred men and boys fishin' from a hundred boats.

As we gits down toward the water, I can smell salt air, and my heart beat harder and harder. I'se hopin' I'll see my boy.

And then we come 'round the corner, and there be these fellers in soldier suits—short blue coats, all old and patched. They's the lads from the Marblehead Regiment, and they's lined up to greet him.

And my heart jess stop, 'cause I see a Negro in the front row.

'Tain't my boy. But they's another Negro, at th'other end. And tha's him. My Matchuko, standin' next to this little white feller with a squinty eye. And right next to Matchuko is a little black boy, mebbe five year old. And I tell you, I jess start to cry.

I'se standin' at some distance, so none of them see me, but the General hear me snuffle and give me a funny little look. Then I see somethin' in his eye, like he know. Then he go down the line of men, lookin' at each of them. But I has to stay with the coach, when all's I want is to run to my boy.

Then he stop in front of my son, look hard at him, and I'se worryin' cause even if Massachusetts outlaw slavery, this here be the President. If he want a slave back, he can have him.

But all he say is, "Victory or . . . ?"

And Matchuko smile and say, ". . . death, sir."

Then the General jess move to the next man. By and by, he go in a tavern for to have somethin' to eat, and he tell me to go down and buy some salt cod to bring home. He love that salt cod, see. He say for me to git a good price on a barrel. He say, "There's a Negro fisherman, one of our veterans, with a little boy. He might be a good one. Go and talk to him."

Well, suh, I go runnin' back down to that dock, with my heart all poundin' in my throat. I see the little boy first. Then I see Matchuko, mendin' net, and the white feller with the squinty eye be watchin' him.

And Matchuko, when he see me, he drop his splicin' awl and stand real slow . . . and, well, tha's the happiest minute of my life.

After we hug and all, I say to the white man, "Thank you, mister. Thank you for givin' my boy a job."

And the white man say, "I didn't give him nothin'. Him and me's partners."

"Partners?" I say. "A white man and the son of a slave? Partners?"

"Why, hell and damnation," he say, "your boy saved my life."

C.D.—*In general, the first year of the presidency was a time of gentle breezes.*

*It remained Washington's hope that there be no political parties—factions he called them. He hoped instead for consensus achieved through rational discussion. But in April of 1790 a vote was taken in the House.*

*Alexander Hamilton had made his first proposal to put the infant United States on a paying basis. He wanted the federal government to assume all the war debts of the states. But many of the states, mostly southern, had already paid their debts. So what to do?*

*The vote, in April, showed twenty-nine in favor of assumption, thirty-two against. In the struggle between a strong federal system and states' rights, the first cold gust had blown. And May brought a crisis that showed the fragility of the leader who would seek to calm the winds.*

## Thomas Jefferson:

I had been heartened greatly for our Constitution when a Bill of Rights was amended to it, and so I willingly joined Washington's administration when I was asked to be secretary of state.

However, I had only been returned from France and in my position a short time when I was taken with the headache. All my life, and especially at times of great loss or great stress, I had been gripped by paroxysms of the most excruciating pain. When such a headache came on, there was nothing for it but to retreat, preferably to a darkened room, and to avoid reading, writing, and almost thinking, my only medicine a dose of Peruvian bark.

The stresses that brought on the headache may well have arisen from the debate which had been raging in the House of Representatives over the matter of debt assumption. But I was brought quickly from the bed of my own sickness by something far more stressful—the news that Washington was dying.

A mild May cold had degenerated into pneumonia. It was put about that he was only slightly indisposed, but New York is a city where there are no secrets, and word passed quickly from one place to another that he was *in extremis*.

## Hesperus Draper:

Yes, I heard the bad news about the President, but I didn't print it. 'Twasn't something to print without knowin' for certain.

I had a spy in the Senate, by the name of Will Maclay, from out in western Pennsylvania. He was about the most radical Republican you could find.

He wrote me, "I have been to the President's dwelling to express my solicitations. Mrs. Washington accepted them, but the news was apparent by the redness in her eyes and the distracted nature of our talk. More to the point were the words of one of the physicians, that death was imminent. I will inform you better as soon as I have news, so that you may be the first to publish."

## Abigail Adams:

I dreaded his death for reasons that few persons, and only those who knew me best, would believe. It appeared to me that the union of the states depended, under Providence, upon his life. At that early day, when neither our finances were arranged nor our government sufficiently cemented to promise duration, his death would, I fear, have had the most disastrous consequences. I feared a thousand things which I prayed I never might be called upon to experience. Most assuredly, I did not wish for the highest post for my husband.

## Thomas Jefferson:

I was convinced that, without him, the whole structure would topple. He had brought us together and would hold us together. If he could be preserved for a few more years, till habits of authority and obedience were established, we would have nothing to fear from the forces of either monarchy or anarchy.

I rushed to his side, the intensity of my own pain forgotten.

One look at him, at his gray hair untied on the pillow beneath his head, his eyes sunk deep in their great sockets, and I was in despair.

But then, about four o'clock, a successful—indeed a miraculous—effort of nature relieved him. A copious sweat came on, his expectoration, which had been thin and ichorous, began to assume a well-digested form, his articulation became distinct, and in the course of two hours, it was evident that he had gone through a favorable crisis.

Three weeks later I received a most unusual invitation from him—to go fishing.

## Jacob, Mount Vernon Slave:

Well, I'se a slave, so I don't know much, but I tell you that they's plenty you can know about a man, jess by watchin' him fish.

The General take Mr. Jefferson and Mr. Hamilton fishin', see. He sail down to Sandy Hook on this nice little schooner, and he fish for bass. Spend three days fishin' and puttin' in to shore each night.

Now, I don't know what all those men talk about, 'cept that they's goin' on 'bout words like "assumption" and "refunding," and one time I hears Mr. Jefferson say how they all has to give a little and take a little in such a government as this.

And the General, he say, "Not a compromise of principle, but a compromise in the interests of harmony, in the interests of the nation."

Me, I jess watch these two fellers, Hamilton and Jefferson, and I git the feelin' that they ain't gonna be too friendly for too long.

With Jefferson, what you see first is his smile, all gentle and nice. With Hamilton, you look at them eyes, all sharp and smart. Jefferson talk soft and slow, like a southern man. Hamilton talk fast and you can hear him over the strongest wind. Jefferson's tall and angly. Hamilton ain't.

And when the sea start to run, Jefferson jess stay

put. Hamilton go from this side to that, lookin' down, actin' as nervous as a cat on a runaway cart. When I bait a hook for Jefferson—we's usin' sea worms—he don't ax agin till the worm's gone. He jess sit, with his line in the water, lettin' 'er dangle. Hamilton bounce his line up and down, up and down, and after a while, he say that mebbe we should change worms, seein' as he ain't had no bites. And I say, "You ain't catchin' anything cause you's jiggin' too much. Sit still, mebbe you catch a fish."

The General catch the most, 'cause he know just when to jig, jess when to sit. He bring in bass and blackfish, too. And it bring him back to feelin' good, though he still seem weak for a long time after that sickness.

Tha's about all I 'member, 'cept that the General, when we's sailin' back in, he say to me, "I just turned those two men into friends."

"Yassuh," I say, "nothin' to make men friends faster than fishin' with 'em."

"And, Jake, I'll always remember that it was you who taught me to fish."

And that make me feel good.

## Hesperus Draper:

You remember that me and my wife bought up some promissory certificates from old soldiers. But we always told those boys to hold on, hold on, that things might get better. But most boys sold when they needed money. Hell, I sold sometimes. I even heard that Washington did once in a while.

So we should all have been happy with the plan Hamilton come up with to settle the debt, because it redeemed those certificates at full value. But Virginia had already paid off her war debts. Massachusetts hadn't paid a nickel. Worse than that, it always seemed like 'twas northern speculators comin' south to buy up the certificates at ten cents on the dollar, so cash-strapped Virginia farmers could pay their taxes, so Virginia could pay off its war debts.

'Twasn't right.

And I said so in my paper.

James Madison, who'd been Mr. Constitution, was a strong opponent of the Hamilton plan. He wrote to me that he was tryin' for a different system to pay off the certificates. Those who were original holders would be paid face value, the speculators would be given only what they had paid.

I liked that even if it would cost me money. 'Twould keep all that money from concentratin' in the hands of the northern speculators. Because you know, money is the root of all evil. It's also the basis of all power, and Hamilton liked to see power in the hands of the men he thought could wield it. No power for the common folk in his world, no sir.

## Thomas Jefferson:

We had discussed the business of assumption on the fishing trip, quite briefly.

Later, Hamilton met me one day before the President's house. He was looking somber, haggard, and dejected beyond description, even his dress uncouth and neglected, and he asked to speak to me. It became plain that he was desperate to make assumption work or he would resign.

I thought that bringing Congressman Madison together with Hamilton, so that they could share their plans, would move us toward a conciliation, and so I invited both of them to dine with me. And there, in the candlelight of my home, an agreement was reached.

The new federal government would assume the debts of the war, including payment of the soldiers, the money to be raised by higher tariffs and excise taxes on such things as whiskey. But as an anodyne to the South, the new federal capital city would be located there. The government would move to Philadelphia for ten years, then establish itself in a place, most likely on the Potomac, that would be selected by a commission.

As my friend Madison said, those who are most adjacent to the seat of legislation will always possess advantages over others.

## Alexander Hamilton:

My business with Jefferson would not remain so cordial, but at that moment we had arrived at an agreement that would go far to making America respected in the eyes of other nations. Our debts would be paid, our securities, even the soldiers' certificates, backed by the full faith and credit of our government.

I considered it a complete victory and a vindication

of our maneuverings back at Newburgh, especially as I had expected all along that the capital would end up in a southern state.

The President had not spoken his support publicly. He preferred to keep his opinions close when he could, as a way of discerning the opinions of other men, but in private he said to me, "The war was incurred as a common cause. If the invaded states had believed that they would receive no financial support from their neighbors, opposition in them might very soon have turned to submission."

It was plain to me that he understood the principles of the Federalism I hoped to inculcate. They were the principles of order upon which a government had to be based.

## Hesperus Draper:

Here's what Patrick Henry said about assumption: "It is repugnant to the Constitution of the United States, as it goes to the exercise of power not expressly granted to the general government."

And here's why: Hamilton opposed the Madison plan, which would have taken a cut from the speculators, because Hamilton believed that the best way to build an economy wasn't to pass out the money in little dribs and drabs, so this farmer had a few dollars and that shopkeep had a few more—you know, the men who fought and bled and earned the money.

No, Hamilton liked it that speculators held so many certificates, because he believed that they were the ones who'd do somethin' with the money. Reinvest. Build ships. Build manufactories. Create wealth—for themselves first, and maybe then for everyone else.

It sure sounded good, such pure Federalism, but government was cuttin' out the little fellers right from the start.

So I decided to print Henry's speech verbatim, and I added this from the Protest of Virginia: "This bill will concentrate and perpetuate a large monied interest in opposition to the landed interests and lead to a change in the present form of the federal government, fatal to the existence of American liberty."

I know Washington read a lot of newspapers, so he knew what I was thinkin' and writin' about assumption. And senators like Maclay spoke their minds too: "The President has become in the hands of Hamilton the dishclout of every dirty speculation of every variety. His name goes to wipe away blame and silence all murmuring."

But Washington wouldn't stoop to answer me or Maclay or anybody else, at least in public. 'Twas always his way. Knew that if he did stoop, he might lose control of himself. Couldn't let that happen. Not answerin' also saved him from sayin' a single public word about this assumption business.

But he wanted it. He'd led an army backed by a government that had no cash, no credit, and nobody's confidence; he wasn't about to lead a government that way. And he wasn't about to damage his reputation if he could let Hamilton catch the criticism.

## Thomas Jefferson:

I was duped in our dealings with Hamilton. It did not take me long to realize it. While our capital would be in the South, all of our money would be concentrated in the North, in the hands of speculators and paper-money men. The farmers of the South, men of independent spirit and pursuit who were the true strength of the nation, would be left cashless.

## Nelly Custis Lewis:

My grandfather was happy with assumption, and he was happy that the capital was moving to Philadelphia. My grandmother was even happier, as it was that much closer to Mount Vernon.

Sometime during our last dinner in New York a messenger arrived, bearing a package.

My grandfather's eyes brightened to see the name of the Marquis de Lafayette on the package, and opening it, he discovered a key and a painting.

The key, flaking rust onto the tablecloth, was as large as any I had ever beheld, something to open a portal rather than a mere door. The picture was an engraving of what looked like an ancient battlement fallen into ruins.

"What does the note say?" asked my grandmother.

Grandpapa read, "Dear General, Enclosed you will find a gift from the free people of France—the key to the Bastille and a picture of the building, as it now appears."

"Oh," I said, "this is wonderful."

But my grandfather's face darkened. "Do not be too certain, Nelly. Every revolution is a leap into the dark."

C.D.—*That key gave reality to revolution. A sea breeze was lifting, though it must still have felt gentle at the back of a man who was, by now, aging rapidly. After two serious illnesses, his hair had gone gray, his jowls had drooped, his step was slower, his teeth gone but for one. Worst of all for an accomplished horseman, he could no longer spend a day in the saddle.*

*But he was optimistic. "Public sentiment runs with us," he wrote, "and all things hitherto seem to succeed according to our wishes."*

*It was easy to enjoy the breezes. But they foretold of stronger winds in Washington's first term. Ahead lay a fight over funding the Bank of the United States, Hamilton's next step in centralizing the American economy. The furies would rise in France. And there would be Indian troubles, too.*

# Joseph Britain,
## known as Silverheels:

We of the six tribes had been blown to the four winds. We had lost our power. We had lost our lands. So we made treaties. We were now "good" Indians.

The "bad" Indians lived farther west. The Miamis

and the Chickasaws. They let the British run them—the British who were still at Fort Niagara and Fort Detroit. The British wanted the Ohio River to be the place where the new United States ended. They wanted everything beyond for themselves.

But Caunotaucarius did not want to let them have it.

Our treaty came from Caunotaucarius himself: "Let it be heard by every person in your nation, that the President of the United States declares that the government is bound to protect you in all the lands secured to you by treaty."

These were good words. But only words. Not days later, Christian Senecas were attacked and killed by bands of drunken whites.

Our chief, Cornplanter, had grown in wisdom, but he believed he had to protect his people, so he went after the whites. There were fights. There were deaths. Things never changed.

Cornplanter cried to Caunotaucarius, "Our father and ruler, now speak and tell me, did you order our men to be killed? If so, you struck the innocent first. We hope you will not blame us, as your people have first broke good rules. As for our people, they are as friendly to you as ever."

Caunotaucarius said he would protect us from bad whites and bad Indians, too. Thing had changed, that we could not protect ourselves any longer. But I was not surprised. I knew this would happen.

I stayed with Cornplanter. I gave counsel, because I was now old. This meant I was wise. But I did not feel old, and nothing I had seen had made me wise.

At least Mary Britain kept me warm on cold nights,

and sometimes she warmed my cold heart. But when I thought of Caunotaucarius, who came to us as a stupid, disrespectful boy, who sent the army that destroyed our towns in the war between the mother country and her children, when I thought that he was now our greatest protector, I felt very cold.

## Alexander Hamilton:

B y 1792 the government of revolutionary France was claiming that we were still bound by our 1778 treaty and should support them in their wars with their neighbors. I asked the President, "Of what good could it be for us to support a revolutionary government, when it might be replaced by another a month hence?"

Washington said, "Have you discussed your attitude with the secretary of state? This is his purview, after all."

To which I responded, "We see the world in different ways."

I did not tell him what I thought of Jefferson's womanish attachment to France or his womanish resentment of Great Britain. Jefferson would draw us into the closest embrace of the former and involve us in all the consequences of her politics.

He wanted us to give special trading provisions to a renegade government that he believed was advancing, rather than retarding, the exalted rights of man.

I told Washington what I told Jefferson: "My commercial system turns very much on giving a free course to trade, and cultivating good humor with all the world. I see no reason to hazard anything which may lead to commercial warfare with any power, for a worse kind of warfare may result."

"That," said Washington, "is the answer that I would give myself."

Washington saw the world as I did. I can say that with confidence. And because of his support for my programs, our economy was secure by the end of the first term. Would that our secretary of state had done his job as well.

## Thomas Jefferson:

For the good of the nation, I bore with Hamilton all through the first term, through economic debates and through our growing disputes over France.

Then, in the spring of 1792, Washington told his cabinet that he was intending to step down a year hence, at the end of his first term. We all were shocked.

A short time later I took breakfast with him. Ostensibly, my purpose was to convince him that control of the postal service should be removed from Hamilton's Department of the Treasury.

I said, "Treasury already possesses such an influence as to swallow up whole executive powers. And the next president, without your weight of character, will not be able to make headway against such entrenched interest."

He raised his hand, "You and Mr. Hamilton will—"

And I informed him directly that I had no political motivation for my position, as I intended to resign as well.

The muscles in his jaw relaxed enough that his

mouth was forced open by his dentures. Then he looked into my eyes and said, "I'm leaving because, were I to return, people might say that I cannot do without the sweets of office. You know yourself 'tis whispered about by some and written about by newspapers inimical to me."

Indeed, certain newspapers had begun to criticize him, however obliquely. I said, "It is the nature of what we are engaged in, that we should inspire strong opinions and that they should find their way into print."

But he kept on. "I feel myself growing old, Jefferson. My health is less firm. My memory, which has always been wanting, grows worse. And perhaps other faculties of my mind are decaying and I don't even know it."

"I can assure you, sir, that it is not the case," I said. "I can also assure you that I have resolved to retire when you do."

When he mentioned newspapers inimical to him, he was making reference to a gentleman on my payroll at the Department of State, a man named Philip Freneau, the very one famous for bringing orangutans to New York Harbor.

Remember that by now the cleavage between my positions and Hamilton's was distinct.

Hamiltonians had the support of the *Gazette of the United States*, a paper of pure British Toryism, which took many an advertisement from Hamilton's Treasury Department.

Mr. Freneau was a firm Republican who owned the struggling *National Gazette*. I employed him, and though I admit giving him so little to do as not to interfere with any other calling he might choose, I did not attempt to control his thoughts or his paper. His words were apt enough without me.

For example, he saw the national debt, which had been created out of Hamilton's debt assumption and the Bank of the United States, as a boon only to the moneyed classes: "Artifice and deception has brought about one revolution in favor of the few. Another must and will be brought about in favor of the people."

## Alexander Hamilton:

Mr. Philip Freneau of the *National Gazette* deserved no better than the company of orangutans. He was a vile attention-grabber and a troublemaker.

In the *Gazette of the United States*, I asked rhetorically why such a captious critic of our efforts would be taken into the employ of one of our governmental departments as a language expert, though he knew only French. "Why?" I wrote. "So Freneau's patron, Thomas Jefferson, can gain influence over Freneau's paper. Jefferson has hitherto been distinguished as the quiet, modest, retiring philosopher; as the plain, simple, unambitious Republican. He shall now, for the first time, be regarded as the intriguing incendiary that he is."

Then I wrote to Washington that his declining the second term would be the greatest evil that could befall the country. More importantly for such a man, I reminded him that to decline would be "critically hazardous to his reputation."

## Thomas Jefferson:

Washington wrote to me: "How unfortunate, and how much to be regretted then, that whilst we are encompassed on all sides with avowed enemies and insidious friends, that internal dissensions should be tearing at our vitals."

I told him the truth, that I supported him, that Hamilton was the root cause of our difficulties, that he would prostrate the credit and honor of this nation, and that I had never attempted to influence Philip Freneau.

## Alexander Hamilton:

Washington wrote to me, seeking to ameliorate the conflict between me and Jefferson. I pledged my honor to him that I would not do a thing to engender a feud. And it began to become clear that he would stand a second time. How could he not, considering the factions within the administration?

## Nelly Custis Lewis:

I would have to say that we all knew, even before Grandpapa did, that he would stand a second time. He was never a man to evade a hard task.

But all through the summer at Mount Vernon, he was reluctant to make a decision. Finally, Mr. Jefferson came to Mount Vernon to talk with him.

It was early morning. It was raining, and on such days Grandpapa took his exercise by walking back and forth on his piazza. Sometimes, when I was awakened by the sound of the rain, I would hear his footfalls and the sound of his voice as he counted each circuit of the piazza.

On that morning I heard his conversation with Jefferson.

I admit that I was taken with the man. He was one of the few men I had ever seen who was as tall as Grandpapa, and he had a smile that conveyed all the benevolence of Lafayette. Perhaps it was something one learned in France, Jefferson having spent many years there. But if you go to the theater, you know of the villainous character called the Smiler with a Knife. That is what I now think of Jefferson.

Grandpapa asked, "What is the talk in Philadelphia?"

"That North and South will hang together only if they have you to hang on."

"And what is the voice for your own continuance?"

"Less resounding," said Jefferson. "I must see to my own home."

For a time, all that I could hear was the falling of the morning rain.

Finally, Grandpapa said, "Thomas, we are engaged in an experiment in the practicability of republican government, to see what dose of liberty a man can be trusted with for his own good. I need the check of your opinions, to keep things in the proper channel."

"You're the only one who can keep things in the proper channel, sir," said Jefferson.

"I will not make my decision until a month before the electors gather. But I urge you not to harden yourself."

This was interrupted by the call to breakfast. I hurried down to join the meal, hoping that I might hear some further discussion. But all they talked about at the table was the difficult business of growing things in poor Virginia soil.

I felt bad that Grandpapa was forced to beg and that he seemed so concerned to keep Jefferson. But in looking back, I could see how shrewdly he balanced himself, even in a small conversation like that.

## Hesperus Draper:

Oh, but 1792 was a juicy time to own a printing press or two.

No matter whose side you were on, there was always something to print, though Charlotte insisted we not print anything we couldn't verify.

'Twas a strange proposition. How, I asked her, could we verify that there was a revolution in France? None of us had seen it.

"None of us saw you fight at Monmouth, either."

"Well," I said, "I can't confirm the truth of what people say, but I can confirm that they've said it."

"So what have people said?"

"That Hamilton is an adulterer. And some have said his adultery led him to conspire with the adultress's husband, who then went into the hill country of Virginia and bought up soldiers' certificates, months before debt assumption."

"Do we have names?"

"If we do, the world doesn't know them, but . . . it's been said, and it wouldn't surprise me, considerin' where all the assumption money ended up."

"If you print that," she said, "I can print what Hamilton said about Jefferson in the *Gazette of the United States*."

"Which is?"

"That he's 'a secret voluptuary, an intriguing incendiary, an aspiring turbulent competitor.'"

I licked my lips and said, "A secret voluptuary? Like me?"

I was sixty by then, but I still kept those youthful juices flowing.

She just looked at me over her spectacles. "A secret voluptuary, I think, is one who lies with his slaves. 'Tis one of your virtues, Hesperus Draper, that you've never felt the need to own slaves."

"No," I said, "but I defend the rights of those who do."

We printed our rumors about Hamilton, and the *Gazette of the United States* kept on Jefferson. The opposing papers threw mud back and forth like furious little boys, and it splattered all over Washington's white stockings. But he stood above it all, as always, and told people that he had no doubts about what he called "the infinite benefits resulting from a free press." He said it, but I don't know that he believed it.

I think that disunion—his favorite word when he wanted to frighten us—frightened him, too, and that's what he saw comin' when he read the papers, or when he thought about Hamilton and Jefferson. So he stood again, to keep us together, and he was elected again. Unanimously.

'Twould be the last unanimity we'd know, from that day to this.

\* \* \*

One thing Charlotte always wanted to do was go to a presidential levee.

I said, "Why would you want to do that?"

"Because this Freneau calls it a grand show of monarchical display, and I simply can't believe it. The Martha Washington I knew was a woman who would never let pomp and display turn her head."

"The George Washington I knew was a man to whom such things came as naturally as pissin'," I answered.

"Then maybe it's his natural inclination to look like a king and act like a king. But you know yourself that he doesn't want to be a king."

She was right about that, or he would've been king already.

So I kept promisin' we'd go some time. But how would I be received, considerin' the things I'd written? I'd been the first to call the city of Washingtonopolis "that swindle on the Potomac." In '92, I'd supported all the anti-Federalist candidates, who were now callin' themselves Republicans, for the House of Representatives. And I'd hit at Hamilton's pro-British policies on trade, pointin' out that republican France might prove a better business partner.

But I'd never attacked Washington directly. Maybe I respected the old dog more than I wanted to admit. Maybe I knew he could still bite. And old dogs are snappish when you step on their tails.

Besides, nothin' I could write would equal the things Philip Freneau was now puttin' into print. Just after the presidential election, he leveled this at Washington's levees: "They are the legitimate offspring of inequality, begotten by aristocracy and monarchy upon corruption. Washington would blind us with the glitter of distinction. The freemen of America understand their rights too well to surrender them for the gratification and ambition of any man, however well he may have served his country."

## Thomas Jefferson:

Publicly, Washington feigned indifference to written opinions. Privately, he seemed truly bewildered. And I was sincerely sorry for him.

He said angrily, "These late attacks upon me for the levees, I cannot fathom. I must appear presidential, but I must appear accessible as well. To whatever the public wants in this regard, I will cheerfully conform."

I did not offer him my opinion on the levees.

I believed that, naked, he would have been sanctimoniously reverenced; the rags of royalty that enveloped him should be torn off.

## Nelly Custis Lewis:

I went to his office on the night before his second inauguration. It was well after eight. My grandmother had already gone to bed. My grandfather had just finished writing his speech and was now reading it to himself.

I asked him if he would read it aloud.

"Only if you will promise to play the spinet for me afterward," he said.

You know, he loved for me to play the spinet. This had been the cause of more than one dispute, when I preferred not to practice or to play in public.

"I shall play 'Over the Hills and Far Away' for you, Grandpapa."

"Then turn your back for a moment."

I obeyed, and when he told me I could turn back, he was wearing his teeth. He assumed a properly grave position behind his desk, held the words beneath the lamp, and read, "Fellow Citizens," followed by a short introductory paragraph.

Then he went on, "Previous to the execution of any official act of the President, the Constitution requires the oath of office. This oath I am now about to take, and in your presence, that if it shall be found during my administration of the government, I have in any instance violated willingly, or knowingly, the injunction thereof, I may (besides incurring constitutional punishment) be subject to the upbraidings of all who are now witness to this solemn ceremony."

And that was all. I sat back, shocked. Where were his words of inspiration? Of hope? Had he not done a good job? Our country now had an economy, funds, commerce, a future.

People say that he had a thin skin. Never was it more apparent.

C.D.—*The domestic wind was now steady and strong. And even as spring arrived, the gusts from across the Atlantic promised a cold political winter.*

*Just after his second inauguration, Washington learned that the king and queen of France had been beheaded. Lafayette had fled to Austria, but in that*

*he had recently led French troops against Austria, the*
*Austrians threw him into a cell, where he would re-*
*main for four years, much to Washington's distress.*
*And Great Britain, unable to stand by any longer, had*
*declared war on France.*

*It seemed, in that turbulent spring of 1793, as if ev-*
*ery American made a choice. Was he a lover of France*
*and Republican radicalism? Or was he a supporter of*
*Britain and the Federalism that looked to copy British*
*models?*

## Hesperus Draper:

In May of 1793, Charlotte and I finally went to Philadelphia to see one of Washington's levees for ourselves.

We'd just bought the *Spectator*, so there was business to tend.

And I didn't think I'd ever again be so far on Washington's good side, considerin' that I'd written in support of his Neutrality Proclamation, by which he hoped
to keep us out of the war between England and France.
We could recognize the new French government, and
we could keep payin' our war debt to France. But that
didn't mean we had to keep other agreements we'd
made with a French monarchy that no longer had a
head, and I mean that literally.

There was another reason for goin', too.

Life is a voyage. Sometimes the sea is calm, sometimes 'tis rough. But in the end, the ship always sinks.
And my Charlotte's fine voyage through life was comin' on toward its end. She'd been coughin' for some

time. And she'd got skinnier. And . . . well, the consumption takes a lot of people. And who knows why one gets it and another don't?

Dr. Craik sure couldn't answer the question. But he give us the name of a doctor in Philadelphia who might help.

We got there in the season of fine weather and flowerin' shrubs and riots in the streets. That's right. Folks had gotten so fired up over things in Europe, 'twas all anyone talked about. And most folks had taken to wearin' cockades—red, white, and blue for them who backed France, black for the lovers of Britain, like they was wearin' the colors of their favorite racin' horse.

Charlotte and I planned to stay in a fine boardin' house near the City Tavern, where I didn't expect such foolishness. But when we got there, the young feller who opened our chariot door looked in and said to me, "Good afternoon, Citizen." Then he turned his eye to Charlotte. "And to you, Citess."

"Citess?" I said. "Citizen? Whatever happened to Mr. and Mrs.?"

"The Republicans say that such words are too high-flown. So we're takin' up the French way in Philadelphia." Then he pointed to the red, white, and blue cockade in his hat. "We've even adopted the French colors."

"What's next?" I asked. "The guillotine?"

He just scowled. As I say, everyone was takin' sides, even doormen.

We arrived early for the levee at the President's home on Market Street.

We were ushered into what they called the presentation chamber, which sounded a little frightenin' to me. From that point, every step was as carefully planned as a piece of theater, which I suppose wasn't surprisin'.

Two liveried servants in powdered wigs bowed to us at the door. They were both as white as their wigs, because here in the North, Washington didn't let his slave help be seen in public, which I thought was somethin' hypocritical.

Tobias Lear, the secretary, asked our names, though he knew them. Then he whispered them to a servant, who announced us in a fine loud voice. A few heads turned, but most everyone kept talkin'.

Over in a corner, John Adams was goin' on about somethin'. Hamilton was in another corner. If Jefferson had come—though he never did—he'd've gone to a third corner. Henry Knox was fillin' half the floor. And right in the middle, wearing a fine black suit, holdin' the whole room together just by standin' there, was Washington.

He was speakin' with one of the handsomest women I had ever laid eyes on: Mrs. Elizabeth Powel. I'd met her before in my travels. She was a little heavy now, but she still had that strawberry-colored hair, sharp eyes, a mouth that always seemed like she was about to give out with some fresh remark.

'Twas rumored that she'd written a letter to Washington that convinced him to stand for President the second time. 'Twas also rumored that if he ever spent time with a woman other than Martha, 'twas Elizabeth. Seein' how hard he was listenin' to her, and how close he come to smilin' at whatever she was sayin', I knew where folks could find such notions.

But when a man's doin' things with a woman in private that he don't want the world to know about, he usually avoids her in public, or he gets so dewy-eyed around her that a blind man could tell he was diddlin' her nibblies behind closed doors. And neither of those described Washington.

Lear offered his arm to Charlotte and led her toward Lady Washington. The ritual said that the husband was supposed to wander off into the crowd, but I stayed close, because Charlotte was weak after the trip, and gettin' gussied up for this gatherin' had made her even weaker.

She'd rouged her cheeks, put lip grease on, brought in a hairdresser who combed out her hair and did it with pearls and a bandeau. And we'd had her fitted in a fine blue silk dress. She was so skinny, didn't spend but pennies for the silk.

As for Lady Washington, my first thought was that she sure had gotten old. Grown herself a nice full saddlebag beneath her chin. And that hair of hers, there was so damn much of it, looked like 'twas all standin' on end. But she loved to wear these big caps that they'd stopped wearin' in Europe twenty years ago. And . . .

I could have kept my mind headin' in this sarcastic direction, but I'd always liked her. Could always sense a good heart.

Martha gave Charlotte a hard look. 'Twas plain she didn't recognize the fadin' woman standin' before her, but with the sickness, there was plenty who didn't recognize my wife anymore.

Charlotte was supposed to dip a curtsy to the President's lady. That's what we'd been told, but she wobbled a bit, and Martha's hand went out to her immediately, and by God, from beneath that silly cap of hers, Martha pulled out a memory. "Why, Charlotte, 'tis a pleasure to see you after all these years. How can any of us forget Valley Forge?"

"Oh, I can't," said Charlotte.

And with that, followin' the ritual, Lear led her to a chair nearby, where she should sit, "without noticing any of the rest of the company, to await the attention of the President."

I wasn't plannin' on leavin' my dyin' wife alone for anything, but she give me the eye, the way a woman can do it. Give it to me two or three times, as if to say, Move away.

And I'd no sooner turned to the tea table than Washington was at her side. He offered a slight bow of the head. Never shook hands at these things. And said, "If there were dancing here tonight, Mrs. Draper, I would hope that you would consent to join me, as once you did."

Charlotte's face, which was flushed anyway, burned a bright scarlet. "Mr. President, I would give anything to dance with *anybody* again."

Washington may not have gotten the full meanin' of that remark. But he said, "Madam, we would all give anything to be fifteen years younger." Then he offered her his arm. "Now, let me guide you toward the refreshments."

And all eyes turned, because this was not part of the ritual. Usually, after his conversation with a lady visitor, she was then free to take herself to the tables of cake and tea, coffee and ice cream. Washington must have known. But how?

Mrs. Elizabeth Powel came up beside me. "Your wife is honored. He seldom offers his arm to any woman."

"Perhaps he knows how sick she is," I said.

"Perhaps," said Mrs. Powel. "He has a sixth sense about people."

"I taught him," I joked. "Back when we was boys, down in Chotank."

Mrs. Powel laughed at that. "No one taught him what he knows."

"He learned in *The Rules of Civility*," I said.

"No one taught him, nor any book," she said with more insistence. "Abigail Adams put it best: 'He's polite with dignity, affable without familiarity, distant without haughtiness, grave without austerity. He leaves Royal George far behind.'"

"Don't say that too loud, about Royal George," I warned. "I'm a Republican, don't forget."

"But are you a Jacobin, too? Do you favor removal of Federalist heads?"

"Only a few." And I cast my eyes toward Hamilton.

Washington was back now, carefully leadin' my wife to a chair, helpin' her to sit again, holdin' her cake plate till she was settled. Washington knew instinctively what was needed. He gave her the plate, and with a small bow, he left her to conversation with the other ladies.

Now he was comin' toward me. This ought to be interestin', I thought.

I offered a small bow of my own. "Mr. President."

He responded with the same. "Mr. Draper. Your wife looks well tonight."

"Thank you, sir."

Elizabeth Powel said, "I was telling him how quickly the news has spread that the Drapers have bought a paper in Philadelphia."

Washington gave me that flat stare. The face had grown old, the dentures looked like they hurt like hell, but those eyes were still the same. Eyes to take the measure of you, to pin you to your own lie, to make you squirm if you betrayed him. "I have read what you've written."

"I hope you read my support of the Neutrality Proclamation."

"Such support may not leave you in good stead with your more radical readers."

"Like Mr. Freneau?" I asked. "Mr. Orangutan?"

Washington said nothin' to that. Never named names in polite company. Instead he said, "Now that you've seen one of our levees, simply say what goes on here. Say that any may attend, no matter their beliefs. Say that what . . . *pomp* there is in all of this . . . perhaps it consists in my not sitting."

As we left, I thought of something Freneau had written: "A certain monarchical prettiness must be highly extolled, such as levees, drawing rooms, stately nods instead of shaking hands, titles of offices, seclusion from the people."

He wasn't the first newspaperman to get it wrong. Nor would he be the last.

A few days later, I caught up with Jefferson. He greeted me as "Citizen Draper" and invited me to join him in his daily stroll through the garden behind Independence Hall.

We walked for a time. I talked about Philadelphia doctors. Jefferson commented on this flowerin' shrub and that buddin' tree. Said the smell of the boxwoods reminded him of home.

"So," I said, "is that why you're leaving? You miss your boxwoods?"

"Ah, Citizen—"

"Call me Mister or Draper. Leave 'Citizen' to your French friends."

"But you misunderstand the meaning of the term. We're no longer moving toward the tassels and baubles of monarchy. We're getting back to a just mean: a government of laws addressed to the reason of the people and not to their weakness."

"Does that mean you're stayin'?"

"Somewhat longer. How long, I cannot say . . . Ah, Philip!"

A feller came around the corner. Had a dark brow and wore a devilish grin, as if 'twere his natural state to go about lookin' amused by all the sin he saw around him. He was Philip Freneau.

"Draper!" he cried. "It's been years."

"Hardly recognized you without your apes."

The grin grew a little wider. "I was disappointed that your papers supported this Neutrality Proclamation."

I give Jefferson a little jerk of my head. "He supported it, too."

"I signed it," said Jefferson. "I do not support it."

Another fine bit of sophistry from the secretary of state.

"And," Jefferson went on, "I've resisted the President's implication that I should somehow silence Mr. Freneau, perhaps by withdrawing my appointment."

"A position much appreciated," said Freneau.

"Draper, take a lesson from Mr. Freneau." Jefferson—a tall scarecrow of a man—slouched a little closer to me and said, "I believe that his paper has saved our Constitution from galloping into monarchy."

Freneau gave a shrug, as if to ward off praise too high. "When I wrote that Washington signed the Neutrality Proclamation so that our pro-British faction would not chop off his head, I wrote the truth."

I laughed at that. Washington signed the proclamation because he was no fool. He knew we didn't belong in a European fight.

As I watched the scarecrow walk off with his court jester, I wondered if Jefferson ever asked himself how it looked to be payin' a man to criticize the administration he worked for. But Jefferson was a man who could marry a dozen contradictions in his mind and make them live happily ever after.

Look at how he married the name "Genet" and the word "diplomat."


Citizen Edmund Genet, envoy of revolutionary France, and the biggest fly in Washington's soup during the year of the French crisis. Short, redheaded, not much to look at, but fluent in more languages than I had fingers and thumbs. He had typical Gallic charm, which is gracious; typical Gallic arrogance, which is audacious; and a typical Gallic heart, which is devious.

Instead of comin' straight to Philadelphia to present his credentials, he got off the boat in Charleston and outfitted several French privateers to sail against Great Britain. 'Twas a plain violation of the Neutrality Proclamation, but true to that Gallic nature, Genet thought he had the right to do it, by virtue of our old treaty.

Then he traveled north to the ovations of simple Americans who remembered, or were reminded, that France had helped them during the Revolution. By the time he reached Philadelphia, Genet was afloat on a cloud of joyous American frenzy.

Everywhere you went in Philadelphia, you heard that damn "Marseillaise," all about bloody flags and armed *citoyens*. Everywhere you went, tradesmen and mechanics strutted in the streets, wearin' the red, white, and blue cockades, and if you were wearin' a black one, you'd be jostled or challenged, or worse.

Me, I didn't wear any damn cockade, but even that could cause problems.

One day as I was on my way back to our rooms from the paper, two half-drunk rowdies stopped me and said, "Citizen! Hey, citizen!"

I tried to step around them, but they blocked me like the bullies they were.

"You ain't wearin' a cockade, there, Citizen. And that's a fine suit of clothes you're wearin', too. Could it be that you're a rich monocrat?"

"A what?" I knew what it was, but I just wanted to make these apes try to explain it.

"A monocrat," said one. "A man who believes in the rule of the . . . the . . . mono."

Well, I had taken to carryin' a walkin' stick. I didn't need it for walkin', but I liked havin' a place to slip a little tube-like flask, and the brass head concealed an excellent dagger.

Two quick swings and I was on my way again, embarrassed to call myself a Republican.

# Thomas Jefferson:

I brought Citizen Genet to meet the President shortly after his arrival.

In the streets, where "La Marseillaise" was sung and French cockades were worn, it seemed that the old spirit of 1776 had been renewed. But our government—our President especially—was all cold caution.

Washington even made a point of receiving Genet in his drawing room, beneath the portraits of the late king and queen of France.

But Genet acted as if he did not notice this affront, executing a deep bow, offering his papers, and saying, "It is a pleasure to meet America's first citizen."

Washington bowed in return. "I am proud to be called citizen. It is the highest compliment one can pay to any man in any country."

"Then," Genet began, "as a citizen you know that when treaties speak, the agents of nations have but to obey."

This had been my own position.

But the President simply stood, staring flatly, saying nothing, delivering a gaze to unnerve an ionic column, let alone the garrulous Citizen Genet.

At length Genet felt compelled to ask, "Do you not agree, sir?"

And Washington responded with cool diplomacy: "The treaty we made was with a different government, and while we were the first nation to recognize the French Republic, we must honor neutrality."

"But, sir," Genet said, "that is an annulment of the sacred treaty between our two nations, made in 1778. Consider the anger of good Americans. Consider the opinions of your own gazetteers."

The President raised his chin slightly—his only sign of annoyance—and said, "I do not read the gazettes, and it is of very slight importance to me whether my administration is talked about."

"But, sir—"

The President went on: "It is the sincere wish of the United States to have nothing to do with political intrigues or the squabbles of the European nations; but only to exchange commodities and live in peace and amity."

The talk went on for some time longer. It seemed to me that Genet promised everything and asked for nothing. But the President would not commit us to anything. More than ever, I felt that he was in the thrall of the Anglophile Hamilton, that he should take this position.

I will admit that a more subtle diplomat than Genet might have conducted himself more gracefully and achieved more for his nation. But Genet was hotheaded, and so disrespectful toward the President that he was soon heard to boast that if he did not get the kind of cooperation he wanted from "Old Man Washington" he would go through the gazettes to the American people.

This struck Washington's sensitive temper. He warned me, "I'll allow no one, British or French, to threaten the executive. What would the world think of such conduct?"

Then we received alarming intelligence: Genet had raised an army to attack Florida, a possession of Spain, which was an enemy of France; he continued to defy the President by outfitting American privateers to seize British merchantmen in our waters; and he had boasted that the French of Canada might be induced to rebel. He would plunge our whole continent into war. Nevertheless, I was determined that we should continue to conduct our business with France as one friendly nation to another.

To that end, I was most pleased that the President called a meeting of his cabinet.

The atmosphere in the meeting room that August day was warm, despite a gentle breeze lifting off of Market Street, and it grew warmer under the influence of Hamilton. True to his inclinations, and seeing the advantage the Federalists had got, he announced that we should publish an account of Genet's doings and reveal them to the American people.

This may have been the first time in his life that Hamilton had demonstrated any confidence in those to whom he usually referred as rabble.

I feared that publication could compromise the friendship between our nation and France. So I made my position clear, stating it in cool contrast to Hamilton: "Friendly nations, gentlemen, negotiate little differences in private."

"This," answered Hamilton, "is no small difference. We are discussing the honor of the United States. We must go to the people."

"Sir," I told Hamilton, "everything you say here is calculated to force the President to make himself head of a party instead of the head of a nation."

The President said nothing. He simply listened, as was his habit, his eyes shifting, his mind turning slowly.

And Henry Knox raised the temperature in the room even more, delivering a foolish, incoherent sort of speech regarding a recently published satire by Freneau. It was called "The Funeral Dirge of George Washington."

## Alexander Hamilton:

As Knox described the latest excrescence from the pen of Freneau, Washington's face reddened and the springs of his dentures squeaked, a sure sign that he was clenching his jaw to control his anger. Across the table, Jefferson's placid, freckled face reddened as well, perhaps from embarrassment.

Freneau's doggerel described Washington as a monarchist, presenting his neck in the guillotine for his sins. The effect on the President, as one would imagine, was volcanic. Not since Monmouth had I seen such fury.

He roared suddenly, "I am sick of this personal abuse! I've never repented but once that I did not resign this office, and that's been every moment since. I'd rather be in my grave than here." He slammed his great hand on the table. "My reputation is assailed—"

Though I attempted to inject a soothing word, Washington would hear none of it. "They charge me with wanting to be a king. But I turned down kingship at Newburgh. And that rascal Freneau"—here Washington shot an angry look at Jefferson—"sends me three papers a day, as if he would like me to distribute them for him!"

Jefferson said, "I doubt that."

"I don't," roared Washington. "I am sick of all of this. Sick to death!"

## Thomas Jefferson:

He had gotten himself into one of those passions in which he cannot command himself. And it went on, louder and louder, until finally he had no more energy and slumped back in his chair, his head down, a trickle of perspiration carrying hair powder down his cheek.

For a long moment no one spoke.

Finally I said, "Mr. President . . ."

And he raised his head like a man just awakening. He straightened himself, made a small motion of his mouth to straighten his dentures, and said, in a voice almost supernaturally calm, "We will let events show whether an appeal to the public will be necessary in this Genet business."

I considered this a small victory, especially as Hamilton was overruled.

But Hamilton had his newspaper, as we did ours. And under pseudonyms, he was soon revealing Genet's plans to ignore "le vieux Washington," the old Washington, and take his case to the American people. This was something the American people resented.

As if to prove Hamilton's contention, as if with enough rope he might hang himself, Genet went about the country, visiting Republican clubs, delivering speeches, and, when a French fleet paid a visit, he hurried to New York, where he proclaimed that he would now have 1,500 French sailors with which to outfit privateers in America. Even the staunchest Republicans were unnerved by his arrogance.

Then a letter appeared in American newspapers: "Mr. Genet, the French minister, has said he will appeal to the American people certain decisions of their President." This was not signed by some Hamiltonian pseudonym, but by John Jay, chief justice of the Supreme Court.

Americans turned against Edmond Genet.

And I felt compelled to withdraw my support, as one would quit a wreck which could not but sink all who would cling to it, though I would not quit my support of France and her revolution. Rather than have it fail, I should have seen half the earth desolated.

*C.D.—No doubt, Jefferson counted his Virginia hill-top in the half to be spared.*

*As for the Genet business: Washington was still the first man in America, and no French wind would blow him down. But when Genet was recalled that autumn by a new French government, which most surely would have executed him, as the Reign of Terror was then in full cry, Washington gave him political asylum.*

## Hesperus Draper:

In the middle of August, the rain came on Philadelphia—heavy, soakin', steamin' rain that finally put out the pro-French fire set by Genet. But soon after, folks started feelin' a worse heat. 'Twas yellow fever.

Nobody knew what brought it, though I think 'twas the summer rain. Or maybe those French refugees from the Dominican Republic, driven out by revolution. Or maybe, as Dr. Benjamin Rush said, 'twas a load of coffee left to rot on a Philadelphia dock.

But it spread across Philadelphia like a crock of molasses spilled over a table, slow and steady and unstoppable. Hamilton and his wife caught it early. Henry Knox and his wife fled north, but they were quarantined outside New York, for fear that they were carriers. Elizabeth Powel lost her husband. Federalist or Republican, it made no matter. The death carts came for every family.

All about the city you could smell the stink of burnin' gunpowder and hot vinegar, which were supposed to cleanse the air. And the only folks you saw on the streets were the nigras, who were immune to the fever, or so 'twas claimed. They were left to drive the carts and dig the trenches that passed for graves, and strange enough, but plenty of them died, too.

I sprinkled hot vinegar on all our windowsills. I made Charlotte keep a camphor handkerchief at her nose, even in the house. But none of it done her any good. When the fever struck and her eyeballs turned yellow and she spit up black vomit, I knew 'twas the end. Didn't even send for a doctor to bleed her. Why should she survive this, in order to cough her lungs up in a month?

So I let her go. Held her skinny little body close. Told her I loved her. Held her and let her go.

'Twas hard, but sometimes, lettin' go is for the best. I let go and buried her. Then I got on my horse and headed home.

# Nelly Custis Lewis:

The whole city was dying.

One of the first deaths came right there at 190 Market Street. Mr. Lear's wife, Polly, died in an upstairs room, leaving us all in a deep valley of grief.

Added to grief was fear, made all the sharper for us children by Grandmother. Each day she would go from window to window, her eyes watering in the haze of hot vinegar, and she would stare out and proclaim how she wished that the rain would end.

We were, as Grandpapa said, blockaded by the fever. But when the time came for us to leave, as we always did for a time in late August, he refused to go.

So Grandmama said, "If you stay, I'll have to stay. And that means the children will have to stay."

"Patsy," he said, "I can't run and frighten those who must stay."

"You will do what's best for your family," said Grandmama.

"But—"

And she would hear no *buts*, for once. "Think of your family, George," she said. "Think of Nelly and Little Wash. I won't bury them as I did my children. If I do, you'll soon be burying me."

And my grandpapa, who never ran from an enemy, ran from the fever, and from the anger of his wife.

## Dr. James Craik:

That fall, we who were of the Masonic order gathered in the new federal city, just across the river from Alexandria. Washington, a former Worshipful Master of the order, led us in procession from the new president's mansion, which was no more than a foundation hole, down the muddy trail that would soon be called Pennsylvania Avenue, then up Jenkins Hill, to the place where a single sandstone block hung suspended above a foundation wall. All around was vegetation as thick and scruffy as any to be found in the Great Meadows of our youth.

A god gazing down would have laughed at our small ceremony, and the feeble sound of the celebratory cannon shot, once Washington had lowered the stone into place. But to us, Washington's presence had lent dignity to the proceedings. And even as I considered the ravages of time and political troubles upon his face, I realized that he had achieved the objective that had driven him for forty years. He had built his reputation. He would have the esteem of generations yet unborn. And he still understood the principle of a thing better than any man I ever knew. I was proud to have known him.

## Hesperus Draper:

That fall, I let go . . . let go for longer than I'd planned.

Me and Eli headed out like we done when we was young, headed west for that Ohio country, for those bonus lands we'd never even bothered to visit. I reckon I went to . . . to heal my soul.

'Twas a beautiful season, all gold and red and bright. Nothin' dark or wet about the woods that year. Long before the snow flew, we had us a fine cabin. Did some huntin'. Did some drinkin'. Did some thinkin', too.

Washington had gotten more of this land than I did, but truth was truth. He was the one who did the hard work. Maybe he deserved the best bottoms, the way he'd always said. As for me, well, I liked that hillside. Not much for farmin', but it had a nice view of the Great Kanawha, windin' through the valley.

That winter, some Seneca Injuns come through and tried to trade some parched corn for a little liquor. And I'll be damned, but one of them—he traveled with a white woman—he sure looked familiar.

I asked him, "Where do I know you from?"

He looked into my eyes in that dark way that Injuns have, and he said, "I tell you for two gills of whiskey."

Well, I always like a man who bargains. I offered him one gill, he took it, and he told me his name. "I am Silverheels. You are the one who fucks women in the bushes."

And I just had to laugh.

Like I've told you, the country was big, but it was a small, small world.

That Injun talked good English by then, and he liked our whiskey, so he stayed for about a week. Helped us hunt. Asked me to teach him how to read. Said he wanted to be able to read treaties so that he could understand them. Thought that was a laugh. Most white men couldn't understand treaties, because most treaties were written by lawyers. But I did my best to teach him his alphabet.

For two years I stayed out there. My shippin' business run itself. Had growers in America and clients in Europe. So long as the British and the French didn't interfere with our trade, everything moved along. As for the gazettes, Charlotte had built that staff of smart young men, who weren't so young anymore, and they jumped at the chance to run the two papers.

I knew next to nothing about the struggles of George Washington to hold the country together. Figured he'd done well enough up to that point, he'd finish the job. And I sure knew what he meant about land bein' the only thing that mattered, the most permanent estate. I loved that far country. So did Eli.

And Silverheels and his woman visited us every few months, while wanderin' from place to place. One spring day we went fishin' in the river.

Silverheels caught a big bass and said, "My wife gave me that fish."

"Your wife? What do you mean?"

"Number two woman. She rides this river. She rides it to the next life."

I looked at the water. "So does my number one woman."

"Your woman with the yellow hair and the red hat? I tried to save her that day in the river. I made three good shots, but I could only save you."

"'Twas you?" And I remembered wantin' to die that day, with Bee's bloody head in my lap. But I didn't. My life hadn't been easy after that, but I was glad I'd lived it, and sure glad I'd known Charlotte Spencer Draper. And I had to thank that Injun.

And what did I miss while I was livin' out there?

Well, some farmers in western Pennsylvania, who took their grain to market in the liquid form, they decided they didn't want to pay Hamilton's excise tax on whiskey. So they burned a few barns, tarred and feathered a few tax collectors, and Washington called out the army. 'Twas known as the Whiskey Rebellion.

Some people considered it the greatest challenge yet to the Constitution. Washington put on a uniform and, with Hamilton trottin' along beside him, rode halfway across Pennsylvania, but he didn't have to go all the way. Those farmers didn't want trouble from the militia that came rollin' out as soon as they saw a chance to relive the old days by marchin' with the great Washington.

Jefferson called the President's response "an armament against the people at their plows." He'd resigned by then and enjoyed the luxury of shootin' off his mouth any time and place. At least Freneau had lost his patron and his paper.

And Jefferson wasn't the only one who resigned.

Henry Knox left, sayin', "All my life, I have been pursuing elusive bubbles which burst on being grasped, and 'tis high time I should quit public life and attend to the solid interests of my family."

I thought old Fat-Ass Henry didn't give himself enough credit. He'd stood by the President through thick and thin. And I always pictured him that day at Monmouth, drownin' in his own sweat, firin' grapeshot over the hedgerow.

I missed all the fury over the Jay Treaty, one of the most complicated, troublesome things that ever has happened in this country. 'Twas a treaty with England and a bad one by most folk's lights. The British agreed to leave the northwest territory, which was fine by me. Meant the Injuns wouldn't have the British eggin' them on along the frontier. But the British still reserved the right to close foreign ports to neutral ships wherever they wanted.

Jefferson called it an outrage. So did most Americans.

But Washington was just keepin' us out of war. He knew we were weak. He'd sought neutrality in the Genet business. Sought it with the Jay Treaty, too. 'Twas all tied together in his mind. He knew that wars are the way to poverty, and poverty is the way to impotence. And America was impotent enough already.

The cabinet became even more impotent when Hamilton left. He said, "Public office in this country has few attractions. When balanced against the jealousy of power and the spirit of faction, the opportunity of doing good is too small to warrant a long continuance of private sacrifices."

I didn't come back permanent till late 1796. 'Twas time to live in the world again. Time too for the next election. I threw my support behind Jefferson, but Adams won, with Jefferson takin' the vice presidency. Adams said he was happy about this. But the two of them reminded me of America's Cain and Abel.

c.d.—*For eight years the winds had blown and abated and blown again, and many an American believed that for all the buffeting he had taken, only one man could have stood the early blasts. Now there were two distinct political parties, for good or ill. But there was a policy toward the powers of Europe. And there was financial stability at home.*

*And while critics like Freneau had continued to carp about his decisions, America's Cato would have no need to fall on his sword. The wind would be gentle at his back, all the way home to Mount Vernon.*

## John Adams:

It had been sure punishment for a man like me to preside over the Senate for eight years, to listen to men talk five hours a day, and not be at liberty to talk myself.

But my victory in the 1796 election I saw as a vindication of all we had pursued and suffered. As for Vice President Jefferson, I suppose that somewhere in my mind, I thought that the job would serve him right.

On the day of the inauguration, I arrived wearing my best pearl-gray suit and my sword. Naturally, I came in last, and as I entered the hall, I saw that most of the senators and representatives were crying.

Later everybody talked of the tears, the full eyes, the streaming eyes, the trickling eyes, etc., etc. No one described the particulars to say the why or wherefore. I was therefore left to suppose that it was all grief for the loss of their beloved Washington.

But there was no grief on Washington's part. I took my seat between Jefferson and him, and I was puzzled by the expression on Washington's face. It was as if he enjoyed some triumph over me.

I inclined my head, gave a polite nod, and methought I heard him say, "I am fairly out, and you are fairly in. See which of us will be the happiest."

It was a strange remark. But in truth, here was a novelty in the history of man, in the history of governments. One sun was setting in full orbit, and another rising, though admittedly less splendid.

I will say that my speech was well received. Then I marched out to polite applause, assuming the whole time that Washington was behind me. Upon reaching the door, I glanced over my shoulder, only to see that Washington and Jefferson were still on the dais enacting a small scene.

Once, then twice, Jefferson refused to exit ahead of Washington.

Finally, Washington made a distinct gesture for Jefferson to leave first, which Jefferson obeyed. Only then would Washington descend after him.

Ever the actor, he knew well the role he now played. He was no longer President Washington or General Washington. He was merely, to borrow a Republican phrase, Citizen Washington.

And a good actor always knows that the last performer to leave the stage will hear the loudest applause.

This scene was played out in silence, with a few sniffles serving only to enhance it. Jefferson reached the foyer, looking more placid than he had a right to. Then Washington strode down the aisle, past the senators and representatives, so many of whom had assailed him for eight years. But he looked neither left nor right as he came. Gods are not expected to make eye contact. But neither do they cry, and it was true that his eyes filled with tears.

As he stepped into the foyer, joining me and Jefferson, the door closed behind him, like the curtain descending after the play, and it was as if every cannon in the Revolution were firing at once in the Senate chamber, such was the sound of the roar.

## Abigail Adams:

Shortly after my husband's inauguration, I asked him what he thought would be Washington's legacy.

He responded, "A tall stature. He was like the Hebrew sovereign chosen because he was taller by a head than the other Jews."

I cannot deny that my husband envied Washington's fame. And none could deny that Washington had been well-served by my husband, who constantly supported his measures but scrupulously avoided all improper interferences.

But I felt that my husband missed the point of his predecessor's greatness. Washington had such presence, such a proud demeanor, and so happy a faculty of appearing to accommodate another person's opinion while carrying his own point, that if he had not really been one of the best intentioned men in the world he might have been a very dangerous one.

# Jacob, Mount Vernon Slave:

We's headin' south agin. Me and Alice be happy of that, you can be sure, but they ain't as many slaves to go home as they was to come here.

You know, the General's cook, Hercules—big strong boy, like the name make you think—he run off a few months earlier, and the General jess let him go. And then they's Oney Judge, Miz Washin'ton's favorite slave, a girl Miz Washin'ton raise up like one of her own. She run off a little while later.

They track her all the way to Portsmouth, New Hampshire. They's rcady to haul her back, till the sheriff up there, he tell 'em that they be a riot if they try. So the Washin'tons write to her and beg her, 'cause Miz Martha truly love Oney . . . tha's what she tell my Alice. But Oney love her freedom more.

You know, over the years, I hear some bad things 'bout them New England folks, but I don't believe none of it.

Anyways, the General come in the room jess when me and Alice is packin' up.

He say, "Is everything going along?"

We say, "Oh, yassuh."

"Don't forget the pets, or I shall never be forgiven by the grandchildren. On the one part, I'm called on to remember the parrot; on the other, to remember the dog. For my own part, I shouldn't pine if both were forgot."

"Oh, we won't forget nothin', suh."

Now he lowered his voice and stood closer to us than I reckon he ever done since we was kids. "I have told some of the other servants that I am prepared to forget something else."

"What else, sir?"

"Perhaps I should say some*one* else." And he started to back away. "I just want you to know. If you wish, you can stay. If you wish, you can go north. I know that Massachusetts has some towns you might like." Then he go off.

I look at Alice. "Is he sayin' what I think he is?"

And she say, "I think he givin' us our freedom." But she don't have a big bright smile on her face. She look more worried than anything. Then she say, "How old you reckon you is, Jake?"

"I don't rightly know. Seventy, I thinks."

"If we go free, who gonna give two old broken-down horses like us a job?"

"Who gonna give us somethin' to eat?"

"Let's go home," I say. "Home to Mount Vernon."

## Hesperus Draper:

About a year after he left office, a notice was posted in my paper: "For Sale, Acreage on the Great Kanawha, contact G. Washington, Mount Vernon."

He'd leased some of his bonus lands. He was sellin' the rest. By rights, he was still land-rich and cash-poor. Just how poor was something I wanted to find out.

'Twas a fine warm June afternoon when I rode up.

Washington and his wife were on the piazza. Two old folks, enjoyin' the breeze. She was knittin'. He was watchin' two of his pet deer down at the edge of the woods. He'd long ago gotten rid of his hounds so that he could keep the deer and let them wander on the grounds. Quiet pursuits for a quiet old man.

I hadn't seen the Washingtons since my Charlotte died. So they both had kind things to say. They liked her more than they liked me. But that was the story of my life in that woman's shadow.

Then, since I'd come on business, Mrs. Washington excused herself, leavin' me alone with the great man.

"So," I said, "I've come to buy your land on the Great Kanawha."

"Do you think you can afford it?"

"I have cash in hand."

"Many Americans have cash in hand. Many more than in 1787."

"You did the job, General. I have to admit it."

That warmed him some, so he called for Madeira. Then he asked, "So why has your paper opposed me so often?"

I shrugged. "'Tis the way men are made."

"Disunion can grow from opposition, and disunion will be the end of us."

A slave brought the Madeira.

After a sip, Washington got to the business at hand. "Why do you want the land, Draper? You have no heirs."

"Neither do you."

"'Tis why I ask. You might point me toward some truth."

"I want the land because I want to hold a piece of the future." I thought 'twas a good answer.

He must have thought the same thing. He nodded a bit, then sucked his mouth around to straighten his dentures. "Is the future worth ten dollars an acre?"

"Ten?" I said. "It's worth about four."

"Then you can't value it too well."

He was askin' too high. I was biddin' too low. The

fair price was about seven. But I didn't need the land. Had all I wanted right there in the two thousand acres I held, thanks to him.

So we sat like that for a bit, each tryin' to freeze the other into sayin' somethin', and both too stubborn. If there was to be a counteroffer, it would have to come from one of the deer out on the lawn.

Finally he said, "The future . . .'tis a good reason to do things."

"Do we have a deal, then?"

"The future will be worth far more than four dollars an acre. We have all of us made it invaluable by our sacrifices."

"The future is always invaluable to old men, George."

"Then perhaps I should keep the land."

"Until someone comes along who's willin' to pay for it." I finished my Madeira. "I have to warn you, I won't back down in my attacks on Adams. You know what Franklin once said about him? 'Always an honest man, often a great one, but sometimes absolutely mad.'"

"I agree with points one and two. After Mr. Adams has been president a while longer, he himself may agree with the third."

"I'd say he's mad already. He loves monarchy. He lets the Federalists stifle complaint. He's bad-tempered."

Washington raised his chin slightly. "Freedom of the press is important. So is restraint, which is the best medicine for a bad temper."

'Twas plain I wouldn't be invited for supper, so I stood up to leave. He stood with me. Didn't shake his hand. Knew he didn't like to shake hands. And I found that I didn't have any restraint, even after all these years. I just had to tweak him once more. So I

leaned close and I said, "You know, George, the bonus lands, they were . . ." I wanted to say "a swindle."
But I didn't. Couldn't bring myself to do it. I just said,
"They're beautiful. But us enlisted men, we deserved
more."

And he didn't get mad. Didn't even get red around
the neck. He just said, "Draper, I did my best."

I rode back down the drive, with him and his tiny
wife watchin' me. Were they sorry to see me go? Or
were they just makin' sure I was leavin' the property?
I didn't rightly know.

I give him a wave as my horse went into the woods.
I think he waved back.

## Nelly Custis Lewis:

W hen I was married at Mount Vernon in the spring
of last year, my grandfather gave me away. He
looked happy and robust, and never did I feel more
joyful in his presence.

You know, we had enjoyed a special warmth. I had
always been able to make him laugh, even when he
entered a room and all talk, all laughter, ceased because of the gravity of his presence. So my wedding
was an event of great happiness, especially as my
grandparents invited me and my husband to build our
home on the Mount Vernon property, which we are
now doing.

As nature decrees these things, I was soon with child,
and brought to bed at the end of November, and delivered of a baby girl.

As Dr. Craik decrees these things, I was not allowed

from my bed to see Grandpapa during his dying hours, even though he was a few feet away, separated by no more than the wall that separates their private wing of the house from the rest of our quarters.

And neither was I allowed to come downstairs to see him in the three days following his death, when his body was laid out in the large dining room on the north side of the house.

But I had to bid him farewell. I awoke during the night before he was to be placed in the family tomb. The moonlight came through the windows on the west, so I knew it to be quite late.

I tiptoed downstairs, filled with a mixture of grief and fear, a strange, cold feeling at the back of my neck. I was very weak, not so much from the childbirth, which now was no more than a memory, as from having been abed for so long.

I slipped through the little parlor, past the spinet that Grandpapa had bought for me in New York and which I had played for him so many times. Then I stopped in the doorway. The coffin was on the opposite side of the room, under the Palladian windows where the sideboard normally stood.

Cold moonlight fell in long shafts through the west windows.

I stepped into the room, my toes like ice on the wood boards.

I went toward him. He looked, in his best black suit, as placid and peaceful as one is supposed to look who has died in bed. But my emotions were all of fear and loneliness.

The great body, which had endured so much, the great mind, so steady in its operation, so sure in its conclusions, was all stilled. Here was no more than an empty vessel, drained for the subsistence of a nation. It was only after these thoughts passed that I could reach out to touch him.

And a voice came from the darkness behind me. "Evenin', Miz Nelly."

I withdrew my hand in fright.

Old Jake was sitting in one of the chairs along the wall. "You ain't s'posed to be out of bed, is you, ma'am?"

"What are you doing here, Jake?"

"Just settin'. Settin' a last time with the massa." The old Negro came over and looked into the coffin, then reached out and touched his hand. " 'S cold."

"You must have loved him very much," I said.

He chuckled. "Oh, no, ma'am. I like him, for a massa, 'specially seein' as how, in his will, he's freein' his slaves. I like him plenty. Never love him, though."

I was shocked. "He loved you."

"All's I know, he treat me better 'n I would've been treated anywheres else. And I'se sure gonna miss him. So I'se settin' with him some." And the old slave took me gently by the arm. "I reckon you better set, too, ma'am, 'fore you fall down."

And we sat together in the moonlight, with the body of the greatest man in America before us. Even though Jacob was an unlettered slave, his presence comforted me.

# EPILOGUE

So the story had been told.

But copies of two letters still lay before me, in my room at Gadsby's, and they vexed me. They were letters that Washington had written to Sally Fairfax.

What could I make of them? Was there enough here to besmirch a great man? Enough to bring down one of his successors? And did I want to?

Sally Fairfax had shown me three letters. I had inserted one that came from the middle of her life. But her youth and old age still lay before me. One letter was written when she was unattached, one when he was unattached. I turned to the simpler of the two, written in old age. I set down Sally's name in dark letters, and shaped her narration, as I had done with so many others:

## Sally Fairfax:

*In the late summer of 1798, I received a letter from him that filled me with . . . something. I'm not sure what. I've tried to read between the lines, as they say, to put it all in context. But even as an old widow, I hesitated, like the young girl who hesitates because she is uncertain of a gentleman's intentions. Does his interest derive from her warmth of personality . . . or her other charms?*

*His letter talked of the five and twenty years that had passed since I left Belvoir, and of all the great events that had transpired. Then he wrote: "None of the events, nor all of them together, have been able to eradicate from my mind the recollection of those happy moments, the happiest in my life, which I have enjoyed in your company."*

*This, even when coming from a sixty-five-year-old man, and even with a chatty addendum from his wife, had an impact. You can be sure.*

*He went on: "Worn out in a manner by the toils of my last labor, I am again seated under my vine and fig tree, and wish to spend the remainder of my days (which cannot be many) in rural amusements, free from those cares which public responsibility is never exempt."*

*And then he invited me to return to America and spend my last years there among my friends in a country that, as he said, "bids fair to be one of the greatest and happiest nations in the world."*

*I did not return. Though I would dearly have loved to see him, and I wish now that I had . . .*

C.D.—Unrequited love. Poets found many truths in such fertile soil. Men might rise to greatness in spite of it or because of it, or simply because they were destined to be great.

Poets also found truth in an old man's dreams of youth.

I looked again at my notes from the Paris meeting with Sally Fairfax:

Says she wrote to him just before his marriage to Martha, congratulated him on impending wedding, tried to joke with him about becoming a husband.

She says to me, "It is strange, Mr. Draper, but whenever a woman jokes with a man, she is seen as a coquette. George, however, did not take his feelings lightly. Here is the letter that he wrote back to me."

It is in Washington's unmistakably large, spacious, and careful hand:

Camp at Fort Cumberland, 12th Septr 1758
'Tis true, I profess myself a votary of love. I acknowledge that a lady is in the case, and further I confess that this lady is known to you. Yes, Madam, as well as she is to one who is too sensible of her charms to deny her power over him. I feel the force of her amiable beauties in the recollection of a thousand tender passages with her that I could wish to obliterate, till I am bid to revive them. But experience, alas! sadly reminds me how impossible this is.

You have drawn me, my dear madam, or rather I have drawn myself, into an honest confession of a simple fact. Misconstrue not my meaning, nor expose it. The world has no business to know the object of love declared in this manner to you, when I want to conceal it. One thing above all things in this would I wish to know, and only one person can answer me or guess my meaning—but adieu to this, till happier times, if ever I shall see them.

Her eyes fill with tears. She wipes them away, saying, "Oh, silly woman . . ."

After a moment, she explains, "I keep this letter to remind myself of the life we knew, back at Belvoir, *back in those wonderful days. I show it to you to show you how ... how good he was."*

*I ask, "Did he love you?"*

*"The ocean between love and infatuation is a wide one, Mr. Draper. I think we both sailed upon it."*

*"So ... you loved him?"*

*She gives me a little smile, a twitch of her brow, flicks her eyes toward the carriages clattering by on the Champs-Élysées. A coquette still....*

Not even the most rabid French-loving Republican would attempt to make something of Sally Fairfax's connection to Washington. Far more in keeping with his attitudes about love was his letter to Nelly Custis before she married: "Love is a mighty pretty thing, but like all other delicious things, it is cloying, and when the first passion of love subsides, remember that love is too dainty a food to live on alone. Do not forget good sense and a good disposition."

While I was considering this more practical advice from the ever-practical Washington, there came a knock on my door. Answering it, I was shocked to see Miss Delilah Smoot, wearing the same dove-gray cape she had worn the first time I saw her, in my uncle's office.

It seemed a lifetime since she had told the story that first set me traveling.

I said, "Delilah ... it's good to see you."

"Lost my job, thanks to you."

"I'm sorry."

"Don't matter. Found a better one. Found a master who pays in land."

"Well ... I should say I'm ... I'm ..." Her presence

unnerved me so, the best I could muster was "I'm happy for you."

"Be happy for yourself. Be happy for this." And she withdrew from her cape a letter. She did it with so little fanfare that I was not prepared for what she said next: "I saved one from the fire."

I was shocked and almost speechless. "Are you . . . are you talking about one of George's letters to Martha?"

"The first one. Thought it might be worth somethin' someday."

I waited, as they say in the boardinghouses, for the other shoe to drop, in the manner of seeking a price.

Instead she went on, "Don't seem fittin', somehow, sellin' such a thing."

And she handed me the letter. I'm certain that my hand shook. How could it not, considering what I held? The ancient wax seal was stamped with a *W*. It was a letter to Martha, written in December 1758, from Mount Vernon. I scanned it quickly, and phrases leaped out at me:

"I profess myself a votary to love. I acknowledge that a lady is in the case, and further I confess that this lady is known to you . . . but adieu to all this, till happier times, which I know await us in the years ahead, my dear madam, when we shall see our estate grown to maturity, our family grown to honorable adulthood around us."

I flipped back through my manuscript to December 1758 and found that the letter would have been written after Washington came back from the French and Indian War, after he and Sally Fairfax had their last private talk, after Washington promised to play Juba to Sally's Marcia, Romeo to her Juliet.

So many of the same phrases filled the letters. So many of the same sentiments. But the letter to Martha looked ahead; the letter to Sally looked back. One was melancholy, the other filled with hope.

It has been said that life is simply an accumulation of dreams and memories, and both were there, in those two letters.

"I think that what he wrote, it's a fine sentiment," said Miss Delilah when I was done reading.

Washington may have yearned for Sally. He may never have stopped loving her in some corner of his heart. But what would I learn about him from an exploration of such a truth? What good could come from the exposure of it? Perhaps the restraint he learned in controlling his passion for Sally may have taught him how to restrain the other emotions that boiled in him. Perhaps . . . but there was so much in his life of greater importance.

I could not doubt, after following their lives together, that he grew to love Martha for more than her money. As for the burned letters, I could only speculate that Martha had decided to keep something of her life to herself. And there, I determined would be the end of it.

These letters would be left to privacy, not posterity.

I went over to the table and wrote a few final sentences. I bundled up the manuscript and was done. Then I invited Miss Delilah to accompany me to my uncle's office, to deliver the manuscript.

It was a short walk from Gadsby's to the Draper offices, where I found a large crowd milling around in the street.

Upstairs, a tall man with a badge was reading a warrant to my uncle: "For making false and malicious statements against the government and its agents, I—"

"You're arrestin' me?" demanded my uncle.

"Now, Hesperus," said the marshal, "I been warnin' you ever since they come out with this law. Will you come quietly, or do I have to manacle you?"

"No manacles," grunted Eli.

My uncle now spied me. "Well, Christopher, meet the federal marshal."

The marshal did not bother to look at me. He just said, "Stop the palaverin', Hesperus. I'm just doin' my job. Now, will you come quiet or—"

My uncle spied the bundle of manuscript under my arm. "Is that it? Is that your book?"

I said that it was.

"Did you find the secret?"

"There were no secrets," I said. "Miss Delilah is certain of it."

He gave Delilah that lascivious old squint. "Did he pay you, darlin'?"

"I ain't . . . I'm not lookin' for pay, Mr. Draper."

"Not lookin' for pay?" My uncle turned his eye to me once more. "Don't believe her, son. Don't believe anyone who says they're not lookin' for pay." Then he swept my manuscript from the desk, "Readin' matter for my night in jail. Now, Christopher, sit down at my desk and aim your pen right between Adams's eyes." My uncle seemed almost joyous. It was as if this arrest were a kind of victory.

And with a flourish of coattails, he and my manuscript marched out in custody of the federal marshal, with the rest of the newspaper staff following like hens after the rooster.

Once the noise of the crowd had receded and silence enveloped us, Miss Delilah said, "I'm headin' for the Ohio country in a few days. I sure could use some company."

I caught her meaning. I was more than flattered. I was sorely tempted. And I told her as much. But I also told her that I could not leave my uncle, not as the battle moved toward its climax.

"Well," she said, with no touch of disappointment in her voice, "Come visit me in Pittsburgh sometime."

I told her I would come in the spring. I watched her from the window as she crossed Market Square. Then I sat down to the business of attacking the Alien and Sedition Acts and the Federalist Congress that had passed the bills. Those acts, passed by one party out of fear of another, were a blot on our shield far uglier than the worst words ever written by Philip Freneau or Hesperus Draper.

And I said so, in a screed that took me the whole night to write.

The next morning I went to the jail to see my uncle, and it looked as if he, too, had been working all night. His eyes were bloodshot, his hair had fallen from its queue and draped the sides of his face. A pile of manuscript sat on the table before him and loyal Eli Stitch nodded on a stool by the cell door.

But when he saw me, my uncle smiled. "Ah, the great author."

*Author.* I must admit that I was truly flattered to hear that word applied to me. "You've read it, then?"

"Yes, I have."

"And?"

"There's one thing certain, son. I've had a hell of a life . . . a hell of a life."

"And?"

Just then the marshal came in with a ball of twine. "Don't you go hangin' yourself with this, Hess."

"Don't worry, Tom." My uncle took the twine and wound it around the manuscript several times, first horizontally, then vertically. Then he had me reach through the bars and press my finger onto the place where the twine crossed itself, so that he could knot it.

With a penknife—this was a very friendly jail—he cut the twine and hefted the manuscript in his hands. "A fine package."

"Are you sending it to the printer?" I asked, my belly filling with pride.

"No . . . no," he said. "But it'll fit just fine in the back of my safe."

It was as if someone had pulled a cork somewhere below my belt. All the pride went pouring out of me, and the bile of shock rushed in to replace it. "Uncle, what are you saying?"

"Printin' this won't do us any good at all," said my uncle. "When you come right down to it, you like Washington. I reckon I do, too. And the damnedest thing is, he didn't ask us to like him. He just did what he thought he was supposed to do—most of the time, anyway. You have to like a man for that, or at least respect him."

He shoved the manuscript through the bars to Eli Stitch. "So this goes to the back of my safe . . . till we need it."

I watched the big, brain-broken bodyguard going out the door with my manuscript and I tried to think of a way to rescue my career as a writer. "Uncle," I asked, when I finally found my voice, "what about the election? The presidential caucuses?"

"I've decided that showin' Washington with all his warts won't do us any good. We'll just have to show Adams with all *his*."

Exactly what I had thought at the beginning. "But what of my manuscript?"

"It's *my* manuscript, son. You took my money. I own your work. Argue if you want, but better that you turn your attention to Adams and make yourself some more money. Makin' money is the quickest way to make yourself feel better. So down with Adams, up with Jefferson."

"Uncle," I said, "I think Jefferson's more devious than Adams."

"So he is. So he is. But he won't arrest me if I say so."

That was fifty-eight years ago, sir, but it seems like yesterday. It's hard to believe that most of those people have turned to dust . . .

I worked for my uncle all through the 1800 election. And what a bloody mess it was. Newspapers became inked brickbats, and pens were knives flying through the air. The Republicans assailed Adams as a monarchist, the Federalists charged that Jefferson was an atheist so depraved as to be lying with his own slaves—a charge I suspected was true. And just as my uncle predicted, the Federalists sought to link Washington and Adams like political brothers. But that did Adams little good.

The electors fragmented their votes among Adams, Jefferson, Aaron Burr, and Charles Pinckney, so that the whole business was thrown to the House of Representatives. After twenty ballots and six days of arm-twisting, Jefferson was elected. This meant the end of the Alien and Sedition Acts, which were scheduled to pass from law on the first day of the new administration, unless the president signed an extension. This also meant the beginning of the end of the Federalists.

As for me, I'd had enough of the scribbler's life. If a publisher could bury my work in a safe, I needed a new line of work. So I headed west.

I never found Miss Delilah, not that I looked very hard. I was more interested in taking a lesson from Washington: I was buying land. I bought my way from Pittsburgh right across the prairie. When I got here to Chicago, I bought here, too, though back then, it was no more than a village around Fort Dearborn.

It wasn't until 1826 that my dusty, half-forgotten manuscript reached me by mail, along with the news that Uncle Hesperus had dropped in his traces at the age of ninety-four while dictating an editorial against, of all people, President John *Quincy* Adams.

I put the manuscript into my own safe, and there it's stayed, until now. Here—let me brush the dust off so it doesn't get your fine, lawyerly black suit all dirty—take it and read it and think about it.

If I were to add another narrator, I'd write the name of Napoleon, and below it, these words, uttered on his deathbed: "They wanted me to be another Washington."

The greatest military genius of his age, who literally snatched an emperor's crown and placed it on his own head—he knew the truth: An American general who had never grasped for power, who used it judiciously, who surrendered it willingly, was by far the better man.

Washington feared the dictatorship that Napoleon

stood for. But he feared disunion even more. He often said that disunion was the only thing that could ruin our American experiment. It was a lesson he never forgot as President.

Remember the lesson, sir. An Illinois lawyer running for the Senate from our new Republican Party should never forget it, especially in these dark days.

So, good luck, sir. Turn your face to the future, as Washington did, and remember the words of Hesperus Draper, words that Washington must have carried in his own head, considering how he responded whenever his countrymen gave him another insurmountable task: "Learn by doin', and do by finishin'."

# JOANNE FLUKE

# FATAL IDENTITY

*You only
die twice...*

# Don't Miss These Other Chilling Thrillers!